HEAD WOUNDS

Mitch Mitchell has just been told that Radio Brum are dropping her programme for the summer. Her dream home, a chapel conversion, is proving disastrously expensive and Mitchell and Orient, the detective agency she co-owns, is making a loss. So it seems like good news when celebrity cook Sissy Childe asks her to find her missing half-sister. The trail leads Mitch and her partner Tommy to Devon, where the body of a young woman wearing Rosie's jacket is found, but it is not Rosie. Now there are *two* mysteries – who is the dead woman, and where is Rosie?

HEAD WOUNDS

HEAD WOUNDS

by

Valerie Kershaw

Magna Large Print Books
Long Preston, North Yorkshire,
BD23 4ND, England.

British Library Cataloguing in Publication Data.

Kershaw, Valerie
    Head wounds.

    A catalogue record of this book is
    available from the British Library

    ISBN   0-7505-1740-9

First published in Great Britain 2000 by
Constable, an imprint of Constable & Robinson Ltd.

Published in Large Print 2001 by arrangement with
Constable & Robinson Ltd.

Magna Large Print is an imprint of Library Magna Books Ltd.

Printed and bound in Great Britain by
T.J. (International) Ltd., Cornwall, PL28 8RW

1

'...I barely remember bomb sites in England after the war so it was a great shock to see so much damaged property. People are living in places with plastic wrap stapled to the windows. Packs of stray dogs are running the streets. Lots of abandoned cars which had served as cover for snipers. There are bullet holes in walls and you can trace where they come from, the angle of the firing. Then to meet the folks, all of whom seem so amicable. I live in a house. I've got the whole ground floor. He's a Croat, she's a Serb, living in a Muslim community and managing to get by. Their kids fled to Holland during the Bosnian war and to my endless satisfaction I was able to get the parents a visa to go and visit them. They'd been trying for four years, unable to break through the red tape. Then some crazy outsider storms in and gets it for them – sadly, all it took was one phone call to a woman I met in the Dutch Embassy at a party and the right papers were signed. But though I was very glad to help, how can they live in a country with so little regard for them?

'Anyway, I set up shop and recruited characters, some journalists, some not, and trained them to do talk show radio, pull in the guests, discuss issues at a grass roots level. This is apparently a novel idea for Bosnians because most stations are so biased that only one opinion is ever heard. We get lots of callers and the shows are doing really well. We've already had lots of good issues aired. They've gained so much confidence they've even turned on us. We've had one show about how awful the Red Cross soup kitchens were (I was shitting bricks because I thought this was crossing the line ... the unemployment rate is seventy-five per cent, so do we really want to take on the Red Cross? But in the interests of democracy...). It turns out the criticisms were entirely accurate and the food that was designated was being side-tracked. The Red Cross acknowledged the problem and set up a different way to distribute ... wow... We did another one with the women from Scbrenica...'

Mitch, turning to the next sheet of Ellie Peters' letter, caught a glimpse of her watch. She rammed the pages into a plastic Tesco bag bulging with boxed tapes and scrawled programme notes, grabbed her coat and tape recorder and shot out of the front door into March sunshine. The roar of city traffic, more in her bones than her ears, the slight flavour of burning carbon monoxide and something else, too, this being pumped rhythmically through all the chambers of her heart: spring. Even her left knee joint, which she suspected of becoming arthritic, this morning moved with honeyed ease. Before she snapped the front gate behind her, her body redesigned itself, shoulders back, buttocks tucked in, steps pinging on elastic. She ignored the strange fruit bursting on the nude limbs of the lilac bush: a weathered piece of plastic food tray, a Mars bar wrapper and the sloughed-off skin of a used condom.

What a day, she told herself, a day to even rejoice in the detritus of the city, get high on the sulphur-tinged atmosphere. Oh to be in England and all that stuff. But wasn't that April? Anyway, Ellie Peters seems to be enjoying herself too much at the moment to have any home thoughts from abroad.

Didn't she feel even a little bit envious?

Yes, I damn well do, Mitch decided, reviewing the day before her at Radio Brum.

Not enough to stop her whistling as she unlocked the door of her grey Escort, a car so inconspicuous that she always had to memorise the spot she'd parked it in so she could find it again.

2

Arthur Trimble had battled fiercely against
the temptation to wash the sock he'd stolen
from the corpse's left foot. He'd noticed
already that he'd compensated for this by
becoming even more meticulous in other
spheres of his life. One of his wife's friends,
on seeing his garden full of ranks of present
and correct tulips, had wanted to know:
'Who is the sergeant-major in your house?'
Coral hadn't laughed. 'Need you ask? I'm
particular about things myself. I admit it.
But I don't go about realigning the tooth-
brushes. Or turning the front garden into a
parade ground.'

He'd long recognised that obsessiveness
was wired into his structure. Not being a
slob was a good thing, wasn't it? It had been
what had drawn Coral to him. 'I couldn't
make love to a man who wasn't nice, you
know?' she'd told him. 'They do say op-
posites attract but I think that's really silly. I
just couldn't live with a dirty devil.' She'd
pulled a face, smelling the stench of the
unregenerate male. 'I can't abide mucky
sods.'

As Cory, their son, grew older, Arthur first

watched the boy regiment his blocks of Lego and later the sea shells he collected. A spark off the Trimble ancestral soul. Did that please him? Yes, it did.

One of the things which had attracted him to Coral was that she was a bit dim. She knew where Turkey was, of course, but would certainly have trouble in pin-pointing Vietnam. He liked putting her right. It confirmed him in his opinion of himself. Top of the form, ten out of ten, first class. However, he soon learned to exercise a degree of caution. He didn't think of her as sensitive but if she felt he'd gone too far his punishment could be surprisingly brutal. She'd given him some shiners over the years. Arthur had found he'd had to refrain from telling her quite a few things she really ought to know.

After some enforced reflection, he'd decided to confine her education to what he considered to be proper subjects, like history and geography; he'd taught her how to write a decent business letter, a little about music, architecture, plants, even art. He'd learned to live with serviettes, desserts, television sets in fake Georgian cabinets and candlewick covers on the lavatory lid. He'd never even considered mathematics. Coral, as far as he knew, had never come into contact with algebra and geometry, though he'd been surprised to discover her bent for fiscal management. Even in the worst of the recession she'd managed to increase the profits from her dress shop. It was certainly hard to visualise her or any of her swanky clientele being seen dead in a pair of well-washed and worn white towelling socks. Were they sports socks? he wondered. But the corpse had not been kitted out for games, not even for hiking.

As a boy Arthur had come down one morning and found his mother's tabby cat dead, railing stiff, whiskers almost looking as if they'd leapt to attention. She – he was already romanticising her rather, sometimes thinking of her as, oh, she of the virgin sock – wasn't like that, but she hadn't looked as if she were asleep either. He'd known she was dead all right. Even now, just thinking about it again, he recaptured some of that frisson of excitement.

He hadn't even thought of telling Coral. Secretiveness was his nature. As a very clever middle child marooned in a very ordinary family he'd learned the benefits of being what he was not – like them. But when the time came to choose a career he'd decided he was old enough and big enough to assume his true colours. He would be a schoolmaster. His family had thought he was acting out of character. When he continued to act out of character his mother, father and two sisters had, in many ways, shown their displeasure. One nephew, he suspected with tacit parental approvement, had openly tried to bully him. He'd taught too many youngsters not to know how to handle the situation. Now, on the very rare occasions he let himself be dragooned into a family occasion, his father joked in a fake Welsh accent: 'Look you, there's posh then. Sure you've nowhere better to go, boy-o?'

Coral, though she was no brighter than most of the Trimble tribe, played more subtle games. She both encouraged him and pulled the rug out from beneath his socks. He might plan their little educational trips to Greece and South America. She paid for them. Work and increasing success had transformed his baby bride into a woman of sterling worth. He suspected that she felt she carried a lot more weight than he did now. Strange in a woman who didn't even know where Vietnam was.

But there were a lot of things about Coral that didn't quite add up. For instance, more than once a woman had buttonholed him at a party and told him what marvellous taste his wife had. If you wanted something really elegant to wear you had to go to Coral's. How could a woman who stuck a candle-wick cover on her lavatory seat be described in those terms? It had struck him that there was a remarkable similarity between his mother-in-law's interiors and his wife's. Yet the clothes they chose to wear were totally different. Coral, unlike her mother, really did dress well. He defined this in his mind as 'almost discreetly'. Discretion would have been boring; not quite managing it carried an erotic charge. He wondered if having to make money at something had made Coral challenge and then set aside her mother's idea of what fashionable women should wear.

There was, of course, nothing fashionable about the white sock, and the erotic charge *that* carried sometimes blew his eyeballs out. He kept seeing it as part of one of his wife's tasteful window displays. He let it crawl out of a black evening purse, let it burrow into the nest of pink silk chiffon he imagined the purse lay on. The picture made him sweat with anxiety.

Saying he felt compelled to exhibit it, just as he'd felt compelled to steal it?

Dear Lord, he thought. What is happening to me? I'm not like *that*.

There was no doubt in his mind that the woman had been shot. She was face down and a buzz of bluebottles were settled in a small crater clearly visible beyond the crown of her skull. He thought it must be the exit wound for it seemed unlikely someone had fired into the top of her head. Both her feet had been lifted out of her brown slip-on sandals. My God, the bullet had not only blasted her upwards, but made her spin. She'd landed first on her left elbow. The arm was in such an unnatural position he was pretty sure it was broken. Whack, he'd thought, and that's that. He had to try quite hard to refrain from smiling. After all, it was a very dreadful thing. Wasn't it?

But perhaps the most dreadful thing of all was that he'd not been repulsed. He'd certainly shivered. At one point he'd had the crazy notion that someone was playing a comb covered with paper and then he'd realised the zitherish sound was the chattering of his teeth.

When his teeth quietened, he became aware of burning. It was a squealing heat as if his flesh were the rubber tyres of a crashing car he was desperately trying to control. When he smashed into stillness his bowels had loosened and he was gulping for air.

He wasn't sure afterwards, but he thought that he'd first felt the heat when he'd decided to steal the sock. When he'd pocketed it he'd realised he wouldn't be able to call the coppers. That was all right. It was a relief really. He couldn't afford to come under the spotlight anyway. He'd his probity to think of. As a male teacher in a private all girls' school one just couldn't be too careful. The last thing he wanted to do was become a target for gossip.

Yes, better all round to keep mum. After all, she was beyond human help. Someone else would stumble over her. They could set the wheels in motion. In time she'd be decently laid in her coffin, that crust of bluebottles settled in her black hair dispatched back into Mother Nature's womb.

Arthur Trimble had crossed his fingers and then crossed himself. Words sighed in his head like a spring breeze. 'Give sentence with me, O Lord, and defend the cause of my soul against ungodly people; deliver me.'

Even before the incantation ended he was also hearing a squeaking, like the noise of a rat, as he felt the wheel of his fortunes turning.

Among all the other things he was aware of when he pocketed the sock was the knowledge that he was betraying his baby bride. Of course, he knew that in reality this seventeen-year-old, still in charge of his heart, was no longer there. He hadn't realised quite how adult Coral now was, what a successful *woman*, until she'd produced the money to buy the cottage in Coombe Foot. This was the picturesque and genteel Devon village she'd been born in. Tom Hook and his wife Rita had brought up Coral and her sister Pat in one of the two pairs of council houses on the straggling road out to the west of Coombe Foot.

Arthur would have preferred to remain in Newton Abbot. He'd chosen the bungalow they'd lived in there, drawn both by its neatness and by the fact that it was on the right side of town for his journey to work. Now he faced the daily bottlenecks she'd faced when travelling to her shop in Torquay. It seemed to him that for a long time now he was being pushed, usually gently, in directions he didn't want to go. And yet he'd settled into village life very comfortably and wouldn't think of moving.

And, if he were honest, he'd have to admit that the early years of their marriage hadn't been as idyllic as he often pretended. His baby bride had now grown out of tantrums and bouts of sulking and the ear-splitting pop music he'd tried to make himself like because he didn't want to appear to her as being too daddy-ish. At least he hadn't had to hide his dislike when his son Cory started blasting out hip-hop or heavy metal.

The truth was that Arthur felt himself incapable of real happiness because, throughout his life, he'd experienced something as being missing. What he lacked he'd found impossible to pinpoint.

Until he found the sock.

Or until he'd found a woman dead?

She was freshly murdered because rigor mortis, something he only knew about from seeing the dead cat, had not set in. But perhaps it had come and gone? After all, when people got as far as being humped into their coffins they surely didn't look as if they were in the process of being electrified?

He had pushed up the left leg of her jeans to her calf and, being very careful not to touch her flesh, transferred the bunching denim to his left hand, leaving his right free to peel off her sock. So horrified was he of touching her body, he'd inserted a stick down the heel and had worked with that to lever off the sock, aware he was scratching almost pellucidly white skin, the friction of his movements fizzing deliciously in his bloodstream. And yet he was frantic with anxiety, too. What if someone stumbled on him? What would they think? Why was he doing this? The other thing he was acutely aware of was the buzz of bluebottles in his ears. He knew nothing of their habits. Were they dining on her blood or her brains?

It very nearly didn't happen. He could practically count on one hand the times he'd taken the footpath through Coombe Woods to Bishop Coombe. If he hadn't lent Coral his car to do the weekly shopping because hers had broken down, he'd have driven round to see how poor old Woody Woods was. Woody, head of the maths department, was one of the few friends Arthur had made at St Ursula's. Five years older than he was and all her weight hanging in front of her, as if a sack of live rabbits swung from her neck, she was nevertheless of a similar temperament to him; hard-working, conscientious and meticulous. She'd been released from the cardiac unit at the local hospital the week before. 'Fit as a flea, sweetheart,' she'd boomed down the phone. 'Just a little warning. A slow-down signal. That's what the doctor said. The feller didn't look a day older than my girls in the Sixth. But there you are. Tempus will fugit and all that tommy rot.'

It was March, a fine, late afternoon, too warm for the time of year. His and Coral's cottage was opposite the church, on a bend of the gently rising lane which lay at right angles to the main road swirling through the village like a river bed. He clicked the gate shut and had walked no more than twenty yards before he was halted by Paul Maugin, who was turning his old Volvo estate car into the driveway of his house. Arthur, a man used to living by timetables, was intrigued to see the bonnet nosing in rather than out of Good Hope Cottage for late on Thursday afternoons Maugin drove off to play bridge then have dinner with the Childe family at Coombe Grange. But hadn't someone told him that Childe and his partner Penny Gilbert were off jaunting about France?

His next-door neighbour answered his salute with an almost imperceptible nod of his long, thin head. Though Maugin was a tall man with wide shoulders, he always gave him the impression of being squeezed in, of not having the room to move about properly, as if he inhabited a bottle. Maugin's speech was curiously restricted, too. At times Arthur found himself possessed with an urge to physically pull the words out of his throat, so slow were they in coming. The upper class drawl fascinated him and he occasionally stole bits of it. Just as Arthur's father used a Welsh lilt to throw a humorous cloak over the aggression he felt for his son, so he used Maugin's upper class drawl in some of his exchanges with Coral. 'Where are you *orf* to now?' What really irritated Arthur, though, was the supposition in the village that Maugin was the clever one, not him. They might ask him in the pub which country Zaire was before it became the Congo but it was Maugin they thought of as erudite. This rested, as far as Arthur could tell, on the belief that Maugin had been a diplomat. Some said something in the Foreign Office. Arthur would question the supposition that one had to be bright to have a hand in the balls-up which was England's foreign policy. But even Coral, when talking about him, sometimes tagged on to the end of her sentence, '...but then I suppose he's what people used to call an egghead.'

Arthur could now hear the door of Maugin's estate bang. He turned to look back but his view of his neighbour's driveway was blocked by the straggly yew which also, he knew, cut out most of the light from Maugin's sitting-room. Alfie, Maugin's cat, streaked over the wall to the car.

The schoolteacher carried on walking down to the main road and crossed it by the Pilgrims' Inn, then walked by the high whitewashed cob garden walls and gable end of Manaccan House. The converted barn next door was now the home of Coral's solicitor, Clive Upjohn. Attached to one end was a small row of thatched cottages. He took the fork that led up to Coombe Woods.

He listened carefully for engine noises as he climbed up the winding single-track lane; cars tended to shoot the corners, throwing threatened walkers on to the impaling branches of lethally trimmed hawthorn hedges. Rounding a blind bend he saw, four hundred yards in front of him, on the brow of a steep incline, a figure blackened by the setting sun; a giant beetle shape reared up on a pair of tine-thin appendages. A small segment detached itself, a loop of umbilical cord unwinding. The whole suddenly resolved into a man and a dog on a leash. An instant later Arthur recognised Clive Upjohn. A gaberdine boater was shading a

21

baking potato of a face on which were wedged round wire-framed glasses. 'Quite a warm afternoon,' said Clive as he approached. 'Not bad weather we're having. Considering.' He turned to look at the lurcher uneasily moving at his feet. 'Jo-jo's had quite a good run. Oh yes.'

'Bit early aren't you? To-day?'

'Doing a bit of tricky paperwork at home, old son. It's Bedlam in the office at the moment. Incidentally, we were hoping you'd pitch in and help with the fete this year. Can sometimes be a bit of a drag, I know. But it always raises lots of lolly. Considering.'

'The exams are starting then. Always a very busy time.'

'Good try. But no banana. Who's not busy? Cecily will be in touch with Coral. And I warn you. My wife's never been known to take no for an answer. Well, we must be pushing on, eh Jo-jo? Enjoy your walk. Nothing like blowing the cobwebs away.' The dog, aware that Upjohn was going to move before he lifted a foot, suddenly sledged ahead.

Turning, Arthur trudged on up the incline and then took the fork down to Coombe Woods. They lay in private, well-fenced land but Oa Bone, the pop star owner, had cunningly hidden a stone stile behind what looked like, on first sight, an impenetrable hedge of mixed hawthorn and coppiced

22

beech. He'd no objections to locals taking a short cut to Bishop Coombe but didn't want hordes of picnicking holiday-makers driving out animal life.

Arthur carefully circumvented the hedge and levered himself over the stile. He found himself sniffing. Not just damp, he thought, but not quite as bad as the smell of household rubbish. Woods, his soul told him, always needed a jolly good wash and brush up.

He'd followed the looping path for five minutes before he came to the small clearing. There he saw, just beyond bracken on a rising rim of grassland, a baby adder's tongue and went to investigate the rarity. The single, short frond of the fern barely rose above the top of the coming spring grass. It had divided to form a leafy oval and the tongue-like spike was starting to rise almost rudely into the softening evening light. He straightened up and looked around him.

The grasses clothed the top of a small outcrop of rock. Ten feet below him was another dish of grass and then the woods began again, marching down the hill to grazing land. She was on her stomach, her left arm at an unnatural angle. Her hair was splayed about her thin shoulders, the faded denim jacket rucked over the waist of her jeans, a line of scarlet shirt showing. A tiny halo of black danced through her hair. He felt nothing but puzzlement as he scrambled down to her. She didn't look asleep but he hadn't arrived at the point when he knew she was dead. He was mistaking the blood for muck. Even then he'd been very much aware of the white socks. He could see one slip-on brown sandal three feet in front of a widely flung leg. Looking back, he thought of the woods as being deafeningly quiet, of no birds calling, but he wasn't quite sure if he'd made that up because he felt it was proper for the dead to bring silence.

Later, when he'd reached Miss Woods' cottage, he dressed up the image of the corpse in the tune of a hymn.

Though the cause of evil prosper,
Yet 'tis truth alone is strong,
Though her portion be the scaffold...

And he was disconcertingly aware he was smiling again as his thumb stroked the sock in his pocket.

Smelling humus, he suddenly noticed that Woody was wearing her gardening shoes and that a tiny lip of soil protruded from the left one. 'You've not been out weeding, have you?'

'Of course not! Cross my heart and hope to die. Just a bit of pruning. A little light exercise. That's what the doc recommended, you know. Mustn't wrap oneself in cotton wool.' She was holding a glass of whisky.

'And should you be drinking?'

'Oh, fal-di-riddle,' she said as she led the way into her lounge. She went up to the sideboard to pour him a drink. The chintz covers of the easy chairs were rather greasy and as he chose among them he was trying not to let that disturb him. None of Woody's furniture shone, though not much of the tops of the surfaces could be seen. They were covered in flowers which she'd stuffed into casserole dishes and milk cartons when her vases had run out. Get well cards fluttered like pennants among the petals.

He found he liked nursing his secret. He looked her straight in the eye as she handed him his drink. The small, eight-year-old boy he'd once been wanted to shout: 'I know something you don't! I know something you don't!'

What would teacher say? 'That's quite enough from you, Arthur.'

She wouldn't believe him.

What Woody actually said was: 'People have been so wonderfully kind. But one does rather suspect some of them of simply being morbidly curious. And one can't help wishing the vicar would wait until one was well again before turning up. When one's feeling really badly a visit from a chap in a black skirt puts one in mind of one's funeral. Silly, I know.'

'Such a frightful thing to happen. We were so shocked,' said Arthur, the overpowering scent of flowers in the room reminding him of all the services for the dead he'd ever been to. Which made him think of the corpse again. It occurred to him for the first time that nothing about the body suggested that it had been 'interfered with' – that's how he phrased it in his mind.

Her jeans had been up.

No bonking?

'...to be honest, I didn't think she'd ever be on our screens again...' Miss Woods was saying. He stared at her blankly.

'You know. Sissy Childe. Our other local celebrity. The one that's not Oa Bone. The telly cook, for goodness' sake! Are you all right, Arthur? In the words of the horrors we teach, you look spaced out.'

'Indigestion.'

'In my case that turned out to be a dicky heart. Why didn't you say? You could have had brandy.' Sitting there in her chair, she looked almost like a belly-up breeding toad, watery eyes stiffened by the translucent carapace of her spectacles.

'Whisky will do the trick.'

'Have another.'

'In a moment, if I may. You were saying...'

'About Sissy. Word has it she's been signed up by one of those independent telly programme makers they go in for these days. A new half-hour series. I don't suppose it will be actually broadcast for twelve months or more but there it is. A new Sissy,' She slowly shook her head. 'I never could understand her success. You'd think that all her piggy fatness would put people off eating anything she made. I don't mean that unkindly, of course, I'm hardly sylph-like. Did you know she's let Manaccan House for the whole summer? So we won't be seeing her, unless she stays with her father and Penny at Coombe Grange. For goodness' sake, get yourself another one. And pour me one too while you're up. Can't say I've ever been fond of my body. Never was much of a beauty. But letting me down like this ... a dicky heart, indeed. Really, I can't tell you how put out I am. I was scared stiff for a while, I can tell you. I like my Maker as well as the next but I don't want to see him today, thank you very much.'

'Come on, Woody. Cheer up. At least you've been let out of school early. If you're really lucky you'll miss out both on Easter and the summer term.'

'I know. I mustn't whinge. Though I jolly well feel like it. But I'm still here. That's the main thing. Thank you, sweetheart.' She took her refilled glass. 'Oh and I haven't told you the really hot gossip. To be honest, rumour would be a more accurate description. We're going to have some refugees in the district. Kosovars. A chap is pitching all the old dears out of his nursing home and putting in these Muslims.'

'Really?'

'They're only just about to clear that site which housed those Poles after the Second World War. Catholics. Indians. Muslims. You start to think that if all the world was C of E there would be far fewer conflicts. Tepid. That's the heat of a tip-top religion. Too much drama's no good for anyone. When I was wired up to this monitor thing and I kept listening out for the blips ... well, you know ... it's jolly unnerving thinking that if they stop you're a goner. I know it's pathetic, Arthur, but there you are. Ping, ping, ping. It turns into a regular Chinese water torture. Oh, it's so nice to see you. I'm fed up with being so cheery with all my other visitors. I can moan as much as I like to you. We've always been able to have a good old moan together. One of the reasons we get on, I've always thought.'

'Must say I've never quite looked at it like that.'

She was eyeing the whisky bottle again. 'No, no. Better not. Now tell me about yourself. What have you been doing?'

Arthur, to his horror, found he was starting to blush. He got up hastily. Hands clasped behind his back, he stared out of the small dusty window at Woody's back garden. 'Lawn needs cutting. I'll pop round and do it after school one evening soon. It's amazingly early to be so high. Bet you didn't cut it at the back end.'

'That's kind of you. Don't quite fancy doing it myself. I mean, I know one's supposed to run up hills and pole vault after a heart attack. Well, it seems all wrong. It really does. There's nothing like a brush with death for putting the wind up you, I can tell you. Anything a bit more than light exercise and you're in a sweat of anxiety wondering whether you're going to keel over again.'

'So I should imagine.' He found his finger surreptitiously stroking the towelling sock in his pocket.

Hadn't he had a little collection of socks before?

But those had come off the feet of live girls.

Each of them had been a possible baby bride. But they were all as old as Coral now.

'I suppose we all *do* have to die,' Woody was saying. 'But one doesn't want to go before one's time.'

'I suppose not.' He was again caught in a frisson of excitement, a web of delight sheathing flows of honey. Whack, whack. That's that.

3

'...the women from Scbrenica, a very militant bunch of old Muslim ladies who were quite prepared to stone UN tanks and take hostages. The Internationals were scared to death of these women so it took quite a bit of sweet talking to get top officials into the studio live for a debate with them. It turned out they had very legitimate reasons for believing their husbands, sons and brothers were being held illegally and secretly in Serbia and as a result a massive effort got under way to sort it all out ... heady stuff! ... I've been offered a trip to Kosovo. That's in the south, towards Greece. There's a possibility I'll be taking the refugee route over the border into Albania. I found myself saying yes even though I'm as fond of my skin as the next... Well, they are expecting all hell to break loose in the province at any minute. Maybe even pitched battles or NATO air strikes...'

'It's spooky,' said Digger Rooney, his fingernails clutching each side of his head, focusing attention on his new butch hair-style. 'Wasn't it supposed to go quiet like this in the First World War? Before bombardments and things began? Before you got blown to bits?' He had been flicking through the pages of *Sight and Sound*, the in-house magazine produced by the large media group Radio Brum was part of.

Mitch looked up from her letter. 'Was Ellie Peters before your time, Digger?'

'Who she?'

'One of the best damn radio journalists we ever had, that's who,' said Quentin Plunkett. Taking off his cans, he picked up the spool of tape he'd been editing and dropped it in the pouch at the front of his fisherman's sailcloth top. Yellow leader dribbled over his portentous belly. 'Married some Yank. Ten years ago, was it? Quite a turn-up. Pretty much an old boot in the looks department, our Ellie.'

'Rubbish. You think any woman's ugly if she doesn't kowtow. If she's knocking spots off the chaps,' said Mitch. 'Anyway, she's in Bosnia at the moment, apparently setting up a radio station or showing the locals how us lot do it. She seemed to sink without trace for years and then her husband died and now this ... back in harness and having a whale of a time. God. I wish I knew more about the situation there. The only thing I remember about the old Yugoslavia is going on holiday with my daughter Cassie when she was a little kid and the men chucking cigarettes at me. I mean, lets get real. What's so scary about Kosovo, for instance?'

'For a start British troops are to be sent to the borders of the region. The idea is that they'll help to stop any civil war there from starting a wider Balkan conflict. Most of the population are Muslim Albanians with a few Roman Catholic Albanians thrown in and that's the language spoken. However, the Serbs, who are Orthodox and a tiny minority, regard Kosovo as the cradle of their civilisation. It's always been pretty remote, mostly surrounded by mountains, a sort of cracked plateau bisected by hills.'

Mitch and Digger turned to stare at Quentin. He said: 'It's only what any half-educated person would know.'

'I always went out of the room when any part of the Balkans came up on the news. I still go out of the room when the IRA beam up,' said Digger. 'Always seems the perfect time to put the kettle on or do the washing up. I mean, talk about yawn.'

'I suppose starving babies make you yawn, too.'

'To be truthful, yes. I mean, the world is saturated with bombs and starving babies and torture and all these berks trying to make me feel guilty about something I've had no part in. Just pisses me off. I'd rather wash the pots.'

'Pilate washed his hands.'

'Yeah. Well. Christianity would have had a

hard time if he hadn't.'

'Digger!'

'Come on, Mitch. When did you listen to some crap about the peace process on the news? I bet, like most of the nation, you just tune out.'

'You are appalling.'

'You can get bored rigid with anything if it's shoved down your throat in never-ending bucketfuls. That might be a long way from being politically correct but it *is* the truth.'

Mitch decided to ignore him. 'Come on, Quentin. How come you know so much about what'sitsname?'

'Kosovo. The so-called lost heart of the Balkans. My grandfather was a mining engineer with a British company working in the region in the twenties. Lead and zinc. It's mineral-rich. My grandmother did coloured sketches of the people. You know, gipsy women with plaits and baggy pants with knee-length aprons over them, patriarchs in cylindrical hats and long black robes. They were all round the walls of my nursery. I grew up in a sort of Student Prince never-never land.'

Mitch found herself staring at Quentin. It seemed grotesque to her that any child could become Quentin Plunkett, the pompous Colonel Nobody of a provincial music scene. Mother Nature at her bitchiest and trickiest. But who would recognise me as the five-year-old I once was? Truly, that is some other person.

'I got Christopher Robin,' said Digger. 'You could say I never stood a chance. And Peter Pan collars and bar shoes. Everyone else's mother was into Paddington Bear. Tough little guy in Wellington boots and anorak. A hot-shot boysie traveller from Peru.'

Mitch ignored him. 'Muslims. Two sorts of Christians. I always found the religious thing confusing. I thought Yugoslavia was Communist.'

'When I was there for a couple of vacs during my student days nothing seemed to have changed much outside the capital. I actually went to an Orthodox saint's day festival. Outside the church the women laid the food out for the men and then retired. When the chaps had had their fill they ate the leftovers. Sacks for carrying. That's the phrase they used about women. Their only use was to breed the next generation of men. No matter what the religion, it's a fiercely patriarchal society. I don't know what they'll make of our Ellie.'

'Times might have changed,' said Mitch.

'I wouldn't bank on that,' said Digger. 'I'd stick to rainy days in Brum if I were you. Even if you're a chap words like patriarch aren't good news unless you're seriously into sado-masochism.' Digger dropped his nose back in the company's magazine. 'Listen to this. Management are spending two million quid on a new logo. If we've got any queries we can – among other people – contact Guidelines and Information, Vehicle Delivery, Radio Design, Legal, Corporate and General Stationery and Finance and Budgeting. Do you think that all bureaucrats are crackers? Or is it just me?'

'If you'd been committee-oriented, you wouldn't be sitting here. You'd be somebody,' Quentin said.

'Who?' Mitch asked herself.

Quentin, turning to her, said: 'Someone who didn't have to produce programmes for Toytown radio and run a half-baked detective agency to make up the jolly old pay cheque.'

'Well, you work down in the salt mines with the rest of us,' said Digger.

'Just goes to show.' The music producer stood up.

'What?'

'The sheer hell of not being a committee man. Are you going bald?' Quentin began to examine Digger's head with all the suspicion of an old-fashioned nit nurse.

'That's a lie. That's more than being economical with the truth. That's slander.'

'In my experience incipient baldies go in for these close-cropped butch hair-styles.'

Quentin flicked his head and a flashing heavy wing of hair dipped in Digger's direction. 'Anyway, I shouldn't have thought butch was you. Fairies aren't supposed to be butch.'

'Fat lot you know.'

'Children, children,' said Mitch.

'And I'm not going bald!'

'If the organisation's shooting for a new image I don't see why Digger shouldn't,' said Mitch, and then to Digger: 'What's his name? Come on. Give.'

'Trevor, actually.'

'I knew it! You're entitled to a different hair-style when you get a new lover.' Mitch ruefully ruffled her own hair. 'Can't remember the last time I changed my barnet.'

'Well before my time.' said Quentin. 'And I've been here over ten years. Mitchell, you're so far past your sell-by date you're almost retro.'

'Listen to him! The last time you blew your trumpet you screwed up your granny's gas lighting.'

'Mitch...'

She swung round to face the opening production office door, her flying boots almost hitting a boxed pile of old *Mitch Mitchell Investigates* tapes. She conjured her body into a working position, legs demurely under her desk. 'That's me.'

'Have you a mo? In my office?' The station

36

manager was wearing a white cotton polo-necked sweater under a pink pinafore, cut in the fashion of maternity wear. Most of the clothes Freya Adcock chose suggested that she was three months pregnant, though her belly had never got any larger. 'Of course, we don't know the gestation period of were-wolves,' Digger had said. 'Nor flying pigs, for that matter.'

'Sure,' Mitch answered her. Her heart seemed to slip in its bony frame.

'Five minutes, kiddo. I want to pop into the studio first. All right? OK?' she said, looking at Digger and Quentin. 'Keep up the good work.' The door banged behind her.

'What's it all about?' Mitch wondered.

'Behind closed doors? Bad news, I'd say,' said Quentin.

'She usually comes straight out with it. If it's a minor offence,' said Digger.

'Thanks. Thanks a bunch.'

'She's already doing the summer schedules,' said Quentin. 'I'm supposed to record some brass bands. "Oh, we do like to be beside the seaside." That sort of stuff. Jolly hols music.'

'Birmingham's at least a hundred miles in any direction from the coast,' said Digger.

'Who in their right mind would take a jolly hol in Brum?' Mitch asked.

'There's the lake in Cannon Hill Park. I

suppose they have boats. There's the Floozie in the Jacuzzi in the city centre. We could take over her bath. Though shifting a statue might prove difficult,' said Digger.

'She can have wall-to-wall sitar music if that's what it takes to keep *More Maestro Please* on air in the dog days of summer. No one stops sending in bills just because it's August,' said Quentin.

'You think she might take some of the regular programmes off the air in the holiday months?' Mitch was aware her voice was rising. She made an effort to control it. 'She's never done that before. She believes in continuity. She's always on about continuity. You know she is.'

'She went on that programme schedule training thing after Christmas,' Digger said. 'She came back full of words like strands. Strands this. Strands that. Seriously strands.'

'Oh God. That's right.' Mitch considered this. 'But strands have been the in thing for years. So that's all right. Isn't it?'

'You've got to be honest, Mitch,' said Digger. 'Things about care in the community and inner city schools are hardly August progs.'

'If we're seriously into audience building they aren't the sort of stuff to broadcast at all,' said Quentin. 'The only people who listen are those in them. And they only tune in to hear what they sound like on radio.'

'Do you seriously think the TWGP Workers' Band playing "We do like to be beside the seaside" pulls in the punters?'

'You'd be surprised.'

'I would,' said Mitch, standing up. 'I certainly would. Anyway, this station is supposed to be committed to making some serious investigative stuff.'

'I read the publicity hand-outs, too. But who does what they say these days?'

'Trevor,' said Digger. 'And on top of that what you see is what you get. Oooooh, oooh, ah-ah-*harh*.'

'God. You're a dirty devil,' said Mitch.

'Envy will get you nowhere.'

'Thank God,' said Quentin.

Mitch, opening the production office door, was already wondering what she could come up with if Freya cut off her life support systems. Could she turn a penny being an on-air agony aunt? Maybe a series on really gruesome illnesses? People would love that? 'Sure they would,' she said to the door as she walked into the cloakroom. 'But would I be able to stomach it? Oh, if only the detective agency were doing better.' She dumped her handbag on the tiled ledge in front of the wall-to-wall mirror above the wash-basins. She got out her armoury. A little bit of glitz on her eyelids, a more scarlet shade of gloss on her lips, fingers then pushing her hair up, teasing it out, making her head bigger. 'Quentin's right. Why, oh why, didn't I become a committee-type person? I'm too old to be scratting around for the equivalent of dog ends. Why didn't I go the bureaucratic politicking route? Whatever made me think *working* was the way?'

Suddenly she snapped her shoulders back, adjusted her scarlet waistcoat, resettled the cream floppy bow at the neck of her soft satin blouse and looked herself in the eye. 'Do shut up whingeing,' she told her reflection. 'Get out there and perform.'

'Aye, aye, captain.' She snapped a salute. But her black-trousered bum rode the air like a heavily laden cargo boat as she made her way down the corridor to Freya Adcock's office. Out of strategically placed orifices in the ceiling the station's output dripped over her head, chilling rain.

The door to Freya's office was open. Mitch knew that this was supposed to convey to the staff that the station manager was not the station manager at all, but a member of a team who could be called on to help out at any time. But as the workers wished to appear super-efficient, in order to keep their jobs, any problems they had they kept to themselves.

'Close the door,' Freya said without raising her head from the papers she was studying. She was sitting behind an executive-sized mahogany desk, papers and boxed tapes of programmes neatly stacked about the outer rim. Two large plastic clip-on earrings sat by the phone. 'Take a pew.' Frequently she came round to the front of the desk and, hoisting her buttocks, sat on a corner, signalling this was going to be a friendly chat. This afternoon she not only remained behind it, but continued reading, leaving Mitch to view the pictures on the wall, all artistically distorted computer images of Birmingham's landmarks. Mitch crossed her legs and then uncrossed them.

Freya took a yellow marker pen, ran it through some of the print and then pushed the papers away. 'Sorry about that,' she said, leaning back in her chair and surveying Mitch. Her baby-soft hair, threaded with pink ribbon, bobbed as she nodded to herself. Mitch felt as if she'd been sized up for her coffin by a funeral director tricked out as a 1930s female child star. 'And how is the Mitchell and Orient Detective Agency going? If only I had a second string to my bow. Broadcasting is so very uncertain.'

'We've been very busy but it's quietening down a bit now.'

'And Tommy Hung? What a dear man. You're so lucky to have found such a super business partner. That's half the battle, I should think.'

'He's fine.' Mitch found she'd picked up her handbag and placed it firmly on her lap, bang in front of her heart. She was holding on to it as if it were a shield.

'That's excellent. Jolly good.' Freya was drawing another sheaf of papers towards her. She briskly patted them into a neat shoe box shape. 'This summer I've decided to try out one or two new voices. Ring the changes so to speak. One hardly wants doom and gloom in the holiday months. Though, of course, we'll always examine the big issues. When the time is right.'

Mitch wondered whether to jump in with proposals for an agony aunt pilot, or maybe live shows from the back of a vice squad car or a casualty department, for it was obvious that the schedules were in front of Freya and Mitch, adept at reading upside down, saw *Mitch Mitchell Investigates* wasn't among the names of the programmes. The schedules themselves were somehow different, too, and then Mitch realised they were combined. She was reading 'Spring' and 'Summer'. Two of her heartbeats crashed into each other.

Has the bitch dropped me for two seasons?

Better not start pitching now, though, the general in Mitch warned her. I need to *think*. Then plan a proper campaign.

A long silence developed between them.

Mitch found she wasn't going to ask about her show. Let the bitch tell her. And may she choke on it.

Freya leaned forward. 'I've decided to take *Mitch Mitchell Investigates* off the air.'

'Permanently?' It was Mitch who choked. Half the word was trapped in her throat.

Freya had no difficulty in understanding her. 'I haven't made up my mind about that yet. It has been running for quite a while now. Maybe some new thoughts are necessary? But one doesn't want to be rushed into making a decision, does one?'

Mitch became aware that her fingers were itching. She'd have liked to lean over, grab Freya by the neck of her sweater and whack her across the cheek. The explosion of rage took her by surprise. Freya was oblivious to it. She leaned even further forward. '*Mitch Mitchell Investigates* has had a really good run, kiddo. You must agree there. Still, *The Mousetrap* went on for ever. One mustn't be too hasty. I do see that. We'll think about it. Plenty of time, after all. Anyway, not to be despondent. There's a possibility of other work coming your way. Do you remember Sissy Childe?'

'The television cook?' Mitch's head was filled with a vision of a woman the size of a Sumo wrestler dressed in a silk tent patterned with dazzling optical illusions. Her arm was locked round Freya's waist

43

and the pair of them were high-kicking their way across the production office floor.

'We are ... the girls from Higher Cheam,
We have ... the most terrific team,
We are ... the girls who always score,
More and more and *more!*
Re-ra, re-ra, ra-ra-ra!

'We went to school together,' Freya said.
'I remember.'
'She was very taken with you, you know.'
She was even more taken with Marco Rice, Mitch remembered and almost groaned. That woman had practically snatched her lover from out of her bed. But whatever made you think you could get away with having a toy boy? she asked herself. And what a little shit he turned out to be.
'Is Marco Rice still working for her?'
'Who?'
'You know. He used to work here.'
'Oh, him. The one with the bad back. No idea. The thing is she's in Birmingham at the moment. She's doing a pilot for a new series with one of these little independent producers. They're thinking of using Stratford for some outdoor location work. You know, ye olde English recipes. But easy ones. Not stuff twelve blackbirds or anything gruesome like that.'

'What a politically correct Hamlet may have had for his dinner?'

'Exactly. Got it in one. She was very impressed, you know, with the Mitchell and Orient Bureau's work on the Late Knights' case. To come to the point, you'll be hearing from her.' She corrected herself. 'You should be hearing from her.'

'I'm no cook. Honestly.'

'Oh, you don't have to convince me of that, kiddo.'

'I'm not that bad!'

'Whatever makes you think it's about cooking, anyway? I got the impression it was some sort of investigation she had in mind. Anyway, this is all beside the point. What I was thinking of was that we'd run *Mitch Mitchell Investigates* to Easter. That's when your contract ends, isn't it? Haven't the builders almost finished converting that canal-side chapel of yours? I expect you could do with a bit more free time to move in and get settled down. Quite a project you took on there.'

'Maybe I could do a bit of interviewing for the breakfast show. Or some lighter stuff for *Hometime*.'

'Well, you could ask their producers. But they are running very tight budgets. And there's no shortage of odd bods to help out. Experienced personnel are so hellishly expensive. Anyway, that's up to you, kid.'

'I won't hold my breath, then.'

'Much the best attitude to take. Get a bit of the old leisure time in while you can. Life's not all work, you know.'

4

'When did he start?' Mitch Mitchell was anxiously looking at Tommy Hung's closed office door. 'God, how I hate figures. I hate my fleshly figure. I really *loathe* my bum. And I hate figures that are supposed to add up and make a profit and never do.' She'd known as soon as she'd woken up that this was going to be a bad day which was why she was wearing scarlet. Black was for good days only.

'You're not usually a pessimist,' said A.J., who was sorting through Mitchell and Orient's post. 'We may be having a bit of a lull now but we've been really busy. Look!' She was pulling a cheque out of an envelope. 'Isn't that just gorgeous!' She bent a dark head, her pony tail splaying over the shoulder of her white shirt as she kissed it. 'Who said detective agencies never made money?'

'Tommy. And he's the only one who's been keeping the remotest eye on the pennies. If it turns out we're just about breaking even ... well, that's not bad is it? For the first year in business?'

'I do know we were in profit for the month

before last. He told me,' said A.J. 'Then there was that lovely big cheque from the Glick Hope Institute.'

'It sounds OK when you put it like that, but the truth is, honeypot, I've never been in profit. It's God's way of keeping me humble.'

'Cheer up. Anyway, isn't Monday your day at the radio station? Just think of it. If we *are* in the black you can give up your broadcasting job.'

'Broadcasting might be giving me up. Freya's dropping me from the spring and summer schedules. She's trying out some new voices. I've a gut feeling this may be the parting of the ways. It couldn't be happening at a worse time. God. Do I need the money. Do you have any idea of how much dense aggregate block is? These are hideous apologies for proper bricks, right? Sort of baby breeze block. Forty-five pence *each*. Not mentioning seventeen and a half per cent VAT on top. Now they've found death watch beetle in the roof timbers. I thought that was some kind of myth to do with church towers. Whatever made me think turning a chapel into a house was a good idea? I sold my home so I could raise more working capital for the detective agency. Now I find the price I got for it and more is likely to be sunk into this conversion.'

'I thought it was all going so well.'

'Well, the builders are certainly getting on with the job and even the architect is not moaning about the quality of the workmanship. But every time they unpick another bit of the fabric they find a horror story. The price of the job just keeps notching up. It's scary. It doesn't help to know that the guy I bought the place from went bankrupt. I'll never forget seeing all the oblongs of lighter colour on the floor where his printing machinery had once stood. Sometimes I even get to thinking God is seriously displeased. He's putting the monikers on anyone who has the brass neck to try anything but hymn-singing in what was once a place of worship. Crackers, I know. But if you saw some of the bills landing on my doorstep you'd start to lose it.'

'Maybe it's what happened there that's getting to you. I wouldn't live there. Not after that.'

'You mean the mad doctor and the night I nearly got shoved off my perch? To be honest, I don't remember much about that.' But suddenly the doctor was there, his giant shadow flickering in the candlelight. He was whispering in her ear: 'This is case clickety click. The body is that of a well-developed, well-nourished fifty-year-old Caucasian female with black hair and brown eyes. The body is sixty-four inches long and weighs a hundred pounds.' *But I'm not dead!* The scream would not come, could not come because her muscles were paralysed.

'Mitch!'

'What? Oh–' She was aware of her feet seesawing, of sweat leaking out of skin dissolving in fright. She sat down abruptly on the chesterfield couch which was placed at right angles to the agency's reception desk.

'Are you all right?'

'That's never happened before.'

'What?'

'Well, I've never been able to remember anything. Not about what actually happened in there that night. It's always been a blank.'

'You mean, you've had some kind of flashback?'

'I'm OK. Just took me by surprise, that's all. I mean ... really...' Goosepimpled now and looking around the reception area of the detective agency, needing to construct her world again. Her eye found out the oil painting of the stern female Victorian, bequeathed to the newly fledged agency by one of Mitch's ex-lovers. She felt her backbone stiffening. Tommy Hung had placed the picture so that it was the first thing prospective clients saw when they crossed the threshold. 'Detectives have a very sleazy image,' he'd told her and their assistant A.J.

'Here, my dears, is rectitude, reputation, reliability.' Totally shameless, he'd ordered the small plaque which had been screwed into the wall beneath the portrait. The legend read: 'H.R.H. Mitchell 1868-1941.' The strange thing was that over the months Mitch had come to realise that the woman looked very much like a great-aunt of hers. With a slight reshuffle of the genes this monster of probity could be her. Tommy had reinforced their ancestry with as much mahogany and button-back leather as he could squeeze into what had once been a terraced house. No one had yet had the heart to tell him that the harem-style lamps were misplaced, more a borrowing from backgrounds in Victorian artists' studies of rotund nudes than furnishings from a gentlemen's club. The whole terrace, which fronted the canal in the Gas Street Basin in the heart of the city, now accommodated small businesses.

She became aware again of A.J.'s anxiety. 'Honestly. I'm all right. No problems. Really. Apart from builders' escalating bills and no money coming in from broadcasting this summer. If only the agency could hook a couple of wealthy clients with the kind of cases which take ages to solve. Good money spinners.' Mitch stared in the direction of her partner's office. 'What's taking him so long? I mean, what are all these electronic gadgets for if not to tell you in two seconds flat what deep shit you're in?'

'Something will turn up. You'll see. In fact, I got a call in from a woman this morning. She wouldn't talk to Tommy or me.'

'Why didn't you say? Give me the phone—'

A.J. was shaking her dark head. 'She wouldn't leave her name or number. Said she'd try again. Talk about cagey...'

Mitch got to her feet. She was glad to find they acted as though a floor was beneath them. 'I'll be in my office.'

'What about the radio station? You're supposed to be there today.'

'You're worse than my dad was. The young aren't supposed to be conscientious. They're all Cool Britannia. You know. Slobs. Oh, if Freya rings tell her I've gone off to interview Roz Parker.'

'Who's she?'

'Doesn't exist as far as I know. If Freya can ditch me I can ditch her. Right?'

'But Mitch—'

'Don't worry. I'll do these last two programmes I'm contracted to do. But in my own way and my own time. She's lucky I didn't duff her up. I felt like it. New voices. What the hell's wrong with the old ones?' However Mitch, climbing the stairs to her first-floor office, knew exactly what was wrong with them. *Old voices were worn-out voices. Right?*

Well, don't say you didn't know it was going to be a shitty day. That's why you're in screaming scarlet.

She opened her office door, kicking it closed behind her. She dumped her handbag and a plastic Tesco bag full of assorted taped interviews, notes, to do lists concerning the building work at the former chapel and two rye crispbreads spread with cottage cheese. Her lunch. She was on a diet again. Perhaps that was another reason she felt so down in the dumps. No blood sugar. She wandered over to the window. Canal waters glittered and frisked, long boats dipping, pennants snapping. On the other side of Gas Street Basin a youth was cleaning down tables on the apron of paving in front of the revamped Edwardian pub. Even though the window was shut, she could hear the distant growl of city traffic, a sound as reassuring to her as any mother's lullaby.

She turned when she heard Tommy Hung's step on the stairs. A.J., though she was slim and her young limbs full of grace, always sounded like an articulated lorry changing gears as she roared up from the ground floor. Tommy didn't quite shuffle, more the steady, rhythmical noise of a plane shaving wood.

He appeared in the doorway, this morning looking like an oriental English gentleman about to step into some exclusive members' enclosure. Mitch remembered that the cricket season was not far off. She watched him appraise her office, the black and chrome Italian leather seating, the blond wood, the palm tree by the window. She knew that he thought it looked like an office in a car salesroom, naff Brummagen glitz. When things were not going well and he felt himself to be blameless, he often let her see him disparagingly survey her habitat. He was letting her know that if she had more taste, if she in some way could only come up to scratch, they could overcome the difficulties they found themselves in.

'Not good news, I take it?'

'No.'

'How bad?'

Over the sound of her heart, which had started to bang alarmingly, he said: 'I think we'll have to make some kind of decision by the end of the summer.'

'That bad.'

'I'm afraid all the expenses mount up so. Rent, rates, wages, electricity, water, phones. You must take a look at the figures.'

'What good would that do? Two and two will still add up to four, won't they? You don't need to be a mathematical genius to get the picture.'

'Things could still buck up. The trouble is that the work is so lumpy. No even cash flow. One just about thinks one's really got off the ground and then as the silence lengthens one realises take-off's been aborted again.'

'Sorry,' said Mitch.

'It's not your fault.' However, he was looking round her office again.

'Advertising? It produced some results last time.'

'It's a possibility.' Tommy was cautious. If he spent money he liked to get something substantial for it, like button-back leather chesterfields. He regarded a three-column ad on a flimsy bit of newsprint a very poor return.

With that in mind, and knowing his yearning to rub shoulders with the toffs, Mitch said: 'What about the glossies? Real quality. Maybe *Country Life*. Even aristos are human. I mean, some of them must be in need of a private detective. Maybe not.' None of the Upper Crust would dream of buying their clothes in Birmingham. Was it likely they'd shop for their private eyes here?

'Actually, my dear, that could be worth considering.' A light bulb had lit up in Tommy's head. His face shone. Looking inscrutable had always seemed quite beyond him. He'd started off as a Chinese laundry boy working below decks in the British navy. She knew a padre had taught him public school English and imbued in him a love of

Sherlock Holmes stories. That was as much as he'd tell her about his past. She guessed that he had jumped ship at some time and surmised he'd gone into the restaurant trade for he was certainly a good cook. Now he presented himself as a prosperous retired seventy-year-old, your late twentieth-century dilettante detective, though he'd always made it clear his purse was not bottomless. She liked him. He was a good guy. She also thought that investigating his past might uncover a real bastard. You didn't start off life in a Hong Kong slum and land up a moneyed gent in an exclusive flat in Edgbaston by being Mr Nice Guy. However, though their partnership had sometimes been stormy, she could never accuse him of being less than a gentleman. In fact his Goody Two-Shoes prissiness often got right up her nose.

As the phone began to ring she stretched out her hand for the receiver.

'Before you leave you must look at the figures,' he told her. 'You are not a little child. You must not hide away.'

'Sure,' she said and at the same time thinking: Not today. The sums may stack up the same tomorrow but I'll be different.

'Am I talking to Mitch Mitchell?'

The voice was familiar. 'Yes.'

'Sissy Childe.'

'Nice to hear from you.' Mitch began

edging a pad towards her. 'How are things? Freya said you might be in touch.' She heard her office door shut, Tommy making his way downstairs.

'Listen, kid, can we meet? I was thinking sometime late this afternoon. I'm up here to do a series. We're based in Stratford-upon-Avon. Antique recipes, that sort of thing. You know, take ten swans–'

'Surely you can't do that. Take ten swans?'

'Can't take a dozen blackbirds, either, and bake them in a pie. Believe me, antique recipes and political correctness don't mix too well.'

'How are you getting round that?' Mitch knew the conversation was going off track, but was nevertheless curious.

'We're strong on things like pike. You'd be surprised at how good pike can taste.'

'If Sainsbury's don't stock it I'm never going to find out.'

'That's exactly the producer's point. Tickle the palate of the food buffs. Nosh out there beyond the supermarkets. Real alternative eating.'

'Glad I'm not a pike.'

'Sweetheart, there are already a blancmange of food shows on offer. You've got to be different. Anyway, all this is by the by. Can we fix up a meet? I'm coming into Birmingham. Be around five o'clock. I've got something on in the city later only don't tell

Freya. She'll be peeved I haven't called her.'

'Sure,' said Mitch. If she were playing hooky the less said the better. 'What about my office?'

'Isn't there a pub across the basin? Teddy's or something? We've met there before. Remember?'

'OK. Teddy's at five. What's this all about, Sissy?'

'We'll talk about it when we see each other, OK? Got to fly, kid. I'll tell you one thing. Antique recipes are the best way yet of losing weight.'

Mitch put the receiver down. She began to restlessly patrol the floor of her office. God, it was at times like this she really missed a cigarette. Why is it that everything you enjoy is bad for you? She remembered Marco Rice, surely young enough to be her son, and that astonishing interlude when they'd been alone together in Radio Brum's production office. He'd been snatched from under her nose by the predatory Sissy and for all Mitch knew could still be sharing the cook's bed. The trouble is that when you're my age, she thought, you've had too much past and a lot of it's very undignified. In fact in her experience dignity and being human just didn't go together. Too much knickers and zips, lavatories, boils, death and tripping over. The order in the chaos was surely an illusion.

It was at this point that Mitch decided, after all, to go and do her stint at the radio station. At least if she swung into the usual routine it would clear her head of all this rubbish. But how to get out of the place without being waylaid by Tommy and a fistful of figures? She glanced at the window, full of a startling image of herself clambering over the sill and down Rapunzel's hair; an escaping back view flitting along the towpath. In the event she descended by the stairs and told A.J. and Tommy, emerging from his office with spread sheets clutched to his heart: 'Can't stop. Fish on the line. Be in touch later.' She slammed the door after her and speeded round the block and up the ginnel to collect her car from the street behind the canal basin. She'd finally held a funeral party for her old TVR and had bought the kind of nondescript car which Tommy said all private detectives must have; it was a completely reliable three-year-old grey Ford Escort. Up to now, Mitch had resisted the impulse to have it sprayed hot rod pink.

The rush hour traffic was over but there was a build-up on Bristol Road even though the resurfacing at Middleway Junction had been completed. As she swung left into the leafy road which led to the broadcasting centre, five storeys built round a courtyard with a bit jutting out of the end like the tail of a squared Q, she saw a sea of people. The centre's security force was out in numbers, herding the crowd into three ribbons, on pavements on each side of the road and fanning down a wide grass strip in the middle. Some youngsters had climbed surrounding trees, one middle-aged woman had brought a short pair of steps with her, not tall enough for her to sit in judgement like a tennis umpire, but high enough to see over the massed heads in front. The security men were low key, laughing and joking with people in the crowd, pretending not to see the tree dwellers. There was a lot of muscle in the gently moving ribbons; too much hassle from an officious policing force could close these rag-tag ranks, form invading battering rams.

'What on earth's going on?' Mitch asked the man who was controlling the car-park gate. She was holding up her security pass.

'Oa Bone's in the building. Doing a bit of a chat for the half-past six telly opt-out. About five hundred people out there. That's more than turned up for the Queen!'

'Well, he is a classic,' said Mitch. 'His songs are part of many people's salad days.'

'Me included,' said the guard. The bar lifted and Mitch drove through to the back of the building. The car-park was full except for slots reserved for radio news cars. Against the rules, she slid into one of the two held open for Radio Brum. If she were lucky, she'd be all right until lunchtime. She gathered herself and her plastic bags together and went into the broadcasting centre by the back way, along a corridor lined with props cages. She emerged into the wider, light-filled corridor which tracked three sides of the inner courtyard. The fourth side, at the front of the building, consisted of reception areas and a large foyer television studio from which lunchtime shows were broadcast.

Today the courtyard itself had been co-opted into a studio and she could see by the state of unreadiness that it was not going to be used for the lunchtime show but Midlands Live, the regional television news magazine which went out in the early evening. From the bustle of figures at one end it appeared they were going to pre-record one item. The figures separated out and between the tracks of cabling, headphones, cameras and clipboards she got a back view of a bending figure wearing elasticated skin-tight jodhpurs, calf-high leather boots with soles like blunt instruments and a white, blouselike shirt tucked in at the waist.

'A bum to die for,' moaned a voice behind her.

'I take it you're not referring to mine,' said Mitch.

'Sorry, angel,' said Digger.

'Shouldn't you be in the studio?'

'Had to nip down and see him. Oh, to be back in the Sixth Form again. All blackheads and yearning. Lusting after the most improbable types.' Digger began to sing softly:

'Well, you've got it wrong,
Hey, you're not my song,
You're just some ordinary babe-ee-ee
Who's driving me craze-ee-ee...'

'Haven't we all been there, honeypot. Much of my life has been spent mooning over men who are nothing more than retread two-year-olds. You know?' said Mitch. 'What's Oa Bone doing in Birmingham? I thought he'd retired or something.'

'He's doing a live charity show tomorrow night at the Exhibition Centre. They're hoping to raise money for Kosovar refugees.'

'I thought the conflict hadn't started there yet. At least, not so's you'd notice.'

'Apparently Muslims are already streaming over the borders into Albania. We're doing a little spot on it on my show. Couldn't get Oa, of course. I'm having to interview some little PR person with an attitude problem. Either that or nothing doing. No pull. That's the trouble with local radio.'

As Oa Bone turned, Digger moved forward, cramming his face into the window. 'It was so *hot*. You know, when you're really young. All those hormones doing somersaults, I suppose.'

'Cool is less cruel,' said Mitch. A bouncing fringe fell across Oa Bone's forehead, wings of curling black hair swinging over his ears to shadow his cheeks. His head was long and lean, like his body. What could be seen of his face appeared corroded, as if he'd lived in acid, not air. 'Imagine what you must have crammed into your life to look like that. Just imagine.'

'I don't dare,' said Digger. 'Far too scary.'

5

Mitch, who wanted to do some research in the city library before she met Sissy Childe, left the radio station early. She'd also promised Digger she'd call at a nearby art gallery to collect some stuff about a forthcoming exhibition. 'I'll eat my hat if someone's actually painted a picture,' said Digger. 'It'll all be installations. Giant mousetraps baited with human dummies. All that kind of gear. Statements made for museum spaces. Nothing for the likes of you and me.'

Mitch, collecting her stuff, like an anxious bird wobbling about with nesting straw, said: 'Art was always élitist, honeypot.'

'It's there,' said Digger.

'What?'

'Your handbag.'

'So it is. See you.'

It was three thirty on a fine March day, full of the external roar of the internal combustion engine, giant skeleton trees dressed in baby buds and the occasional remnant of weathered rubbish drifting through the shiny air. The mid-morning crowds had dispersed from round the broadcasting centre, presumably because Oa Bone was no longer in the building. Mitch, turning the grey Ford Escort towards Bristol Road, thought the practical plan would be to park at Masshouse and walk through the city, stopping off where necessary to do her errands.

Much of Masshouse was at the bottom of a circular cavity, concrete walling and pillars supporting arterial roads overhead. She parked her car, looked up to see the wheels of an articulated lorry roaring along, and then made her way to Dingley Passage. She had plenty of time, she could stroll, she tried to stroll, but this city moved to faster rhythms and she found she was pulled into the hurried pace of those shoulder to shoulder with her. She crossed through the main shopping district, to the small, almost inconspicuous cathedral which lay at the centre of lawns, its Burne-Jones glass shielded by stout wire mesh. If this cathedral had ever embodied Birmingham's spirit, which Mitch doubted, it had been supplanted by the welcoming legs of the bitch of creation in Victoria Square. Here the Floozie in the Jacuzzi lolled in her lotus leaf, her large greeny bottom sunk in juices which cascaded down flights of steps to another pool. The second pool was the dwelling place of a pair of serious-faced apprentice lovers, the kind, she thought, who'd never get the hang of it all. Mitch had long ago given them two out of ten and decided psycho-sexual counselling wouldn't help. The iron man, rearing by bollards near the edge of the square, certainly looked full of power but he'd been trussed up. Problems, problems, Mitch thought. Even statues have problems. Soon she would have to look at hers. But not now. Not on a screaming scarlet dress day.

The library was a series of inverted mucky concrete wedges, like a section of a pyramid stood on its head, a design so brutalised by unsympathetic materials that its art deco inspiration was totally lost. Mitch, who intended to do a programme on what it was like for victims of violence to pick up the threads of their lives again, was there to look at some newspaper reports of trials. Tracking down the VDU towards the end of her research, she came across a three-year-old story about Oa Bone raising money for Bosnian refugee children. 'In a way, this is for Geoff Stark,' he was quoted as saying and Mitch had to search her mind. Hadn't that been the band's drummer who had died in the late eighties? Drugs?

'Geoff was brought up in children's homes and foster homes. In his early years he didn't get the breaks. When you're close to someone you can see how that works out in later life. As the song ... you know ... about money, hey, money can't buy you love. But anything that helps, even a little bit, that's got to be good. Geoff was a bit of a sinner but he'd be comfortable with this. His money is still doing a lot for a home-grown charity. He'd maybe be surprised that I've got round to doing something, too. Sometimes you do the right thing. It's no big deal.'

Bad boys playing saints?

Well, there were times when you had to change your image, she thought. Otherwise, you'd ossify. Isn't it, though, sometimes too late? She remembered Oa Bone's corroding face and wondered if he also had a corroding heart and liver. 'Life tends to find you out in the end,' her mother used to say as those who'd once done her down slid off the bottom of snakes into their coffins. However, it seemed hardly likely that Freya was going to do that in the near future. What kind of move was she going to make if the station manager axed her in the autumn and winter, too? She felt a flutter of panic.

The truth was that even those who thought of themselves as the good guys were shoved off ladders and plunged down snakes. And they hadn't even had the fun of misbehaving themselves.

Mitch sighed and switched off the VDU. She gathered up her notebook and dropped it in her capacious shoulder bag. All this anxiety is probably due to the food I'm not letting myself eat. Dieting might be good for the figure but it puts all those little grey cells in one hell of a crappy mood.

Outside, the sun still shone. Mitch hunched her shoulders as if it were raining. She collected Digger's press pack from the Bright Gallery, a parcel all done up in a plain brown wrapper and for all she knew containing a couple of condoms – wow, aren't we the daring ones, get your head round that – the unwritten message. Mitch pulled herself up. Stop being so cynical, she told herself. OK? What's wrong with kids having a bit of fun? Shake yourself out of this. But she knew she wouldn't be able to. That was the whole point of a screaming red dress day.

She made her way along the processional way – all patterned brick paving and in-your-face statues – to an elegant smoked glass and sea grey reinterpretation of art deco, signalling itself as the International Convention Centre. Under an apex of glass, lit with shards of red neon, she entered the foyer of the Symphony Hall. She was using this as a short cut to the canal beyond. She followed the towpath, passing banded walls of grey and rust brick, clip-clopping on her wedge-heeled shoes under the bridge and into the Gas Street Basin.

She was a little early for her meeting with Sissy Childe. She could drop into the office but she feared a lurking Tommy, hands full of spread sheets and doom. She could see what progress was being made on the conversion. She was reluctant to do that, too. What other horrors had been unearthed? Death watch beetle, for God's sake. *I can't afford it.* There. At last she'd admitted it to herself. Oh, what a mess she'd managed to get herself into. What a truly awful mess. All her affairs in financial disarray. What a time for Freya to pull the plug. Not that the money she earned from Radio Brum would alter the overall picture. The conversion was already running twenty-five per cent over budget and it was still six weeks from completion.

What I really need is a large gin, she thought and made her way to the Basin Tavern, which was known to everyone as Teddy's because of its fake Edwardian décor. She was trying to clear her mind of her troubles for she intended to pitch as hard as she could for the work on offer. Sissy Childe, she was thinking, built like a Sumo wrestler, all that flesh bouncing with life. Sissy, mouth open, in an improbable high-kicking routine with Freya:

'We are ... the girls from Higher Cheam,
We have ... the most terrific team,
We are ... the girls who always score,
More and more and *more!*'

Sissy, a life force who glows so much that everyone, and that includes me, is sort of dimmed. That had certainly always made her feel a little resentful. Not to mention the fact that the television cook had made off with her lover.

Still, she told herself, a job is a job. A gas bill doesn't have finer feelings.

She sighed and pushed open the door of Teddy's. The sweetish smell of beer, the brasswork and blood red wall coverings gently muted by cigarette smoke wrapped her agitated spirit. She moved to the bar, ordered her drink, not yet ready to look around to see if Sissy had arrived.

'Ace!'

That's her. She's here, Mitch thought as she swung from the bar but she couldn't see the cook.

'Ace!'

My God, there she is. A half-size Sissy, hair dyed white and stuck up like a sweeping brush, was sitting in a corner. She was wearing some kind of winkingly bright synthetic fibre suit in baby pink, silver platform shoes and yes, Mitch was not mistaken, there was a very large diamond in her nose. Moving nearer her, she saw that there was a doll-like smoothness about her forehead and cheeks. Had she gone in for cosmetic surgery? Had dieting sucked so much flesh out of her that her face had resembled an empty sugar bag? 'I didn't recognise you at first,' Mitch said. 'You've got a brand new figure.'

'It does throw people. Even throws me at times. I still act fat. You know, I won't push through a shop door with someone else because I think we'll get jammed.'

'How much weight have you lost?'

Sissy was not going to be drawn. 'A lot.'

'It suits you.' Mitch didn't know whether it did or not. It was disorienting.

'I see you're just the same as ever. Recognise you anywhere, soldier.'

'But what happened? I mean, why did you … God … it couldn't have been easy...'

'One day last summer. The phone didn't ring. Let's be honest, it hadn't rung for a while. Show biz cooking and Sissy Childe seemed to have got divorced. You know the game. One minute you're flavour of the month, the next people are embarrassed to know you. Actually, I was thinking I might break back with something like an eat yourself thinner series of shows. After all, I'd made my name by being the gross cook. Didn't work out like that at all, but losing all this weight did sort of get me talked about again. This little independent came up with the antique cooking idea. Niche market stuff but there's super potential here. And none of your crap studio backgrounds. Old money kitchens. Aspirational stuff. Me in this vaguely retro punkish kind of gear which says sort of wow, cutting edge, against these ye olde Jane-Austen-coddling-eggs backgrounds. You know? Syllabub with knobs on.'

'God. Different. Right?' Mitch, who had been desperately hunting around for something to say, had been perilously close to speechlessness. Been too long a broadcaster for that, thank God, she thought, her eye now taken with the large diamond in Sissy's nose which seemed to continually wink at her. Is it entirely *safe*, to wear something like that? she found herself wondering. I've done programmes with socially challenged Brummies who'd think nothing of ripping off her nose to get their hands on that rock, and not all of them druggies.

'Red suits you. You know that? Particularly that – well, what would you call it? Shouting scarlet?'

'Oh, this old thing. Been with me forever. Can I get you another drink?'

'Fizzy water. I see you haven't changed your ways. God. Even the smell of alcohol now seems to turn my stomach.'

'Well, I can't have another,' Mitch decided. She was aware of sagging, bones too glum to bother to hang together properly. 'Driving, you know.' She hauled herself up. She tried to keep contempt out of her voice. 'Fizzy water for two, then.'

When she came back within range of Sissy, the diamond was lowered, winking over the top of a lilac patent leather handbag the cook was fishing in. 'Ha. Here we are. What do you think, ace?' A lot of damson-coloured fingernails seemed to dangle in the air as she gave Mitch a photograph.

Mitch studied the picture carefully. A skinny young woman – late twenties? – stared solemnly back at her, dark hair pulled back and tied at the nape of her neck. She was wearing T-shirt, jeans and trainers. She had a lot of brow, good cheekbones and a long, curly, expressive mouth. Lips turned down just a fraction. Mitch, who was struck by the fact that the woman didn't resemble Sissy, didn't say that. She restricted herself to: 'An attractive lady.'

'Rosie. My half-sister. She's gone missing.'

Mitch waited for Sissy to say something else and when she didn't, she guessed: 'She's done it before?'

'Twice. Well, twice big time.'

'You've been in touch with the police?'

'Yes. But you know... well, doing it twice before... Let's be honest, they're hardly going to pull out the stops, are they?'

'She's not a child. People go missing all the time. How long's it been?'

'A week now.'

Mitch was staring at Sissy. She was finding

it hard to get past all this doll-smooth skin, to judge if Sissy were really seriously worried. But why call in a detective agency if she's not?

'Look...' Sissy stopped. Mitch waited. Eventually Sissy said: 'It sounds so ridiculous... If you were a man I'd never tell you this...'

Mitch waited.

'I had a dream. Oh God. I'm sounding like that American guy. Martin Luther what'sit... Three nights ago. No four now. It was a sort of awful pictorial cliché. It was off shore and Rosie was in the water waving at me. It was England. The water was grey and cold. Not the kind of water anyone would swim in. You know? And then I realised...'

'Not waving but drowning...'

'I can't tell you what kind of feeling came with the dream. It wasn't what I was seeing ... it was the feeling...'

'What kind of feeling?

'Grief. Shattering grief.'

Mitch could hear the murmur of other conversations in the background, some laughter. She said: 'Can you tell me something of your family background?'

'I was born in 1956. And to save you the mental effort, that adds up to forty-two. I'm pretty sure my parents married because I was on the way. People did in those days. At that time my father was trying to make his way as an actor. The Childes are a perfectly respectable family from the south-west who were in the cattle and land auction business for a couple of centuries. There were two sons. My father, the elder, was very bright and went to Cambridge where he got the acting bug. That was OK because Uncle Bobby went into the business. My mother was an East Ender, a Bluebell girl. You know, dancing in sequins and tights with a two-foot headdress on. Freakie or what? She was quite a bit older than my dad when they married but, and I'm guessing here, he didn't know that. As you can imagine, it was pretty much of a disaster but it was helped along for a while because my father was away quite a lot, doing bits and pieces in the provinces. My mother, I learned later, was already an alcoholic when they married and she died when I was eleven.

'The family raised enough money to send me to boarding school. It was at Higher Cheam that I met Freya. It was a good place. Rather prissy. Quaker leanings, but OK. Anyway, a year later Staffy – that's my dad, Stafford Leyton Childe would you believe – married Dee. Dorothy Holbrook. She was nineteen at the time. God knows what she saw in my dad. He was practically forty by then. I was thirteen when Rosie was born and you can imagine how I hated the idea of this little stepkid. Dee was bad enough. Wonderful hair though and this extraordinary porcelain skin. The helpless little I need a man to support me type.

'She'd picked the wrong one in Dad. I mean, he did in the end manage to get a few television parts and all that. But it was all bit stuff. Hand to mouth. It made him bitter. Failure sours people, you know? Like they were being fed little pieces of poison all the time. They get ill with it. He was always thinking the big break was round the corner. A maybe next week life...'

Mitch, who could almost sense a quivering in the air, said: 'Well, his track record didn't stop you. You made it big. You made it very big–'

'You didn't,' said Sissy. 'You were on telly at one time, weren't you?' She was weighing Mitch up, perhaps for the first time: 'But not making it big, it hasn't soured you. Quite the contrary.'

'I suppose it's how you look at it. To me, it's all adventure. Some things come off, some don't. That's what gives life its kick for me. There are no winners. Not in the long run.'

'I wish I had your attitude.'

'No you don't. Anyway, attitude is wired in. You're very focused and that's perhaps another word for obsessional. As long as I'm in there, you know, dancing, doing, well, it's OK.' And then, catching sight of the blazing linen mix of her dress, she added: 'Most days it's OK. I don't know what brought this on. You were telling me about Rosie, right?'

'Rosie...' The timbre of her voice had changed, becoming softer, more full-throated. 'I was set to hate this awful brat. I mean, I pretty much despised her mother. It was the craziest thing. Rosie simply fell for me. Just like a crush. I mean, she'd trot after me everywhere. When she was older she'd sit on the step waiting for me to come back from the shops or whatever. It was very flattering. She simply totally and absolutely demanded that I liked her. It's hard not to like someone who thinks you're wonderful. It really was just the oddest thing. No one could understand it, particularly not Dee. But there it was. This little thing adored me. Actually, she gave me my name. Sissy. She couldn't get her tongue round Feodora and who can blame the poor little sod. My mother must have been pissed out of her head when she named me. Feodora. It sounds like a hat.'

'Fedora.'

'Too true. In one way Rosie's life mirrored mine. Her mother dropped out of her life when she was eleven. She took off with an American. She lives in Venice, Florida now. Around that time Gramps died and Dad made the big decision. He took off with Rosie and went to live in the old family home in Coombe Foot. Uncle Bobby had been killed in a riding accident a couple of years earlier and Dad inherited the lot. He sold the business and they live off the income.'

'They?'

'He and Penny Gilbert. A very sensible woman. Me and Rosie really like her. When they first went down to Devon Rosie became a weekly boarder at St Ursula's. That's a school just beyond Newton Abbot. Penny was quote housekeeper unquote. Now no one cares any more and he introduces Penny to everyone as his partner. How she puts up with Dad day in and day out I don't know. Anyway ... Rosie ... very bright at school, a mathematician. Staffy was so proud of her. She followed his footsteps to Cambridge. Actually, the first time she bolted she was still at school. Fifteen though she'd already got a bunch of O levels. Staffy lost two stones. Not a word for six months. Too cruel.'

'Youngsters can be very cruel.'

'Yes ... well ... something got broken then and it's never been properly mended. Anyway, Rosie came back, did her A levels and went to Cambridge. After that she got a job in the City. Whiz-kid stuff. Lasted hardly any time before she took off again.'

'Did she let anyone know this time?'

'Not on your life. But you can only cry

wolf once, right? We just got on with things. Sure enough we got word some months later. This time she was in what used to be Yugoslavia, helping with refugees.'

'When did she come back?'

'About three years ago. Until recently she shared a flat in London with a girl called Bernice Brody. A wannabe celeb type. Bernice has this place in a Wandsworth high rise. Ex-council. A real crummy location if you ask me. Rosie drifted along doing a bit of this, that and the other. Most of it cash in the back pocket stuff. Barmaiding, working for a crammer at one stage trying to get kids through their GCSE maths. Nannying for a while. I couldn't work out how she and Bernice managed to put up with each other. Talk about chalk and cheese. But, of course, Rosie does have some media connections. Oa Bone for one, me for another. That's what Bernice liked. And I think Rosie enjoyed her bit of power – being able to produce us celebs. Or not. But there was some sort of bust-up there. Rosie told me Bernice was chucking her out. Maybe Bernice thought that Rosie had by now given her all she could. It maddens me, if you really want to know. How could Rosie go along with all this garbage?'

'But you don't know what their bust-up was about?'

'No.'

'Does Rosie do drugs?'

'Well, I'm sure she experimented when she was younger, but the answer's no. That's not the reason she couldn't get her life together. I suppose the real answer is there's too much Dee in her but times have changed. You really are lucky if you can live off a man now. They want someone who can chip in with the household bills. Let's face it, they *need* someone who can help with the finances. Either every member of the family works or none of them do these days. Basically, Rosie was into bumming around. But you're not young for ever. When you're clocking up thirty ... well, you know, it's question time, isn't it? Bum around long enough and there you are, a bum. Only they don't call you a bum. They call you a slag. Anyway, the upshot of all this was that Penny Gilbert, Dad's partner, heard there was a vacancy for a temporary maths teacher at St Ursula's, Rosie's old school. Some old biddy had a heart attack or something. Rosie got the job. The idea was she'd live at my place – I bought a longhouse down in Coombe Foot three years ago, when the loot was really coming in, you know?'

'You've got a cottage in the village your father lives in?'

'It's supposed to be a sort of pension thing ... something in the kitty for later. You know?

So the idea was that Rosie would teach at St Ursula's and live at my place, Manaccan House, this summer. That way I'd hopefully get a bit of rent and she wouldn't be in Dad's hair...'

'Can we back up a bit? When Rosie was fifteen and disappeared–'

'Actually, I may be a bit out there. She could have been sixteen–'

'What happened? Where did she go?'

'London. Look, I'm not too sure what went on that first time. I always assumed she'd gone off with some fellow. She and Staffy didn't talk about it. All I know is that Dad went up to London to fetch her back.'

'Maybe I should have a word with him?'

'I can't see that would help much. Anyway, he and Penny are touring France at the moment. I don't know exactly where they are.'

'OK. Let's leave that, then. This latest disappearance?'

Sissy's patent leather lavender handbag began to hiss.

'Shit.' She opened it and took out her mobile phone.

6

Arthur Trimble was looking out of the sash window of what had once been the first-floor drawing-room of a Georgian house. He was watching all those little white socks bob up and down. Up and down. At St Ursula's only the Sixth Form girls were allowed to wear tights but mostly they preferred black calf-hugging socks and footwear which to him looked like labourers' boots. The day girls were rapidly being swallowed up in their parents' waiting cars and now only a trickle of white socks remained, the last of the boarders making their way to Biddolph House and afternoon tea.

Her white sock was in a cardboard box at the bottom of his wardrobe. Maybe he'd take it down to his greenhouse and hide it under one of his gardenias when he potted up the cuttings. When her gardenia was ready to flower he'd bring it into the house and place it where they could both see it. 'Isn't it lovely,' she'd say. 'The heavenly smell!' On top of the television? The problem was lack of light in that corner of the room. A windowsill would be ideal, but he wanted his treasure to be more central than that. Always within Coral's line of sight, right under her nose.

That was one part of his brain, buzzing with delight, full of a rebirth, a magnificent flowering. He'd choose white, single petals, not a vulgar double variety, a bouquet as delicate as his seventeen-year-old bride had once been.

Another part of his brain was so sick with anxiety that his guts felt constantly stirred. It was just as though a cook were trying to retrieve a pan of runaway custard. Every so often a voice rose to the top, a bursting bubble which squealed: 'Why did you do *that?*'

At first he'd scanned the papers, terrified of seeing her splashed across the page. They said you couldn't leave the scene of a crime without something of yourself remaining behind. What had he left? He'd gone over and over it in his mind. A hair from his head as he'd slyly rubbed the stick up against her tender skin when he'd levered the sock away from the heel? A thread from the beige cotton twill slacks he'd been wearing? They photographed every little bit of the scene. They then did a video. And in his imagination the film developed into a picture of himself.

But I didn't do it.

Who would believe him? How could he

even begin to explain about the sock? He couldn't even explain it to himself.

But sometimes, deep in a lesson about the Elizabethan Poor Laws, he found himself grinning. The knowledge of the sock smiled in his bones, warming marrow like the heat of the sun on a summer's day. He could not now even remember what the dead woman looked like. Her face was that of Coral when she'd been his bride, sweetest seventeen and *his*.

It was now four days since he'd discovered her sleeping with her chaplet of bluebottles clasped about her dark hair. Still nothing in the papers, and he'd scanned both the local and nationals. If he hadn't taken the sock he'd be wondering if he'd somehow fallen asleep on the way to Woody's and dreamed it. The obvious explanation was that no one else had come across her body. He tried to tell himself that this was a good thing. Didn't evidence at a crime scene deteriorate rapidly as time passed? There had been, for instance, heavy rain last night. That must have washed away lots of forensic evidence.

But what and who else was stealing treasure from his beloved? He knew there were lots of foxes up there; vixens with hungry cubs to feed. Such easy prey. Fingers, toes, hands, feet. And what about the scavenging crows? A tasty morsel for any winged predator. He had such an urge to keep her safe. Even though he knew this was ridiculous, the urge not only remained but grew stronger as time passed. It just isn't seemly, was how he put it to himself. The meticulous part of his nature wanted her folded in her shroud, boxed in her coffin and tucked up in the earth. You can't just leave things around. They must be put away.

He wondered if he could ring the emergency services. Not the police. The very word set his heart pounding. But there was the ambulance. Couldn't he put a call in to them from, say, a public box? Didn't people talk through handkerchiefs when they wanted to disguise their voice? Or he could use his father's mock Welsh accent or steal Paul Maugin's grating drawl. *I was orf walking...*

It wasn't Paul Maugin who he'd seen out walking but Coral's solicitor Clive Upjohn, taking out his dog earlier than usual. Could that mean anything? So full had Arthur been of his own concerns that for the first time he found himself wondering who the murderer was and why he'd killed her.

An attempted rape which had gone wrong? Clive didn't appear to be anything but boringly normal. He was a solicitor, for God's sake. But didn't these twisted little deviants always turn out to be the ordinary bloke who lives next door?

And then Arthur remembered being in

Woody's living-room telling himself, 'She hadn't been interfered with...'

Zipped up. Yes. There was no getting round that.

If she had been unzipped, violated, would he have stolen the sock?

Or would he have seen her as spoiled meat?

He found himself clutching his head. What were you thinking of? Why did you do *that?*

'Henry did it.' The voice came out of nowhere. He looked round to see who was speaking to him but there was no one else in the room.

Do I know any Henry? Who the hell *is* Henry?

He found himself thinking that if Henry stole the sock at least no one could blame him. The things some blokes got up to. It was a wonder anyone could sleep safe in their beds.

The large panelled mahogany door opened. 'So glad I've caught you.' Joan Battersby, the headmistress of St Ursula's, was holding a book. 'I saw Woody last night and promised to lend her my copy of *Burke's Mathematical Teasers*. It only takes her fifteen minutes to polish off the *Times* crossword. Doing nothing is one of the most difficult things in the world, don't you find? Especially for someone who is used to being so active. She said you were going round after school one day this week to cut her lawn.' Joan was a tall, sturdily built woman of thirty-five, a year younger than his wife Coral and fifteen years younger than he was. She had good teeth and hair, a lot of jowl and far too much breast for his liking.

'How was she?'

'Well, I was surprised actually. When I saw her in hospital she looked as if all the stuffing had been knocked out of her. I was quite shocked. Not like our Woody at all. But now ... well, it's *her* again. You know? Apparently they're starting to wonder if she had a heart attack at all. Did she tell you?'

'No.' He took the book from her.

'Her little do may be all down to delayed shock. I suppose her case must have had too many atypical features for them to be satisfied with the first diagnosis.'

'She never said anything to me.'

'I think she was waiting for the results of some tests when she first left hospital.'

'But what could this shock be? This is Woody we're talking about. Pretty unshockable, I'd say.'

'Her brother died recently. Don't you remember?'

'That was six months ago. Still, it's got to be good news if it's true. The whole business has frightened the fire out of her.' He was looking at Joan Battersby. School numbers had been falling and there were rumours that she was looking for ways of culling the staff. Was Woody worried about her job, thinking delayed shock a better proposition for an employer than a heart attack? But she is an excellent teacher, Arthur thought. However Woody, like him, would be more expensive to employ than some kid fresh out of college. And there was one thing Woody was really good at. Adding up. 'Any idea when she'll be back?'

'Not the foggiest. It's really hard luck on the Upper Sixth. Of course, if they don't know enough to pass A level maths now, they never will. But it's the feeling of someone being there holding your hand metaphorically speaking, if you know what I mean. And then, of course, the younger girls can't afford to miss a whole term's work. I thought I'd dropped lucky. An excellently qualified person. But it appears to have fallen through. I expect the offer of a full-time job suddenly materialised. We'll just have to make do.'

'Sorry I won't be able to lend a hand.' It was a firm statement of intent.

'We'll *all* have to muck in. Tell Woody if she needs any help, all she has to do is ask.' Joan had transferred her gaze to the walls, decorated in a dingy cream eggshell paint which was stained under one of the sash windows. 'If this place wasn't such a colander we might be able to get a fund together for some decent IT equipment.' Her cube-shaped heels thunked rapidly across the wooden boards to the door. 'Night, Arthur.'

He grunted, waited long enough for her to clear the corridor and then went down to the staff room to collect his briefcase and anorak. As he crossed the wide entrance hall to the porch the door to the Upper Fourth classroom flew open and a child barrelled into him.

'No running in the corridors!' he roared.

The girl skittered away from him. A pair of very bright black eyes surveyed him. They seemed curiously void of human expression. It was as though some animal warily viewed him. The child was backing and he found his eyes straying to her feet and the rather droopy towelling socks flopping over her unpolished lace-up shoes. 'What do we do while we're in school, Jones?' Even as he said it he was aware of something happening in his heart. Something which made it swell, hurt. The beginnings of a heart attack? Was he going to keel over, just like Woody?

Ishbelle Jones put a hand up to her riotously curly black hair and pulled a strand down towards her mouth as if she were preparing to suck it. Behaviour, he thought, more appropriate to a five-year-old than someone rising fourteen.

'Walk,' he said. 'We walk, Jones.'

She said nothing.

He found himself staring at her moist little mouth, trying not to seek out the slight swell of tenderly budding breasts. He shook himself a little. 'Right. Let's see you do it.'

She almost broke into a run as she went through the set of swing doors which led to the porch, an enclosed structure which became a portico in the school's brochure. He found himself looking at the plasterwork on the ceiling so Henry would not be tempted to stare at white ankle socks and marvellously slender, almost stick-like legs. He himself reached the steps leading down to the gravel drive just in time to see her bounding over to her waiting friend, a stocky little kid with gingery blonde hair. They did not link arms but Ishbelle Jones gave a few skips and a jump like a welcoming puppy and then she and Alice Rice raced towards the school gates.

Ishbelle Jones, he found himself thinking. I've never really noticed her before. I'm sure I haven't. Such a moist little mouth. Moist little vulva, too. And those baby animal eyes.

He would not allow himself to think such things.

He hurried to his car. He'd change into his gardening gear and have a cup of tea and then do a bit of digging. Get some vigorous exercise. Oh yes.

He was not quite ready to let himself know

that he was not going to do any such thing. Oh no. He was really planning to take a brisk *walk*. Treat himself to a little peek at that female in the woods.

Henry could spring that on him later. Henry was the kind of bloke most people wouldn't want to know, including Arthur. Where the devil did he spring from? he wondered again. And smiled.

It was only as he was driving towards Coombe Foot that he realised a dull, grey morning had become a soft blue afternoon. He began to whistle. He listened to his merry tune. Long time since I whistled, he found himself thinking. Getting to be a gloomy old sod. Mustn't let that happen.

Coral was in the sitting-room when he got home, her feet up on a footstool. She was reading one of her books. They tended to have one-word titles resembling those of cars, *Cavalier, Polo, Princess, Escorts*. He'd forgotten it was Monday, the day she left her assistant Terrie in charge of the shop. In the morning she cleaned the cottage even though she could well afford to have a woman in. But a woman would not go down on her hands and knees and, using a stiff-bristled hand brush, sweep up the fluff between the skirting board and the fitted carpet before hoovering up, nor clean under the bowls of wash-basins nor, taking a rag in both hands and pulling it taut, rub vigorously round the base of taps to ease out any dirt. On Monday afternoons she usually drove over to her health club in Torquay, but obviously she'd decided against it today.

'Oh, it's you, Arthur,' she said, sooty eyes looking over the cover of her book. Illustrated was a willowy waisted woman in a large straw hat before beach and waves and in the background a mansion on a cliff. He made out the title: *Astra.* Since stealing the sock, he'd found it difficult to meet her gaze. It was as if, until that moment, the years hadn't touched his baby bride. But now the spell was broken. He saw this thirty-six-year-old stranger and, although she'd looked after her face and figure, the bloom of youth had long gone. His sumptuous dark rose had disappeared leaving this artificial one in its place. Touch her and you touched plastic. He felt bereaved and like most bereaved just a little bit glad the dearly beloved had departed. *F-r-e-e-d-o-m.* He'd certainly stretched the odd limb or two as he'd shaved that morning and that while noticing eyes moist with not quite formed tears.

'Had a nice day?' All solicitous because he was alarmed at the slight feelings of revulsion she now invoked in him. 'What about a cup of tea?'

'Sure.' Her eyes had dropped back to her book.

He felt a small spurt of anger. Not even a thank you. By rights she should be off her backside and making him a cup of tea. She'd been at home all day, hadn't she, while he'd been slaving away in a classroom.

When he came in with the tray her eyes were closed. The pages of the book lay across her chest, her pearly sheened fingernails steepled over the cover. Her eyelids didn't even flutter as he put the tray down by her side.

'I'm off to Woody's when I've had this,' he said. That was a lie so it was Henry who had said it, wasn't it? He bit into the cheese sandwich he'd made himself.

'We're low on milk. Stop off somewhere. Don't bring back any of that full cream stuff.'

'I'm not going in the car. I'm walking,' he said. Why should I run round after the bitch? Never a please. Never a thank you. Good job he'd not changed into his gardening gear. He couldn't walk through the village in those clothes.

She opened her eyes. 'Christ. You can be an awkward sod. You know that? We need some milk. It's not much to ask, is it?'

'I've got needs too. I need some fresh air after being stuck in a classroom all day.' He bit into the remainder of his sandwich.

'Please yourself. It's you who has cereal in the morning.'

He carried on chewing. Silence, as he'd learned in his dealing with schoolchildren, was a very potent weapon. She grew the silence, little miss dolly bird in her navy blue skirt and white apron-collared jumper, a teen queen going on forty.

'Why can't you get it?' he asked eventually.

'Because I've got to go back to the boutique in a few minutes, that's why. The paperwork's been piling up. And before you start, there's a salad in the fridge though God knows you're old enough and big enough to sort out dinner for yourself.' She had now taken her feet off the footstool and was sitting upright, the book half hanging off her left hip.

His control cracked. 'Christ. You've turned into a real hard cow. You know that?' He was itching to get his hands on her. He could feel his face growing ugly. She'd change her tune if he got hold of that gold ring pinned through her ear and tugged until half the lobe came away. Talk about ringing the changes.

'Who the hell do you think you are? I don't have to put up with you, Arthur Trimble.' *Astra* dropped on the floor as she sprang up. 'You're pathetic, you know that? A pompous little git with an attitude problem.' She leaned closer to him. 'Mr Big Brain! But you can't *think*, can you? It's easy to know where Jakarta is. It's not easy to figure out what stock to buy to keep your customers and the money rolling in. You think you're clever? You're a pin-head!'

She was going to slap him. He was sure of it.

'Shut up or...'

'What? You'll give me a detention? Knock off some house points? I'm not a little girl, I'm specially not your little girl. You need to get your head round a few facts that matter. Like it's the end of the twentieth century. More women work than men. You know? Things move on and if you don't you move out.'

He recoiled then, almost as if she had slapped him. 'What the hell do you mean?'

He was aware that she was as shocked as he was. 'Don't push it. OK?'

'Push it? Christ. All I said was I couldn't pick up a bottle of milk.'

'Believe me, you said much more than that. And so did I. Why don't you *think* about it?'

He was aware he was smiling foolishly, panic suddenly robbing him of speech.

Henry wasn't tongue-tied. He asked Arthur: 'Are you going to put up with this?'

But he was too frightened to listen to this other guy in his head.

Move out?

She'd turned away from him, but not before he noticed the tremor in her hands.

Her limbs bristled as she walked out of the sitting-room. There was a bit of blue throbbing in her calf. Is that a varicose vein? he wondered and suddenly Ishbelle Jones' legs came into his head, thin as stamens on a newly opening bloom, perfectly unblemished.

He looked down at the tray of tea, untouched. 'Don't push it,' she'd said. But hadn't she been doing just that for a long time now? 'More like shove,' Henry told him. 'Who faces the traffic jams in the morning now? Not to mention making the tea she doesn't drink?'

'Oh, put a sock in it,' he told the voice in his head but he didn't call goodbye as he walked round the cottage to the gate. He was hot and seething so much he was glad to be moving. It was almost as if his anger was a rolling ship and he had to dance about a bit to rebalance himself.

He was so caught up in fury he didn't realise the gate to Manaccan House was open until he found himself shutting it. Someone too lazy even to shut a gate! Well, at least there was nothing of a sloven about his Coral. Credit where it's due.

His temper improved as he climbed towards Coombe Woods. A few sharp words shows we've still got a marriage, he was telling himself. We're talking to each other, and how! Indifference, now, that really is serious.

'Balls,' Henry told him but he was cheerful because he was going to get an eyeful of this cold-blooded lovely spark out on her belly in this crooning spring glade. There was one good thing about the dead. They didn't answer back. They did as they were told. In fact, you could make them do anything.

'Who killed her?' Arthur wondered.

'I wonder what it's like? Killing someone?' Henry wondered.

Overhead a blackbird began to sing, the liquid notes painful in his ears.

Soon the dungy smell of the woods was around him, not quite an under armpits, unwashed body smell, cooler than that, more rotten altogether.

He began to feel anxious. What if he couldn't find the spot? One bit of wood looked very much like another. He shouldn't have left her for the foxes to snack on. He should have taken more care of her than that. And then there was the glittering jet halo of bluebottles. He really ought not to let them get in her brain. They might start to lay eggs, make little nests or do whatever they did. He'd have to look up stuff about their life cycles, get them sorted.

There it was. The single short frond of fern. My adder's tongue. Got you. And he trotted across, feeling his chest swell, his sinews ping. I will look after you, sweet-heart, he vowed.

97

And there he was, legs straddling the grassy-topped skull of rock, out of leafy gloom into brilliant sunshine and blinking.

But as he gazed down he saw her bed of green was empty. He found his knees sagging under the sick weight of her loss. Clawing at his heart he almost tumbled as he plunged down the incline to the flattened grass which had once felt her weight.

Someone's found her, he thought. They've taken her away.

But surely the discovery of a murdered woman in Oa Bone's woods would have been on the television news, in all the papers? His name guaranteed worldwide headlines.

For a moment Arthur wondered if he had gone mad. Shock brought him down to his knees. A swoon of white particles filled his vision. As it cleared he saw a small piece of denim stuck to the bristling stem of a bramble. He plucked it off. Staggering to his feet, he looked about him. Both sandals were gone. A dragged body would have made track marks through the uneven clumps of quickly growing grass, but he could see none. A slight flattening here and there. Did the pattern fit the feet of a man heavily laden with a body?

Had the killer come back, intent on giving his victim an unofficial funeral?

That night he dreamed of the corpse. She

was there in the woods, as he'd found her, but suddenly she turned her head and one eye looked up over her shoulder. A baby animal's eye.

Ish-belle.

A sound like the tenderest of spring breezes.

Beside him Coral was snoring, not heavily, light snorty noises.

7

Drifting in through the partly opened window was the noise from the pub across the basin, murmurs, laughter. Canal boats clanked and yawed at their moorings and Mitch dipped her nose in an oily city whiff which she particularly liked, childishly thinking she could capture it on the tip of her tongue if she stuck it out. Now in the panes was a dimmish orange for the lights had been switched on above Teddy's doors. Suddenly, and for no reason she could discern for the problems she'd woken up with remained, a screaming red dress day had turned mellow. She got up, shut the window, and sat low and so deeply in her office chair that her belly was pushed up into comfortable hands which were laced above it. Her legs were splayed out in front of her. Her breathing and the slow clunk of her heart were creating an almost hypnotic ease. Probably that double gin I had, she thought. Tommy was settling himself into a chair opposite, an upright, prim old yellow gent, who tonight looked a little tired. Mitch hauled herself into a more businesslike position.

'How did it go?'

'I think we got the job.'

Almost imperceptibly, he relaxed in his chair. 'I left the spread sheets on your desk.'

Mitch looked at them. 'I'll go through them. Give me the bottom line.'

'We're not quite breaking even.'

'Isn't that really good for a young business like ours, Tommy?'

'All my ventures make money *immediately*.'

She didn't say anything, letting him work through it. He said eventually: 'I don't have hobbies.'

'I don't either.'

'We'll see. We'll see. Take another look in the autumn. I know you're against the idea, but I think we'll have to do some serving of legal papers. That sort of thing. The work could well lead to more interesting stuff. Anyway, we'll leave that for the moment.' Tommy looked at her. 'You only think we've got the job. What is the fly in the ointment?'

When Tommy used a cliché he often emphasised the first word in the phrase and Mitch had a mental image of him constructing the picture, in this case the fly frantically wriggling to free itself from sludgy death. Perhaps this trick of his stemmed from the days when he was learning the language and he was having a little chuckle to himself as he saw the appropriateness of the words.

'Sissy wants someone down in Coombe Foot immediately. She doesn't want us to start looking into the disappearance of her half-sister sometime whenever. I'm sure Freya won't hold me to being physically there at the radio station until the end of the month. But she will want the last two pro-grammes in the can. Working like the clappers that's at least two days. There're lots of interviews to set up, people to see, never mind the editing.'

'I don't see a problem there. I can go down.'

'She wants to see you first.'

'Look me over?'

'Sure.'

'You've all got a bad racial memory of ancient oriental gentlemen. They were called something like Chung Foo and were villains in thirties detective stories.'

'Or the laundry man Mr Woo.'

Tommy laughed. 'I'll be a wow with the villagers, my dear, I promise.'

'First you'll have to be a wow with Sissy,' Mitch said bluntly. 'You're due to have breakfast with her at the house the film company hired down in Stratford. Right. I'll fill you in with the details of Rosie's dis-appearance, such as they are, and then the family background. Sissy has a Devon longhouse in the village and that is where

Mitchell and Orient will be temporarily setting up shop.

'They were built sideways into the hill, you know. Longhouses. The farthest portion of the house was for the farmer and his family, the bottom bit for the livestock. All the animal muck could then be swilled down the hill away from the domestic buildings. Primitive hygiene at work.'

'How on earth do you know that?'

'One picks up these things.'

Mitch grunted and waited for Tommy to settle himself with his notebook and a pen banded in gold. If she knew her man, the gold would be eighteen carat. 'Well, Rosie was hired as a temporary maths teacher at her old school. St Ursula's is private, on the north side of Newton Abbot. There's a mix of day girls, weekly and full-time boarders. By coincidence, the woman she is replacing used to be Rosie's old maths teacher. Miss Woodward had a heart attack. She lives in Bishop Coombe and might be worth a visit. She should know things about Rosie the family don't.

'Eleven days ago, that's a Friday, Rosie went down to Sissy's house which had been lent to her for the summer. She arrived late morning and in the afternoon went to St Ursula's and saw...' Mitch glanced at her notes, 'a Joan Battersby, the headmistress.

'On Saturday Rosie goes into Torquay to

103

an upmarket dress shop owned by a woman in the village called Coral Trimble to get kitted out. She apparently only owns jeans and T-shirts. The school rule is that the women teachers wear skirts or dresses. No trousers. Sissy is picking up the tab. The arrangement is that Rosie will refund her when her pay cheques start coming in. She certainly bought some clothes – so at that point she was still intending to start work on the following Monday. She rang Sissy and told her what she'd spent.

'That was mid-afternoon on the Saturday. That evening Rosie went to see her old maths teacher, Miss Woodward, who by then had come out of hospital. On Sunday afternoon she went to see an old school friend in Newton Abbot, Hazel Rayburn, now a local GP. They had lunch together and then Dr Rayburn drove Rosie back to Manaccan House, that's Sissy's place. That takes us to ten past three and, as far as Sissy knows, that is the last time Rosie was seen. Sissy has been down. As far as she's able to tell Rosie's clothes are still there, well, most of them. Certainly the clothes she bought from Coral Trimble's shop. If Rosie had done a runner – and she had done twice before in her life – she took nothing, or very little, with her.'

'What kind of an impression did you get of Rosie?'

'A bit of a bum, to be honest. Appeared to have everything going for her. Nice-looking, top-class brains, but blew it. She'd worked in the City, cleared out and did some aid work in the old Yugoslavia, came back and for the past three years appears to have been drifting. Doing a bit of this and that as it turned up but basically I should imagine, though Sissy didn't say this, existing off benefit. Before this temporary job came up she was living in a high rise in Wandsworth with another girl, Bernice Brody. Apparently this girl's a bit of a jill-of-all-trades, too. Some modelling, some extra work in films, a gofer on fashion shoots, a sort of clinger-on to the outer rim of the glamour trade. We'll have to see her. If we get the job, I could do that.'

'I take it Sissy has contacted this Bernice Brody?'

'No dice. Bernice hasn't heard from her since she went down to Coombe Foot.'

'Lying?'

'It's got to be a possibility, hasn't it? You ought to be in Coombe Foot. By the way, I've agreed that we'd live at Manaccan House. Sissy is going through leanish times at the moment. She'll cough up our daily rate, but wants to keep the expenses down.'

'Won't their father chip in?'

'He doesn't know a thing about it. He's travelling round France with his girlfriend.

Anyway, Rosie has done this twice before. He'd probably think she'd just turn up again.'

'Why doesn't Sissy think she will?'

'You're not going to believe this...' and Mitch told him about Sissy's dream.

'You shouldn't be so sceptical,' Tommy said when she'd finished.

'The funny thing is, I wasn't when she was telling me. I mean, it obviously frightened the life out of her.'

'For many years I've had a recurring dream. I am lying there and I know I'm dying and though I can't see my hands I know I'm wearing gloves but I also know it's ... odd. Not cold enough.'

'You've never told me before.' Even as she said this, Mitch realised that though they'd now been in partnership for months she really knew very little about Tommy Hung. She had, of course, been to his flat in Edgbaston but because of his love of acting out his fantasies – the living-room of the flat was done out like an English gentlemen's club – it was difficult to get a line on the real Tommy. Had he told her of a relative in their first investigation? A nephew? She'd certainly never met any of his relatives though he had no qualms about introducing her to his women friends.

'Well, you know, people are wary,' said Tommy. 'Freud gave dreams a very bad name. What an extraordinary fellow he was. But whichever way you look at it, Sissy's dream was so strong she's acting on it. We have to respect that.'

'I think of myself as being a fairly intuitive sort of person, but I've never had a dream like that. The nearest sort of experience I've had isn't very near at all.'

'What's that?'

'Cassie, my daughter, had her nose literally pushed out of joint when she fell off her bike as a kid. When the casualty doctor snapped it back I felt it right through my body and out of my toes. I almost fell over. For a moment I was living in her flesh. Now she's been in America for so long some days pass when I don't even think of her.'

'Right. Onwards,' said Tommy. 'You were going to tell me about Rosie's background. And these two runners she did previously.'

Fifteen minutes later Tommy snapped his notebook shut.

Mitch, yawning, got up and stretched. 'My car is over at Masshouse. You couldn't give me a lift?' She opened her handbag, extracted a letter and took it out of its envelope. She waved the envelope at him. 'Here we are, honeypot. Sissy's address in Stratford and a little map. No doubt you'll hit some rush hour traffic but you will be driving out of the city. It'll be an early start.'

'Best bib and tucker?'

'The whole English gent bit you do so well.'

'What's Sissy like?'

'Seriously over the top. The pair of you should get on famously.'

Tommy, quite unable to conjure up any Asian inscrutability, looked hurt. Mitch, thinking of the Chinese water torture he was about to inflict on her – the spread sheets seemed to loom larger and larger – was unrepentant.

In spite of lecturing Mitch on the advisability of a detective having a nondescript car, Tommy drove a Jaguar. Mitch had thought it politic not to complain. He was such an Anglophile that she felt she was lucky he didn't turn up for jobs in a Rolls Royce. She looked at him sideways now as he drove through light late evening traffic. In the city's flickering glare the flat planes of his face had an almost lavender hue, his skin crazing a little, like an ancient pot. What she would give for half an hour inside his flat-backed head. Perhaps, she thought, I'd be disappointed. All his little ploys and tricks might camouflage the depressingly mundane. Tommy circled the city centre and then dropped down by Aston University into Masshouse. 'Thanks, Tommy. You're an angel,' she said as she got out of the car.

'I'll give you a call and let you know when I'm off to Coombe Foot.'

'You're sure you'll get the job then?'

'Ladies like me,' he said. 'They certainly do not see *me* as a laundry man.'

Well, thought Mitch as she watched him go, that puts me in my place. As usual, she had difficulty spotting her car. It's as memorable as a semi in Great Barr, she thought. Why did I let myself be talked into it? She would not want a Harrods green Jaguar, like Tommy's. What she craved was a sunflower yellow one she'd seen with a black roof and mudguards. Oh, she could most certainly picture herself at the wheel of that little number. It was like something out of the twenties jazz age, all trumpets and drum rolls.

She fastened her seat belt, turned on the engine and began to fiddle with the radio. Down the crater which was Masshouse was not the place to fine tune so she waited until she'd driven out and was on her way to the Bull Ring. She suddenly heard a familiar voice. She twiddled. '...the excrement was liberally festooned about the gut-wrenching lavatories, no running water, no electricity, but did you want it? When it was light enough you could see blood on the walls. In half a sniff I decided that this Albanian hotel was not the place I wanted to be in and I hadn't the courage to try any more. It was, I had been informed, the best place in town...' Ellie Peters, Mitch realised. She must have been commissioned to do a piece for Radio Four.

'...refugees from Kosovo come to Albania over the mountains. Below the tree line there is mined no man's land, wide as a motorway. It ploughs through forests where bear and wolf still roam. The countryside is magical but dangerous. Serb patrols don't open their mouths. They talk with their machine guns. But neither bears nor Serbs are as dangerous as kith and kin. This is the land of the blood feud. There are valleys where there is not a male in evidence. Their way of life is hiding from nephew, brother, son-in-law. Revenge killing is as endemic as hunger. After the fall of the Communists, the old lawlessness flourishes...'

Mitch pictured Ellie as she'd last seen her, her plumpness disguised by floppy clothes, thick, curly hair cropped about a surprisingly delicate face, bangles jingling above child-sized hands. A comfortable figure, inhabiting comfortable spaces. Rivals often misjudged her, as Mitch had to begin with. '...out of the magic spaces you descend into a town. This one. And here I am pussy-footing through piles of broken bottles, plastic wrap, disintegrating cans. But where does anyone get most of the stuff which finds its way into these heaps? It is a list of nos. No proper shops. No buses. No taxis. No petrol stations. What there is are diseased concrete tower blocks with plastic-chewing livestock wandering between. Ill-nourished, shaggy Pied Pipers, these goats trail swarms of flies behind them. As you walk along the street there's a quiet scream-ing between your shoulders you describe to yourself as an itch. Any moment could be one moment away from dynamite explod-ing, bullets tearing into pock-marked walls or tender flesh ... foreigners, after all, are a time-honoured source of plunder...

'My fear, a squeal which seems to emanate from my flesh rather than my brain, is a novelty. Because of the endless vendettas, an inheritance of the Kanun, the tribal con-stitution, fear never leaves many of this society's males. Numbers of Albanian women appear to live in daily dread. In this fiercely patriarchal society they must, at every moment, please the male, serve him and – their prime function – bear more males. I was told that girls of fifteen ask to be sold into a life of prostitution in Italy rather than be wed to men their fathers have sold them to...'

Albania, what's Ellie doing there? She said in her letter she was going to Kosovo. Must be trouble brewing in that region, Mitch thought. War?

Mitch pulled the car up in front of her rented flat and listened on. Ellie, she thought, had lost none of her skills during the intervening years in America. There she was, a women who surely must be nearing sixty now, braving Albanian lavatories – to Mitch, bullets were a lesser evil. Would I do it, she wondered, or have I reached a point in my life where comfort is a necessity? One thing is for sure, she told herself, I'll stop whingeing about the horridness of my rented flat. She turned off the radio and collected her gear from the passenger seat.

In the hall was the familiar whiff of slowly decaying building, dry rot, wet rot, degenerating plaster, mould, old meals. The light from a sixty watt bulb presided over wallpaper bulging at the seams and what was once a multi-striped carpet made from the factory's left-over yarns and now an almost uniform sludgy grey She opened the treacle brown door into her flat. She never now put on the overhead light in her living-room but switched on two red-shaded side lights so she would not have to confront the large yellowish stain spreading down from the coving round the ceiling. The lamps also threw shadow on the photographs of the chapel she'd pinned to the door, pictures taken before the conversion work had started and the bills had begun to soar above initial estimates.

She dumped her stuff on the floor and was mixing herself a gin and tonic when the phone rang. She fell on to the couch, receiver in one hand and glass in the other.

'Mitch?'

'Just got in and poured myself a drink. Hang on while I gulp.'

'Well, hurry up. Trevor's coming over in half an hour and I must have a shower,' said Digger. 'I want to smell appetising. Did you drop off at the Bright Gallery and get my stuff?'

'Sure. It comes in a plain brown wrapper. Yawn, yawn, yawn.'

'That's not such a bad gag. Don't be so cynical.'

'I'm not cynical. I just find it deeply boring.'

'I might have to plug a hole in my afternoon show and it'll do for that.' Digger had obviously looked down at his watch. 'Goody, I've still got twenty-five minutes. Just time to tell you. Oh blossom, such drama...'

'Give.'

'I've just come back from the bar at the Holiday Inn–'

'My God, Digger, that's a bit posh for the likes of us.'

'I was meeting an Arts Council grandee. You know how it is with them. Location, location, location. If Perrier is not costing twice as much as a good malt... Anyway, we'd done the biz and were walking into the foyer when who should we see? Well, I saw him but the grandee pretended not to. Who does a pop megastar think he is? Way below *me* in the scheme of things ... you know the attitude of these Arts Council bods–'

'Do get on with it, Digger. I take it we are referring to seeing Oa Bone?'

'Didn't I say? Charcoal grey pin-striped trousers, beige jacket in a wider pin-stripe in some naff material like polyester, purple bishop's shirt with a purple dog collar, hair à la Simon Rattle electrified genius curls standing up all over his head – and track shoes, soles starting to come adrift from the tops. Not leather. Two henchmen, Savile Row suits doing the businessman gold Rolex bit, hovering–'

'Got the picture.'

'My Arts Council contact, working over-time at not noticing, goes out. He thinks I'm still with him and is talking to me. But I see someone vaguely familiar coming towards Oa and his cronies. It takes a while for me to get her number. It's the television cook, the gross one who's a friend of Freya only she's demi-gross now. Lime green glittery dress, skirt just covering her bum–'

'We used to call them pussy pelmets.'

'In the days when five-pound notes were white and big enough to wipe your bum on? Electric blue clogs. You know, they have wooden soles? The wooden bit was lime green. Dirty great diamond stuck in her

114

nose with little black legs sprouting from it. You know, painted on her skin so it all looked like a jewelled beetle was clambering over her nose. Never again call me over the top, petal.'

'What do you mean, *again?* When it comes to style, on a scale of one to ten you're two and a half could try harder.'

Who's talking? Like you, I've grown out of the *Look At Me* stage.'

'What happened?'

'She waltzes up to Oa and she obviously thinks that now she's with them the party's complete and is starting to push off towards the doors but one of the henchmen has a word in her ear. By which time this other woman is walking towards them, all ash blonde hair and this muslin stuff clinging to her as though it's wet, though it's not, sort of arranged so that tits and pussy are not visible but look as though they might be if she makes one wrong move. I mean, wow! The grandee, of course, is through the doors and out by now, head so crimped he thinks theatre is something that doesn't happen in real life. You know your Digger. He's bagged the best seat in the house.'

'And who is this vision in muslin?'

'How should I know? Some wannabe celebrity, I expect. Anyway, a henchman introduces her to Sissy and they do a bit of chat, Sissy well at a disadvantage. She's a foot shorter than La Muslin and all that lime green has turned her toadlike. But they seem friendly enough. Maybe even knew each other. Then wham! Sissy smacks her across the face. I've never seen a woman hit someone before–'

'You've led a sheltered life.'

'She doesn't put her shoulder into it, like a man would, but all the action comes from her elbow. I have seen it happen on these old black and white films, when I think about it, but, of course, Sissy isn't wearing an elbow-length glove. Not a lot of noise. Like a plash of water hitting the harbour wall. Can't see if it makes a weal because La Muslin is blushing like fury. Sissy turns on a blue and green clog and marches off, back to her room, one supposes. Suddenly her shoulders do a sort of forward roll and she starts to shake and then almost falls flat on her face as she speeds up. I mean, what La Muslin has said has seriously upset the cook. This is mega gulp stuff. When he sees how distressed Sissy is, Oa turns on La Muslin and says something. Her head goes back like this–'

'I can't see you, Digger.'

'Not like when Sissy slapped her. Wafts more, like a bee has got too near her chops–'

'But what did La Muslin say to Sissy? What did Oa Bone say to her?'

'No idea, blossom. No one was projecting

116

their voice. This wasn't a real stage, after all. Life is never wholly satisfactory, don't you find? But it has its moments. At this point in time all mine are with Trevor. Must dash. Do not, on any account, forget to bring in the stuff from the Bright Gallery. Under plain wrapper, eh? Well, one can travel hopefully.'

Mitch dropped the receiver back in its cradle and took another sip of her drink. She was worrying at something, as if it were a sore. Ah yes, she could make out the stain below the coving if she really studied the shadow. Sissy, she decided after pondering on the interview, had not lied to her but she was beginning to feel there was much she should have told her and hadn't.

She decided to get out of her red dress and have a shower.

8

Mitch, who had been editing her programmes till midnight in the deserted
studios of Radio Brum, decided she wasn't
going to drive down to London to see
Bernice Brody, Rosie's former flatmate. If
she went by train, she could at least pick up
on some of the sleep she'd missed. She'd
take a taxi from Euston station.

Tommy Hung always sounded like the
Duke of Edinburgh when he spoke to her
on the phone; he sometimes walked like the
Duke of Edinburgh, too, one hand lightly
clenched behind his back as if this were an
appendage he couldn't find a use for. He'd
reached her before she'd started her mara-
thon editing stint. 'One can't help being
impressed by Coombe Foot,' he'd said.

'You can't,' said Mitch, to whom villages
were only useful for illicit weekends. Wine in
hand, lover hovering behind trickling a
forefinger down towards the nape of her
neck, the view of the fourteenth-century
church from the hotel's Georgian sash
window was likely to quiver deliciously in
the tenderest parts of her anatomy; she
especially liked to gaze at the bell tower. Too

long since she'd enjoyed such a weekend. Ageing bones made few new lovers, she thought sadly.

'On the outside Sissy's place is all it should be, a typical Devon longhouse. Roses round the door. But, my dear, one goes into the lavatory and finds a Buddha, made of concrete with some kind of shiny specks in it, staring down at one from the windowsill ... well, it is rather disconcerting. Do you think it's meant as a joke?'

'I've no idea.'

'I find it in very questionable taste. My bedroom, the most restful at Manaccan House, had lime green glass vases on the windowsill – I removed them – and mirrors and pictures propped up rather than hung. One had a fake leopardskin thing at the end of one's bed. I removed that, too. What can you think?'

'Sissy is a follower of fashion.'

'But what is wrong with a few horse brasses?'

'You have to clean them.'

'Well, there you are. I've seen Miss Woodward, the maths teacher Rosie was supposed to be taking over from. She remembered the old Rosie well. She said that if they're lucky, teachers get a pupil like her once in their career. The girl had an exceptional talent for maths. She was marked out as Oxbridge material from the word go. Took all her O levels a year early. Then something went wrong. Miss Woodward doesn't quite know what, so she says. But she has thoughts about it. When Rosie was fifteen Oa Bone – you know, the pop star – bought this Victorian pile between Coombe Foot and the next village, Bishop Coombe. It was said that some of the young girls in the neighbourhood went to wild all-night parties there when the band came down. There was a lot of ill feeling. One farmer went up with his twelve bore and shot out half the windows. In the end it was all hushed up and the parties stopped as abruptly as they'd begun. The band obviously decided on more anonymous premises for their rave-ups.'

'Well, that might begin to explain how Oa Bone acquired his face.'

'What do you mean?'

'Seriously Dorian Grey. Had Miss Woodward any idea where the fifteen-year-old Rosie vanished to when she did her bunk? I mean, it was months before she turned up again.'

'It was assumed she'd run off with a chap. It was quite a scandal at the time. The Childe family are prominent in the community. When she was admitted back into the school everyone was expecting the worst, that she'd do it again or get into drugs if she wasn't already doing them. Give

120

a dog a bad name stuff. But she surprised them all. Kept her head down and herself out of trouble and then, as you know, went up to Cambridge. I think we've got to find out what she did when she vanished.'

'If Sissy knows, she's not saying. My guess is we'll have to dig pretty deep to find out.'

'There's this woman who is a doctor who was a contemporary of Rosie's at St Ursula's. I'm seeing her on Thursday afternoon. She might know.'

'What does Miss Woodward think of Rosie now? It was the Saturday evening before she disappeared she saw her, wasn't it?'

'She said she wouldn't have known her. The Rosie she remembered she described as "vital". This Rosie appeared almost cowed, Miss Woodward said. As if the stuffing had been knocked out of her. Importantly she said she'd wondered how Rosie would cope with a class of lively schoolgirls. "I wouldn't say I was astonished when Rosie didn't turn up. It was probably for the best, you know."' Tommy was reeling off from his notebook.

'What did she feel about Rosie just taking off without letting anyone know?'

'She'd done it before and turned up again. The bad penny. But she did admit that Rosie could meet a challenge well enough when she chose. The first time she'd come back she'd completed her schooling and gone on to get a good degree. I gathered –

between the lines – she'd been looking forward to this meeting with Rosie and had been disappointed about how it turned out.'

'Perhaps Rosie was the one who was disappointed and Miss Woodward had picked that up. When Rosie was a kid she might have thought of Miss Woodward as her guru. I mean, her talent was for maths and Miss Woodward was the maths teacher. There might have been quite a strong relationship going. Sissy did say that Rosie could get fervently attached to people. Sissy had wanted to hate her new half-sister but Rosie had simply demanded to be loved.'

'That's all very well but Miss Woodward is one more name on the list of people who are not surprised – and not worried – that Rosie has gone missing.'

'Do *you* think she's just done a bunk again? After interviewing one or two people you usually get a feel for a case.'

'Something awful's happened. But I put that feeling down to Sissy's dream. How often have you had a dream you've acted on?'

'Never.'

'Before you get down here on Thursday I hope to see all the people we know have had contact with her since she came back to Coombe Foot. That's still on, is it?'

'When I get back from interviewing Bernice Brody I intend to wrap up my Radio

Brum work. I'll probably set off for Devon after lunch. At least, that's the plan.'

'It's a little over three hours' drive so you should be here around tea-time. I'll cook dinner and we'll spend the evening going over what we've got.'

'Well, I must say you sound very perky, Tommy.'

'Getting out of the office does one good.'

'Amen to that,' said Mitch. 'I'll be splicing tape till midnight. And Chancellor Brown needn't worry his little head about me getting a rise above inflation.'

Now, settling into the crowded train at New Street station, Mitch took out her London A to Z. Though she'd take a taxi to Selwyn Gardens, it was likely she'd have to find her own way back. The nearest tube was at Southfields on the District Line. She'd have to change to the Metropolitan Line at Edgware Road. She jolted back in her corner seat as the train started moving. The growing colonies of buddleias among the scrub on the gravelled embankment began to blur. The increasing rhythm of the train's wheels rocked her to sleep.

She was dozily awake half an hour later. She told herself she was not going to review her worry list which, she thought gloomily, was about to jump category into the phrase: 'Abandon hope all ye who enter here.' For some time now she'd had to will herself to go down and see the builders doing the conversion work on the chapel. It was like having to keep revisiting the scene of a major traffic accident only instead of blood oozing from limbs she viewed fungus leaking from planks.

Not to mention the likelihood of Freya booting her out of her broadcasting job.

And although she'd promised herself she would have a holiday from thinking of ways of trying to solve her problems, she nevertheless found herself wondering if Ellie Peters might provide the key to a bit of work. But how? For a start she was not even going to contemplate going near an Albanian lavatory. She didn't much fancy taking a trip to Romania, either, and meeting the sewer children. Or reporting on any of the world's desperate lives.

Am I getting too old to be a broadcaster? Is that what I'm saying?

Am I getting too old to live?

Gloom blew out of her mouth and ears. Behind this dense fog she retreated further and further back in her seat. Beyond the window the semi-detacheds of England flashed by, lit by fitful sunlight. By the time the train was reaching the outskirts of London, Mitch's constitutional ebullience was reasserting itself. She saw a gaily striped sun umbrella on a balcony looming over the rail track, a child waving from his bedroom window. Yes, she was leaning forward again.

When she stepped down on to the platform she stopped long enough to take in a good lungful of air. A little oily, a hint of fast food, warm beer and the right sort of muck, city muck. Everyone going somewhere, doing something; importance about its business. And I've got to catch my taxi to Selwyn Gardens. I'm going to see what'sername. What was her name? For a moment Mitch's mind was completely blank. A hanger-on to the outer rim of the fashion world, she remembered. Irish-sounding. Bridget? Bernice Brody. Stepping out now, shoulders set at a good angle, bum perky. Back on track.

'Wandsworth? Selwyn Gardens? Tower block?' The driver's face was as white as the underbelly of a slug, but not as moist.

'I never get to go to top destinations,' said Mitch as she climbed into the back of the taxi. 'That's the story of my life.'

'Yeah, yeah.' The cab pulled away from the pen of tubular steel. There was silence as he jousted with another taxi as they came up from Euston to street level. He said: 'I always get south of the river. You know?'

With something approaching elegance, he slid the car between the traffic. She delved in her handbag for the number of the flat.

'It's off Augustus Road. Right?' he asked.

'No idea.'

'That's the feeling in my water.'

They were silent for the rest of the journey.

As she paid him, he said: 'Bottom of Augustus Road is where they line up the cabs for the Wimbledon tennis punters. Out the tube at Southfields, one pound fifty to the courts, at least four sharing.'

'Better than eight quid. Keep the change.'

'There's more action in a tower block than on a tennis court. I'd bet money on that.'

'I wouldn't know, honeypot.' She put her purse back in her handbag before she climbed out of the cab.

She stared round her. There was landscaping and good quality wrought-iron railings and the looming towers looked reasonably well cared for. The parked cars all had their wheels on and the windows were intact. Some youths loitered by the railings and when they raised their heads their eyes had that bright, detached, adolescent look. The flats started on the first floor. Garages, undercover bin areas and the entrance were located at street level. Mitch was about to buzz through to Bernice's flat when a young Asian family came out through the swing doors and let her in. Most of the tiles were still on the entrance walls and had been sprayed with some kind of speckled green plaster. The rubber flooring in the lift had been swilled out and was damp. Mitch, missing something, realised she'd as yet seen no graffiti. She went up to the seventh floor and found herself in a U-shaped corridor. She was aware of an agitating flapping. Turning down the left leg of the U she saw ragged strips of plastic wrap teasing free from wall-mounted horizontal glass grating.

She rang the bell of number four but removed herself from the vicinity of the Judas hole. She didn't want to have to confront a disembodied eye looking into her eye. The door, on a chain, opened a few inches. 'Mitch Mitchell. I rang yesterday, Miss Brody.'

The chain was shot back and the door opened. Bernice Brody was six inches taller than she was and had a smart starved model shape. Her hair had been tucked under a red cotton scarf. She was wearing a snow white T-shirt and her well-washed jeans, though no trouser crease had been pressed in, looked newly ironed. On her feet were fur slippers shaped like cats. 'I'm decorating in the kitchen. Come in. I'll make some coffee. No word?'

'No.'

'I really don't know what I can tell you.'

Mitch followed Bernice down a yellow hall which just had room for the radiator on the wall and the watercolour of sunflowers above it. The partitioning in the flat was only as thick as the top joint on Mitch's little finger. The kitchen partition – Mitch couldn't think of the rooms as having walls – had an internal window of ribbed glass. The small aluminium step ladder took up half the space in the room and each rung was as spotless as Bernice herself. She was painting a floor to ceiling cupboard which butted at right angles to a tiny sink. The kitchen was yellow and the cupboard soon would be. The only spots and spills were on the window overlooking other tower blocks. These were a dirty white and had been made by pigeons. Seeing Mitch look at it, she said: 'I've had to net the balcony in. Otherwise I'd be knee deep in pigeon droppings.' She showed Mitch into the lounge, also yellow. Though it was a cheery colour, by now Mitch was beginning to think she'd dropped into a bowl of custard. The carpet, curtains, nets, and sixties furniture had obviously been supplied by Bernice's landlord. The three-piece suite, navy blue, green and claret striped, was nearly new. 'They brought in some new regulations about the foam in chairs so the landlord had to replace the old one. Fire risk or something. I try not to think about fire. I mean, on the seventh floor with a lift shaft and stairwell to draw the flames? I'd get out tomorrow if I could afford to.' She left Mitch settled in a chair and went to make the coffee.

Looking round, Mitch confirmed that yellow did not go with beige, but the room was immaculately tidy. The glittering eyes of a row of small cats, some ceramic, some made of fur fabric, watched her from the top of the teak which surrounded an electric fire. Pine shelves, so different from the rest of the furniture that Mitch guessed they belonged to Bernice, held not only books but what looked like an overflow of jars from the kitchen. Glucosamine plus chondroitin, she read, pure evening primrose oil, ginkgo biloba, cod liver oil. Bernice came back from the kitchen with one cup of coffee and a glass of water. 'It's filtered,' she said and Mitch assumed she was talking about the coffee and then, after taking a sip, realised she meant the water.

Bernice put her glass on the coffee table. 'I don't want to be ... well ... it's obviously all very worrying ... but the thing is that most of Rosie's gear is still in her bedroom. There was someone called Penny who has access to a van and she and Rosie were going to drive down here and clear the room out. She's rented it till the end of the month so that still leaves almost two weeks. But another girl has arranged to move in. I need the money, you see. Of course, I'd much rather not share at all but it isn't an option. I have to have the income.'

'Perhaps you should talk to her sister?'

Bernice pulled a face. 'Sissy and I aren't on any sort of terms. You know?'

'Why not?'

'Things weren't going too well. I had to ask Rosie to leave. Rosie was all right about it so why should her sister kick up a fuss?'

'Well, I'll be getting in touch with Sissy. I'll mention it if you like.'

'Would you? It's all very awkward. I don't want to be at all pushy but you can see there's absolutely no space to store things here.'

'How long has Rosie been sharing with you?'

'It must be a year now. At first we got on quite well as flatmates but I can't tell you much about her social life or anything. We weren't what you'd call friends. You know?'

'Did she have a boyfriend?'

'There was someone called Julian Small but I gather he was a friend rather than a boyfriend if you see what I mean. I think she met him while they were doing aid work in Bosnia. He was working in hostels for the homeless in London but he's somewhere in the West Country now. I might be wrong, but that could be one of the reasons she decided to take this teaching job down there.'

'Do you know how I could contact him?'

'No.'

'Do you mind if I look in Rosie's bedroom? There might be letters, a contact book even.

Come too, and we can carry on talking. What about girlfriends? Was she working anywhere while she was living with you?'

'She did some work down at the hostels. Cooking, I think. Barmaiding. Some stuff at a crammer. What turned up. This is her room.'

Mitch was decanted out of custard into dingy magnolia and found she was relieved. The same beige curtaining and the floor covering, between the piled cardboard boxes, was beige, too. She made for packets of correspondence secured by elastic bands, which were stacked in a shoe box on a white melamine dresser. She was about to pick the box up when, in the crevice where the carpet met the wall, something glittered momentarily in fitful sunlight. Mitch saw it was a small needle, no longer than a fingernail. 'I wouldn't pick that up if I were you,' Bernice said. 'I'll put some rubber gloves on and get rid of it later.'

'What's it all about then?' Mitch asked.

'None of her family know. I wouldn't have known if I hadn't caught her at it.'

'It's a funny sort of needle.'

'You use it to inject into the skin. The stomach in her case. It was when I started buying disposable plates and cutlery that I knew she'd have to go. I just couldn't cope. She'd got Hepatitis C. Apparently there is only a tiny, tiny chance of catching it. But she'd caught it, I kept thinking, so why not me?'

'I've heard of Hepatitis A and B. But never C.'

'It was only named at the end of the eighties. It's a sleeper. She thought she'd caught it fifteen years ago. Sharing needles.'

'She was only a schoolkid then,' Mitch said. 'No more than fifteen years old!'

'Heroin, she said. But she managed to get clear. Start her life over.'

'Sissy never told me.'

'Her family didn't know. I know that sounds astonishing but that's what she said.'

'I wonder if that's why she went missing the first time?'

'I don't know. We didn't talk about that. As far as she was concerned, that part of her life was over and done with. And then this came back to haunt her. She only went to the doctor for some iron tablets. She thought she must be anaemic. She had a blood test and the virus was found. When they did a liver function test at the hospital they found she was suffering from some fibrosis. She said she'd been told that the fibrosis – I think that's something like scar tissue, you know? – may eventually lead to cirrhosis and possibly liver cancer.

'Anyway, she went on this drug – Interferon – and had to inject it three times a week. She said she was tolerating it better than many. No night sweats or hair loss. But she was very tired a lot of the time.'

'Didn't she worry that she might pass this virus on to one of the schoolkids she was about to teach? Though you said the risk of contagion is very slight ... still, it might have built up in her mind. That might be why she didn't turn up at St Ursula's to start teaching that Monday. And she knew she couldn't come back here, didn't she?'

'She *did* see it from my point of view. She knows how terribly squeamish I am. I mean, it's not as though we're real friends or anything. God. It was giving me nightmares. She might talk blandly of hair loss and night sweats. It literally gave me the shivers. I'm sorry. I didn't want any part of it.'

'Who else knew?'

'No one, as far as I know. Except her doctors, of course. I mean, if people found out they might want to steer clear of her. Like me. She still had to live, didn't she?'

'And she was still on this drug? Interferon?'

'Sure. You're on it for a year. I believe it improves the liver function though she said you were lucky if it killed off the virus completely.'

'And she told you no one knew about it.' Mitch was talking more to herself than Bernice. She turned: 'Are you sure she'd given up street drugs?'

'That's what she said and I saw no sign of anything like that. She couldn't even tolerate alcohol any more. Apparently, that's one of the signs that you've got Hepatitis C.'

'And if she was tired all the time it could be she didn't have the stamina to hold down a full-time job for any length of time. I asked you about girlfriends?'

'She did mention one or two girls' names but I don't know where they lived or anything.'

'Julian Small might know. If I can track him down. Do you mind if I take the correspondence with me?'

Bernice didn't answer straight away. 'OK,' she decided. 'I can't really believe anything awful's happened to her but if it has I'd never forgive myself if I didn't help you ... I mean...' and her hands spread out. 'All this does put me in a very awkward position, you know? You will speak to Sissy?'

'Sure. I'll get it sorted as soon as I can. In the mean time, do you think if I have a quick look through the boxes ... something might jump out at me...'

Bernice sat on the bed and watched her work. Mitch eventually gave up. 'Doesn't seem anything here to help me but we'll go through it properly when we get the stuff down to Devon. Well, I think that's all. Thank you very much for being so cooperative.'

'Just a minute...' said Bernice as Mitch retrieved her bag and the box of letters.

In the hallway they knocked into each other as Bernice gave her a plastic carrier bag to put the correspondence in. 'And it's possible this may help.' Bernice held out another letter. 'She sent it to me last year. I mean ... oh well ... you never know... As I said, I don't want to hustle anyone but I'd rather like to get that room decorated before the new girl turns up. There's one thing about yellow. It does let in the sunshine. You know?'

Mitch was looking down at the letter she'd been given.

'There is one other thing. Something and nothing. Just after she'd gone I did get a phone call for her. Some girl with a foreign accent. I told her Rosie's new address.'

'What was the girl called?'

'She didn't give her name. Just said she was an old friend but they'd lost touch recently.'

'Can you remember anything else about the call?'

'Not really. No. I mean, it was no big deal, was it?'

Mitch shoved the letter in the bag with the others. As Bernice opened the door for her she asked: 'Is it safe round here?'

'It's not safe anywhere,' said Bernice.

9

There was always something teddy bearish about him. It was a quality, she was sure, which earned him a good living. People liked his air of solid, warm comfort and talked to him. He was interested in them, they felt. Actually, it usually wasn't personal. He was a man with a great deal of curiosity. Coral had first talked to him about buying the shop premises in Torquay and then about the cottage in Coombe Foot. That was the time he'd first met Arthur. It was much, much later she'd talked to him about her husband and then she hadn't intended to. After a discussion about buying the shop premises next to hers and extending into it, Clive Upjohn had said what about a drink and a bar snack lunch.

When he'd come back to the table with their drinks he'd caught her watching a young couple. 'First I started watching people to see what the women were wearing, you know? That was before I was absolutely sure in my mind what kind of a fashion boutique I wanted to run. Most women have no style at all. Some, and this is bad, too, try over hard. Sort of like painting by numbers. With one or two very rare women you're left thinking: Is this going to be the fashion? Is this what's coming in? They may not look nice but there is something incredibly stylish about them. If they were wearing cement bags you'd be thinking cement bags were about to happen.'

'You are looking for trend setters?'

'At first I was just looking at women. And then I became more specific. I started looking at shapes and what suited those shapes and what garment and colour went with what. I built up my business by not selling women the clothes they thought they wanted to buy. I work my bum off selling them clothes that suit them. You only have to say, "No, I don't think that's quite you", but you don't guide them to what suits them. You let them choose and choose until you can honestly say, "You look seriously good in that" . . . and other people say that, too – friends, family – so they come back and their friends start coming in. Selling people clothes they look nice in is very good business.'

She sipped her spritzer. She had never told Arthur about why she bought the stock she did and how she sold that stock to her customers. He was a man who was obsessed with being top of the class so that any skills he didn't command he tended to denigrate.

She would always be a foolish little 'see me' girl to him. Unless he woke up one day and saw her through new eyes. Saw her in the way other men did, men like Clive Upjohn.

She told Clive: 'I've got into the habit, now, of watching people. Have you noticed how some couples, particularly young ones, seem joined even when a room separates them? It's as if they were caught in some honeyed spider's web. Their backs may be turned to each other, their minds full of someone else, but then a slight shift exposes the thread between them.'

She amazed herself when she said: 'I can't believe that Arthur and I were ever like that.' She paused. He did not seem worried or shocked by what she said, simply interested. She went on: 'Though at one time I do remember *needing* to say his name and I'd work it into any conversation. You know, "Arthur says...", "Arthur does...", "Arthur thinks..."' She then remembered something which shocked her now: 'Secretly, in my mind, they were sort of enchanted words, "with my body I thee worship"... I honestly can't believe that now but I know it happened. In the beginning, you know?'

'You were little more than a child when you met. Well, actually, you *were* a child.'

'I liked sherbet,' she remembered. 'I wonder if you can still get that?'

Months later, in his office, she told him: 'I

am not saying I'm thinking of leaving Arthur because I'm not, you know. It's sort of … well … I'd just like to know, that's all. If we parted could I still keep my business and the cottage? I need working capital, too. Would he be entitled to half of my money? I simply want to know what the legal position is…'

It was when they were eating dinner at the Carlton Arms in Ashburton that she said: 'Things really seemed to change when my son went to university. It was almost as if I'd suddenly become colour blind. Well, not quite that. Not so obvious as that. More a toning down to an interminable dimness. Dinginess. Do you know, I put it down to the house needing repainting. We had a fresh coat of magnolia. The decorators did the inside of the house from top to bottom.'

He began to laugh and she did, too. She laughed so much that tears came into her eyes.

Later, perhaps a month later, when they walked through the woods with the lurcher off the lead, chasing in front, she said: 'This evening over tea…' She paused. Should she have said tea? Well, she and Arthur had eaten at half-past six. No one had dinner at half-past six, did they? Nor supper? But she didn't feel really anxious about it, she discovered. 'Well, I said "due to" and he corrected me – should have said "owing to..." I think he has knowledge like other people have Jaguars or gold cards or street cred.' She considered. 'It doesn't get me mad any more. It sort of bores me. He bores me so much it's almost a physical thing. I can't bear to look at him. I try not to look at him any more. Blot him out, I suppose.'

Walking on, she thought about it. She certainly wasn't bored when they rowed, and that was becoming scarily frequent. 'I don't think that's quite right, really. Of course, he does bore me...' and then she managed to dig out the thing that really worried her: 'He frightens me.'

'Has he ever hit you?'

'Not really. Actually, it's the other way round. I've slapped him when he's really, really got up my nose.'

'If he ever hits you get up to the hospital. That's evidence.'

'What if he *killed* me?'

'You're not seriously suggesting–'

'No,' she said. 'I'm just being stupid.' Her hand was in his now and she'd not quite known how it got there: 'I suppose it's because he's so strong. Built like a little bull.'

'If there's any violence you must get out.'

'I don't know why I said that. He's never knocked me about.'

'Jo-jo!' he'd called, and the dog had come to heel.

The next weekend his wife Cecily went to Kendal to see her mother and he sneaked her in through the back door of his house. Though the wine had yet to be opened, they were both intoxicated by the knowledge that all this was happening in the centre of the village, right under the noses of their neighbours. He took the wine up to his and Cecily's bedroom. He got undressed, propped the pillows up on the bed and lay watching her as she examined the peach chintz curtains Cecily had chosen, picked up her scent bottle, opened her wardrobe, dressing-table drawers. She took out Cecily's nightgown, a white floaty affair, the neck trimmed with rosebuds. He watched her undress and put it on. He did not move from his sitting position as she came over to the bed. She bunched the front of Cecily's nightgown, lifted it and straddled him, she as soft and warm as sun-warmed water, he as hard as granite.

Later she carefully smoothed the creases out of the nightgown and slipped it back in the drawer while he, still in bed, opened the wine.

'Now when Cecily wears that I'll always remember you,' he said.

'Will you?'

'Arthur doesn't know what he's lost.'

'I'm too old for him. Have been for a long time now,' she said.

'*What?* You're hardly in your thirties. You, my dear, are just the right age.'

'He likes teenagers. Though maybe, even when I was seventeen, I was a little old for him. I found that out by watching. You know? The kids he teaches at school.'

'You're not saying–'

'No. I'm not. I shouldn't think he's let himself know. He only knows about un-important things. Where Vietnam is, for instance.'

He handed her a glass of red wine. 'And the difference between "due to" and "owing to".'

'You remember that.'

'Of course I do.'

They silently toasted each other. Both knew there would be other times. Both knew it would never again be as good as it was this first time. 'Will you change the sheets before Cecily comes back?' She was curious.

'No. I don't want her asking questions.'

'Do you often ... well, you know...'

'Not for quite a while. Come here.'

But Coral shook her head. She knew she'd always remember what had happened tonight and she didn't want to spoil it with what might be less than perfect. Besides, she wanted to leave him needing more.

When she got home she found herself slyly looking at Arthur Trimble and then biting back her laughter. Sitting in a chair, a finger trailing along her belly. In her mind that finger was stroking Clive Upjohn's seed, those jewels hidden in her flesh.

Cecily was back from visiting her mother, but, fortunately, the weather had turned warmer. After her tea, at six thirty, and before the Upjohns' dinner at eight, they met twice under a large oak tree, three hundred yards away from the boundary of Oa Bone's land. Jo-jo, the lurcher, was let off his lead during the coupling, each moment of which was spiced with the fear of being discovered by others enjoying the spring woods. Though these occasions had only been two in number, Coral had now evolved the ideal outfit. She had dispensed with bra and knickers, wore black floral-sprigged pants, cut wide in a crinkly crease resistant fabric and with an elasticated waistband. The matching sweater and top fleece were jumbo-sized. There was plenty of room for hands to delve and dive. She didn't want to be caught naked in the woods. In this outfit he could fuck her with slight, easy adjustments to her clothing. He, seeing how well her outfit worked, took to wearing jogging pants which also had an elasticated top. The fact that their buttocks froze over was part of the fun; ice in the gin.

'But you do plan it all wonderfully well,'

he'd told her. 'I don't know why I'm surprised at that. It's inventive planning which has made your business so successful.'

Shortly after this second rendezvous he'd rung her at the shop. 'Have you seen the weather forecast?'

'The outlook's none too clever.'

'What about getting one more in while we can?'

'Why not?'

'It's a bit inconvenient because we're having people over to dinner tonight.'

'But Jo-jo will have to have his walk.'

'Quite.'

'A quickie then.'

Coral rang Arthur when she knew he'd be on his lunch break. In the hearing of her assistant she said: 'Terrie and I are going out to the flicks after work. We're going to go and cry buckets at *Out of Africa* again.'

'When will you be back?'

'Not late. Around nine. There's a quiche in the freezer.'

When she put the phone down Terrie said: 'He's going to cotton on. It's a wonder he hasn't already.'

'Not him,' said Coral though she felt her stomach suddenly tighten. 'I wish I could wake up tomorrow and find Arthur just not there. Sort of magicked away.'

'My old man would magic me away if I got up to what you're getting up to.'

'Well, I like that! The way you've played around.'

'Not since I've met Darren I haven't.'

Coral, who was always smartly dressed while she was at her business, was looking through the racks for an outfit similar to the one she wore when she met Clive in the woods. 'Red's definitely not my colour,' she said, 'but I think this one's going to have to do.'

'Are you and this solicitor serious?'

'What do you mean?'

'Well, is he going to leave his wife for you?'

'I doubt that. She's got money. Or she will have when her mother dies. Anyway, it's not that kind of a relationship. You know? Nothing heavy. Honestly, Terrie! The look on your face. It's such a long time since I've had any fun. I'd clean forgotten what having fun was like. I don't want to get hitched up to anyone else. I seem to have spent all my life hitched up to someone. I'm not so old. I just want to live a little before it's too late.'

'If that's what you want, you're really going to have to dump Arthur then. And I can't see him going quietly.'

'He might. If I handle him right.'

'You've got a very good lifestyle. He won't want to give that up and go and live in digs.'

'God. You're such a ray of sunshine.'

'It's not as easy as you think. I should know. I've been through one divorce.'

'Well, I've got to do something. I'm only thirty-six!'

The shop door opened and Terrie turned with a smile to the customer. Coral unhooked the red outfit and took it into the back with her. She changed into it after they'd closed the shop for the day and topped it with the fleece, a favourite garment of hers. She had an hour and a half to kill before she met Clive so she strolled down to the promenade and sat outside a café. She ordered a cheese sandwich and pot of tea. She'd almost finished when an old woman who obviously recognised her strolled towards her. Coral couldn't place her. She supposed she must be a customer. The woman said: 'Well met. At least for me, that is. You are going back to Coombe Foot? I don't suppose you could give me a lift?'

Coral was just about to say no when she realised the situation could escalate if she weren't careful. She'd placed the woman. 'It's Mrs Bone, isn't it? You're over to see your son? Sit down and we'll order more tea.' Oa Bone's mother looked so ordinary that many people had difficulty linking her to her flamboyant son. Her basic shape was square, chubby, freckled flesh rolling slightly on her blunt bones. A thick white fringe of hair almost touched the top of glasses looped about her neck by a long fake gold chain. Her clothes, Coral was pretty

146

sure, came out of Marks and Spencer. Nothing about her told anyone that her son was a multi-millionaire.

When the waitress came out Mrs Bone spoke to her in a foreign language. Not French, not German. Coral knew enough to realise that. The waitress was laughing and talking very rapidly. When she'd disappeared, Mrs Bone said: 'Evie was born in Czechoslovakia, just like me. She came over here when she married an Englishman.'

'You'd never know. I mean, you speak perfect English.'

'I was born in Sudetenland on the Czech-German border. The Allies hoped to appease Hitler by giving it to him and thousands of us fled into the Czech interior. I suppose you could say I'm here, sitting in this chair, because of a young English stockbroker. The British Refugee Office was set up in Prague. Three months before the Germans marched in, a man called Nicholas Winton organised children's transports. Trains taking us children to sponsors in England. I was nine and my cousin was seven. My mother and father, all my other cousins, everyone except an aunt, died during the war.'

Coral stared at her.

Mrs Bone laughed. 'Norman calls me a bit of ancient history.'

'Norman?'

'Oa is a stage name, of course. He kept the Bone bit because he said it had the right sound. Mr Winton and his friends saved over six hundred of us children. We even had our own school in the heart of Wales during the war.'

They rose from the chairs and before they left Evie came out again. 'Sorry about that,' Mrs Bone said as they walked away. 'We don't get much opportunity to chat in our own language. Actually, in Sudetenland we were supposed to speak German but Czech was a point of honour when I was a child. Czechoslovakia was only founded in 1918, after the break-up of the Austro-Hungarian empire, and my parents were very fierce about speaking in our own mother tongue.'

'Did you ever go back?'

'Yes, after the war. There was my aunt, you see. But a butcher and his family were living in her old flat in Prague and she was allocated just one room. There was a lot of bad feeling. I shared the room with her for a while and then came back to England. She wouldn't join me but she did come over for holidays.'

'My mother remembers the war a bit,' said Coral. 'She thought that when it was over it would stop raining for ever! Of course, she was only a little kid then.'

It was dark by the time she dropped off Mrs Bone at the security gate to Oa Bone's house. The property was screened by high walls and trees and most of the people in the village had never seen it. Those who had were, on the whole, disappointed. She'd heard it was a very pleasant two-storey Victorian villa with a verandah running along the front and a fine conservatory at the rear. 'But you couldn't call it a mansion,' one man said. 'And that's the least you'd expect, isn't it?'

There was a narrow single-lane road to Coombe Foot from the centre of the small village of Bishop Coombe and another, equally narrow road half a mile beyond Bishop Coombe. This was situated near the estuary and the seaside town of Teignmouth. It was off this second road that Oa Bone's property lay, extending through woods and pastureland almost to Bishop Coombe. Clive and Coral met a few hundred yards beyond the boundary of Oa's land in denser, more private woodland owned by a local farmer. Clive approached this spot with his dog from the road nearer the estuary, she from the village of Bishop Coombe. She ran her car off a bend in the lane and parked it on grassland under a stand of young elms. When she'd been a child the village had been full of venerable elms but they had succumbed to Dutch Elm Disease and the saplings, as they approached maturity, also died off, leaving small, desolate pockets in the verdant landscape.

Clive was there before her but he wasn't sitting under their tree waiting for her. He was deep in greyish pools of bracken. His dog, out of sight, was sending up crackling fronds and dead leaves as he dug through undergrowth. Bursts of whining yaps, soft, almost purring growls rose as a second level of detritus, heavier, just cleared the fronds: grit, soil, a clunk of pebbles.

Half turning, Clive said: 'I don't know what he's found.' His boater-shaped gaberdine hat, brim well down, hid the upper part of his round face. The dog's yaps began to rise; frenzied, piercing, almost a squeal. 'Jo-jo. Quiet! For God's sake—'

The dog suddenly shot through the ferns, something between his jaws. 'He's got a dead mouse,' Coral said.

'Disgusting creature.'

The animal lifted salivating jaws higher, showing off his prize. Coral intuited rather than saw. There was a trembling at the back of her knees, making the joints collapse a little as if the bone had suddenly become friable.

'What on earth's he got?' asked Clive.

'Is it a finger?'

Clive waded out of the ferns. Jo-jo trotted over to him and dropped his find. Clive squatted.

'It's a finger,' she insisted. She was suddenly afraid he'd lie to her.

He quickly snapped on Jo-jo's lead. The dog began barking, twisting his body in an effort to break free. 'Hold him, will you? I'll have a look-see. Better use both hands. He's a devil when he wants to get at something.'

One hand on the leather part of the lead, another on the chain, she watched Clive plunge back into the ferns, a black figure against lighter night. He bent down and she lost sight of him. Jo-jo, transferring his attention from the finger to his master, stopped barking. In the sudden silence, far away, she heard singing. A man's voice. She could not make out the words but knew them from the tune.

Well, you've got it wrong
Hey, you're not my song
You're just some ordinary babe-ee-ee
Who's driving me craz-ee-ee...

Jo-jo started barking again and now both she and the dog were looking at the finger, lying on the top of a tussock of grass, seemingly pointing towards them. Was she mistaken? Could it be one of those sheaths used to protect an injured finger? But this, she knew, was a bloated finger.

The tussock began to sway in her vision, running towards her like an incoming tide.

The finger grew, pointing her out, filling her vision. She closed her eyes. From the crown of her head to her heels hair stiffened, her skull, her spine, tibia, fibula, scaphoid, covered in quills of dread. Toes rooted in dread.

Clive rose up from the bracken, bubbling in shadow. 'I don't want to disturb the site.' He had to raise his voice to be heard over Jo-jo's barking, steering the words over the spaces between them. 'It looks like Jo-jo's found a body. A woman, I would judge. She must have only just been buried.'

She had opened her eyes. She formed her words with equal care. 'Why do you say that?' Rigid, dread now trickling out of her hide, down the soft, ripe inner sides of her legs.

'We were here two – was it three? – nights ago. Jo-Jo didn't dig up a finger then, did he?'

'What are we going to do?'

He was wading back out of the bracken. She found herself looking at his hands, capable hands, each digit flexed, ready to snap the necks of fronds which waved before him. She didn't look at the finger two yards from her feet though now she knew it well enough. One from a pair of middle fingers.

'I shall go back home and call the police.'

'What about *us?* There's Cecily and Arthur.'

'I was alone, walking the dog. You're not here.'

Understanding was very slowly forming in her mind. 'I'm not here,' she said, having to capture words and surprised when she heard each one because she thought of herself as speechless.

'Coral...'

She experimentally broke one foot free from the earth beneath it. She raised her head and looked up at him. He was six inches taller than she was and standing too far from her, the intimacy between them streaky with darkness. 'I can't smell her,' she said, though she was wrinkling her nose up as if she could.

'He's only unearthed a hand. But it looks as if it's attached to an arm. Hey! Steady...'

'I'm all right. I'll go home now.'

'I'll come down to the car with you.'

'No. We might be seen together. From the road.'

'Coral–'

'Shocked. That's all.'

'Look. We can't be in touch. Not for a while.'

She knew they'd never be in touch again, not in any intimate way, and now other concerns were filling her mind. The most prominent was loneliness. She began to shiver.

'You've got to get a grip.'

'I *will* be all right.' She turned from him and, walking very carefully through the lively darkness, wanting to be sure each limb was functioning normally, negotiated bracken and tufts of grass until she came back down the path. Now she knew her bones were articulating correctly she dared to look into her mind. To her relief she discovered the labyrinth was bunged up. 'And we don't want to get our finger out, do we?' It was only as levity bubbled up she realised she'd been catapulted to the edge of hysteria.

Behind her she could hear the dog barking.

She was finding it difficult to subdue laughter.

10

'Tommy? Hi, there!' Mitch dropped her bag and transferred the receiver to her right hand. 'I've only just this minute walked in. I've been in the studios most of the morning pulling together the last of my stuff for Radio Brum. Thank God I've wrapped it up. Minus the pink ribbon, it's all on the station manager's desk. Well in the can. W-o-n-d-e-r-f-u-l. When I've snatched a bite to eat I'll hit the road. I should be down in Devon around teatime.'

'I've tried to reach you on the mobile, too.'

She looked round, wondering where her mobile phone might be.

'My dear, that's why the agency got the mobile phones. You know. Instant contact.'

Mitch passed a weary hand across her brow. 'I fucked up. Right?'

Tommy, who didn't like to hear her swear, said nothing.

'I've simply been so colossally busy. I went down to London to interview Rosie Childe's flatmate yesterday. Remember? It was midnight when I got back. OK, OK so I forgot to take the mobile.' It didn't seem politic to mention she'd spent the afternoon shopping in London. Apart from anything else, she was not in a position to afford any of the six items she'd bought. A queasy sickness, gone almost before it registered, fluttered in her stomach. She hadn't even opened the last builders' bill. 'I got up with the *lark* to finish off my radio work.' The righteousness which had underpinned the sentence evaporated. 'Something's happened.'

'A body was found in woodland on the edge of the village. I heard it on the radio. just a brief statement.'

'Rosie Childe?'

'No one knows. Not yet. Sissy rang before she started the journey down from Stratford. She doesn't think it can be her sister. They found a funny sort of needle in the jacket pocket of the victim. The kind used to inject drugs under the skin.'

'Oh my God. They've found Rosie all right.'

'Why do you say that?'

'Bernice Brody. The flatmate. She told me Rosie had contracted Hepatitis C. She was on Interferon. Injected with this little needle. Into the skin over the stomach, I think Bernice said.'

'Sissy doesn't know that.'

'Nobody knew. Bernice found out when she spotted her injecting one day.'

'You are sure of this?'

'Well, Bernice was so worried about contracting the virus she told Rosie she'd have to leave the flat.'

'So Mitchell and Orient have a murder inquiry on their hands.'

'We have?'

'The victim was shot.'

Mitch was silent.

'Do you think I ought to get hold of Sissy? Tell her?'

'No, Tommy. No. She'll find out soon enough.'

'Listen, I'm going to have to go over to Bristol this afternoon. A guy called Julian Small. He and Rosie met in Bosnia while she was doing some aid work.'

'Bernice – the flatmate – she mentioned him, too. Not a boyfriend. At least she didn't think so. You've tracked down his address? Good for you. Bernice hadn't the faintest... She came up with some interesting stuff but it'll keep until we meet up. When will you be back at Manaccan House?'

'Hopefully, I'll be there when you arrive. But I'm not sure how long it will all take. Look, I wonder if you could interview this doctor that Rosie had Sunday lunch with? She lives at Newton Abbot. It's on your way. I'd fixed an appointment for four thirty but I'm not sure how my day will pan out.'

'Sure. That's OK. Hazel Rayburn, wasn't it? So we're just going to press ahead.'

'Until we're pulled off the case, yes.'

'You are positive this isn't an accidental death? People do shoot themselves, you know.'

'Women don't shoot themselves, do they? But no, I'm not sure. I mean, I don't know if the post-mortem's been done yet. Sissy didn't say and I didn't ask. I didn't ask her anything, actually. I only know what she told me. She sounded – well, only just about in control. I'm going to push off to Bristol now. We'll know a lot more by this evening.'

'Will Sissy be staying at Manaccan House with us?' She was wondering how they would cope. In Mitch's opinion, Sissy was a seriously over the top character; a distraught Sissy might turn into a localised typhoon.

'I don't know.'

'Well, we'll just have to manage her somehow,' said Mitch.

'I know you're not at all cold-hearted, my dear, but every now and then you really do sound it, you know.'

'One's got to survive. Sissy at full stretch would not be a human being. We're into a phenonemon.'

'Oh, I see.' Tommy didn't like the sound of this. 'If the worst comes to the worst there must be a village GP. He'll have something in his bag of tricks. I must be off, Mitch. Bring your mobile down.'

'Sure. Hey. Hang on just a minute. I need

this doctor's address and any directions she gave you...'

Mitch, directions on the back of a supermarket receipt, put the phone down. She began looking round the lounge of her flat. Her back was already aching a little with weariness – 'and a betting person would put good money on you bashing back up the motorway tomorrow, case in the hands of the police, and you with no broadcasting work, nothing to do but rearrange unpayable builders' invoices...'

Ho-hum.

She found the mobile phone on the bread board, scattered with crumbs, next to a dried-up heel of bread. Where's warmth and order, she wondered, the Aga, the checked red table-cloth, dogs in baskets, dishy home-made soup and equally dishy men taking off game jackets after hot country pursuits and now in pursuit of scrumptious totty, i.e. me?

In your dreams.

What she wanted, to make up for it all, was a good slug of gin, but as she had a three-hour plus drive ahead of her she settled for a hot shower and a cheese and pickle sandwich washed down by coffee. By one o'clock she was smoothly on her way south, the nondescript grey Escort, she had to admit, without the vices of her old TVR. For one thing the floor beneath the pedals seemed quite secure.

It was only when she eased her car on to the M42 that she wondered why Tommy had chosen to do the Bristol interview. She would be passing through the city in a couple of hours and it made much more sense for her to stop off than for him to make the long round trip. It won't be because he's got into a muddle, as I might have done, she thought. He'll have his reasons. Some line of inquiry which hasn't quite yet crystallised in his mind?

She liked Tommy but he did have this way of making her feel inadequate. Circumstances always seemed on top of her and she dodging around them, trying to turn to her advantage a little bit here and a little bit there, aware always of the precariousness of life. He was Mr Control, spread sheets filed in correct order in his office, knives lined up in his kitchen. Whatever happened in Tommy's world, he'd never find his mobile phone sitting next to stale bread.

She'd always had this worry that one day events might really run away with her and she'd topple into catastrophe; now she saw that this was an ever-growing possibility. As soon as this case was over, probably by tomorrow morning, she'd have to face some hard decisions. A decision.

Halt the conversion work on the chapel and try to sell?

This was the first time she'd asked herself that question.

She was now on the M5. She'd seen cloud building up over the Malvern Hills and, as she approached Tewkesbury, she was running into squally showers.

She first turned on the radio and then the windscreen wipers. Soon she was singing along with the music, amusing herself by pretending to be a baritone. 'Deep in my heart ...' Altering the words: 'Down in my boots...'

Suddenly she was completely making up words and tune as she bowled along.

'Oh, I'm a splendid bit of totty,
Why are you so goddamned
     snott-e-ee-eee...'

This in a high, wailing squeal she imagined imitated some female pop stars.

Mitchell, you've been in some frightful financial holes before, she told herself. You've always pulled out of them. You'll do it this time, too.

'I'll hop out of my kit
For any boy who's fit...'

She made good time, coming off the A38 at the all-singing, all-dancing roundabout at Newton Abbot not long after four. Shuffling lanes, shuffling through traffic lights, she headed into the small town, branching off when she saw the sign to the railway station. The station came up on her right, an imposing, two-storey Victorian building with an apron before it large enough to accommodate six or seven horse-drawn carriages; now at least twenty cars were parked in front of the brick and granite façade. The distant, mournful hoot of an incoming train floated through her opened window.

Pubs and shops appeared on either side of the Escort. She came to a crossroads, more shops on the far side but on the nearside almost a mirage, a gathering of solid, pastel-washed villas. Victorian, she guessed, though they looked Georgian. A small, calm oasis just above the newsagents, charity shops and discount stores, occasional empty windows showing that the recession of the early nineties was still lingering.

She found her way through to the villas and eventually spotted Townend. It was detached, though separated by only a few yards from neighbours, washed in Wedg-wood blue, windows and quoins trimmed in white-painted stone. A small front garden had a box hedge. The rest was gravel and a grey Rover was parked just beyond the entrance. The sun came out as Mitch drew alongside the kerb. After she'd locked the car and stretched, she found herself watching light explode on the fanlight above the white panelled door. Mitch's old house had been built of red brick but in style it resembled this one and she felt a little tweak of yearning. That house was the one in which she and her husband Max had brought up their daughter, Cassie. And then he'd died and Cassie had gone off to America. It had been hard adjusting from a warm, family life to her present solitary existence. Occasional lovers might spice things up for a time but none replaced the teasing bear of a man who, she realised, still claimed a central part in her life. Her day-to-day activities were now measured against his absence as once they'd been measured against his presence.

Still fighting to be her own person. Whatever that might really mean. After all, the only people who could live in a vacuum were the dead.

She rang the domed brass door bell and stood admiring the rather gruesome knocker, a severed cast-iron hand. A large-boned woman appeared on the step above her, tall but with a small, rather delicate freckled face, a lot of frizzy yellow hair balancing the figure. She was wearing a nut brown dress in lightweight wool. It was sprigged with tiny lavender roses and her large feet were thrust in matching lavender boots. 'Hello there' – a voice with some boom in. Mitch was reminded of games mistresses and long ago hockey fields. 'You must be Mitch Mitchell. Your chappie rang.' Mitch found herself looking up into grey eyes with a knees-up sparkle lurking in their corners. She felt small, which she physically was, and not quite to Hazel Rayburn's taste. If she wanted Dr Rayburn's approval she'd have to fight for it. This made her tense for Mitch always had the childish desire to please people and she had to work quite hard to ignore it. Dr Rayburn is twenty years your junior, she told herself, and yet here you are seemingly reduced to a recalcitrant schoolgirl. She squared her shoulders. 'Nice to meet you.'

'We'll pop into the morning room. Mummy's in the lounge.'

The hall was a comfortable place with a coat flung across a Victorian spoon-back chair, keys and letters strewn across the top of a mahogany chest of drawers near the bottom of a wide, white-painted stairway. Dr Rayburn opened a door just beyond the rising banister rail. She did not step aside to allow Mitch to enter first.

Mitch said, while the back of the woman was still towards her: 'I suppose you have heard they've found a body at Coombe Foot?'

'Do take a pew, Miss Mitchell.' No

refreshments were offered, Dr Rayburn's leisure hours perhaps too often interrupted for her to bother about social niceties. A decision she'd consciously taken, Mitch guessed.

She and the doctor settled themselves in large comfortable chairs by an empty black marble fireplace. It was a cheerful room, pink-beige walls, pinky sludge fabrics and an old Persian rug with a navy ground on the floor.

'Rosie's disappeared before, you know. She's never been found dead. I can't believe it's her. I mean, that woman was shot. That's got to be murder. Before you ask, Rosie's not my patient. I make it a rule not to have friends on my list. I was about to get her on a colleague's list when she did her bunk. I have to say, though, I do find it rather odd that she's upped stumps just now. She certainly led me to believe she was looking forward to working at St Ursula's.'

'Did you know that Rosie had Hepatitis C?'

'Yes. She told me she was taking Recombinant Interferon Alfa. It's a drug which interferes with virus reproduction. It had been used with another drug called Ribavarin but, although the majority of people don't suffer too many side effects from Ribavarin, she became severely anaemic and her specialist had discontinued it – at least

165

for now. She said she'd got so tired that even going to the lavatory felt like climbing Mount Everest.'

'Do you think she was fit to go to work?'

'Oh, yes. By the time I saw her the red blood count was back to normal.'

'Should she have thought of working in a school at all? Hepatitis C is infectious.'

'Research indicates that the risks of catching it are negligible. Most people do one or two very stupid things in their lives and get away scot free. Rosie was very, very unlucky.'

'You said that you didn't think the body they found could be Rosie's because the victim had been murdered ... but, well, correct me if I'm wrong, I got to feeling...'

'You are very perceptive, Miss Mitchell. Interferon by itself can have very debilitating side effects, too, and one of them is depression. Another is exhaustion. In Rosie's case the exhaustion was caused by her low blood count and when that returned to normal her energy came back. In fact, she had enough energy to think of taking this job.'

'By the same token she'd also have enough get up and go to kill herself. If she were depressed, that is. You think she was.'

'Well, in one way it was perfectly natural she should be depressed. Wouldn't you be if a serious illness had been diagnosed and you were on drugs which, in her case, had produced at least one very unpleasant side effect? At one point it did cross my mind. In some cases clinical depression is a devil – the mood need not be low in a conventional sense. If you remember Sylvia Plath's novel about depression ... it's a feeling, say, of a pane of glass between you and the world. Plath called her novel *The Bell Jar* if I recall correctly... I was going to mention it to the colleague I hoped would agree to become her GP. But to be honest, Miss Mitchell, I could have been quite mistaken. I hadn't seen Rosie for a long time. She was so different ... not in looks, not that. It's hard to put a finger on – the old Rosie just wasn't there any more.'

'You're not the first person to mention that.'

'Look, the odds are totally against her committing suicide. Most people just don't. I simply wanted you to bear that in mind with all the other possibilities.' She leaned forward a little, opening her legs and placing the heels of her hands half-way along her thighs. The material of her dress pooled. Her posture was almost aggressively masculine and yet the soft material of her dress sensuously draped ripe, feminine curves. 'Of course, the changes detected in Rosie by her friends could all be down to Hepatitis C. In my experience, suffering is not ennobling. Seriously bad for the character in most cases.'

'Where did you first meet Rosie? At St Ursula's?'

'We were in the same class though she's a year younger. She's very bright. To tell you the truth, I was always a bit envious. I had to really slog at it, you know? My father was a doctor – he's dead now – and I terribly, terribly wanted to follow in his footsteps. I got through to medical school by the skin of my teeth, though after that I never looked back. Round peg in a round hole. Rosie sailed into Cambridge, no problem. And she had a year out from school.'

'I was coming to that. Why did she vanish? Drugs, boyfriend?'

'I didn't find out until years later, when we were university students, in fact. I used to have a boyfriend at Cambridge – not at the university – and went over from time to time. When she was very drunk one night, she told me she'd had a baby. She was too out of it for me to get more out of her. Later she said she'd gone to London, done bar-maiding work, all sorts. Her father only found out when she was in hospital, giving birth. And that was the time he found out where she *was*, too. There'd been a tremendous police search for her. The baby was put up for adoption and Rosie came home. All very hush-hush. She told me even

Sissy didn't know.'

'Who was the child's father? Could it be Oa Bone?'

'She didn't say. Wouldn't say.' Hazel Rayburn eased back a little. 'But she'd certainly been to some of those wild parties they held at Bishop Coombe at that time. And before you ask me, I never went.'

Mitch was thinking. 'It is amazing that even her sister didn't know about the baby.' She was also wondering why the doctor had told her. Mitch decided that Hazel Rayburn was far more worried about Rosie and her disappearance than she pretended.

'Could Rosie and her father count on Sissy's discretion? Maybe that was the sticking point. Rosie said no one at the school knew though it seems probable to me the headmistress was in on the secret. I mean, Rosie was allowed back, wasn't she? Having a baby is different, say, to someone with a drugs problem. I mean, the headmistress would know she wasn't about to find brown *et al* in the classrooms.'

Mitch moved on. 'These vanishing acts she's sprung on family and friends – it's a very cruel thing to do, isn't it? Torturing those who love her. But then her mother did that to Rosie when she was – eleven, wasn't it? At any event, she dropped out of her life. Some might think it a form of acting out.'

'Not such a wild speculation, but nevertheless speculation. However, the pattern is that Rosie Childe, like a bad penny, always turns up again. I mean, why is her sister employing detectives this time round?'

'Sissy had a dream.'

'We all have dreams, even if we don't remember them the next morning.'

'I usually remember my dreams but I've never acted on one. Sissy's says she hasn't, either. Not before the one about her sister.'

'One knows one can never wholly rely on logic. That's the problem. Makes fools of us all.' Dr Rayburn got up. 'Of course, there is always the possibility that Sissy doesn't want to say why she's worried about her sister. I do find this all ... unsettling. The body they found ... well, of course they haven't identified it yet or we should know...' She didn't look to see if Mitch had got to her feet. She opened the door. 'But perhaps the police can't reach Rosie's father? Isn't he touring in France? With his partner?'

As she walked down the hall Mitch heard a soft, rhythmic wheezing. It took a moment for her to realise it was snoring, a sound coming from the direction of the drawing-room.

'Mummy's obviously got her tootsies up again,' said Dr Rayburn as she opened the front door. 'She never used to when Daddy was alive. But then he didn't approve of females snoring.'

'Thank you for your help.'

'I can't see I've been of help. But then, I suppose you know your job.'

'May I ring if there is something else?'

'Only if it's important,' said Dr Rayburn and shut the door.

11

Though no more powerful than a hand-held sparkler, the glare forced Mitch to shut her eyes. The momentary windscreen dazzle on the passing car was gone. She leaned further back in the driver's seat and, in order to concentrate, closed her eyes again. She was parked two hundred yards down the road from Townend.

She carefully went through her interview with Dr Rayburn, sometimes going back to round up a stray fact and insert it in its proper context. She opened her handbag and fished out notepad and biro. She quickly jotted down the salient facts under varying headings.

Why am I doing all this? she thought, suddenly irritated. Rosie is dead. As far as we're concerned, the case is closed. She reached in her bag again and took out the mobile phone. She rang Tommy.

'Hung speaking.'

'Any more news?'

'Mitch? Sissy's not been in touch but she did say we must leave it to her and she would get hold of us as soon as practicable. Before the day's out at any rate.'

'Where are you?'

'Actually, I've just turned into the driveway at Manaccan House. A four-hour round trip. Quite the soddest of sod's law ... it turns out Julian Small's down this way tomorrow. Tavistock – on business. He's left me his mobile number in case something urgent comes up. Where are you?'

'Newton Abbot. My interview's done and I'm just about to start out for Coombe Foot.'

'I've got some very interesting stuff. Apparently Rosie saw someone else before she went missing. Someone from her past. Julian Small was pretty cagey on the phone which was why I thought it worthwhile bashing up the motorway.'

'Dr Rayburn came up with loads of interesting stuff, too. I thought she'd be far more cagey. A bit tricksy really. She was sure the body they found wasn't Rosie's and, because it's not official yet, I couldn't say different. Could I? But there's no point in getting excited about anything. We'll be on our way back home tomorrow.'

'I forgot to get some milk. If I'm out when you get here I'll be at the village store. It's only five minutes' walk from the house and I need to stretch the old pins. I'll pop the key under the mat. The door everyone uses is at the side of the house in what one supposes was once a track which led to the farmyard. Just pull your car in. There's plenty of room.'

'Look, I'll pick up some milk if you like—'

'The store is where you get to know what's happening in this village. They might have some news. They know me now. We're on very good terms.'

Mitch didn't doubt this. Tommy had a talent for getting people on his side. It was why, rather to her surprise, she'd found herself in business with him. 'OK, honey-pot. See you soon.' She tucked the mobile phone in her bag and started the car. She threaded her way back to the roundabout and had to go round twice before she worked out which lane she needed to pick up the road to Coombe Foot. She decided she must be whacked. She'd had a heavy day before she even began her drive south.

The road climbed steeply ahead of her and by the time she'd crested the hill the houses had petered out. The tarmac ribbon in front of her narrowed abruptly as the car plunged towards the sea. There were shimmering glimpses of the wide estuary and then trees closed overhead to form a green tunnel patched with light. She swung out into corkscrewing bends and through more tunnels, passing colour-washed cottages standing in the dips of fertile, rolling countryside. She came down into another valley and saw by the sign that this was

Bishop Coombe. Cottages snaked along either side of the Escort. Tiny windows glinted.

Following the sign to Coombe Foot, she turned right when she came to the centre of the village. The road climbed and, by the time she'd driven past cottages and a pub, narrowed to a single track unevenly beaded by passing places. She held the centre of the tarmac so she could see more clearly when she came to the bends. The hill was steep. She nudged the vehicle round another bend and then moved up a gear as she went down through woodland. When the car unwound from a Z bend she was suddenly confronted by a policeman, an armless neon jacket over his tunic. He was waving her down.

She poked her head out. He leaned towards her. 'Can you tell me if you drive down this lane regularly?' He held a clipboard, pencil attached with a string. In the distance she could hear a search party moving through the woods. A dog howled. Roots of hair stiffened; gossamer threads of frost at the nape of her neck.

'The dead woman who was found? I heard about it. Has she been identified yet?'

He didn't answer her question. 'If you could just–'

'Afraid I can't help. This is the first time I've used the road. I'm going to stay in the village.'

'Sorry to have bothered you.' He stepped back.

She put the car into first gear. The trees thinned as she plunged towards the valley bottom. Modern houses appeared, scarcely visible through verdant greenery, and then a long cream wall. She arrived at a crossroads and a jumble of thatched cottages with uneven cob walls. She turned into the eddying main street and spotted Manaccan House almost at once, a short high garden wall with an inset wooden gate, a cream-washed gable end and a farm gate on the farther side, fastened back to admit vehicles. She swung on to a wide stretch of gravel. Tommy had backed his Jaguar in and left it at an angle, leaving her a parking space he could ease round. She cut the Escort's engine and wearily stretched herself. Shower first, she promised herself, a glass of something after.

No one answered the bell so she groped under the coir mat and fished out the key. She opened the door wide and then emptied the boot. The suitcase she'd brought was large; clothes for all occasions, including a funeral. There was also the plastic shopping bag containing Rosie's correspondence, which she hadn't yet been through, and a couple of reference books. Inside one of the books was the letter Bernice Brody had given her. This she'd read and her first conclusion was that Bernice had handed her the wrong one.

Pushing the door wider with a wedge-heeled shoe, she lugged the suitcase through. She found herself in a large kitchen, a cream Aga built into the chimney breast at the far end. She dropped the suitcase on old, well-polished terracotta tiles and went to examine the cooker. It emitted a gentle heat. She peered down at her reflection in one of the shiny chrome lids. She then turned to examine the rest of the room. Old pine table and chairs in front of a french window which overlooked a cobbled yard on the other side of the house, pine dresser filled with modern blue and white earthenware, blue gingham curtains, a yellow plant pot with an African violet in it. This, she thought, is seriously unSissy. Where's the industrial steel fridges and worktops, the *batterie de cuisine?* This isn't a cook's kitchen. In other ways, too, Sissy seemed entirely missing; no sign of purple and scarlet cocktail sticks, no gold-plated dishes, nothing over-the-top glitzy.

And then Mitch remembered Tommy complaining about the Buddha in the lavatory and the leopardskin at the end of a bed. She'd obviously been at work in other parts of the house. Mitch found the kitchen warm and comfortable; it made her think of cats lapping milk and fresh eggs with bird shit on them. Am I going to go all twee in my old age? she wondered, somewhat un-nerved. Mitchell, if you ever start feeling tempted to buy brass horseshoes I'm going to divorce you.

She noticed that beside the Aga there was a mini-oven on a worktop with a grill setting, a microwave, toaster and electric kettle. Before she went to hunt for the shower she decided to have a cup of tea. She found the teabags, switched on the kettle and went to explore the rest of the ground floor.

A door from the kitchen led straight into a large beamed sitting-room. Chintz, old furniture, an inglenook. Tommy would love all this, she thought. French windows led out into the enclosed cobbled yard which had been half turned into a courtyard garden. The work appeared to have been left off some time ago. Another door led to an enclosed glass porch on this side of the house. Added in Victorian times, Mitch guessed. There were etched patterned panes, one cracked, surrounded by a border of ruby coloured glass. And that was it. The two rooms were large but from the outside Mitch had supposed the house to be bigger.

She turned back to make her tea. There is something seductive about the place, she thought, rather like landing in the middle of a Beatrix Potter illustration. It has all the properties a hard-headed radio journalist cum detective should scorn. It's endearing.

Yes, well up Tommy's street all this ... letting her partner admire the place for her because she liked to think herself too much a design aesthete to be bowled over by cosy. She brought her tea into the sitting-room, sat on the William Morris patterned linen union, her yawn so big her jaw twanged. She bent and tugged off her shoes, pulled up a footstool and settled her feet on the well-upholstered top. Drinking her tea, she wriggled her toes, admiring the candy floss pink nail varnish and thinking that if they made some money out of this case she'd buy herself some silk knickers. Interlock were sturdy and more comfortable but to conjure up that glint in the eye that aroused a chap's interest you had to invest in silk next to the skin. At least, she thought as she yawned again, it's worth a try.

She woke slowly, at first not opening her eyes, her brain nesting drowsily in her skull. Then a dark blurred world before her, sharpening into Sissy's sitting-room. Sudden anxiety made her sit up straight. She switched on a lamp, glanced down at her watch and saw she'd been sleeping for almost an hour. Where was Tommy?

'Tommy!' She lurched to her feet, hoping for a shouted reply from the kitchen or a bedroom. 'Tommy!'

Where was the man?

'Tommy!'

Switching on the lights as she went, she started in the kitchen and then climbed the stairs. Three bedrooms with beams and ceilings sloping at all angles, a pink shower room with girls and boys in Roman gear looking statuesque on tiled walls, a bathroom with a Buddha on the deep window-sill.

No Tommy.

She went out and checked the cobbled yard which was surrounded by high walls and then the gravelled driveway. His Jaguar was still there but there was no sign of Tommy.

A little quiver of anxiety which she made herself dismiss. What could happen to an ancient Chinese gentleman in a quint-essential English village?

Well, for a start police with dogs were searching woodland for clues to a corpse.

Mitchell, for God's sake.

She looked down at her watch again. It was gone seven o'clock. The village shop would be closed. Anyway, how could you get lost on a five minute walk down a main street? He must have heard something, gone somewhere close by, for he hadn't come back for the Jaguar. But why didn't he ring to let me know?

Perhaps he had. When you're asleep you wouldn't hear the Last Trump, would you?

Mitch's anxieties were not fully allayed. But what can you do, honeypot? You can't scour the village as if he were a lost five-year-old. He's fully grown up and he's only been adrift for an hour. If he went looking for you in similar circumstances he'd spend most of his days trying to round you up.

He'll turn up soon enough, she told herself, and went back into the house. She lugged her suitcase upstairs. Tommy had chosen the best bedroom which had windows looking over the front and back of the property. His alarm clock was on the pine bedside cabinet, the office laptop computer on the chest of drawers. Behind it an oil painting of yachts at sea was propped up and she remembered Tommy complaining about some of Sissy's pictures not being hung on walls.

She chose the next best bedroom – one window, long and very thin with dipping ceilings. There was a wardrobe built into a recess and Sissy had just managed to get a double bed in. She'd had to use compact disc shelves, presumably because she could get nothing narrower, as a bedside cabinet. On top of them was a bedside lamp and Mitch, who liked to read before she went to sleep, nodded in approval. A pine chest was beyond the bed. On one of a pair of lime green glass candlesticks swung a little white pillbox hat, a crest of vivid blue feathers sticking up at the back, short matching veil of blue. A very Sissy touch, she thought. She was quite relieved. She was beginning to wonder if the place really belonged to the cook. She drew the curtains, stripped off and went for a shower.

She put on dilapidated grey sweats and went to explore the kitchen. Tommy had remembered the wine. She opened a bottle of rosé and lifted her glass to him. 'But where are you, you rat? What are you up to?'

Had he and Sissy met up? Was he at Sissy's father's place for some reason? For a moment she was tempted to ring. She resisted it. She had to trust his judgement. Tommy didn't do things on impulse, as she was inclined to. Whatever the explanation for his absence was, it would be a good one.

She fried up some eggs and bacon on a gas hob she found sunk into the worktop. She didn't trust herself with the Aga which, to her, looked as if it had been built to run a steam train or small cargo boat. She sat at the kitchen table, using a hunk of dry bread to soak up the juices. The meal, she had to admit, didn't lend itself to wine but when she'd finished it and washed up she felt a great deal better.

Not wanting to hang around wondering what the hell Tommy was up to, she opened the reference book and took out the letter Bernice Brody had given her. Might as well do a bit of work, she thought.

First she turned to reference works and some maps of what had once been Yugoslavia. She felt she needed to orientate herself. The land lay east of Italy across the Adriatic Sea, not quite as long as the leg of Italy, but fatter. To the north it was bordered by Austria and Hungary, with Romania and Bulgaria further east and Albania and Macedonia to the south, then Greece. Looking at the redrawn boundaries within the old Yugoslavia, Mitch saw that Slovenia, Croatia and Bosnia all took in some of the Adriatic coastline. Serbia was inland, Belgrade not too far from the Romanian border. Far south, butting against Albania and Macedonia, was the Serbian province of Kosovo. Most of the population here were Muslim, she learned, ethnic Albanians. The few Serbs who lived in the region were Greek Orthodox Christians but, as Kosovo was part of Serbia, they ruled.

Mitch studied the map for a few more minutes before turning back to the letter Bernice had given her. It was dated June of last year. Rosie hadn't flown into Belgrade as Mitch, in her hasty first reading, had supposed, but Sarajevo, which was in Bosnia.

'Did you know that Archduke Ferdinand was assassinated in Sarajevo and that was considered the motivating factor in starting

183

the First World War?' Rosie had written. 'Sarajevo is Muslim although no veils are visible and folks don't go to the mosque much. Most dress as if they are supporters of some local football team. But five times a day the call to prayer can be heard in every street. It's sort of part of life like the limited food supply and the erratic power and water supplies. Of course things are better than they were. When I was an aid worker out here people ate grass, dandelions, paper. They even exchanged recipes in the hope of making them tastier! Still, every inch of every garden is used for growing vegetables and they use anything, including old tyres, as planting boxes. I wonder if it was like this at the end of the Second World War? Buying and selling is seriously weird. There are no personal accounts at banks, no cheques, credit cards. It's all cash in hand, generally German marks because no one seems to be able to agree on a mutual currency. I seem to notice everything really sharply now though that might be because you focus on different things when fighting is going on...'

Mitch found herself frowning. Just *why* had Bernice Brody given her this particular letter? What possible bearing could it have on Rosie's disappearance?

She got to the bit in the letter about how Rosie had gone to Zagreb to meet Julian Small and how, quite by chance, they'd come across Yolanda Hadri. 'Actually, fell over her would be a more accurate description. She's a cleaner at the airport there and all these cleaners wear these grotty shoes, sort of high platform things with laces and heels cut out.

'Reading between the lines, I think she's the breadwinner. Musa will hate that. Man and wife things here tend to be pretty State of the Ark – pardon the pun. And, of course, Musa does come from a remote Kosovar mountain village originally. Seriously Muslim macho. But, oh boy, is he beautiful. I thought I'd got over him but there you go! I think Yolanda was a bit hurt, but I thought it better to stay well clear. Of course, I'm always telling myself that me and the Musa Hadri thing was all down to lust. Anyway, on to safer things. I'm always fascinated by communist style. People always think it so drab. Tell me, are bright yellow and orange drab? That's what we're into at the airport.'

Mitch read through the passage again. She wondered if Bernice were telling her in a roundabout way that Rosie and this Musa had an affair?

But what could that have to do with Rosie's disappearance from Coombe Foot? How could it be connected to her death?

I don't yet know for sure she *is* dead, Mitch told herself.

But I actually saw one of those needles

185

Sissy told Tommy about. How many other people use them?

She turned back to the letter.

'Julian was as shocked as I had been when we eventually got back to Sarajevo. I know it sounds ridiculous when we'd both been out here working. But ordinary life takes over when you get back to England and, though you don't really forget, the images get sort of neutralised. That's the best way I can put it. Sarajevo is shocking. Huge skyscrapers – all built on a shoestring – gutted but people living in the ruins. The windows are repaired with plastic stapled to whatever still hangs together. The roads look as if they've been used as giant dartboards. They're well pitted with bullet holes and the poverty is awful. You can get some inkling here as to why they call it grinding. Yolanda, and she's a university kid, is lucky to be a cleaner. Lucky? There'll be some deal going on in the background, I bet. Sexual favours? She's a knock-out looker. Something Musa won't know about, that's for sure. Everyone, but everyone, dreams of getting out. There's an enormous black market, Mafia, three groups of people living side by side who loathe each other – Serb, Croat, Muslim–'

The letter broke off. Mitch, who had scanned it the first time with her mind full of Radio Brum work she had to finish, hadn't realised there was one, possibly

186

more, pages missing.

'You booby,' she told herself and got out her contact book. She used Sissy's phone to call Bernice Brody. No reply.

She poured herself another glass of wine and then put the bottle back in the fridge. Three glasses, she told herself, were more than enough. It was then she noticed a plastic bottle of milk. She stared at it. She couldn't remember seeing it when she found the bottle of wine but it must have been there.

She thought back to what Tommy had said. He must have been at the shop when she arrived because the key was under the mat. But as the milk was here now he must have come back.

You were asleep. He decided not to wake you. OK?

But if he had to go out again why didn't he leave a note for her? The unease she'd felt earlier returned. I'm not seriously worried, she told herself.

But she was.

For once he's acted out of character, that's all.

And then she thought, well, maybe not. If he's not left a note it must be because he's somewhere very close.

She remembered that the gravel drive where they'd parked their cars led to a farm-yard.

Time to explore, she thought. She rooted through her bag for a torch.

The driveway stopped at the rear gable end of the house. There was a cattle grid, an open tubular five-barred gate and a disused concrete farmyard. Weeds higher than she was, perhaps rooted in an old slurry pit, were on one side. In front of her, at the top of a short incline, was a cob barn with a rusty corrugated iron roof. More outbuildings of various widths partly butted on to the gable end of the house and climbed to meet the barn at right angles.

A breeze had got up, stirring the tops of the shooting weeds. She padded up to the barn. The corrugated iron doors were padlocked and it looked as though they hadn't been opened for some time. Behind her she heard two bumps and then a stuttering grating noise. As she turned, the beam of her torch illuminated one of the doors in the row of outhouses. It was swinging into the yard. Something monstrous and rubbery yellow, like a giant duck's foot, emerged. A primitive noise, not quite a grunt. The fat splat of yellow stopped moving.

Mitch found her left hand had crept to her throat. Her body was a bell for the sound of her heart. She pushed unwilling limbs across the cracked concrete. As she neared the open door the yellow blob resolved into a hand in a rubber Marigold glove, splayed now and still.

'Tommy?'

She pushed the door further back.

He was on his belly, one arm stretched out and now almost touching her foot. She had a foreshortened view of the top of his head, the flat back of his skull, his short hair, though grey, almost schoolboyish in the way it stood up round the crown. Half hidden in shadow was a bloodied ear. His legs, behind his neat trunk, had a detached look about them, as if they weren't Tommy's, not any more. They'd somehow come adrift, been discarded.

Juggling with the torch, Mitch propped the door wide with a stone. She knelt down and carefully slid her fingertips under his chin. Her heart was banging so wildly it was some moments before she discerned a thready pulse. 'Oh, Tommy...' she murmured, words almost lost as she expelled a lungful of pent-up air.

He appeared to be unconscious but something was happening, something so quick she couldn't gauge what she'd seen. She was suddenly sure he knew she was there.

Her fearful fingers turned his head to the side to make sure his airways were placed in the optimum position. When she released him there was blood on her thumb and index finger. 'I'm just going to phone for the ambulance. OK? You're fine. You're going to be fine. You hear?' Tears filmed her eyes. 'Oh, honeypot...' and suddenly she was running back to the house.

It was while her fingers were tapping out 999 that she remembered what Tommy had told her about the recurring dream he had.

I'm lying there and I know I'm dying and though I can't see my hands I know I'm wearing gloves but it's not cold enough to have them on.

12

'Mr Upjohn, please.'

'Who's speaking?'

'Coral Trimble here.'

'Just one moment, Mrs Trimble.'

Coral, who had come into the shop's stockroom to make the call, up-ended the biro and then began nervously to walk it through her bony fingers.

'I'm sorry, Mr Upjohn is in a meeting at the moment. Would you like to leave your number?'

She gave Clive's secretary the number and turned to see her assistant Terrie looking round the door. Terrie mouthed: 'Sorry. It's Mr Lucas, looking for a birthday present for his wife. He wants you.'

Coral patted her hair and went back on to the shop floor. During the day she tried twice more to reach Clive Upjohn. He'd just popped out, he was with clients, sorry, his secretary had no idea when he'd be free.

Coral pretended to herself that it didn't matter. No big deal. He was really busy, OK? She was scared by the way her flesh was becoming charged with anger. Intermittently there was a scream of rage somewhere in her stomach; not her throat, that was as silent as the grave. The noise she occasionally allowed was a hum, acting this was just a normal day.

Late in the afternoon she felt she had enough control of eight stones of turbulent meat to voice some of what was troubling her. 'He's avoiding me,' she said to Terrie, very low key. She had been awake for long stretches during the night. There was no problem keeping well away from the soapy, fragrantly scented Arthur, who showered just before he turned in. He seemed to need to keep a distance from her, too. Smells wove confusingly in and out of her mind during these dark hours. There was something distinctly nauseous. Fee, fi, fo, fum-ish.

But the smell of human death, she remembered from childhood, was not pongy like a dead mouse. It was sweet enough to befuddle your senses; white lily sweet, the bloom of ritual decay. Sometimes, the worst times, she was not at all confused. Fright made her scuttle to the lavatory.

Over the breakfast table she tried not to meet Arthur's eyes for fear of what he would read in her face. But why should she feel guilty? She had nothing to do with that corpse. It wasn't her fault.

The police had parked a caravan in the pub car-park.

People could go and tell tales.

'You're in a right state, you are. Ants in your pants. You know that? Must be l-urr-v-vv. You had a row or something?'

'No. No, it's not like that, Terrie...'

'What's up then?'

'Nothing's up!'

'You just said. You said he was avoiding you.'

'Well, I don't–'

'Maybe his wife's found out. What'ser-name? Cecily-face.'

'That woman's too off the wall to see an elephant in her living-room.'

'I wouldn't be too sure about that.'

'I really need to get hold of him, you know? What a time to arse around playing hard to get–'

'Look, if you two really are still hot for each other he's got to have a damn good reason for not returning your calls, right?'

Coral sat down on the chair reserved for the reluctant males women sometimes managed to drag into the shop with them. *Maybe the police were there?* That was ridiculous. Why should they be? All he'd done – all his dog had done, not even him – was find a body.

In her mind's eye she saw the finger. It seemed to float above the tussock of grass. Sometimes it was the size of a finger, at others it was as big as one of those old-fashioned Zeppelins. And it never stopped pointing at her, marking her out. The guilty one. 'Oh, shit,' said Coral.

'Look, you can't rely on men, can you?' said Terrie. 'They've always got their own agenda. I mean, I know they're supposed to be the logical ones but they never are, are they? They're just good at justifying themselves. There's always a save-the-world reason for the shitty things they do.'

'You don't understand...'

How had the finger got detached? Had Jojo just tugged it off or was the woman in a whole lot of little bits and pieces? 'I've got the runs,' she'd told Arthur as she'd scuttled to the lavatory again, and she might have, too, the way her stomach kept yawing.

Sometimes the finger was joined by complete hands. Clive Upjohn's snapping off the necks of ferns, Arthur's strong, gardener's fingers stretching wire, tying up plants. 'Christ! You've turned into a real hard cow. You know that?' The afternoon he'd found her in the sitting-room reading and he'd wanted her to go to the shop for something, she forgot what. Square-ended, muscular fingers itching to inflict damage.

But he didn't know about Clive and her. She was sure of that.

What was there to bloody well know? The man wouldn't even return her calls.

'I hate men. You know that?' she said to Terrie.

'That's why you've got a shop full of clothes so women can dress up to attract them.' Terrie said. 'Honestly, Coral! If you're going to go in for a bit on the side – well, things are going to get really crappy now and again. You're talking to an expert. Worn *out* the T-shirt. I'm glad to be out of that scene, believe me. Sure, it's fun, it's exciting, but it comes with its own barrel loads of shit.'

'It's not like that!'

'What's it like then?'

But Coral couldn't tell Terrie about the dead woman, that what she really wanted Clive for was to find out what the hell was going on, that not knowing was sending her right round the twist. She needed to talk about it, then maybe her anger would go and she wouldn't feel like screaming and her stomach would stop cramping up.

She wanted to feel safe again.

'I need him. You know?'

'You poor cow.'

The weight of Terrie's pity almost brought tears to Coral's eyes. She went to the lavatory again though by now it was a ritual, like putting hands together in prayer.

After that she rang Clive. She was told that he'd gone home early and by now Coral could detect the hint of triumph in the secretary's voice. Relaying piss-off messages could put a bit of interest in a boring day; it could be serious fun being extra specially nice about it.

Coral, tidying the shop floor after the day's work, studied her problem. There was no way she wasn't going to get to see Clive Upjohn so, short of knocking on his front door and pushing past Cecily, how was she going to do it?

Well, he always took Jo-jo for a walk, usually in Oa Bone's wood. 'What if he sees my car?' In her mind's eye she saw him turning and hurrying away. She could park it, as she usually did when she met him, on the other side of the woods and then slip under the wire into Oa Bone's land and hang around by the stile. Chances were he'd turn up sooner or later. But what if the police had widened their search area? No one would be looking after dark, would they?

After Terrie had gone she rang Arthur: 'I'm having to stay a bit late to sort out some new stock. I won't be much more than an hour. Do you want to hang on for tea?'

'You're never home these days.'

'You should be pleased that business is booming.'

'If you say so.'

'Oh, go stuff yourself.' Anger, at last finding release, almost blew her head off. The receiver made a wonderful noise as it crashed back against its cradle. 'Dick head!'

She burst through to the shop floor. 'You hear that!' But hundreds of garments heard nothing at all; an empty yell in an empty shop, but all the same she felt a bit better.

She went to titivate herself, making herself nice for Clive.

Plenty of war paint.

She reached the woods not long after six o'clock. Too early. She leaned back and closed her eyes. She found she was ill with tiredness. It was like mild flu. She was light-headed but weighted with draggy limbs. Nobody said that finding corpses was exhausting, she thought, but it is.

When she woke it was quarter to seven. Clive, a man who was as regular in his habits as Arthur, would be setting off with Jo-jo at seven. She'd better get a move on, she told herself, head congealed with uncompleted sleep. She'd tumbled into unconsciousness practically sitting bolt upright, her seat belt fastened. Clumsy fingers eventually released the belt. She climbed out of the car.

The wind had dropped, but there was a slight rustling all the same. The darkness seemed to move. She locked the car door. It was only when she reached the first pools of newly shooting bracken that she realised she was wearing high heels and negotiating the uneven, shadowy terrain was not going to be easy. 'Shiter-ooo,' she muttered as a twig slapped into her face.

She had to bend double to get under the wire into Oa Bone's section of the wood. When she straightened she suddenly remembered Jo-Jo stopping barking.

Well, you've got it wrong
Hey, you're not my song

But it wasn't music in her ears now. What she was hearing was feet floundering through undergrowth. Hair on her arms prickled as it hardened.

A haphazard jigsaw of lightish cotton trousers, the toe of a trainer, a whiff of good quality perfume and then a square, shadow streaked female figure emerged, a thick fringe playing footsie with the upper edge of wing framed spectacles. The ground was rising steeply so Coral had to crane her neck as she tried to identify the foreshortened figure. She felt she knew the woman but couldn't put her together with a name.

'You out too? Can you see the place? Are the police still there? Is it obvious where they found her?'

'Mrs Bone...' Coral had scrambled forward and was level with her.

'Olga, please.'

Coral was panting, feeling hot and foolish but grateful that Mrs Bone had found a reason for her being in the woods. Eventually, she said: 'You have to get under the wire.'

'I expect the place is marked off in some way? I suppose many would call it idle curiosity. What is idle about curiosity? A woman said my father had been shot in woodlands. But I don't know whether it's true or not. She could have been lying. I know about my mother. She survived the war, you know. They'd liberated the camp she was in. Typhus got her a few days later. Lots of them died of typhus.'

Coral didn't know what to say. She'd made sure she never read any stuff about death camps and nor had she seen any Hollywood version. 'It's just not nice,' she'd told Arthur when he'd wanted them to go and see *Schindler's List*. 'I like a bit of gore,' he'd said. 'It all happened. It's based on truth. Anyway, it's about people being saved.'

'My memories of my mother are good,' said Mrs Bone. 'There's a picture of her in my mind choosing fish from a barrel. A live, beautiful carp. It was for our Christmas dinner and we kept it in the bath tub in the mean time. I never really see my father. The woods are there but I don't go in. I've never been able to find out if the woman lied.'

'But why should she?' Coral was beginning to feel embarrassed, as if a stranger in a bus had suddenly pushed up a sleeve and waved a pus-running arm in front of her.

'Before my mother left she gave family things to friends in the village to look after for us. When I went back after the war two families gave me stuff without me having to ask, another family wasn't too pleased but I got the stuff anyway. This woman denied she was looking after my mother's furs even though she'd been seen walking about in some of them. She was mad at me. Mad fit to burst at me for coming back. It was she who told me about my father. No one else in the village knew anything about it. You have to understand that some people hoped their Jews wouldn't come back and then they'd get to keep the things. She might have told me that about my father to spite me. Mightn't she?'

Why is she telling me this and without a by-your-leave? – itching to get away and yet acutely aware of the old woman sizing up ranks of dark tree trunks and not her. I'm going to miss Clive if I'm not careful. Trying to recall her attention, Coral asked: 'Do they know who the dead woman was?'

'They think it might be Rosie Childe. You know, the cook's sister. She went missing and Sissy's gone as far as paying a private detective to find her. Some old Chinaman. Really rum but then that's Sissy, isn't it? But you don't pay out good money unless you've reason to believe – well, something horrible's happened, do you?' Mrs Bone had turned to her. 'And really, one never knows, does one?'

Coral opened her mouth and then shut it. When she opened it again she said: 'She came into my shop. Seriously. She was in my shop looking for some business-y clothes. She was starting a new job. Very alternative she was, if you know what I mean. All over jeans. She had this most gorgeous man with her who sat and waited. Foreign guy. What did she call him? I can't remember. Is it her? Is that the one?'

'You must go to the police.'

Coral was thinking her way round what might prove to be a problem. 'But it needn't be Rosie, need it? I mean, it could be someone else. For a start we get an awful lot of walkers down here. You don't want to get involved, do you, particularly if it's a waste of time. If it is Rosie I'll tell them.'

Mrs Bone was beginning to look at the wire fence. 'I'm glad it wasn't on Norman's land,' she said.

'I'll lift the wire up a bit for you if you like.'

'That would be kind. I suppose people would say I'm being morbid. My son would certainly not approve.'

'Maybe it's not a good thing to do?'

'It'll be all right,' said Mrs Bone. 'There'll be nothing left to see. Anyway, it's dark.'

Coral, unable to pick her way through Mrs Bone's contorted logic, but without time to argue, hiked the wire up and the old woman, surprisingly nimble, scrambled through to the other side. She looked back at Coral anxiously then with thumb and index finger carefully adjusted her glasses. 'I feel rather foolish, you know,' and when Coral didn't reply, she added: 'There it is.'

'Be careful, won't you?' Coral wagged her hand, an almost royal wave and turned to push her way up through the woods, not looking back. To her the Second World War inhabited the same space as the Battle of Hastings even though her mother had been a child then.

It slid from her mind, immediate physical discomforts taking over. Skin was now being rubbed raw on the inside of her right shoe. My stockings must be in shreds, she thought. She was hobbling as she reached the path that led down to the stile. She looked at the illuminated face of her watch. It was just after seven. She must hurry.

There was no sign of Clive when she reached the stile. Perhaps she'd been foolish to suppose he'd carry on walking Jo-jo through the woods? 'Now when Cecily wears that I'll always remember you,' he'd said as she'd slipped his wife's floaty nightgown over her head. He'd been keen enough on her then. 'Arthur doesn't know what he's lost.'

Well, I don't care about all that, she

thought, I just want to *talk* to him. She bent back through the protective branches of an oak tree. She had to shuffle a bit to find a place she could see out of. I mean, I don't love him. He's really quite flabby. At least Arthur's always kept himself in trim. Not that she fancied Arthur any more. She couldn't now think of a time when she had wanted him. At least he didn't fancy her either. There was no undignified shoving him off.

But what would she tell her son?

He's got his own life now, she thought. A divorce won't be nice though I'll try to do it all nicely.

And then she found herself thinking that if the dead woman was Rosie Childe Arthur wouldn't be involved. No way. Even if Rosie had been a looker, which she wasn't, she was too old for him. Why, the woman was her age or more.

Suddenly there was a picture of Rosie in her mind, a thin woman who didn't hold herself well, who stooped rather, as if she couldn't be bothered to be upright. She'd been unprepared for catching Rosie's eye, darkly bright with life...

Through the veiling twigs she saw movement and then, out of nowhere, Jo-jo was at her feet, wagging his tail, licking her leg. She pushed back branches.

'What the hell are you doing here?' Clive

203

Upjohn was so near she almost bumped into him as she came out of her hiding place.

'What do you think? Why didn't you call back?'

'I thought we agreed we wouldn't get in touch. I thought we agreed that. What's the matter with you? The cops are crawling all over the place, poking, prying, turning up stones. Do you want them to know you were there, too? That we were out for a bit of nooky? Do you want to say that in court, have everyone read it in the papers?'

'I just wanted to know what the hell was going on. You don't know how dreadful it is. I hardly slept at all last night and now I've heard people think it's Rosie Childe and she was in my shop!'

'I don't know yet who it is but I'd say it's unlikely to be her. From what I've heard this is more like an execution than anything else. One shot through the back of the head. Rosie Childe certainly wasn't a member of the IRA and she didn't do drugs. And lots of people saw Rosie before she did a bunk, not just you. Oa Bone was expecting her the Sunday night she vanished. Look, Coral, you've got to start thinking straight. You've got to snap to.'

'I feel so awful!'

'You've got to see this as something to be tackled. If you don't keep your wits about you the pair of us could become the focus of some crap tabloid story or something. Do you want that? If you're not too worried about Arthur, think of your son. Think of your parents.'

'Oh, God...' Coral could feel the tears gathering.

He had his arms around her now and she did feel a bit safer. 'It's knocked you sideways. It's knocked me sideways.' She could feel his hand smoothing back her hair. 'At the moment it's like you're in the middle of a burning house, going frantic, right? You've got to place yourself outside the house. Make sure you don't burn, OK? The bottom line is that it's nothing to do with us, we just happened to find the body.'

'Jo-jo did. We didn't.'

'Jo-jo did—'

'I just needed you so badly. I was so frightened.'

'But you understand what I'm saying? You're a good businesswoman, Coral. You know how to be detached. This is a problem to be solved. Think of it like that. If you go to pieces we're all in the shit.'

'OK.'

He was disentangling himself. 'You're going to be all right?'

'It'll be OK.'

'Don't get in touch again. If you feel you can't hold the line get yourself out of the village. Go and visit an aunt or something.'

'I'll be all right now. I–'

'Sure you will.' He bent down and kissed her, not a lover's kiss and somehow she knew he'd never kiss her like that again. Maybe, because of what they'd found, they'd even find reasons for disliking each other.

'If only it hadn't happened–'

'But it has, so we go on from there. That means you must be off before we get spotted. You'd better hurry.'

She reached up and kissed him on the lips, rubbing herself up against him; because of the way he dressed he always seemed to her to have a bit of the schoolboy about him, someone who could be tempted into mischief. He was all lawyer tonight, almost roughly disentangling himself. She felt hot, slightly ashamed, and turned away quickly before she was tempted to say anything. Hurrying back along the path, she was glad her feet hurt so much; if a tear did manage to escape she could point to popped blisters. What a silly cow you are, she thought. Oh, the mess I've been landed in.

She was shimmying back under the wire at the boundary of Oa Bone's land when, to her left and higher up in the woods, she heard movement. That ghoul of an old woman, she thought, what Mrs Bone had told her hovering about in the back of her mind, loathsome, like uncovered slugs. She increased her pace. I was a fool to try and see Clive. What good has it done? It's upset me more.

But none of it is anything at all to do with me. Clive was right about it. I've got to start thinking straight. She was too tired and confused to try now. She'd make a start on it tomorrow.

It was only when she'd parked her car in the drive that she started to worry about facing Arthur. Oh, balls to it, she thought, pushing back her shoulders as she went into the hall. She knew before she reached the lounge door that he wasn't in; these days she seemed almost to smell his presence. She immediately went across to the drinks cabinet and poured herself a whisky. Lowering herself into her armchair, she took a sip. From the empty armchair opposite his disapproving eyes watched her. He didn't think whisky a suitable tipple for women; he implied it released their vulgarity, made them lascivious in terrifying ways.

She heard the front door open. She tipped the rest back in one gulp and stooped to hide the glass under the frill of the peony-patterned loose cover.

'You're back then,' he said and as he came into the lounge she realised there was something different about him: she sensed him as being bigger, as if he'd thrown off a large shadow and was growing into it.

'Where have you been?' she asked and then she noticed him looking at the wreckage of her shoes.

It was then she saw grass stains on his trainers, a piece of bracken sticking out by his ankle bone.

'I'll give you three guesses. Where have *you* been?'

13

'There is no specific medical treatment in many instances.'

'You can't do anything?'

'I didn't say that. Strokes usually do their maximum damage within twenty-four hours. If the patient survives there is usually a rapid recovery in the first month as swelling dies down et cetera. Hopefully, speech returns. Leg movements begin to occur, arm... Expert nursing in the early period, rehabilitation...'

'The blood ... I thought, well, he'd been bashed over the head.' Mitch was looking up at the doctor who seemed almost naked in youth, tall and hovering about as if he didn't quite know where to put all his limbs. 'Hit, you know.'

'We think he banged his head when he fell.'

'He had a stroke and crashed to the deck? I was talking to him on the mobile hardly any time before!' She could hear her voice rise, she could discern the note of anguish, but at a distance; intellect had detached itself, was as cold as the hospital's sodium glare.

'We'll give Tommy a scan tomorrow. Look, I think you'd better sit down.'

'It's such a shock–'

'There's no pain, you know. The brain is not supplied with a pain receptor.'

Painless apocalypse. Mitch, sinking into the moulded plastic chair, didn't know whether she'd spoken her horror out loud or it was in her head. 'How bad?'

'Well, as these things go, it's pretty severe.' The youngster in a maroon shirt, wearing a stethoscope instead of a white coat, sat down beside her. 'Loss of consciousness. Deep paralysis ... arm and leg ... one side. Difficulty swallowing. There usually isn't any what you might call medical treatment that will help – drugs, you know – but we can deliver expert nursing care, rehab...'

'What are his chances?'

'A third of all people who suffer an acute episode will die within three weeks.'

'He's over seventy.' Mitch said, more to herself than him. 'But I never really thought of him as old. You know? Tommy wasn't an old man.' She corrected herself. 'Isn't an old man.' She was searching her memory and coming up with bits of information garnered when she'd been interviewing experts for a programme during a National Stroke Week. 'A bad sign is incontinence, right? A brain completely deprived of blood will die in four minutes... It's all so sudden ... he was on the phone hardly any time ago.' She was hearing the wail in her voice rising windily higher and was embarrassed. Like an opera singer, she thought. 'What about his relatives? I'm his business partner, you see... I don't know of any...'

'Relatives should be informed as soon as possible.'

'I'll get A.J. on to it the first thing in the morning.' Something stuck at the back of her mind from their first case together. A nephew? Some connection with a Chinese restaurant in Birmingham. Nothing more came to her. 'I think there is someone somewhere. I mean, we were close in some ways, but not close at all. God. We didn't often row but when we did... I mean, we were business partners.'

'You've said. Would you like to see him now? Before he goes up to the ward?'

Mitch found she didn't want to, she needed to shield herself, but all the same she rose to her feet. But what can I do for him? The hospital glare was itself so aggressive as to be near inducing a grimace; chalk-scratching sounds shrivelled her ears as she passed a curtained cubicle. The squish of rubber soles, chatter between unseen people, and then a curtain made of pennant-bright material being rattled back. Tommy on his side on a trolley, a neat white cellulose blanket hiding most of his slight form, a crest of grey hair sticking up round the crown of his head. She saw his face only too clearly, though it was sideways on to her and she was looking down. It was split in two. One half was comedy, the other tragedy. A tear slowly began to swell in her eye. 'What have you gone and done?' she whispered.

'You think it's broken?' A voice fluttering through the walls of curtains.

'We'll know after the X-ray.'

'If he's broke, dear, you won't be able to drive.' A limb was obviously a he in this part of south Devon.

The voices played over Mitch, not distracting her enough to stop another tear forming. Very gingerly she felt under the blanket for his hand, dry, like kindling for a fire. 'It's me, Tommy,' she whispered, feeling a fool, for it was plain Tommy wasn't there. 'You've had a bit of an accident, OK? You'll be all right, you'll see. I've got to go now, but I'll be back tomorrow, you bet. Now you get a good night's sleep. You'll be pole vaulting next week, you see if you're not. Tommy, darling, you will do your best, won't you?' She gave the twiggy lumps of fingers a hard squeeze and then stepped back.

He lay inert, stripped down to fundamental lines, almost like a cartoon. The miseries of man. Offered up on a wheeled altar.

A small feeling of revulsion passed through her, driving a splinter-thin wedge between him and her.

'I'll be in tomorrow, you bet. You're going to be just fine.' She turned and firmly shut the curtain after her and walked through the rows of cubicles. The chalk-scratching sounds had ceased. There was a sudden, ear-splitting squeal coming from the centre of a tight knot of Asians towards the back of the waiting area. Mitch pushed through the first set of swing doors and now, frantic to get out into fresh air, dived towards the second set just in front of her. She stood at the top of the steps for a moment, not quite sure whether she was still in tears. The night was stained with orangeish brown which pooled the wide apron of tarmac in front of the casualty unit. One parked ambulance, a handful of cars, but no people. It must be late, she thought. A small breeze was rustling in a bed of shrubs marking the far boundary of the emergency parking area. Not quite confident enough yet to move, half jarred out of herself, she continued to study the terrain. Not quite in her clothes, either, she realised, fiddling to get the collar of her tracksuit top to settle. Knocked off centre by a too sudden shift in events.

Tommy's world had changed and hers with it.

The next thing she was aware of was sitting behind the driving wheel of her car. The Jade Dragon. The name dropped into her mind. Their first case together and Tommy had carried out some inquiries there because he knew the owner. Sung something Chin. Perhaps he would know if Tommy had any relatives in England?

She remembered her first meeting with him in his flat off Sir Harry's Road in Edgbaston, the lounge pretending it was part of some traditional Englishmen's club and the bookshelves full of Sherlock Holmes adventures, Ethel Lina White, A.E.W. Mason, hardly a jacket without a corpse, a bloodied knife, a smoking gun.

Then she'd thought him well into his seventies. He'd simply got younger and younger in her mind as their acquaintance lengthened.

He could be eighty, she thought now, stunned.

He had been, he'd told her that day in his flat, an Unofficial. 'It was twenty years before I came ashore and went into other enterprises.' Chinese laundry man to the Royal Navy. 'I was recruited in Hong Kong as were so many others. Ten of us manned an aircraft carrier, two a destroyer.' All in that crystal-cracking accent, fashioned for him by the ship's padre who had taught him English.

An unimaginable life, she thought now; little Hong Kong slum boy to the dapper English gentleman.

A man who travels so far travels light, she further thought. There will be no relatives, at least in England.

How will we bury him?

How can we know what he is?

She'd always treated him like the perfect English gent he'd set out to be. But she also remembered him telling her on their first meeting: 'I find much that is odd about the occidental mind. Bizarre even.'

And what if he lives? Who'll take care of him?

Somehow or other I'll make sure he's all right. A stranger in a strange land needs extra special care for surely the horrors of aloneness are worse for him.

'Oh, Tommy...' She fisted away a tear and started the engine. Trying to bring back the shape of her everyday life, she turned on the radio and cosiness came through the ether.

She swung out of the hospital driveway and headed with a thin stream of traffic towards the A38. Playing with the dial, she landed in the middle of a news.

A deep brown voice told her: 'Ministers will activate plans to deploy several thousand British troops in the former Yugoslav province of Kosovo if Nato goes ahead as expected with a campaign to bomb Serbian forces.

'This follows a hardening of purpose after the discovery of scores of slaughtered ethnic

Albanian men, women and children, apparently murdered by Serbian forces crushing a Kosovar rebellion. Over ninety per cent of the people in the region, part of Serbia, are of Albanian descent.

'Meanwhile, the influx of Kosovar refugees into this country is sharply up and the social service director of one London borough has proposed tented camps in London's parks. He said many asylum seekers were choosing Britain rather than other countries because certain law firms in the capital were touting for trade in the streets of Kosovo. In his borough up to sixty refugees a day were demanding asylum and accommodation. A Conservative councillor said she'd been told flyers were being distributed and even the Kosovar government had got wind of them. She said solicitors receive thousands of pounds for each asylum seeker who signs up with their firm.

'Britain looks after destitute refugees until a legal process has reached a decision as to whether or not they will be allowed to stay. The Home Secretary attended an EU crisis meeting in Brussels last week to discuss the escalating problem. It has been reported that empty MoD barrack blocks may be used to house the refugees. It is thought that thousands of refugees bypass officialdom altogether, afraid that, at the end of the day, they will be deported. They simply arrive in

216

the backs of lorries ferrying goods across the Continent, usually without the lorry driver's knowledge, and slide away to join a network of family or friends already established over here. England is favoured because citizens do not carry identity cards.

'London alone supports 40,000 known refugees at a cost to the taxpayer of £550,000 a week.'

Suddenly a picture of a younger Tommy Hung formed in Mitch's mind, leaving the ship he was working on when it was docked in Portsmouth or Plymouth and never returning. An Unofficial who unofficially became part of the British population?

But he's lived here for so long, she thought. Surely he must now be completely official, just like me.

And then another picture of him came into her mind, sitting in a much-painted Lloyd Loom chair in the conservatory of her old house. His fingers were steepled over his stomach and his ankles were crossed, small toe tucked against his left foot which, as always, led the way. It was a characteristic pose. Alert, yet something self-satisfied about him, as dapper as Hercule Poirot interpreted by a Chinaman could be. Tears washed her eyes. The road was dissolving in front of her.

Did she love him because really he was quite ridiculous?

She felt the ache in her bones, as if she were in for a bad bout of flu.

She used the cuff of her old tracksuit top to wipe her eyes.

There was a female voice filling the car now and Mitch realised a slug of regional news was being broadcast. She wiped her eyes again before reaching towards the knob. Her hand stayed and then curled round the driving wheel again as she listened.

'Rival consortiums bidding for the new south Devon radio franchise will hear tomorrow who the winner is. The two front runners are believed to be Harry Jessop, the man who runs Cornish Sounds, and the pop star Oa Bone who has joined up with George Grigson, a founder of London Fidelity. Oa Bone lives locally and both consortiums have a range of local backers.'

Mitch reached out again to turn off the radio and then thought better of it; she didn't want silence, afraid it would be filled with Tommy, that she'd go to pieces. She felt so strange she wasn't entirely sure a nose wouldn't drop off, an ear. What if a heart forgot to beat?

And now she was wondering about hands, her hand holding Tommy's little bundle of sticks and thinking there was something, some connection, she was missing. There were the pennant-bright curtains, Tommy's

218

prone doll figure, all that sodium light, no shadows to hide in. No. She couldn't think what it was she should do something about.

She was now driving through the lanes, headlights playing on the road in front of her, momentarily turning trees and branches into calcium white stalagmites.

Her body, which still seemed half disconnected from her, sighed. A turning, a shifting, a creaking; a vessel being swung to face a different direction. Even the stale air she was breathing felt a little different; emptier.

Nothing stays the same, she thought, intuitively knowing that the course of her life would be, was being, dramatically reshaped. The sigh now a shiver, fright pitting her skin.

Oh, Tommy.

What have you gone and done?

She turned right towards Coombe Foot, the dipped headlights washing cottage walls. She began threading the car like a needle up the single-track lane which was knotted with passing places.

'...People are always staring at me,' Tommy was telling her. 'Amazing, really. You'd think they'd be used to an oriental chap by now. They never look at Asians like they look at me and those chaps really *are* odd. I don't think it at all fair.'

She told him: 'Perhaps it's because you

sometimes walk with one hand clenched behind your back like the Duke of Edinburgh. Now that is odd.'

She was almost laughing at the sight of him doing just that when she was blinded by light filling her windscreen. She floored the brake pedal, hearing the screech of rubber against road as she spun the wheel; the bump of grass, a wild tilt as she seemed to rise upwards in the seat. The glare was wheeling away, she could see the mouth of a driveway towards the left and then she was on it, the car rocking.

She leaned back in the driver's seat, perfectly still. What the hell happened back there? she found herself wondering, too numb to care about the answer.

She sat there longer, assessing her body. Nothing seemed to hurt anywhere, she could see the fantastical pattern of calcium white leaves and twigs and now she could hear an urgent rapping on the passenger window. It was then she realised that the driver's side of the car was wedged too closely to the hedge for anyone to get through. Very slowly she released her seat belt. She fumbled with the lock on the passenger side. All the movements she made were curiously timeless.

A head ducked in, a man, lots of hair spilling over a narrow jut of face. 'Are you all right?'

'Think so. How about you?'

'Shaken. And stirred. Let me help you out and we'll look at your car. I somehow managed to make a passing place. God knows how.'

Mitch very slowly bumped herself over the steering wheel and then swung her legs out of the car. As she pushed herself up the world revolved and she began to totter. A firm arm pulled her towards a steady body. 'Sorry...' she heard herself say.

'Sit back down and put your head between your knees.'

'It's all right. Things are starting to come the right way up again.'

'You're sure?'

'Yes.'

'You've had one hell of a shaking but I don't think too much damage seems to have been done. The car appears to be in one piece. Maybe there'll be some minor denting and scratching. Whooo...' Mitch, trying to stand on her own, felt her legs start to give way. 'Better sit down,' he said.

'It's probably more to do with the hospital than this,' she said. 'Tommy, my partner, he's had a stroke. It's knocked me for six.' She paused. 'God. That sounds awful. As though I'm the one that's *in extremis*.' She was on the seat now, feeling muscles contract as if she'd been shot through with electricity.

'That wouldn't be the little Chinese chap, would it? Staying at Sissy Childe's place?'

'Yes.'

'How terrible. He came to see me. Charming man. Funny thing to say about a person these days, isn't it? Listen, I wouldn't worry too much yet, you know. My father had what seemed a catastrophic stroke when it happened. But he recovered very well. Lived to be eighty-nine. You're Mr Hung's assistant?'

'Partner. Mitch Mitchell.'

'How extraordinary. Oa Bone was talking about a Mitch Mitchell just tonight. I had dinner up at his place. You aren't by any chance a broadcaster?'

'That's me.'

'Sorry. My name is Paul Maugin. I live opposite the church in Coombe Foot, next to the Trimbles. Have you got round to them yet?'

'I haven't got round to anybody or anything in Coombe Foot. I arrived, fell asleep and then found Tommy. But what could Oa Bone be saying about me? I don't know him. We've never met.'

'Oh, yes you have. When he was Norman Baron, lead singer with the Blue Barons.'

'Never heard of them.'

'They apparently sank without trace in the middle seventies. From their ashes rose Oa Bone and the Roller Blades. Perhaps you don't remember? But you did do a radio piece on what it was like to start a rock band, the kind of gigs the band got, what it paid, how a song could change from week to week. Oa Bone said it was the first and best piece that anyone had ever done about him. He's still got the tape. We were into a bit of nostalgia. Scenes from early youth. At least he and his mother were. I passed.'

'Really?' Mitch, searching her mind, could come up with no memories. 'It rings no bells but then I suppose I must have done a few thousand radio packages in my time. I mean, most bands are like last Monday's lunch, totally forgotten.'

'What made you give up broadcasting?'

'I haven't. I set up the detective agency with Tommy to run alongside my broadcasting work. Freelancing tends to be feast or famine. When it's quiet on one front it's busy on the other. At least that's the theory.' Mitch found she was tentatively stretching out her hand. 'Well, I really do seem to be in one piece.' She pushed herself up again from the passenger seat. 'Fairly steady on the old feet now. The first thing I knew about you was when the windscreen filled with light.'

'It really is a bad bend. At night you can usually spot headlights zigzagging towards you through gaps in the hedges but because of farm buildings this is a dark bit. There are surprisingly few collisions considering the road snakes like hell. What I'll do is drive a little further down. There's a grassy patch there I can run the Volvo on. You can then back out into the passing place and align yourself with the road. There shouldn't really be much traffic at this time. We were unlucky.'

'What time is it?'

'Getting on for eleven. I thought I'd try the all-night supermarket. Save me a journey tomorrow. I've got a really busy day on. If the option's there, why not go for it? Though I might think twice in future.'

Mitch had been looking at the bodywork of the car. 'Well, the light's not good but no real damage seems to have been done.' She turned, studying him for the first time. He was tall, thin, long bony face, a wedge of white shirt showing above a V-necked sweater. Her curiosity roused because of his interest in her? Something between them in the chalky striped night?

But we can't even see each other properly, she thought and then thought she might be too close to him and backed off a little.

'Right. I'll move my car.'

She got back into hers and wriggled over to the driver's seat. Suddenly she was aware of being fully back in her body, hot and perspiring a little. Right, concentrate on your driving, she told herself. You don't want him to think you're a complete idiot, do you? The car was so near the hedge on her side that if she turned too sharply away as she backed, the front nearside would be badly scratched. She moved the wheels inwards, towards the hedge, giving herself a better angle to work from. Adjusting the mirror, she saw him pull out of the passing place across the road and after dipping her headlights twice in farewell backed up.

Five minutes later she was pulling into the driveway of Manaccan House. She was reminded of the cottage night light she'd had as a tiny child. Every window blazed with light.

She cut the engine and scratched her head.

There were no lights on when she'd left, she was sure of it.

She found she didn't care who had broken into the house. I mean, she thought, this is just getting silly. Let anyone dare have a go at me and I'll smash his head in. She'd already survived so much in the last few hours that she felt immortal. Not hesitating for a moment, she walked across to the door and let herself in.

'Is that you, ace!' The shout came from the sitting-room.

She found the new diet-sized Sissy Childe sitting up straight in one of the loose-covered armchairs. Her dyed white hair stood up like a coxcomb, giving her the look of an exclamation mark; a screamer, Mitch thought, for that was what some journalists called them. She glittered in a white suit made of some sort of fluorescent material. A pair of purple strappy high-heeled sandals, which she had pulled off as she'd walked across the carpet to the chair, were sole up. A matching handbag, perhaps thrown at the ceiling, was precariously balanced on the top of the back of a chair. There was a feeling of chill frenzy about her, as though at any moment hysteria would burst through her skin.

Sissy in her mortuary-attending outfit was a sight Mitch thought she'd never forget.

The diamond in her nose flashed. That purple-painted mouth opened. Like a parent confronting her child, she asked in a voice which would freeze vodka: 'Where the hell have you been?'

It didn't freeze Mitch. 'It was Rosie?'

14

Sissy Childe had put on a large navy and white striped butcher's apron over her white fluorescent suit. The edges of her, where the suit was exposed, twinkled, giving her the look of a human eclipse. She now began chopping onions and potatoes on a big wooden board.

Mitch, still in her tracksuit, was sitting on one of the stick backed kitchen chairs in a loose lotus position, insides of her feet resting on shin bones. She nursed a glass of white wine. The diet-diminished Sissy had a half-glass of water on the table near her. '...though I desperately want to get drunk,' she'd told Mitch.

'Why don't you?'

'I'm out of here before six in the morning. There's a meeting to organise a shoot. We've got the garden of – is it New Place? Anyway, the pad Shakespeare retired to. We're going to do black pudding?'

'What's that?'

'You don't want to know. Believe me.'

Mitch, easing her buttocks on the wooden chair bottom, said now: 'You must be so relieved.'

Sissy's chopper suddenly burst through the disciplined rhythm she'd set. 'Anger. I'm so bloody angry with her. All this ... this...' and now the chopper was high, glinting, Sissy's coxcomb of white hair quivering, '...for want of a phone call. Sweet Jesus!' The chopper missed a half-dissected onion and hit a potato, which jumped over the table and disappeared under it. 'Oh, shit.'

'If you look at it from Rosie's point of view she'd never suppose you or anyone else would think a body found in the woods near the village was *her* body. Why should she? *She* knows she is alive.'

Sissy looked at her. Her face was flushed, puffy. Breath came down her nose in little snorts. By the time she'd laid the chopper down, out of harm's way, Mitch found she was sweating a little. The cook ducked under the table. She picked up the potato and, in her stockinged feet, marched over to the sink. She had her voice under control. 'The thing about tortilla is that you cook it slowly. Everyone thinks that if you're doing omelette mixture you whack up the heat.' She swilled off the potato under the tap and took it back to the table. She was now looking at the chopper as if wondering whether she dared pick it up again.

Mitch searched for something to say.

Sissy said: 'How come the jacket they took off the corpse was Rosie's? Answer me that,

OK? She must know something. For a start she must know who the woman is, don't you think? And the jeans, the rest of the clothes, didn't really fit the victim. The police said it was quite probable they were Rosie's too.'

What can you suppose when the corpse and the clothes don't match? Mitch's brain spun. She took a gulp of wine.

'Oh Christ. You just don't want to see such things. I couldn't ever do it again. You know? Oh, shit.'

Mitch averted her gaze.

'Well, soldier. I hope you're hungry.' When Mitch turned back to her the cook seemed quite normal. The chopper was in her hand again.

'Peckish. Decidedly peckish.'

'Why the hell didn't she phone me? I mean, she called to say how much the new gear she'd bought at Coral's had cost me.'

'Do you phone people when you're going to behave badly? She was letting a lot of people down when she did a bunk.'

'But why has she disappeared?' Sissy was silent for a moment. 'What do I know about her anyway? After the things you've told me. The sister I have in my mind has nothing to do with the real Rosie.'

'The relationship you formed when you were young, that's always there. You told me yourself that you were determined to hate her before she was born but you couldn't.'

'She had this God Almighty crush on me. I was flattered. OK?'

'She taught you how to love her. That's what is true about you and Rosie and you have to see that when you see the rest.'

'Bullshit.'

Mitch carefully unwound her legs, lowered them to the tiled floor, and went over to the dresser. She poured herself another drink.

'You're nothing but a drunken cow. You know that?'

'Not as drunk as I'm going to be,' said Mitch. 'You'd better get a move on with that Spanish whatjermacallit.'

Slivers of potato began to leap through Sissy's fingers. 'She had it all, you know? Brains, not bad-looking. Comfortable background. What the hell went wrong? And don't give me a lot of guff about her mother going off. I lost my mother, too, didn't I? Lots of kids have to deal with far worse things and they make out.'

Mitch was thinking of something else. Sissy padded over to the two-ringed gas hob, dropped the vegetables into sizzling olive oil and then turned the heat down. She sat herself at the kitchen table. 'I can't get used to your new size,' said Mitch. Was she really thinking of Tommy, shrunk to nothing on the hospital trolley? 'Weight suited you.'

'Fat cooks are out. They aren't politically

correct. They carry this subliminal message. Greed is good,' said Sissy. 'I like to work. I'm not natural dole fodder. That's what I found out. Doing nothing drove me nuts. Christ, I'd have had a bolt shot through my neck if it meant I got a job.'

Mitch found herself looking at the diamond which had been driven through Sissy's nose.

Sissy got up and turned the onions. 'Well, ace. You've had time to think about it. What the hell was Rosie's clobber doing on a woman who was murdered?'

'I can't come up with an answer that makes any sense. I keep thinking of daft things like Rosie's gear was stolen from a clothes line. But why would anyone make off with an old denim jacket? It's perverts who steal from lines and they're male and they usually go for underwear. Did Rosie give the stuff away? Don't snap my head off, but I suppose there is no doubt this kit is Rosie's?'

'The jacket certainly is. I've seen her in it loads of times. The jeans and shirt – well, who could know? They're universal, aren't they? Anyway, it was you who told me about the kind of needles Rosie used to inject Interferon and one of them was in the jacket pocket. I suppose I'll have to pass that bit of information on to the police.'

'It would be impossible for you to say if

the dead woman had, in life, looked anything like Rosie? You did say the remains were pretty far gone...'

'I'd say this woman was in better shape than Rosie, not so thin. But, of course, I've only just learned that Rosie's suffering from this hepatitis variant. I mean, this woman had a completely different kind of body than Rosie's. More womanly. Rosie always did look rather angular and boyish. Her hair was dark, much the same colour, but coarse and thick. Abundant. Rosie's is fine, on the thin side.'

'But as this woman was wearing at least one garment of Rosie's we do know the two women weren't too dissimilar as far as size goes.'

Sissy was following her own line of thought. 'Is it so easy to get guns now? Well, if it is, anyone could have done it. You don't think the killer could have supposed it *was* Rosie? Shot this other woman by mistake? Could that have sent Rosie off into hiding?'

'Why would Rosie go into hiding?' Mitch asked. 'Why wouldn't she go to the police?'

'Like an execution ... that's what the police said. The woman was shot at close range. The bullet entered around the nape of the neck and went upwards. Came out at the crown of her skull.'

'So she was shot from behind?'

'Yes.'

'The killer following, below her perhaps, not seeing her face. Maybe they were on a hill. Must have been steep.'

Sissy placed both hands on the top of the table and pushed herself up using her arms. 'My legs go a bit wobbly every now and then,' she said. She moved a little unsteadily to a cupboard and took out a mixing bowl and then opened the fridge. 'Eggs. Eggs. Ah. Here we go.'

'Of course, none of it may have anything to do with Rosie at all. A woman was escaping from a violent man, stole the clothes because she needed clean clothes or dry clothes. The killer catches up with her and, well, there we are.'

'And where's that? Even in this day and age I still would have thought most English husbands or boyfriends don't have access to a gun.' Sissy cracked six eggs into the bowl with one hand and began to whisk them up with the other. Mitch, watching her, thought there was something very import-ant to remember about hands. Whose hands? Nothing came to her. Sissy said: 'It's so soothing, don't you find? Cooking?'

'No.'

'We are on the coast here. Could be a drugs-related thing.'

'If that were so, I'd think that definitely excludes Rosie. With this hepatitis thing all drugs and alcohol are out. Of course, she did work in the old Yugoslavia for a bit and while she was there she didn't know she'd contracted this virus. A lot of drugs come through eastern Europe.'

'One woman dead in Rosie's clothes and Rosie missing. You'd think there really would have to be a connection.' Sissy tipped the egg mixture into the pan, shaking it from side to side.

Mitch found herself moistening her lips. 'How much longer?'

'A good twenty minutes. Tortillas are slo-mo omelettes.'

Mitch pulled a face.

'It's the smell of the gently frying onions. It sort of stirs all the digestive juices,' said Sissy. 'I've often thought it would make a corpse sit up. Sorry. Sorry. Oh God. What am I saying? That poor woman. The thing that really horrifies me ... well, I won't be able to forget how she looked. How she smelled. I'll tell you one thing. I'm going to be burned, soldier. Christ. It's disgusting.' Sissy sat down at the table. 'Perhaps Rosie saw sights like that all the time. I mean, when she was in Bosnia. Don't you think? If she did, she never mentioned it to me. But then, she never told me she'd had a kid.'

'There's always the possibility that her disappearance is connected with that baby. The child must be thirteen, fourteen now? I mean, Oa Bone does live down here. Maybe he had the kid traced?'

'You think Oa Bone is the father?'

'Just speculating. I suppose there'd be quite a lot of studs at these parties held at Oa's house. If the kids were drunk or drugged or both would Rosie even know who the father of her baby was?'

'Are you going to tackle Oa Bone about it?'

'I think I've got to.' Mitch thought about it. 'There's going to be no easy way to put it to him.'

'And we're talking about a guy with a mean streak.'

'You've had some dealings with him?'

'It's Rosie who really knows him. If fact, that girl she shared a flat with in London often acted as Oa's armpiece.'

'Bernice Brody?'

'Sure. Rosie introduced them. Bernice acted as a decoy so he and whoever was his latest girlie could carry on their affair in peace. And then this Bernice chucks Rosie out of the flat! I had words with her.'

'My God. The row in the hotel in Birmingham? Bernice was with Oa that night? Quite a scene. I heard all about it.'

'It *is* a small world. Of course, I didn't know Rosie was ill then and that was why Bernice wanted her out.'

'She also wants Rosie's stuff out.'

'I know. I know. We'll let Rosie deal with

that when we find her.'

Mitch heard her stomach grumble. Another glass of wine, she thought, would help settle it. As she poured, she said: 'I ran into someone coming back from the hospital – quite literally, you could say – who'd been to dinner with the Bones tonight. Mother and son. The chap I met was Paul Maugin. You know him?'

'Not so's you'd notice. He plays bridge with my father and Penny and a woman called Cecily Upjohn. She's the wife of Clive Upjohn, a solicitor who lives in the village. Paul turned up here about three years ago, bought old Archie Mole's place after he died. General gossip says he was in the Diplomatic Service, some say the Foreign Office. But in this village, I've found, if you don't tell people about your past they're liable to invent one for you. It goes like this. Upper class accent. Some sort of toff. But he bought old Mole's place, didn't he? Not much money left in *that* family's kitty. Must have had some sort of job. When the French come on a twin town exchange he jabbers to them like a native, doesn't he? Got to have lived in foreign parts. Foreign Office. Diplomatic Service. Bob's your uncle.'

'Hasn't anyone asked?'

'Perhaps he's not telling.' Sissy got up again and eased a knife round the omelette, levering it up from the sides of the pan. She put two plates in the Aga's bottom oven, found some brown bread and began to cut it up.

'Paul Maugin knew me as soon as I mentioned my name. Tommy had been to see him, mind. It could be the death is a totally village affair. What do you think?'

'Well, I do know Coral is having an affair with Clive Upjohn, the solicitor. Cecily's husband.' Sissy paused. 'Clive's the man who found the dead woman.'

Mitch took a sip of wine. 'Yes?'

But Sissy was shaking her head. 'If the woman with a hole in her head had been Coral Trimble I suppose that could have maybe stacked up. But as it is ... Christ. You must have some ideas.'

'Not at the moment. Tommy was going to tell me something but I don't know what.'

'I'm really sorry about him, you know? He was – is – pretty far out and all that. God. That dates me,' said Sissy. 'When did people stop saying far out?'

'When you start saying spiffing, that's the time to worry.'

'You say that?'

'I try not to.'

'Good.' Sissy put the knife between frying pan and its contents, eased it round, lifted the pan and neatly tossed the omelette.

'You're showing off,' said Mitch.

'Listen, this is nothing. I can juggle four plates.'

'If you've got it … flaunt it.'

Mitch watched Sissy put a piece of the omelette on a warmed plate and then unwound herself from the lotus position once more and, fingers under the wooden seat of the kitchen chair, used its back legs and her feet to rock herself to the table. She picked up her knife and fork as Sissy put the plate in front of her. 'It always seems to make me hungry. Disaster, I mean. When Max – he was my husband – died, I stuffed myself with fish and chips. Tommy looked so *small*.'

'I'm always hungry. Even when I had blubber on my blubber I was hungry. I'm not more hungry now than I was then. I mean, in the end, there are some things you have to learn to live with, right? Like little Rosie and her hepatitis.' Sissy cut a minute sliver of omelette off her portion and began to chew it. She had small teeth, Mitch noticed; a small mouth for such a large appetite.

'This is a nice place,' Mitch wolfed another piece.

'Mistake. I'm going to sell it. I bought it when the money I was earning from the last series of cook shows was rolling in. My pension pot, I thought. Then the whole shebang hit the buffers and it didn't seem like such a good idea. I'm going to sell, pay off the mortgage on my London pad and let the State look after me in my dotage. Everyone else does. What about you?'

'Don't talk to me about money.'

'Bad? Listen, ace, to one who knows. When you're down a hole stop digging.'

'Someone else said that to me. But it's easier said than done.'

'No. It's not, actually.'

'You're right. You're right. Shove the wine over, will you?'

'Are you going to drink the whole bottle?'

'Why not?'

'Is Tommy going to die?'

'Looks like it.'

'Well, he is knocking on.'

'I know.' Mitch, stuffing her face and catching sight of another forkful of yellow, suddenly remembered a yellow blob which had resolved into a Marigold glove. 'Why was he wearing rubber gloves?'

'What?'

'That's it. Someone at the hospital must have taken them off. He wasn't wearing them when I held his hand. But he was certainly wearing them when I found him. When Tommy's in his role of detective he's all detective. *He would wear rubber gloves to handle evidence.*'

'What are you talking about?'

'I think that just before Tommy had his

stroke he'd found something in one of the outhouses attached to the house. Something he thought was evidence. Something he'd only handle with gloves on. Don't ask me what. I mean I was in there with Tommy. So were the paramedics. But we were all so concerned about Tommy. I mean, if a giraffe had been in there none of us would have noticed.'

'Right, soldier. We'd better go and look.'

'Where the hell did I put my torch?'

'I've got one.' Sissy got up and began to search in a cupboard. 'Here we are.'

Suddenly they looked at each other. 'Rosie?' Sissy whispered.

'What would Rosie be doing in the outhouse?' Unless she's dead, Mitch thought.

Sissy was getting a queer look, as if she'd lost a dimension, was pasted to the kitchen wall.

'Come on.' Mitch's voice was rough. 'It'll be something and nothing, you bet.'

'Sure it will.'

Mitch went ahead of Sissy, opening the back door. Light leaked out into the night. A full moon had risen, illuminating long furrows of clouds. It was as if the world had been turned upside down and ghostly ploughed fields were looking on them from the sky. A soft breeze lifted a strand of Mitch's hair. 'Give me the torch,' Mitch said.

Sissy handed it over and shut the back door. Mitch switched on and swung the beam to the rim of the gravel driveway. The light illuminated the cattle grid and the opened tubular steel farm gate. It jumped forward as she moved, picking out dock weed thrusting through the concrete yard. 'I've got no shoes on,' Sissy said behind her. She was crossing the cattle grid.

'Go back and get some.'

'Not on your life.'

The beam touched a patch of corrugated iron roofing on the cob barn directly in front of them. Mitch swung the torch to the outhouses at the side. 'That's the one.' To the left of them weeds began to whisper.

'That's what could have caused his stroke.'

'What?'

'What he saw in there.'

'Shut up,' Mitch told her. Her head dipped fractionally as her spine frosted. She suddenly found she had to push her legs forward. She was already trying to sniff out what might be in the outhouse. The torch picked out the wide flung door, spider threads looping between splinters of wood, old paint flaking round the knob. Cracking concrete rode up beneath her feet. She stepped over the threshold on to a brick floor. Uneven cob wall leapt at her.

'Found anything?'

The torch settled on a white plastic bag in

one corner. Resting on top of it was a pair of platform shoes made of black canvas. Sissy pushed past her.

Mitch asked herself: 'Don't I know something about platform shoes?'

'My God, they're weird. Who'd wear such monstrosities?' Sissy had squatted in front of the bag. 'Move that light.'

'Clothes,' said Mitch.

'We'd better get hold of the police.'

15

'Can I have a word with you about Ishbelle Jones?'

Lorraine Pickles, form mistress of the Upper Fourth, looked up from the battered armchair she was sitting in. Shadow chasing light streamed in from two sash windows; the unseasonably hot afternoon sun was behind copper beech trees. Most of the teachers in the staff room had finished their tea and there was a clink of mugs being stacked on an aluminium tray. 'What's she been up to?'

'Well, I'm not sure whether it's important or not,' said Arthur Trimble. 'There seems to be a falling off in her work for me. Quite a steep one.'

'I've not noticed anything,' said Lorraine. 'But then she was never very good at French.'

'Trouble at home? She's a day girl, isn't she? What's her background?'

'Not our usual girl. Her mother runs a bed and breakfast place. One of those monster Victorian houses in Newton Abbot. I think there was a messy divorce but that is a few years back now. Not drugs? You're not thinking drugs, are you? Girls do tend to go a bit ... well, distant ... when they first start menstruating, you know.'

'Family financial problems? I mean, how can you afford to send a kid here on the profits from B and B?'

'I have a feeling I heard somewhere that a relative pays the fees. Grandparent perhaps.' The school bell began to ring and Lorraine Pickles started to get up. She was an angular woman and though she was well into her thirties wore her fair, thick hair in two short plaits. It gave her the look of a Heidi doll which has seen better days. Bony fingers dived towards her purple chunky knit cardigan. She plucked away a tiny piece of whitish gauze-like stuff. 'I left a paper hankie in the pocket when I put it in the wash. *D-ISSS*-aster. You think I should keep an eye on her?'

'Something and nothing, I expect. Ishbelle is one of my better pupils.' Arthur Trimble had reached the stage when he found himself almost impelled to talk about her, say her name. *I-s-h-b-el-l-e*. A gentle swish of a sound, like a wavelet washing over sand. *I-s-h-b-el-l-e*. He was almost in physical pain when, in his mind's eye, he saw her running out of the school's doors into the sunshine. He'd felt like this when he was young and in pursuit of baby brides. Oh, those cherry-picking days. Each success had carried its trophy: one white sock. And then he'd grown older and the pickings were slimmer. He'd decided to settle down, to marry a baby bride. But now their child was older than Coral when they'd wed. Now he could no longer deny to himself that Time, the most wicked of the Furies, had turned his baby bride into an old hag.

He was aware of the eyes of the battered Heidi doll and realised he could find himself in a very dangerous position if he weren't careful. Like a penitent who denies himself pleasure, he must discipline himself not to say that miracle of a name out loud. He found his body tautening sickeningly at the prospect of such self-denial. 'Back to the coal face, eh?' he said.

'How's Coral these days?'

Now why had she asked him that? 'Actually, she's thinking of expanding the shop. It's doing really well. But it would involve quite a big financial outlay. I mean, you never know what's round the corner, do you?'

'Too true.'

Arthur, desperate to get away with his little store of information about Ishbelle, skipped towards the corridor. Like some butterfly enthusiast out with a net, he'd been collecting bits of stuff about her all afternoon. In the lunch break he'd risked a confrontation with Joan Battersby, the head, when he'd stolen into her outer office and looked into the part-time secretary's files for the girl's address.

His last class of the day was a group of Upper Sixth girls who were taking Economic History at A level. They had been revising for the last two months, Arthur presenting them with questions from old examination papers and guiding them through framing their answers. He was an old hand at this. The number of girls taking the option at A level was always large for he was known for producing good examination results.

He began with a look at the Victorian Factory Acts and, when he judged concentration had waned too far, went into some of the tricks of producing the material they'd learned on the page. When he'd got them fashioning the first paragraph in an essay on the subject, he was free to look out of the window.

Events had moved dramatically since he'd found the body of the dead woman in Oa Bone's woods and stolen the sock. Before that he'd supposed himself to be a reasonably conventional man. If he'd imagined discovering a corpse he would have seen himself stifling a scream, being sick, perhaps crying as he ran to call the police. Acting in a way he pictured any decent man would.

What had happened was that in stumbling

over that corpse he'd stumbled over things he'd hidden away from himself. The discoveries shocked him. For the first few days his predominant emotion had been fear. With newly opened eyes he saw things he didn't want to see. The baby bride in his bed was an old bag with effluent running through the sewage system which had once been her veins. The reincarnation of his baby bride danced before him: dazzlingly pure, and at the centre of this whiter than the whitest vision inky black hair, inky black eyes. The white sock he'd stolen from the corpse a tangible proof of the moment his whole world swung upside down.

This morning he'd asked his shaving mirror: Who am I?

Who am I *now?*

Some of the answers had been simple.

Not the husband of a bag of pus. That's for sure. He'd seen her near the stile leading into Oa Bone's woods, Clive Upjohn's arms round her. He'd not felt any of the emotions countless television dramas had led him to suppose he would. He'd been relieved. Objective evidence that the woman *lying next to him* was the slag he'd suddenly realised her to be. How could he have been deceived in her for so many years? Seeing the woman dead in the woods, *smelling* her, had finally broken the spell more effectively than any abracadabra.

To be absolutely truthful, he wouldn't have minded seeing Coral and Clive shagging. That hadn't occurred to him until they'd parted after kissing and cuddling. He'd been disappointed they hadn't gone all the way.

But this confirms it, he thought. I am right about her.

And in his mind's eye it was her body he discovered, her sock he pried from dead flesh.

He'd taken to waking in the small hours of the morning and looking at the lump which was putrefying hardly more than six inches away from him. Sometimes he was sure he heard the buzz of bluebottles in his ears. If that thing raised its dark head off the rose-sprigged pillows and turned to him, flaps of rotten flesh would be hanging off cheekbones. Eyes teetering from their sockets.

Gap-toothed, she emptied evil greenish bile on him; baptising him in her loving blessing.

It should be buried.

Or burned.

It was the only way to get rid of the *smell*.

After school he intended to track down his baby bride to her lair. It had to be today because his car was in for its service and he was using the courtesy vehicle provided by the garage. If this car was spotted outside her house he thought it very unlikely anyone would connect it to him.

Of course, he didn't want his Ishbelle in that house but in his house, the one across from the church.

'Never in a month of Sundays, old son,' Henry had told him. 'Ishbelle's real. She's not a figment of our imagination, now is she? You can't just wave the old magic wand.'

And sometimes in his dark confusion Coral's image turned into that of Cory, his son, and he felt something which he'd decided, astonished, was grief.

'Just go along with it,' Henry had advised. 'Something will sort itself out, you'll see.'

But he didn't see. Sometimes he felt so disorientated he was literally dizzy and grabbed out to hold on to something. Talk about falling through the looking-glass.

'Oh, stop being so prattish. You'll have her, never you fear,' Henry told him. 'Well, I'll have her. And that's the same thing, isn't it?'

Arthur liked to hear Henry's voice in his head. Henry was always so calm and sure, so *encouraging*. He'd certainly turned up at the right time.

'Best to attack on all fronts,' Henry said. 'Sorting Coral's not going to be a doddle, no way. But the main thing is, while we think of something, we're *nice* to her. The loving hubby. Then if an opportunity arises we can't say no to, well ... at this stage of the game, we keep all options open. Right?'

Are we going to kill her?

Are you out of your tiny mind?

Arthur, though he'd no intention of killing his wife, even though she was a bag of pus, was disappointed. The kind of life he fantasised for him and Ishbelle involved lying on decks of yachts and coral beaches with palm trees swaying overhead. That cost money and if he and Coral went through a sticky divorce how much would he get? Nowhere near his fair share, that was for sure. Coral may not know where Vietnam was but she'd certainly locate places to hide their money from the courts.

Henry said: 'Accidents, though, do happen.'

Arthur saw the corpse again, Coral's hair, Coral's clothes. Face down and the bluebottles settling in a small crater beyond the crown of the skull. Whack, he'd thought, and that's that. Glee was rising; deep-bellied gurgles of laughter.

Might as well admit it. There were times when he could hardly keep his fists under control. He'd like to push Coral's well-flossed teeth right down her throat before squeezing the life out of her.

If only finishing off the bitch was that simple. But you only had to see the village full of coppers asking questions to realise it wasn't. They said there was even some old

Chinaman, a private detective, poking about and people might tell things to him they wouldn't tell the police. Nasty, private things they didn't want to sign their names to.

What did you get for murder? What tariff was that?

'God gave all of you in this room a good brain,' he now told the Sixth Formers in front of him. 'You use it like a good general would and you'll be able to pick off any prize you fancy. Now Gillian, we'll start with you. Read what you've got. Everyone in on the comments. You've all got a good grasp of the subject. How you present it is at least half the battle.'

'Are you teaching them how to bullshit?' Henry asked.

'How you present yourself is what you are.'

'Make sure you're a loving husband then,' Henry told him. 'You don't want people to say it was you who did the pushing if Coral happens to fall off a cliff.'

Arthur felt his stomach turn.

Still, he thought, no gain without pain and there would be little treats to pull him through. Like hunting down sweet Ishbelle to her lair. He was already cocking his ear to hear the bell which marked the end of the school day.

By keeping a sharp eye out, Arthur had

discovered that Ishbelle was part of a school run, mothers delivering and collecting kids on a rota basis. When he'd learned that, he'd thought better of trailing her to her lair; instead he'd risked sneaking into Joan Battersby's outer office. His plan was to hurry off as soon as the bell rang, climb into the courtesy car, find her address and lie in wait. 'Maybe do a recce,' Henry said. 'Could be useful to know the geography.'

Arthur knew it was Henry who was licking his lips, even though it was his tongue which was moving. Arthur was beginning to believe Henry was the ghost in his machine.

As soon as the bell began to ring, Arthur's jacket was off the back of the chair, his briefcase was in his hand and he was off, the first out of the classroom. The fewer people who saw him climb into an unfamiliar car the better. He had the entrance door in his sights when he heard a shout from behind him. 'Mr Trim-*bulll*...' Miss Battersby shouted, though she knew perfectly well how his name was spelt. 'Have you a moment?'

He turned to see her in the entrance of the outer office, aware that each and every particle of his flesh was a guilty thing and hoping she wouldn't see this. 'Not really!'

'It won't take a moment.'

'Really, I–'

'Just a moment.'

252

And though he was walking back to her it felt as though she was reeling him in.

'Yes?' he said.

'Let's pop in here and shut the door. Little ears, you know...'

The door of the outer office clanged behind them.

'You are in a rush?'

Choose your lie with care or you could be found out. 'Something's cropped up.'

'Ah...' and Joan Battersby, using all her heaviness of jowl and breast to remind him of the weighty authority figure she was, waited to be told more.

'What is it you wanted?' He had no intention of going beyond 'Something's cropped up.' Anyway, that was the truth in a way. His new baby bride had cropped up.

'Lorraine tells me you have worries about Ishbelle Jones. Much better to nip things in the bud, so to speak.'

Arthur was aware that Henry was looking at all Joan's good teeth, just as well flossed as Coral's, and flexing his hand, Arthur's hand, itching to knock them down her throat.

Be brazen in a lie which can also be seen as a value judgement. 'There has been a falling off in the work she's been doing for me.'

'One has a perpetual worry about drugs.'

'Lorraine told me it was more likely to

have been caused by her periods starting. Look, I'm afraid I really do have to dash. Perhaps we could set up a meeting for tomorrow? Or we could just keep a watchful eye...'

'A watchful eye, I think, at this stage.'

'Sorry to be in such a rush.' Arthur headed to the door and, to give the nosy bitch something to watch and wonder about as much as anything else, ran down the corridor to the entrance. Underneath his bluster his heart was thumping. He was curving towards panic. Had someone seen him watching Isabelle Jones? Smiling that unmistakable bemused lover's smile? Seen the light in the lover's eye?

How could he court his future baby bride under that dragon's nose?

'You don't have to teach at this school,' Henry said.

'Oh yes? And what do I do for cash?'

Henry did not need to answer that one. Coral owned her business premises and what with stock and goodwill there was a tidy sum there, not to mention a fairly hefty bank balance. And when money passed between a deceased wife and her widower even the government didn't come in and steal inheritance tax off the top.

Suddenly the old Arthur Trimble was back. He was so frightened his guts loosened.

It doesn't mean anything, he thought. It's just thinking. But he didn't stop running as he headed across the staff parking area to the dark blue courtesy car.

Fairlands, Roseberry Lane.

That's where his love nestled in her virgin single bed.

'Some hopes,' said Henry. 'They lose their cherry before they're twelve these days. Still, if she's broken in there'll be no squeals, will there? No messy spilling of blood. Virginity is overrated, my son.'

There is something about white interlock knickers that even the blackest, flimsiest of panties can't touch. Henry and Arthur were quite agreed about that.

'Not to mention short white socks,' said Henry.

Too right.

Henry gunned the car out of the school gates. Arthur took over after a wild right turn. He didn't want to be flagged down by a police car.

'OK, OK' said Henry. 'God, you are an anorak. You know that?'

Arthur thought that if he were caught for what he was about to do he could plead insanity. Didn't schizophrenics hear voices? Of course, he knew he wasn't mad. He was just after one last baby bride before old age set in. One last, glorious fling before he, like Woody, was pole-axed by a heart attack or worse – and there was a lot of worse that didn't even bear thinking about.

Much of Fairlands was hidden from view by great horse chestnut trees but between their massive trunks he could see expanses of pebble-dash, painted white, and an entrance canopy supported by Doric columns. Three wide stone steps led down to a pink gravel drive. At one side of the gable end was a glimpse of a small car-park. Driving a little further up the steeply rising lane, he saw there was a castellated parapet behind which were the shallow slopes of a Welsh slate roof.

He found he was delighted. His Ishbelle should live in a castle, even if it was a mock pebble-dash one. He drove a little further up Roseberry Lane, swung the car round and came back down past other Victorian villas, each well set back from the lane. He turned again when he'd passed Fairlands and made his final approach, parking a little below the house. He now put on the black baseball cap and the pair of glasses he'd bought and got out the town map he was going to pretend to study. Later, when the time was just right, he intended to light up a cigarette. Neither of them smoked and when Arthur had first thought of this Henry had objected strongly: 'It's not healthy.' 'Everyone knows I don't smoke. A guy smoking in a car can't be me.'

Arthur was already seeing in his mind's eye Ishbelle getting out of a car and shouldering her bag before walking up the drive to the front door of Fairlands. Where do we go from here? he was wondering.

'What goes in must come out again,' Henry said.

'She'll be with all her mates.'

'You're such a wimp, you know that? Leave it all to me, old son. Today we're just scouting the ground, OK?'

Arthur was just about to ask Henry what he had in mind when a car drove past and parked a few yards further up on the same side. Henry made a funny little noise in Arthur's throat, almost a purr, and Arthur busied himself lighting a cigarette, then he pretended to look at the map. No clumsiness. All neatly done before Ishbelle had dragged her bag from the floor of the car.

She was the last but one kid and she turned to wave to a girl in the passenger seat next to the driver and then, almost hypnotised, Arthur watched as his prospective baby bride sauntered across the road.

Bless her little white cotton socks, he thought reverently.

It was at that point he saw a man walking along the tarmac towards her. He was young, shoulders well back, heels in their big white trainers driving so hard down he was bouncing along, light, unzipped anorak in a slipstream behind him and sometimes spreading as if he were about to soar skywards. Quiff of black, thick hair vibrating slightly as he headed down his flight path. He had practically reached Ishbelle when she turned to him, gawky limbs splaying in confusion. Laughing, they headed up the drive towards the entrance of Fairlands.

'One of the lodgers,' Arthur told Henry. 'Absolutely nothing in it.'

'Totty's all the same,' said Henry. 'Screaming for it. Better get in while the going's good.'

'She's not like that.'

'Yeah, yeah. What I want you to do is to buy a nice big joint of mutton.'

'*Mutton?*'

'You can put it in that bloody greenhouse of yours. I want to know what it smells like when the maggots set in.'

'No way,' said Arthur. 'You're sick. You're scaring me, you really are.'

'Me? Get away with you. If you're thinking what I think you're thinking, you're wide of the mark, old son. Me kill someone? What do you think I am?'

'Accidents can happen.'

'You said that. Not me.'

16

'The sister said he had a comfortable night.' Mitch's shoulder was hunched to form a cradle for the phone, a cup of black coffee in one hand and aspirins in the other. Her eyes were squeezed into a thin line to shut out glare. It was mid-morning and the sitting-room at Manaccan House, which faced south, was full of poles of light-splintered shadow on wavering cob walls.

'He's not going to die,' said A.J.

'I hope not.'

'He's such a sweetie.' The sentence seemed to run into an invisible barrier. The last word concertinaed. Mitch had a vivid mental image of A.J., thin and feminine in businesslike pinstripes, in the reception area at the Mitchell and Orient Bureau. Her free hand would be searching for something solid among Tommy Hung's idea of furnishings, leather-buttoned chesterfields, a fake Victorian ancestor on the wall – an Anglo-Saxon female dragon – and electrified oil lamps which bellied in and out like harem dancing girls.

Sweetie... Mitch had never thought of Tommy like this. She quickly popped the aspirins in her mouth, swallowed coffee and put the cup down. Fingers free, she caught the slipping receiver.

A.J. had to repeat her question. 'What do you want me to do?'

'I don't know if he's got any relatives in England. Any relatives period. He simply never talked about anything like that. Isn't that odd?'

'Well, *you* don't, not really. I know you've got a daughter in America. But I don't know her name. I do know you were married because sometimes mail comes addressed Mrs. I don't know what the E.E. stands for, Mitch.'

Mitch was startled. 'My daughter's called Cassie and I'm a widow.'

'And the E.E.?'

'I'm not going to say. Too sad. I think my mother was wondering until the day she died how the hell I managed to turn up in her prim little nest. However, back to Tommy. The only thing I can come up with is a Chinese restaurant called the Jade Dragon and a chap called Sung something Chin. On our very first case I went round there to ferret out some information. Tommy organised it. Said this man was a friend, I think. Maybe a relative? Anyway, he might know something.'

'Right. I'll see what I can do. Just how bad is Tommy? I mean, what shall I tell him?'

Mitch had dreamed of Tommy, not raised on a hospital trolley but offered up in her arms, the dust of him blowing away in a great wind which was deathly silent. 'Bad,' she said. And then said: 'I think. Just say serious. Seriously ill.'

'I'd like to come down,' said A.J.

'I really need you in the office. I'm going to see him this evening. Look – just leave it for now, will you? For a start, we have to try and reach any relatives he may have. If ... well ... the situation gets worse ... well, of course...'

'What about the investigation?'

'The murder victim wasn't Rosie. So we're still in business. Sissy and I were up half the night. We found some clothes in an out-house here and had to call the police.' Mitch, in bringing A.J. up to date, was surprised her grasp of detail was not diminished by the leaden sickness souring her brain.

'But why would the dead woman change her clothes? Why did she dress herself in Rosie's kit? And did the killer then think he was finishing off Rosie Childe?'

'All good questions,' said Mitch, feeling the pressure in her head increasing, a stirring up of the acid sludge of indulgence. 'Very shortly I'm off to see Julian Small who is down in Tavistock today on business. He's the chap who went with Rosie Childe to

261

Bosnia last year. Tommy said he'd got some very interesting stuff from him but I don't know what. I'm seeing Miss Woodward, an old teacher of Rosie's, after lunch on Saturday. I also rang Oa Bone to see if I could fix up an appointment. No joy there. I just got a cow of a woman who said she'd pass the message on. And if I ring a hundred times I'm sure I'll get the same answer.'

'Why do you want to see him?'

'Well, the theory seems to be that Rosie got in the pudding club at one of his parties. It's a long shot, sure, but what if he's the father of her child? As far as I know, he's never been married so has no legitimate children. He's at the time of life when people have stopped feeling immortal. At this stage houses aren't bricks and mortar but flesh and blood.'

'But what could that have to do with this other woman's death and Rosie's disappearance?'

'No idea,' said Mitch. 'But it's ground which has got to be covered. You could help a bit there. Find out what you can about him. Digger at Radio Brum should be a big help. Will you also ask him to pull a few strings with his producer chums? I want to know how to get hold of an old friend of mine called Ellie Peters who is out in Bosnia at the moment. Network radio have been broadcasting some of her pieces.'

'You're spelling that the normal way? Anything else?'

'Nothing you can help with. I want to get hold of Bernice Brody again, the woman Rosie was sharing a flat with in London. There are one or two things I'd like to know more about. But I've not been able to contact her yet.'

'What's Sissy's reaction to it all?'

'Unprintable when she came back from the mortuary. But as far as I know she doesn't want to pull the plug on the investigation. She'd gone by the time I'd crawled out of bed. There was a planning meeting for a shoot in Stratford-upon-Avon. You can get me on the mobile, A.J. But not in the next ten minutes. I got totally ratted last night. I'll be in the shower working on rising from the dead. I'm never going to do this again. If Sissy can stick to water when all hell breaks loose so can I.'

'Pull the other one,' said A.J. and Mitch heard her assistant put the phone down. Her eyes, more used to the glare, were now wide open and she saw Sissy's strappy purple sandals were still where they'd fallen when the cook had pulled them off as she'd walked to an armchair. The matching handbag, which had precariously come to rest on top of the back of a chair, had gone. She then noticed that the glass panes in the french windows badly needed cleaning and that weeds were growing through some of the cobbles in the courtyard beyond. None of this affected the charm of the room. Mitch found that she was rearranging the furniture in her mind, removing the brass from around the inglenook fireplace, adding a mirror which would reflect not the courtyard she saw now but one drenched in roses. Am I going soft as I trundle along to old age? she wondered. This is not my scene. Not my scene *at all.*

Upstairs and under the shower, water running through her hair to her scalp, sliding down the nape of her neck to her buttocks, trickling between her thighs, trembling on the edge of painted toenails, she tentatively tried a whistle.

Suddenly she was singing.

Oh, I'm a splendid bit of totty
So don't you be so snotty...

Suddenly she clamped her lips shut. How can you? she found herself thinking. When Tommy's going to die?

Tommy is *not* going to die, she told herself firmly.

And if he doesn't, *who will look after him?*

I can't be expected to. Alarm tensed her muscles. I'm just his business partner. I don't really know him. Oh Tommy. Why couldn't you be more careful?

And who will look after you when the time comes, Mitchell? Not Cassie. She won't even come back to England to see you. You have to go and see her.

Well, I haven't landed on a hospital trolley yet, she thought. I'm still up and running. What's the point in thinking about things which may never happen to you?

O-h-h-h...
I've got legs up to my ears,
Jolly jugs which have no peers,
I'm a syncopated lady
Built to drive you crazy!

Singing her demons away.

Dressed conservatively for her, oatmeal linen slacks, matching knitted silk sweater, canvas shoes, no ear-rings, nothing to startle the horses – how could Sissy have visited a mortuary looking like the queen of tarts? – she bounded down the stairs. It was when she reached the bottom she realised her headache had practically gone. Must be pretty sturdy stuff, the Mitchell flesh, she reassured herself.

The ship's bell hanging outside the back door clanged. She turned and opened it to find Paul Maugin standing on the step. He had to stoop to come in. Mitch didn't like thin men because their bones stuck into you; making love could feel like being the cheese in a grater. She didn't like men who were too tall because awkward gaps could open up between erogenous zones. She wasn't keen, either, on top drawer voices. Former public schoolboys, in her opinion, sat too high on the shelf, were too unsure of themselves, to jump down and become the equals of women. They also retained a prankish sense of apple-pie bed humour she found deeply unfunny. But here she was standing on the terracotta tiles of the kitchen floor swimming, but not drowning, thank God, in Old Adam's delight. His eyes were blue. He said: 'Came to check up on you. I don't often drive people off the road, you know.'

'Well, we didn't quite crash into each other, did we?'

'I can see you're in fine form. Could you manage dinner on Sunday night?'

'Sounds super.' She was shocked to discover her voice had suddenly acquired a Sloaney edge.

'Nothing you don't like?'

'I'm easy to feed.' To look into his eyes she had to tilt her head back. All her life she'd been forced to look up to men.

'Are you? How's Tommy doing?'

'OK, I think.'

'That's good. Good Hope Cottage, opposite the church.'

When he'd gone Mitch found her feet

doing a twitchy little dance round the kitchen table. The best thing you could do is put a cork in it, reason told her. You don't want another disastrous affair. Especially with an upper class git who thinks you're just a little bit of easy under-bred totty.

You can shut your mouth, she told reason. I can go out to play if I want to.

But she'd come back down on to her heels by the time she collected her jacket and handbag. She stuffed the mobile phone in a pocket.

Outside was a child's picture book day, baby white clouds, great big sun and cartoon sheep on the high, dipping hill above Manaccan House. Unseasonably hot for the time of year.

Paul.

She was trying the name out.

She'd never had a lover called Paul.

He's not your lover. Honestly. Some people.

He might be.

Hey, kiddo. Stop dreaming. Let's go. She swung into the car and studied the map before switching on the engine. She lowered two windows so she could create a cross breeze, let in the clutch and began to think of the questions she'd ask Julian Small. On the phone he'd sounded rather prim, more like a town hall bureaucrat than a trouble-shooting aid worker used to being in dangerous parts of the world. She thought he'd expect her to be serious and low key which was why she'd chosen the outfit she had.

She battled through the snaggles in the traffic system which almost throttled Newton Abbot and hit Ashburton as she came off the A38. The town was guarded by rows of pastel-washed council houses cut into hillside. The road through the centre, flanked by handsome Georgian buildings, led to wooded terrain which rose to the granite outcrops of Dartmoor. Mitch followed the signpost to Princetown.

She passed through wooded country, smelling pine resin. The Tavistock Inn loomed and vanished and she suddenly found herself dipping through a swell of bracken washing into gorse. Jaunty cloud above, dazzlingly white, an underbelly of darkness plunging over waves of moorland. She heard a mew; full-throated, hungry. Startled, she cocked her head. There it was again. Buzzards, she thought. The cry rode on a peevish whining. The stone walls which lined the road were so loosely knitted together that wind swilled in fist-sized gaps. And then the moor itself butted the road; in the lee of granite outcrops were straggling groups of ponies.

She passed the turn-off to Princetown and soon, to her left, the gaunt blocks of Dartmoor Prison rose. They reminded her of the cotton mills of the north, though she knew they were of a much earlier date, originally built to house French prisoners of war at the turn of the eighteenth century Many years ago she'd gone there to research a package for network radio. Like a great house, or a public school, the prison had its Latin motto. Spare the vanquished. Good words, she'd thought, seeing the human buzzards in the prison's public car-park, binoculars astride noses, hunting for glimpses of gaol-birds.

Her handbag began to keen. Mitch dipped in a bunch of scrabbling fingers and came up with the mobile phone. 'A.J.?'

'Actually, it's Darcy Moran, Mr Bone's assistant. Mr Bone has got some free time on Saturday afternoon. Could you make it around three thirty?'

'Excellent.'

Darcy Moran gave her the directions and then said: 'Till tomorrow.'

Mitch dropped the phone back on to the passenger seat. Shows how wrong you can be, she thought. I imagined I'd have to scale a couple of mountains to gain access. 'Well, don't get too cocky,' she told herself. 'You've still got to find a polite way of asking him if he's the father of Rosie's kid.' She decided there wasn't one and it was a pity she'd left her running shoes in Birmingham.

Tavistock lay beneath her, the railway viaduct looming above roofs and canopied by gently billowing hills. The old copper mining town snoozed in its hollow, pits closed, civic buildings baronial tombs to the wealth amassed by last century's dead.

She parked just past the plundered ruins of the twelfth-century abbey and walked back to the centre of the town which, she found, had an airy handsomeness, wide roads, old trees casting bony shade and a wash of space before the market building. The rearing, neo-Gothic edifice, steep-roofed, castellated, chimneys soaring like lances, had been mentioned by Julian Small. 'You can't miss it,' he said. 'It looks like a Victorian railway station.'

Mitch glanced at her watch. She'd just about make it. She didn't increase her pace. She liked to sniff out somewhere new to her. Tavistock, she decided, had the feel of being stuck in the fifties, and she couldn't decide whether this was due to the granite pavement slabs under her feet or the thinness of the traffic stream. The town, on the western edge of Dartmoor, was a long way from most places people needed to get to.

She crossed by the police station, a castellated annexe attached to the market complex, and walked round the back of the building. There, next to a butcher's in a narrow alleyway, she found the café she was looking for. Green tables with richly patterned laminated table-cloths were arranged along the walkway. On this fine March day most of the chairs appeared to be occupied. The smell of warming dishes and coffee. Mitch, who earlier had thought she'd never want to eat again, found she was hungry.

'Miss Mitchell!'

She looked along the row of tables and spotted a man sitting alone. But surely he was the wrong man? His head was shaved from his neck to the top of his ears, the pelmet of hair left woven into a rat's tail plait at the back. A rich claret and green brocade waistcoat was worn over a wool polo-necked jumper. Jeans, big boots, four rings in his left ear.

'Over here.'

A very alternative businessman, she thought, and felt ludicrously overdressed as she walked across. She was smiling brightly and he managed a vinegary grin. Though he couldn't be more than mid-thirties, his face was scrunched like a dried-out window leather. Worrying for the world.

'Hi there. Lovely day.' Mitch dropped into the chair beside him. Fearing he wouldn't be up to it, she caught the waitress's attention. 'On me,' she said. He didn't demur.

While waiting for their cheese and rolls they stirred their coffee. His was black.

They'd talked about Tommy, the weather and his business meeting with the Friends of Lichen, which had its national head-quarters in the town. 'I've moved on, right? Getting the head wrapped round green issues, OK?' he said. 'I've come to realise that's the important thing. No world, no people. Simple. All that stuff in Bosnia, you know? Changes people. Changed me. I had to get into my inner space. Do some serious stuff. Brood the choices.'

'Quite,' said Mitch, aware of the peda-gogue 'see me' tone in her voice. She'd always had the urge to discipline the woolly and to her New Age speak came into that category. She tried to loosen up and told him about Ellie Peters setting up a radio station in Bosnia.

'Yanks,' he said, dismissing over two hundred million people in one wave of nail-bitten fingers.

'Actually, she's English,' and then Mitch realised that Ellie wasn't, not any more. Before too many hackles could splinter the conversation she thought she'd better get down to the nitty-gritty. 'We're still no nearer to finding Rosie,' she said and brought him up to date on the story.

'The dead woman was wearing Rosie's clothes? Tommy didn't tell me that.'

'He didn't know.'

'I believe in people doing their own thing,

you know? But Rosie... Well, you had to watch out for Rosie. She's like a little kid in many ways.'

'What do you mean?'

'Well, take this guy Musa Hadri she met when we were working over there. He's a Kosovan – I see some papers go for Kosovar, but what do they know? – from some remote bit of mountain on the Albanian border, right? He came down to Bosnia when his cousin died. Went to help his uncle in this bicycle repair shop. This was before the war. Of course, when the shooting match starts he's in the thick of it. We're in 1992 when Serbia decides to fight to the death to prevent a Muslim state springing up in their midst. We bunked down in Sarajevo, attached to a group helping out with the UN aid vehicles. Bread queues were quite often mortared, you know. People killed. But then this bomb was fired into the market place, not much more than a stone's throw from the Presidency. I missed out on it, thank God. Nearly seventy dead. Two hundred wounded. That was where Rosie met Musa, among the blown-off limbs and puddles of brains. They worked until they dropped into each other's arms. It was all big deal Hemingway stuff, you know? Though when they hit the sack I don't think they gave a shit about the sun also rising. She really got bound up in that guy in other ways, too. I don't know this for sure, but certainly it was suspected by more people than me that she began to mess with guns as well as bread. She certainly helped to ferry people across the lines. And then I hear she's going to marry this kid Musa. He'd be in his late teens then.'

'But why shouldn't she? Marry him, I mean?'

Julian Small looked at her; the beam in his small, worried eyes was so intense she felt he'd reached through to her brain to see if all the grey matter in there were dead. 'With Musa you're into the male Muslim customs from a remote region which is in a time warp, right? These guys may tote Kalashnikovs or some such shit but I doubt they're much out of the Dark Ages. Women are your basic body servants. They're not even allowed out of the house without male permission. I mean, believe me, they make an Anglo-Saxon male chauvinist pig look politically correct.'

'Sacks for carrying,' Mitch remembered.

'What?'

'Someone told me that some of the men there think that's all women are. Sacks for carrying.'

'And some. A lover's one thing. It bears no relation to being a wife. Right? Luckily for Rosie there was a British United Nations commander in Bosnia at the time. After a bit of top people liaising she suddenly found herself in the company of some Coldstream Guard types and on the plane back to England.'

'She was hijacked? Were they allowed to do that?'

'I shouldn't think so for a minute.'

'But they did it.'

'Lots of things happen in a situation like that. War is different. Believe it.'

Mitch suddenly had a mental picture of an excavated mass grave of torture victims. Bosnians or Serbs? Pictures not quite black and white. Mud and shapes and a news-reader's neutral grey voice. She found herself staring at a woman strolling along the alleyway, tomato-coloured sweater, cropped sand jeans, cork-soled shoes. She said eventually: 'Didn't Rosie think of trying to get back?'

'Musa married almost immediately. A kid called Yolanda who worked as an interpreter at that time. I should think that had been arranged for quite a while. Yolanda was a good catch for him. Her father's one of their intellectuals.'

'So Rosie, was really a bit on the side? Why did he want to marry her, then?'

'Passport out of the place.'

'Anyway, you felt relaxed enough about it to go back to Bosnia with her last year?'

'Sure. It was unfinished business for her

and I had a bit of research to do for a relief organisation.'

'But she saw Yolanda.'

'How did you know that?'

'Her flatmate gave me a letter Rosie had sent to her.'

'She saw Musa, too. I was not aware of *that* until we were back in England.'

'You think they got back together again?'

'Like as in item? She said not.'

'Do you believe her?'

He tapped the side of his shaved pate. 'Rosie's got no discipline. Can't get herself centred. Know what I mean?'

'Could he be over here? Could she have funded him?'

'How do I know?' He was silent. They were both now watching the passers-by.

'From what you hear Kosovars seem to be coming over by the lorry load.'

'War and refugees go together.'

'Can Rosie fire a gun?'

She followed his gaze. He was watching a little girl's red ribbon dance through the sunshine. 'From what she told me she'd learned how to use a Kalashnikov.'

'She could be a killer.' Mitch realised she'd spoken the thought aloud.

17

Miss Woodward's cottage was one of a small row built along the narrow corkscrewing lane which bisected Bishop Coombe. Mitch started to pull into a dirt and grass alley at the end of the block when she read the notice. 'Private Land. Strictly No Parking.' She straightened the car and drove on. There was a T-junction just before one of the more vicious twists and a war memorial set up on a small irregular patch of lawn. Mitch turned up the hill at the junction and eventually, ignoring the 'Patrons Only' sign at the entrance to the village pub's car-park, left the grey Escort there. Every other conceivable space, and some inconceivable ones, had been taken.

Though it was only March, climbing roses sprawling along pastel-painted walls were sprouting leaves. Down from the moor, in the deep valleys, warm sunshine slipped through greenery as heavily as sediment gliding to a river bed.

Mitch sauntered back down the hill, letting the sun play on her, pushing fingers up through hair at the nape of her neck and shaking out the exuberant black curls.

Unfurling herself after a bleak winter of anxieties about her radio job, the viability of the detective agency, builders' bills and what she thought of as 'general shit'. She felt a tingle at the bottom of her spine and yes, there it was, the waggle had come back to her bum. Splendid, she beamed. Excellent, and she inhaled the perfumes of the afternoon.

Number six was second from the end of the short row of brick Victorian cottages which sat uneasily in a village of cob walls and thatched roofs. There was a tiny, shady front garden in which self-seeded ivy and ferns had been left to run riot about a fuchsia bush which obscured part of the front window. Long trails of spiders' webs netted the bush to the glass. The acid orange curtains were unlined. She rang the unpolished brass bell button and listened out for footsteps. There weren't any. She rang again and then stepped back to the other side of the road and looked up at the bedroom window. Nothing stirred. She recrossed the road and explored the back of the alleyway. Long thin strips of garden ran towards a boundary stream. Outhouses, perhaps once privies, bordered the water. There was no sign of life in any of the gardens.

She'd try one more time. She was just turning when a red Golf swung into the alleyway, lifting small stones as it swirled to a stop just beyond the no parking sign. The man opened the car door cautiously, making sure it didn't bang into the gable end wall. He manoeuvred himself out. They looked at each other over the top of the car door; the one who had obeyed the sign indignant, the one who hadn't apparently oblivious to it.

She opened her mouth to say something and then shut it. What she needed, if he could give it, was information, not an argument. Easing down, she studied his spade-shaped face and the wire-framed glasses. His hair, the colour and texture of dead grasses, receded unevenly from his brow and splayed out about his ears to spikily frame a button-shaped nose and moist, pursed mouth. An air of the pedagogue about him, she thought, and then noticed his hands through the car window, big, blunt and powerful. On the back of one was a discolouring bruise.

'I was looking for Miss Woodward.'

'She can't be far,' he said. 'I've come to cut her lawn. She's probably nipped up to the post office.'

'Haven't we met before?' Mitch knew they hadn't but liked to name all those who drifted within her sphere when conducting an investigation. '"You never know" should be the Mitchell family motto,' A.J. had once told her.

He was saying: 'Probably in connection with St Ursula's? Arthur Trimble. I teach there.'

'Coral's husband,' said Mitch and studied him more closely.

'Actually, yes.'

Mitch had no intention of questioning Miss Woodward with him hanging around. 'I'll try again later.'

'I'll give her a message if you want.'

'No need.' There was not enough room to squeeze by him. She had to thread herself between the passenger side of the car and interwoven fencing.

'You are a friend of my wife's?' A distinct waspiness. She turned towards him and realised she was about to be handed one hundred lines. *Coral is a word no educated person uses.* Is my imagination running riot, or does he know his wife's having a bit on the side?

'Acquaintance is perhaps putting it too strongly. Well, I'll leave you to your labour. I'm sure it's much appreciated.' Mitchell the diplomat. She was aware of him staring at her as she walked down to the T-junction. She glanced back once. He was not eyeing her shape, the waggle in her bum. He was watching, she could swear, to make sure she didn't run down the corridor. And yet he was the one who had parked his car cheek by jowl to the sign: 'Private Land.

280

Strictly No Parking.'

Back in her car, she stared at the steering wheel and considered the gap which had suddenly opened up in her schedule. I'll get Tommy over with now, she decided, pictures in her head of free time in the early evening. She was seeing herself in the sitting-room at Manaccan House, sprawled in an armchair, a glass of gin and tonic near her right hand. *Get Tommy over with.* As if her partner were a dreaded chore. Maggots of guilt began to pick holes in her thought. But what can I do? It's not my fault his brain's blown a gasket. Christ. I couldn't be more sorry. It leaves me in a tremendous hole. Though not as big a hole as Tommy. She trembled on the brink of imagining the place he now inhabited; she pulled back. Bleaker than the grave, she thought, and had not the courage to enter it.

Why hasn't A.J. rung? Where are his relatives?

She fastened her seat belt and started the car. She knew A.J. would be in touch as soon as she had news. Maybe there would be none. Tommy, a pilgrim from a distant era, a distant land, might long ago have lost touch with his relations. Anyway, wouldn't any self-respecting Chinese family disown a relative who modelled himself on the Duke of Edinburgh? Mitch found herself smiling even as her bruised heart swelled.

The hospital was a different place in daylight. The complex was built on a steeply rising hill, Victorian granite blocks nearer the road, stuccoed buildings squeezed into dug-out space at the rear. Tommy was on Barlow Ward, the preserve of geriatric males. Mitch, who had never thought of him as geriatric, was alarmed to find her perspective changing to accommodate the institutional view.

First she waylaid a young nurse, a neat Chinese girl who said: 'Saw' when Mitch asked to speak to the ward sister. It took Mitch a moment to realise the girl had said: 'Sure.' She found she was brimming over with a tender pride for Tommy who never swallowed his rs, who hit his ls off the front of his palate like any Anglo-Saxon. He was so special.

The ward sister told her: 'He spent a comfortable night.'

'Ah,' said Mitch, weighing what had happened to Tommy with this official pronouncement. 'He's doing well then. Might fully recover?'

'It's too early to say. But we mustn't be too optimistic. It was a severe episode.'

'He'll need care when he comes out?'

'It could make all the difference.'

'I'm still trying to track down his relatives.'

'Please let us know when you have.'

Mitch, suddenly aware of her anger, began

to back off. It's not her fault Tommy's had a stroke, she thought. Well, the bitch could be more positive. And then a little check in her step. A quiver in her flesh. *His situation is hopeless.*

She spotted him in a bay of beds near the entrance to the ward, six old men with their heads cranked up above their feet, three facing towards the other three. They seemed to her as if they'd died and been laid out. She almost jumped when a reedy voice said: 'Whatcha, darling.' She found herself looking under beds to see what live creature lurked in this still place.

She sank into the chair next to Tommy, suddenly hot and blushing, realising she'd forgotten to bring anything for him. 'Honeypot,' she murmured, aware of the old Tommy and the new Tommy simultaneously, as if a line had been drawn from his brow to the tip of his chin. Half of his features looked as if they'd melted, slid out of place. His tipsy eyes were open but it was difficult to know if he saw her or, indeed, anything. The covers went up and down but not quite regularly; he seemed to quietly shudder rather than breathe. Mitch looked beyond him to the curtains which had been drawn partly across the window, cutting out most of the sun's rays.

'Tommy?' Did his head turn a fraction? Could he hear her?

Probably not. She took a deep breath and, ignoring the other men in the bay, some of whom, she realised now, were fully *compos mentis* and would hear every word she said, she brought him fully up to date on the investigation so far.

She drew some conclusions. 'It's got to be a reasonable bet that the body found in the woods is that of a refugee. Maybe even young Yolanda. There is one hell of a connection. The corpse was wearing Rosie's clothes, for God's sake. Rosie Childe did have an affair with what'shisface – Musa? – the guy who became Yolanda's husband. Rosie could even have killed Yolanda. She could handle firearms. I found that out yesterday. And the rumour is Rosie was seen in Coral Trimble's shop with a foreign guy. Musa? Maybe he got rid of his missus. Maybe that's why Rosie bolted. I know, I know. At it again. Making two and two add up to five. But what else have we got?' She considered. 'I've always had a feeling that Rosie's kid – the one she had adopted – has got something to do with all this. What's my evidence? Zilch. Sweet FA. It's a hunch. I know you don't go big on hunches but I can't stop having them, can I? And sometimes instinct is right. OK? I'm off to see Oa Bone when I leave here. I've got him down as a maybe daddy. But how am I going to ask him? I mean, politely? He's going to stick one hell of a big boot up my backside. Well, there it is. Not much nearer to finding Sissy's half-sister really, but I've got an idea things are starting to shape up even if I can't see quite what that shape is yet.'

She leaned back in the chair. She realised her hand had crawled towards Tommy's right hand which lay palm down on the white bedspread. Not quite touching, not quite daring to touch. She took a deep breath and placed his hand in hers. Dry, the texture of over-cooked fish. And then it began to happen. At first she thought she must be imagining it but no, her hand was beginning to be squeezed. Oh Tommy, she thought, the ache in her bordering on pain. Her breath became short, almost as laboured as his.

After two long, silent minutes, she was beginning to wonder if he'd ever free her. She needed to get out of here. Didn't she have places to go, people to see?

It was as if she'd told him this. His hand tightened. He tried to pull his shoulders from the pillow. 'Aaah-runk,' he seemed to say. 'Yah-sar-uk.'

'Tommy?'

But now his hand had slipped from hers.

'Tommy, what did you say?' Had he heard her analysis of the investigation so far and tried to point up some glaring omission? Or was it something else? When she'd reached him on her mobile after she'd seen Dr Hazel Rayburn he'd said: 'I've got some very interesting stuff.' He was going to tell her when she arrived at Manaccan House.

Looking down at her partner, she knew he'd faded from her. She stood up. 'I'll be back tomorrow,' she told him.

The voice she'd heard before piped up. 'Bring 'im something next time you come, missus. Never seen no one come empty-handed before. 'E needs a bit of something. 'E's not up to swallowing yet, not proper, but 'e could manage a bit of orange juice maybe. 'E a chink, then?'

'He's called Tommy Hung,' and she located a man in the bottom bed with purple lips and gooseberry eyes. 'At least that's his English name.'

'Ticker,' he said. ''Ell of a state, my ticker.'

Before he could settle into his tale of woe, she said: 'Must dash.'

In the sunshine again, she walked briskly to her car, checking out her body's performance. Everything seemed in good working order. Oh, honeypot, may you forever be a visitor and never a patient. Her thumb and forefinger gave the end of her nose a sharp tug. She couldn't quite seem to get rid of the ward's smell.

Oa Bone's house was not the sort of place Mitch would have expected a multi-millionaire rock star to live in, nor did it have the Bondlike security systems she'd imagined. There was a high stuccoed white boundary wall topped with wrought-iron work which featured a march of spear-like points and only one entrance, at the east side of the house. She parked the car on a verge and approached tall double wooden gates. Cut into the left one was a door. As she lifted the latch and stepped over the bottom rail a dog began to bark. She found herself in a working stable yard, though some of the buildings had been converted to garaging. The smell of dung permeated the air. There was a path, edged with a mossy run of scalloped Victorian terracotta tiles, and she followed it round to the front of the house. Two deckchairs and a small table were set under a huge cedar tree on an expanse of lawn which sloped downwards towards huge banks of rhododendrons and camellias. Oa Bone got up and walked towards her. His companion, an elderly woman, picked up her book off the table and began to read.

Mitch turned to look at the house. It had a slightly down-at-heel air, in need of a new coat of paint. It was a cream-stuccoed, comfortably sized Victorian villa sited on a small knoll. A glass-roofed verandah, supported by wrought-iron columns, wrapped round the front and west sides. On the first floor long windows were protected at the bottom by intricate grilles in which window boxes had been placed. Winter pansies bloomed in profusion.

'It dates from 1840. Built by Captain Lucas Brown when he came back from India. I suppose he got the idea for the verandahs while he was out there.' Oa Bone had come up behind her. 'He was responsible for the design. He obviously liked pretty houses. Probably liked pretty women, too.'

'It's splendid,' Mitch said. And it was, though not the million-plus pad she'd thought he'd own. 'It's very good of you to see me.'

'I know,' he said.

She looked up at his face. The skin fitted loosely, almost like a spongy rubber mask, a big swell of elasticated lip, clown's eyes, a mop of black tinted hair falling over his forehead. Even though his body was almost brutally thin, his jeans were tight. He wore a white sweatshirt and no shoes. His nails had lost the pinkness of youth; thick yellow horns which needed clipping.

He led her through the open front door into the house. A plain hallway with polished oak floor, one or two pieces of Georgian furniture, no pictures. He stood to one side to let her go first into a finely proportioned room she decided must be the drawing-room. A large, worn rug on the wooden floor, battered chintz-covered sofa, old leather armchairs, thick, faded linen curtains, Georgian bookcase and two fine inlaid Dutch marquetry cupboards. It all evoked an air of a gentleman who has come down in the world. From what Mitch recalled of Oa Bone's background, he was an Erdington Brummie who had made good. She suspected that all this dressing down cost as much as, if not more than, dressing up.

'Would you like some tea?'

'Yes, please.' She expected him to ring a bell or pull a tapestry ribbon and she spotted a device at one side of the marble fireplace. It was a white round pot disc haloed by filigree gilt work with a small handle which she thought he would pull up and down. But, whistling softly, he went to get the tea himself.

He turned as he reached the door. 'Sugar? Milk?'

'Just milk.' As he opened the door she heard female laughter from the back of the house. She found she felt relieved. It had upset all her preconceived notions when it appeared that the bad boy icon of rock was going to make her tea. He could be my maiden aunt, she thought. The image isn't the person, she reminded herself. But then you don't get to look like Dorian Grey without having some seriously wicked habits, do you?

She began to pace the floor. If he was into horses he could also follow other country pursuits. Like shooting.

You're just some ordinary babe-ee-ee
Who's driving me craze-ee-ee...

He must have had more totty than you've had hot dinners, she told herself. Why would he start putting holes in women's heads now?

There was a flickering on the periphery of her vision. She turned and noticed that the centre of the three single french windows was open. Hems stirred. Motes of dust were illuminated by a rising shaft of sunlight. She was reminded of the puff suspended in the air after her mother had beaten rugs on her clothes line.

She went over to a small table at the side of the windows and began examining family photographs. Among pictures of his kin there was just one publicity shot of Oa and members of his band, young men with big hair and bell-bottomed trousers. Oa backed through the door. There was a mug of tea in each hand. 'Park your bum,' he said. She chose a chair by the fireplace. 'So what's all this about Rosie Childe? How am I supposed to be able to help?'

It was then she realised that this was as

much a fishing trip for him as for her. To give her time to reflect on this she didn't answer him directly. 'I hear you're heavily into raising and giving money to charities in what was once Yugoslavia. Why did you choose that sort of charity? I mean, above all others?'

He sat on the chair opposite her, lifting his fifty-year-old legs up and crossing them in a semi-lotus position. The sharp triangle formed at the knee joints appeared to give the chair fledgling wings. 'I'd been looking for something for a while. I'm one of the trustees of the Geoff Stark Fund.'

'Your drummer? The one who died at the end of the eighties? I thought the Stark Fund had set up a clinic for drug users who wanted to ditch their habit?'

'Actually, it's a psychiatric unit for anyone who needs to sort their head out. People pay according to their means. The fund picks up the rest of the tab. Nowadays we have quite a few wealthy clients. We actually make a profit out of them. It all goes back into the fund, of course. But that's Geoff's thing. He thought about it all before he died, made sure everything was in place.'

'So he knew he was going to die?'

'Towards the end his liver was shot. To be honest I thought Geoff was wasting his money but over the years I got to realise it worked. In part.'

'How do you mean?'

'It's not all success but there's certainly enough success to make it good. You know? And I got to thinking I'd like to do something similar.'

'Why Yugoslavia?'

'Rosie Childe wrote while she was working out there. Four years ago? Something like that. She told me what the situation was and would I contribute something to the aid programme. You may imagine the amount of begging letters I get but in this case I decided to take a look.'

'Why?'

'Olga. My mother. She's Czechoslovakian.'

'The lady in the garden?'

'That's Olga. Anyway, I wouldn't be here now if the British Refugee Office in Prague hadn't got her out on one of the children's transports just before the Second World War. The rest of the family was wiped out. I mean, all this had been staring me in the face for years but it took Rosie's letter to get me going. I went out there.'

'You met Rosie?'

'Basically she's one of the good guys.' He pointed to his head. 'Just one or two missing links up there. Could drive you crazy.'

'That's in your song.'

Suddenly he laughed. '*That* song. Anyway, when I arrived home I started to organise things.'

'Did you see Rosie when she came back to the village?'

He hesitated. 'I was supposed to see her here the Sunday evening before she was due to start work at the girls' school – St Ursula's. She never showed. She often did that kind of stuff. Nothing like raising other people's blood pressure to raise the level of attention, too. I wasn't surprised when someone told me she'd not turned up at the school, either. What I can't understand is why Sissy Childe has employed a detective to find her. She'd know better than me what Rosie's like. I mean, this kid has always been into letting people down. Pissing them well and truly off. Does Sissy know something that we don't? Why does she think it's different this time?'

And this, Mitch thought, is what is behind his fishing expedition. Is he afraid for some reason? Had Sissy got an ulterior motive for employing the bureau? 'She thinks this time it's different enough to hire me. Did you know that when she was a teenager Rosie had a child which was subsequently adopted?'

He didn't answer her question. He said: 'What can that possibly have to do with what's going on now?'

'The general feeling seems to be that Rosie got pregnant at some bash held here. She was around fifteen at the time. She did a bunk, faced up to all the shit alone. She wasn't found by her family until she was in hospital having the kid.'

'I didn't know that. That takes a lot of guts.'

'But you did know about the child?'

'Only recently. And if you're thinking what I think you're thinking forget it.'

'You're saying it's not your child?' Mitch was suddenly aware of a shadow by the open window. It drained away.

'Of course it's not my child.'

'In words from a famous court case, "You would say that wouldn't you?"'

'Oh, come on. Is this what it's all about? You're trying to chase down the paternity of this child? It's nothing to do with Rosie slinging her hook? I understand from Rosie that this child of hers was legally adopted. She's no idea where her little girl is now. Furthermore, it is none of her business.'

'The baby came up in the course of the investigation. I have to cover all the angles.' Mitch saw the shadow again. It shrank away as the curtain billowed gently into the room. The sun's ray shivered over Oa Bone's head.

'Well, I think you've got things seriously out of whack. How can something so far in Rosie's past have a bearing on the present?'

'The past has everything to do with the present.'

Oa Bone suddenly laughed. 'If you want to

talk philosophy, OK. But if you really want to find Rosie all I can say is that you're seriously off course.' He began to unwind his long legs. 'If you want to know what I think ... my guess is that bitch Sissy is up to something. Altruism isn't her bag. No way.' He stood up.

'Was there any special reason you were seeing Rosie that Sunday?' She put the mug down and looked towards the open window again as she rose from the chair. She'd wondered if someone had been out there, listening in to their conversation. The shadows were small, mice with tails of light. Nothing now to suggest a figure.

'If she'd come we'd have probably talked about the situation in Kosovo. Things like that.'

'Well, I appreciate you seeing me, Mr Bone. And let me congratulate you on winning the radio franchise.'

'Pretty much touch and go, that. We were sweating right down to the wire. Jesus. I wouldn't like to go through that again. I don't know what you're doing messing around with investigation work. You're a broadcaster, Miss Mitchell. I mean, you're seriously good. You did a piece on an early band I was in.'

Mitch still couldn't remember the interview. She supposed it must be one of the many she'd done which were so unremarkable to her they'd been erased from the memory bank. 'Broadcasting is a fickle employer. I needed another string to my bow. Life on the dole just seems too surreal for someone like me.'

They had now reached the front door. Both chairs under the cedar tree were vacant. There was no sign of Oa Bone's mother. 'Well, it's nice to have met you again.'

'Sure,' said Oa Bone. 'Rosie Childe is very good at looking after number one, you know. I'd start looking over your shoulder if I were you. Look at Sissy. I mean, talk about flaky...' He dipped back into the house before she could reply.

She stood on the step for a second. Is he trying to put me off track or is he right about Sissy? she wondered. *Has Sissy reason to think Rosie is dead? Was what shocked her at the mortuary the fact that a stranger lay on the slab?* She walked round the side of the house. A dog began to bark again as she crossed the stable yard. It was only when she'd stepped over the rail at the bottom of the door inset into the massive wooden gates that she saw the elderly woman. Oa Bone's mother had her bum firmly parked against the bonnet of the car. Her feet were crossed. The side of one navy blue canvas deck shoe rested across the other. Sun glinted off the lenses of her spectacles. 'Mrs

Bone?' The woman was wearing an old Paisley patterned skirt and an even older woollen shirt and Mitch found that it irritated her. In Mitch's opinion a family with several millions should rise to the challenge and spend it.

'I'd try Roseberry Lane in Newton Abbot, my dear. A house called Fair or Pear something or other. It puzzled me. I never did think he was sliding off to see one of his women when he went there. When he plays he always plays away.'

'It was you by the window. You were listening.'

'If I've got a grandchild I want to know about her.'

'Why don't you ask him? Why wouldn't he tell you? You're his mother!'

'He tells me what he wants me to know and that is rarely what I want to know. Even if it is true, if he thought he had good enough reason he'd deny it.'

'He'd lie?'

'Everyone lies all the time. Unless it's a great big whopper most people don't even realise they're at it or they think of it as white lies. Lies are like oil in the knee joints. Without them society would be crippled. How good you're looking, how young you're looking, you can't come because you've got a previous appointment, what a bore, of course I love you darling, well, it didn't cost much at all... Life moves on big lies, small lies and, of course, we lie and say it doesn't. I can't be bothered with all that. I lost my first family, Miss Mitchell, they were wiped out during the Second World War. That's not true. There was one of my mother's sisters left. The boring one. Since my husband died it's practically been just my son and me. As far as I know he hasn't produced any offspring but if he has I want to know.'

'The possibility is a very, very remote one.'

'I know that. However remote, I've got to find out.'

'Do you always try to listen in to your son's private conversations?'

'No. Only if I'm really full of beans. I've sort of to psych myself up for it. Besides, he told me you were a detective and you have to wonder, don't you? He's been up to an awful lot in his time so it wouldn't be surprising if some chickens came home to roost. Would it? I'll ring you in a couple of days or so and you can tell me if you've found out anything. I'll pay you, of course.'

'I don't want money. I already have a client.' And then, worried that Mrs Bone would start investigating herself, she found herself saying: 'I'll see what I can do.'

'I'd take my money if I were you,' said Mrs Bone. 'You don't look as if you can afford to have principles.' She leaned up off the car's bonnet. 'I was very surprised when my son said he was going to see you. I wondered what on earth was going on. He's not at all keen on nosy parkers.' She was trotting back across the lane. She let herself in through the door and banged it shut.

Well, thought Mitch, that's a turn-up for the book. At least I've never listened in to other people's conversations. Well, not often. And strictly in the line of business. I wouldn't like to have her as my mother but then, Mitch reflected, she'd not much liked her own. It had been rather like loving Mrs Prune. But she had sometimes thought – though not until after her mother was safely dead – that there was a naughty Mrs Prune who had been desperately struggling to get the hell out from under, and eventually did so, in the form of her daughter.

Thank God, she thought now, you only have to go through childhood once.

Then she thought: there's something seriously out of whack here. *If Oa does have a child, why isn't he acknowledging the fact?*

She climbed into her car and as she backed up she decided she'd go and see if she could winkle out Miss Woodward before she called it a day.

This time when she knocked at the door of number six she heard footsteps behind the solid Victorian door. A woman whose clothes seemed to be springing gaps everywhere, like a bursting bedspread, said:

'Well, what is it?'

'Miss Woodward? It's about Rosie Childe.'

'Missing,' said Miss Woodward. 'Missing indeed. It's about time people learned to get their facts right. I saw her yesterday in Queen Street. I did think of having a word with her. She really ought to know about all the fuss she's causing. But she was too far away. I can't run, can I? I've just come out of hospital. Let me tell you, Rosie Childe isn't worth dying for. She was with two girls from St Ursula's. Alice Rice and Ishbelle Jones. Now that *is* odd.'

18

Ishbelle Jones was in her bedroom, sitting at the small pine table she did her homework on. Her diary was unlocked and open. She sucked the end of her biro, curls falling over her forehead. In the end she wrote: 'It's difficult to describe him because he's all over the place. Serious energy. He sort of jumps out of himself. I can hear Alice laughing at me. "Ready to catch you in his arms, you mean?" Haddi's mega attractive, I mean really, really, not like that awful Justin Bannerman she goes on about. Justin's pathetic. I can't think why Haddi is with that woman. She's so old and there's something creepy about her, the way she keeps on looking. Alice says the woman's probably a dyke but then why is she with Haddi? My mum thinks there's something wrong with her, that she's ill or something. She says that makes people look older than they are. Me and Alice bumped into the cow in Queen Street on Friday and she took us to Mr Bertie's. She bought us a bag of chips each and a Coke. I thought she was nosy, the questions she was asking, but Alice says she was just trying to be friendly...'

Ishbelle stopped writing. She had begun picturing Haddi in her mind, hearing him whispering: 'Pr-eety babe-eee...' She was smiling as she thought of how she'd teach him to speak English properly. Her lips, patchy with partly sucked off lilac frost lipshine, traced the sound for him. The hair at the back of her neck tickled her spine. The sensation was exquisite. 'Uuuoooh! I'm hot for him.' She remembered the words from one of the books that she and Alice kept at their secret place. God, if her mum knew the half about the stuff in their *X Files.* Even they didn't fancy some of the antics the characters got up to. I mean, in your mouth ... ugh ... she thought. That's disgusting. She just knew that Haddi wouldn't expect her to do anything like that.

She heard a noise in the garden below her window. She got up and went to investigate. There was that woman, thin as a coat hanger, all droopy-haired, hanging about on the lawn. She was wearing the same things she always did, jeans and a polo necked jumper. A navy blue cardigan was tied round her scraggy bum. No sign of Haddi. The woman seemed without purpose but gradually drifted over towards the back of the lawn and there rooted herself in. She shook her hair back and looked up at Ishbelle's bedroom window. Ishbelle withdrew behind the curtain. She's spying on me. She really is, she thought. I wish she'd go. But if the woman left her mother's B and B so would Haddi.

What can he see in her? She knew she was living in a different world from her mum and that of all the other adults she came into contact with. She and Alice had discussed this at length. 'Women are from Venus and men are from Mars and it's us kids who are from planet Earth,' Alice said after describing to Ishbelle some of her dad's inexplicable behaviour. Ishbelle had to admit that Alice's Justin Bannerman was a kid, one of them, whereas Haddi was over the divide and why he did some of the things he did – like have a relationship with that woman – was beyond her.

What could the creepy cow think she was doing, staring up at her window for God's sake? Perhaps she really was a dyke and went around with a dildo stuffed in her handbag. 'An object used as a substitute for an erect penis.' Alice had found the definition in a dictionary. 'Do you think it means something like a banana? A large one, of course?' Ishbelle had looked at her, her jaw dropping slightly and then they'd rolled around with laughter. They'd later decided a rolling pin was a more likely object because a banana would split its skin. 'I mean,' said Alice after they'd stopped laughing 'yuk.' 'Yuk yuk yuk...' Ishbelle agreed. 'How can they?'

But reading through their growing *X Files* they'd discovered that their elders did weirder things than that. Alice had said: 'If you weren't careful it could seriously put you off. Know what I mean?' Yes, Ishbelle did.

Cautiously Ishbelle extended her neck and peered round the sprigged lilac curtain. The woman was drifting away again towards the front of the house. She thought: Is she or isn't she mega creepy? Perhaps she was mad, like the women who stole babies from maternity units or prams. It's me who's mad, thought Ishbelle. Whoever heard of a thirteen-years-old baby!

She's just a sad old bag. What *can* Haddi see in her? On the wall over her pine bed-head Ishbelle had a poster of Five and until Haddi had danced into her life Spiky Scott had been the object of her desire. His hair stood up in little stiff pyramids over the crown of his head. Her mother called them worm casts but a fat lot she knew about the fashion scene. She even thought St Ursula's school uniform was nice. The chores her mum had lumbered her with just so she could earn enough for a pair of bootcut hipsters. She was wondering whether going for a combat body warmer would be worth all the hassle. Alice's parents gave her a clothing allowance. She didn't have to spend her Sunday mornings hoovering and ironing in return for the clothes on her back. She didn't discuss this with Alice, nor any of the other girls at school. She knew most of their families were much better off. She told herself that she didn't mind but, of course, she did. Everyone looked down on people who had no money, even if they pretended not to.

She looked at the small alarm clock on her work table. If she didn't get a move on, she'd miss the bus. She unclasped the silver chain at her neck. There were two keys on it, the gold-coloured one locked the diary, the Yale key was for her and Alice's secret place. I think I'll write poetry, she suddenly thought. I don't see why not. But how could she net the dazzling Haddi in words? All the stuff about tigers and bright eyes had been used. And let's face it, other people's love affairs were a big yawn.

But you're not having a love affair with Haddi.

That withered spy of a witch is.

She just couldn't get her head round it. Maybe he was her long-lost son or something. But then he'd have to look a bit like her, wouldn't he? A half-starved mouse couldn't produce a tiger.

God. Just look at the time. She took a packet of cigarettes and a lighter from under her mattress, stuffed them in the pocket of the canvas jacket, buttoned the pocket and slung the jacket over her shoulder. The wide landing was flooded with buttery afternoon light, some spilling down the stairs from the second floor, some washing through the arched window illuminating the half-landing leading to the hall. The sound of her flying feet was deadened by the turkey patterned carpet. She ran up the hall and flung open the kitchen door. 'Mum, I–' The rest of what she was going to say piled into a little grunt of surprise. Her eyes grew.

Elaine Jones was by the kitchen sink turned towards Mr Trimble. His arm was round her waist and his hand was moving up towards her breast. Just before all Ishbelle's sentence had piled up her mother had jumped and Mr Trimble's arm had been pushed away. Elaine was blushing. Mr Trimble was grinning. 'You do look different out of your school uniform.' He sounded different, not at all like the man who droned on about eighteenth-century land enclosures.

Was that a shadow of a wink? Ishbelle was speechless. She lowered her gaze, avoiding him, avoiding them.

'Henry's just popped round to tell me about the school outing to St Ives,' Elaine said.

Ishbelle found her tongue. It felt thick, awkward. 'He's not called Henry'

'To my friends I'm Henry,' he said. 'My

very close friends, that is.'

Ishbelle lifted her head. 'He's called Arthur, Mum,' and now she was blushing, embarrassed for her mother. How could she let that seriously yukky man paw her?

'You're off out then? Where to? Perhaps I'd better make myself useful. What do you think? Do you want a lift?' he asked her. He turned back to her mother. 'Never know who's about these days, do you?'

'I don't need a lift. I'm meeting Alice at the bus stop.'

Now he was not so much looking at her as finding her out, all the hidden places, making her wriggle as if she were guilty of something. He had discovered the keys hanging from the silver chain round her neck. In desperation she looked to her mother to rescue her.

'You are so rude,' Elaine Jones told her daughter. 'You just say thank you.'

Ishbelle looked from one to the other of them. Her mother's lips, buttered red, were thinning as she waited for her to apologise. His face had disappeared into a gigantic grin, strong yellow teeth bordering a moist U-shaped line. She turned and ran. She banged the heavy front door after her. Gravel flew off the soles of her trainers as she hurtled down the drive. She rounded the stone gateposts and pounded along the tarmac pavement. The growing stitch in her side began to make her bend. She halted when she was almost at the main road. She was gasping, hands under her budding breasts, hot breath blowing off hotter cheeks. On the other side of the main road she could see Alice at the bus stop, one strap of her small purple backpack over her combat body warmer. Alice didn't notice her until she was half-way across the road and then she waved. 'I was beginning to think you wouldn't make it,' she said when Ishbelle, snorting for breath, reached her. 'You look like a boiled beetroot.' She swung her backpack off her shoulder and pulled the flap far enough back for Ishbelle to see the top of a bottle of wine. 'You got the ciggies?'

Ishbelle had to wait a moment for her lungs to find enough air. 'Course I have.'

'I've told Mum we're at your place, right? Just in case she asks,' said Alice. 'She's gone quite soft in the brain since they found that body in the woods. She thinks a rural Jack the Ripper's on the loose.'

'God, don't say that.'

'Do you believe in heaven?'

'Too dead boring for words.' Ishbelle had stopped heaving. Her hands were dug into her hip bones, trying to squeeze away the stitch.

'I wonder what that woman thought? Just before he topped her?'

'She probably didn't think at all,' said Ishbelle. 'She probably shit herself.'

The truncated orange coach with Minirunner emblazoned in gold along its sides pulled in. The doors swung open and the driver, a pretty girl whose hair stuck out in bunches on each side of her head, took the fares. All the other people on the bus were pensioners.

'Anyway, there are two of us,' said Ishbelle. 'Killers always go for one, don't they?'

'Not many. Think of that mum and her two kids.' Suddenly Alice was laughing. 'If you could see your face!'

'It's not funny.'

'God. You're so easy to wind up. You know?'

As the bus moved off Alice began to talk about Justin Bannerman. Ishbelle was listening with half an ear as she replayed the scene in her mum's kitchen. She was tackling the whole thing as if it were a problem in arithmetic. Surely she'd made a mistake somewhere? Had she multiplied when she should have subtracted?

The bus threaded through lanes on a busy roundabout and then the metal panels vibrated as the driver changed gears to tackle the steep incline which led out of the town into the countryside. Soon all they could see were dense hedges on each side of the road. They emerged on to the rounded brow of a hill and had their first view of the Teign estuary. The water was bound by wooded tussocks of land which swelled into grazing land. Beyond were the roofs of houses, dipping downhill towards a small dock, built on drained marsh where sea and river met. This evening the waters were flat and had a silvery gleam, like the back of the salmon which swam up the river to spawn.

The bus plunged between steep wooded banks. They got off at Bishop Coombe near the war memorial and then swung up a hill towards the outskirts of the village. By the time they had climbed over a stone wall and tramped up the rake of a bank they were breathless. They paused at the top. The water below them was hidden by the canopies of trees but they could hear it, not the sound the sea made but the quieter rhythms of the estuary.

'Well, are you going to tell me what's wrong?' Alice suddenly asked her.

'What do you mean?'

'Come off it. You've hardly said a word. Let's sit down and have a drag.'

They settled themselves in a hollow on the other side of the bank, the sun warming their bodies.

'Well, give,' said Alice after they'd lit up.

'You're not to tell anyone.'

'When did I ever grass you up?'

'Sorry.'

'Oh, for God's sake. Spill it out, will you?'

'I just can't get my head round it, OK? Talk about gross. Just before I came out I went in the kitchen and there's Tinker Bell feeling up my mum.'

'You're joking.'

'And the crazy thing is he was calling himself Henry.'

'You do mean Arthur Trimble? The one and only? You do mean *him?*'

'It was Tinker Bell all right. I almost died with embarrassment. I mean, how could she? Just imagine him touching you up.'

'Let him try...' But she said it absently and Ishbelle knew that she was thinking. Alice shifted her backpack into a pillow. Cigarette smoke was drifting from her sharp little nose. 'How long's it been going on, do you reckon?'

'I didn't know anything was going on. I didn't even know they knew each other.'

'Of course she knows him. There's parents' evenings and stuff like that.'

'I mean, out of school. Elaine said he'd come about the school trip.'

'You're reading too much into it. That's my bet. I mean, he *could* have come about the day out at St Ives. What do you mean when you say he was feeling her up?'

Ishbelle placed one hand on her rib cage and then extended her thumb so it began to

311

rub against her breast. 'And then she jumped away and she was blushing.'

'Well, if someone barges in on you ... well, you can sort of start and feel guilty even if you are doing nothing. I mean, you may think people are bound to come to the wrong conclusion. And, then again, maybe he was trying it on and she thought it totally gross.'

'I could have got it all wrong.'

'Well, you could. Couldn't you?'

'Why did he say his name was Henry?'

'How do I know!'

'He sounded sort of different.'

'What do you mean?'

Ishbelle took a last drag on her cigarette and then crushed it out on a stone. The filter tip had a little bit of lilac frost lipshine stuck to it. 'He sounded sort of – well, you know – breathy, somehow. Like a dirty old man.'

Alice heaved herself up. 'And how many dirty old men do you know?'

Ishbelle laughed. 'You think there's nothing in it then?'

'Well, you do get bees in your bonnet. You know you do. I mean, you should just listen to yourself sometime when you're on about Haddi's girlfriend. To hear you she's just a piece of over the hill totty! She's not like that at all. She's quite attractive, really. I'd die and go to heaven if I were as thin as she is.' Alice flicked the end of her cigarette through her fingers, watching it whizz through the air. 'Come on. I've brought some sausages, too. I thought we could light a little fire—'

'You're not being fair!'

Alice looked at her from under thick blonde lashes. It was a long blue gaze she'd been cultivating for the benefit of Justin Bannerman. Now there was a glint of malice. 'You're just a jealous little cat, Ishbelle Jones.'

'No I'm not!'

'Are.'

'Not.'

'Are.'

'Not.'

'All right. All right. All right. Pax.'

'She is a sad cow.'

'Sure. Mrs Mega Sad.'

'You're just saying it—'

'What more do you want? Come on. My stomach's rumbling.' Alice, swinging her backpack over her right shoulder, was leaping down the hill. 'Alice is coming, hurrah, hurrah!'

'Alice came in her forty-eight bra!' shouted her friend, breathless behind her.

'I'll get you for that!'

But Ishbelle, though slightly shorter than Alice, was a natural athlete. She peeled off at an angle and then surged ahead, arms flung out for balance as she jumped from rock to tussock and then charged under a lattice of branches and leaves. 'Sausages!' Her cry was exultant.

Sure-footed, black curls leaping, she emerged on to a curving stretch of pebbled muddy shingle. In the middle was a two-storey boathouse. Stout padlocked doors guarded the lower level. Above was a railed wooden balcony and behind it a long room which even had a rudimentary kitchen. It was Ishbelle who had found the key to the upper level, neatly tucked into a gap between the riser and tread of the bottom step. They had searched in vain for one to open the padlocked doors.

They hadn't immediately moved into what they christened 'the boat room'. Alice, who was keen on detective stories, had done some investigating first. She found out that the property, which also included a house higher up the wooded hill, belonged to a German family who used it as a holiday home. They usually came in August but hadn't been seen for the past two years. Ishbelle was delighted. 'We're like mice,' Ishbelle had told her friend.

'Come again?'

'Well, you know. They live in other people's houses. That's where their hidey-hole is.'

Alice had stared at her. 'Sometimes, Ishbelle, I think you're bonkers. Mice are vermin. People set traps for them.'

'Well, I know what I mean...' Ishbelle was thrilled because sneaking into someone's property and setting up their very own nest could land them in trouble. It was dangerous, she thought, but more exciting than scary.

Suddenly Alice burst out of the wood on to the shingle, face pinkly filmed. 'You could have waited for me.'

But Ishbelle was already off, jumping up the wooden steps to the boat room. She undid her silver chain and put the Yale in the lock. It was dark, only the light from the door illuminating the room. French windows which led on to the balcony were protected by wooden shutters and both sets opened from the inside. She and Alice had oiled all the hinges and now they moved back easily. The room was striated with bars of lemon light. She went out on to the balcony and leaned her elbows on the stout wooden rail. The muddy shingle formed the boot of a long-legged inlet, bent at the knee. Trees and reeds restricted vision so Ishbelle, brushing all the curls from her face, could still only see a small patch of the estuary beyond. Alice, below her, was already hunting about for kindling for their fire. Her gingery blonde head was bent and she was intently examining ground; she might have been peering over her school work. Suddenly she looked up. 'Get some water, will you!'

'Aren't we going to drink the wine?'

'We'll have coffee later.'

They were grinning at each other, happy to be bustling about in their secret place and yet, at some deeper level, as indolent as sun-warm cats. Ishbelle collected the chipped enamel pan from the top of the mini-sized Calor gas cooker and bounded down the steps. She took the steep path behind the back of the boathouse which led up to the house, a gloomy Victorian yellow and red brick affair. They used a stream which bounded towards the beach for neither knew if the river water was safe. They had no idea how far the salty tidal wash ran.

The empty windows of the house, white-flecked from droppings of gulls and hazed by storm-driven grains of sand and soil, looked down at her as she kneeled by a miniature waterfall and filled the pan. When she scrambled up she saw a heron rising in the sky, perhaps startled by their arrival from a nearby bank.

By the time she got back Alice had the fire going. She'd brought down the frying pan from the boat room and was tucking a string of sausages into it. She thrust the pan through the thick smoke billowing from the heart of the blaze. Ishbelle felt her stomach yaw. Oh, the delight of woodsmoke-singed sausages. She carefully set the pan of water by Alice for she was the cook. Her friend was now kneeling, bottle in the left hand, corkscrew in the right, frowning in concentration as she pressed down. Ishbelle stretched out by her side, idly watching the billow of smoke drift away to the west, hearing the first sizzle and pop from the frying pan, nose not yet detecting the smell of cooking sausage meat. Alice now sat, bottle wedged between her knees, and yanked. The cork flew out. She drank some of the wine, tipping her head back, the bottle high, imagining she was some male movie hero. She passed the bottle to Ishbelle, who was daintier and would have preferred to drink it from a glass.

When they'd eaten the sausages and the wine had sunk to half a bottle, Ishbelle produced the cigarettes and they lit up. 'Shall I raid the *X Files?*' Alice asked.

'God. Is that crap all you ever think about?'

Alice had perceived Ishbelle's almost imperceptible shudder and intuited its cause. 'You really think Tinker Bell and your mum are an item. What makes you so sure?'

Ishbelle considered. 'When she's up for it she wears too much make-up. Sloshes it about. You know? And he was really smarming up to her. Telling her just what she wanted to hear.'

'God. Gruesome. You wouldn't have thought old Tinkers had it in him.'

'I don't mean lovey-dovey stuff. What my mum wants to hear is that I'm included. Elaine's into playing families with her men. When he starts on about giving me a lift, I'm not safe out on my own, I mean, she's lapping it up. This man is kind, this man is caring. She feels it's safe to go to bed with him.'

'I can't imagine it.'

'What?'

'Tinker Bell doing it.'

They began to giggle.

'I'm pretty sure he's got a wife. My mum sometimes buys stuff from her dress shop. Coral's,' Alice said.

'That doesn't stop them. The one my dad went off with was also married to someone else at the time.'

'I somehow always thought ... well, your mum and Oa Bone?'

'Don't be daft. Elaine just does some secretarial work for him when his assistant is off or they've got a lot on. Oa goes for chicks in their twenties though how they can do it with a man old enough to be their grandad ... You wouldn't want to write poetry about him, would you?'

'Write *poetry?*'

'Well. You know what I mean. It'd be like

celebrating a lizard.'

Alice drank some more wine and passed the bottle to her friend. She had been thinking. 'We could always ring Coral. Tell her what her old man's up to. That should put paid to it.'

'Oh, I couldn't!'

'I could, though. Why not?'

'Let's just hang on for now. See if Tinkers really plans to get his feet under the table. Elaine's taste in men is truly gross. Talk about serial embarrassment. You know?' Ishbelle conducted a mental review. 'But going with Tinkers. That's the pits.'

'Give me the bottle. I'll finish it. If we don't get a move on we'll miss the bus. Come on, Ishy. It's not as bad as all that. If it all gets too heavy we'll think of something.'

They struck camp as quickly as they'd set it up. Ishbelle produced some peppermints. For a while Alice walked with exaggerated care. It was dark by the time they boarded the little bus and settled sleepily on to seats. 'My mum thinks it's the cleaning lady who makes off with the old vino,' said Alice and they began to giggle. Ishbelle got an attack of hiccups and pinched her nose. They swayed into each other as the Minirunner braked hard before swinging on to the four-lane roundabout on the edge of town.

'God,' said Alice, as they clambered off at

the next stop, 'I can't take you anywhere,' and she began to bang her friend's back.

'You cow! That hurts!'

'You really are a softy. You know that?' Alice, swinging her backpack over her shoulder, suddenly began to walk as she imagined someone really drunk might do.

Ishbelle split. Even when she'd put the width of the road between herself and her friend she could still hear Alice's squawk of laughter. She increased her pace. Alice clowning around sometimes got right up her nose. 'See you tomorrow!' she yelled and turned into Roseberry Lane.

Big Victorian houses, most of them stuccoed and painted in pastel shades, sat comfortably behind trees and shrubberies. The orange glow cast by street lights was patterned with the shadow of twigs whose shifting sounds tickled her ear-drums. The sound rose, almost becoming the swish of a car as she walked under the canopy of horse chestnuts up to the front door of Fairlands. When light flooded the bottom of the drive she realised it was a car, a taxi. Someone was getting out of it and was now bending to pay the driver. She rooted around in her pocket for the front door key. She inserted it and then swung back to see Haddi emerging from the splashes of bright light and gloom. She had such a sensation of her heart falling over that she automatically braced herself.

She could feel herself blushing and was glad it was dark. By the time she'd opened the door he was beside her. She quickly switched on the light. The hall with its cream dado and the big sisal mat cut into the turkey red carpet transported her back into the safety of the everyday world. As she slipped the front door key into her pocket she was aware of his hands, one hovering over her budding breasts. He took hold of the silver chain about her neck and flipped up the Yale key. 'And theez guy? What izz-z for?'

'Our place. Alice and me,' she heard herself saying.

'Alice?'

'My friend.'

'Ah. The ginger blonde. I seen her. What izz place?'

'Den. Secret. Our place.'

'You play houses?'

'No.' She was shocked he could think her so young. 'We hang out there. Play music. You know. Chill out.'

'The romance? Boyfriends?'

'No!'

Light flooded down the stairs. They both looked up, hearing the footsteps. The woman appeared on the lip of the landing. She was wearing a glimmering white dressing-gown, her hair wrapped in a towel. The woman didn't at first move or say anything.

'You show Haddi theez place.' His lips brushed her ear. 'You say dan?'

The woman began to walk down to the half-landing. Haddi suddenly bounded past Ishbelle and took the stairs two at a time. He reached out to the woman. Hand in hand they climbed upwards.

Ishbelle felt unbalanced. She leaned back against the front door. Excitement, guilt, for she and Alice had sworn never to tell another of their secret place, fear and a sense of falling into some unknowable void. The future?

'Mum!' she bellowed. 'Mum! I'm home!'

There was no answer.

She ran down to the kitchen. The light wasn't on. She tried the dining-room. Gleaming in the darkness were three white cloths on separate tables laid for breakfast. She knew now that her mother wouldn't be in her office or the residents' lounge but she tried them anyway.

Elaine's gone out with Tinker Bell, she thought. She found it so absurd she almost giggled. Then a tight knot of panic. She won't expect me to do the happy families bit with that slimy creep? Suddenly she was drenched in tiredness. She could hardly lift her feet to trudge the stairs to her room. Though there was nothing she wanted to see, she turned on the television which sat on her chest of drawers. She slid into bed, covering herself with her duvet. Later, she switched off the set, climbed out of her clothes and pulled the duvet over the top of her head.

She woke once. She'd moved in her sleep and through a gap in the quilt she could to see a wedge of light shine in through her bedroom door. The light grew narrower, the door clicked shut. 'Mum...' she murmured and dug further into her bed.

In the morning she found one of the socks she'd been wearing the day before had vanished. It was only later she discovered her diary had disappeared, too.

19

'At last.' Mitch had picked up her mobile phone from the passenger seat of the car. 'Honestly, A.J. I was beginning to think you'd dropped off the planet.'

'Sorry. But I'm hitting a big blank when it comes to finding any relatives of Tommy. How is he?' asked her assistant.

'Not good.'

They were silent, Mitch thinking of Tommy shrunk against the dazzling white of the hospital bed. It was as if something had hoovered all the innards out of him and left just the husk.

'I didn't manage to get hold of this guy at the Jade Dragon you told me about until today. He didn't know anything about Tommy's private life but he said he'd ask around in the community and see if he could come up with anything. I got hold of Tommy's solicitor on Friday. Fat lot of good that did.'

'How did you know who it was?'

'The lease on our offices. It was Tommy who dealt with all that stuff. Remember? Anyway, it's Carstairs and Fry. Posh offices near Birmingham Cathedral. They apparently hold some private papers of Tommy's – I suppose the guy means his will. He was going to check with the hospital and then take a look and see if he could help. I don't think old man Carstairs intends to get back in touch with us. He'll let the hospital know. Looks like we're into serious red tape there.'

'Shit. But you've done well, A.J. God. What a mess. The investigation down here may be coming to an end. But I can't leave Tommy in Devon on his own. Can I? On the other hand I've got to keep earning. I'm already knee deep in the financial you-know-what.'

'Why don't you put that place of yours on the market? The conversion's nearly complete. It's in a prime spot. Should fetch a packet. The whole thing's turned into a nightmare.'

Mitch was astounded when she heard herself say: 'Maybe you're right.'

A.J. was silent. Being diplomatic after making her point, Mitch thought. And wondered whether she was going to fall head first into a hole which had suddenly opened up in her stomach. She'd put so much work into the project. For her it had represented a new beginning. She sighed. This was not the moment to contemplate what she thought of as the enormity of her failure. Was there really no possible way she could make it come out right? 'I'll get this case wrapped up and give it some serious thought.'

'You think you've found Rosie Childe?'

'I'm watching a house called Fairlands, a B and B place. I found out from the newsagent's at the bottom of the road it's run by a woman called Elaine Jones who has a kid called Ishbelle. Around thirteen years old, he thinks. Rosie was seen on Friday with Ishbelle and her schoolfriend Alice. How I arrived where I am at the moment is a bit of a convoluted tale. And I could certainly be jumping to the wrong conclusions. It wouldn't be the first time. But I think Rosie Childe is staying here because she's the natural mother – or thinks she is – of Ishbelle Jones. She wants to clock her kid.'

'Wow. Are you sure?'

'No. And I don't want to go up to the house and start asking pointed questions. If I'm right it's quite possible I'll scare Rosie into doing a runner and we'll be back to square one. I thought I'd keep obs for a while and see if anything gives. Hang on, something's happening. Look, I'll be back in touch tomorrow. Sunday's supposed to be your day off.' Mitch clicked off and picked up the office camera from the passenger seat. She'd heard a front door crash and now there were rapid crunching sounds. Someone running. A girl came barrelling through the gate. Mitch had only time to get off one frontal shot and then another snap of a back and furiously pumping arms and legs.

Ishbelle Jones?

Mitch leaned back in the driver's seat. She'd have to admit that the kid in no way resembled Oa Bone. She opened the glove compartment and fished for the photograph she had of Rosie Childe. Was there a likeness? Maybe. Maybe not. It certainly didn't jump out at her. But something had. There was something utterly familiar about Ishbelle. Mitch pictured all the people she'd talked to and one by one ruled them out.

God, you've got to start performing. You must put Tommy and everything else to one side and *concentrate*. She again began to visualise all the faces she'd seen since the beginning of the investigation.

No luck.

She then saw shade-dappled figures begin to emerge through the trees down the drive. A couple. She picked up the camera again. She recognised one of them. Arthur Trimble was now almost at the gatepost. With him was a woman in her late thirties. Elaine Jones? The woman was dressed in a navy blue jacket which she wore over a flowered wrap over skirt. Mitch, who liked to slap on the make-up herself, nevertheless thought the woman had been too heavy handed. She wove about her companion as if she were knitting him to her. Mitch thought he seemed rather glum. He unlocked the red Golf she had seen on Saturday afternoon, settled into the driving seat and then opened the passenger door. She gracefully folded herself as she lowered herself in and neatly arranged herself by his side. I bet she's wearing scent, Mitch thought. Not too much and nothing too sweet. By then she'd knocked off three shots. As the Golf drew away from the kerb Mitch dropped the camera back on the passenger seat.

Everyone except the person I really want to see, she thought. How long am I going to sit here? Well, I'm certainly not going to give up my dinner with Paul Maugin. He's the goods.

Suddenly she was singing softly to herself:

'One was frightfully naught-ee
Stuffed out of sight-t-t-t
By a big boy in blue jeans–'

Oh, for a chance, she thought. The only thing my love life's been notable for recently is its absence.

But things could buck up.

Couldn't they?

Should she wear scent? Or did it over-power those almost unsmellable natural odours which were said to turn on a chap? Oh, come on, will you? You've hardly met this guy. Just loosen up and play it casual. A bit of fun, hopefully. That's the weight of it, isn't it?

Her mobile went again. 'Mitchell.'

'Well, you needn't blow my ear off, blossom. I've had a bad enough weekend as it is, thank you very much. I don't need you screeching at me.'

'Digger? You're getting to be a serious whinger.'

'Oh, well, if you're going to be like that. I've been working my butt off for you, you know that? I wouldn't care but I'm not even an employee of this crap outfit you run. The Mitchell and Orient Bureau. Sounds like a ticket office. Some tacky tour operator–'

'All right. All right. All right. Sorr-r-eee...'

'No you're not. You never are. You just pay lip service so you can use me–'

'Digger, darling, honeypot, snooky pie, what the hell's the matter? You're coming on like a hysterical hamster.'

'I've lost my job at Radio Brum. That's what's the matter. Just like you. The station manager can't stop firing people. She's gone ape shit.'

'You're not serious?'

'She had me in on Friday afternoon. I'm out next week when my contract ends. She's turning my slot over to a new voice after Easter. The new voice she's hired to replace you belongs to some kid not long down from university who is so super-efficient it's frightening. Though you wouldn't know it to look at her. A thin border of bright red hair round her chops. The rest is black and never seen a comb.'

'As far as I'm aware Freya Adcock is rehiring me after the summer.'

'What an optimist you are, blossom. She's telling everyone she's going for a new sound. Young, vibrant, voices for the millennium. We're to be dumped like the century. History. Am I thoroughly depressing you?'

'Yes.'

'Good. People screeching at me down the phone is the very, very last thing I need. I want – I need – resuscitation. The breath of life being pumped back into my lungs. A nurse doing nursey things. Male and gorgeous preferably. Strong tender arms to hold me when I'm well enough to weep. Telling me how terrific I am and meaning it.'

'No one ever tells me how terrific I am.'

'Well, most of the time you're so – what's the word?'

'What *is* the word?'

'Bossy. You will keep sweeping people into doing what they don't want to do. Like all this stuff you've landed me with. Well, blossom, I've come across for you once again. Why do I do it? All I hope is that you appreciate it. A dinner wouldn't come amiss. Or a bottle or two of bubbly. Anyway, I've dug out all that News Information could give me on Oa Bone and some stuff I had, too. Far too much for me to send by any other means than the good old-fashioned post. It should reach you to-morrow. As for this woman Ellie Peters, the one in Bosnia or wherever – well, I got through to the network radio producer who's been commissioning one or two packages from her. Your friend is now in Kosovo, somewhere up on the hills near the Albanian border. The producer will get a message through when Ellie contacts her again. You'll have to wait for Ellie to get hold of you. I sort of got the feeling you shouldn't hold your breath.'

'You really are an angel.'

'I must be. I'm not wringing the station manager's neck at this moment in time, am I? I'm sat here telling myself it will be wonderful to be on the dole. I'm going to totally adore collecting my giro or whatever it is. I need some space, some time for myself. You wouldn't believe the bullshit I'm telling myself.'

'You really think this is curtains as far as Radio Brum goes? And for me, too?'

'Yes. You know what Wonderkid is calling the airtime which used to be yours? *Fast Forward.*'

'No Brummie granny is going to switch on

to a programme called that. They're into rewind.'

'I told you. Freya Adcock's gone ape shit.'

'I know the world is supposed to keep changing but sometimes it changes far too much. Do you really think I'm bossy?'

'Yes.'

'No one's ever told me that before.'

'You come in three stages!' It was Digger Rooney who was bellowing now. Near to tears, she was sure. 'Bossy, bossy and bossy!' He slammed the phone down.

He really doesn't think he's been taken off air just for the summer. He thinks Freya Adcock isn't going to re-employ him ever.

Or me either.

The bitch has actually fired us both.

Mitch, who had been fired once before by Freya Adcock and who had led a very precarious existence at Radio Brum since, found she was unmoved. I suppose I'm lucky it's lasted so long, she thought. My God. It certainly never rains but it pours.

And then she got lucky.

Hearing the front door of Fairlands closing, she picked up the camera again. Two people. A man in his early twenties, not physically big but full of zap, or was it sap, Mitch wondered as she clicked off the first shot. He burst about the space surrounding the tall, bone-thin woman. She was not pretty but interesting-looking, hair swinging across her cheeks as she walked, the movements delicate, almost careful. Rosie Childe was easily recognisable from the photograph Sissy had given Mitch, and yet she was surprisingly different in many ways. She commanded attention, for instance, but not because her presence was dominating; more because she was so etiolated. If she were a plant Mitch would have given her a good watering.

Click, click, click.

Gotcha.

The moment was one of the sweetest Mitch had ever tasted. A hunter's delight when the prey was in the bag. All her work could have yielded nothing, all her suppositions could have proved wrong. But this time she was not wide of the mark. Bull's-eye, honeypot, she thought, her joy flooding from the chambers of her heart, whacking her shoulders back, raising her chin, nose tilted, scenting her victory.

And then she was working again. Click, click, click. The pair were now standing between the gateposts. Rosie Childe reached out skinny fingers and took the hand of the man. His thumb turned inwards and massaged the artery running through her wrist. No doubt about it, Mitch thought. They were lovers. Good at it, too, she thought. I bet those two know how to make a body sing.

Rosie Childe turned back towards the house, the man walked down the incline towards the main road.

Gotcha!

Mitch picked up the mobile and tapped in Sissy's number. She was told to leave a message and she did. She was still elated, but frustrated, too, because there was no one to share this moment with. Still, it was good. The first bit of good in what seemed ages.

She turned on the engine, swung the Escort round and drove back to Manaccan House. She parked neatly beside Tommy's Jaguar. If only it weren't such a posh green, she thought. That's so Tommy. He would go for a car the same colour as top people's carrier bags.

She entered the house built of mud and chopped straw with a dollop of dried grass on the roof. She felt wonder, touching an undulation in the cob wall. It sounds so improbable, she thought, as if Manaccan House should be out in the African jungle instead of a clotted cream village in England.

The first thing she discarded were her shoes. Most of the rest of her clothes floated down to the landing carpet. She assembled her body in the shower, standing on alternate legs as she soaped her feet and then slowly worked her way upwards.

Breathe through the heats of our desire
Thy coolness and thy balm,
Let sense be dumb, let flesh retire–

Now why am I singing that hymn, she wondered as the words sprang full-throated from her strict Nonconformist childhood. I don't want my flesh to retire. It's been in retirement far too long as it is.

She did not dress at all retiringly, but she was not too heavy with the make-up. She'd always loved to slap it on with a few extras like false eyelashes and a sprinkle of glitter on the lids. But now she was older she was more careful because the realist in her told her there was a thin line between looking good and coming on raddled. For Mitch getting older was one of the hardest things she'd ever done. It took a lot of working at.

But when she finally inspected herself she found herself not too displeased. The cashmere top and long skirt fitted her well, her thick black hair shone and her neck – that signpost of ageing – was holding up well. As it ought to be, she thought, considering how much cream I slosh about.

She looked at her watch.

Time she was off.

She was as excited as she had been as a teenager when meeting a new date.

Some things never die, she thought.

Thank God.

She slipped into a pair of new forties-style sandals, wedge-heeled, peep-toed, which would no doubt cut her flesh into strips of julienne, and clattered down the stairs.

It was no more than three minutes' walk to Paul Maugin's place. She'd left her mobile phone, along with everything else, on the kitchen table. The rest of her world could go hang.

God, I'm hungry, she thought.

Paul Maugin's cottage was in Church Lane. The church was floodlit. Above the round, castellated spout on top of the tower was the undulating line of the top of the hill, then a wash of lighter night.

Mitch spotted the yew which marked out Paul's cottage. It had a weird moustache-like shape, probably because it had been chopped about in an effort to keep it within bounds. The various prunings had not been a success. It shadowed most of the cottage, a poky-looking place with witchy little windows. A dingy brass bell with a bit of rope attached swung by the fading yellow door. She pulled it. Paul, like some giant in a fairy story, bent to squeeze his head under the door frame. He was surrounded by the smell of cooking flesh and herbs. All her taste buds were popping. 'How did you know the way to a woman's heart was through her stomach?'

'You've got the look of someone with a healthy appetite. Loin of pork with apples.'

'Roast potatoes?'

'All the bad things which are so good for you.'

'Wonderful...'

'We're going to eat out at the back. I know it's only March but it's still amazingly warm. That's if you don't think it quite mad.'

'Absolutely not.'

The front door opened into the lounge, a shadowy lair of a place with a monstrous inglenook fireplace. He led her through it to a large kitchen, where an old Aga cooker was set into another huge fireplace. A cat was sprawled on a wide shelf above, front leg negligently dangling over the edge, whiskers dipping into the steam rising from pans. 'Alfie's favourite place,' Paul said. 'He likes to be at the heart of the meal-time action.' Alfie stretched out and stiffened the dangling leg, splaying pads, uncurling claws. His face disappeared into an enormous yawn, the upper jaw adorned with the tips of his ears.

'You'd think he'd get too hot.' Mitch was now being regarded by marmalade eyes, black pupils vertically slitting the irises in two, letting out a gleaming intelligence.

'Alfie likes heat. The airing cupboard, the hearth, under the duvet if he gets a chance. But best of all he likes to be on that shelf when I'm cooking. Keeping an eye on things. Working on his appetite. Gin? Wine? I thought we'd have a drink before we ate.'

'Gin and tonic, please.'

'Go on through. I'll be with you in a minute.'

Outside lamps lit a patio of uneven cobble stones beyond the kitchen door and an old wooden table was laid for two. The garden was walled in cob, with a single-storey building, possibly an old pigsty, enclosing the rear end. Herbs and climbing roses flourished. By the back step two old barrels and a battered milk churn were planted with winter pansies. Paul, emerging with drinks, said: 'I never intended to stay here. But places like this sort of get into your soul. Everything to hand, really, including the church to receive your body when the time comes. I can't believe I once used to be ambitious. The most exciting thing I do here is pop over to France and bring back a few cases of decent wine for friends and acquaintances. Cigarettes for those who won't give up smoking.'

'You're a smuggler?'

'I wouldn't go so far as to say that. I'm more a man with pastimes. My main income comes from a flat I rent out in London.'

'What other pastimes do you have?'

'Fishing. Helping a guy who grows flowers

for the market with his books. A bit of French translation. That doesn't pay at all well. If it turns up and I fancy doing it, well, I'm your man. And what about you?'

'Oh, you know about me. In between broadcasting I try to earn a bit extra doing investigations for people.'

'Will Tommy being ill change things for you?'

'Yes. But I don't know how yet. I've not really had time to think about it. How did you land up down here?'

'Initially I trained as a lawyer but it didn't suit me. I married a girl whose family owned a small chain of hotels. We did all the usual things, including having a couple of kids, and then it all went to the bad and we divorced. I had a friend in the wine trade and went into business with him in Wimbledon. I met up with what I thought was the love of my life but she eventually left me for my business partner. I initially came down here to think things over. But in reality you don't think. Events happen and you get on with it. Alfie decided I was just right for him and moved in almost immediately and the chance to do a bit of this or that turned up. Life simply went on.'

They sat in comfortable silence, he sipping his whisky, she gin. 'My husband died. We had a daughter but she's in America. I go out to see her. She never wants to come to England. It seems to suit her out there.'

'So you're on your own?'

'Not so bad.'

'No.'

'Is that Arthur Trimble's cottage next door?'

'Yes. You've run across the schoolteacher, have you? Arthur's a bit of a rum bugger. The sort who counts his nails and lays them out in regimented rows in the tool shed. But they say he's a very good teacher and his wife Coral, as you know, runs a very successful dress shop. I don't suppose they're odder than most.'

'It was Coral's lover who found the body, wasn't it?'

'Clive Upjohn, the solicitor. Of course, the rumour in the village is that they were in the woods together when that dog of his found the grave. The other rumour – well, this is more than a rumour – is that someone's discovered something in Oa Bone's woods. It's led to a breakthrough in the case. They now believe she could have been done in on his property. Police are going up there in force tomorrow with dogs.'

'But why would anyone kill in one part of woodland and then move the body to another bit?'

'The theory in the taproom of the local is that's down to Oa Bone.'

'He killed her?'

'He found her in his woodland and shifted her over his boundary. At the time his consortium was bidding for the radio franchise. It was a very close-run thing. A body on Oa's land, the prospect of a murder inquiry, was likely to tip the decision the other way. But, no, I don't think anyone here seriously believes he killed her. There's not much shit money won't buy you out of. Why kill anybody? People round here have quite a lot of time for Oa. He's never flash with his dough, just the opposite. Supports local events.'

'Well, someone killed her.'

'They reckon it was some kind of execution. I suppose you've heard that theory? She was shot in the back of the head at quite close range. Locals think the murder's to do with drugs or the IRA.'

'The IRA doesn't seem at all likely. There's this cease-fire. The government is freeing terrorists. Is there much of a drug scene here?'

'Sure. I would guess quite a bit is smuggled in across the briny, too. There are lots and lots of little vessels and quite a stretch of coastline. By the way, I was told Inspector Jain came knocking on your door late this afternoon.'

'We found some clothing in an outhouse and handed it over to the police. It'll be about that.'

'I expect they'll want to know where Rosie Childe is in case she knows anything about it.'

Mitch looked at him. She hadn't thought of that. She'd have to try and raise Sissy as soon as she got back to Manaccan House. Sissy needed to be down here, now, if she wanted to see her half-sister before the coppers poked their noses in. Mitch had no intention of lying to the police.

Alfie had appeared in the doorway, tail up, its tip curling over his back. His jaw seemed to rock on its hinges as he screeched. 'Dinner-time,' said Paul.

'I thought cats were supposed to mew.'

'He can do that, too. When he decides it's appropriate.' Paul stood up. He was tall, thin bones knotty at the joints, greying hair sprouting over a pointy forehead. It seemed to Mitch surprising that such a deep voice could come out of all the narrow spaces. And that unmistakable public school accent. She idly wondered where all the family money had disappeared to. Whatever the story, his down-at-heel lifestyle suggested it was all long gone.

He appeared with wine, home-made salmon pate garnished with lemons, brown bread and then followed with pork. They ended with fruit and liqueurs in their coffee. Alfie was served with both first and second courses, tiny portions nicely arranged on a white china bowl at the side of the steps. Their meal came on earthenware dishes.

'That is one hell of a spoiled cat,' Mitch observed as she sipped her coffee.

'It is impossible to spoil a cat. Correction. It's impossible to spoil Alfie. He lets me know what he requires and makes sure I provide it. Usually he's out on the tiles at night and sleeps in the morning.'

'I hope he's properly grateful.'

'Alfie? He knows I'm the lucky one because he's chosen to live with me.'

They heard a car's engine, a roll of wheels on gravel and then silence. 'Arthur's home.'

'Not Coral?'

'You get used to the different engine sounds. More coffee?'

'Without the alcohol. I won't even be able to totter home if I have any more.'

They sat chatting and then, as Mitch rose to go, there was a bang next door, followed by furious voices.

'They're at it again,' said Paul. 'At one time it was very occasional but now...'

There was a searing ripping sound followed by a thunderous bump. A screech, a wail. A series of staccato crashes, each higher than the last. A roar. Mitch thought the thatch was going to fly off the roof and rain on the village.

Alfie was hiding between the barrels of winter pansies, only a very small patch of his bum exposed. Mitch's hands were becoming fists, almost as if she thought the fight would spill over the garden wall. Paul was braced.

Silence.

Mitch unfurled her fingers. 'My God. Do you think he's killed her?'

'I've no idea what goes on but it's usually him who is sporting the bruises.'

And Mitch remembered the dark patch she'd seen on the back of Arthur Trimble's hand when he'd rested it over the top of the door of the Golf. Had he got the bruise while protecting himself from Coral's blows?

'Come on,' he said. 'I'll walk you to your door.'

'He lets her beat him up?'

'Well, I don't know, do I? I'm not in that chocolate box cottage. Thank God.'

Alfie suddenly shot past them, making for the safety of Paul's kitchen.

20

Coral Trimble was sitting on a bench over-looking the sea. An east wind had risen in the early hours of the morning. The collar of her navy blue coat was up and her hands were deep in its pockets. The wind whipped up strands of her black hair. The grey sky, streaked with bars of livid sunlight, was as watery as the ocean. Wheeling gulls swooped down to perch on iron railings. Behind her, the promenade was almost deserted though the thoroughfare was full of traffic and beyond the buses and cars people were hurrying in and out of shops.

She knew she should be thinking, planning, but her mind was curiously empty; not static, though, dipping and planing, like flotsam. Shock? Her whole body ached. She was the one who had sprung at him and at first she'd given as good as she'd got, but he'd cornered her in the end. He'd not used his fists but the flat of his hands, rhythmically, as if he'd been knocking down dough.

Then he'd taken her there in the kitchen.

When he'd finished he'd kicked her twice, quite lightly, in the cleft between her buttocks.

He'd made them a cup of tea. 'Henry's not all bad, you know,' he'd said and momentarily he'd sounded anxious. She, her face bulging and raw with tears, had not raised her head. Her sweaty body heaved with nauseous pain. He'd whistled as he'd gone to bed. For her benefit, she'd thought. There was a defiant note to it. She knew the words.

Now the labourer's toils are o'er,
Fought the battle, won the crown...

A hymn for the departed. They'd sung it at her father's funeral.

Surely he couldn't have remembered *that?*

Her bones had crouched over wincing, soft tissue, sheltering as much vulnerable flesh as she could.

Night in the kitchen drifted in and out of her pores, a slight, greasy edge to the chill. Bones tried to settle in more comfortable positions.

In all their married life, nearly twenty years, he'd never hit her before though she'd had a go at him more than once. She'd known that little by little things had been changing since Cory had left home and gone off to university. Their one joint enterprise, this son they'd nurtured, had overridden their own needs. Now they were an ill-matched pair in a chocolate box cottage prison.

She disliked him.

But he hated her. She'd deceived him, hadn't she? His tender child bride had become a raddled old bag.

As the dawn came she furtively dragged her beaten limbs to the spare bedroom. She didn't want to be there when he came down for his breakfast.

Now she was scared of him.

And when she'd looked in the mirror that morning she'd seen what he saw, this haggish shrew, and knew it to be her because he knew it to be her. That she was more than ten years younger than he, that she was pretty enough to be wanted by other men, seemed to count for nothing.

Do you turn permanently into what you are perceived to be? The thought had horrified her though not as much as the knowledge that he would feel justified in killing the hag in his house.

Every so often, behind her kneecaps, a violent trembling occurred. If she were upright it forced her back to the ground.

When he at last got up, when she heard his movements through the doors and walls of their cottage, she positioned herself so that she was sitting upright on the bed, feet on the carpet, head up.

How he whistled. Blowing up a storm.

He didn't, as she'd hoped he would not, have the nerve to face her.

Though she'd not been aware of planning, she had been very active; consciousness, this drifting flotsam, had simply sailed over strong, forceful currents working beneath.

Now she saw her lover walking briskly towards her. Clive Upjohn's old-fashioned heavy overcoat flapped about his chalk-striped grey trousers. Too burly to look dapper, his glasses enormous, the eyes behind the lenses schoolboyish, he nevertheless had a slightly pompous, smug air. Born prefect material and she found her lips almost remembering how to smile.

'Hello, sweetie,' the solicitor said and sat down beside her. 'I've found you a man who'll handle it all. He's good. Richard Green. He'll fit you in at eleven. You said you've got photos?'

She carefully took her hands out of her pockets and gingerly raising one opened her shoulder bag. She winced a little as she withdrew the Polaroid snaps. 'I couldn't take them myself, of course.'

They studied them, she detached, as if this was not her body they were studying, as if these bruises had nothing to do with her. He struggled for detachment. 'You should have gone to the hospital like I told you.'

'Why? Nothing's broken.'

'It could be used in evidence.'

'I've got these.'

'Who took them?'

'Terrie. You know. My assistant at the shop.'

'She could be called on to give evidence.'

'She'd do that.'

'What the hell started it all?'

She knew that really wasn't the question he wanted to ask. 'Look, I'll certainly keep you out of it if I can. He does know about you but he can't prove anything. I've always denied it and I'll continue to deny it. You've nothing to worry about, Clive.'

He settled back on the bench. 'I didn't mean–'

'You want to know where you stand. I'd want to know if I were in your circumstances.'

'You seem to be very calm about it all.'

'Weird. Shock, maybe. But it's not stopped me doing things. The locksmith's coming this afternoon. Handy that the appointment's for eleven. This Mr Green of yours–'

'Sorry, but in the circumstances ... well, it had to be a stranger.'

'Look, I understand. You don't have to explain. Honestly. Anyway, as soon as I get back to the cottage I'm going to put all his stuff in suitcases out on the drive–'

'Listen, do you–'

'I don't care about any legal niceties so you can shut up, Clive.'

'You didn't even think it worthwhile going to the hospital. You should–'

'I couldn't. I simply couldn't face it.'

'Coral–'

'It's the humiliation. I'm OK in this little light-headed world of mine ... I can't *feel* anything, you know? Bob, bob, bobbing along. Of course, there're the physical aches and pains. That's different. I could have slid down a hill or something.' Then she said: 'I couldn't stand anyone pawing me. Being nice to me. OK?'

'But–'

'You can't understand. And why should you?'

'Doing things your way you're in control again?'

'I never thought of that. Getting through is all I want to do. But he's not ever sleeping under my roof again. Period.'

He was silent, wanting to say something, to advise her, she thought, but in the end he asked: 'What about your son?'

'Well, it's one step at a time, isn't it? Look, I'm going to get through this, OK? But in my way. And the first thing is that bastard's out the door. Any legalities can piss off.'

Suddenly he was laughing. 'You are the most surprising woman...'

'For a dress shop owner?'

'I didn't mean that. Just there's a lot more to you than first meets the eye. But what did start it all? You told me he'd never laid a finger on you.'

'I think he's gone bonkers. No. No, I'm not just saying that. There's this chap Henry who has suddenly cropped up.'

'Henry? Christ, you don't really mean he's what we used to call AC DC? I mean, he fancies a bit of male totty now and then?'

'Well, I could be way, way off beam but I wouldn't be surprised if Henry didn't exist.'

'I've lost it.'

'When we were first married he used to call ... well, you know, down there ... my private parts ... well, he called them Henry's toolbox. As he's Arthur I'd got to wonder about this Henry, hadn't I? He told me that when he was a kid he'd had an imaginary friend. Lots of kids do. His was called Henry.'

'I don't suppose it's that odd–'

'Then suddenly this Henry pops up again after all these years. It was as if this Henry were beating me up, not him. That's what he tried to imply. I mean, what is balmy? Oh, he'll be as right as rain while he's teaching this morning – it will be as if last night hadn't happened – but I'm telling you, he's lost the plot. I've never been scared of the man. Not till last night.'

'My God ... you don't suppose...'

'Suppose what?'

'Well, the woman that was killed...'

'Wasn't she shot? Didn't someone tell me she was shot?'

'He could have got hold of a gun, couldn't he?'

'From where? They don't exactly grow on trees, do they?'

'It's you that's telling me he's gone off his rocker–'

'But she was a woman. She was too old.'

'What do you mean?'

'I was a child bride, remember? He's always liked – well, not little, little girls. More teenagers. Why the hell do you think he teaches in that girls' school?'

'You're not suggesting–'

'No. I'm not. Honestly, Clive. As far as I know he's always been absolutely scrupulous. Lots of teachers must fancy their nubile pupils but they don't do anything about it.'

'Well, whether you're right or wrong, no one has suggested, as far as I know, that the killing of that woman was some kind of crime of passion. From what I hear, it looks more like an execution.'

'Why would he just go out and kill some unknown woman, anyway?' Suddenly she heard a quiet, almost discreet rattling. Her knees were knocking.

'Coral...' He reached out and took her hand in his. She winced as bruised muscle moved. 'You're scared of him. That's why you want him out of the house, isn't it?'

'It's different. He hates me. He wouldn't

kill anyone else. Just me. I mean, if things got out of control. Really out of control.'

'What would you do if he comes back, finds himself locked out, and smashes his way into the house?'

'I'll have the mobile phone in my hand. I'll make sure he sees it through the window. I'll call the police.'

'You hardly need me at all.'

'Yes. Yes, I do, Clive. You've no idea how frightening all this is. I mean, if I let any of that come into my head I wouldn't even be able to stand up. I'd be a jelly.'

'Well, the least I can do is deliver you into good hands.'

'Mr Green? We'd better get on with it then.' She pushed herself upright and, in spite of the pain she felt, thrust her shoulders back. He adjusted his steps to hers and she knew it was difficult for him. He could have been shepherding a very old woman. Not a lot less direct than a snow plough, he used his burly shape to make a way for her along the busy thoroughfares. One or two passers-by looked at her curiously.

He stopped outside a men's outfitters. Beyond the window was a wide doorway with three highly polished brass plates, one above the other, fixed just beyond the stone pillars which supported the pediment over the entrance. 'This is it.'

She looked up at him. She knew they

would never be lovers again, that what they'd had together was over and yet, and she found this surprising, she did not feel rejected or bitter. This was partly to do with him, with the way he'd handled what he'd found to be a very tricky situation, but also because it wouldn't be *fun* any more for either of them. Real life had grotesquely intruded.

'I'll always be here.'

'I know.' And that was surprising, too, she thought. He *would* be there.

'Good luck,' he said after she turned away and was climbing the step to the entrance. But she'd not felt luck had helped her much in business. Honest appraisals of situations had been what had kept her in profit while many in her trade had gone to the wall.

Though he was smartly turned out, Coral thought there was something rather hole in the corner about Richard Green. Ambitious parents, almost the right schools, not quite the right morals. He would have to do but he'd need careful handling and that in spite of the fact it would be she who was footing the bills.

He called their meeting a preliminary chat and, when she'd finally handed over the photographs, she'd felt rather embarrassed. Violence in the tasteful neutrality of his office seemed decidedly off colour. He'd been efficient enough then, made her roll back her sleeves so he could check the bruises on her arms against those on the Polaroids. 'You'll be happy to know we can take the rest as read. But if I need to corroborate I can now do so. And if you could give me this Terrie's full name and address...'

In the end she told him she would be staying with a friend that night. Why pay anyone for anything when you know you're going to do just as you damn well please? she asked herself as she was leaving his office half an hour later.

Well, you can't get divorced without a lawyer poking his nose in, can you?

And she marvelled that Richard Green, without question, had accepted the idea that she'd vacate her house while lawyers fought their clients' corners. To her, her home was as vital to her self-esteem as a freshly bathed body, her make-up, the clothes she wore. Even football team members felt they were more likely to win if they played the opposition on their home ground.

But would Arthur let her stay in the cottage? In her mind's eye she saw glass tumbling out of windows.

I'm going to stand my ground, she thought. If there are any consequences I'll have to do the best I can.

And that light bubble, her consciousness,

slid painlessly over the hunch of bones which protected punished flesh. It was as if the one were not connected to the other.

She collected her car from near the shop. She had trouble extending her left leg to push the clutch pedal down. She put on some music, syrupy stuff. It helped a bit.

Driving the car into the garage, she collected her bag, herself, and slid carefully through the passenger door. At the front door she checked her watch. The locksmith was due to arrive in half an hour.

The cottage closed around her. She knew that some people thought it twee and contrasted it unfavourably with the clothes she stocked in her shop. Arthur had even said once: 'It's as if your mother had bought most of our furnishings.' It had shocked her. She'd not believed him and then gradually she'd let herself know he was right. But she hadn't changed much. These were the things she was comfortable with. It was not merchandise which had to be moved at the right margins.

Her mobile phone went. 'How did it go?' Terrie asked her.

'OK, I think. I'm at home now, just taking my coat off.'

'Look, why don't I just close the shop and come over? Help you–'

'I'd rather you didn't–'

'Look, I don't want to put the wind up

you. But is he going to just pick up his suitcases from the drive and push off?'

'I've got my mobile–'

'He's knocked the shit out of you once. He could do it again. Listen, Coral–'

'In front of all the neighbours?'

'It was pretty much in front of the neighbours last night. Wasn't it?'

'I'm not going to live my life in fear of that crappy little bastard. If you are here what's to say he won't come for me tomorrow or the day after that? I've got to front him. OK? I'm sort of up for it at the moment. Tomorrow I'll probably be some pathetic wet sobbing little mess.'

'Christ. I think you're marvellous–'

'Don't be nice to me! You start being nice and I'm going to crack.'

'OK, OK. You said he'd be home early tonight, didn't you? Around four? What I'm going to do is ring around half-past–'

'I'll ring you, Terrie. Don't worry. I'll be all right. If it all goes pear-shaped I'll be locked in the bedroom, a chest of drawers in front of the door, waiting for the police–'

She heard a smothered wail at the end of the phone. A pause. 'Sorry...' said Terrie.

Coral clicked off the phone.

Right, she thought, let's get cracking. She took in a very long breath and then let it out slowly. She climbed up the stairs, wincing a little as she shrugged off her coat. She went into their bedroom and stared at the bed.

Could she smell him?

The first thing she did was open the window wide, strip off the bedclothes and take them down to the kitchen. She shoved them in the washer and mixed disinfectant with the soap powder.

The suitcases were in the top section of floor to ceiling wardrobes. She'd have to climb on to a chair to get them out. It wasn't easy but she did it and then kicked them into a line on the rose pink sculpted carpet. She'd bought the suitcases last year, forest green canvas trimmed with real tan leather. Two were oblong box shapes, the other a grip.

The front door bell rang. Her heart leapt right out of her body. It's only the locksmith, she told herself and went to open it. To her astonishment she found herself looking down on a man, a large, solid, bony skull, a plump, compact body. Not quite a dwarf, she told herself, suddenly afraid the world was careering beyond her grasp. 'Mr Lester?'

'That's me.' The eyes which looked up at her were very dark blue but light with mischief. She suddenly realised he'd guessed the situation and this was not the first time he'd been called at short notice to change all the locks in a house. 'You want the garage done, too?'

'I do.'

'Well, I'd better get the bag of tricks then, hadn't I?'

'I'll leave the door. I'll be upstairs. Just give a shout if you want anything, Mr Lester.'

'A cuppa wouldn't come amiss.'

'OK,' she said and went into the kitchen. She wondered about making a sandwich for herself but found the prospect of eating nauseating.

Not all Arthur's belongings would go into three suitcases, she'd known that. She would pack for him as if he were going on an extended holiday. The rest of the stuff she'd put in boxes and store in the garage until, as she put it to herself, 'things quieten down a bit'.

She was very methodical, not just remembering his shaving kit, but his passport, medical card, driving licence and even his constipation tablets.

She found her spirits rising. Hysteria? *You're leaving home* ... a song, wobbling round her empty head.

Two boxes were at the back of his wardrobe. One was a shoe box and when she opened it she found a dirty white sock pinned to his best silk scarf as though it were a medal on a breast pocket. She stared at it in increasing astonishment.

'Mrs T...' The locksmith was calling her from downstairs. 'All done and dusted,' said the smiley little man when she arrived on the door mat. 'New five lever locks in the front door and back door.' He handed over to her two keys shaped like those her father had used to secure his shed. 'And this is for the garage.' A key she was more used to, one with a short, unevenly toothed edge. 'Should do you. If you pay by cash now there's twenty per cent off.' He touched his nose. 'And mum's the word.'

'Hang on,' she said and went to get her bag.

'What the VAT man doesn't see his heart doesn't grieve over?'

'Why should I pay for a lot of idle gits doing coke and sticking buns in silly girls' ovens?' He checked the ten-pound notes. 'This'll do nicely.'

'Thank you, Mr Lester. For coming so promptly.'

'Any time,' and he was off down the drive at a fast clip. She found herself wondering how those dancing feet managed to reach the pedals of his van. Her mood changed, became grimmer. Well, that's that done. Suddenly a shudder took her shoulders. It passed through her spine, her leg muscles. It grounded in her heels. The chill shrunk her skin.

I'm really doing this.

'Mum...' She heard Cory's voice in her head.

She shut him off. Later. She'd think about her son later.

Glancing at her watch, she gasped. It was already half-past three. She flew up the stairs, shut and locked the bedroom window, back-tracked and took two towels from the linen cupboard and squashed them into the grip. The cases kept hitting the back of her calves as one by one she bumped them down the uneven cottage stairs. She dragged them along the hall to the door and then raced into the sitting-room. Her hands scattered bills and papers as she looked for notepad and envelopes. She used the window ledge as a desk top, ears straining to hear the noise of an approaching car engine. The blank paper loomed up at her. Short, she thought. Low key. Nothing for his solicitor to get his teeth into.

She put the address and the date at the top. 'Dear Henry...'

She tore off the top sheet and started again. 'Dear Arthur...'

What was dear about a man who had violated the most tender parts of her?

She let it stand. That's how you always began letters, wasn't it?

'For my own safety, I cannot let you come in. All the locks have been changed. If you wish to contact me you can do so through my solicitor...' She ran to the cloakroom and rummaged in the pockets of her navy blue coat. Where was the wretched man's card? She found it and raced back. She copied the details out in block capitals. She saw that Clive had been right not to take the case himself. What would Arthur have done if he'd seen her lover's name printed out? Suddenly what she was going to put next went out of her mind. She placed her fingers on the windowsill, driving down on them, steadying herself. She picked up the biro again. 'I will not answer any calls from you. I will not see you in person. From now on I plan to cut you out of my life. I have already started divorce proceedings and you may find it convenient to employ a solicitor of your own.'

She reread the letter. It was Arthur who had taught her to write her business correspondence. She thought he ought to be proud of her. It was certainly detached, short but nevertheless said all that needed to be said. But how to finish? She wasn't his faithfully. She sucked the end of the biro even though she knew time was speeding past. 'Coral'. She'd reasoned it was not a letter, but a note.

God. Wouldn't it be wonderful to be rid of a husband who was a schoolmaster. What she did and how she did it need not be circumscribed by a prissy little voice in her head. Arthur crappy see me Trimble.

She wasn't there yet.

Sealing the note in the envelope, she wrote: 'For the attention of Mr Arthur Trimble.' The first four words made it all look more official somehow. She glanced at her watch again. Ten minutes to four. Her flesh sweated. She raced back into the hall, opened the front door and one by one hauled the bags out on to the drive. She ranged them so they blocked the gate. He wouldn't be able to swing his car on to the drive unless he moved them. A gust of wind caught her in the small of the back. Black hair tipped into her eyes. She wiped it away, worrying about the note sailing off. She knew it would be difficult to find suitably sized stones in his meticulously kept front garden so she raced back inside. She eventually weighed the note down with a tin of chopped tomatoes.

Done.

She looked wildly around her. Everything seemed so quiet, as if she'd suddenly gone deaf. And now it was profoundly still, too. This was in spite of the fact that she could see the wind worrying at Paul Maugin's straggly yew tree and ranks of Arthur's tulips swaying. It was as if she had been subtracted from her surroundings, as if she weren't really there.

But she knew she was there and if she didn't get a move on her aching flesh might be subjected to another rain of blows. Last night she had pleaded with him: 'Don't hurt me any more...'

Last night she'd been completely pathetic.

Now, wrapped in lightness, in a bobbing balloon of air, she glided ghostlike back into the cottage. She locked the front door, the back door, and tried each window in the house. All secure. It was when she took the mobile phone out of her bag that she burst through the protective skin of the balloon. Momentarily she went blind with panic. The beat of her heart was ricocheting; soon pellets of flesh would explode through her ribs.

She heard the noise of a car engine.

Her vision cleared.

It's OK. It's only Arthur, she told herself. *The devil I know.*

Wobbling legs picked their way back into the sitting-room. The mobile was in her hand, at the ready. She saw him swerving to turn into the drive and then stopping the red Golf as he saw the barricade in front of him. She'd never thought of him as a big man, but he looked very large as he got out of the car. For a moment he stood there. Dumbstruck.

Even though she had to wedge her knees together to stay upright she found she was smiling. You really thought you'd get away with it, didn't you? Who *is* the dummy in this family?

Now he was striding purposefully across

the drive. A key seemed to jump into his hand. Involuntarily she stepped backwards, her back against the cob cottage wall.

She heard the scraping and scratching of the key. 'Coral! Coral! What the devil are you playing at?'

Her spine indented into a curve in the wall. His footsteps going round to the back of the house. The rattling of another key in another lock. 'Open this door! At once! At once! Do you hear me? Now!'

Moments of silence.

She sighed, letting out breath she'd not known she was holding.

Feet tramping round to the front of the house. And then there he was staring in through the sitting-room window at her, bending down, thrusting his face forward, the skin cut into diamonds by the lead latticework. His mouth opened wide, lips lifting clear of teeth. The hole got darker. The rest of his features seemed to disappear. She held up the mobile phone, forefinger already touching, but not pressing, a pad. As she did so his balled fist appeared over the window ledge. Joints whited as it squashed into the glass. Segments haloed a porcelain shepherdess on the inner windowsill.

She hiked the phone higher, placing it in front of her breast, showing it like a cross.

His mouth was opening and shutting, hurling obscenities.

She didn't move a muscle. She was beginning to feel safe.

He didn't walk back on the drive. He tracked straight across the garden, smashing through the tulips. He stopped when he came to the suitcases. Headless and part-headed stems lurched and oozed behind him.

Still not moving, she waited to see what he would do. One by one he put the suitcases into the boot of the car. He removed the letter from under the can of tomatoes and made a great play when he ripped it in two. Instead of throwing it away he stuffed it in his pocket. He picked up the tin of tomatoes and hurled it at the garage door. It was when he dropped his arm she realised he was shaking, irregular little eruptions.

For the first time she moved, walking stiffly to the windowsill.

He was looking straight at her now. He began shouting something. His lips seemed to form: 'You'll be sorry...'

She toppled into the grip of glee. She wanted to shout back, to wave.

Letting herself do none of these things, she moved back a little. You don't poke a stick at a wild bull. But she did sidle out of the line of his sight and then she allowed herself to smile.

It was when she heard him start the engine of the car that she slowly slid to the floor.

Later she rang Terrie, much later she stripped off her clothes and had a shower.

Naked, carrying fresh sheets and towels, she paused at the door of her bedroom. There, on the floor, she saw the two boxes, one opened and the dirty sock staring up at her. She put the linen on the bed, pulled on a bathrobe and squatted down before the other box, a tin that had held the special assortment of biscuits she'd bought last Christmas.

She pulled off the top. It contained another sock, not so dirty as the first, and a diary.

Leafing through it, she paused to read: 'Alice says she wants two kids, one of each. And I told her she was mad. You won't catch me wiping shit off bottoms. But what will I do? Working sounds dead boring...' She turned back to the fly leaf. 'Ishbelle Jones, her private book. If you reach this far, you are cursed. Read further and look upon your hearse.' On the opposite page was a photograph cut out of a magazine. A young man wearing one gold ear-ring, a gold chain, smirked out at Coral. His hair, shiny with gel, was divided into small squares and teased up into numerous points. The effect, she thought, resembled the pattern on a cheese grater.

The diary suddenly fell open at a page which was bulkier than the rest. Three snaps had been glued to the paper. They were of a location, distance shots of a boathouse and, higher up through trees, glimpses of a Victorian house. Though it looked vaguely familiar to her, she couldn't place it. Somewhere on the river nearby, though. She was sure of that.

Rocking back on to the soles of her feet, knees scissoring wide, she again looked at the boxes. Did this girl live there, this Ishbelle Jones?

She had to be no more than a young kid. That little rhyme. A child's work? How had he managed to get hold of her diary? Was she a pupil of his, some girl from St Ursula's?

Well, there was nothing innocent about young kids these days, but at the same time she was thinking surely not, he must look like her grandfather.

She found she was relieved. So, he'd got a little girlie, had he? Collecting her socks as if he was collecting marbles! More evidence for her solicitor.

She ought to have known.

Nothing but a dirty old man.

Did he tell his little tart his real name was Henry?

Henry.

Arthur.

What did it matter?

Nothing mattered so long as she could get rid of the ratbag.

21

Mitch had already had a long day when she began to nose the grey Ford Escort out of the driveway of Manaccan House, on her way to visit Tommy. Suddenly she saw Arthur Trimble's red Golf, heard tyres squeal as he threw the vehicle out of Church Lane and on to the village street. Metal shuddered and then the vehicle powered up the incline, rounded the bend and vanished from sight. Wow, she thought. Who rattled the schoolteacher's cage?

Later, on her way back from hospital, she caught sight of Ishbelle Jones as she was driving back through Bishop Coombe. A claret hat, the shape of a bashed-down topper, was pulled to the tips of her ears. There was a heavy rucksack on her back, what looked like a large soft-covered book of road maps funnelling out of the neck, and a bag of groceries perched on top of the stone wall she was climbing over.

'...for the first time Cruise missiles smashed into targets in central Belgrade...' Mitch, who had been listening to the car radio, switched off the news.

What the hell was that child doing?

None of my business, she told herself. She clicked on the news again...

She'd first heard about the bombing when she'd been listening to the radio while drinking her breakfast cup of black coffee in Manaccan House. She'd clicked it off then because her inner eye had been disturbed.

An important memory had been stirring.

In her mind she had been revisiting the husk of Tommy, and then thought had slid to the husks of empty black canvas platform shoes resting on top of a plastic bag in the corner of the barn. That was it ... the letter given to her by Bernice Brody, Rosie's ex-flatmate. The letter which said they'd come across Yolanda Hadri. 'Actually, fell over her would be a more accurate description. She's a cleaner at the airport there and all these cleaners wear these grotty shoes, sort of high platform things with laces and heels cut out...'

Was it Yolanda who had been shot through the head and dumped? she asked herself again. One thing was certain. Though during the last Balkan conflict they'd eaten dandelions and paper to keep starvation at bay, the thing which never seemed to be in short supply was guns. And bullets.

A man from Kosovo, for instance Musa Hadri, might not realise that Englishmen don't tote Kalashnikovs or whatever and bring one with him when he fled his homeland, especially if he meant to enter the country illegally.

But why give someone some nice clean clothes and then kill her? To put the police off the scent if the body is later found? Surely the killer would have known that though the corpse was dressed in Rosie's clothes that would only temporarily have caused confusion? Further investigation would quickly show the dead woman wasn't Rosie.

Say, though, the killer was a foreigner from a Third World country. He might suppose no one would bother much with an investigation. Musa Hadri, for instance, was born in a remote village in the land of the blood feud where life appeared to be the same kind of throwaway commodity as a polystyrene cup.

What did go on in the mind of a Muslim ethnic Albanian male?

Not much to comfort a woman, I'll bet, Mitch thought, missing Tommy, needing to bounce her ideas off him. She remembered briefing him as he lay in his hospital bed. His fleshless fingers had suddenly tightened round hers. He had tried to raise his death's head from the dazzle of the pillows. He said something. Not in English, she was sure. Cantonese? Ahh something? Yah something? Just a noise, she thought now. Something indecipherable in her ear.

Had she missed the ridiculously obvious?

The phone went. As she picked up the receiver she suddenly became aware of the difference between her hand and Tommy's. Sunlight was bouncing about on her re-assuringly fleshy fingers, blue veining on the back of the palm standing a little clear of cream flushing pink around plumping knuckles.

'Mitch? This is Sissy. I'm sitting in the car outside Fairlands.'

'You've made good time. It's not nine o'clock yet.'

'I started out just after five. The traffic was fairly light most of the way. Look, can you stay in? I want to come over as soon as I've seen Rosie. One or two things to talk over.'

'Sure.'

'You think she's shacked up with this lad you saw her with?'

'Seemed like that to me.'

'And you really think Ishbelle Jones may be Rosie's kid?'

'Rosie hasn't had a child since she signed the adoption papers. If she is the kid's natural mother or thinks she is that is a scary situation in there. Rosie's got to let go. Get out.'

'Do you think I don't know that?'

'Sorry.'

'Have you managed to come up with anything more? Is this lad Rosie's with Musa Hadri?'

'I don't know. But it's got to be a strong possibility. I've been told, Rosie was seen with a foreign guy in Coral Trimble's dress shop. Those funny platform shoes we found with the clothes at Manaccan House ... well, I've cross-referenced them with a letter Rosie sent from the former Yugoslavia ... something about Musa Hadri's wife wearing some which sound like them... Look, all I wanted was for you to go in there with an appraisal of some of the things which might be going on. I didn't want you falling arse over tip.'

There was silence for a moment. 'Well, you've really put the wind up me,' Sissy said. 'What a mess. I've got no talent for walking on eggshells. You know?'

'Who has?'

'I'm terrified I'll have this mother of a bust-up with her. When I don't know how to tackle something I start to rant and rave and chuck things.'

'I don't think that will help.'

'No.'

'Look, you can only do your best.'

'Thinking before I open my big mouth has never been a Sissy Childe talent.'

'There are some things she really needs to know. For a start, I'm sure the police will want to question her about the pile of clothes we found. I mean, if you put every-thing else aside, a corpse has been found wearing her kit.'

'Well, let's hope I hold myself together. I was going to ask you to have a great big gin ready for me but I don't suppose I can start drinking in the morning.'

'It's the thin end of the wedge. Anyway, you've given up spirits.'

'OK, ace. This is me out of here and up that drive.'

'Good luck.' Mitch put the phone down. Thinking of what was before Sissy, she found her heart beating more quickly.

But what could you do about someone like Rosie who, though she didn't seem to be a bad woman, created a lot of bad scenes about her? She remembered her dead husband Max once describing a colleague as 'the seemingly good chap at the heart of chaos'. There was one thing about Freya Adcock, Radio Brum's station manager and her boss, you knew she was an absolute bitch. Or was Freya now her ex-boss? Thinking of the situation she and Digger were in – forced to watch youngsters take over their jobs, forced to agonise over whether they'd get those jobs back at the end of the summer – she saw it as a typical Freya manoeuvre. But at least Freya was fully aware of what she was doing – even relishing the pain she was causing? –

whereas the Rosies of this world never seemed to let their right hand know what their left was doing.

Maybe that was the way to self-destruction and the harm done to others who were in the way was incidental?

Oh, Tommy, I miss someone to talk to. Someone to *hear*.

Well, he wouldn't let you get away with all this airy fairy theorising, she thought. He'd be looking at the facts.

But perhaps she was doing him an injustice. He let her take on that role and concentrated on another because they really were a team. He would know that the facts were those facts because the people were those people. Nothing stood alone.

And what has Arthur Trimble to do with all this? Her mind had taken another sudden leap. She placed him at Miss Woodward's and then at the Joneses' house. He was a teacher at the school Rosie should at this very moment be working in. His wife's lover had discovered a corpse and at first sight the victim had been thought to be Rosie.

Mitch felt herself go dizzy. It was as if the situation was a house and, instead of going though the front door, she was suddenly entering from the back.

It all looked different.

My God, what do I mean? What am I thinking?

Everything's changed so much I don't recognise a single thing.

The ship's bell at the door clanged and she went to answer it. A large man in a misshapen polyester suit stood on the gravel in front of her. He did not quite have the jowls of a bloodhound but he was getting there. Pixie ears shone pinkly from a scalp of reddish grey stubble. 'Miss Mitchell? I'm Inspector Jain.' Not a West country man, she thought. Someone from the north. 'Can I have a word?'

'You'd better come in.'

He followed her into the kitchen and suddenly the big, comfortable room seemed a lot smaller and the place was more dangerous, too. She sensed a cack-handedness and suddenly found herself worrying about Sissy's pots. 'Please sit down,' she said, trying not to keep an eye on his large hands. In her imagination he now sprouted six pairs, like an Indian god.

'Pleasant room, this.' He'd ambled over to the Aga and was using the chrome rail in front of the ovens to warm his backside. 'I hear you've been engaged by Sissy Childe to look for her half-sister Rosie.' His eyes, sunk in overhanging lids, in fleshy cheeks, were bird small, bird bright. 'Have you found her?'

'Yes.'

'Why were you looking?'

'Sissy was worried. Rosie had come down here to start teaching at St Ursula's but she never turned up at the school.'

'A missing person.'

'Right.'

'And the police were informed.'

'Sure. As far as I know. But she had gone missing before.'

'So why was Sissy worried this time?'

'Sissy told me she'd had a dream about her sister being in difficulties.'

'Ahh...'

He waited for her to say more, for her to justify this maybe, but Mitch knew all there was to know about interviewing and said nothing.

'You and Sissy found the clothes in the barn, didn't you? Have either of you yet worked out who they belong to?'

Mitch reached across the pine table to the pile of letters given to her by Bernice Brody. She gave him the one on top.

He took out half-moon spectacles from his inside jacket pocket and propped them on his nose. He was a careful reader. When he'd finished he said: 'The sandals...'

'Are there any refugees in this area?'

'As a matter of fact there are. Sixteen Kosovars. They're living in what used to be an old folks' home in Teignmouth while their requests for asylum are being investigated.'

'Could the victim be one of them?'

'Not one of *them*. The head count tallies. But it looks like she's an eastern European, all right. We've got an interpreter questioning the refugees to see if they know anything about her. If you don't mind, I'll hang on to this. Take a copy.' He'd taken his glasses off.

'Help yourself.'

'What really puzzles me is why the victim was wearing Rosie Childe's clothes, why Rosie made off in such a hurry and what really worried her sister enough to pay someone to find her – no doubt at very great expense.'

'I wish. Anyway, you can ask her yourself. She's with her sister now at a place called Fairlands – here, I'll write down the address...' Mitch reached out for a used envelope.

'You seem in a great hurry to see the back of me. What else do you know about the affair?'

'I don't know who killed that woman or why. I was hired simply to find Rosie and I've done that.'

'OK,' he said and took the envelope. He was leaning up from the rail. 'Better get cracking then. We don't want her to vanish again, do we?'

When they reached the door he wondered aloud: 'What aren't you telling me?' He was on the gravel now and turned abruptly.

'Withholding information carries penalties.'

She looked up to his bulky face. 'I want you to catch this killer just as much as you do.' She closed the door and went back to her coffee. It was cold and she made some more.

And, of course, he knows more than he's telling me, she thought. But what do I care? She suddenly yawned and stretched. Job done. Now she should be thinking of Tommy and what to do about him.

But what could she do?

She finished her coffee and idled into the lounge. She thought again how Tommy would love all this, the chintz, old furniture, inglenook. He had such a romantic idea about the English; she suddenly saw him sauntering about, hands behind his back, a copy-cat of the Duke of Edinburgh, not walking but *progressing*. But you can't give everything up to look after him, she thought. He could linger on for years, bumping at your ankle like a flesh-biting ball and chain.

Why doesn't he get it over with and die? The thought which popped into her head appalled her.

Stop thinking about him. Just stop now. It's doing no good. She opened the french door into the courtyard beyond. It was full of early morning sun. The air was crisp, northern and cool. She looked about her, at the cobbles, the old granite walling. She remembered Paul Maugin telling her: 'I never intended to stay here. But places like this sort of get into your soul.'

Come on, Mitchell. You're a city type. You actually love to sniff a hint of sulphur dioxide in the air. Get a shot of neon light. Hear the buzz of the city, play queen bee at the heart of the hive. It's you. Isn't it?

People come down to places like this to *die*.

And maybe do a little smuggling in the meantime. She smiled when she remembered Paul telling her about the wine. Last night he'd escorted her as far as the door, given her a chaste kiss on her cheek and left her. Alfie, eyes poking holes in the dark, had waited at the gate to collect him. Was she sorry or glad he'd not taken up her invitation to come in? Well, let's be honest, she thought. You were whacked. You couldn't have kept your eyes open five minutes more. That was one heavy day. And isn't it time *you stopped making love to strangers?* Think of that disastrous interlude with Marco Rice. Performing with him in the production office at Radio Brum, for God's sake, and Sissy coming along and whisking him out of your embrace and into her bed in the blink of an eye. Is that good for the ego? Maybe it's time to grow roses and do a bit of smuggling. Fishing, even.

Fishing?

Well, maybe not fishing.

She heard the back door open and hurried inside to the kitchen. There was Sissy in acid yellow top and pants which flared into tulips at the bottom, holding a small fuchsia pink canvas overnight case. 'Get that coffee pot going, ace. Is my head still screwed firmly down on my shoulders?'

'Looks like.'

'I felt it come loose more than once or twice. Rising pressure. You know?'

'You blew it.'

'No. I was an angel. It was more than difficult.' She looked around her for a moment, eyes unfocused, like someone coming out of the dark.

'You'd better have some breakfast, too.' Mitch had set the water on to boil.

'I am hungry,' Sissy discovered, surprised. 'When you're dealing with Rosie you always need to keep fuelled up. As soon as you've got through one scene, the curtain's up on the next. By the way, there's a parcel on the doorstep.'

'Oh, that'll be from Digger Rooney. Some stuff I asked him to send on Oa Bone.'

'Digger's a lovely guy. I do like 'em to look butch. Pity he's gay. He'd be ideal for the odd afternoon after lunch.'

'Tea and crumpets to follow.'

Mitch was being sarcastic but Sissy took

her seriously. 'I'm on a diet, you know,' and she watched Mitch open the door and bring in a crammed jiffy bag. 'Have you ever had a go with women?'

'No.'

'You're really missing out. You know that? Very different.'

'Well, come on. What happened? What's the curtain risen on?'

'Well this guy is Musa Hadri. The one she's with. Haddi, that's what Rosie called him. Anyway, he was there when I turned up. And to be fair, this is one attractive kid. Forget Helen. He'd launch more than a thousand ships. And doesn't he know it.' She smiled at some memory. 'What a little tinker. Anyway, I arrived when some barny was going on. Not between Haddi and Rosie but this kid Ishbelle and her mother. Talk about over the top. It was all about a lost sock, for God's sake. Never have kids.'

'I've got one.'

'Right. I remember. But she's in America, isn't she?'

'Yes.'

'So you're all right. Thumping. Banging. Running about. Screeching. Christ. This was in aid of a lost sock.'

'Maybe it was an excuse to have a row,' Mitch said, remembering some of her run-ins with Cassie. 'How about scrambled eggs? I might do some for myself, too.'

'Should hit the spot. Anyway, where was I? Well, we retreat to the residents' lounge, OK? Nice stout door, no one in there. This foul turkey patterned carpet on the floor. *Artificial* flowers. Still, I don't suppose they charge much. Anyway, Haddi politely makes himself scarce and Rosie and I have our little confab. I'm topping the Angel Gabriel and she's into her mulish routine. She's heard about the corpse they found in the woods, of course, but she really was astonished when I told her the victim was wearing some of her clothes. That I had to view the remains to make sure it wasn't her. I mean, bug-eyed. She doesn't know anything about the clothes in the barn. I told her that it must be down to Musa then. It was too far-fetched to believe there was an A.N. Other in all this.'

'What did she say to that?'

'She went ballistic and I have to say I nearly lost it. I felt like whacking some sense into the silly little bitch. There is no one more determinedly blind than Rosie when she wants to be. I then tried to get into the Ishbelle issue but she clammed up. I started in on how she was financing her B and B idyll with Haddi and met another blank wall. But I have a few ideas of my own. Well, one. Oa Bone.'

'But why would he do that?'

'He's into helping Kosovar refugees, isn't

he? And though he can't stand the sight of me he's got quite a lot of time for Rosie. Or seems to have. There's some link between them she's not letting on about. That's my bet for what it's worth. Anyway, as you can see, I wasn't getting too far–'

'Two pieces of toast?'

'That sounds good. But Rosie and me, Rosie and anybody, never seem to get too far. There's a lot she's never going to let you in on. I came to the conclusion long ago that she simply couldn't tolerate plain, unvarnished friendship. Not with a sister, a lover, or Lord God Almighty.'

Mitch put two plates of scrambled egg on the table and poured the coffee. Sissy picked up a fork. 'Well, anyway, here is me and Rosie not getting very far when I happen to glance out of the window – the residents' lounge is at the front of the building – and I see Haddi hoofing it down the drive with a tartan travel bag in one hand and a bulging plastic carrier bag in the other. And is this Haddi character moving. And if you think all this stuff about people going white is all my eye and moonshine ... it was like Rosie had had a head-on tussle with a vampire. At first I thought she was going to dash through the bay window but then she turned and sprinted out through the front door. He was well out of there by then and by the time I'd got to the gates he was nowhere to be seen. I've never seen anyone disappear so fast. She was so stunned she could hardly speak. I made her go up to their room. All his stuff had gone and I guess what money they had but she wasn't going to tell me that.'

'What made him take off?'

'If I'd found them other people could, couldn't they?'

'Like the police?'

'Well, he is an illegal. I did get that much out of her. The game plan was for them to marry.'

'*Marry?*'

'He'd be a British citizen then, wouldn't he?'

'But he's got a *wife.*'

'According to him, Yolanda was killed by the Serbs.'

'And Rosie believes that?'

'Sure. She's nuts on the guy. She gets these really crazy passions on people. She had one on me when we were kids. I told you. I remember once or twice finding it quite scary. It seemed to me she loved me for everything I was not. When someone keeps looking at you and seeing someone else entirely it sort of knocks you off centre. And it gets wearing, too. You feel like you're covered in golden syrup. You feel so gooey. You just want to wash it all off. Get clean. You know?'

'No. No one's ever felt like that about me. When some-one loves me they're in there trying to correct what they see as my faults. Telling me to come off it, pul-eeze, when I go too far.'

'I'm not talking about love, ace. Passion. It's a kind of madness.'

'More toast?'

'Better not.'

'So what happened then? He's done a bunk, you reckon wiped out her cash. To get down to practicalities, who's going to pay the B and B bill?' Mitch had begun tearing little bits off the corners of the Jiffy bag.

'Can't say that's crossed my mind. I tried to get her to come on here but she wouldn't. She thinks if she stays put she'll be there when Haddi gets a message to her.'

'What do you think?'

'No way. I'd say he won't be short of bride material in England if that's what he wants. It's hard to keep your hands off a guy like him, you know.'

'The police have been here,' Mitch said and gave Sissy the gist of what was said.

'I bet the bastard killed her.'

'Who?'

'Haddi. Killed his wife, of course, so he could marry Rosie and get his British passport.'

'That's got to be a strong possibility. But why not just commit bigamy?'

386

'Well, his wife found him, didn't she? She could make trouble. That's my bet. Will you stop fiddling with that bloody parcel and open it.'

Mitch did. On top of a pile of clippings was a photograph of Oa Bone's band, taken just after it had been formed. Looking down through the years at the young faces, she pursed her lips. Her whistle was silent, Sissy's was not.

'That's got to be Ishbelle's dad.'

'I knew she resembled someone and I went through all the people I'd met that day,' said Mitch. 'I never thought of photographs. There's one on Oa Bone's desk. But it's not as good as this one. And I only sort of glanced.'

'He's dead, isn't he? The drummer. What'sitface...'

'Geoff Stark. Ages ago. Oa Bone helps run a trust fund in his name. The money goes to some place where alcoholics and druggies go to get rehabilitated.'

'Ishbelle really is the spitting image of Stark. It's almost uncanny,' said Sissy.

'It explains an awful lot. Oa Bone must have found out about Rosie's child, used maybe a private investigator to track her down. There's only mum and daughter now. He helps them get installed in Newton Abbot and pays for Ishbelle to go to St Ursula's. After all, he is running Geoff

Stark's charity and charity *does* begin at home.'

'Maybe Rosie got to know and decided to take a look at her daughter. That's why she took up the teaching post at St Ursula's. But then this old flame of hers from the Balkans turns up. He's an illegal. He'd stick out like a sore thumb in a little community. They decide to flit to where they could blend into the background but before they do Rosie wants to get to grips with Ishbelle...'

Sissy and Mitch stared at each other.

'Well, it all seems to fit. Give me the photo. I'm going to go back over there.'

'I'd wait awhile. The police will be there by now. My guess is it will be a very long session.'

Sissy considered this and then pushed her coffee cup away from her, yawning. 'Good thinking, Batman. Besides, I need some more kip. Anyway, I'm fed up with dancing to Rosie's tune. When she gets herself into a mess it's always mega. And she's always in messes.' She'd pushed the chair back and picked up her pink bag. 'Get that. I'm an aunt.'

'No. You're not,' said Mitch.

'That's what I mean. Rosie and messes always go together. What are you planning to do?'

'See Tommy.'

'Give him my love.'

Mitch, left alone in the kitchen, wondered if Tommy were capable of receiving anything. Glad to get out of Manaccan House, get Sissy and Rosie out of her hair, she went shopping for things to take to the hospital. She had lunch, pottered about Newton Abbot, putting off the moment she'd see him propped like some ancient mummy in his NHS tomb.

She was in her car and almost at the hospital when she realised she'd left Tommy's spare pair of pyjamas at Manaccan House. 'Oh shit...' she moaned and drove back to the village. Sissy wasn't around – presumably, Mitch thought, she's back doing her St Gabriel bit with Rosie. Mitch shoved the pyjamas in a bag and was at the bottom of the stairs when the phone rang.

It was Ellie Peters speaking from a border town in Albania. The line was so good she could have been in the room with her. Ellie wanted Mitch to get hold of her mother and give her some messages. 'God knows where she is and it'll be some time before I can get hold of another line.' Mitch promised to relay the information.

'Now, darling, what can I do for you?'

Mitch, briefly outlining the situation, asked: 'What does it all look like from a Kosovar lad's point of view?'

When Ellie told her Mitch said flatly: 'That's unbelievable.'

'Most of what happens out here is unbelievable,' Ellie said. 'The unbelievable is happening right now.'

But it was unbelievable. Mitch, driving to the hospital with Tommy's stuff piled up on the passenger seat next to her, found what Ellie had told her had shown her lives so dark she couldn't get any sort of handle on it.

She was relieved to lay Ellie's information to one side when she entered the hospital. In the corridor, outside the ward, she met the Chinese nurse. 'Something wolly him. About a teacher,' the nurse told her. 'You know about a teacher?'

Mitch shook her head. 'How is he?'

'He all light.'

Tommy was not all right. For one gasping moment Mitch thought he was dead. And then the breathing resumed, chopped up in uneven lengths. His eyes were open but he appeared not to recognise her. Although he was clean there was a faint rancid odour about his flesh.

Mitch put out the stuff she'd bought on the top of his locker, taking a long time in arranging it.

'Don't look so chipper, do 'e?' said the man in the next bed. 'How come you know a chink then?'

'Oh, you know...' Mitch sat down, breathed in deeply and took hold of

Tommy's fingers, now as cold as tines. 'They say you're doing fine...' she said brightly. And then her hand pushed further, palm against Tommy's palm, and she found herself relaxing in the wooden chair, settling into the silent ebb and flow of contact between them.

Later, she thought she'd never concentrated so hard in her life but she felt better about the situation, almost relieved.

They were still a team.

22

Mitch was staring now at the rear of Ishbelle Jones as she struggled over the top of the wall. A sleeping bag was rolled up and secured by straps at the bottom of the rucksack on her back, the map book had been rolled up and formed a funnel which stuck up through the neck by nine inches. The Tesco bag, ballooning with groceries, was squat between valerian which sprouted out of the top of the granite wall. Black hair was escaping from the claret velvet hat. A car honked. Mitch swung back to the wheel, pulling her grey Escort sharply to the nearside. The driver of the passing car honked again. Her heart raised its beat. She rounded the corner, looking for a place to pull in. She had to drive through a series of sharp bends before she found a safe place by a farm gate.

She relaxed back in the driving seat. What would a schoolkid want with that map book, a pile of groceries and a bedding roll? She reviewed what Sissy had told her about the row the girl had had with her mother that morning. Would even the most sensitive child run away over a missing sock? But had the row been about that or was it just a trigger for something much more serious? She looked down at her watch. It was nearly five o'clock. That seemed to indicate Ishbelle had been to school before setting off with all that gear. Surely the youngster would have split this morning if that's what she intended to do?

And this guy Haddi was missing.

Hey, not so fast. Aren't we letting our imagination run away with us here?

We sure are, she thought, and turned the key in the ignition.

She turned it off. A picture of Haddi had sprung into her mind, this dancing Lord of the Summer. More oomph than rocket fuel. Any kid was going to fall for that, wasn't she? Even Rosie, who ought to have had more sense at her age, had thought nothing of ditching a job she hadn't even started yet and doing a bunk with him.

He was a man with the equipment to enchant all the senses. He could easily have bewitched Ishbelle into helping him with some scheme or other.

Even if he hadn't murdered the woman found in the woods, he wouldn't want to stick around after his hidey-hole had been discovered. He was an illegal immigrant, wasn't he? And who in their right mind would want to be sent back to a war zone? He must have seen the pictures on the television news. Hundreds of thousands of his fellow countrymen were being shoved over the borders of Kosovo with guns pointed to their heads.

If he really is a killer what's to say he won't put a bullet through that kid's dreaming little mind?

But in all of this, no one has mentioned that Haddi *had* got a gun. Certainly not Rosie.

Suddenly Mitch picked up the mobile and phoned her assistant, A.J. After they'd talked for a moment about Tommy, she outlined the situation. 'It's probably all a lot of my eye and moonshine but I'm going to have to go after that idiot child. Damn it, I really could do without this.'

'Mitch. For God's sake call the police or something. This is not our business. We're not being paid for this.'

'But I'm more than likely right up a gum tree about it all. Say this kid's just out on some kind of teenage jaunt with her pals? I don't want to drop Ishbelle in a load of shit. Frighten her to death or anything.'

'Haddi could be a killer. Might have a gun. It was *you* who pointed that out.'

'I'm just going to have a look-see. I'm not going near, believe me. I'll take those binoculars you made us buy–'

'Now, listen, Mitch–'

'Honeypot, stop fussing, will you? I'll have

my mobile phone with me, won't I? I'll keep well out of sight. Believe me, I'm in no hurry to meet my maker. I'll just try and take a look at what's going on, if anything. Things appear a bit nasty and I'm a bleep away from the cops.'

'You still act as if investigative work is cowboys and Indians in different outfits. It's a business, Mitch. You know. Sifting paperwork, working the phones, putting out the bills. It's not tearing about the countryside leaving yourself wide open for a stray bullet or God knows what—'

'You sound like my mother. You really do. If she were alive she'd be rabbiting on like this. If there's no fun to be had out of working you might as well be on the dole. Or whatever they call it these days. Feet up, gin in hand, watching the roses grow.'

'I don't think your giro would pay for gin.'

'Where there's a will, there's a way.'

'OK, OK. As soon as you see anything you're on the blower to me. Just keep yourself out of trouble's way. I've enough on my plate worrying about Tommy.'

'A.J....'

'What?'

'Oh, well. You know. It's nice to have someone worry about you. Even when there's no need.'

'Keep in touch.'

Mitch clicked off the phone, slid out of the

car and opened the boot. She changed her jacket for an anorak, her shoes for trainers, picked up a small navy blue backpack and checked. Binoculars, camera, notepad, biro. She transferred her purse and mobile phone from her handbag, fastened the pack and swung it over her shoulders.

Ishbelle, she knew, would be long gone by now but she was fairly confident of picking up her trail. Some of the country was well wooded but there was a lot of open ground, too. Every now and again the girl would have to break cover.

Trudging along twisting tarmac, she examined her feelings. She pin-pointed her unease. The kind of map book, she thought. We're into footpaths and bridleways here. Not motorways. As she came out of the last of the series of bends and worked out the spot where she'd seen Ishbelle, the wind began to rise. Her hair suddenly blew up round her face, a writhing, black halo. She shivered and pulled up the collar of her anorak.

She swung herself over the wall and began to trudge up the hillside. Reaching the top of an outcrop of rock, she looked about her. The land plunged into a basin of trees. Most of the branches were bare though some saplings were greening. Still, she should be able to spot Ishbelle from here, unless she were temporarily shielded from sight by rising rockshelf or crevice. There was no sign of her. She scrambled down the hill, balancing herself with plunging and planing arms. Her foot caught in the extending root of a gorse bush. She tripped, falling backwards. 'Shit,' she swore as she landed on one buttock.

Just what do I think I'm doing? As A.J. said, nobody's paying me for this. Moaning to herself and rubbing her thigh, she suddenly became aware of movement in the trees below her. She swung off her backpack and took out the binoculars. She steadied herself, legs scissoring out in front of her, feet pointing skyward. She trained the glasses on the trees. 'Got you,' she whispered. The girl had put the Tesco bag down. She was bent, her hands squeezing into her waist, as if she had a stitch. 'You *are* going to meet someone. Haddi?'

She made another sweep with the binoculars. She couldn't see anyone else. Ishbelle was straightening. She picked up the bag of groceries again and plunged on. Mitch scrambled to her feet, binoculars swinging on their strap. Wind-whipped rain began to sting her cheeks, flattened waves of distant grass to the right of her. A rabbit hopped out from behind a shoulder of red sandstone and scuttled for cover.

Small pebbles sliding from under the soles of her trainers, she scrambled down to the treeline. She lost sight of Ishbelle completely. She traversed a hillock with clumps of primroses nestling between spurting new growth and then paused when she caught a glimpse of water. It was muddy grey in colour and chill-looking, the surface cracked with agitated rills. Above she heard the cry of gulls as they swooped up the estuary. She went deeper into the wood, now circling upwards, skirting the side of a hill.

Where are you?

She spotted an outcrop of rock and climbed it. From this vantage point she could make out the general shape of the inlet, a distant boathouse and something else higher up through a stand of skeleton trees... A house?

She was startled by a pop, pop, popping just above her head. Like little water bubbles bursting. A bird? Do some birds make noises like that? Even though she was a townee, even though she thought in terms of trilling, she found she knew a bird when she heard one.

Almost immediately there were other sounds. Crack, crack, crack. Gunshot, she was sure. Someone after rabbits?

She spotted patches of red just by the stand of trees. A parked car? She adjusted the lenses. Much of the shape was hidden by what looked like a rhododendron bush, but she became sure it was a car. As far as she knew Haddi and Rosie didn't have a vehicle. Red. Into her mind came a picture of Arthur Trimble, the upturned plant pot shape of his face, receding dead grass hair, moist, pursed mouth. Big, blunt, powerful hands, one with a bruise on the back. I can't believe it, she thought. Why, he's old enough to be her grandfather. No, no, I've got this wrong. No way.

But he did drive a red Golf, didn't he? Ishbelle's mother's boyfriend?

Were mother and daughter really rowing about him? I mean, she thought, who rows about a missing sock?

But he's repulsive.

He's got a bullish shape. Lots of women go for that.

Coral's husband.

A sense of unreality possessed her.

He can't be having it off with mother *and* baby Jones. Can he?

What kind of monster has that woman let into her house?

She remembered the Chinese nurse. She'd said Tommy was worried about a teacher. Had he suspected something and was that what he was going to tell her when she arrived at Manaccan House after interviewing Dr Hazel Rayburn? How long ago that seemed. And what a complicated case this was turning out to be.

Not at all. Not if you'd stuck to what you were being paid to do. You found Rosie, didn't you?

Mitch trained the binoculars on the boathouse. There was something on the railed balcony above the great double doors, just to the right of the french windows. Green, tan. She adjusted the lenses again. Suitcases, she decided. Two suitcases.

The chill in her stomach shrank her flesh. He can't be running away with Ishbelle, she thought. He's a schoolteacher. He'd never be so foolish. Would he?

She saw Ishbelle moving out of the treeline and on to the muddy shingle near the boathouse. She stopped and transferred the Tesco bag to her other hand. She began to look about her. Mitch immediately tugged the zip of her anorak down and shoved the binoculars in. Stray light might reflect off the lenses. She didn't want the girl to know someone was watching her. At that moment a flash of late afternoon sun pierced a brew of cloud. The landscape exploded into colour. Clouds boiled white, yellow, a lurid purple. The light went out. The wind had a sharper edge to it, needling Mitch's hair into scarecrow ribbons, sliding chill between her neck and the collar of the anorak, icing her backbone. She rubbed reddening hands together, trying to decide what to do.

I could have got hold of the wrong end of the stick, she thought. Really, that's the most likely thing.

If she hadn't she knew that she was witnessing the beginning of a tragedy below her.

What kind of a relationship is left when a daughter runs off with her mother's boyfriend? And this kid was no more than fourteen. Apart from anything else, the law was being broken.

There was still a chance that she'd figured it out wrong. She would wait a little longer, see what was going to happen next.

Her attention was caught by the red car, some movement. She trained the glasses, increasing the magnification. The vehicle was so heavily obscured it took her a moment to work out that the boot was being opened. She could see what she thought was a bit of a hand, an arm. Something being lifted out.

A stirring in bushes. Someone appeared to be circling above and round the back of the boathouse, perhaps following a path she couldn't make out. Suddenly she saw him. The schoolteacher was wearing a tweed jacket and rumpled pants. Corduroys, she guessed. In his right hand was a grip, a piece of luggage matching the suitcases she'd seen on the balcony above the boathouse doors. He was carrying two plastic grocery bags in the other hand. His tie was suddenly whipped up in a gust of wind and flapped behind his ear. As far as she could tell he wasn't aware of the approach of Ishbelle Jones and Mitch worked out that the back of the boathouse was blocking off his view of the apron of sand and shingle. Had the girl spotted the suitcases? Her head was down, tail of hair springing from beneath the velvet hat. Her rucksack was jutting out from her waist as she curved under the weight of what she carried.

But surely the teacher wouldn't be taking suitcases and groceries out of the Golf if they were planning to do a runner in his car?

Did they intend to hole up together in the boathouse?

The girl was now plodding along wet, brownish sand. The trail of her footprints was getting longer.

Again Mitch's eye was alerted by movement. Something stirring well above the house which nestled towards the bottom of the wooded hill. She made several sweeps with the binoculars but could make nothing out.

Ishbelle Jones was now climbing the steps which ran up the side of the boathouse to a door. If she had spotted the suitcases on the balcony at the front of the building she'd given no sign. She'd not paused in her trudge across sand and rock. She now put the Tesco bag down on the top step, swung off the rucksack, unlocked the door and went in. In Mitch's heart there was the tenderest of icy quivers. She's so young, she thought. Not much more than a baby. How can that bastard take advantage of such a silly little innocent?

She looked to see if she could spot Arthur Trimble but thick rhododendrons grew behind the boathouse. There was little open ground. But she knew he couldn't now be more than a minute away from the child. Studying the layout more closely, Mitch realised that at the top of the steps was a walkway which ran round to the front of the stone building and the balcony which overlooked the inlet. The tide was coming in. The cracks of agitated rills were swelling into waves, some frothing white as the wind whipped up through the water.

Mitch swung off her backpack and took out her mobile. 'This is what I think is going on ...' and she told A.J. what she was seeing.

'You've got to be joking.'

'I can't believe it myself. But it does look like Mummy let in the big bad wolf when she started to play around with this guy.'

'No sign of Haddi?'

'None. I could have made sense of that. Haddi's got enough sex appeal to launch any female into orbit round Venus. This creep's the pits. In my view.'

'What are you going to do? Call the cops?'

'Well, she's a minor, isn't she? And getting in well above her head. But do I want to make it a police matter? That's got to make a shitty situation worse.'

'Maybe you should ring this Mrs Jones? Let her deal with it. It is her daughter.'

'That's probably the best way out. If I go in and confront them they might do a runner. His car's parked up by the house above the shore. I couldn't follow. The Escort is over the hill. Look, A.J., I'm going to work in a bit closer. Try and make sure I've read this right. I mean, it all seems so unlikely, honeypot. Don't you think?'

'Love does do unlikely things. Shakespeare wrote a play about it. Remember?'

'How could I forget? I did that one for School Cert. It was supposed to be a comedy.'

Mitch now saw the french windows which led on to the balcony being opened. She also saw Arthur Trimble, three strides away from the boathouse's steps. 'Have to go. I'll ring you in about five minutes. We'll make the final decision then.'

'For God's sake be careful–'

Mitch quickly stowed the mobile phone and nimbly worked her way off the outcrop of rock and down towards the shoreline. She tried not to hurry, fearing she would slide, fearing the noise would alert them to her presence. But anxiety was sheening her skin. The path she took blocked off sight of them. Her trainers thumped on to damp shingle. Still she couldn't see the boathouse. She worked her way behind a shelf of rock which projected out into the inlet. The squeal of gulls seared through the agitated pluck and plash of estuary water. She pushed the binoculars over her shoulder and wriggled her way up the damp incline of rock. A fissure near the top split the sandstone, an eye for her to look through. She eased the binoculars back over her shoulder and trained them on the balcony.

First she saw the wine red hat, swerving through the air. Now it was half blocked off by Arthur Trimble's head. There was a scramble of limbs, kicking, sliding feet. An animal squeal peeled apart the valley. *Jesus.* Mitch's fumbling hands tore at the straps of the backpack. A flash of trainer between Arthur Trimble's driving legs. Mitch's hands slithering over the mobile. His shout of anguish. 'A.J. Get the cops. The bastard's attacking her–' Ishbelle up over the balcony railing. He on his knees but his body suddenly flung out towards her, hands spreading wider and wider, big as mechanical grabbers. Ishbelle off balance, toppling towards the shingle below, hat spinning away, legs wide apart and bent, momentarily sitting on air. Arms sprouted before her head. From where she was Mitch heard the sickening crunch of the girl's body hitting the ground. Small particles of sand and shingle spat upwards. Arthur Trimble was already racing back through the french windows. Mitch had rid herself of backpack, phone and binoculars. She was racing across to the boathouse, feet slithering over wrack and green-slimed rocks.

Ishbelle was picking herself up, in a daze, turning round on herself, reaching for the hat, jamming it back on her head. Suddenly she dipped sideways, prising a piece of driftwood from between rocks. 'Run!' Mitch was surprised by the scream in her throat. 'Run! Run!'

Arthur Trimble appeared round the boathouse. Ishbelle brandished the piece of driftwood. Suddenly she dropped it, her ribs ratcheted over her stomach. The yelling seared through the pounding of Mitch's heart. 'Mummy! Mummy!' Trying to shield her thin body with upright forearms, small fists, Ishbelle made a break for the hill. Arthur Trimble was before her, blocking off retreat. He was not running now but dancing to the right and then the left, like a boxer waiting for an opening, arms pumping. She shot off to the right. He was there, cutting the distance between them. She whirled about and ran towards the water. Suddenly spray shot up. 'M-mummy!

Mummy!' Knees coltishly high, arms flailing, the wailing lower than the screech of the gulls but longer, grating slivers off Mitch's ears. She was now closing in quickly but he was so focused he appeared completely unaware of her. He was ankle deep in water, splish, splash, splish, splash, not moving quickly, sure of himself, knowing the girl was his. She had her back to him, hands now over her ears, sliding towards her eyes. He began calling to her. 'I won't hurt you. Why in the world would I hurt you? I won't hurt you...' Slow and honeyed, trying to coax her into turning to him. Trying to get her to present herself to him. She plunged deeper. He followed. Mitch hit the water at a gallop, her feet springing through the agony of her winded body.

Shoulder deep and Arthur Trimble had caught Ishbelle, wrapping his great arms about her. Mitch, half swimming, throwing herself on to his back, digging in with her knees, clawing her way up. She grabbed his ears, feeling them elongate as she pulled with all her strength. Harder, harder, straining against his resisting flesh. Harder, harder and harder. Her teeth grinding, eyes rounding. She could feel him letting the child go. He began pumping back his arms, half dislodging her. She held on. She saw a balled fist coming towards her over his shoulder. A rill of knuckle-bones shone through wet skin and sluicing water. Instinctively she moved a hand holding an ear. She felt her body turn, spray hailing her horizon, splintering her vision of the child who was charging towards the beach. The waters closed over her. She rose, sea streaming off her head, mouth wide, screaming. His hands pounced to close round her neck. Fingernails dug in at the top of her spine. A strong buttock rammed into her side, unbalancing her. She could feel first her trunk and then her head turning until she faced down. One of his hands twisted her hair, using it like a rope. Getting extra grip, more leverage. His knee found the small of her back. He was pushing her down, under water. Eel-like, she twisted, beginning to gasp for air.

Pain grew, slowing her fighting limbs, paralysing them. The pressure turned her breastbone into a dagger, bending it slowly inward. It seemed to cleave apart her heart, grind through the pulping discs of her spine. And then the pain began to ease and she found herself thinking that this was what drowning felt like. It felt like being crushed to death.

She didn't at first think *she* was drowning and when she did she was incredulous, the knowledge laking in a brain which didn't know how to drown though a darkness was appearing at the edges of consciousness. A camera whose aperture was slowly closing.

But this can't be right. It's Tommy who is dying. It's his funeral we should be going to.

And then all questions vanished. Forming in the sudden preternatural calm was a picture of her daughter at three, sitting looking up at an Alsatian and crying, herself at nineteen in a wooden chair, covering an inquest in the fly-blown solicitor's office. Eighty-seven seconds. Break point is reached at eighty-seven seconds. That's what the podgy pathologist is saying.

Then you breathe in water.

Eighty-seven seconds.

But time had stopped. This was for ever.

She had all the time in the world to see wet city pavements, crowds eerie but jolly, shining in pools of neon lights. She recognised someone, her husband Max, coming towards her. He should be older than her but he was younger.

Dead longer than me, she thought.

She opened her mouth and began inhaling the sea.

Water, pitted with rain. And then she realised she was in water and the rain was on her face. There was something else, too, something slimy.

I'm breathing. Incredulity made her open her eyes, blink. How can lungs full of water take in air? She monitored. In, out, in out, painless, pure, life.

And as she took in a long breath she felt her rib cage expand.

She was astonished.

But where's the man? The girl? What's happening?

Very carefully she raised her head out of the water and turned it. She was inches away from Arthur Trimble. He was belly up, three limbs spreadeagled, one arm banging into his side. Something dark was trickling down from the left side of his forehead. A splodgy stain growing, making its way over his eye. Something, too, darkening the dark wavelets, creeping over her, a lot of it. She realised that came from the banging arm, high up, she thought, perhaps his shoulder. Her eyes closed, the back of her head flopped down in the water.

She was listening to herself breathe again.

Opening her eyes she saw a head dripping in red bending down towards her. Clear dark eyes were regarding her.

'Haddi shot him,' Ishbelle Jones said.

'Is he dead?'

'I'm not touching him!'

The dripping red head reared back in alarm.

'Ishbelle?' And then Mitch realised that it was dye from the hat which was running down the girl's face, puddling on her shoulders.

'I've got to get you out of here.'

Mitch didn't move.

'You've got to stand up. Put your arm over my shoulder.'

'Sure...' Mitch slowly raised her head again.

'Come on. He's *moving*.'

Water cascaded from Mitch's body as she struggled upright. The girl was suddenly still and Mitch was, too. In the distance they heard a car engine start. 'Haddi's got to go. He's afraid he'll be caught.'

'He saved my life,' Mitch said. She swayed as she pushed her way through the sea and then they were on the shingle. 'I died?' Again incredulity shook her. She sank on to the pebbles.

'You are all right?'

Mitch let her breath out slowly.

'Did he really *move?*'

'Maybe it was the sea.'

Mitch closed her eyes.

23

Mitch lay on the settee in Sissy's lounge. Beneath her head was a damp towel. She'd put it there to protect the cushions against her wet curls. A rug covered most of the old tracksuit she was wearing. Her chin was raised a little so she could tilt nostrils. A faint smell of woodsmoke. She drew in the air and let the tinge of burning pine logs inhabit the most delicate tracery of her lungs. A slow sensuous pleasure began to suffuse her being, strung along like dew drops on a spider's web of nerve. She was becalmed in delight.

In the kitchen Paul Maugin was whistling. A pan clattered on the Aga. Her eyes half closed. She took in another breath and lungs which should be full of water, which should no longer be able to leech oxygen out of the air, sweetly formed the patterns of life.

It had been a terrible night.

Not long after she'd been admitted to the casualty department at the local hospital the diarrhoea began. 'Getting rid of the whole of the estuary by the looks of it,' the nurse had said and Mitch, too racked to speak, had found her teeth gritting. No sooner were the spasms beginning to ease than uncontrollable tremors began, her body flickering like a dying fluorescent tube of light.

She was admitted to the ward for 'observation'. There was a rubber sheet under her and the sides of the bed were raised. She slept some of the time.

Eighty-seven seconds, she dreamed and the coroner behind his desk eerily flickered in and out of her vision, a black and white wartime movie hero going down with his burning ship. She could hear Morse code clickety clacking through smoke.

She found herself amazed to have survived the hours of darkness, to return to the crisp but restless ward, the clang of trolleys, the noise of water rushing through distant taps. The surreal ordinariness of rain on windows, magenta roses on curtains.

Can I raise a limb? she wondered. She could.

Inspector Jain made an early visit. 'Are you sure you're up to this?' He had been clearly taken aback by her appearance. Mitch touched a slightly sore jaw. There was a soreness throughout her body. No pain.

The doctors thought she looked fine and dandy.

'You've had a narrow escape. You've been incredibly lucky,' said one, a young woman with a crew cut and a wide smile.

Mitch thought that being held under water until you drowned could hardly be described as lucky. She was going to ask the woman why, in fact, she'd *not* drowned but, after her interview with Inspector Jain, felt too tired to hold another tricky conversation.

However, judged not too tired to get up and go.

Sissy, located on her mobile, was about to drive off to see Rosie, who was still at the Joneses' waiting for Haddi to get in touch. 'I suppose it's what they call the triumph of hope over experience but really I could smack her. You know?'

Mitch did know.

Sissy was thinking the problem through. 'I'll give Paul Maugin a ring. I saw him at the shop earlier. He said to get in touch if there was anything he could do. Anyway, ace, someone will fetch you. Rely on it. Only it won't be me.'

'I suppose I could get a taxi. Only I need some clothes. I have a memory of them cutting mine off me.'

'As good as done. Don't worry about a thing. Someone will be there in half an hour. How are you, by the way? Well, of course, you must be OK or they wouldn't be letting you out.'

'I feel like shit.'

'Well, I suppose you would, wouldn't you? When you *really* think about it. Rosie's not too good either. Dr Rayburn's been round to see her. She's just got to come back to Manaccan House and that's that.'

Mitch carefully put the phone back on its cradle which stood on a trolley by her bedside. She leaned back into the pillows, a sheen of hot tiredness overtaking her. Is that Sissy's way of telling me I've got to get out of her house? She suddenly found she was near to tears. Self-pity, she thought, will get you nowhere. Though a good wallow in that trough, she'd found in the past, did a lot to ease the soul.

I wonder if I can use my legs? Well, I can use my arms. Stop being so pathetic, Mitchell.

She was woken by a nurse bringing in two plastic carrier bags bulging with clothes. 'There's a nice-looking man waiting for you,' the nurse said as she drew the curtains round the cubicle. 'We've had two calls from the Press, too, but we told them we'd let you go. Which we are doing, of course. Just thought I'd warn you. They can be persistent little devils. Hey, careful. I'd better give you a bit of help.'

Mitch, who had almost toppled as she tried to swing her legs out of bed, said: 'Just a bit dizzy.'

'You'll be as right as rain in two or three

days. You've had quite a shock to the system.' And then hearing a shout further down the ward: 'Hang on in there, dear. Be down in a minute.'

Mitch, who suddenly realised she was going to be glad to get out of the place, began to concentrate on getting dressed.

Paul Maugin had bent his arm at the elbow and fitted hers in above it, taking much of her weight. He organised her in the passenger seat of his car, adjusting it so she could lean well back, fastening the seat belt for her. Her legs had begun to tremble, gently, like the mechanism in an old lift before it descends to the next floor.

On the drive back to Manaccan House he said: 'He's in the intensive care unit. That's the floor above your ward. Did you know?'

'Inspector Jain told me.'

'The bad don't die,' he said. 'Not in my experience.'

Sissy had made up a bed on the settee for her. Logs burned in the grate and rain-streaked sunlight formed small, moving patterns on old furniture and cob walls. Though she could hardly stand, Mitch had insisted on a shower. She'd had to fight waves of nausea to manage it, but minutes later she was in her tracksuit, the towel was over cushions and she was sinking on the William Morris patterned linen union which covered the settee.

It was when she woke she heard Paul Maugin in the kitchen, sniffed the wood-smoke in the air. He bent to come through the sitting-room door, the house a size too small for him and he as awkward as a lad who'd outgrown his suit. 'So you're awake. Good. Lunch won't be long. I've made some soup.'

'Who is looking after Alfie?'

'Alfie is looking after Alfie. Anyway, he sleeps in the morning after his night out on the tiles. The local quack is coming in later. Make sure you're doing OK.'

'Have they caught Haddi yet?'

'Not that I know of.'

'You wouldn't think it that difficult. He did take off in Arthur Trimble's car. According to the inspector.'

'Ditched it if he's any sense. Taken a train or something. Once he's in a city he's going to be very difficult to trace.'

'If he hadn't shot Arthur Trimble I'd have been in the mortuary, not up on a ward. Haddi saved my life. Inspector Jain said one bullet scraped Trimble's skull. The other lodged in his shoulder. They've dug that one out. Everyone's betting it will match the one which killed the girl found in the woods. He told me she'd been identified. Yolanda. Haddi's wife.'

Paul told her: 'Sissy said that Rosie believed Yolanda had been killed in the

Balkans, before Haddi came to England. That he and her half-sister were planning on marriage.'

'Inspector Jain's theory is that Yolanda followed him, traced him through friends. I think he's right. The woman Rosie used to share a flat with told me about a phone call from a woman who spoke good English but with a foreign accent...'

'If he married Rosie he'd have English citizenship, wouldn't he?' Paul Maugin said. He sat down on a chair opposite her, unfolding his long legs. 'Yolanda tracked him down here. Probably she was in this house, had a shower and Haddi gave her a change of clothes, Rosie's clothes–'

'The theory is he sent her on to Oa Bone's place on some pretext. She actually did know Oa, had met him in Kosovo. She knew he ran a charity for the Kosovar refugees already in Britain.'

'Money, you think? She was sent to ask for money?'

'Haddi went after her and killed her. He wouldn't have considered that wrong. Or I don't think he would. I've got a friend, a journalist, working out there at the moment. Ellie Peters told me about something called the bride's bullet.'

He stared at her.

'It's a fiercely patriarchal society, you know. In the countryside things haven't changed much since medieval times. Sacks for carrying. That's how women are regarded. When a girl marries, her family give the bridegroom a bullet. If she doesn't behave he's at liberty to shoot her.'

'I don't believe it.'

'Nor did I. Well, nor do I now, really. It *is* unbelievable. The practice is supposed to have died out but Ellie Peters reckons it still goes on. Haddi was born, you know, in a remote Kosovar village though Yolanda was a city girl. Her father is a professor, so Inspector Jain told me.'

'If chaps like me could fall back on an old custom like that our ex-wives would cause us so much less trouble.' Suddenly he was on the brink of laughter and so was she. 'Though it's not funny,' he told her. Neither let the little bubble of hysterical mirth break. And then: 'Of course, I've heard of Muslims killing their wives in some parts of Pakistan.'

'Well, whatever he's done or not done, Haddi gets my vote. He saved my life,' said Mitch.

Paul got up and threw a couple of logs on the fire. Sparks flared. Rain pattered on the french windows. The phone rang.

'Tommy,' said Mitch. Paul was already on the way to the door. He looked back. Mitch's face was turned away and in shadow. This can't be right, she'd thought, when she'd realised she was drowning. It's

419

Tommy who is dying. It's his funeral we should be going to.

But who would go?

As far as she knew A.J. had not unearthed one relative. Perhaps, when he left Hong Kong all those years ago, he'd not been going on an adventure in which he hoped to find a new life so much as fleeing from the horrors of the old. He had never spoken to her of his childhood, of the life he led as a very young man.

Paul came back in with a large tray. There were two bowls of steaming soup. 'Leek and onion, and I made some potato cakes, too. Not elegant but sustaining.'

'Smells delicious,' said Mitch though she wasn't hungry. He put hers on a coffee table by the settee.

'It was Sissy. Rosie really isn't at all well but at last she's got her to agree to come back to the village. They're going to use their father's place. She's hoping Penny Gilbert will take over the nursing of her sister. They're due back from France tomorrow and Sissy's got to get back up to the Midlands to finish filming this cook show.'

'That's Mr Childe's partner? Penny Gilbert, I mean?'

He nodded. 'You are to stay at Manaccan House as long as you need to. Sissy says she'll be over to see you as soon as she's got Rosie settled.'

'That's really kind of her.'

'The least she could do, I should think, after getting you embroiled in her family's affairs.' He paused, stirring his soup round with a spoon. 'I expect Tommy looks worse than he is. Lots of people do remarkably well after a stroke.'

Mitch was thinking as she sipped her soup. Eventually she said: 'We're going to have to be his family. I mean, the Mitchell and Orient Bureau. I'm beginning to believe he doesn't have anyone else. Though I've no idea how we'll work it.'

'It's going to be tough.'

Mitch didn't say anything. Somewhere in her being she was already trying to test out the weight of Tommy, wondering whether, even when fully well, she'd be able to cope with such a burden. You don't have to do it, she thought, as she quailed a little.

But who else was there?

Unable to even think about it further, she went on tackling her soup. This was the task of the moment and it was a big one. She fell asleep again before she finished the coffee he brought in later.

She woke to an awareness of breathing perfume. The scent seemed to sit above the hint of woodsmoke in the room. Voluptuous, she thought – lilies, she decided and very cautiously raised her head and looked about her. There they were, a great bunch of them in a square Bristol blue glass vase. Yellow stamens, green veining staining white petal, trumpets hanging from stems which seemed suspended in the air. There was a return of the pleasure she'd felt earlier. She seemed to draw the whole of the grey cool light of the room into her. Bubbles of life pinged at her nerve ends.

In the kitchen beyond she could hear the phone ring, hear someone answer it. Paul was still here. She was now carefully and slowly mapping out the contours of her body as it lay passively on the cushions, the delightful weight of being. No sooner had the phone clicked back than the bell at the back door sounded.

She found she liked the noise of things going on outside the room she was in, the feeling of being caught in an extending web.

The door opened. 'Dr Savage here to check you over.' Paul's voice, though she couldn't see him. A man in his thirties entered carrying a traditional black bag but wearing jeans and an anorak which was stained across the shoulders with a spattering of rain. His eyes were a warm brown, large and very round. Mitch was reminded of a spaniel. The door was closed by Paul's unseen hand.

'Hello there. How are you?'

'Actually, I feel a lot better,' Mitch discovered. 'I've done nothing but doze all day.'

He dropped the bag and checked her pulse. 'Nothing wrong there. You seem to have come through your ordeal remarkably well.'

'You wouldn't have thought that if you'd seen me in the early hours of this morning. There's something I wanted to ask you. You do know *something* about drowning, don't you?'

The grin was wide. 'A bit.'

'Well, the pain I was in when I was underwater was terrible. Like being crushed. Believe me, if you want a way out of this vale of tears don't ever think of drowning. Then I seemed to get through that and everything was calm and pleasant. I knew I was going to die but it didn't bother me. The thing is I know I opened my mouth. I breathed in water. Not a drop seems to have got into my lungs.'

He stared at her and then he sat down in the chair opposite.

'You're asking me why you aren't *dead?*'

'If it's not too silly a question when one is patently alive and kicking. I mean, you don't want to believe in miracles, do you? They sort of seem embarrassing. Sunday tabloid stuff.'

'It really bothers you, doesn't it? Most people are just glad they've made it back. Anyway, there is one of two reasons. If you're holding your breath for any length of time carbon monoxide builds up in the blood and the brain doesn't function properly. One becomes confused.'

'I might have thought I breathed in sea water but in fact I didn't?'

'And then there is the ten per cent of people who drown when in fact no water gets into the lungs. In these people when a breath sucks water into the windpipe so it touches the vocal cords there's an immediate contraction of the muscles around the larynx. It's called laryngospasm. It's really terrifically powerful and it overcomes the breathing reflex.'

'But they still die? I mean, eventually?'

'They suffocate. OK?'

'OK.'

He grinned. 'Though I have seen one or two miracles since I began doctoring. I put them under the heading of unusual phenomena.' He got up. 'You look as though you'll last a good few years yet. I'd put it all out of your mind and get on with things.'

'I expect I shall.' And then, almost to herself: 'It was such a shock to find myself still alive.'

'Well, I must be off. Good luck.'

Mitch's eyes turned to the great bunch of lilies. Paul, coming in after showing the doctor out, told her: 'They're from Ishbelle and her mother. I expect Sissy told them you were out of hospital and staying here.

There's a card.'

'He's a schoolteacher, for God's sake,' Mitch said. 'It was awful.' Ishbelle at first seeming so grown up and then that bone-juddering squeal: 'M-mummy!' 'What the hell got into him?'

'Do you remember that terrible row we heard next door? When we were having dinner?'

'Sure.'

'The next day she had all the locks changed and stuck his suitcases out on the drive. That's the story going round the village, anyway. When she was clearing out all his stuff Coral found Ishbelle's diary. She and her friend used the boathouse like a ... well, a sort of den I suppose. The really odd thing was that with the diary were two non-matching socks.'

'Sissy told me that she was shown the clothing worn by the corpse. There was a sock missing.'

'Really? Well, all the stuff is now with Inspector Jain.'

'This was a simple case. You know? Find Rosie. But all sorts of other events kept overtaking things.'

'Other bits of life. And death.'

'And crazy people. Arthur Trimble's got to be crazy. Hasn't he?'

'Don't ask me. Maybe not much more than your usual dirty old man in a raincoat.

He had just been thrown out by his wife. I can tell you from experience. That makes you seriously furious.'

'You're saying I almost got done in because at the time I was a handy substitute for Arthur's wife? At least Haddi killed the woman he intended to kill,' Mitch said.

'I'm going to make us some tea in a minute,' said Paul. 'But there is something you should be starting to think about while I'm doing it.'

'I don't want to think.' Mitch was again aware of the scent of lilies.

'Oa Bone was on the phone while you were sleeping. He wants me to sort of sound you out. Wonders whether you'll consider working for him.'

'Really? I can't think why.' Mitch was non-plussed.

'He did buy a radio station. Remember?'

'My God. So he did.'

'Look, Mitch, you'd better realise it. You're a bit of a hero round here. The local shop has sent up some scones and clotted cream for your tea. A basket of eggs has turned up on the doorstep. And a bunch of tulips. Don't look so astonished. People can like you if they want to, can't they? There's no crime in that. Is there? You saved the life of that young kid. At least you won't persuade others you didn't.'

'Well, there you go...' and she was still

astonished. She hadn't got round to thinking about that bit yet. 'A.J. will have something to say about it all. She's not into danger and all that stuff. She doesn't seem to think it respectable somehow.' And Mitch, still full of her journey from a watery death, saw that the life she'd come back to could be very different from the old.

Born again, she thought. Can that ever be true? 'With strawberry jam,' she said.

'What?'

'The scones. Cream. And strawberry jam.'

'You want jam on it?'

'Why not?'

The publishers hope that this book has given you enjoyable reading. Large Print Books are especially designed to be as easy to see and hold as possible. If you wish a complete list of our books please ask at your local library or write directly to:

Magna Large Print Books
Magna House, Long Preston,
Skipton, North Yorkshire.
BD23 4ND

This Large Print Book for the partially sighted, who cannot read normal print, is published under the auspices of

THE ULVERSCROFT FOUNDATION

International Financial Aid

International Financial Aid

WOLFGANG G. FRIEDMANN

GEORGE KALMANOFF

ROBERT F. MEAGHER

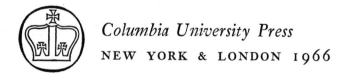

Columbia University Press

NEW YORK & LONDON 1966

c

237508

Ecows.

Preface

THE PRESENT BOOK is the end product of a five-year research project directed by the undersigned, on behalf of the Columbia University School of Law.

The problems and issues discussed in this volume are only to a minor extent of a legal character. They are essentially problems of administrative structure and economic policy. But a knowledge of the great edifice of international development institutions and of the major issues of development aid is today a vital part of the equipment of the international lawyer. Neither the policy-maker nor the administrator nor the corporation counsel can be content with a study of the strictly legal aspects of investment and aid. Institutional and policy problems have become part and parcel of the complex decision-making processes concerned with the flow of capital and other forms of assistance from the economically developed into the economically less developed countries.

Like our previous research projects, on legal aspects of foreign investment and joint international business ventures, the present project has been made possible by a grant from the Ford Foundation to Columbia University. It has given us opportunities for contact and exchanges of views with government officials, scholars, and businessmen of many countries on problems of vital concern to us all. I should like to mention specifically the three-day Conference held at Columbia University's Law School and Arden House in March, 1965, at which some fifty senior representatives of the United Nations, the World Bank, and many other national and international institutions concerned with the giving and use of aid came together to discuss a draft of the materials which are presented in this book in their final form.

At a time when there is a great gap between the increasing needs of the developing countries and the readiness of the world's richer countries to continue, let alone increase, aid on the scale of the last decade, it is hoped that the present study may make at least a modest contribution to the understanding of this overwhelmingly urgent problem.

WOLFGANG G. FRIEDMANN

Acknowledgments

IN THE COURSE of the research, which was carried out during the period 1961–65, twelve interim reports were issued. The authors of this book, who constituted the headquarters staff of the research project, had the assistance of officials and persons in private life in many countries who are too numerous to list completely. Our thanks are due to them all for the invaluable cooperation we received.

Individual reports were prepared by the following authors:

1. Public International Development Financing in East Africa (Kenya, Uganda, and Tanganyika), January, 1962. Robert F. Meagher.
2. Methods and Policies of Principal Donor Countries in Public International Development Financing: A Preliminary Appraisal, July, 1962. Wolfgang G. Friedmann.
3. Public International Development Financing in Turkey, November, 1962. Osman Okyar and Cihat Iren, assisted by Robert F. Meagher.
4. Public International Development Financing in Thailand, February, 1963. Robert F. Meagher, assisted by Paul Sithi-Amnuai.
5. Public International Development Financing in Israel, March, 1963. Chaim Ben-Shachar.
6. Public International Development Financing in Colombia, June, 1963. Prepared in cooperation with Raymond F. Mikesell, Associate Director, Institute of International Studies and Overseas Administration, University of Oregon, in connection with a Ford Foundation grant to the Institute for studies of foreign aid and technical assistance; Jorge Franco Holguin, coauthor, Economic Development Studies Center, University of the Andes, James Anthony S. Ternent and Rafael Isaza, assistants.
7. Public International Development Financing in Senegal, November, 1963. Robert F. Meagher.
8. Public International Development Financing in Chile, March, 1964. Prepared in cooperation with Raymond F. Mikesell in connection with a Ford Foundation grant to the Institute for studies of foreign

aid and technical assistance; Felix Ruiz and Alfonso Inostroza, assistants, Institute of Economics, University of Chile, Alejandro Escobar Cerda, Carlos Hurtado, Juan Braun, and Flavio Levine, assistants.

9. Public International Development Financing in India, July, 1964. R. K. Hazari and S. D. Mehta, assisted by Robert F. Meagher.

10. Public International Development Financing in Greece, September, 1964. Greek Center of Economic Research—Diomedes D. Psilos and Richard M. Westebbe.

11. Public International Development Financing in Sudan, April, 1965. Robert F. Meagher, assisted by Gloria Gaston and Rashid Abdel Wahab.

12. Seminar on Policies and Experiences in International Development Financing, 1965, held at Columbia University Law School and Arden House, March 12–14, a summary, April, 1965.

George Kalmanoff acted as editor for all of the above-mentioned studies.

W. G. F.

Contents

Tables

Abbreviations of Agencies and Organizations

AID	Agency for International Development
CDC	Commonwealth Development Corporation
CDFC	Commonwealth Development Finance Company Ltd.
CD&W	Colonial Development and Welfare
CIAP	Inter-American Committee for the Alliance for Progress (Comité Interamericano para la Alianza para el Progreso)
CMEA	Council for Mutual Economic Assistance (used by Communist countries)
COMECON	Council for Mutual Economic Assistance (used by Western countries)
CORFO	Corporación de Fomento de la Producción
COPERE	Comité de Programación Económica y de Reconstrucción
DAC	Development Assistance Committee of the OECD
DEG	Deutsche Gesellschaft für Wirtschaftliche Zusammenarbeit (Entwicklungsgesellschaft) mbH
DTC	Department of Technical Cooperation
ECAFE	Economic Commission for Asia and the Far East
EDF	European Development Fund
EEC	European Economic Community
EIB	European Investment Bank
ERP	European Recovery Program
EXIMBANK	Export-Import Bank
FIDES	Fonds d'Investissement pour le Développement Économique et Social des Territoires d'Outre-Mer
FIDOM	Fonds d'Investissements des Départements d'Outre-Mer
FAC	Fonds d'Aide and de Coopération
IBRD	International Bank for Reconstruction and Development
ICICI	Industrial Credit and Investment Corporation of India
IDA	International Development Association
IDB	Inter-American Development Bank
IFC	International Finance Corporation
IFCT	Industrial Finance Corporation of Thailand
IMF	International Monetary Fund
KW	Kreditanstalt für Wiederaufbau

NEDB	National Economic Development Board (Thailand)
OAS	Organization of American States
OECD	Organization for Economic Cooperation and Development
OECF	Overseas Economic Cooperation Fund
OEEC	Organization for European Economic Cooperation
OSAS	Overseas Service Aid Scheme
OTCA	Overseas Technical Cooperation Agency
SATI	Sudan American Textile Industry Co. Ltd.
SUNFED	Special United Nations Fund for Economic Development
TTEC	Thai Technical and Economic Committee
UEB	Uganda Electric Board
UNCTAD	United Nations Conference on Trade and Development

1. Introduction

THE PROBLEM of development of the less developed countries, which now constitute a substantial majority of the family of nations, is second in importance only to the future of mankind itself. The question of the goals and methods of development raises many complex and interconnected problems. Sociological, political, economic, and institutional aspects are closely intertwined. It is too late, in this day and age, to ask whether the disturbance of settled and static ways of life in so many non-Western communities will ultimately prove beneficial or detrimental to them.

It was the nations of the Western world that, for their own purposes, disturbed these ways of life by political conquest, by economic penetration, or by a combination of both. Economically, their chief objective was the exploitation of raw materials and agricultural produce needed for their own fast-growing economies. Together with the disturbance of the settled ways of life, these intrusions awakened new aspirations and ambitions, and they exposed a limited elite from the newly opened-up countries to the influence of Western ideas and standards.

When a variety of circumstances, in the postwar period, encouraged the claims for political independence, the new nations, long made aware of the stark discrepancies between aspirations—modeled upon the standards of their former masters—and available resources did not—and probably could not—choose to return to their former static ways of life. Development became the universal ambition. This did not mean only the improvement of living standards, it meant, more importantly, the diversification of the economies of countries that for the most part had depended on either self-sufficient agricultural economies or on the exportation of staple

commodities and raw materials. The goal now becomes a more or
less ambitious industrialization as a means of raising the general economic level and satisfying the growing size and sophistication of
economic aspirations. The noneconomic effects of these new
economic goals—generally formulated in development plans—were
of no less importance than the economic ones.

The new aspirations imply a shift from agricultural and village
communities to towns and cities; they imply many other profound
changes in the ways of living, and they create above all an urgent
need both for capital necessary to build the new factories and utilities and for the skills necessary to transform a generally agricultural,
static, and unsophisticated people into one that can supply the needed
scientists, technicians, teachers, managers, doctors, and administrators.

Because, overwhelmingly, the developing countries are desperately short both of the necessary capital and of the needed skills,
they had to look more and more to the outside world for assistance
and to that extent had to temper their ardent nationalist aspirations.
And it is one of the more significant and hopeful phenomena of our
deeply troubled world that the more advanced and developed members of the family of nations have by and large accepted the challenge and the responsibility to assist in development. Out of the
beginnings created by the establishment of the International Bank
for Reconstruction and Development in 1944 and the Marshall Plan
in 1947, as well as British and French governmental aid organizations
set up in 1946, there has developed a complex system of both international and bilateral aid-giving institutions and mechanisms. These
now form part of the fabric of international life.

The present study is concerned with only one of the many major
facets of the development process, i.e., the comparative analysis of
the methods and policies in international financial aid to the less
developed countries.

International capital movements, which augment the resources
available for investment in the less developed countries, take place in
both the private and the public sectors. Earlier research carried out
in the international legal studies program of the Columbia University
School of Law was concerned with various aspects of *private* international capital movements. That research resulted in the publica-

tion of *Legal Aspects of Foreign Investment* [1] and *Joint International Business Ventures.* [2] A subsequent five-year research project —of which the present book is the end product—is mainly concerned with *public* international capital movements to the less developed countries, i.e., with resources that leave the donor country or institution as public funds and reach the recipient through public agencies.

The private sector, however, may also be involved at the donor or the recipient end. In the last analysis, the private sector is, of course, the ultimate source for all public funds, even those which become available as governmental appropriations out of tax revenues or as a result of the government's power to tax, except in "centrally planned economies," where all major economic activities are carried out by public enterprises. A distinction must, however, be made between private funds which are tapped by taxation and those which are voluntarily invested for public aid purposes in response to official guarantees or inducements. Examples of the latter are private purchases of World Bank bonds, the proceeds of which are loaned for development projects in less developed countries, or in private direct investments made in less developed countries, under U.S. government investment guarantees. On the recipient side, international funds of public origin may either be directly invested by public agencies in electric power or other projects or administered by public agencies as a supplement to the recipient country's general pool of foreign exchange, but, alternatively, international loans of public origin may be extended directly to private enterprises or indirectly through development banks.

Although such qualifications make it difficult to establish an absolutely clear differentiation between public and private international capital movements, the phenomenon with which we are here concerned is that of international capital movements to the less developed countries which arise as a result of international public efforts designed to expand the resources for investment in such countries. The efforts may result in indirect effects on the private sector—and indeed, for the most part, they are designed to stimulate activity

[1] Wolfgang G. Friedmann, ed., and Richard C. Pugh, asst. ed., *Legal Aspects of Foreign Investment* (Boston, Little, Brown, 1959).
[2] Wolfgang G. Friedmann and George Kalmanoff, *Joint International Business Ventures* (New York, Columbia University Press, 1961).

ultimately in the private sector—but for the present the efforts result mostly in the movement of capital through public channels.

In the two decades which have elapsed since the end of World War II, international financial aid for development has steadily expanded in volume and has increased in complexity. A considerable variety of new institutions have been created to carry out the policies which have evolved in this field. Briefly and simply stated, the purpose of our research has been to survey comprehensively and comparatively the policies and methods pursued by the numerous national and international aid institutions on the donor side, to analyze the overall operations of these institutions in a selected range of aid-receiving countries and their participation in selected cases of projects and programs, and to bring into better focus the elements which must be weighed in resolving the policy issues in international financial aid.

An overall picture of international financial aid is first presented in a chapter which summarizes its quantitative dimensions and principal characteristics as they have evolved during the postwar period. This picture is drawn from official sources that have assumed the responsibility for keeping a continuing account of the flow of aid, principally the Organization for Economic Cooperation and Development of the Western bloc powers and its subsidiary Development Assistance Committee. Trends in the total magnitudes of aid, based on certain definitions which are used in these responsible official agencies, are examined. The principal characteristics of the flow of resources which falls within these definitions are viewed in terms of the principal countries and international agencies by which it is provided, the forms or categories into which it may be classified, the terms and conditions on which it is supplied, and the geographic pattern of its distribution around the world. This overall background makes it possible to appreciate better the particular roles played in the process by the individual institutions and countries.

The succeeding chapter presents a comprehensive and comparative account of the aid methods and policies of the countries and institutions on the donor side. A preliminary monograph issued in July, 1962,[3] analyzed for the most part the bilateral aid of the

---

[3] Wolfgang Friedmann, *Methods and Policies of Principal Donor Countries in Public International Financing: A Preliminary Appraisal*, Columbia University School of Law, Report No. 2, July, 1962.

principal Western bloc powers. This has been brought up to date and expanded to include aid of the Sino-Soviet bloc, aid administered by international and regional agencies, and the mechanisms which have evolved to coordinate the aid dispensed by the numerous national and international sources. Thus, the bilateral foreign aid machinery of the principal donor countries—the United States, France, the United Kingdom, West Germany, Japan, and the Sino-Soviet bloc—is viewed comparatively. The World Bank group of agencies—the World Bank, the International Development Association, and the International Finance Corporation—constituting the only multilateral development financing agencies of worldwide scope, are analyzed with respect to their membership, sources of funds, volume of loan operations, types of activities financed, loan terms and conditions, and other activities which support and supplement their primary financing functions. The only other multilateral aid available on a worldwide basis is that of the technical assistance and preinvestment financing programs of the United Nations, which are described in the chapter. Analyses similar to those of the World Bank group of agencies are made of the regional financing institutions—the Inter-American Development Bank and the development financing agencies of the European Economic Community, consisting of the European Development Fund and the European Investment Bank. The nature of the additional regional financial institutions which have recently been established (the African Development Bank) or are in the process of being established (the Asian Development Bank) is also described. The discussion of the network of donor institutions is completed by consideration of the various types of coordinating mechanisms which have been developed—the consortia, consultative groups, and coordinating groups for aid to individual recipient countries; some loosely knit attempts to coordinate aid to groups of countries or on a regional basis; and the Development Assistance Committee to coordinate the broad, overall aid policies of the major sources of aid in the world, namely, the Western bloc powers. This chapter, therefore, affords a thorough view of the policies, institutions, and methods of international financial aid on the donor side.

A large part of the work conducted under our research project consisted of original field studies of the experiences with international financial aid of selected countries in Latin America (Colombia and Chile), Africa (East Africa, i.e., Kenya, Tanganyika, and Uganda; Senegal; and the Sudan), Asia (India and Thailand), and the Middle East and South Europe (Israel, Greece, and Turkey). These studies were carried out wherever possible in cooperation with agencies or individuals in the respective countries, and monographs were issued for each of the ten countries or groups of countries mentioned above. The studies included aid to the respective recipient countries from all sources and so serve to illustrate in a concrete way the operations of virtually all the donor institutions, national and international, whose overall policies and practices are analyzed in Chapter III. The details of the recipient country studies are reduced to their essential features in Chapter IV by an analysis of the aid experience of each of the ten countries in terms of the particular type of development problem faced by the respective country, the nature of the aid it has received, its administration of aid, and its principal problems in aid. These country summaries show the kinds of national situations in the various regions of the world which are encountered in international financial aid and the role played by international aid in relation to the total national efforts and problems.

Further illustration of international financial aid in practice is afforded by the seven cases of projects and programs assisted by external financing, which have been selected from the detailed recipient country studies and are presented in Chapter V. The picture drawn here supplements that of the role of aid in relation to total country programs and problems by showing how it has been provided and administered in a variety of individual situations. The cases illustrate in detail the manner of operation of various types of national and international donor agencies in different specific projects and programs around the world.

Following the comprehensive analysis of the institutions, policies, and methods of international financial aid on the donor side and the selective analysis of how it has worked out in practice in individual recipient countries and cases of financing, the principal policy issues faced by the international community in this field are discussed in Chapter VI. Some fifteen different aspects of the subject which emerge from the analyses on both the donor and the recipient sides are reviewed. For each of these aspects, which, of course, overlap to some extent and are not necessarily mutually exclusive, the principal considerations and forces at work are set forth. The purpose has been to put into better focus the elements that must be considered in resolving the issues. There has been no pretense at offering facile solutions to these highly complex problems. We have been assisted in our effort to define the issues by the discussions at an international colloquium held at the Columbia Law School and at Arden House in mid-March 1965, in which some fifty senior aid administrators from international aid agencies and from national donor and recipient aid agencies participated. Drafts of most of the chapters in the present book were presented as background documents for the conference. A summary of the discussions at the conference was issued in April, 1965, as the final monograph of our research project.[4] That monograph constituted a point of departure for the discussion of the principal policy issues in international financial aid which is contained in Chapter VI.

Finally, a postscript on the future of international development aid is presented in Chapter VII.

A bibliography of selected references for the principal chapters is found at the end of the text.

[4] Seminar on Policies and Experiences in International Development and Financing held at Columbia University School of Law and Arden House, Harriman, N.Y., March 12–14, 1965. Report No. 12, *A Summary*, April, 1965.

II. Overall Magnitudes and Characteristics of Aid

Magnitudes

INTERNATIONAL financial aid for developing countries has come to represent one of the most important positive efforts in international relations since the end of World War II. It has steadily grown in volume, and the pace of its growth has quickened in recent years as greater emphasis has been placed on the need to bring the poorer nations up to acceptable standards of living. Representative of this emphasis are the designation by the United Nations of the 1960s as the Decade of Development, the organization in 1960–61 of a coordinating Development Assistance Committee (DAC) by the twenty-one-nation Organization for Economic Cooperation and Development (OECD) of the Western powers, and the setting in motion of machinery by the UN Conference on Trade and Development held in the spring of 1964 to work out ways and means of meeting the financial requirements of development through trade.

It is not our purpose to go into any elaborate analysis of the quantitative aspects of international financial aid to developing countries. As background, however, for our survey of the policies, institutions, and methods involved in the carrying out of the international aid effort, it is of interest to have an idea of its general orders of magnitude in recent years. For this, we resort to the compilations of the authoritative agencies in the field.

The body most comprehensively concerned with international financial aid for developing countries is the DAC of the OECD. The OECD itself is made up of twenty-one powers of the Western bloc, including the United States, eighteen European countries, Canada, and Japan. International financial aid for the developing countries has come overwhelmingly from the economically advanced countries in this group, though some of the OECD countries themselves, namely, Greece, Spain, and Turkey, are in the category of developing rather than advanced countries. The DAC, in turn, is made up of the thirteen most important capital-exporting countries of the OECD and Australia.[1] These are Austria, Belgium, Canada, Denmark, France, Germany, Italy, Japan, the Netherlands, Norway, Portugal, the United Kingdom, and the United States. The economically advanced countries of the OECD which are not in the DAC are Sweden and Switzerland.

The total flow of international financial resources to the developing countries is kept under constant review by the DAC and the OECD, even though they do not have jurisdiction over all the sources of the flow.[2] This review covers resources that are available on a bilateral basis as well as those that are channeled through multilateral institutions. And, with respect to the ultimate sources of the flow, it includes the members of the DAC itself, the industrial countries of the OECD which are not DAC members,[3] three industrial countries which are not OECD members (Finland, New Zealand, and the Union of South Africa), and eight countries designated as being in the Sino-Soviet bloc (the Soviet Union, Bulgaria, Czechoslovakia, Hungary, Poland, Rumania, mainland China, and East Germany). The developing countries are taken to mean all countries other than those mentioned, i.e., in Europe, Greece, Spain, Turkey, and Yugoslavia (which is not classed as a member of the Sino-Soviet bloc); all in Africa except the Union of South Africa; all in Asia except Japan; all in the Middle East; and all in Latin America. Some developing countries such as Israel, Egypt, Kuwait, and Yugoslavia are also providers of aid, but they are classified as

[1] Austria joined the DAC on March 8, 1965, and Australia joined in March, 1966. The statistics presented in the present chapter for DAC countries as a group do not include data for Austria or Australia. In any case their aid contributions are quite small.

[2] The United Nations also maintains and publishes such statistics. For example, see its *International Flow of Capital 1959–1961* and *World Economic Survey 1963*. UN data on official capital are virtually identical with those of the OECD, although there are some statistical and conceptual differences with respect to private capital, which are now in the process of being reconciled. See OECD, *The Flow of Financial Resources to Less Developed Countries, 1956–1963*, pp. 28–29.

[3] Plus the multilateral contributions of Iceland, Ireland, and Luxembourg.

recipients in these reviews. With some thirty donors and seventy-seven recipients and numerous categories of international financial resources, the question of just what is the magnitude of aid is bound to involve some complications.

Besides the matter of which are donor and which are recipient countries, the question arises as to what is meant by the flow of international financial resources. This is considered by both the DAC and the OECD to refer to actual transfers of resources (except military), whether in cash or in kind, net of repayments of the principal amounts of any previous loans or investments. Commitments of loans or of resources in other forms are, of course, important as indications of current policies, but it is the actual disbursements by which the flow is measured.

By virtue of the existence of multilateral agencies, a distinction must be made between flows from donor countries and flows to recipient countries. Flows from donor countries on a bilateral basis are naturally always identical with flows to recipient countries. In any given year, however, there is no necessary identity between the flows from donors to multilateral agencies on the one hand and from multilateral agencies to recipients on the other. Resources are collected by multilateral agencies in various ways without any direct relation to all the specific uses to which they are to be put. They are gathered in advance of the granting of commitments. There is always at least some lag between commitments and disbursements. And some of the donors (of inconvertible currencies) to multilateral agencies are in the general category of recipients, while some of the recipients of multilateral agency loans are in the general category of donors. The matter of the magnitude of aid handled through multilateral agencies therefore involves some specific definition.

Resources flow to recipient countries from both official and private sources in donor countries. There are various motivations behind the flow, connected to a greater or lesser extent with aiding development. Governments may grant surplus foods or sell them for local currencies primarily to rid themselves of a problem. They may grant loans to promote their own exports and to maintain their own domestic employment. They may, for no reason except the granting of aid, donate the services of technical experts gratis, or they may extend loans which do not have to start being repaid for ten years and then are repaid over a thirty-year period. They may guarantee credits granted by private sources, which might otherwise not be available. Private interests may make direct investment or buy bonds exclusively for reasons of profit. In all of these aspects, the line cannot easily be drawn between what can be considered aid and what resources would move to the less developed countries even in the absence of an international aid effort. In any case, it would seem to be the effect rather than the intention, i.e., the actual movement of resources in certain forms, that really matters.

It is thus obvious that, in any case, some arbitrary definitions have to be adopted to determine the actual magnitude of financial aid that flows to the developing countries. Whether one definition or another is adopted is of less importance than having the terms clearly defined, so that the magnitudes can be interpreted meaningfully. The definitions adopted by the DAC and the OECD are identical with one exception: the OECD includes all loans and guaranteed export credits with a maturity of more than one year, while the DAC includes only loans and credits with a maturity of more than five years. Otherwise, they both include official capital in the form of grants, in cash or in kind, including indemnification and reparation payments; grantlike contributions, such as loans repayable in recipients' currencies and sales of commodities for recipients' currencies; official loans repayable in foreign exchange; official contributions to multilateral agencies; private bilateral direct and portfolio investments and loans; private portfolio investments in multilateral agencies; and government-guaranteed private export credits.

Using the broadest type of definition, the DAC estimated the total flow of financial resources to the less developed countries to have amounted to close to $10 billion in 1963.[4] This included the flow from all donor countries, including the Sino-Soviet bloc, and all loans and guaranteed credits with a maturity of more than one year. Loans and credits of more than one through five years of

[4] OECD, *Development Assistance Efforts and Policies, 1964 Review*, p. 31. Hereafter cited as *DAC 1964 Review;* also *DAC 1961, 1963,* and *1965 Review.* Note that the word "billion" is in accord with American usage, i.e., a thousand million, throughout this book.

maturity, however, amounted to only slightly more than $200 million. The total included somewhat more than $2 billion of private capital invested for profit and $300 million or more of grant assistance provided by private nonprofit institutions. Making allowance for the International Monetary Fund, which is usually not included with the multilateral organizations in DAC-OECD reviews because of the short-term nature of its assistance, disbursements from multilateral organizations amounted to an estimated $800 million or more. Official bilateral assistance from all sources, including only their loans of more than five years, thus accounted for some $6.6 billion, of which $5.7 billion came from DAC members.

The figure of close to $10 billion for 1963 represented an increase of about a third over 1959.[5] The movement of the principal components of the flow is discussed below.

Data compiled by the OECD show that the flow of official financial resources in recent years from its fifteen "industrial members," i.e., the twelve DAC countries mentioned above plus Austria, Sweden, and Switzerland, to less developed countries and multilateral agencies was about three times the annual average in the period 1950–55:[6]

Year	Billions of Dollars
1950–55 annual average	1.9
1956	3.3
1957	3.9
1958	4.4
1959	4.3
1960	4.9
1961	6.1
1962	6.0
1963	6.0

Furthermore, most of the increase was in real terms, since price increases during the period were moderate. While no precise price index for aid-financed imports is available, the OECD points out

[5] OECD, *The Flow of Resources, 1956–1963*, p. 25.
[6] *Ibid.*, p. 18. The figures include contributions to multilateral agencies by three OECD members, viz., Iceland, Ireland, and Luxembourg, besides the fifteen "industrial OECD" countries.

that the average unit values of exports of manufactured goods by eleven major OECD countries increased by about 4 percent from 1956 to 1963.[7]

These figures, as previously indicated, include loans of more than one through five years of maturity, besides longer-term loans. Gross official loans of one through five years maturity amounted to $62 million in 1956 and by 1963 had risen to $109 million, or by about 75 percent. The deduction of these figures would therefore reduce somewhat the upward trend noted, but the absolute amounts involved are small compared with the totals.

The upward trend is confirmed in data compiled by the DAC, which relate to twelve donor countries (all DAC members except Australia and Austria) and include loans only to the extent that they exceed five years in maturity. The total official flow of financial resources on that basis during the period 1956–64 was as follows:[8]

Year	Billions of Dollars
1956	3.2
1957	3.8
1958	4.3
1959	4.2
1960	4.9
1961	6.1
1962	6.1
1963	6.1
1964	5.9

The foregoing figures, both of the DAC and of the OECD, relate to the amounts of official contributions by the respective doner countries covered. They include their contributions to multilateral organizations as well as their bilateral contributions. As previously noted, however, the flows from the multilateral organizations to the developing countries do not necessarily equal the contributions of the donors to the multilateral agencies. The foregoing figures are therefore subject to some adjustment to obtain the actual flow of resources to the developing countries, although the adjustments are usually not large. These have been calculated by the DAC for the period 1960–63 as shown in Table 1.

[7] *Ibid.*   [8] OECD, *DAC 1965 Review*, p. 127.

TABLE 1

DAC Members' Contributions to and Flows
from Multilateral Agencies, 1960–63
(*Millions of Dollars*)

Year	Official Contributions by DAC Members to Multilateral Agencies	DAC Share (80%) of Flow of Resources from Multilateral Agencies to Developing Countries	Excess of Contributions over Flow (−) or of Flow over Contributions (+)
1960	655	307	−348
1961	811	342	− 469
1962	602	466	−136
1963	396	618	+222

Source: OECD, *DAC 1964 Review*, p. 30.

Thus, to adjust the figures of the flows *from* the donors to the basis of flows *to* the recipients, the sums of $348 million, $469 million, and $136 million should be subtracted from the $4.9 billion, $6.1 billion, and $6.1 billion, respectively, for the years 1960, 1961, and 1962; and $222 million should be added to the $6.1 billion for 1963. The net result over the four-year period 1960–63 is that the developing countries received some $731 million less than the previous figures indicate. It must also be borne in mind, however, that part of the flow from the multilateral agencies to the developing countries is attributable to private rather than official capital, since agencies such as the World Bank and the Inter-American Development Bank raise capital by selling their bonds to private investors. The net amount of such private portfolio investment came to $454 million in 1960–63, as shown in Table 8.

The first substantial disbursements under the aid programs of the countries of the Sino-Soviet bloc were made in 1956. Their amounts from 1956 through 1963, as quoted by the OECD, are shown on the following page.[9]

Whether private capital flows, except for grants by nonprofit organizations, should be included in a discussion of the magnitude of aid is, of course, highly questionable. There is no doubt, however, that some private capital flows occur in response to special official

[9] OECD, *Flow of Resources, 1956–1963*, p. 56. Estimate for 1963 by OECD secretariat.

Year	Millions of Dollars
1956	107
1957	87
1958	205
1959	161
1960	186
1961	294
1962	391
1963	425

incentives such as investment or export credit guarantees, tax concessions, or the subscription of capital on call to back bond issues by multilateral agencies. And, in any case, all private capital flows add to the financial resources available to the recipient countries. It is therefore significant to bear their magnitudes in mind in comparison with the flows of official capital.

The statistics and time series available on private capital flows to developing countries are not so reliable as those on official capital flows, obviously because the sources are not as easily identifiable and subject to control. They do not include private grants for development and welfare purposes. They are net of loan repayments and capital repatriations, but they relate only to capital movements originating in the industrial countries; they do not take into account investments abroad made by nations of the less developed countries. They include bilateral direct and portfolio investments and loans, government-guaranteed export credits,[10] and the purchases of securities of multilateral agencies.

The trend of private capital flows to the developing countries is the same whether the OECD series, with its broader coverage with respect to countries of origin as well as maturities of loans, is taken or whether the DAC series is taken. The trend is downward, or at best stationary, in marked contrast to the upward trend of official capital flows. The result is that private capital flows to the developing countries now amount to about a third to a fifth as much as official capital flows, while about a decade ago they were about equal to one another. The OECD series and the DAC series on net

[10] Changes in the outstanding volume of guaranteed export credits are taken to represent the flow of private export credits in the absence of adequate data of any other type.

flows of private capital to the developing countries are shown in Table 2.

TABLE 2

OECD and DAC Estimates on Net Private Capital Flows
to Developing Countries, 1956–64
(*Billions of Dollars*)

Year	OECD [a]	DAC [b]
1956	3.0	2.5
1957	3.7	3.4
1958	2.9	2.7
1959	2.8	2.3
1960	3.0	2.5
1961	3.1	2.7
1962	2.5	2.1
1963	2.4	1.9
1964	n.a.	2.7

[a] OECD, *Flow of Resources, 1956–1963*, p. 19.
[b] OECD, *DAC 1965 Review*, p. 127.

The total flow of international financial resources to the developing countries is thus estimated to have risen sharply in recent years, to a total of close to $10 billion per year, mostly because of an increase in the flow of capital from official sources. To give some perspective to this figure, it is of interest to relate the level which has been attained to the overall quantitative terms in which the central balance of payments problem of the less developed countries was presented to the UN Conference on Trade and Development in the spring of 1964. The UN Secretariat, in its preparatory analyses for the conference, found that the developing countries had a current account balance-of-payments deficit of $5 billion in 1959, which was financed by a net inflow of capital and official donations of the same amount.[11] The projected deficit for 1970 was estimated to be $20 billion, assuming the achievement by that year of the Development Decade target of a 5 percent per annum economic growth rate and a continuation of past trends and relationships of exports and imports and invisible current transactions. It was this gap of $20 billion (in 1959 prices) which would have had to be closed by a combination of trade, aid, and other measures if the growth target were to be achieved. With the net flow of capital

[11] UN, *World Economic Survey 1962*, pp. 6–7.

having reached close to $10 billion by 1963,[12] the problem of closing the gap by 1970 in these purely aggregative terms does not seem unmanageable. However, the growth target itself is a modest one,[13] there are of course many uncertainties about such projections, and the achievement of a desirable rate of economic growth is obviously not automatically assured by any given level of capital inflow.[14] The relationship between the most recent achievement and the target is nevertheless of some significance.

The Sources of Aid

Financial aid to the developing countries comes overwhelmingly from the members of DAC. As previously noted, the only other donors in the Western bloc are smaller countries, such as Sweden, Switzerland, and New Zealand, whose aid contributions are also necessarily relatively small. And the magnitudes of aid flows from the Sino-Soviet bloc, with a recent annual peak of somewhat more than $400 million, constitute only a fraction of the flows from the Western bloc industrial powers.[15]

As shown in Table 3, aid from the DAC countries is dominated by the United States. These figures relate to all long-term official capital as defined by DAC, including both that which flows on a bilateral basis and that which is channeled through multilateral organizations. The United States still accounts for about 60 percent of the total despite efforts in recent years by that country to have other donors increase their shares. Indeed, there has been somewhat of an increase, rather than a decrease, in the United States share during the last five years.

[12] Except for the flow of capital from nationals of the less developed countries to the industrial countries, estimated at somewhat larger than $300 million anually during the last few years. See OECD, *Flow of Resources, 1956–1963,* p. 30.

[13] The rate in 1950–59 averaged 4.65 percent per year.

[14] In the view of the chairman of the DAC, there is "no one figure which could purport to give expression to the needs for assistance by all the less developed countries. These needs differ greatly from country to country and are susceptible of rather rapid change within each country. They are a function not only of the degree of modernization but much more so of the relative ambitions and determination of the development planners and leaders, and of the existence and employment of the domestic resources necessary to make the foreign assistance fully operative." See OECD, *DAC 1964 Review,* p. 14.

[15] On the difficulties of comparing the flow of resources from the Sino-Soviet bloc with that from the Western bloc, see further below, Chapter III.

TABLE 3
Net Flow of Long-Term Official Capital to Developing Countries, by Principal Donor Countries, 1956–63
(Values in Millions of Dollars)

Year	TOTAL DAC COUNTRIES Value	%	UNITED STATES Value	%	FRANCE Value	%	GERMANY Value	%	UNITED KINGDOM Value	%	JAPAN Value	%	ALL OTHER DAC COUNTRIES Value	%
1956	3,206	100.0	1,996	62.3	648	20.2	149	4.6	205	6.4	61	1.9	147	4.6
1957	3,753	100.0	2,083	55.5	819	21.8	300	8.0	234	6.2	58	1.5	259	7.0
1958	4,285	100.0	2,388	55.7	884	20.6	278	6.5	276	6.4	254	5.9	205	4.9
1959	4,232	100.0	2,310	54.6	832	19.7	337	8.0	375	8.9	112	2.6	266	6.2
1960	4,898	100.0	2,850	58.2	842	17.2	324	6.6	406	8.3	125	2.6	351	7.1
1961	6,074	100.0	3,535	58.2	943	15.5	589	9.7	458	7.5	214	3.5	335	5.6
1962	6,043	100.0	3,713	61.4	977	16.2	427	7.1	418	6.9	165	2.7	343	5.7
1963	6,060	100.0	3,842	63.4	843	13.9	422	7.0	414	6.8	172	2.8	367	6.1
1964	5,908	100.0	3,534	59.8	841	14.2	460	7.8	491	8.3	178	3.0	404	6.9

Source: OECD, DAC 1965 Review, p. 127.

The other four major donors are France, West Germany, the United Kingdom, and Japan. The United States and these four countries together account for somewhat more than 90 percent of total DAC countries' official aid.

France, although the second largest, is well behind the United States. It now accounts for about 15 percent of total DAC aid. Its share has gradually moved down from a level of about 20 percent. The amounts of official aid from West Germany and the United Kingdom are of about the same order of magnitude, and their shares have held fairly steady at about 7 percent of the total for each. Japan's share, at about 3 percent of the total, is somewhat less than half that of West Germany or the United Kingdom.

The overwhelming proportion of aid continues to be dispensed on a bilateral basis, although some progress has been made recently in having a larger portion move through multilateral agencies. The relative standing of bilateral and mulitilateral aid is reflected in the data of Table 4, which relates to the countries of the DAC. These data establish a comparison at the point of flow to the developing countries between the bilateral aid from DAC countries and the aid received from multilateral agencies which is attributable to DAC countries. The multilateral flow on this basis accounted for only 10 percent of the total flow in 1963, but there has been a noticeable increase since 1960. During this period new agencies, such as the International Development Association, the Inter-American Devel-

TABLE 4

Flow of Official Bilateral and Multilateral Capital to Developing Countries Originating in DAC Countries, 1960–63
(*Millions of Dollars*)

Year	Bilateral Capital [a] (1)	DAC Share of Capital from Multilateral Agencies [b] (2)	Total (1) + (2) (3)	(2) as % of (3)
1960	4,210	307	4,517	6.8
1961	5,214	342	5,556	6.2
1962	5,334	466	5,800	8.0
1963	5,679	618	6,297	9.8

[a] OECD, *DAC 1964 Review*, p. 105.   [b] *Ibid.*, p. 30.

opment Bank, and the United Nations Special Fund, came into being or into full operation, and older agencies, such as the World Bank, stepped up their volume of activity.

The multilateral agencies included in the foregoing data consist of the World Bank group, i.e., the International Bank for Reconstruction and Development itself and its affiliates, the International Development Association, and the International Finance Corporation; the Inter-American Development Bank; the European Development Fund; and the UN technical assistance and relief agencies, comprising the regular and expanded programs of technical assistance, the United Nations Special Fund, UNICEF, the Relief and

TABLE 5
*Disbursements and Commitments by Multilateral Agencies
to Less Developed Countries, 1963
(Millions of Dollars)*

	Gross Disbursements		Commitments
IBRD loans	462.1 [a]		648.1 [b]
IFC loans and participations	11.6		13.5
IDA loans	104.6		209.9
IDB loans [c]	75.1		211.8
European Development Fund grants	67.5		84.6 [d]
UN Technical Assistance and Relief Agencies' grants	242.3		200.0 [e]
of which UNEPTA		38.5	n.a.
UNTA		27.7	n.a.
UNSF		38.4	n.a.
UNICEF		35.8	n.a.
UNRWA		34.4	n.a.
UNHCR		0.5	n.a.
UNFC		10.7	n.a.
Other		56.3	n.a.
Total	963.2		1,367.9 [e]

[a] Repayments to IBRD were $144.9 million.
[b] Less cancellations as of Dec. 31, 1963.
[c] Excluding loans and grants from the Social Progress Trust Fund.
[d] Includes $23 million of loan commitments to Greece by the European Investment Bank and an interest subsidy of $5.5 million for the five-year period of the loan.
[e] Estimate by OECD Secretariat.

Source: OECD, *Flow of Resources, 1956–1963*, p. 159.

Works Agency for Palestine Refugees in the Near East, the High Commission for Refugees, the Fund for the Congo, and the Korean Relief Agency. The relative importance of these agencies is suggested in the figures of Table 5 on their disbursements and commitments in 1963.

The origin of the long-term private capital that flows to the developing countries is shown in Table 6. The pattern is similar to that

TABLE 6

Net Flow of Long-Term Private Capital to Developing Countries, by Principal Country of Origin, 1960–64
(Values in Millions of Dollars)

	1960	1961	1962	1963	1964
Total DAC countries					
Value	2,532	2,608	2,079	1,945	2,726
%	100.0	100.0	100.0	100.0	100.0
United States					
Value	1,040	1,099	804	737	1,315
%	41.1	42.1	38.7	37.9	48.2
United Kingdom					
Value	432	386	213	213	309
%	17.1	14.8	10.2	11.0	11.3
France					
Value	367	347	310	336	447
%	14.5	13.3	14.9	17.3	16.4
West Germany					
Value	221	212	255	136	284
%	8.7	8.1	12.3	7.0	10.4
Italy					
Value	86	185	215	208	104
%	3.4	7.1	10.3	10.7	3.8
Japan					
Value	100	157	137	114	99
%	3.9	6.0	6.6	5.9	3.6
Netherlands					
Value	170	124	49	107	73
%	6.7	4.8	2.4	5.5	2.7
All five other DAC countries					
Value	116	98	96	94	95
%	4.6	3.8	4.6	4.7	3.6

Source: OECD, *DAC 1965 Review*, pp. 128–33, *DAC 1964 Review*, pp. 102–3, and *DAC 1961 Review*, p. 17.

for official capital, but there are some differences to be noted. The five principal donors of official capital also figure prominently in the private capital flow, but here there is a somewhat greater dispersion. The United States accounts for only somewhat more than 40 percent of the private capital instead of its 60 percent level for official capital. The United Kingdom and Japan, on the other hand, are somewhat more important as sources of private capital. And Italy and the Netherlands also figure much more prominently as exporters of private capital.

Categories of Aid

About 70 percent of bilateral aid, according to the DAC definitions, consists of grants and grantlike contributions (e.g., sales of commodities for local currencies), while 30 percent consists of loans, as indicated in Table 7. The increases in such aid that have been effected in recent years, however, have occurred mostly with the loan component. As recently as 1960, loans represented only 15 percent of total aid. Net loans from DAC countries repayable in foreign exchange, with maturities of more than five years, almost tripled from 1960 to 1964, having increased from slightly more than $600 million to more than $1.7 billion. The principal donors of aid all figure prominently as lenders, but their relative importance is somewhat different than with respect to the total of aid. West Germany is now the second most important lender after the United States, while France is less important as a source of loans than either West Germany or the United Kingdom.

Bilateral grants, including indemnification and reparation payments, increased only slightly, from $2,501 million in 1960 to $2,511 million in 1964, and their share of the rising totals consequently dropped appreciably. They include development grants to help finance infrastructure projects, budget support grants, and technical assistance grants. Indemnification and reparation payments constitute only a small part of bilateral grants. Such grants still constitute close to half of total aid and, looming as large as they do, have a representation of donor countries similar to that for total aid. The United Kingdom is, however, a substantially more important source of grants than West Germany.

Loans repayable in recipients' currencies, which are in effect akin to grants, have held fairly steady at about 5 percent of total aid. This technique has been adopted almost exclusively by the United States. It was eliminated in general development lending by the United States when the Development Loan Fund of that country was replaced in the fall of 1961 by the Agency for International Development, and the policy of lending with repayment in local currencies was replaced by a policy of lending with repayment in foreign exchange, though at very long terms. The technique was continued in loans to Latin America made out of the Social Progress Fund entrusted in mid-1961 by the United States for administration by the Inter-American Development Bank, but, as explained in a later chapter, the Social Progress Trust Fund is not to be replenished.

Sales of commodities for recipients' currencies, on the other hand, represent a much more sizable portion of total aid. They amount to about $1 billion annually, exclusive of the small portions of the sales proceeds available for use by the selling government. This category of aid is also provided exclusively by the United States, except for very small amounts supplied by West Germany. For example, in 1963 German aid of this type amounted to about $2 million. The local currency proceeds of the sales are either loaned or granted for investments in the recipient country, except for minor portions used in the recipient country for expenditures of embassies and other establishments of the donor country.

In the flow of funds from the multilateral agencies to the developing countries, on the other hand, loans are the dominant feature rather than grants. The volume of operations by the lending agencies, such as those in the World Bank group and the Inter-American Development Bank, is substantially larger than that of the agencies that extend grants, such as the UN technical assistance agencies and the European Development Fund. As indicated by the data in Table 5, loans, even on a net basis, accounted for somewhat more than 60 percent of the total flow from the multilateral agencies in 1963, compared with the 25 percent of loans in bilateral aid for that year. Furthermore, the activities of the multilateral lending agencies are expanding at a higher rate than those of the granting agencies, and the European Development Fund, which has hitherto extended grants only, will be making loans in the future as well.

TABLE 7

Flow of Official Bilateral Capital to Developing Countries from DAC Countries, by Categories, 1960–64

(Values in Millions of Dollars)

	1960		1961		1962		1963		1964	
	Value	%	Value	%	Value	%	Value	%	Value	%
Total, net	4,236 [a]	100.0	5,111 [b]	100.0	5,388	100.0	5,680	100.0	5,555	100.0
Bilateral grants	2,501	59.0	2,757	53.9	2,739	50.8	2,644	46.5	2,511	45.2
of which indemnification and reparation payments	133		143		157		140		126	000
Loans repayable in recipients' currencies, net	217	5.1	277	5.4	414	7.7	306	5.4	229	4.1
Sales for recipients' currencies [c]	901	21.3	895	17.5	871	16.2	999	17.6	1,056	19.0
Loans repayable in foreign exchange, for more than five years, net [d]	617	14.6	1,182	23.2	1,364	25.3	1,731	30.5	1,759	31.7

[a] Later revised to $4,210 million.
[b] Later revised to $5,214 million.
[c] Net of resources realized by donor country by use of these currencies.
[d] Including consolidation credits with maturities up to five years where the original and additional credit periods reach more than five years.

Source: OECD, DAC 1965 Review, pp. 128–33, DAC 1964 Review, pp. 106–9, and DAC 1961 Review, pp. 18–19.

The still heavy concentration of aid in the form of grants reflects particularly the activities of ex-colonial powers such as France and the United Kingdom.[16] Grants help finance economic and social infrastructure projects, current budgetary deficits, and technical assistance. This is particularly true in the poorest of the less developed countries and especially in many which have recently emerged from colonial status. In order to create the conditions in which productive economic enterprises can flourish, much investment is needed in transportation, power, water supply, educational, and health facilities. Although revenue-generating projects of this type are financed to a considerable extent by loan assistance, many are financed by grants because of their non-revenue-generating character or their slow yield or because of the balance-of-payments situation of the recipient country. The budgetary support type of assistance is found as a transitional phenomenon, especially in newly independent countries. Technical assistance, on the other hand, is an expanding area of assistance, in recognition of the need to make more effective the utilization of financial assistance.

No complete breakdown is available of grants for these various purposes. However, the flow of technical assistance to less developed countries in 1963 amounted to close to $1 billion, or 15 percent of the total disbursements by DAC countries for both bilateral and multilateral assistance programs. This level was a fifth higher than in 1962. Bilateral technical assistance in 1963 amounted to $848 million, or 32 percent of bilateral grants.

Loan assistance is provided to help finance specific capital projects as well as for more general purposes. The specific projects assisted are both in the public and the private sector, although there is a marked trend toward assisting projects in the private sector through more general loans to intermediate credit institutions in the recipient countries, such as development banks or other specialized financing agencies. The United States, France, the United Kingdom, and West Germany are all channeling increasing amounts of loans through development banks. This is also true of the World Bank group and the Inter-American Development Bank. Other types of general international loans provide overall balance-of-payments sup-

---

[16] For the differing philosophies of the principal donor countries, see Chapter III.

port or finance the importation of broad categories of capital goods or raw materials and semi-manufactured goods to permit the full utilization of existing plant capacity.

The sale of commodities for local currencies, which is done with agricultural products in surplus supply in the United States, such as wheat and fats and oils, is akin to grants for general balance-of-payments support. The recipient countries are able to consume these commodities without any expenditure of foreign exchange and can devote the foreign exchange thus saved to other imports. The payments by the purchasing country in local currency which are then loaned or granted back by the seller to the purchaser mean in effect no payment at all or the indefinite deferral of any repayment in the future.

The several categories that make up the flow of private capital to the developing countries are shown in Table 8. From 60 to 80 percent of the total is in the form of direct investment. The trend of such investment, around which there have been considerable fluctuations, tends to be more or less a level one. Direct investment has come to represent an increasing share of the declining totals of the private capital flow. The trend of bilateral portfolio investment and non-government-guaranteed lending, on the other hand, had been downward in absolute as well as relative terms, but there was a substantial recovery in 1964, when this category rose to some 20 percent of total private investment. There has been a steady rise in private export credits guaranteed by the governments of the capital-exporting countries. Private investment in the securities of the multilateral agencies has been subject to wide year-to-year fluctuations. Over all, the flow of private capital to the developing countries has probably been kept from declining still more than it has by official guarantee and inducement measures.

Terms and Conditions

International financial aid to the developing countries has been hardening in its terms by virtue of the relative decline in the share of grants and grantlike contributions. Aid in these forms is the "softest" of all, since it does not require repayment by the recipients. Furthermore, aside from the fact that grant aid has been generally declining, the grant aid is unevenly distributed around the world,

TABLE 8

Net Flow of Long-Term Private Capital to Developing Countries from DAC Countries, by Categories of Investment, 1960–64
(Values in Millions of Dollars)

	1960		1961		1962		1963		1964	
	Value	%	Value	%	Value	%	Value	%	Value	%
Total, net	2,532	100.0	2,751[a]	100.0	2,088	100.0	1,949	100.0	2,728	100.0
Direct investment	1,848	73.0	2,095	76.2	1,387	66.4	1,570	80.1[b]	1,630	59.8
Bilateral portfolio investment and other lending[c]	408	16.1	404	14.7	214	10.2	162	8.3[b]	560	20.5
Portfolio investment in multilateral agencies	174	6.9	77	2.8	219	10.5	−12	. . .	153	5.6
Guaranteed private export credits	102	4.0	175	6.3	268	12.9	227	11.6[c]	385	14.1

[a] Later revised to $2,608 million.
[b] Percent of gross positive total of $1,961 million.
[c] Excluding guaranteed export credits.

Source: OECD, DAC 1965 Review, pp. 128–33, DAC 1964 Review, pp. 106–9, and DAC 1961 Review, pp. 18–19.

and the terms of loans are therefore of particularly critical importance in the cases of certain recipient countries.

As loans repayable in foreign exchange have been assuming greater importance, the terms of the loans-interest rates, maturities, and grace periods have been made more lenient. There has been a recognition of the prospective problems for the recipient countries of repaying external debt, especially as the volume of borrowing has increased in the growing international effort to promote world economic development. Much consideration has been given by the DAC and its predecessor, the Development Assistance Group, to the terms and conditions of aid, in connection both with the equalization of contributions on the donor side and with the debt-servicing problems on the recipient side. The concern of the DAC is reflected in the Resolution on the Terms and Conditions of Aid which it adopted on April 3, 1963.[17] The Resolution calls for a continuing study of the subject and recommends to members, "that they relate the terms of aid on a case-by-case basis to the circumstances of each underdeveloped country or group of countries" and "that they make it their objective in principle to secure a significant degree of comparability in the terms and conditions of their aid, and so far as possible to eliminate or reduce discrepancies between them."

The progress that has been made in easing loan terms is shown in the characteristics of loans committed during 1963. There was some further easing of terms in 1964.[18] The proportion of bilateral loans with an interest rate of 5 percent or more committed by DAC members as a whole was not quite 40 percent in 1963, compared with 70 percent in 1961, while during this period the proportion of loans with interest of less than 3 percent rose from 19 to 40 percent. Repayment periods also lengthened. The portion committed for more than twenty years increased from one-third in 1961 to over one-half in 1962 and 1963. And the use of grace periods increased substantially.[19] At the same time, the share of "soft" loans from the multilateral lending agencies has been increasing. The World Bank has eased its own terms, and the volume of operations of its soft-loan affiliate, the International Development Association, has increased markedly. The Inter-American Development Bank has con-

[17] For the text of this Resolution, see OECD, *DAC 1964 Review,* pp. 97–99. [18] See OECD, *DAC 1965 Review,* pp. 84–89.   [19] *Ibid.,* p. 44.

currently developed plans to expand lending at soft terms out of its Fund for Special Operations.[20]

The terms of assistance extended by DAC countries are reflected in the data given in Tables 9 and 10, which relate to commitments made during 1963. Among the major donors, grants loom the largest in the case of France, where they account for as much as four-fifths of the total; this is not surprising, since most French aid goes to present and former colonial areas. Grants are the smallest in the cases of Germany and Japan, accounting for about a quarter of their total assistance and being heavily influenced by their reparations payments. Grants account for a little less than half of UK assistance, where they are also influenced by colonial ties, and they account for slightly more than 60 percent of U.S. aid, where grants include that country's substantial sales of surplus agricultural commodities for local currencies. Some of the smaller donors, namely, Belgium, Denmark, and Norway, also give most or all of their aid as grants, while others, namely, Canada, the Netherlands, and Portugal, give minor portions as grants, with Italy at the extreme end of the spectrum with virtually no grants at all.

The principal sources of loans repayable in foreign exchange, on the basis of commitments in 1963, are the United States ($1.5 billion), West Germany ($524 million), the United Kingdom ($241 million), Japan ($218 million), France ($173 million), Italy ($140 million), and Canada ($82 million).[21] The terms of U.S. loans are clearly the most lenient. Most U.S. loans are at less than 3 percent interest and for more than twenty years. Indeed, the typical U.S. development loan during the last several years has had a maturity of forty years, including a ten-year period of grace. There has, however, been some increase in interest rates though they are still generally below 3 percent. When the United States first shifted from the loan repayable in local currency to the long-term, low-interest loan repayable in foreign exchange, the interest rate charged was only ¾ percent. This was later raised to 2 percent following the grace period. U.S. aid legislation for the fiscal year ending June 30, 1965, raised the rates to 1 percent during the grace period and 2½ percent thereafter.

[20] See Chapter III for a detailed discussion of the loan terms of the multilateral agencies.
[21] OECD, *DAC 1964 Review*, p. 110.

German loans, on the other hand, have much stricter terms, although they are considerably more favorable than purely commercial terms. Almost all German loans have an interest rate of more than 3 percent, and a substantial portion are above 5 percent. About three-fourths of the loans have maturities of five to twenty years, although as much as a fifth are for more than twenty years. Inter-

TABLE 9

Commitments of Official Bilateral Assistance
to Developing Countries by DAC Countries,
Distribution between Grants and Loans,
and Distribution of Loans by Interest Rate, 1963
(Percent)

			LOANS [b]		
	Total Assistance	*Grants and Grantlike Contributions* [a]	*Less than 3% Interest*	*3% to less than 5% Interest*	*Interest of 5% and More*
Belgium	100.0	96.1	2.3	1.6	. . .
Canada	100.0	34.8	. . .	. . .	65.2
Denmark	100.0	100.0	. . .	. . .	. . .
France	100.0	80.1	5.4	6.7	7.8
Germany	100.0	23.8	2.0	43.0	31.2
Italy	100.0	0.9	. . .	1.5	97.6
Japan	100.0	26.9	. . .	1.5	71.6
Netherlands	100.0	38.8	. . .	25.1	36.1 [c]
Norway	100.0	86.5	[d]	[d]	[d]
Portugal	100.0	16.4	. . .[e]	83.6 [e]	. . .[e]
United Kingdom	100.0	47.8	12.5	2.5	37.2 [f]
United States	100.0	61.8	28.1	2.9	7.2
Total	100.0	56.1	18.4	8.0	17.5 [g]

[a] Including loans repayable in recipients' currencies and sales for recipients' currencies.

[b] For more than one year; loans of more than one to five years inclusive amounted to $165 million out of the total of $2,954 million.

[c] Including 6.4 percent of total assistance in the form of loans whose terms are not available.

[d] Terms not available for one loan representing 13.5 percent of total assistance.

[e] Based on 1962 information.

[f] Including 6.0 percent of total assistance in the form of loans whose terms are not available.

[g] Including 0.4 percent of total assistance in the form of loans whose terms are not available.

Source: OECD, *DAC 1964 Review*, p. 110.

est rates on UK loans tend to be somewhat higher than on German loans, but maturities are longer. Japanese terms are considerably stiffer than either German or British terms. None of Japan's loans are for more than twenty years, and its interest rates are mostly 5 percent and above.

The minor part of French aid which is extended in the form of loans is at moderate terms. More than half of the loans are at less than 5 percent interest. Most of the loans are in the category of five-to-twenty-year maturities, but 10 percent are for more than twenty years.

Italy and Canada have offered the least favorable terms, but Canada is undertaking new programs of lending at highly concessionary terms. All or almost all their loans have been at an interest rate of 5 percent or more, and maturities have not exceeded twenty years. Indeed, in the case of Italy, almost 20 percent of the loans have a maturity of no more than five years.

TABLE 10

Distribution by Maturities of Official Bilateral Loan
Commitments to Developing Countries by DAC Countries, *1963*
(*Percent*)

	Total Loans	*More than 1–5 Years Inclusive*	*More than 5–20 Years Inclusive*	*More than 20 Years*
Belgium	100.0	58.1	. . .	41.9
Canada	100.0	. . .	100.0	. . .
Denmark	. . .	. . .	. . .	. . .
France	100.0	2.7	87.6	9.7
Germany	100.0	3.0	76.0	21.0
Italy	100.0	18.7	81.3	. . .
Japan	100.0	13.8	86.2	. . .
Netherlands	100.0	. . .	17.2	82.8 [a]
Norway	100.0	. . .	100.0	. . .
Portugal	100.0	. . .	. . .	100.0
United Kingdom	100.0	1.1	20.8	78.1 [b]
United States	100.0	5.0	24.1	70.9
Total	100.0	5.3	44.6	50.1

[a] Includes 10.4 percent of total loans whose terms are not available.
[b] Includes 2.2 percent of total loans whose terms are not available.

Source: OECD, *DAC 1964 Review*, p. 111.

Most aid is tied to procurement in the donor country. This is, of course, not true of the minor part of total aid which is channeled through the multilateral lending and technical assistance agencies. On the other hand, some bilateral aid is tied by its very nature, e.g., aid in the form of surplus food and technical assistance. And the trend has been toward the tying of other types of bilateral aid as well, primarily because of balance-of-payments problems of the donor countries. About 70 percent of total bilateral aid is now tied. The Chairman of the DAC noted that in 1963 there was "a further increase in the proportion of assistance subject to procurement restrictions."[22] Many donor countries, however, are aware of the possible harmful effects of the tying of aid and have shown some tendency to mitigate them in various ways. These include the waiving of procurement restrictions in special circumstances and a concentration on projects for which the donor country offers competitive advantages. Furthermore, to the extent that aid is furnished for broad programs rather than specific projects, the recipient has a flexibility in the choice of products to be imported, which may reduce the harmful effects of noncompetitive purchasing.

Geographic Pattern

The distribution during recent years of aid from the Western bloc powers among the principal recipient countries is shown in Table 11. These data, available from OECD sources, include loans of one to five years' maturity, but these amount to less than 5 percent of the total and so do not alter the pattern significantly.

In 1963, 44 percent of the aid went to Asia (including the Middle East), 26 percent to Africa, 18 percent to Latin America, 7 percent to less developed countries of Europe, and the balance, 5 percent, to countries in various other areas. From 1960 to 1963, the amounts of aid to Africa increased only slightly, while the increases in aid to Latin America were quite marked. There were also substantial increases in aid to Asia and to the less developed countries of Europe.

The comparison among the various recipient countries and regions of aid on a per capita basis, bearing in mind their need for it

[22] OECD, *DAC 1964 Reviews*, p. 50.

on the basis of their different levels of development, suggests the complexity of the forces that determine the granting of aid. While there is some relationship between the amount of aid per capita to particular recipient countries and their relative level of development, the relationship is by no means a perfectly direct one. There are various motivations besides that of raising the level of per capita welfare that affect the flow of aid.

Asia as a whole has received less aid per capita than the average for all recipient countries, despite its low levels of living. This is in particular true of India, although, in view of its sheer size, India is the largest recipient of aid among the countries of the world. Pakistan, another large recipient, has received a somewhat above-average amount of aid on a per capita basis. South Korea and South Viet Nam, on the other hand, have received much higher than average aid per capita, obviously because of their strategic importance in the politico-military confrontation of East and West. Israel has received a still higher amount of aid per capita, though for different reasons, in this case because of its special access to aid of a semi-philanthropic nature and in the form of reparations, which was needed to keep the country afloat as a new nation with a rapidly expanding immigrant population and a paucity of natural resources.

The better-than-average per capita showing of Africa in aid reflects particularly the large amounts of aid received by North Africa. The French-speaking countries south of the Sahara have also received a high level of aid per capita but nowhere near as much as North Africa. The English-speaking countries of Africa, such as Kenya, Tanganyika,[23] and Uganda, have received aid either much closer to the average or even below the average on a per capita basis.

Following the spurt of recent years, Latin America has received an above-average amount of aid on a per capita basis. In view of its considerably higher level of welfare than that of Asia and Africa, Latin America can thus perhaps be said to have received a more than equitable share of aid. The largest recipient in Latin America has been Brazil, but Chile's showing has been much higher on a per capita basis. During the last couple of years Chile has received the highest amount of aid per capita among the Latin American repub-

[23] Which was renamed Tanzania upon its merger with Zanzibar in April, 1964.

lics. Colombia has been somewhat above the average, while Mexico, with a much better fortified economy, has been well below the average. The principal aid recipients in Europe in recent years have been Turkey and Yugoslavia. The showing of both has been well above average, Turkey because of its endemic balance-of-payments problems and strategic geographic location and Yugoslavia probably because of the special interest of the West in keeping it independent of the Soviet bloc.

TABLE 11

Geographic Distribution of Net Official Financial Flows to Less Developed Regions and Countries from Industrial OECD Member Countries and Multilateral Agencies Combined, 1960-63

	NET OFFICIAL FINANCIAL FLOWS (MILLIONS OF DOLLARS)				Per Capita, (dollars),	Population (millions),
	1960	1961	1962	1963	1963	1963
Total recipient countries	4,559	5,544	5,792	6,317	4.18	1,511
Asia	2,245	2,221	2,373	2,756	3.03	459
India	782	665	743	982	2.14	910
Pakistan	253	266	397	502	5.07	66
South Korea	251	229	236	263	9.74	22
South Vietnam	192	167	180	221	14.73	143
Israel	104	107	114	132	66.00	15
Indonesia	61	106	119	116	1.16	2
Formosa	107	115	80	74	6.17	27
Iran	31	138	64	28	1.27	2
Jordan	70	87	77	80	40.00	100
Thailand	50	42	56	46	1.59	12
Other	344	299	307	312	2.18	29
Africa	1,464	1,651	1,710	1,650	5.89	280
French franc area south of Sahara [a]	314	364	431	422	10.55	40
Algeria and Sahara	405	433	393	295	26.82	11
Egypt (U.A.R.)	201	119	193	201	7.18	28
Morocco	79	117	85	109	8.38	13
Congo (Leopoldville)	90	86	67	87	5.80	15
Liberia	10	27	79	34	34.00	1
Tunisia	62	87	65	74	18.50	4
Kenya	21	65	51	56	6.22	9
Tanganyika	10	40	46	29	2.90	10

TABLE 11 (*continued*)

	NET OFFICIAL FINANCIAL FLOWS (MILLIONS OF DOLLARS)				Per Capita, (dollars),	Population (millions)
	1960	1961	1962	1963	1963	1963
Portuguese overseas						
provinces	35	35	41	53	3.79	14
Libya	43	36	32	26	26.00	1
Uganda	20	25	30	21	3.00	7
Other	174	217	197	243	1.91	127
America	335	877	945	1,140	5.04	226
Brazil	52	342	181	202	2.59	78
Chile	17	130	138	147	18.38	8
Argentina	20	43	98	84	3.82	22
French overseas						
departments ᵇ	73	73	104	130	130.00	1
Colombia	−6	66	73	107	7.13	15
Venezuela	−5	−6	71	61	7.63	8
Mexico	16	64	52	86	2.26	38
Bolivia	12	24	36	53	13.25	4
Other	156	141	192	270	5.19	52
Europe	354	548	468	471	5.23	90
Turkey	128	178	228	221	7.37	30
Yugoslavia	66	169	176	178	9.37	19
Greece	43	68	35	39	4.33	9
Spain	80	102	4	1	0.03	31
Other	37	31	25	32	32.00	1
Oceania	30	38	60	26	5.20	5
Unallocated	131	209	236	274	...	...

ᵃ Including French overseas territories, whose net receipts were $20.2 million in 1960, $24.6 million in 1961, $30.3 million in 1962, and $28.9 million in 1963.
ᵇ Including Réunion.

Source: OECD, *Flow of Resources, 1956–1963*, pp. 44–45.

The main beneficiaries of aid from the Sino-Soviet bloc, on the basis of cumulative commitments through 1963, have been India, Egypt, Afghanistan, and Brazil. Algeria became an important recipient in 1963.[24] All these countries except Afghanistan figure prominently too in aid from the West, as indicated in Table 11. Afghanistan is also a recipient of aid from the West, though the aid is not large, primarily because of the small size and primitive state of the country.

[24] OECD, *Flow of Resources, 1956–1963*, p. 55.

The flow of aid from individual donors to particular recipients is to a large extent a reflection of the past and present political and economic ties among nations and of the special position of certain countries. This is indicated in the distribution for 1963 shown in Table 12. Among the principal donors, the aid of the United States is the most widely spread around the world. West Germany, with no recent colonial ties, also has a relatively wide geographic spread in its aid. The aid of the United Kingdom, on the other hand, is considerably concentrated in British Commonwealth countries and former colonies in Africa and Asia, while that of France is even more concentrated in associated countries, mainly in Africa. Japanese aid goes primarily to countries in Asia.

From the vantage point of the recipients, the showing of the United States is predominant in all major areas except Africa, where France is the main source. The less developed countries of Europe also receive substantial aid from the industrialized countries within the region. Besides its aid from France and the United States, Africa receives aid from a number of European countries and more recently from Communist China. A considerable number of European countries, Japan, and Canada are also represented in the minor part of aid to Latin America that comes from outside the United States. Aid to Asia comes mostly from the United States, West Germany, Japan, and the United Kingdom.

During recent years there has been a definite trend toward a greater geographic dispersion of aid.[25] The concentration by the United States on fewer countries in its aid of recent years, which is discussed in the succeeding chapter, has not involved any reduction in the geographic range. The greater geographic dispersion has occurred through an increase in the volume of aid dispensed through multilateral agencies as well as in the bilateral aid policies of individual donors. The aid of the multilateral agencies, being less subject to special political factors, is widely dispersed. Individual donors, especially those whose aid has been relatively concentrated geographically, are extending their assistance to more and more countries. UK aid has been steadily moving beyond the Commonwealth. And, though it is not as yet reflected to a great extent in

[25] OECD, *DAC 1964 Review*, pp. 39–41, and OECD, *DAC 1965 Review*, pp. 41–45.

TABLE 12

Distribution of Net Official Bilateral Financial Flows from Individual Industrial OECD Countries to Less Developed Regions, by Continent, 1963
(Millions of Dollars)

	Europe	Africa	America	Asia	Oceania	Unallocated	Total
Austria	0.10	0.06	0.10	2.05	...	−1.83	0.48
Belgium	1.60	75.79	...	...	...	−0.89	76.50
Canada	...	1.66	34.86	50.98	...	2.74	90.24
Denmark	−0.10	...	...	−0.50	...	1.20	0.60
France	...	654.50	144.30[a]	10.00	...	25.00	833.80
Germany	40.41	66.39	36.42	193.31	...	62.40	398.93
Italy	38.97	46.06	19.91	1.13	...	3.01	109.08
Japan	1.83	4.54	11.47	143.23	...	0.23	161.30
Netherlands	−0.50	...	16.90	...	...	1.50	17.90
Norway	...	0.43	...	1.42	...	0.57	2.42
Portugal	...	51.12	...	...	...	...	51.12
Sweden	0.20	2.18	0.11	4.60	...	0.11	7.20
Switzerland	−0.03	0.57	1.26	0.71	...	0.47	2.98
United Kingdom	29.01	178.73	28.54	114.77	8.17	10.58	369.80
United States	344.00	463.00	560.00	2,035.00	17.00	121.00	3,540.00
Total	455.49	1,545.03	853.87	2,556.70	25.17	226.09	5,662.35

Source: OECD, *Flow of Resources, 1956–1963*, p. 168.

[a] Of which $127.8 million went to French overseas departments (Guadeloupe, Guiana, Martinique, Réunion).

practice, France has taken policy decisions to increase assistance to countries outside the franc area. As a result, aid recipients are dealing or will be dealing with an increasing number of donors. Thus, as the volume of international financial aid to the developing countries increases, the scope of the assistance widens, and it grows in complexity. With the prospect that the needs for aid will continue to increase substantially before its objectives are realized and with the available resources being subject to limitations, it will be necessary to give concern to the utilization of the resources economically, so that overlapping, duplication, and waste are kept to a minimum.

III. Methods and Policies of Donor Countries and Institutions

SINCE the announcement of the Marshall Aid Plan in 1947—an historic landmark in the evolution of the concept of international economic aid—the methods and policies of economic aid, flowing from the more highly to the less developed countries, have gradually evolved into a permanent feature of postwar international relations. Economic development aid, as a vital aspect both of international organization and of the national policies of the industrially developed countries, has spread from the U.S. concept of the Marshall Plan to many other nations and from the World Bank to a growing number of other international institutions. The International Bank for Reconstruction and Development is now flanked by two affiliate institutions, the International Development Association and the International Finance Corporation. Regional international aid institutions, such as the Inter-American Development Bank and the European Development Fund, supplement the international institutions of worldwide scope.

The United States—still by far the largest single national aid-giver—has developed a permanent institutional structure, whose pillars are the Agency for International Development (AID) and the Export-Import Bank (EXIMBANK). The aid-giving machinery of some of the other major Western countries—notably Britain and France, which have for many years granted aid to their colonial empires and overseas territories—has become transformed, with the emergence of the former colonies as independent and overwhelmingly underdeveloped states; at the same time, their aid mechanisms are becoming increasingly institutionalized through the establishment of permanent agencies of aid administration. In recent years

West Germany—in the immediate postwar period a major recipient of Marshall aid—has become a major aid-giver, reflecting its great prosperity and status as a major industrial and technically developed state. More recently still, Japan has gone through a similar evolution. The policies and machineries of these, and many other nations that give aid on a smaller scale, have emerged out of the semi-secrecy that has enveloped these policies and procedures in the past, and they have become part of international coordinating mechanisms.

The major aid-giving countries, notably the United States, the United Kingdom, France, and West Germany, publish annual or periodic surveys of the institutions, principles, and processes of their economic assistance to the developing countries. Most of the donors meet with some of the major recipient countries through formal consortia under the guidance of the World Bank or the OECD or through less formal consultative groups, thus providing a link between the international aid-giving institutions and the various aid-giving nations.

In recent years the Communist countries—i.e., principally the Soviet Union and the more industrially developed East European countries such as Czechoslovakia and East Germany as well as Communist China—have become an increasingly important factor in international development aid. This is a reflection not only of the growing industrial and technological sophistication of these countries but also of their growing worldwide involvement in international affairs, which means competition for influence in the developing countries of Asia, Africa, and Latin America. The aid-giving methods of the Communist countries—which do not participate in the international lending institutions such as the World Bank—are in certain respects different from those of the Western world.

The present study is concerned with *public* international development financing. This indicates its objectives as well as its limitations. It is a study of the public aid policies of the major aid-giving states and the major supranational institutions. It is not a study of the structure and importance of commercial credit operations, nor does it attempt to appraise the adequacy of the total flow of funds into the underdeveloped world. This does not mean unawareness of the obvious interdependence between public development aid and private investment. If and when private investment from the developed countries in the less developed countries comes to operate in the way in which it does at the present time within the Western world, public development aid will eventually recede and fade away. At the present time, however, the inevitable preeminence of public aid is obvious.

There are, of course, certain twilight areas, certain government operations directly designed to assist private commerce and investment. These take today two major forms. One is government-backed export credit guarantees as they operate in a number of countries, notably in the United Kingdom (Export Credits Guarantee Department), the United States (Export-Import Bank), and in Germany (Hermes Kreditversicherungs A.G.). The first is a government department, the second a government corporation, the third a joint stock company backed by government guarantee. All provide guarantees—essentially of a short and medium-term nature —to private enterprises of their own countries for export credits granted by them to their foreign contractors in the course of ordinary commercial transactions.

While the governments concerned exercise an obviously important auxiliary function in this way, it is essentially an ancillary to private international commerce, and its detailed study, while no doubt a subject of great importance, would lead away from the study of public aid policies.

Another way in which public development policies and private investment are linked is through the direct investment guarantee schemes presently operative in the United States, West Germany, and Japan. These arrangements involve bilateral international agreements between the government of the country that provides the guarantee and any country with regard to which it is operative. The guarantee consists of insurance against certain risks attendant upon foreign investment which may be purchased by foreign investors from agencies of the government of which they are nationals. Although important as a public device to stimulate the flow of resources to less developed countries, these schemes involve flows of private, not public, capital and are on that account also excluded from our study.

Private foreign investment in underdeveloped countries as such, while it may be important to development, is a considerably different phenomenon from public development aid and is responsive to entirely different circumstances. Though, like the OECD,[1] mindful of its importance, we are not dealing with it in this study.[2]

General Objectives of the Principal Donor Countries

The United States—still far and away the largest provider of foreign aid—became involved in international development aid on a major scale principally as a byproduct of the worldwide responsibilities thrown upon it as a leader of the Western world after World War II. The size as well as the direction of U.S. aid is an extraordinary blend of humanitarian sentiment and Cold War strategy. Without the basic and continuing readiness of the American people to help those in need out of a sense of responsibility of the rich for the welfare of the poor—a tradition deeply ingrained in the history of American society—it would be impossible to continue and expand U.S. aid on its present enormous scale year after year. Yet the necessity and direction of this aid is deeply influenced by long-term strategic objectives, especially since the emergence of the Sino-Soviet bloc as an increasingly important factor in international economic development. The presentation to Congress of the Mutual Defense and Development Programs for 1965 lists as the first of three major principles which guide the allocation of U.S. assistance to individual countries: "The importance to the United States of strengthening the country's economy, political structure, social institutions, or security conditions." [3]

[1] The OECD statistics, to which frequent reference has been made, give the flow of all capital funds from OECD countries to the underdeveloped countries but make a clear distinction between official aid and various forms of private investment. In doing so, the OECD reports disavow any intention to distinguish "capital intended primarily to help overseas development" from primarily commercially motivated investment. In the same vein, the British official aid figures (H.M. Treasury, *Aid to Developing Countries*) clearly distinguish bilateral, multilateral, and other economic aid, including technical assistance given by the British Government, from British private long-term investment abroad.

[2] For an examination of a particular type of private foreign investment in less developed countries, see Wolfgang G. Friedmann and George Kalmanoff, *Joint International Business Ventures* (New York, Columbia University Press, 1961).

[3] U.S. Aid and U.S. Dept. of Defense, *Mutual Defense and Development Programs FY 1965*, p. 21.

Economic development aid is a battle for political influence—even if it means only preserving India as a neutralist democracy or preventing the newly emerging African states from becoming economic or political clients of the Communist bloc. Because the political objectives are long-term and worldwide, they cannot, in most cases, be productive of immediate and concrete results. Impatience with the failure of visible political dividends accounts for such gestures as a—subsequently rescinded—resolution of the Foreign Relations Committee of the U.S. Senate in May, 1962, to cut aid to India by 25 percent as a token of protest against India's policies over Goa or the rider attached to the Foreign Assistance Act, 1964, requiring dollar payment for surplus food sales to "Communist" countries. This affected mainly Poland and Yugoslavia, two countries whose independence is, in the opinion of successive American governments, a major interest of U.S. policy.

Humanitarian considerations clash with cold-war strategy over the question of whether to supply surplus U.S. wheat to a hungry Communist China. But whether the usefulness and effect of economic aid will be measured in terms of short-term political dividends—such as alliances or pro-United States attitudes in the United Nations—or in terms of long-term objectives in an immensely prolonged and unending worldwide battle, it is a political conception that prevails in U.S. aid. Hence, it is also inevitable that such aid—despite the repeated assertions made of the preference for private investment and aversion to public involvement in an essentially capitalist economy—should overwhelmingly be public aid, a matter of political decision and of public administration rather than of private business.

A third objective—of domestic rather than of international politics—has become more prominent and articulate in the last few years, as a result of the economic worries of the United States both with respect to the competitiveness of its industry in the world market, and to the strength of the U.S. dollar: official statements before the Congress have stressed that foreign aid will help the U.S. economy and will develop new markets for U.S. industry. The policy of tying aid to procurement in the United States is mainly a result of these new preoccupations.

It is one of the ironies of our time that it is in the United States, the paramount champion of private enterprise, that public aid policy and administration should be an overwhelmingly important factor in the flow of U.S. funds, equipment, and technical assistance to the underdeveloped world. It is not merely a question of laying down policies and providing public funds. Aid policy is buttressed by an elaborate apparatus of public agencies, by a network of government country missions all over the world, and altogether by a predominance of public initiative, even where, as in most cases, private enterprise is brought in to carry out the actual operation and to supply the goods, services, and know-how required.

Despite criticism in the U.S. Congress and elsewhere of the continuing burden of public development aid, as well as of the predominance of public development assistance over private investment abroad, public development aid will most likely remain the predominant aspect of development assistance flowing from the United States and to a lesser extent from other Western aid-giving countries. But there is now growing emphasis on the encouragement of private investment as at least a partial alternative to public development aid and on the strengthening of various forms of public support to private investment in developing countries.

In contrast to the United States, Britain, France, and to a lesser extent West Germany have a long and still-continuing tradition of private pioneering abroad, often in association between industrial enterprises and private banks that have long specialized in international investment. This contrast can largely be explained historically. Britain and France—and some smaller European countries, notably Belgium and the Netherlands—have for centuries ventured abroad and built up political and commercial empires originally explored and exploited by private enterprises of all kinds. American business and industry, on the other hand, have overwhelmingly been preoccupied with domestic development. International expansions and affiliations have been a relatively recent overflow, and only a very few enterprises have had a basic international orientation. Without doubt, American business and industry are at present in a process of transformation and evolution, and with every year experience in foreign operations grows and expands. But the present situation is still one of paradoxes. The predominance of the public effort, in terms of capital, policy, and administration, is resented, but it is there. By contrast, in Britain and France, where private industry and banking have long been actively associated with international economic development, the public-political orientation of development aid is more easily accepted.[4]

Both Britain and France have for decades been used to, and have developed a machinery for, development aid to dependent territories as an inevitable corollary of imperial power and responsibility. Indeed, in the case of France and Great Britain, it may be said that the political conception of development aid is the natural one and only gradually—as more and more of the newly independent countries, such as India or Nigeria, Tunisia or the Ivory Coast, move toward worldwide associations—the political and administrative aspects of development aid will be tempered by commercial and financial considerations, the more so as such aid now will increasingly be given in association with other noncolonial powers or with international institutions whose motivations are different.

In West Germany there is an ambivalent attitude toward international development aid. While of increasing political and strategic importance in world politics, West Germany—still trying to find a balance between the traumatic experience of collapse, physical destruction, and economic paralysis and the hardly less dramatic transformation of defeat and chaos into high economic prosperity, affluence, and political power—still does not see itself as a world leader. The political and industrial leaders and the administrators of Germany now overwhelmingly accept the need and the obligation of a continuing role for Germany in international economic development, though not to the same extent as is true of the prevailing attitude in the United States, and they reject for themselves the strongly political influence which is characteristic of U.S. aid. The

[4] The contrast in the proportion of private capital investment to public financial aid is particularly striking between the United Kingdom and the United States. In the United Kingdom in 1963, the total net flow of private capital through direct investment, export credits, and portfolio investment amounted to $311 million, compared with $413 million of development aid. In the United States, the corresponding figures for 1963 were $882 million, as against $3,844 million, i.e., at a ratio of less than one to four. Moreover, most of the private capital flow from the United States is probably accounted for by investment in oil-producing areas. For France during the same period, the private capital flow at $230 million amounted to more than a fourth of the official flow, which was $858 million. The corresponding figures for West Germany were $136 million (private) and $421 million (public). The private investment of France and Germany in 1963 was, however, substantially lower than in earlier years.

lack of German preoccupation with the problems of world leadership that daily confront the United States is reinforced by the resentment of a country which, for all its prosperity and foreign exchange reserves, still regards itself as relatively short of long-term investment capital. To this must be added the government's aversion to the role of the state in economic affairs, an aversion possibly heightened by the inclusion of the Liberal Democratic Party in the present coalition. Broadly speaking, those presently in control of German aid policies want to see development aid proper confined to social and humanitarian objectives, including help in training and education in the underdeveloped countries, but they reject the mixing of commerce and politics in the extremely "soft" terms of loans for production and industrial development as they are given by the AID.

There is also a strong preference for the flow of international capital on commercial rather than concessionary terms in the attitude of Japan. As in the case of Germany, Japan has a limited concern with the political objectives of aid. In addition, being at a lower level of development, Japan, unlike Germany, is itself in need of capital for investment.

Bilateral Foreign Aid Machinery

UNITED STATES

Development aid from public U.S. sources is still far and away the most important single factor in international development aid. In 1963, it amounted to $3,844 million out of a total of $6,075 million flowing from the twelve DAC countries (excluding Austria), comprising the major part of the industrially developed world outside the Communist bloc (whose contributions to less developed countries in 1963 are estimated at $425 million). The distribution of this aid is worldwide, even though the proportion of aid received by various underdeveloped areas has shifted from time to time, according to political as well as economic and social factors. Thus, Africa has in the last few years emerged as a substantial recipient area of U.S. aid, as more and more states emerge from colonial status to independence.

The universality of the aid effort of the United States is also reflected in the size of its share in and contribution to multilateral agencies. The United States is by far the biggest single subscriber and contributor to the International Bank for Reconstruction and Development, as well as to its affiliated agencies, the International Finance Corporation and the International Development Association. It has also provided the largest capital contribution to the Inter-American Development Bank. Through its membership in the OECD, the United States now also participates fully and actively in the aid-coordinating efforts of an essentially European organization, which Japan has also joined recently.

The contributions of the United States to the multilateral agencies consist, in the first place, of its capital subscription payments to the World Bank and other financial international agencies and, in the second place, of special contributions to various technical assistance, relief, and emergency programs—such as the UN Special and Children's Funds, the World Food Program, UN technical and operational assistance to the Congo, or the UN Relief and Works Agency for Palestine Refugees. The total contributions by the United States to the multilateral agencies, in capital subscriptions and grants, have in recent years amounted to a net total of about $200 million.[5]

Multilateral assistance is still far outweighed by the bilateral aid program. Total official bilateral aid by the United States to developing countries has, in recent years, hovered around a figure of $3,500 million. This is exclusive of military assistance, which has amounted to about $1.2 billion during the last few years. The $3.5 billion of economic aid does, however, include about $500 million of "supporting assistance" and similar emergency assistance which contributes to the military defense efforts of recipients indirectly and is motivated principally by short-term political and strategic objectives rather than by long-term development objectives. The "supporting assistance" is concentrated in countries on the periphery of the Sino-Soviet area, including especially such countries as Korea, Viet Nam, and Laos. "Development assistance," in U.S. parlance, is designed to help "the growth and advancement in freedom of the less developed nations," while military and supporting assistance is "provided to friendly free-world nations to strengthen

[5] OECD, *Flow of Resources, 1956–1963,* Tables IV.2 and IV.3.

their defense against external attack and internal insecurity, maintain economic stability in emergency situations, and thereby help establish a basis for economic and social programs." [6] Military and supporting assistance have been declining in recent years both in absolute terms (from $3 billion in fiscal 1961 to $2.6 billion in fiscal 1962, $2.2 billion in fiscal 1963, and $1.7 billion each in fiscal 1964, 1965, and 1966) and relative to economic aid.

The administration of this huge aid program is, since 1961, essentially in the hands of two public agencies: (1) the U.S. EXIMBANK, a government-owned corporation, though primarily an export-financing institution, has operated as a lender for development aid on essentially commercial terms since 1934; (2) the functions formerly exercised by the International Cooperation Administration and the Development Loan Fund were delegated in 1961 to a new semiautonomous public agency within the State Department, the AID, under an administrator with the rank of Under Secretary. The AID now administers all capital and technical assistance, except for the loan operations of the EXIMBANK and the technical aid provided by the Peace Corps. Besides AID, however, the U.S. Department of Agriculture is involved in the administration of the Food for Peace Program, and other agencies of the government cooperate with AID in various aspects of its assistance.

A new and separate agency for technical aid—whose impact so far has been qualitative rather than quantitative—is the Peace Corps, an organization of volunteers—under official auspices—trained to work in underdeveloped countries which request their aid. The main functions of the Peace Corps have been described in the AID program as the filling of immediate personnel gaps in development activities and as a way to improve the means of international communication. In 1964, a total of 10,000 Peace Corps members were working in forty-six countries, mainly in teaching and a variety of technical services.

About half of the total volume of U.S. economic aid is provided out of the annual appropriations effected pursuant to the Foreign Assistance Act adopted each year. These appropriations are in turn distributed to the extent of slightly more than half as soft-term development loans and the balance as technical assistance and other

---

[6] These definitions are taken from U.S. AID and U.S. Dept. of Defense, *Mutual Defense and Development Programs FY 1965*.

grants. A third of the total aid is provided through the Food for Peace Program of disposal of agricultural surpluses under Public Law 480. And the small balance is made up mostly of EXIMBANK loans. Thus, the bulk of the large U.S. bilateral economic aid program is largely in the form of grants, grantlike transfers, and soft loans. The distribution of bilateral commitments by legislative authority in 1963 is shown in Table 1.

TABLE 1

United States Aid Commitments, 1963
(Millions of Dollars)

Foreign Assistance Act		2,166
Development loans	1,137	
Development grants	352	
Supporting assistance	537	
Social Progress Trust Fund [a]	51	
Administrative expenses	57	
Other AID	32	
Food For Peace Program (P.L. 480) [b]		1,429
Title I	914	
Title II	170	
Title III	290	
Title IV	55	
Export-Import Bank [c]		283
Peace Corps		59
Other		26
Total		3,963

[a] Administered by the Inter-American Development Bank; mostly loans repayable in recipients' currencies ($47 million in 1963); includes a small amount of grants ($4 million in 1963).
[b] Title I represents transfers of resources through sales for recipients' currencies; Title II and Title III represent grants of agricultural commodities for disaster and other relief, as well as for economic development; Title IV consists of loans of agricultural commodities repayable in dollars.
[c] All loans, including export financing of less than five years' maturity.

Source: OECD, *Flow of Resources, 1956–1963*, p. 116.

The fields appropriate for development loans and development grant assistance are defined in the submission to Congress for the fiscal year 1965 as follows:

AID uses Development Loans to provide goods and services needed by the less-developed countries to build the capital base necessary for economic progress. Development Loans are used to finance, for example, road-building equipment, replacement parts for factories, generators for power plants, construction equipment and pumps for irrigation projects; the services of U.S. engineering and construction firms to design and build needed roads, dams, factories; and capital for industrial development banks, or for agricultural credit programs through which farmers can finance better seed, fertilizer, equipment.

AID uses Technical Cooperation Development Grant funds principally to hire experts and technicians to help other countries train teachers, health workers, agricultural extension agents, and other skilled persons needed to achieve economic progress. Experts and technicians are hired directly by AID, or obtained by contract with American universities, businesses, cooperatives and other organizations that have the needed know-how. These funds are also used in part to pay for goods and equipment needed in technical assistance—textbooks for a demonstration school, for example, or DDT for a malaria eradication program.

This means that it is the field of technical assistance in the wide sense—training, education, and basic social services—that is now seen in the United States as the proper field for outright grants. This, as we will see, corresponds broadly to the concept developed in the other major aid-giving countries.

The term "loan" covers, however, a vast variety of terms, including loans of such softness that they are barely distinguishable from grants. AID loans have included terms of forty years at an annual rate of interest of ¾ percent.[7] It is important to stress this conception of capital loans, which differs significantly in particular from that of West Germany. On the other hand, the earlier practice of the Development Loan Fund to make loans repayable in local currency has now been abandoned (except, primarily, for the loans of local currencies received by the United States in payment for U.S. agricultural surpluses; these loans are also repayable in local currencies). This softness is, however, counterbalanced to some extent by the fact that virtually all the aid provided by the AID is tied to procurement for the required goods within the United States.

The reconstruction of the organization of U.S. development aid has been accompanied by a significant evolution—almost a revolution—in the philosophy of aid-giving. The most important aspect

---

[7] This low rate of interest has been raised in a number of successive steps during recent years. The 1965 foreign assistance law provides for a minimum rate of 1 percent during an initial ten-year period of grace and 2½ percent thereafter.

is that the United States has, since the change of administration in 1961, openly and emphatically accepted the need for long-term development planning by the recipient countries as an essential precondition of effective aid.[8] In an article contributed to the *AID Digest* of May, 1962, by its Director of Research, Evaluation, and Planning Assistance, planning is defined as a "process of using scarce resources efficiently, rationally, and totally, to reach certain national goals." It is described as "the really tough and difficult way of insuring that the developing countries use their own resources intelligently and efficiently."

It is essential to mention this evolution in official U.S. thinking because traditionally the concept of economic planning has been associated by the majority of Americans with socialism, and socialism is rejected as an ideology. The new emphasis on the vital importance of long-term planning in conjunction with aid-giving recognizes a distinction between national economic planning and socialism (i.e., public ownership of resources). It does almost inevitably lead to the recognition of a transition from individual "project" aid to a wider concept of aid associated with the overall needs of long-term development. Thus, "about 65 percent of the assistance extended through the AID in the years 1961 through 1963 was for programme financing." [9]

The acknowledgement of the need for long-term development planning as a vital condition of effective progress in the developing countries is accompanied by the reluctant admission that public development financing will, for many years, continue to be the chief source of aid to the developing countries. Despite the traditional American preference for private enterprise and private investment as agents of economic development, and despite the desire to lessen the continuing burden on the American taxpayer—represented by an increasingly restive Congress that judges the continuing annual budget requests for development aid with growing criticism and skepticism—the annual figures of the flow of private capital to developing countries show, year after year, the inadequacy of such private investment for even the barest minimum needs of the devel-

[8] The May, 1962, issue of the *AID Monthly Digest* is entirely devoted to the various aspects of development planning.
[9] OECD, *Flow of Resources, 1956–1963*, p. 121.

oping world. In 1963, the total flow of private capital from the twelve DAC countries to the developing countries, at $2.1 billion, was far less than half the amount of the official resources flowing in the same year ($6.1 billion). By comparison, in 1957 the flow of private capital resources almost equaled that of the official flow. At a time when both the number and the needs of the developing countries keep growing, the proportion of private to public investment —even if private investment can properly be described as "aid"— has almost steadily declined.

In order to counter this state of affairs, and also in order to put increased emphasis on the link of continuing U.S. aid with the demonstrated will and capacity of recipient countries to help themselves, U.S. aid policy has most recently—partly under the influence of the Clay Committee's Report of 1963—emphasized three major objectives:

1. Provide more economic aid for long-term development and less for current budget support.

2. Emphasize the transition of developing countries to self-support wherever possible.

3. Increase reliance on private enterprise for development, and extend the use of private resources in the AID program.

An important practical aspect of this shift is that help is increasingly concentrated on a limited number of countries. In the proposed program for fiscal 1966, two-thirds of AID's development assistance was planned for seven countries, "which are engaged in strong, self-help, development programs": Brazil, Chile, Nigeria, Tunisia, Turkey, Pakistan, and India.

Moreover, U.S. development aid, while relatively stable in absolute figures, is a steadily decreasing proportion of the United States' gross national product. While the foreign assistance program in 1949 totaled about 2 percent of the gross national product, the 1965 program constitutes less than 0.6 percent of the estimated gross national product for 1964.

It is with regard to Latin America that the new U.S. policy has been most articulately defined, in the announcement of the Alliance for Progress by President Kennedy on March 13, 1961, and the subsequent signing of the Alliance Charter by the nations of the Hemisphere at Punta del Este, Uruguay, on August 17, 1961. Under this program, the goal set is a per capita growth in the nations of Latin America over the next ten years of at least 2½ percent per year. Compared with a total inflow of external financing into these countries from all sources of about $1 billion per year or less in recent years, the Alliance called for at least a doubling, to a minimum of $20 billion over the decade. About half of the total amount, or a minimum of some $10 billion, is to come from various U.S. official programs, and a target of at least $3 billion each has been set for U.S. private investors, international agencies such as the World Bank and affiliates and the Inter-American Bank, and European and Japanese public and private sources.

Great emphasis is placed in the program on domestic development strategy in the Latin American republics—involving land and tax reform, improvements in public administration, an emphasis on development planning, and increased investments in projects of a social character such as housing, water supply and sanitary facilities, and education—and on the necessary relationship between external financing and such elements of domestic development strategy. Although the United States took the lead in getting the Alliance for Progress under way, the emphasis is on hemispheric cooperation in the effort, and regional organizations—the Organization of American States, the United Nations Economic Commission for Latin America, and the Inter-American Development Bank—have been assigned important roles. At the same time, efforts are being made to bring donor countries from outside the region into the investment programs, individually as well as through multilateral efforts in the DAC, and through the participation of international lending agencies such as the World Bank complex.

During the first three years of the program, U.S. official financial aid to Latin America met the goal of at least $1 billion annually. A peak of $1.2 billion in such aid was reached during the fiscal year ending June 30, 1964. The international agencies have also generally met the target set for them. There have been shortfalls, on the other hand, in the activity of U.S. private investors and in public aid and private investments from outside the Hemisphere, although there are signs that these situations are improving. U.S. private investments are tending to recover, particularly under the impetus of the U.S. program of guarantees for investments against the political risks of expropriation, currency inconvertibility, and war or insurrection. European and other governments are beginning to respond in a limited way by facilitating bond flotations in their markets by the Inter-American Development Bank (e.g., Italy, West Germany, and the United Kingdom) and by entrusting public funds for lending by that Bank (e.g., Canada, Spain, the United Kingdom, and the Netherlands). Also, an international investment company, the Adela Investment Company, was formally constituted in September, 1964, with an initial subscription of $17 million by private investors from the United States, Europe, Canada, and Japan to make minority equity investments in industrial ventures in Latin America.

Considerable progress has also been made in measures to promote domestic development in Latin America in pursuance of the principles adopted by the signatory states. A major step toward international direction of the program was taken with the constitution in November, 1963, of an eight-man executive committee, the Inter-American Committee for the Alliance for Progress, to coordinate and promote the carrying out of the provisions of the Punta del Este Charter. This committee completed an overall review in 1964 of Latin American development plans and programs, and is concentrating efforts on the problems of external debt, control of inflation, and reduction of barriers to trade in the area.

FRANCE

French economic aid has in the past been almost entirely concentrated on its overseas colonies and, since the independence of its Asian colonies, on the vast and extremely underdeveloped complex of former French West and Equatorial Africa, in addition to Algeria, Morocco, and Tunisia. This accounts for the very high proportion of official grants in the total of French contributions to underdeveloped countries (80 percent in 1963). In 1963, total French aid amounted to $858 million out of a total flow of French capital to developing countries of $1,088 million (including private investments).[10] Since the rather sudden transition to independence of the great majority of the formerly French African territories, there have been many organizational changes, and the present brief account deals with the situation as it has developed in the last few years.

[10] Cf. Chapter II.

The principal organ of administration of French economic aid for the independent countries of French-speaking Africa is the Caisse Centrale de Coopération Économique, except for aid to Algeria, most of which is administered by the Secretariat of State for Algerian Affairs. The Caisse Centrale is a semiautonomous public corporation with competences and functions of remarkable flexibility. The Caisse acts both as a provider of development aid under its own responsibility and as the executive mechanism for the allocation of public aid funds (Gestion de Fonds Publics). In the former role, the Caisse has a permanent "dotation" (25 million F), but its funds derive mainly from additional sources.[11] The Caisse concentrates entirely on loans for economic development and on participations. It is, like many of the postwar public corporations of Britain and France, a business institution but one directed to public purposes, not to profit-making. Its general purpose is to pay for itself and to invest profits in further loan or investment operations.

The range of activities of the Caisse is remarkably wide. The principal activities consist of advances to the states of independent French-speaking Africa, loans to public corporations or other public authorities in those countries, loans to commercial companies with public participations and equity participations by the Caisse in such enterprises, loans to private enterprise, and rediscounting of medium-term loans. In 1963 the total commitments composed of these various elements amounted to 286 million F, i.e., approximately $60 million. Of this amount, 206 million F went to States or public authorities and 80 million F to private enterprises. Typical terms for loans range from 2½ percent and maturity periods of from ten to twenty years (for loans to public authorities) to 5½ percent and maturity periods of from seven to ten years (for loans to private firms).[12]

The Caisse only lends or invests for specific projects, since general development financing is looked after by a special Treasury Fund, Fonds d'Aide et de Coopération (FAC). Its powers would permit loans to a foreign country (i.e., outside black French-

---

[11] These consist of reserves, Treasury advances, loans from the Caisse des Dépots, and excess of reimbursements received over repayments of its own obligations. A. Postel-Vinay, "La Caisse Centrale de Coopération Économique," *Bulletin de liaison et d'information de l'Administration Centrale des Finances,* No. 27, 1964.

[12] See OECD, *Flow of Resources, 1956–1959,* p. 56.

speaking Africa), although the Caisse has not yet operated in this direction. The Caisse also acts as the paying agent both for FAC and the European Development Fund of the European Economic Community (EEC).

Traditionally, the Caisse has enjoyed very considerable autonomy in its lending and investing operations, but it seems that under the de Gaulle regime, and especially since the establishment of the Ministère de Coopération in 1961, this autonomy is somewhat more restricted. There is no doubt, however, that it is in the Caisse that the greatest amount of actual experience with the economic development problems of French-speaking Africa resides.

The link between the Caisse and the French government is constitutionally provided by a Conseil de Surveillance, in which the Ministère de Coopération and the Ministère de Finances are represented, together with the board of the Caisse. Because of the traditionally strong position of the Caisse and the close personal links among the various officials, cooperation in the Conseil appears to work very smoothly. But on questions of policy, the Minister of Cooperation and the Minister of Finance could give directions to the Caisse and, if necessary, forbid certain operations for reasons of general or financial policy.[13] The Minister of Cooperation is specifically responsible for the FAC and the Minister for Overseas Territories and Departments for the funds applicable to these possessions (FIDES and FIDOM).[14]

One of the most remarkable activities of the Caisse has been its encouragment and its financial participation in local African enterprises of all kinds. Generally, the proportion of aid to the public and private sectors of the recipient states has been roughly in the ratio of two to one; in the year 1963, it was on the order of two and a half to one. Aid in the public and semi-public sector has been concentrated on the establishment of and participation in (1) credit societies and development banks, (2) housing and land development societies, (3) electric power utilities, and (4) public institutions (such as local authorities, railway and harbor corporations, and chambers of commerce) concerned with economic and social development of the country.

[13] The Director General of the CCCE (Postel-Vinay) describes this situation as "une double tutelle ministerielle" (cf. footnote 11).

[14] On these, see further below.

The Caisse attaches great importance to the function of development banks in Africa. Generally, the African governments now hold the majority of the capital in these development banks and the Caisse a minority. There is also now increasing participation of other units, mainly of public banks and credit societies. Private participation does not seem to be excluded but has not so far occurred. The French authorities believe emphatically in the necessity of *public* development in this phase of African evolution, given the paucity of private long-term development capital. The development banks, in which the Caisse participates, have great elasticity of movement. They can themselves take equity participations or lend to commerce and industry; they can accept gifts, loans, or subventions and lend them out again.

The Caisse regards as equally important its initiative and participation in the promotion of the generation of electric power and in housing development.

In the private sector, the assistance of the Caisse is now, in almost equal proportions, concentrated on agricultural and forestry development on the one hand and mining and industrial enterprises on the other. But this is still on a considerably smaller scale than the aid given to basic utilities and development banks.

The Caisse also plays an important role in the technical assistance field by supplying advisers to African governments and institutions and by training Africans in France.

The other major source of French aid to the independent states of French-speaking Africa is provided by the FAC. This is not a separate legal personality (unlike the Caisse), but a "budget line." It derives its funds exclusively from the French government and has in the past used them almost entirely for subventions (and not, like the Caisse, for loans and investments). Its principal purpose is to aid social, economic, and scientific development (such as research projects) by way of subventions. FAC Missions, composed of personnel from the Ministry of Cooperation, operate in the African states. The FAC commitments in the African states are divided into "operations of general interest" and "development programs." In 1962, the former amounted to 242.6 million F and the latter to 259.9 million F. Operations of general interest include mineral prospecting, scientific (mainly agricultural) research, and, above all, cultural and educational support. In the field of development programs, the FAC links its support increasingly to development plans,[15] and it divides its contributions among "general expenses," "development of production" (which is nearly half the total), "infrastructure," and "social equipment."

FAC assistance, which has hitherto been entirely in the form of grants, is now beginning to be extended to loans in the case of revenue-producing projects, with an interest rate of ¾ percent per annum and maturities of ten to twenty-five years, including grace periods of three to five years. As French aid becomes more diversified, it can be expected that the present large preponderance of grants will decline. Such aid as has been given in the form of loans in the past has, for the most part, been at maturities of ten to twenty years and at interest rates of 4 percent or more. Judging by the soft loans that have been initiated by FAC and by a recent $30-million loan extended to Mexico at an interest rate of 3 percent, the terms of French loans will probably be eased in the future, especially considering the fact that even soft loans are generally less of a burden on the donor than grants.

The Caisse Centrale acts as the paying agent of the FAC on behalf of the government. It acts in the same capacity for two other types of French aid operations: aid for the *territoires d'outre-mer* and aid for the *départements d'outre-mer.*[16] The principal fund for economic and social aid to the *territoires* is the Fonds d'Investissement pour le Développement Économique et Social des Territoires d'Outre-Mer (FIDES). The agency for the *départements d'outre-mer* is the Fonds d'Investissements des Départements d'Outre-Mer (FIDOM). Neither operates in independent countries, i.e., in the states of *l'Afrique d'expression française.* The latter also participate, as associate members of the EEC, in the aid efforts of the latter's European Development Fund. To this Fund, France, like the other members of the EEC, contributes, and the French Caisse Centrale acts as the Community's paying agent.

On the multilateral level, France is a member of and subscribes to all the international financial agencies, though on a substantially

---

[15] At the end of 1962, Senegal, Mali, Cameroon, and Dahomey had four- or five-year plans.

[16] The former—halfway between independent states and administrative departments—and the latter together have about one and a half million people. They are mostly scattered possessions in the Pacific, West Indian, and Australasian areas.

smaller scale than the United Kingdom. She is a member of the EEC and of the OECD. France's multilateral aid involvement, especially in conjunction with the International Bank for Reconstruction and Development and the United States, may gradually become more important as the newly independent French-speaking African states move for aid from these latter two sources. The visit of M. Houphouet-Boigny, President of the Ivory Coast Republic, to Washington in May, 1962, with specific loan requests to the World Bank and the United States—and, on the other hand, General de Gaulle's visit to Latin America in October, 1964, during which he made certain commitments for educational and technical assistance—illustrate this evolution.

Total French official aid of $858 million in 1963 consisted of bilateral grants of $697 million, $134 million of net lending of more than five years' maturity, and $27 million of contributions to multi-lateral agencies. The decline in French aid from nearly $1 billion in 1962, according to *DAC 1964 Review* of OECD, does not reflect a change in policy but was the product of several accidental circumstances, such as political events in Algeria and the completion of some of the major overseas projects financed by France.

One substantial change will result from the new status of the French-speaking African states, as associated members of the EEC. The French government has, for many years, not only provided a price subsidy for the tropical agricultural produce of French Africa by compelling the French importers to pay a substantial margin over the world price but has also, through the Caisses de Stabilisation, insured the African producers against price fluctuations on the world market. The price subsidies must, under a convention between the EEC and the eighteen French-speaking African states, come to an end within a period of five years, during which certain transitory compensation will be paid to these states.

In 1963 the French government appointed a commission for the long-term review of the entire French aid policy. The report of this commission, the so-called Jeanneney Commission, was published late in 1963.[17] The most important recommendations of the Jeanneney report can be briefly summarized as follows:

[17] *La politique de coopération avec les pays en voie de développement*, Rapport de la Commission d'Étude instituée par le Decret du 12 mars 1963, soumis au Gouvernement le 18 juillet 1963, published by the Ministère d'État Chargé de la Réforme Administrative (Paris, 1963).

1. There should be a greater geographical diversification of French aid.

2. While France should maintain a priority over aid to French-speaking Africa, it should persuade its European partners to cooperate to a greater extent in aid to that region, and, concurrently, a larger share of French aid should go elsewhere.

This indeed is an extension of the view that motivated the establishment of the EEC European Development Fund in 1958. The pattern suggested for 1975 is a reduction in the proportion of total aid going to the franc zone from 87.5 percent in 1961 (excluding the overseas departments and territories, which are not considered *foreign* at all by the Commission), to 60 percent; an increase in the proportion of aid going bilaterally to other countries from 4 percent in 1961 to 15 percent in 1975; and an increase in the share of multilateral aid from 8 percent in 1961 to 25 percent in 1975. Some moves have been made recently in this direction, such as the commitment of a $30-million, 3 percent, ten-year, untied loan to Mexico (which would, however, have to be matched by $120 million in suppliers' credits), but too little time has elapsed to estimate the effect of this policy. France cannot quickly disengage itself in Algeria (which alone receives a third or more of total French bilateral aid) and in Africa south of the Sahara.

French foreign aid, at a level of close to $1 billion annually, continues to be the second largest in the world, second only to the United States. The Jeanneney report suggests that public aid can well rise to keep pace with the growth of the gross national product, to which it bears the high ratio of about 1.5 percent (the highest of any donor country) but considers that it would be unreasonable to expect it to be any higher. The French Premier, on the other hand, in a Parliamentary debate in June, 1964, said that, although foreign aid expenditures would be kept at the present level, they would not rise *pari passu* with GNP, and the ratio to GNP would consequently decline. There has been a considerable amount of public questioning in France during the last few years concerning the value and effectiveness of the country's large foreign aid expenditures. Among the more widely read criticisms were a series of articles in *Paris-Match* by Raymond Cartier.[18] The Premier's state-

---

[18] "Attention: La France Dilapide Son Argent," *Paris-Match*, Nos. 777 (Feb. 28, 1964), 778 (March 7, 1964), and 779 (March 14, 1964).

ment was undoubtedly made in the light of these and other criticisms. If the absolute volume of aid is not to increase and if there is little leeway in present French aid to Africa, there is little likelihood that the policy of a wider distribution of aid will make great headway in the near future.

The high proportion of grants in the total French aid effort—80 percent of bilateral commitments in 1963 [19]—is explained to a large extent by the great importance of technical cooperation and current budgetary support in French assistance. In 1963, French expenditures for bilateral technical cooperation amounted to $295 million, or about 35 percent of total aid disbursements (the only higher figure was $368 million for the United States, representing slightly less than 10 percent of its aid disbursements). France had the greatest number by far of personnel sent to less developed countries—about 50,000 in 1963—the next highest number being 13,548 for the United Kingdom. Of the total for France, about 30,000 were teachers and 19,062 operational personnel; advisers numbered only 1,713. About a fourth of French bilateral aid in 1963 consisted of current budget subsidies.

The recommendations of the Jeanneney Commission concerning aid administration were not published with the rest of its report. No changes in administration have been made since the report of the Commission. It is understood that some of its administrative recommendations concerned a greater centralization of activities, such as the complete integration of the FAC into the Caisse Centrale. As is apparent from the foregoing survey, the responsibility for French aid administration is at present widely scattered. It is possible that France will, sooner or later, introduce a structural reform comparable to that introduced by the British Labor Government in October, 1964, with the creation of a Ministry of Overseas Development. For in France, as in Britain, the multitude of aid agencies and aid funds have developed out of the variegated responsibilities of an imperial power in relation to its colonies and other overseas dependencies. This situation is now rapidly changing.

In any case, French foreign aid is likely to become more diversi-

[19] Comparable figures for other major donor countries are: U.S., 62 percent, UK, 48 percent, and Germany, 24 percent, including grantlike aid such as loans repayable in local currencies and transfers of resources for which payment is made in local currencies.

fied in nature and scope. The proportion of loans to grants is likely to increase somewhat, parallel with a gradual reduction of the present overwhelming direction of the aid effort toward French-speaking Africa and a shift from current budgetary support to capital projects.

UNITED KINGDOM

Like France, the United Kingdom has until recently devoted the overwhelming proportion of its foreign aid effort—financially and administratively—to the development of its vast Empire and Commonwealth. This emphasis is gradually shifting as the remaining colonies are being transformed into independent members of the British Commonwealth, or—as in isolated cases, like Burma—into foreign independent states. At the same time, the increasing number of multilateral international public finance agencies—in all of which the United Kingdom participates—is helping to diversify Britain's aid effort. The United Kingdom is one of the major subscribers to the World Bank and its two affiliated agencies. It is a member of the OECD, whose DAC is designed to coordinate Western aid efforts, and of the aid consortia for India and Pakistan. Important British participations in multilateral aid schemes include the Indus and Volta River development projects.

But the proportion of British bilateral assistance to its total aid remains overwhelming. In the fiscal year 1963–64 (April through March), bilateral aid given by the United Kingdom (gross disbursements) amounted to £158.0 million, a substantial increase over previous years, while multilateral aid (to the UN and its agencies, including the IBRD) totaled £17.2 million (also a substantial increase). The corresponding (provisional) figures for 1964–65 are £172 million and £18 million.[20]

Aid to dependent territories and independent Commonwealth countries continues to account for most of the bilateral aid. In 1964–65, Commonwealth countries and territories received some 87 percent of the United Kingdom's bilateral financial aid; aid to colonial territories has increased, despite the decline in the number

[20] Ministry of Overseas Development, *Overseas Development: The Work of the New Ministry* (August, 1965), Cmnd. 2736.

of such territories, the increase having occurred in loans rather than grants. Aid to independent Commonwealth countries has registered the largest increase of any of the categories, more in the form of loans than grants, although the latter have increased significantly too. Countries outside the Commonwealth have also received more aid, with a significant proportion continuing to be in the form of grants; the proportion of loans relative to grants in total bilateral aid has increased appreciably, from about 20 percent of the total in 1957–58 to about 50 percent in 1964–65. Thus, as the volume of British aid has increased, it has gone more and more to independent countries, including some outside the Commonwealth; and, as might be expected with such a shift away from colonies, loans have come to represent a larger portion of the total relative grants.

Aid Administration. The administration of British development aid has been considerably affected by the new Ministry for Overseas Development, created by the Labour Government in October, 1964. Until then, coordination had been effected through an intergovernmental committee under the chairmanship of the Treasury, the key agency for the determination of overall aid policy. The Treasury is concerned with the effects of aid on the British economy and with its fiscal and balance-of-payments implications. Cooperating with the Treasury, with respect to aid for particular groups of countries, were the Colonial Office, the Commonwealth Relations Office (independent Commonwealth countries), and the Foreign Office (foreign countries). The Colonial Office and the Commonwealth Relations Office, though still separate, are now under a single Secretary of State, as a prelude to the eventual elimination of the Colonial Office. Technical assistance activities for all areas were, since 1961, administered by the Department of Technical Cooperation. Its functions included the administration of the Overseas Service Aid Scheme, of some of the educational and research expenditures under the Colonial Development and Welfare Act, and of the facilities provided under the Colombo Plan and the new (1959) Commonwealth Education Scheme. The Export Credits Guarantee Department, which is a subsidiary of the Board of Trade and which administers the program of government insurance of privately granted export credits, also administers, in cooperation with the

Commonwealth Relations Office and the Foreign Office, public loans granted under the Export Guarantees Act, which, in fact, constitute the major part of all public foreign loans.

The purpose of the new Ministry of Overseas Development, which was established in October, 1964, is to centralize the administration of aid in one department under a cabinet minister. While the Department of Technical Cooperation had already coordinated technical assistance for all developing countries since 1961, responsibility for capital aid still remained dispersed among the various ministries and departments mentioned above. The Ministry of Overseas Development has now assumed responsibility for the economic aid program as a whole. This includes

The terms and conditions of aid; the size and nature of the programme for each country; the management of financial aid and technical assistance; relations with international aid organisations; the British interest in United Nations programmes of technical assistance; and relations with voluntary bodies concerned with aid and development.[21]

But for the dwindling number of dependent territories, responsibilities remain divided between the Colonial Office, which, in consultation with the Ministry, is in charge of budgetary aid, and the Ministry, which, in discharging its responsibility for development aid, acts in agreement with the Colonial Office. The Treasury retains the main responsibility for relations with the International Bank for Reconstruction and Development (IBRD), while military aid remains under the Foreign Office, the Commonwealth Relations Office, and the Colonial Office.

Of the eight divisions of the Ministry of Overseas Development, one deals with general aid policy and international relations in the field of aid and development. Of the other seven divisions, three have essentially regional responsibilities (Asia, Africa, and the Caribbean and Latin America). The other four divisions are responsible for various aspects of technical assistance and thus absorb the functions as well as the organization of the Department of Technical Cooperation. The Ministry has a greatly extended economic planning staff, responsible for the Ministry's work in the economic and statistical fields, and twenty-nine professional advisers on technical subjects.

[21] Ministry of Overseas Development, *Overseas Development*, p. 27.

Besides the departments of the Government involved in the administration of foreign aid—the Treasury, Colonial Office, Commonwealth Relations Office, Foreign Office, and Export Credits Guarantee Department—there is the statutory Commonwealth Development Corporation engaged in lending as well as investing in equities. Though autonomous, it is nominally responsible to the Secretary of State for Commonwealth Relations and the Colonies.

In addition to these agencies and institutions in the public sector, development finance is provided in the form of loans as well as equity investments by the quasi-public Commonwealth Development Finance Company Ltd.[22]

Sources of Funds for Aid and Terms of Aid. The sources of the funds for British foreign aid reflect the pragmatic approach of the United Kingdom to the varying requirements of foreign aid. Grants are made out of the annual appropriations voted by Parliament for the various agencies. The Parliamentary votes are usually not much more than ratifications of the amounts of appropriations worked out by the Treasury. The Colonial Office extends grants out of its annual appropriations for current budgetary support as well as for specific schemes within the framework of the development programs prepared as required by the Colonial Department and Welfare Acts. The technical assistance expenditures made by the Ministry of Overseas Development are also in the form of grants and are provided by annual parliamentary appropriations, as are the amounts of assistance extended in grants by the Commonwealth Relations Office and the Foreign Office.

Annual appropriations are also the source for the few loans granted by individual departments on soft terms, for the financing of local currency requirements, as well as for the assumption by the departments of interest waived on loans granted at the customary rate (the government borrowing rate plus ¼ percent). Most of the loans extended in the British foreign aid program are granted at the customary rate by the Export Credits Guarantee Department pursuant to Section 3 of the Export Guarantees Act of 1949. The device has been used of waiving interest entirely during the first seven years of long-term loans, which can have the effect of reducing the effective rate from, say, 5½ percent to below 3 per-

[22] See below.

cent on a twenty-five-year loan. This approach is said to have been used to avoid differential borrowing rates for overseas and domestic borrowers from the government. While the interest is waived as far as the overseas borrower is concerned, it is paid to the Export Credits Guarantee Department by the Commonwealth Relations Office or Foreign Office out of their appropriations.

Sources other than specifically earmarked appropriations provide the funds for most loans under the foreign aid program. These sources consist of Treasury borrowings or general Treasury surpluses. Expenditures financed in this way are known in British fiscal parlance as "below the line" expenditures, as distinguished from the "above the line" appropriated expenditures. Loans financed from this type of source include the Section 3 loans mentioned above, Exchequer loans to colonies, and Exchequer loans to the Commonwealth Development Corporation. Exchequer loans to colonies have been made since 1959 to offset the decline in the availability of the private capital market in London for loan flotations by colonies. The Commonwealth Development Corporation, which finances itself entirely by borrowing, has obtained its borrowings thus far mostly from the British Treasury. Such "below the line" foreign aid expenditures in total accounted for £71 million in 1963–64, or about 40 percent of total foreign aid in that year.

As previously noted, about half of British foreign aid is still in the form of grants, although this proportion is now beginning to change, since there are fewer dependent territories, and the expansion of the British aid program mainly takes the form of development loans.

Furthermore, close to 80 percent of the loans are for twenty years or more. In its September, 1963, White Paper on Aid to Developing Countries (Cmnd.2147), the Treasury announced that maximum loan terms had been raised from twenty-five years with a seven-year grace period for repayment of principal, to thirty years and a grace period up to ten years. The average interest rate on all UK official loans committed in 1963 was slightly below 5 percent.

The White Paper of the Ministry of Overseas Development, presented to Parliament in August, 1965, strongly expresses the view that even this progressive softening of the terms of development loans is not sufficient to ease the increasing burden of debt of the recipient countries:

The Government believes that the time has come for a new initiative and that we need not be inhibited by our present difficulties from taking it. Useful though the waivers have proved, they do not fully meet the difficulties of the most needy countries, and there is little point in lending more to meet debt service on old loans. We have therefore decided to make development loans free of interest in appropriate cases. This concession, combined with suitable arrangements for the repayment of capital, will give us greater freedom in the determination of terms and, in particular, will enable us to lighten the burden of debt service in the middle and later years of the loan.[23]

In pursuit of this same policy, the government also recently decided to waive the interest on certain loans to the Commonwealth Development Corporation.

The only part of British aid which is formally tied to the purchase of UK goods and services is that in the form of Section 3 loans, which may be used for imports only and now account for about 30 percent of total aid expenditure. Furthermore, much the greater part of these loans is not tied to specific projects and may be spent on a wide range of goods. The rest of the capital aid is not formally tied to purchases in the United Kingdom, although it is, in fact, expended there in view of the close relations of the recipient countries with the United Kingdom. Except for Section 3 loans, much the greater part of British aid is for local currency expenditures, and the recipient countries have available as free foreign exchange the sterling which gives rise to the local currency counterpart. The portion of UK aid for imports by developing countries which is not formally tied is nevertheless subject to the proviso that British industry cannot supply the goods or services required on "reasonably competitive terms."

The Commonwealth Development Corporation. The Colonial Development Corporation was converted into the Commonwealth Development Corporation (CDC) in 1963 to take account of the change in the status of most colonial territories. It can now carry on the full range of its activities in any part of the Commonwealth except those countries which became independent before the initial creation of the organization as the Colonial Development Corporation in 1948. Thus, it cannot operate in such countries as India or Pakistan.

Outstanding commitments of the CDC amounted to £119.3 mil-

[23] Ministry of Overseas Development, *Overseas Development*, p. 35.

lion at the end of 1963, of which £87.3 million was in the form of loans and £32.0 million in equity investments. Slightly more than half of the total commitments (£62.2 million) was in enterprises owned only partially by the CDC, and only a small amount (£12.3 million) was in direct projects of the CDC or in enterprises wholly owned by it. The balance of about 40 percent of total commitments (£44.8 million) was in the form of loans to governments. Total commitments rose to £125 million at the end of 1964.

The CDC is a very flexible organization. It can lend or invest for all developmental projects except hospitals, schools, roads (unless incidental to other projects), and radio or television enterprises. Its funds are not tied with respect to area of expenditure. It works with both public and private enterprises and agencies. In some cases it has granted loans for terms up to forty years. Its commitments at the end of 1964 were distributed in the following types of projects: 52.5 percent in basic development (primarily power and water and housing finance), 21 percent in primary production (mainly agriculture and ranching), and 26.5 percent in commerce and industry (factories, hotels, and industrial development companies in the recipient countries).

The CDC maintains a network of six regional offices. Its commitments at the end of 1964 were quite evenly distributed among the six regions (Table 2).

TABLE 2

Commonwealth Development Corporation Commitments
as of December 31, 1964
(Millions of Pounds)

Caribbean	16.2
East Asia and Pacific islands	23.6
East Africa	22.2
Central Africa	25.9
Southern Africa	23.2
West Africa	13.5
Other	0.4
Total	125.0

Source: Commonwealth Development Corporation, *Reports and Accounts 1964* (London, 1965), p. 12.

The cost of the finance provided by the CDC is limited by the fact that it operates exclusively with funds borrowed at commercial rates of interest (the average cost to the CDC of Treasury money was 5.6 percent in 1964).

Very recently, however, this burden has been somewhat eased by the government's decision to waive the interest on selected projects, during the period "when an investment is fructifying." This concession will apply to agricultural schemes and local development companies, in which the Corporation invests either by way of equity or loan. The CDC has £150 million of long-term borrowing authority, plus £10 million of short-term borrowings. Sums borrowed from the British Treasury are limited to a maximum outstanding of £130 million. Most of its borrowing to date has been from the Treasury.

The CDC is currently committing funds at the rate of close to £10 million a year. Gross Exchequer advances to the CDC in 1963–64 amounted to £5.1 million (compared with the total of £175 million for all UK foreign aid). While thus representing only a small part of total British foreign aid, the CDC has been a highly versatile instrument in the program. It is, however, seriously handicapped in its long-term investment policy by its continuing dependence on Treasury loans and the relatively high rates of interest it must charge to its borrowers to meet its own interest obligations to the Treasury. The recent concession by the government, noted earlier, may improve the CDC's position to some extent.

The Commonwealth Development Finance Company Ltd. The Commonwealth Development Finance Company Ltd. (CDFC) was incorporated in 1953 to finance industrial enterprises in Commonwealth countries conducted primarily by private interests. It does not normally invest in social infrastructure projects or in projects operated by governments. It extends loans and also invests in equities.

The CDFC's authorized capital of £26.3 million is subscribed as to 55 percent by 172 industrial, commercial, mining, and shipping firms and financial houses, including such firms as British American Tobacco, British Petroleum, Courtaulds, Imperial Chemical Industries, Tube Investments, and Unilever. The remainder of 45 percent is held by the Bank of England and by certain Commonwealth central banks. Of total authorized capital, only £7.3 million is paid in, the balance serving primarily as a guarantee for funds borrowed in the market. As of March 31, 1964, CDFC's borrowings consisted of £7.6 million of long-term funds and £2.9 million of bank advances.

Outstanding loans and debentures held by the CDFC amounted to £15.6 million as of March 31, 1964, and equities to £2.7 million. Total commitments as of that date, including those not yet disbursed, amounted to £23.4 million. The total current rate of commitments is about £4 million per year.

The average term of CDFC loans is about ten years, and the interest rate charged by it is about 7½ to 8 percent per year, or 1½ to 2 points above the long-term borrowing rate on the London market.

The CDFC holds investments primarily in industrial enterprises and secondarily in agricultural estates, utilities, and development corporations. Its investments are widely spread geographically in Africa and Asia and also include some small investments in Canada, Australia, and New Zealand.

The CDFC maintains liaison with government departments and agencies in London as well as with such agencies as the World Bank and the International Finance Corporation. In addition to its investment activities, the CDFC provides advisory services through the business experience of its own staff, as well as by access, through its shareholders and others, to experts outside of its own staff.

The CDFC thus performs a function, although limited to the Commonwealth, similar in many ways to that of the International Finance Corporation.

The Future of British Aid Policy. Despite the seriousness of Britain's balance-of-payments position, which severely restricts her capacity to increase capital aid and private investment in developing countries, the White Paper of the new Ministry of Overseas Development, of August, 1965, expresses not only Britain's determination to play a major part in international development assistance but also important reflections on the lines of future aid policy.

Reference has already been made to the White Paper's emphasis on the need to further soften the terms of aid and to give interest-free loans in selected cases—a development opposite to the relative stiffening of terms that the U.S. Congress has recently imposed on an unwilling administration. The White Paper further emphasizes the growing importance of technical assistance. The Ministry has taken a number of new decisions in this field. They include the formation of a corps of economic, administrative, financial, and technical specialists, to be built up to about 100 in two to three years; the encouragement of service overseas by volunteers currently numbering 1,400, for which about £620,000 has been allocated in 1964–65; assistance in the economic planning of the less developed countries; and the stepping up of various educational and training schemes. The White Paper strongly supports more cooperation between the donor countries, mainly through the World Bank and the DAC of the OECD.

It sees the role of government aid not as an alternative but as complementary to private investment, especially through "basic investment in transport and power and in human skills on which industry can draw, and without which it may hesitate to invest." The White Paper stresses the need for cooperation with the recipient countries, through the increasing participation of local staff and capital and through "new forms of joint enterprise, involving cooperation between British private entrepreneurs and local entrepreneurs, or development corporations."

WEST GERMANY

Economic aid to developing countries by West Germany, as an organized and continuing effort, is of fairly recent date; and the institutional machinery has undergone several changes.

On the policy level, the preponderant influence was until 1961 exercised by the Ministry of Economics (Bundeswirtschaftsministerium) with some participation by the Foreign Office (Auswaertiges Amt). This influence, however, has been affected to some extent by the establishment of a special Ministry for Economic Cooperation (Bundesministerium für Wirtschaftliche Zusammenarbeit). The Ministry for Economic Cooperation is primarily concerned with the technical aid and social aspects of development aid, while the Ministry of Economics is predominantly concerned with the capital supply aspects. The economic aid budget is under the general responsibility of the Ministry of Economic Cooperation. The division of responsibilities between the two ministries is far from clear, and cooperation far from perfect.[24]

Coordination is achieved—and basic policy determined—by an

---

[24] See, for a recent appraisal, John White, *German Aid* (London, Overseas Development Institute Ltd., 1964), p. 34 *et seq.*

interministerial committee in which, apart from the two ministries already mentioned, the Foreign Office and the Ministry of Finance are represented. This interministerial committee is, at least in theory, the highest policy-making organ within the West German government for matters of international development aid. Apart from the ministries, the Kreditanstalt für Wiederaufbau (KW) is represented on the Committee in a consultative capacity.

The KW—which is the principal public development lending agency of the Bundesrepublik—is in certain respects comparable to the French Caisse Centrale. Like the latter, it is both the managing agent for public aid funds to developing countries from other sources and an aid agency in its own right, using its own resources. As the name indicates, the KW was originally primarily concerned with the reconstruction of the German domestic economy, and this is a continuing function. With the continued strengthening of the domestic German economy and the growth of its capital resources, however, coupled with the increasing role of West Germany as a major provider of aid for developing countries, the foreign aid function of the KW has steadily grown in proportion to its domestic function. In the year 1963, out of its total commitments of 3,478.1 million DM, 911.6 million DM went to domestic and the remainder of 2,566.5 million DM went to foreign commitments. These commitments were made to the extent of 62 percent of the total from public funds, and the remainder was based on the KW's own funds. (In 1964 the proportion of the KW's own funds—out of a smaller total—increased to 42.8 percent.)

Out of the total public funds made available to the KW in 1963, 750.7 million DM came from the so-called European Recovery Program (ERP) counterpart funds, i.e., from funds originally provided from government sources in local currency as a counterpart of the Marshall aid granted by the United States to Germany. The remainder came from budgetary appropriations of the federal government and those of the Länder. The funds coming from the KW's own resources comprise not only the resources made available from current repayments and from funds transferred to KW reserves but also medium-term funds placed at the disposal of the KW by the European Coal and Steel Community, as well as all funds procured by the KW from institutional investors and in the capital market. In

1963 the KW issued bonds totaling 578.3 million DM, consisting of about three-fifths of long-term bonds.

As to the type of loans provided, a basic distinction is made between commercial transactions and capital aid. The former include loans for establishments and participations abroad, nontied financial loans, and export financing. Capital aid consists of loans mostly for specific projects; the rest are so-called "nonproject" loans. In 1963, out of the total amount of foreign loans committed (2,566.5 million DM), about three-quarters, i.e., 1,858.4 million DM, went to capital aid loans, 411.6 million DM to export financing, 289.8 million DM to nontied financial loans, and 6.7 million DM to establishments and participations abroad. Except for a little under 250 million DM, all of this went to developing countries. This capital aid was divided almost equally between "production" and "infrastructure" projects, the latter mainly in the fields of transport, irrigation, and public utilities. Industrial projects predominated in Asia and infrastructure projects in Africa, reflecting the different stages of development of these two continents.

Foreign aid commitments made by the KW in 1964 were substantially lower than in 1963 and considerably lower than in 1962. Total foreign transactions amounted to 1,655.4 million DM, as against 2,566.5 million DM in 1963. Capital aid was halved (923.5 million DM, as against 1,858.4 million DM in 1963). On the other hand, actual disbursements (1.1 billion DM) increased sharply and, for the first time, exceeded commitments made during the year. Untied financing credits were also reduced (from 289.8 million to 52.0 million DM). By contrast, export finance credits—both to foreign importers and German exporters—rose from 411.6 million to 670.0 million DM.

The principles of German development aid have gradually become clarified and consolidated during the past few years. They are dominated by three basic beliefs. First, there is the definite preference of German governmental aid—which flows through the KW—for clearly identifiable purposes. The German government is convinced that the utility of development assistance can be measured far better against clearly identifiable projects than as general budgetary or other development aid. Hence, the bulk of capital aid goes into specific projects deemed essential to the further development of the recipient countries. In 1963 more than one-half of the total amount represented loans to Asiatic countries. The balance was almost equally divided between African and European developing countries. The biggest single project loan was one of 452 million DM to enable Hindustan Steel Ltd. in India to start work on raising the crude steel capacity of the Rourkela steel works. Nonproject loans—reduced to 31 percent of the total in 1964—have generally been given only in connection with multilateral actions and, in the case of loans granted to countries suffering from strained balances of payments, to enable them to procure raw materials and spare parts in order to insure full utilization of their existing manufacturing plants (so-called "maintenance support").[25] In 1964, out of the greatly reduced total amount for capital aid (923.5 million DM), the bulk went again to Asia (440.3 million DM) and Africa (319.7 million DM).

The admittedly limited granting of loans for the purpose of easing a strained balance of payments represents a certain concession to the belief now held in many aid-giving quarters that such loans may in certain situations help a country over a difficult period. Another limited departure from the belief that aid should be earmarked for specific projects is the granting of loans to development banks. In 1963 these consisted of two loans totaling 45 million DM to Indian development banks, 40 million DM to two Pakistani development banks, 11 million DM to the Thailand Development Bank, and 10 million DM to the Cameroons Development Bank. Such institutions have been chosen as recipients of loans because they are "familiar with local conditions" and because "without this method, it certainly would scarcely be possible within the scope of capital aid to further the small and medium-sized industries within the developing countries' national economies."[26] In 1964 this policy of channeling more aid through development banks continued as the best way of assisting small and medium enterprises.

The second basic principle in German development lending is the differentiation, in terms of aid, between infrastructure projects and

[25] KW Report for 1963, pp. 62–63 (English edition). In 1961–63, balance-of-payments support was given mainly to Latin American countries.
[26] *Ibid.*, p. 61.

industrial projects. This corresponds generally to a distinction between non-revenue-earning and revenue-earning activities. Public utilities, irrigation, and communications come under the former, agriculture, mining, and manufacture under the latter category. Loans for the former are generally granted at a rate of interest of 3 to 3.5 percent and a maturity of twenty years, and the latter at about 5 percent and a maxium of fifteen years. The average rate of interest on new loan commitments in 1963 was 4.3 percent and the maturity nineteen years.[27] This is still a long way from the practice, now increasingly adopted, not only by the IDA and the American AID but also more recently in some French loans, of giving very long-term maturities at nominal rates of interest or—as in the more recent development of British aid policy—interest-free. This, in the German view, is a barely disguised form of grant.

The third basic principle of German aid philosophy is that grants should be given only for technical cooperation activities, indemnification payments, and the German contribution to the Indus Basin Development Fund,[28] while other economic aid should be in the form of loans. This policy is due to the conviction that charity is neither desirable nor in the interest of the developing countries, since it would tend to inflate demands and shield the recipient from the hard realities of economic life.

In the area of commercial transactions, the export credit facilities granted by the KW supplement the export credit program of the German Export Credit Company, a joint undertaking of commercial banks. In 1963 the KW made a major shift from loans granted to German suppliers to loans granted to foreign purchasers. In that sense, export credit financing by the KW became more genuinely a form of foreign rather than domestic aid. In 1964 export credit aid was almost evenly divided between German exporters and foreign purchasers.

The emphasis on project loan financing is underlined by the KW's extensive administrative preparations and supervision in the uses of loans made for such specific projects.

In accordance with the consistent postwar economic philosophy of West Germany, the German aid policy emphasizes the impor-

[27] OECD, *Flow of Resources, 1956–1963*, p. 87.　　[28] *Ibid.*

tance of strengthening the private sector in developing countries. But the 1964 Report of the KW—which gives a statistical breakdown of forty-six current development plans—acknowledges that

development plans have become a fact of economic policy of which the aid-giving countries have to take note, whatever their view of long-term economic planning may be for their own country, and regardless whether their aid is given as a global contribution to a development plan or, as in the Federal Republic, predominantly by way of project financing.

The main criticism is directed to the lack of realism of many development plans.

Another German aid institution, the Deutsche Gesellschaft für Wirtschaftliche Zusammenarbeit (Entwicklungsgesellschaft) mbH, which was founded in September, 1962, has issued a report on its first year of operations (1963). The purpose of the DEG—whose capital of 75 million DM is entirely subscribed by the German Federal Republic—is to encourage private investment in developing countries, mainly by equity participation in a variety of projects. By the end of 1963, the DEG had approved seven projects with a total investment of 7 million DM, representing 29 percent of the capital invested in the enterprises in which the DEG participated. It had under examination thirty-six further projects with a total investment volume of 237 million DM and a DEG participation of about 37 million DM. Apart from that, the federal government made a special contribution to enable the DEG to participate in the Tanganyika Development Finance Company, the development Finance Company of Kenya, and the Development Finance Company of Uganda. In all three of these cases, the African governments concerned and the Commonwealth Development Corporation of the United Kingdom are the other shareholders. The still very modest operations of the DEG are mainly directed to Asia and Africa, with Latin America coming third. By far the most important fields of investment have hitherto been machine construction and textiles. The DEG favors joint ventures with middle- and small-scale enterprises.

While the objectives of the DEG could, therefore, be compared to those of the International Finance Corporation, i.e., the use of public funds to encourage and participate in joint ventures with private business in developing countries, the stimulating effect on German private investment in developing countries has thus far been modest. In 1963 the new German direct private investment in developing countries amounted to only about $50 million.[29]

In the total figures of development aid payments made by West Germany,[30] private funds, not only in the form of export credits but in the form of private investment as well, are listed as a part of bilateral aid. In 1963, such private investments represented 23 percent of the total bilateral aid granted by West Germany—and bilateral aid was 96 percent of the total aid. The unreserved classification of private investments made on commercial terms as development aid raises serious problems with regard to the definition of "aid," which is discussed elsewhere. To some extent it reflects the view in West Germany that private capital flows should be the main means of promoting development and that governmental aid is only supplementary. But even in the figures of official aid only, West Germany, with $421 million of net disbursements in 1963, was slightly ahead of the United Kingdom, ranking third among the major Western aid-giving countries, behind the United States and France.

The drastic reduction of aid commitments by the KW in 1964—and a slightly reduced appropriation for development aid in the 1965 federal budget—appears to indicate that, after a quick and dramatic spurt, the German aid commitment may level off. New capital aid commitments, as distinct from greatly increased disbursements on previous commitments, declined strongly, both absolutely and relatively to credits given for export financing and foreign investments and participations—which are far more commercially oriented.

JAPAN

With total official bilateral and multilateral aid disbursements to less developed countries that amounted to $172 million in 1963, Japan—now a member both of the OECD and of the DAC—follows the United States, France, West Germany, and the United Kingdom in the order of non-Communist countries providing aid on a sub-

---

[29] OECD, *Flow of Resources, 1956–1963*, p. 83.
[30] KW Report for 1963, Table III, p. 23.

stantial scale to the less developed countries of the world. No less interesting, for the purposes of this study, is the institutional pattern of aid-giving that Japan has developed in recent years.

In certain respects, the development of Japanese aid policy resembles that of West Germany. Both countries emerged from World War II shattered and economically exhausted, though with great possibilities of speedy recovery. For the first decade the efforts of Japan, like those of West Germany, were overwhelmingly concentrated on the reconstruction of the domestic economy, in both cases with very substantial help from the United States, which in Japan had also for the initial postwar period the responsibilities of the sole occupying power. The industrial and general economic recovery of Japan has been no less spectacular than that of West Germany. The major difference is that at the start of its postwar expansion Japan was industrially relatively less developed than Germany and her marked economic expansion—a rise of 43 percent in industrial production between 1960 and 1963—absorbed an even higher proportion of capital resources than the corresponding development in West Germany. The needs of an expanding domestic economy are still the main reason given by Japanese official quarters for the still low level of her slowly expanding general aid effort. What is without question is that Japan, though not as affluent as the countries of Western Europe, has in recent years clearly joined the ranks of the major industrially developed countries outside the Communist world and has had to face the problems of living close to a large number of neighbors who are at a much lower level of economic development.

The first major stimulus and necessity for Japan to provide economic assistance to a number of less developed countries in Asia came from the reparations claims made against her after the war. Japan concluded reparations agreements with Burma, Indonesia, South Viet Nam, and the Philippines. While these reparations agreements meant a net financial burden from the point of view of the Japanese government and the Japanese taxpayer, their implementation gave a stimulus to the Japanese economy, since the Japanese machinery and other capital goods and, above all, Japanese technical assistance had to be supplied on a major scale. Asia has remained the major recipient of Japanese development aid efforts. In 1962, Asian countries received about two-thirds of the Japanese official contributions, including nearly all the grants—amounting to $74.6 million, and mostly accounted for by reparations obligations—and about half the gross amount of long-term loans (more than five years), put at $115.1 million.[31] Apart from the reparations-receiving countries, the major recipient of Japanese assistance has been India.

The only other region to which Japanese aid efforts have been directed to any considerable extent is Latin America, which in 1962 received about half the official loans granted by Japan for development purposes, with Argentina as the major recipient.

The still rather modest flow of private Japanese investment—which in 1963 amounted to about $80 million—was almost evenly divided between Asian and Latin American countries. In addition, publicly guaranteed export credits for five years and over were granted in the amount of $13.3 million, mainly in Latin America.

The institutional structure of Japanese aid is complex and in many ways still experimental. As in Britain and West Germany, the policy-making responsibility is divided among several ministries. In Japan these are the Ministries of Foreign Affairs, Finance, and International Trade and Industry. A fourth agency is the Economic Planning Agency of the Japanese government. There is also a Council on Overseas Economic Cooperation which serves as an advisory body for the Prime Minister. The Ministry of Foreign Affairs has the major responsibility for reparations, which still constitute a substantial portion of the total Japanese aid effort.

While in theory these different governmental departments and agencies are supposed to cooperate and coordinate their policies, a recent first-hand study [32] suggests that there is much interdepartmental rivalry, especially between the Foreign Ministry and the Ministry for International Trade and Industry. To some extent such rivalries are, of course, inevitable and have their parallel in other aid-giving countries, since the Foreign Ministry is inclined to look at aid efforts essentially from the foreign policy point of view, while the

---

[31] In 1963 these two figures were little changed, with bilateral grants amounting to $76.7 million, of which $62.1 million represented indemnification and reparations payments, while loans extended for more than five years, gross, amounted to $118 million. Source for all these figures: OECD, *DAC 1964 Review*, Tables 4 and 5.

[32] John White, *Japanese Aid* (London, Overseas Development Institute Ltd., 1964), p. 28 *et seq.*

economically oriented agencies are concerned with financial and economic considerations and particularly with the interests of national industry.

The most important single administrative (as distinct from policy-making) agency for Japanese aid is the Export-Import Bank of Japan, which was established in 1952 and is under the general supervision of the Finance Ministry. In recent years, the Bank's main concern has been with long-term credits to developing countries. But far and away the most important part of its activities consists of the granting of export credits, which by the end of 1963 constituted 86 percent of its total credit activities. Most of these were given to finance the export of ships, shipbuilding having developed into Japan's single most important export industry. While the Bank may give loans both to Japanese exporters and to foreign importers, the former prevails by far.[33] In that sense, the aid aspect of the Export-Import Bank's credit operations is, from the point of view of the foreign recipient, an indirect one.

The aid aspect is further reduced by several limiting conditions imposed upon the Bank. In the first place, it is specifically prohibited from competing with private institutions. In the second place, it will lend funds only if financing is not available on ordinary terms from other sources and if repayment is considered certain. In the third place, the Bank insists on some degree of private participation. But above all, its interest rates have to be sufficiently high to cover the operating expenses of the Bank and the cost of borrowing from governmental funds. The Bank's capital fund is derived from budgetary allocations, and additional funds may be lent to it by the Finance Ministry. According to these provisions, the lending policy of the Export-Import Bank has to be at commercial rates. In 1963, almost all the Japanese official loans—for most of which the Export-Import Bank accounts—were at rates ranging from 5 to 7 percent.[34]

In being compelled to lend at commercial rates of interest, by which it can repay its own loans from the government and meet its operating expenses, the Japanese Export-Import Bank is comparable

---

[33] In contrast to the recent shift in the opposite direction by the German KW, as indicated above.

[34] $132 million at from 5 to 6 percent, $81.4 million at from 6 to 7 percent, and $23.9 million at more than 7 percent. Source: OECD, *DAC 1964 Review*, Table 6.

to the British Commonwealth Development Corporation. The policy is also comparable to that of the World Bank, but the latter has in effect greatly mitigated this policy by coupling its loans with the soft-term loans of its affiliate, the International Development Association, which lends for fifty years at ¾ percent. The average maturity of Japanese official loans was thirteen years in 1963.[35]

In 1961, the Overseas Economic Cooperation Fund (OECF) was established as a second official Japanese lending agency. Its objective is to enable the government to provide credits on easier terms than those of the Export-Import Bank, and the Fund therefore offers credits repayable over twenty years, including a five-year grace period, at 3.5 percent. But the appropriations made from public funds to the OECF and the scale of its operations have remained very modest. Annual appropriations have hitherto been below $50 million. An interesting aspect of the OECF—which is supervised by the Economic Planning Agency—is its ability to make equity investments and to make loans for experimental operations such as mine prospecting and feasibility surveys.[36] On the whole, the OECF indicates a potential rather than an actual modification of Japanese aid policy.

Capital aid policy of the Japanese government, like that of the German government, emphasizes project assistance and is wary of program financing, particularly for the purchase of commodities which would normally move through commercial channels. Nevertheless, "a fairly large share of total Japanese assistance is extended in the form of program assistance."[37] The direction of Japanese aid is closely linked with Japan's foreign trade policy:

In most instances, Japan has a favorable balance of trade with the less developed countries. Consequently, with a view to strengthening long-term economic relations, the Japanese Government gives high priority to projects or programs which are export-promoting or import-saving from the recipient's point of view, and which are in line with efforts to industrialize or diversify the recipient's economy.[38]

The importance of technical assistance in the Japanese aid effort is expressed by the establishment in 1962 of an Overseas Technical Cooperation Agency (OTCA), whose objective it is to coordinate

[35] OECD, *Flow of Resources, 1956–1963*, p. 93.
[36] *Ibid.*, p. 95. [37] *Ibid.* [38] *Ibid.*

all Japanese technical assistance activities except for a part of the program administered by the Ministry for International Trade and Industry. The OTCA operates autonomously under the supervision of the Foreign Ministry. It is in charge of the important program of training foreigners in Japan and sending Japanese experts abroad. It also controls the establishment of technical centers in other countries, and it cooperates with private banks in the collection and exchange of relevant information.

Through its membership in the OECD and the DAC and through its participation in the Aid-India Consortium under the auspices of the World Bank, Japan is now participating more actively in the various Western efforts to coordinate national aid policies among donor countries. This may, in due course, produce further modifications of Japanese aid policy, parallel to those proceeding in Western countries.

SINO-SOVIET BLOC

Only a very minor proportion—estimated by the OECD at 6 percent through 1963—of total Sino-Soviet bilateral aid commitments has hitherto been in the form of grants.[39] The Sino-Soviet countries also contribute to the UN technical assistance and relief agencies, of which all the Communist countries, except East Germany and China, are members. Their total contributions on that account in 1963 amounted to $6.3 million. None of the Communist countries participates in or subscribes to the World Bank or its affiliated institutions.

Volume and Direction of Development Assistance... According to information from Soviet sources,[40] the Soviet bloc (CMEA)[41]

[39] OECD, *Flow of Resources, 1956–1963*, p. 56. The Sino-Soviet countries covered include the USSR, Bulgaria, Czechoslovakia, Hungary, Poland, Rumania, mainland China, and the Soviet Occupied Zone of Germany.
[40] *International Affairs*, February, 1964, p. 71.
[41] Although formed in 1949, the Charter of the Council for Mutual Economic Assistance (CMEA) was not approved until 1959. Its members are Albania, Bulgaria, Czechoslovakia, East Germany, Hungary, Mongolia, Poland, Rumania, and the Soviet Union. Mainland China, Cuba, North Korea, North Viet Nam, and Yugoslavia have attended meetings as observers. The purpose of the Council is to provide mutual assistance, coordinate foreign trade, furnish information about the Members' economies, and exchange views on common experiences. Albania and all the Asian countries except Mongolia have stopped attending meetings. In the West the Council is known as COMECON. See Andrzej Korbon-

countries) as of early 1964 was furnishing economic and technical assistance in the construction of 1,100 industrial enterprises and other projects in forty developing states, including 166 projects in India, 50 in Indonesia, and 178 in the United Arab Republic. By the end of 1962, specialists of CMEA countries had trained about 53,000 workers, engaged at construction sites in the newly free countries. In 1962, CMEA countries sent 7,000 specialists to young states to provide various services. Over 10,000 persons from Asian, African, and Latin American countries are studying in educational establishments of CMEA countries. U.S. sources estimate that over 14,500 Communist technicians were working abroad in 1964 in some thirty less developed countries.[42]

Until a few years ago, the share of the USSR in the economic assistance given by the Sino-Soviet bloc to developing countries amounted to about 85 percent. More recently, the assistance programs of the other Eastern European Communist countries and of mainland China have increased, and in 1964 they represented about 20 percent each of total Sino-Soviet commitments of assistance.[43] The total disbursements made by way of economic assistance to less developed countries by the Communist states in 1963 are estimated by the OECD Secretariat at $425 million. Commitments far exceed disbursements and in 1964 are estimated to have risen to a peak of nearly $1.5 billion.[44] In any estimate of the financial volume of economic assistance from the Communist world, however, it must be borne in mind that, because of disparity of methods and systems, the figures are not easily comparable with those of the Western world. The significance of the volume of Sino-Soviet bloc aid is, of course, affected by the pricing policies of the state trading organizations of these donor countries.[45] The prices fixed by them on

ski, COMECON, *International Conciliation*, No. 549 (New York, Carnegie Endowment for International Peace, September, 1964).

[42] U.S. AID Program Presentation to Congress for Fiscal Year 1966, March, 1965, p. 181.

[43] *Ibid.*, p. 180.   [44] *Ibid.*, p. 179.

[45] As India has been the most important single recipient of aid from the USSR and of important aid from other Communist countries, the following figures, compiled by official Indian sources and reproduced from Report No. 9 in our research project on Public International Development Financing in India, pp. 156 ff., give a more detailed picture.

Up to the middle of 1963, the four principal Eastern European countries that exports financed through credits may or may not be in accord with world market prices.

The level of close to $1.5 billion of Sino-Soviet aid commitments estimated for 1964 represented a sharp increase over earlier commitments, from the beginning of such commitments in 1954 through 1963 (Table 3). Of the total commitments of $5.4 billion, $1.9 billion had been disbursed by the end of 1963.

TABLE 3

Sino-Soviet Aid Commitments, 1954–63

Year	Millions of Dollars
1954	11
1955	149
1956	608
1957	227
1958	556
1959	894
1960	1,165
1961	957
1962	507
1963	319
Total	5,393

Source: OECD, *Flow of Resources, 1956–1963*, p. 56.

---

granted aid to India were the USSR—the only Communist aid-giver up to the end of the Second Plan period—Poland, Czechoslovakia, and Yugoslavia.

Aid Authorizations up to Mid-1963, millions of rupees

(4.76 rupees = U.S. $1)

USSR	3,838.1
Poland	298.0
Czechoslovakia	231.0
Yugoslavia	190.5

These figures exclude minor grant transactions. There were also small credits from Hungary (80 million rupees) for aluminum and chemical plants and from Rumania (52 million rupees) for an oil refinery. The figure for Czechoslovakia excludes a supplier's credit of 170 million rupees.

The greatest part of these authorizations is directed to specific projects in heavy industry—steel plants, oil refineries, heavy machine building, heavy electrical equipment, mining machinery—in the public sector. A small portion is directed to industries such as drug manufacture and optical glass, and another portion is directed to the setting up of power plants in the public sector.

Development aid from Communist China increased sharply in 1964. A large part of it is directed to Africa (including Egypt), for which Chinese aid commitments rose from $73 million in 1963 to $162 million in 1964.[46] Chinese aid consists largely of credits and technicians to build light industries, roads, and state farms, as well as commodity credits for the import of Chinese goods. Most Chinese credits are interest-free and carry generous grace periods (e.g., ten years) and extended amortization schedules (e.g., twenty years including grace period). The Chinese have also agreed to extend some grants in convertible currencies to a number of African countries. It is likely that Communist China will direct its still very limited but growing economic and technological resources to selective projects and countries, with a heavy political orientation.

The principal recipients of Sino-Soviet aid have been India, the United Arab Republic, Afghanistan, and, especially in the most recent years, certain countries of Africa. Algeria has been a particularly heavy recipient during the last few years. In addition, several African countries—the Central African Republic, the Congo (Brazzaville), Kenya, Senegal, Tanzania, and Uganda—accepted Communist economic aid for the first time in 1964.

The foregoing data relate to Sino-Soviet aid to non-Communist less developed countries. In addition, Sino-Soviet economic aid commitments to Cuba are estimated to have amounted to almost $500 million in specific project credits and almost $900 million in general trade credits by the end of 1964, besides technical assistance through the services of several thousand personnel working in government, industry, agriculture, and education. Economic aid commitments by the USSR to Communist countries of Eastern Europe, China, Mongolia, North Korea, and North Viet Nam are estimated at $6.7 billion for the entire period 1945–64 and at $600 million during 1964.

Chinese Communist economic commitments[47] from 1953–64 have been estimated at $2,262 million,[48] of which $754 million, or

[46] African-American Institute, *Africa Report*, X (January, 1965), 40.

[47] W. F. Choa, "China's Economic Aid to Developing Countries," *The China Mainland Review* (Hong Kong), I (June, 1965), 13 ff. Most of the following information is summarized from this article.

[48] Value of assistance was given in Chinese yuan and the conversion rate used here is $1 = 2.46 yuan.

approximately one-third, has been to non-Communist countries.[49] North Korea and North Viet Nam have been the recipients of the greatest amount of assistance, equal to 25.4 percent and 27.3 percent of the total, respectively. Other major recipients have included Albania (5.4 percent), Mongolia (4.1 percent), Burma (4.0 percent), Egypt (4.0 percent), Cuba (3.6 percent), and Indonesia (3.1 percent). On a regional basis most of the total assistance has gone to Asia (71.9 percent) followed by Africa (15.1 percent), Europe (6.6 percent), Latin America (3.6 percent), and the Middle East (2.8 percent). From 1958 to 1964 the Asian share dropped to 52 percent, while the African share has climbed to 25 percent. This is in line with a discernible trend in recent years of an increasing proportion of Chinese aid being directed to non-Communist countries. Thus, in 1961 they received 40 percent of the total, in 1963 they received 70 percent, and in 1964 they received almost 100 percent. The level of aid shows no consistent pattern on an annual basis. In 1961 it was estimated at $395.2 million; in 1962, a year of difficult economic conditions on the mainland, commitments dropped to $11.7 million; in 1963, it recovered to $125.3 million; and in 1964 it stood at $292.1 million.

In 1955 virtually all the Chinese aid was in the form of grants. Since then emphasis has shifted to loans, and today almost all Chinese assistance is in the form of credits. These credits have generally had low interest rates varying from 1 to 2½ percent. More recently these credits have been interest-free, with a ten-year period of grace and extended amortization schedules (e.g., twenty years, including grace period). As a rule, repayment is in local products or local currency. Although credits are generally tied to purchases of Chinese goods and services, there have recently been some grants in convertible currencies to a number of African countries.[50]

Aid Methods and Policies of Communist Countries. In methods and objectives, the economic aid offered to developing countries by Communist states differs from that of the non-Communist world in a number of important respects.

There is no dichotomy of public assistance and private in-

[49] *Ibid.*, p. 17.
[50] African-American Institute, *Africa Report*, X (January, 1965), 40.

vestment—in so far as the latter can be considered as a form of development aid. As the Communist economies are centrally planned and directed, economic assistance offered to developing countries is part of the overall public economic planning and administration. There can be no private foreign investment, because there is no private entrepreneurial capital and enterprise of any major dimension. As a consequence, the economic aspects of development aid can be and are, far more directly than in the West, part and parcel of overall political strategy. While in the Western world the political objectives of public economic development assistance, both in its military and in its nonmilitary branches, play an important and acknowledged part, the public assistance is supplemented by nonpolitical private capital movements and investments.

The ideology of private enterprise limits, in particular, the ability of Western governments—and most notably that of the United States—to assist state and other forms of public enterprise in the developing countries. Assistance to public enterprise is reluctantly accepted in the domain of infrastructure (transport and public utilities), but it is frequently not extended to industrial state enterprises, even if these are a basic feature of the developing country's economic system and planning. By contrast, Communist aid favors state enterprise. In the words of a Soviet writer,

It is a distinguishing feature of economic assistance from the Soviet Union . . . that it is being used for building State-owned enterprises. . . . The State can more successfully protect national industry from foreign competition. . . . Strengthening of the State sector curbs the arbitrariness of foreign monopolies, serves as an impediment to the growth of local monopoly capital, which furnishes the material foundation for the reactionary forces that, as a rule, are allied with imperialism and feudalism.[51]

A practical illustration of this difference of approach is the issue of economic aid to the proposed new Indian steel plant at Bokaro. India first sought massive loan assistance for this big project, with strong support from the Kennedy Administration, from the United States, but abandoned the request in view of determined congres-

[51] Kapranow, article in *Trud,* quoted in *News and Views from the Soviet Union,* USSR Embassy, New Delhi, Feb. 10, 1962, p. 8.

sional opposition to U.S. support for this State-owned plant. Negotiations were then opened with the USSR, which promised massive loan and technical assistance.

Aside from aid in the form of credits and technical assistance, assistance to developing countries through the purchase of their exports is emphasized by Communist spokesmen. They also contend that Soviet exports to the developing countries, unlike those of the capitalist countries, which respond to their own commercial interests, help these countries to build up their economic system as their own interests require. Particular emphasis is being placed on increased trade with the less developed countries. A typical statement is that

foreign trade is a basic and most promising form of economic cooperation between underdeveloped countries of Asia, Africa and Latin America and the Soviet Union and other socialist countries. This is due to the fact that internal sources are the chief factor in the development of any country; foreign aid is just a supplementary factor.[52]

In the USSR, the Ministry of Foreign Trade is in charge of the planning and control of trade with foreign countries. Under the supervision of the Ministry, the USSR has some twenty foreign trade corporations which have responsibility for trade in specific commodities or in certain cases for the trade in any commodities within a specific area. In addition, a State Committee for Foreign Economic Relations, with the status of a ministry, develops economic contacts with all foreign countries and supervises technical, economic, and scientific collaboration. This Committee must coordinate its operations with those of the Ministry of Foreign Trade. The supervision of this coordination is carried out by a policymaking State Commission for Foreign Economic Affairs, which is attached to the Presidium of the Council of Ministers.

Forms and Terms of Aid. The great majority of loans by the Soviet Union and the Communist countries of Eastern Europe carry an interest rate of 2.5 percent and are repayable over twelve years

[52] Quoted from Russian sources by W. Malenbaum, *The East and West in India's Economic Development* (Washington, D.C., National Planning Association, 1960), pp. 43–44.

from the time of the last delivery of goods. In certain cases, repayment maturities are much longer, even up to fifty years.[53] In the case of Soviet loans to India, the repayment period has gradually risen from twelve to seventeen years. Although in the case of State-directed economies, commercial and noncommercial rates of interest cannot be easily distinguished, it is clear that an interest rate of 2½ percent is, by international standards, well below the commercial rate. To that extent, the loans offered by the USSR and other Communist countries are genuine aid.

A common repayment provision in Soviet aid agreements provides that the funds will be put into a bank account in the recipient country and be utilized for local purchases for export to the Soviet Union.

The credits granted on these terms are for the most part project-tied i.e., they are linked with a specific industrial project such as the construction of the Indian Bhilai steel mill. The credit has to be used for the purchase of Soviet machinery and the payment of the services of Soviet engineers and technicians. Most of the Communist aid has hitherto been concentrated in the field of ferrous and nonferrous metals, engineering, and metalworking industries.[54] The concentration on heavy industries tends to coincide with the preferences of many less developed countries with respect to the sectors to be developed in their economies. Other major projects have been concerned with power development and irrigation, such as the Aswan High Dam in Egypt and a hydroelectric plant in Afghanistan. The overall responsibility in these large projects usually resides in an agency of the less developed country.

There are also numerous projects involving light industries and social welfare facilities such as hospitals. In these smaller projects, especially in Africa, the Soviets have increasingly assumed total responsibility and have turned them over as functioning units on a "turnkey" basis, in the interest of doing what they regard as a proper job. While technical assistance is essentially provided through the services connected with the construction of an industrial plant for which a loan has been granted, there is also an extensive program for the training of personnel from the less developed

[53] OECD, *Flow of Resources, 1956–1963*, p. 56.   [54] *Ibid.*, p. 55.

countries in the USSR and in other industrially developed Communist countries.

Recent aid by Communist China, as previously noted, is even somewhat more liberal than Soviet aid in the terms of repayment and in the tying of funds by purpose and by country of expenditure.

The World Bank Group

The "World Bank group" of international financial agencies consists of the World Bank itself, formally designated as the International Bank for Reconstruction and Development (IBRD), and its two affiliates, the International Finance Corporation (IFC) and the International Development Association (IDA). Although the three institutions are separate legal entities, they are in fact closely linked. All three agencies have the same Board of Executive Directors. The President of the Bank, who is selected by the Executive Directors, is ex officio President of IDA and Chairman of the Board for all three agencies. The President of IFC is technically appointed separately by the Board, but, in fact, the President of the World Bank and IDA is now also President of IFC. Although the other officers and staff of IFC are for the most part different from those of the other two agencies, the World Bank and IDA are managed by the same officers and staff. Despite its separate legal personality, IDA is, in fact, operated as an integral part of the Bank. Its funds, however, are kept separate from those of the Bank, as provided by its charter, in view of differences in the proportion and manner of contributions by members and, to some extent, in the membership itself.

The World Bank was created, along with the International Monetary Fund (IMF), at the Bretton Woods Conference of 1944 to meet international financial problems that were envisaged for the postwar period. The IMF was to finance temporary balance-of-payments deficits, while the Bank was to provide long-term finance for the reconstruction of economies damaged by the war and for the development of the less developed countries. The Articles of Agreement of the Bank came into effect on December 27, 1945, and the Bank opened for business on June 25, 1946. The only major one of the forty-five countries that participated in the Bretton Woods

Conference that did not join the institutions created was the USSR. Poland withdrew from the Bank in 1950, Czechoslovakia in 1954, and Cuba in 1960.

IFC was created in 1956, following several years of international discussion, to supplement the activity of the Bank by providing risk capital and financing projects in the private sector without government guarantees. Loans made by the Bank, if not made to governments, require the guarantee of governments according to the Bank's charter, and this factor inhibited the extent to which the Bank could work with the private sector. In April, 1955, the Bank formally submitted a proposed charter for IFC to its member governments, and IFC came into being in July, 1956.

IDA was founded to provide development financing to less developed countries on terms more flexible and bearing less heavily on their balance of payments than those of loans of the World Bank, which fixed its terms in light of the fact that its major resources for lending came from private capital markets. As in the case of IFC, the idea for a soft lending institution was discussed for several years. The discussions culminated in the submission by the Bank to governments of Articles of Agreement for IDA in January, 1960, and the institution was formally created in September, 1960.

These agencies are the only multilateral agencies that provide capital funds for investment in the less developed countries on a global basis. Other multilateral agencies providing funds of this type are regional in scope, such as the Inter-American Development Bank, the European Development Fund, the European Investment Bank, and the recently created African Development Bank. And other multilateral agencies which are global in scope provide technical rather than financial assistance. This, of course, is true of the UN technical assistance program and even of the UN Special Fund. To the extent that the latter does provide assistance akin to capital assistance, the capital is for "pre-investment" activities, such as surveys of resources, rather than for capital investment projects as such.

THE WORLD BANK AND IDA

Membership and Capital.   Only members of the World Bank are eligible for membership in IDA, although there is no compulsion on

World Bank members to join IDA. Thus, all members of IDA are also members of the World Bank, although there are some World Bank members who have not joined IDA. Membership in the IMF is a necessary condition for membership in the World Bank. The feeling at Bretton Woods apparently was that the long-run financing to be provided by the World Bank for reconstruction and development could not be effective without the reasonably stable standards of international exchange to be fostered by the IMF.

World Bank membership has grown rapidly in recent years as numerous newly independent nations have joined. For example, seventeen countries joined the Bank during the year ending June 30, 1964. The number of members as of June 30, 1964, was 102. As of the same date, all World Bank members except nine (Belgium, Guinea, Indonesia, Jamaica, New Zealand, Portugal, Trinidad and Tobago, Uruguay, and Venezuela) had joined IDA. Thus, IDA had ninety-three members.

The initial capital of the World Bank was fixed at $10 billion, with only 20 percent to be paid in: 2 percent in gold or U.S. dollars and 18 percent in the members' own currencies, and the use of these currencies by the Bank was subject to the consent of the respective member. The balance of 80 percent of the subscribed capital was to be subject to call in order to honor the obligations of the Bank that might arise in connection with its borrowings or the guarantees issued by it. The Bank envisaged obtaining most of its resources for lending by borrowing in private capital markets with the backing of this large amount of capital subject to call. In September, 1959, the Bank's capital was raised to $21 billion, but only a part of the $11-billion increase was to be paid in; most of the increase was in the form of capital subject to call to permit the Bank to expand the volume of its borrowing.

As of June 30, 1964, the Bank had $21.2 billion of subscribed capital, of which $229 million had been paid in as gold or U.S. dollars, $1.5 billion had been paid in as national currencies available for loan disbursements (including $572 million by the United States), and $19.1 billion was on call. Of the capital subject to call, the share of the United States was $5,715 million, and that of the sixteen other countries that are classified as economically advanced for IDA purposes amounts to $7,675 million.

The terms of the Bank's loans—interest rates, maturities, and to some extent even the risks it has been prepared to assume—reflect its primary dependence on private capital markets for its resources. In view of the different function it was to perform, the nature of IDA's financial endowment was also different. The essential point is that its resources for lending consist exclusively of its own funds, rather than private funds borrowed against the backing of its capital. This makes it possible to extend soft terms.

IDA's initial capital was fixed so that it would amount to $1 billion if all World Bank members joined. The members of IDA are divided into two groups, the economically advanced countries and the less developed countries (Part I and Part II members, respectively), and the terms of the capital contributions differ for each. Part I members contribute capital on a fully convertible basis; 23 percent was to be paid initially and the rest in four equal annual installments. Part I members are not eligible to borrow from IDA except for their dependent territories. Part II members contribute only 10 percent of their capital subscriptions on a convertible basis, half initially and the rest in four equal annual installments; the balance of 90 percent is payable by each member in its own currency on the same payment schedule as applies to Part I members, with the currencies to be used for the most part only with the consent of the member concerned. Part II members are eligible for IDA credits.

IDA's lendable resources amounted to $782 million by mid-1964, including $10 million of supplementary contributions by Sweden, although total subscriptions came close to $1 billion. With the lendable resources virtually all committed by mid-1964, it became necessary to provide for an expansion of capital, and an agreement was reached to this end which became effective on June 29, 1964. An additional $753 million in convertible currencies are to be provided thereby, to be paid in three annual installments beginning in November, 1965. These additional resources are to be contributed entirely by Part I countries. A third supplementary contribution of $5,045,000 was also committed by Sweden.

The country quotas for capital contributions to the World Bank and IDA have been fixed on the basis of formulas that reflect their economic strength. Voting power is based on capital subscriptions, though not entirely. Each member has a certain minimum number of votes plus additional votes based on capital subscription, with the result that voting power is somewhat less than directly proportional to capital subscriptions.

The five largest shareholders of the World Bank as of June 30, 1964, and their share of total capital subscriptions and votes are given in Table 4.

TABLE 4

World Bank Capital Subscriptions and Voting Shares
of Five Largest Contributors
(Percent)

	Share of Total Capital Subscribed	Share of Total Votes
United States	29.97	26.86
United Kingdom	12.27	11.06
France	4.96	4.53
West Germany	4.96	4.53
India	3.78	3.48
Total	55.94	50.46

Each of these five largest shareholders appoints one Executive Director. The Board of Executive Directors of the Bank consists of twenty members, with the remaining fifteen elected by varying groups of member states. This is, in effect, the working board of the Bank, to which the Board of Governors, which meets only once a year with one Governor representing each member, has delegated most of its authority. All loans are submitted to the Executive Directors by the Bank's management for decision. The Executive Directors meet at least once a month at the Bank's headquarters, and most of the Directors work as such on a full-time basis. The President of the Bank is selected by the Board of Executive Directors and serves as its Chairman, having no vote except the deciding one in case of an equal division.

Four of the five largest shareholders of the Bank are economically advanced countries, and they hold 46.98 percent of the total votes. With the addition of one other economically advanced country, such as Canada (3.26 percent of the votes), or a few such as Belgium (2.00 percent of the votes), Italy (1.62 percent), and Japan (2.91 percent), this group has a majority of the voting power. In the case of IDA, the same four countries plus Canada and twelve other economically advanced countries that make up the Part I membership hold 64.4 percent of the voting power.

Resources for Lending. As noted, in the case of IDA it has been the convertible capital which has been paid in, primarily by the economically advanced countries, which has determined the volume of its lending, although some new resources have been made available recently to IDA out of World Bank earnings and Sweden has made supplementary contributions over and above its participation in IDA's capital.[55] In the case of the World Bank, on the other hand, by mid-1964 it was possible to make total loan commitments of about $7.8 billion and total loan disbursements of close to $6 billion, on the basis of only about $1.7 billion of paid-in capital freely available for lending. The $1.7 billion consisted of "free" gold or dollars plus national currencies released by members for lending or conversion to other currencies. Borrowings and earnings have added to this original resource for lending.

The largest resource has been the proceeds of Bank bond issues. As of June 30, 1964, Bank bonds outstanding amounted to $2.5 billion. Somewhat more than half of the bonds were held by non-U.S. investors, including some denominated in dollars. Of the total, $1.9 billion were payable in U.S. dollars and the balance in Canadian dollars, Swiss and Belgian francs, pounds sterling, Deutsches Marks, Italian lire, and Dutch guilders. The scope for additional borrowing is quite large; it will be recalled that as much as $13.4 billion of capital from economically advanced countries is subject to call.

The Bank has also recouped funds by selling portions of its loans, usually the early maturities, to other investors. Such sales amounted to a total of more than $1.7 billion by mid-1964. Besides, repayments of principal on loans disbursed by the Bank had accumulated to $773 million by the same date.

Finally, certain reserves accumulated by the Bank out of earnings have added to the pool of funds available for lending. The Bank has maintained two reserve accounts, a Special Reserve and a Supplemental Reserve. The Special Reserve has been built up from the

[55] Amounting to $15,135,000, added to its initial subscription of $10,090,000, and its subscription of $15 million in connection with IDA's June, 1964, increase of capital.

earmarking of 1 percentage point of its total interest charges, designated as a commission, and must be kept in liquid form to meet liabilities arising out of borrowings and guarantees. By June 30, 1964, the Special Reserve amounted to $288 million. After that date the earmarking practice was discontinued, and all earnings, with minor exceptions are now subject to disposition by the Executive Directors.

The Supplemental Reserve resulted from all other net income and is a cushion against losses on loans and guarantees but is also available as a resource for lending. It amounted to $558 million on June 30, 1964. All net income earned by the Bank, except for the 1 percent commission, had been allocated to this Reserve up to June 30, 1964. An interesting innovation was introduced with respect to the net earnings of fiscal year 1964: of the total of $97.5 million, only $47.5 million was allocated to this Reserve, while $50 million was transferred as a grant to IDA. This action was taken in July, 1964, and the Bank's Supplemental Reserve increased from the June 30, 1964 figure of $558 million to $605.5 million with the allocation of the $47.5 million.

World Bank net earnings increased to $136.9 million in the fiscal year 1965. The sum of $61.9 million was transferred to reserves, boosting them to a total of $956.5 million. As for the remaining $75 million, the Bank's directors recommended its transfer to IDA, as had been done with the sum of $50 million a year earlier. Approval of this action was expected at the September, 1965, meeting of the Board of Governors.

A proposal for new resources for IDA to be obtained in private capital markets was made at the March–June, 1964, United Nations Conference on Trade and Development (UNCTAD).[56] The proposal, on which the conference requested a study by the World Bank, called for the constitution of an international "interest equalization fund" by economically advanced countries to finance the difference between commercial interest rates on borrowings and concessionary interest rates on lending. The borrowings would take place, as they do now by the IBRD, in private capital markets, and

---

[56] The proposal is known as the Horowitz Proposal, since it was made by David Horowitz, Governor of the Bank of Israel and head of the delegation of Israel to the conference.

the proceeds would be used for IDA-type lending. There are various precedents for this type of operation, some of which have been cited elsewhere in this chapter, e.g., the assumption by various agencies of the British government of interest waivers granted by the Export Credits Guarantee Department and the assumption by the European Development Fund of part of the interest charges of the European Investment Bank.

In February, 1965, the World Bank published a report by its staff on the proposal.[57] The report does not make any recommendations regarding the adoption of the proposal. It is not a policy document representing the views of the Bank as an organization but rather a technical staff study. The study merely analyzes and brings to the attention of governments the possible effects and policy implications of the proposal, although it does include definite positions of the Bank staff on certain of the technical aspects.

The proposal as originally presented to UNCTAD contemplated a scale of borrowing of some $2 billion a year for a ten-year period, but it was later reduced for purposes of initial study to $600 million a year for a five-year period. The essential point of it is to tap private sources and to minimize recourse to government budgets for an increased volume of loans to less developed countries on concessionary terms. The proposal was flexible with respect to the institutional arrangements through which it might be carried out.

The Bank staff study points out that there are serious limitations on the prospects for borrowing in private capital markets, particularly in view of balance-of-payments problems in such important potential markets as the United States and the United Kingdom and because of alternative claims on such borrowed funds, including those of the World Bank itself. With respect to possible types of government guarantees to back the bonds that might be sold, the Bank staff took the view that the capital on call and the reserves of the Bank itself should not be used for this purpose, since "it would be prejudicial to the Bank's credit standing and to its reputation for sound and businesslike financing if it were to borrow against its own credit in order to lend to IDA." [58] Furthermore, from the institutional point of view, the judgment of the Bank staff was that "it would be

[57] IBRD, *The Horowitz Proposal: A Staff Report* (Washington, D.C., 1965).
[58] *Ibid.*, p. 20.

preferable that IDA borrow for itself" [59] rather than for the Bank to borrow on its behalf. The idea of the interest equalization fund, the report points out, of course involves the important issue of a long-term commitment by governments to contribute to it because of the interest differential that must be made up each year for the duration of the bond liabilities and of the long-term loans made out of the proceeds.

As indicated in the Bank report, the proposal can be used as a supplementary, rather than as the principal, device for increasing IDA's resources. And mention is also made of at least two other approaches to the problem: governments individually could lend funds to IDA, which they could obtain either by borrowing themselves and/or by budgetary appropriations; or they could underwrite and subsidize the interest charges on loans to particular countries.

In remarks made on the Bank study at a meeting in March, 1965, of the Committee on Invisibles and Financing related to Trade of the UN Trade and Development Board, Horowitz reaffirmed his support of the proposal bearing his name, and pointed out that the problem is one of alternative ways of raising resources for concessionary lending. He expressed the view that

if the project is a high-priority one, the apparent difficulty of some technicalities can be overcome and the Horowitz Plan . . . may be considered, in the present circumstances, as a practical plan to a substantial expansion of assistance to developing nations on realistic terms, with a relatively minor allocation from budgetary resources.[60]

Volume of Lending. During the year ended June 30, 1964, the World Bank and IDA together approved loans in the amount of close to $1.1 billion (World Bank, $810 million; IDA, $283 million) and disbursed close to $700 million (World Bank, $559 million; IDA, $124 million). That fiscal year represented a peak of activity in both loan approvals and disbursements for IDA and close to a peak for the Bank. The rate of loan approvals increased still more

---

[59] *Ibid.*, p. 24.
[60] United Nations Conference on Trade and Development, TD/B/C.3/1/ Add.1, March 26, 1965, p. 5.

during fiscal 1965, when the Bank committed $1.02 billion in loans and IDA committed $309 million.

The volume of loan commitments and disbursements by the World Bank has increased steadily during its eighteen-year history. The trend is reflected in the averages for successive three-year periods (Table 5), which smooth out the somewhat fortuitous fluctuations that occur from year to year.

TABLE 5

World Bank Loan Commitments
and Disbursements, 1947–49 to 1962–64
(Millions of U.S. Dollars)

Fiscal Years (Annual Average)	Commitments	Disbursements
1947–49	217	175
1950–52	254	117
1953–55	304	268
1956–58	498	372
1959–61	657	508
1962–64	714	555

The peak of commitments was 1.02 billion in fiscal 1965; and the peak of disbursements, $620 million, occurred during fiscal 1963 following the year of the previously recorded high for commitments.

Thus, the rate of World Bank lending has reached an average level recently of somewhat more than $700 million per year in commitments and somewhat more than $500 million in disbursements. As previously suggested, this level has been reached without any strain at all on the Bank's resources. Indeed, the Bank is in a highly liquid position and has not added at all to its outstanding funded debt during the last couple of years.

Most of the Bank's loans go, of course, to the less developed countries. Its first operations consisted of some $500 million of loans for postwar reconstruction in France, the Netherlands, Denmark, and Luxembourg, but the task of European reconstruction was taken over in 1948 by the Marshall Plan, and the Bank at that time turned its attention to the "development" rather than the "reconstruction" part of its functions. However, a minor, though by no means negligible, part of the Bank's loans has continued to be devoted to projects in economically advanced countries. In fiscal 1964, for example, out of the $810 million of commitments, $125 million was committed to Japan and close to $100 million to New Zealand, Denmark, Finland, and Norway.

As previously indicated, the rate of IDA commitments has reached over $300 million per year. IDA's brief history of lending activity is shown in Table 6.

TABLE 6

IDA Loan Commitments and Disbursements, 1961–65

(*Millions of U.S. Dollars*)

Fiscal Year	Commitments	Disbursements
1961	101	. . .
1962	134	12
1963	260	56
1964	283	124
1965	309	222

The recent increase in IDA's resources of $753 million, to be paid in three equal annual installments, plus the $50 million granted to it by the IBRD, are calculated to permit a continuation of the present rate of activity for some three years more, assuming that the rate of disbursements moves closer to the rate of commitments. IDA's credits have, of course, gone exclusively to less developed countries and especially to the poorest ones or those in the most difficult balance-of-payments positions.

PURPOSES OF LOANS

The World Bank has granted its loans primarily for electric power and transportation projects. Its cumulative commitments up to June 30, 1964, as indicated in Table 7, have been for electric power to the extent of 35 percent of the total and for transportation to the extent of 33 percent. IDA's loans have also gone primarily to economic infrastructure projects, especially in transportation, but agriculture has figured to a greater extent in IDA than in World Bank loans, and IDA has financed non-revenue-producing water supply and education projects, which, until recently, have been totally absent from World Bank lending.

TABLE 7

Cumulative Loan Commitments of the World Bank and IDA, by Purpose, as of June 30, 1964

	WORLD BANK		IDA	
Purpose	Millions of dollars	Percent	Millions of dollars	Percent
All purposes	7,793	100.0	778	100.0
Electric power	2,711	34.8	58	7.5
Transportation	2,575	33.0	354	45.5
Agriculture and forestry	556	7.1	133	17.1
Industry	1,203	15.4	106	13.6
General development	205	2.6	. . .	. . .
Telecommunications	46	0.7	42	5.4
Water supply	. . .	. . .	63	8.1
Education	. . .	. . .	22	2.8
Reconstruction	497	6.4	. . .	. . .

The small degree of differentiation between the World Bank and IDA on the basis of the purposes of their loans is likely to be reduced even more in the future. In liberalizing its lending policies, the Bank too has entered fields in the social sector, such as education. The essential difference between the two is consequently emerging as a matter almost exclusively of repayment terms. IDA is the fund to be used for countries whose balance-of-payments situation requires terms that involve less of a repayment burden than those granted by the Bank, although the projects financed will be mostly of the same type. Indeed, in some countries, the two sources of funds are being combined in the same projects to achieve a blend of hard and soft repayment terms.

Both the World Bank and IDA expect to continue emphasizing economic infrastructure projects but to pay greater attention in the future to projects in the fields of agriculture, industry, and education. Cooperative agreements have been worked out with the UN Food and Agriculture Organization and with the UN Educational, Scientific, and Cultural Organization to help identify and carry out projects in agriculture and education, respectively.

Most agricultural projects to date of the World Bank and IDA have involved the financing of agricultural machinery, irrigation, or land reclamation. It is hoped to place more emphasis in the future on assistance to agricultural credit and extension agencies, on loans for the development of crop storage facilities, and on the financing of farm-to-market roads.

World Bank financing for industry has included relatively few large projects in such fields as iron and steel and pulp and paper. These projects, while requiring government guarantees, have been in the private sector. The Bank has not extended loans to industrial projects in the public sector. Furthermore, the substantial amount of financing it has provided to industry via intermediate credit institutions has been almost exclusively to privately controlled companies of this type. By June 30, 1964, the Bank had committed $267 million of loans to privately owned development finance companies for relending to specific private industrial projects. IDA had committed $10 million of loans for such companies. And IFC, which takes the lead for the World Bank group in assistance to development finance companies, usually providing equity capital while the Bank and IDA lend to them directly or indirectly, had invested $17 million. The World Bank group has also provided much technical assistance to such companies and assisted in the creation of a number of them, such as the Industrial Development Bank of Turkey and the Industrial Credit and Investment Corporation of India. Future industrial financing by the World Bank group will continue to emphasize assistance to these intermediate credit institutions.

All IDA loans for industry have been of an indirect type. Besides the $10 million in loans for development finance companies, it has granted a loan for the development of industrial estates, and two large loans ($90 million in June, 1964, and $100 million in August, 1965) to India to permit certain industries to import components, materials and spare parts in order to overcome the shortage of foreign exchange that has limited their imports and, consequently, the utilization of their capacity. The latter loan is more in the nature of a general program loan, in contrast to the usual World Bank–IDA practice of lending only for the construction or expansion of specific projects. It is illustrative of the greater flexibility that is being introduced into their lending policies.

The World Bank hopes to expand assistance to industry also by enlarging the financial resources available to IFC. The charters of both institutions are in process of amendment, pursuant to action taken by their Boards of Governors in September, 1964, to permit the Bank to lend money to IFC in much the same way as it does to national development finance companies.

The more flexible approach of the World Bank toward the financing of industry is also finding expression in a modification of its hitherto strict policy of not lending to state-owned industrial enterprises. In an address on March 26, 1965, to the UN Economic and Social Council, the President of the Bank stated:

We have been reluctant to finance State-owned industrial enterprises primarily because of the great difficulty of assuring that they would be managed on a businesslike basis, free of political pressures. We are quite aware, nonetheless, that in some of our member countries, and especially in the newer ones, a shortage of private savings and of industrial entrepreneurship harshly limits what purely private capital can accomplish. We are therefore embarking upon a re-examination of our policies as applied to such cases to see whether there are ways, other than through completely private ownership, in which effective management of industrial ventures can be assured.

The emphasis in World Bank–IDA lending for education is to be on vocational and technical instruction. As of June 30, 1964, loans for education had been extended to three countries, Pakistan, Tanganyika, and Tunisia, all by IDA. The World Bank made its first education loan in October, 1964, for a College of Agriculture in the Philippines. In doing so, the Bank granted somewhat more lenient repayment terms than usual in its loans—an amortization period of thirty years, including an initial grace period of ten years.

Loan Conditions and Terms. World Bank and IDA loans have generally been limited to the foreign exchange requirements of the projects financed, although there have been some exceptions to this general rule. For example, in January, 1962, the Bank granted a $95-million loan for electric power to Argentina, of which $60 million was for local currency costs in the project. Furthermore, these institutions have recently recognized that they should legitimately be expected to provide more local currency financing. Their annual report for the fiscal year 1964 states (p. 8) that their "Executive Directors have confirmed the principle that the Bank and IDA should be prepared to provide finance for local expenditure on high-priority projects in cases where lending only funds needed for direct imports would not provide adequate support."

World Bank and IDA loans are, of course, not tied with respect to country of purchase. Loan recipients are free to spend the proceeds of loans in any member country or in Switzerland (which, though not a member of the World Bank, has opened its capital market to Bank bond issues). Indeed, World Bank–IDA loans are strictly supervised to insure that the terms of international competitive bidding are fairly observed.

World Bank–IDA loans have at times been subject to compliance with administrative or financial conditions imposed by the lending agency on the projects to be financed. These have been concerned, for example, with the creation of autonomous government corporations or other administrative changes for the management of officially owned railways in order to free them of political influences or to place them on a more commercially oriented basis or with the establishment of higher rates by public utility enterprises in transportation or electric power to permit them to service Bank loans and to accumulate reserves to finance expansion. At times, such conditions have understandably created frictions, but they have by and large been accepted as desirable reforms that might otherwise be politically difficult to achieve.

As previously indicated, the essential difference between the World Bank and IDA hinges on the repayment terms of their loans. The World Bank is the relatively hard lending agency, while IDA is in fact the soft-loan "window" of the same Bank and is the resource used to ease the external debt repayment burden for poorer countries. The Bank charges an interest rate which reflects the cost of its own borrowing in private capital markets. Its rate held at 5½ percent per annum from September, 1962, to early in 1966, when it was raised to 6 percent. IDA charges no interest rate but only a "service charge" to defray administrative expenses, which has uniformly amounted to ¾ percent per annum. World Bank loans have had to be repaid during periods ranging for the most part up to a maximum of twenty-five years, with an initial grace period of two to five years. IDA has uniformly granted a repayment period of fifty years, including an initial grace period of ten years, with amortization of 1 percent of the principal per year during the first ten years of the repayment period and 3 percent per year thereafter for the remaining thirty years. IDA credits, nevertheless, must be repaid in convertible currencies.

World Bank and IDA loans have been combined in the programs for particular countries to achieve a repayment schedule somewhere between the hard terms of the former and the soft terms of the latter. In some cases, there has been joint financing by the two in individual projects as well.

The difference in repayment terms, in turn, arises from differences in the types of resources for lending used by the two agencies. The use of government contributions by IDA permits it to give concessionary terms, while the use of resources raised in private capital markets makes it necessary for the Bank to limit itself to "conventional" terms.

The soft terms of IDA are granted only to governments. They are not intended to subsidize revenue-producing projects, either in the public or the private sector. Whenever IDA loans are re-lent by governments to such projects, IDA insists that conventional terms of finance be applied in the subloans.

Although IDA is the principal device of the World Bank group for making soft loans, the World Bank itself, in selected cases, has recently liberalized the terms of its own loans as well, in view of its strong financial position. Some loans have been granted for more than the usual maximum of twenty-five years. In February, 1964, a thirty-five-year term was granted in an electric power loan to Colombia, and in October, 1964, a thirty-year term was granted in the Philippine education loan. Longer grace periods than the usual two to five years have also been granted, as in the case of an eight-year grace period in a highway loan to Liberia granted in January, 1964, and a ten-year grace period in the Philippine education loan. Also, the Bank commitment charge of ¾ percent per annum on the undisbursed portion of loans was reduced, effective July 1, 1964, by one-half, to ⅜ percent per annum.

TECHNICAL ASSISTANCE AND OTHER ACTIVITIES

In carrying out its central function of supplying loan funds for development projects, out of its own resources and those of IDA, the World Bank has provided a considerable variety of other services in support of this primary activity. These have included taking the lead in the coordination of international assistance for selected countries, making available advisory services to assist countries in preparing development plans and investment projects, conducting studies on various problems of world economic development, and providing training facilities.

The Bank's role as a leader in the coordination of international financial assistance for development is discussed elsewhere in this chapter. It has included its chairmanship of the aid consortia for India and Pakistan and of the consultative groups for Colombia, Nigeria, Tunisia, and the Sudan. The Bank plans to increase the latter type of activity. In his address of March 26, 1965, to the UN Economic and Social Council, the President of the Bank stated in this connection,

We have recently come to a decision in the Bank to redouble our efforts in this respect. We plan to take the lead, insofar as practicable, in organizing consultative groups where they promise to be of some advantage, and we have started conversations with member governments on this subject.

Akin to the lead it has taken in these international development financing groups is the role played by the Bank in bringing about a settlement of the Indus River dispute between India and Pakistan and in forming and administering the related Indus Basin Development Fund for the construction of facilities in Pakistan to carry out the agreement and to utilize the resources of the river.

The Indus, with its five main tributary rivers, comprises one of the great river systems of the world. The sharing of Indus waters was a cause for dispute between provinces in India even prior to independence and partition. Following partition, the dispute was raised to the international level. Pakistan had become the downstream riparian, and the headworks of the two main irrigation canals in Pakistan were left on the Indian side of the border. The sharing of the waters was a principal cause of strained relations between the two countries.

In 1952 the two governments accepted the offer of the President of the World Bank to use the good offices of that institution to resolve their differences over the use of the Indus waters. After years of Bank-initiated studies, analyses, and negotiations, the Indus Waters Treaty and the Indus Basin Development Fund Agreement were finally executed in 1960.

The arrangements provided for a division of the waters over a transitional ten-year period. During the ten years Pakistan was to construct a system of works to permit a relinquishment of old sources of water and the receipt of new sources and, in addition, to provide for irrigation development, development of 300,000 kilowatts of hydroelectric power, lowering ground water levels in water-logged and saline areas, and flood protection. In order to finance this program, an Indus Basin Development Fund, consisting of the equivalent of $894 million in both convertible foreign exchange and local currency, was created. The Fund received its money from seven countries besides India and Pakistan and from the World Bank in loans and grants as shown in Table 8.

TABLE 8

Contributions to the Indus Basin Development Fund

	Foreign Exchange Grants, millions	Foreign Exchange Loans, millions	Local Currency Grants and/or Loans, millions [a]
Australia	£A 6.96		
Canada	Can.$ 22.1		
West Germany	DM 126.0		
India	£ 62.1		
New Zealand	£NZ 1.0		
Pakistan	£ 0.44		£ 9.85
United Kingdom	£ 20.86		
United States	U.S.$177.0	U.S.$70.0	U.S.$235.0 [b]
World Bank	. . .	U.S.$80.0	

[a] An equivalent amount in Pakistan rupees.
[b] To be either loans or grants.

Source: World Bank Press Release No. 650, September 19, 1960.

Each of the parties agreed to make semiannual payments into the Fund up to the amounts pledged. The Indian contribution was fixed in the Water Treaty. The Bank acts as administrator of the Fund. Disbursements are made to Pakistan by the administrator exclusively to finance the cost of equipment, supplies, and other property and services required to construct the system of works agreed to by the contributors to the Fund. In April, 1964, the foreign exchange contributors to the Fund agreed to increase their contributions by an additional $315 million, including a $58.5-million loan from IDA.

To assist countries in drawing up national development plans, the World Bank has sponsored comprehensive survey missions. The first such mission was organized in 1949 to help Colombia establish the basis for a national development plan. General survey missions of this type have worked to date in some twenty-three countries. These missions have conducted one-time studies to permit the countries to see their development problems in better focus and, as a byproduct in many cases, have led to later Bank financing of specific projects.

Besides the general survey missions, the Bank has also provided resident advisers to help in national planning and project preparation. Toward the end of 1961 it established a Development Advisory Service to administer this type of activity.

The Bank has also assisted in the organization and financing of particular project and sector studies. It has done this on its own as well as in cooperation with other international agencies. Mention has been made of the Bank's cooperative arrangements with the FAO and UNESCO to develop projects in agriculture and education. The Bank has also acted as Executing Agent for surveys financed by the UN Special Fund.

Besides the studies and advisory services for individual countries, the Bank has carried out various studies of general interest in connection with economic development. These have included studies of international commodity trends of special interest to the less developed countries, studies of the external debt servicing capacity of such countries, and studies for the possible creation of a system of international investment insurance on a multilateral basis. The UN Conference on Trade and Development, held in March–June, 1964, requested the Bank to study the proposal for creation of an "interest equalization fund," which has been mentioned, as well as the feasibility of a system of financing to offset persistent adverse movements in export earnings, and the use and term of suppliers' credits and credit insurance.

In March, 1965, the Bank submitted to its members a convention for the creation of an International Center for Settlement of Investment Disputes between foreign investors and host governments by conciliation and/or arbitration. The Center, to come into being upon ratification of the convention by twenty governments, will operate as an autonomous international institution under the auspices of the Bank. By September 1, 1965, there were ten signatories to the Convention.

The Bank started a program of training as early as 1948. These activities were expanded in 1956 with the establishment of an Economic Development Institute. The Institute has conducted general six-month courses on economic development for officials from developing countries and specialized courses on project evaluation. Courses have been given in English, French, and Spanish. By September, 1964, a total of 342 officials from eighty-five countries had participated.

IFC

Membership in IFC is open only to members of the World Bank. The authorized capital of the corporation was fixed at $100 million. Capital subscriptions are generally to be paid in within thirty days of date of subscription, in gold or U.S. dollars. As of June 30, 1964, seventy-eight countries were members of IFC, and their subscriptions, all paid in, totaled $99 million.

Of the total membership of seventy-eight, eighteen economically advanced countries accounted for 80.98 percent of the subscriptions and 71.45 percent of the total voting power. The five largest shareholders as of June 30, 1964, with their shares of total subscriptions and voting power, were as shown in Table 9. As in the case of the other institutions of the World Bank group, India figures among the first five shareholders because of its sheer size.

The basic resource of IFC for investment is its capital, supplemented by the net earnings and profits it has realized on its investments and loans. Furthermore, when it sells its investments, it has

TABLE 9

*Subscriptions and Voting Power
of IFC's Five Largest Shareholders*
(Percent)

	Subscriptions	Voting Power
United States	35.54	29.90
United Kingdom	14.55	12.37
France	5.88	5.12
India	4.48	3.95
West Germany	3.69	3.30
Total	64.14	54.64

the proceeds of these sales for new investments. The representation of these various sources of funds in its cumulative commitments as of June 30, 1964, was as follows:

	Millions of Dollars
Capital	99.0
Net earnings	18.9
Net profits on portfolio sales	1.3
Repayments on investments	6.0
Sales of investments	22.4
Acquisition by others of securities covered by underwriting commitments	7.4
Total of funds available	155.0
Gross commitments made	111.4
Less cancellations	8.3
Net commitments made	103.1
Excess of funds available over net commitments	51.9

Thus, as of June 30, 1964, IFC had uncommitted funds available for its operational activities in the amount of $51.9 million. Furthermore, by virtue of action taken to amend its own charter and that of the World Bank, it had the prospect of being able to borrow from the latter organization several times the amount of its own capital.

IFC investment commitments made during the year ended June 30, 1964, reached eighteen in number and $20.8 million in value. Its disbursements amounted to $15.6 million, which was close to the peak of $15.9 million reached the year before. The rate of commitments increased to 22.7 million during fiscal 1965. Average annual commitments and disbursements during the five years ended June 30, 1964, were about $17 million and $13 million, respectively. The record of IFC's commitments and disbursements since its establishment is given in Table 10.

TABLE 10

IFC Commitments and Disbursements, 1957–64

(Millions of Dollars)

Fiscal Year	No.	Commitments	Disbursements
1957	1	2.0	. . .
1958	8	9.6	3.3
1959	10	14.7	6.6
1960	12	21.7	12.8
1961	9	6.2	10.4
1962	9	18.4	11.9
1963	11	18.0	15.9
1964	18	20.8	15.6
Total	78	111.4	76.5

IFC investments can be made in any member countries, but they are in fact concentrated in the less developed countries. All the $111.4 million of gross commitments were made to such countries except for $4.2 million committed to Australia, Finland, and Italy, including $1 million to Italy for an enterprise in the less developed southern region of that country.

IFC investments have gone almost entirely to manufacturing enterprises, directly or indirectly, with only a small amount having been devoted to mining. The indirect investments in manufacturing have been via IFC's assistance to development finance companies. Total IFC investments in such companies amounted to $16.7 million as of June 30, 1964, and this type of investment has been growing in importance. About 30 percent of IFC commitments in fiscal 1964 was for such companies. The IFC has helped in the capitalization of thirteen different development finance companies throughout the world.

According to its original charter, IFC could not make equity investments. At the same time, it was supposed to turn over its holdings by selling them to private interests whenever it could do so on reasonable terms. But private investors were frequently not interested in purchasing merely loans with a fixed rate of return. The IFC attempted to overcome this by making loans through the purchase of convertible debentures or by having features in them such as stock purchase options, contingent interest provisions, and other equity-type arrangements, to make them as attractive as possible to potential private buyers. It could thereby also carry out its objective of minimizing fixed charges in the financing provided to enterprises. Later, in 1961, its charter was amended to permit it to make equity investments.

IFC investments in the form of subscriptions to capital shares have been growing in importance relative to loans. During fiscal year 1964, more than half ($12.1 million) of IFC's total investment commitments ($20.8 million) was in the form of direct investments. By June 30, 1964, 30 percent of IFC's portfolio was in equity.

IFC can also underwrite the issuance of shares by corporate enterprises or give standby commitments for their purchase. Underwriting and standby commitments accounted for $2.9 million of the total commitments of $20.8 million made during fiscal 1964.

IFC does not make conventional loans or charge uniform interest rates; the conditions vary with the individual project. Most investments have been made at a fixed interest rate of 7 percent per annum plus other features such as additional interest contingent on profits. The usual loan term is from about seven to fifteen years, with serial maturities after an initial grace period.

IFC does not invest in government-owned or -operated enterprises, although it is not precluded from investing in enterprises which have some public financial participation. Its role is essentially that of a mobilizer of private investment, both domestic and international, in manufacturing enterprises in the less developed countries. Besides its financial assistance, it also helps projects by giving technical, managerial, and financial advice and by recruiting capital from other sources. Its $21 million of commitments during the fiscal year ending June 30, 1964, are reported to have been joined by commitments from other investors, including the World Bank, of nearly seven times that amount.

Inter-American Development Bank

The Inter-American Development Bank (IDB) came into existence on December 30, 1959, when the agreement for its establishment was ratified. The year 1960 was devoted to organization and preliminary operations by the Bank, and it made its first loan in February, 1961.

The Bank, whose membership consists of the United States and all nineteen Latin American republics except Cuba (Cuba did not ratify the agreement), came into being shortly after the United States announced, in August, 1958, its willingness to participate in such an institution. The ensuing period of a little more than a year and a quarter until the Bank's establishment was taken up with the drafting of its charter by a special committee representing the prospective members, which completed its work on April 8, 1959, and with ratification of the charter.

The decision of the United States to participate represented a reversal of the negative, or at best neutral, attitude it had always had toward the creation of an inter-American bank. A proposal for such an institution was made as early as the first Inter-American Conference held in 1889–90. A charter for an inter-American bank was actually drawn up in 1940, but it was never ratified in view of the preoccupation with World War II and the creation of the World Bank at the Bretton Woods Conference. Thereafter, the United States consistently held the view that economic development in Latin America could adequately be financed by its own Export-Import Bank and the World Bank. It was not until 1958 that the United States changed its attitude, as a reaction to the low point in United States–Latin American relations symbolized by the animosity expressed toward Vice-President Nixon during his tour of Latin America in that year.

The IDB was modeled after the World Bank in much of its organization, and in the fact that only part of its capital was paid in and a larger part remained as callable capital to guarantee bond issues which were to be floated in private capital markets. Furthermore, it anticipated IDA, which was to be created later, by having a Fund for Special Operations as a soft-loan "window," in addition to its ordinary capital resources. A unique feature of the IDB was the granting to it in June, 1961, for administration by the U. S. government, of a Social Progress Trust Fund for Latin America.

Membership and Capital. The quotas for the subscription of capital by countries were fixed in accordance with their economic capacity, on the basis of criteria similar to those used for the IBRD. The voting provisions also follow the IBRD system, consisting of a small, fixed number of votes for each member country, to which are added votes proportionate to capital subscription. Thus, the United States, like all other members, starts with a base of 135 votes, but its total number of votes is 35,135. The share of the United States is 43.04 percent of total capital subscriptions and 41.82 percent of total votes.

Like the IBRD, the IDB has a Board of Governors and a Board of Executive Directors to which the Governors delegate their authority for continuing operations. The Board of Governors is composed of one Governor and Alternate named by each member. It meets once a year on a rotating basis in the capital cities of the members. Its meetings are held in April; the Bank's fiscal year is the calendar year. This compares with IBRD annual meetings in September, related to a fiscal year that ends June 30. The Board of Governors names the President of the IDB.

The Board of Executive Directors consists of seven Directors, one of whom is named by the United States. The Executive Directors have their offices at the Bank's headquarters in Washington, where they hold their meetings. The authorization of loans is a function of the Board of Executive Directors.

The authorized capital of the Bank was originally fixed at $850 million, including Cuba's quota. The initial capital actually subscribed, with Cuba's failure to join the Bank, amounted to $813,160,000. Somewhat less than half of the initial authorized capital was to be paid in, with the balance of it subject to call as a guarantee fund as in the case of the IBRD. On the basis of the amount of capital initially subscribed, the paid-in portion was to total $381,580,000 and the portion on call $431,580,000. Payments were to be made half in gold or U.S. dollars and half in the currency of the subscribing country. The initial payments of $381,580,000 were completed, according to a schedule that had been established, by October 31, 1962.

The U.S. subscription amounted to $350 million, of which $150 million was paid in and $200 million was on call. The capital paid in by the other countries in gold or U.S. dollars came to $115,790,000. Of the total of $381,580,000 initially paid, the Bank therefore had $265,790,000 in gold or U.S. dollars and the balance of $115,790,000 in Latin American currencies.

The Bank has since taken action, which became effective January 28, 1964, to increase the callable portion of its capital by $1 billion and to raise its authorized capital by an additional $300 million for subscription by possible new members. The U.S. portion of the increase in callable capital, proportionate to its original subscription, is $411,760,000, and the sum of $43,340,000 is unassigned. Subscription to the additional $1 billion of callable capital was to be effected half by December 31, 1964, and half by December 31, 1965. Excluding the unassigned portion, the halves come to $478,330,000. As of December 31, 1964, nineteen countries had subscribed a total of $471,825,000. This brought the total of the Bank's callable capital which had been subscribed to $903,405,000, of which $405,880,000 had been subscribed by the United States.

RESOURCES FOR LENDING

The resources available to the IDB for lending consist of proceeds derived from three separate funds: its Ordinary Capital Resources, its Fund for Special Operations, and the Social Progress Trust Fund turned over to it by the United States. The Bank's ordinary capital, as noted, provides paid-in capital that can be loaned out and capital on call that serves to guarantee the Bank's bond issues, the proceeds of which are another resource for lending. There have also been participations by private banks in IDB loans and sales of IDB loans out of its portfolio. The Fund for Special Operations is made up of contributions by the member governments, which are kept entirely separate from the capital of the Bank. The Social Progress Trust Fund consists, of course, exclusively of contributions by the United States.

As noted above, the paid-in capital of the Bank amounts to some

$380 million, of which $265 million is in gold or U.S. dollars and $115 million in Latin American currencies. In addition, subscriptions to capital on call now amount to some $900 million, including $405 million of subscription by the United States. When present arrangements for increase of the Bank's callable capital are completed by the end of 1965, it will have a total of such capital, without the admission of any new members, of close to $1.4 billion, including somewhat over $600 million from the United States.

With a sixth bond issue offered in the United States on October 28, 1964, the total sum raised by bond issues of the Bank came to the equivalent of $272.6 million, of which $225 million had been sold in the United States and $47.6 million in Europe. The latter consisted of $24.2 million raised in Italy, $15 million in West Germany, and $8.4 million in the United Kingdom. The proceeds of all of these issues are freely convertible. There is considerable scope for additional borrowing on the basis of the recent increase of the Bank's capital on call.

Loan participations and portfolio sales amounted to a total of some $22 million by the end of 1964. These participations and portfolio sales thus freed a small portion of the Bank's funds for further lending.

Contributions to the Fund for Special Operations were originally fixed as $150 million but actually came to $146,316,000 without Cuba. The contributions were to be paid, as with the paid-in portion of the ordinary capital, half in gold or dollars and half in members' currencies. Payment of the contributions was completed by October 31, 1961. The United States' contribution came to $100 million, or 68.35 percent of the total, which was a much larger share than its share in the ordinary capital of the Bank. Total gold or dollar resources of the Fund amounted to $123,158,000, consisting of the U.S. share plus half of that of the other countries.

At the same time that the Bank took action to increase its capital, it also increased contributions to the Fund for Special Operations by 50 percent. This increase of $73,158,000 was to be paid on the same basis as the initial contributions, i.e., half in gold or dollars and half in member countries' currencies. The U.S. share was $50 million. When the action is completed, the Fund will total $219,474,000, of which $150 million will be from the United States and $34,737,000 will be in gold and dollars from all other sources. The cumulative total paid into the Fund came to $218,921,000 as of December 31, 1964.

The Social Progress Fund, entrusted in 1961 by the United States to the IDB for administration, amounted to $394 million. This was part of a total amount of $500 million intended to finance social progress in Latin America under the Alliance for Progress. Besides the $394 million entrusted to the IDB, $100 million was allocated to bilateral programs of the United States and $6 million to the Organization of American States (OAS) to strengthen its technical cooperation with member countries. The sum of $131 million was added to the Fund by the U.S. government in February, 1964, to raise the total to $525 million.

The Bank recently increased still more the resources available to it for soft loans. Its Board of Governors recommended at the April, 1964, annual meeting an increase of $900 million in the resources of the Fund for Special Operations, to be paid in the currency of each member country in three equal installments. The recommendation became effective on March 31, 1965. The U.S. contribution is $750 million. These increased contributions are to be effected in three installments on or before June 30 and December 31, 1965, and December 31, 1966. No further contributions will be made to the Social Progress Trust Fund. New lending of the Social Progress Trust Fund type will be made out of the Fund for Special Operations.

The IDB has also taken steps to obtain funds from the governments of certain nonmember countries. The United Kingdom and the Netherlands have recently announced their intention of channeling funds through the Bank in the amount of $11.6 million and $10 million, respectively. On December 3, 1964, the Bank signed an agreement with Canada to administer a fund of $10 million to finance economic, technical, and educational assistance projects in Latin America. Specific financing proposals are to be agreed on by Canada and the Bank, as are the terms of financing, which may be free of interest and up to fifty years in maturity, although repayments are to be made in Canadian dollars and loan proceeds are to be tied to purchases in Canada. On March 29, 1965, the Bank signed an agreement with Spain under which the Spanish government is to provide $20 million at a term of twelve years and an interest rate of 4¾ percent per annum, to be used for the "ordinary capital resources" type of loan by the Bank. Of the total, $7.5 million is tied to purchases in Spain. On June 27, 1965, Canada agreed to make an additional $15 million available for economic development projects in Latin America. Like the earlier $10-million fund, the proceeds are tied to purchases in Canada, but unlike the earlier allotment, in this case the terms are "hard": interest rates are to be at commercial levels and repayment terms up to twenty years.

Volume of Lending. From the beginning of its lending in February, 1961, to December 31, 1964, the IDB authorized loans from its three funds of close to $1.2 billion. Slightly more than 45 percent came out of its ordinary capital resources, slightly less than 40 percent from the Social Progress Trust Fund, and the balance out of its Fund for Special Operations. Close to 35 percent of the total authorizations had been disbursed by December 31, 1964.

During each of its first two years of operations in 1961 and 1962, the Bank authorized loans at an annual rate of about $300 million, representing about a quarter of all public international development financing in Latin America (the major portions coming bilaterally from the United States and from the World Bank group). The rate of loan authorizations declined somewhat in 1963, principally because of the approaching exhaustion of the Social Progress Trust Fund but rose again in 1964, following the renewal of the Bank's resources in all three funds early in that year.

The rate of disbursements has risen steadily as the accumulated authorizations have come to be translated into effective expenditures on projects. In 1964, disbursements moved up to about $200 million.

The record of the Bank's loan authorizations and disbursements is shown in Table 11.

During the first half of 1965, loan approvals amounted to $88.7 million: $35.2 million out of ordinary capital resources, $21.6 million out of the Fund for Special Operations, $28.9 million out of the Social Progress Trust Fund, and $3 million out of other funds. Disbursements during that period came to $80.1 million: $38.8 million out of ordinary capital resources, $13.4 million out of the Fund for Special Operations, and $27.9 million out of the Social Progress Trust Fund.

The Bank anticipates a rate of loan disbursements in the near future of about $300 million annually, of which one-half will be hard loans out of its ordinary capital resources and one-half soft loans out of its special funds for this purpose.

TABLE 11

Inter-American Development Bank Loan Authorizations and Disbursements, 1961–64
(*Millions of Dollars*)

	Ordinary Capital Resources	Fund for Special Operations	Social Progress Trust Fund	Total
	LOAN AUTHORIZATIONS			
1961	130.0	48.1	115.6	293.7
1962	83.7	40.8	204.9	329.4
1963	179.3	32.5	47.1	258.9
1964	164.0	49.4	85.9	299.3
Total	557.0	170.8	453.5	1,181.3
	DISBURSEMENTS			
1961	3.2	2.5	0.9	6.6
1962	28.0	8.8	21.8	58.6
1963	59.8	15.3	65.9	141.0
1964	106.6	24.6	66.9	198.1
Total	197.6	51.2	155.5	404.3

Purposes of Loans. Like the World Bank group, the IDB lends mostly for specific projects. Its loans have been more widely distributed among economic sectors, however, and it has devoted much more resources to projects in the social sector, particularly in view of its administration of the U.S. Social Progress Trust Fund.

The distribution of total IDB loan authorizations by purpose during its first four years of operation in 1961–64, classified for each of its three sources of funds, is given in Table 12.

The Bank's own "ordinary capital resources" have been devoted mostly to industry and agriculture and only to a minor extent to economic and social infrastructure facilities. The distribution of the loans from its Fund for Special Operations is similar, though with a greater concentration on agriculture relative to industry. Much of the lending for agriculture and industry has been via intermediate credit institutions in the recipient countries. Almost 45 percent of the Social Progress Trust Fund loans have been for low-cost housing. Water supply and sanitation have accounted for a little more than 30 percent. Land settlement and higher education have made up the balance.

TABLE 12

Inter-American Development Bank Loan Authorizations, by Purpose, 1961–64

(Percent)

Purpose	*Ordinary Capital Resources*	*Fund for Special Operations*	*Social Progress Trust Fund*	*All Three Funds*
Industry and mining	43.3	29.2	. . .	24.6
Agriculture	30.0	38.9	17.1	25.8
Electric power and transport	17.3	14.5	1.2	10.8
Export financing	2.0	. . .	. . .	0.9
Planning	0.1	0.6	. . .	0.1
Water supply and sanitation	7.3	16.8	31.1	18.0
Housing	. . .	. . .	43.9	17.1
Higher education	. . .	. . .	6.7	2.7
Total	100.0	100.0	100.0	100.0

The composite results for aggregate Bank lending out of its three funds show agriculture and industry together accounting for half of the total, with agriculture only slightly ahead of industry. Social infrastructure projects account for close to 40 percent of the total, with housing and water supply and sanitation being of about equal importance. The balance of some 10 percent is for electrical power and transport, which by contrast are the fields of predominant importance in the loans of the IBRD and IDA.

The IDB lends to or for private enterprise as well as for investment by government agencies. Loans out of the Social Progress Trust Fund, intended for social infrastructure facilities, are, of course, for official or quasi-official projects. On the other hand, almost half of the Bank's total authorizations out of its own resources by December 31, 1964, were for private enterprise. Loans for private enterprise came to $324 million out of the total of some $725 million. The bulk of this lending, however, was via intermediate credit institutions. The total granted to such institutions came to $243 million. Unlike those of the World Bank group, the IDB loans to intermediate credit institutions have been mostly to public institutions of this type, although they are, of course, for re-lending to the private sector. Although the Bank will not lend for a project to which the host government objects, it does not require government guarantees of its loans.

The Bank has placed great importance on the support of economic integration in Latin America. Wherever possible, projects contributing to this objective have been favored. The Bank has granted loans to the Central American Bank for Economic Integration and for a coordinated program of the national universities of the five Central American countries. In September, 1963, the Bank instituted a special program to finance intraregional exports of capital goods within Latin America. It earmarked an initial amount of $30 million of its ordinary capital resources for this purpose, to be lent to specialized national credit agencies. By June 30, 1965, loan authorizations of $12 million had been made to finance such capital goods exports. Assistance has also been granted for the integrated development of border zones. In August, 1965, the Bank established an Institute for Latin American Integration, with headquarters in Buenos Aires to engage in training, research, and advisory work related to the integration process.

Besides its provision of capital assistance, the Bank has placed much emphasis on technical assistance with the general objective of increasing the capital absorptive capacity of member countries. It devoted $33.9 million to this purpose during the period 1961–64, about two-thirds on a reimbursable basis and one-third in the form of grants. Grants have been financed out of the net income of the Fund for Special Operations. About a third of the funds committed for technical assistance has come out of the Social Progress Trust Fund and two-thirds out of the Bank's own resources. The major part of the assistance has been to strengthen general planning activity and the conduct of feasibility studies. In August, 1965, the Bank granted to Chile a $3-million loan out of its Fund for Special Operations to help finance a continuous program of pre-investment studies. This was the first in what was expected to be a series of loans to member countries for this purpose.

LOAN CONDITIONS AND TERMS

The conditions and terms of IDB loans vary to some extent for each of its three loan "windows." Loans out of the Bank's own resources are generally for not more than half of the total cost of the projects financed. Like the World Bank, the IDB for the most part finances only the foreign exchange requirements of projects, although in special cases some of the local currency costs may be financed as well, either in foreign exchange or in the local currency which has been paid into the Bank by the borrowing member. Loans out of the U.S. Social Progress Trust Fund are, of course, not limited to foreign exchange requirements (as has been noted, housing, in which the foreign exchange component is usually quite minor, has received most such loans), although there must be an appropriate contribution by the borrowing country.

IDB loan proceeds are not tied with respect to country of procurement. Indeed, by the end of 1964, over 50 percent of the imports and import commitments arising from the loans out of the Bank's own funds were from countries outside of the Western Hemisphere which were not members of the Bank. U.S. Social Progress Trust Fund monies, however, can be spent only in the United States or the borrowing country or in other IDB member countries if the Bank deems this to be advantageous to the borrowing country.

Loans out of the Bank's ordinary capital resources are on hard terms. Maturities for private sector projects generally vary from eight to twelve years and go up to twenty years for public infrastructure projects. The interest rate, based on the experience of other hard lending agencies such as the World Bank and the European Investment Bank, had been 5¾ percent per annum, but this was raised to 6 percent in July, 1964, in view of the expansion in Bank borrowings at increased costs in Europe.

The "special circumstances" that determine whether the soft terms of the Fund for Special Operations are to be applied are related to such criteria as the debt-servicing capacity of the borrowing country, the revenue-generating characteristics of the project, or its balance-of-payments effects. Maturities range up to thirty years, including substantial grace periods, and the interest rate has been 4 percent in most cases. It is possible and usual for repayment to be effected in the borrower's own currency even if the currency of the loan was dollars or some other foreign currency.

Social Progress Trust Fund loans may also be repayable in local currency and most of them have been, though with a maintenance of value provision. Maturities have been mostly thirty years, and interest rates range from 2 to 3½ percent, including a commission of ¾ percent payable in dollars.

The Bank as a Regional Instrument. The IDB limits its loans to Latin America, but it is by no means the major source of finance for the region. The Bank still accounts for only about 30 percent of public international development financing in Latin America. It was intended to supplement and not replace existing sources of such finance, whether bilateral or multilateral. In a similar fashion, while the IDB has become an important participant in cooperative assistance efforts of all types for Latin America, it has not done so as the exclusive chosen international financial instrument of its members. In October, 1963, Ecuador designated the Bank as financial agent for its Ten-Year Economic and Social Development Plan, but the first and only other international financing consultative group organized in Latin America, that for Colombia, was set up under the chairmanship of the World Bank. The IDB is, of course, a member of the Colombia group. The consultative group for Ecuador, with the participation of nineteen nations and nine international agencies (the World Bank group, the IMF, the UN Technical Assistance Board and Special Fund, the OAS, CIAP, and the Panel of Nine Experts of the Alliance for Progress), was constituted by the IDB in June, 1965. Included among the nineteen nations are five Latin American republics and Israel, who were to participate particularly in providing technical assistance.

The IDB cooperates closely with the various inter-American agencies which are working toward economic development in the region and has taken the lead in attempting to increase the participation of sources of finance other than the United States. It cooperates particularly with the OAS, with the UN Economic Commission for Latin America, and with the recently created Inter-American Committee for the Alliance for Progress. It has been pushing for more financial assistance for Latin America from countries besides the

United States, directly with the governments concerned and via the DAC of the OECD. It supported the formation of the ADELA Investment Company by leading corporations of Europe, Canada, Japan, and the United States for joint venture investments in Latin America. The IDB thus has served to give an emphasis to international development financing in Latin America, which would undoubtedly not have been as great in the absence of this regional instrument.

Development Financing Agencies of the European Economic Community

The Rome Treaty of 1957 that established the EEC provided for two development-financing mechanisms, the European Development Fund (EDF) for financing in overseas countries and territories associated with the EEC and the European Investment Bank (EIB) for financing in member countries on the European continent. The purpose of the EDF was to distribute more widely among the member states of the EEC the burden of financing development in the French-speaking territories and countries of Africa. Such financing had been carried out hitherto almost exclusively on a bilateral basis by France; with the achievement of independence by these territories and their association with the EEC, it was considered appropriate and equitable that the burdens be more widely shared along with the benefits of the new preferential arrangements, which now were to be on a Communitywide basis rather than merely two-sided. The EIB, in addition to financing projects of regional interest in the Community and the modernization of industries to prepare them for competitive Common Market conditions, was to finance projects for the development of the less developed regions within the six member countries on the continent itself. In fact, it was designed to a large extent to help in the process of developing the south of Italy.

Upon completion of the first five years of operation of the EEC and of its two development financing institutions, a number of important changes were introduced. A new Convention of Association between the EEC and the overseas associated states in Africa became effective on June 1, 1964. This Convention provided for an increase in the volume of operations of the EDF, a diversification in its methods of financing, and a greater emphasis on technical assistance related to its financing. In connection with the entry of the EDF for the first time into the field of financing through loans, a link was established between it and the EIB with respect to both administration and resources for the financing. Thus, both institutions became involved in development financing outside the European continent.

In addition, the EIB expanded the scope of its operations from the less developed regions of the six European member countries themselves to other less developed countries on the continent by virtue of the achievement of associate membership in the EEC by Greece and Turkey. The associate membership of Greece took place in November, 1962, and that of Turkey became effective on December 1, 1964.

EUROPEAN DEVELOPMENT FUND (EDF)

The First Fund. The EDF does not have a separate juridical personality. It is operated as part of the administrative structure of the EEC. The EEC (which is the European Common Market organization, separate from the other two European communities, namely, those for coal and steel and for atomic energy) is administered by a commission of nine members named by the six participating states, subject to the policy directives of the Council of Ministers representing the states. Each of the nine Commissioners is at the head of a "Direction Générale" with particular functional responsibilities. One of these, the Direction Générale VIII, is concerned with Overseas Development. The "Direction Générale" of Overseas Development is, in turn, divided into four "Directions," one of which administers the EDF (the other three being concerned with Trade and Exchange, Research, and Training).

The EDF during its first five years, or the "First Fund," as it is referred to, had resources available to it amounting to $581.25 million. These resources were contributed by the member states in the following proportions: 34.4 percent by France, 34.4 percent by West Germany, 12.0 percent by Belgium, 12.0 percent by the Netherlands, 6.9 percent by Italy, and 0.3 percent by Luxembourg.

The First Fund made grants exclusively, all on a project basis and to governments and governmental agencies, for non-revenue-generating social and economic infrastructure purposes. There were no allocations by countries, and those countries whose administrations permitted them to present acceptable projects naturally were most favored. Only toward the latter part of its operation did the First Fund take the initiative by way of providing recipient countries with technical assistance designed to help them prepare projects for investment. An example of this is the comprehensive economic survey mission sponsored by the Fund for the Republic of the Congo (Leopoldville).

By August 31, 1964, the resources of the First Fund which had been committed amounted to $489.3 million, of which $303.7 million was for economic projects and $185.6 million for social projects. The economic projects were primarily in the field of transport (roads, ports, and railways) and secondarily in agriculture and the modernization of rural areas. The social projects included education and training, health, water-supply systems, and town planning. Principal recipients were Madagascar ($53.5 million), Cameroon ($44.5 million), Senegal ($37.6 million), Mali ($33.0 million), Ivory Coast ($33.1 million), Chad ($28.2 million), Upper Volta ($26.4 million), Niger ($26.0 million), and Algeria ($20.4 million). Total disbursements amounted to somewhat less than $200 million, or about 40 percent of the total commitments. In all, close to thirty independent states and dependent territories received financing, primarily in French-speaking Africa. By June 30, 1965, total commitments amounted to $563.5 million and disbursements to $255.9 million.

The First Fund maintained a procedure of exchange of information outside the EEC with other sources of aid, principally the United States, which maintains a resident mission to the EEC in Brussels. Contact was also maintained with the World Bank group of financing institutions and with the United Nations, although less regularly, since these agencies do not have offices in Brussels. The Fund was also represented as a separate agency on the Development Assistance Committee of the OECD in Paris. There was, however, only one case of joint financing by the Fund and other sources of aid, namely, the Trans-Cameroun Railway, for which the Fund committed a grant of $16 million, the FAC of the French government a grant of $8–9 million, and the AID of the U. S. government a long-term loan of $9 million.

The Second Fund. For the five-year period commencing with the effective date (June 1, 1964) of the new Convention of Association between the EEC and the African states, the EDF has been endowed with $730 million of resources, compared with the $580 million of the First Fund. The proportionate contributions of the six members of the EEC are similar to those for the First Fund, although the shares of Belgium and the Netherlands have been reduced and that for Italy has been increased; the shares are as follows for the Second Fund: France, 33.75 percent; West Germany, 33.75 percent; Italy, 13.7 percent; Belgium, 9.45 percent; the Netherlands, 9.05 percent; and Luxembourg 0.3 percent. In addition, the European Investment Bank is to provide $70 million out of its own resources, to make a grand total of $800 million for the five-year period. Besides this total of $800 million, provision is made for EDF advances to the commodity stabilization funds of recipient states up to a maximum of $50 million.

The associated states in the new Convention consist of eighteen African states, all of which are former French colonies except three —Burundi, Republic of the Congo (Leopoldville), and Rwanda, which are ex-Belgian. In addition, there are thirteen dependent territories and departments that qualify for Second Fund aid by virtue of a determination by the EEC Council of Ministers.

The distribution of the total of $800 million by type of financing and type of recipient state is shown in Table 13. Thus, the EDF grant program is $100 million more than in the First Fund, and $120 million is added in the new loan programs.

The grants are to be used for the same purposes as in the First

TABLE 13
Proposed EEC Aid under Second Convention with the Associated African States, 1964–69
(Millions of Dollars)

	Independent States	Dependent Territories	Total
EDF grants	620	60	680
EDF special loans	46	4	50
EIB loans	64	6	70
Total	730	70	800

Fund, plus the following new purposes: technical cooperation, linked to investment projects as well as those of a more general nature, subsidization of the interest rate charged by the EIB, and aid for "production and diversification."

The EDF special loans are to be made for revenue-producing projects as well as for the purposes of "diversification." They will be at a maximum term of forty years, including a ten-year grace period, and an interest rate of $1\frac{1}{2}$ to $2\frac{1}{2}$ percent per annum. They may be granted to private enterprises by special decision of the EEC. The EIB will administer these loans as well as the loans it makes out of its own resources.

The EIB loans are to be made for purposes similar to those for which EDF special loans are to be granted. Their terms will be harder than those of the EDF special loans and will conform to the general terms of EIB lending—maximum maturity of twenty-five years and interest rate dependent upon the rate at which the EIB borrows funds in private capital markets (the interest rate charged by the EIB in mid-1964 was $5\frac{7}{8}$ percent per year). The EEC may decide, however, at the request of the recipient, to assume the payment of 3 percentage points of the interest, so that the EIB would receive the full amount of the interest while the recipient might be paying only $2\frac{7}{8}$ percent. As indicated above, EDF grant money is available for such payments of interest. The first EIB loan under the new EEC–Africa Convention was announced in May, 1965. It consisted of a $1,015,000 loan to the Ivory Coast for a banana-processing plant, at a term of seven years and an interest rate of $5\frac{3}{4}$ percent.

As noted above, grants under the Second Fund may be made as "aids to production," and all three types of financing, i.e., grants, soft loans, and hard loans, may be extended as "aids to diversification." These classifications relate only to aid to the independent states and have their origin in the gradual elimination of the system of purchases by France of commodities from its former colonies at prices above world market prices as a form of subsidy. A maximum of $230 million out of the total of $730 million for independent states is to be used in this way and is allocated in certain amounts, country by country. There are eleven countries eligible for "aid to production" as a means of financing improvements in the productivity of existing output in view of the elimination of the higher than world market prices paid by France. At the insistence of other members of the EEC, a maximum of $130 million was fixed for such "aid to production" to the eleven countries. The remaining $100 million was distributed as a minimum "aid to diversification" for the remaining seven countries which are not eligible for "aid to production." Thus, the system of country allocation for the $230 million of "aid to production and diversification" was the result of a compromise with the original French position that the full amount be made available to improve the competitive position of certain countries whose exports were being subsidized by France. Since the country allocations of "aid to production" were made in advance, inequities were likely to arise, depending upon the course of world market prices; subsidies were established before knowing what they should actually be; they would be excessive to the extent that actual prices turned out to be higher than anticipated and insufficient to the extent that prices turned out to be less than anticipated.

The remaining $500 million in aid for the independent states was not allocated by country and was to be expended, as with the First Fund, for projects as they came in. It was expected, however, that the Second Fund would take much more initiative in granting technical assistance for the preparation of investment projects.

Assistance under the Second Fund, like that under the First Fund, may be used to finance local currency as well as foreign exchange requirements. It may not be used, however, to cover current administrative, maintenance, or operating expenses and so is entirely for capital expenditures. Although the aid is not formally tied to expenditures in the EEC and associated countries, it has in fact been expended almost entirely in those countries and is likely to continue being so expended.

All projects are subject to the approval of a committee made up of representatives of the six member states of the EEC and are then passed on by the EEC Commission; disagreements between the projects committee and the EEC Commission are resolved by the Council of Ministers.

With the approval of thirteen projects on July 28, 1965, total authorizations under the Second Fund came to $161 million, or close to a fourth of the Fund's total resources in little more than a year of operations.

THE EUROPEAN INVESTMENT BANK (EIB)

The European Investment Bank operates as an entirely autonomous institution of the EEC. Its total subscribed capital amounts to $1 billion (France and West Germany, 30 percent each; Italy, 24 percent; Belgium, 8.65 percent; the Netherlands, 7.15 percent; and Luxembourg, 0.2 percent), but only $250 million has been paid in. The balance of the capital is, in effect, on call as a guarantee fund for bond issues placed by the Bank in the private capital markets of Europe. About $155 million had been raised by the Bank in this way up to the end of 1964. With respect to the sources of its funds, the Bank thus operates in a similar way to the IBRD, and it is correspondingly also a hard lending institution like the IBRD.

By the end of 1964, after some six years of operation, the Bank had granted a total of $465 million in loans, of which two-thirds went to Italy, mostly for the development of the southern part of that country; 15 percent to France; 7 percent to West Germany; 1 percent each to Belgium and Luxembourg; 8 percent for projects in Greece; and 1 percent to Turkey. Total loan commitments in 1964 amounted to about $107 million.

The sectoral distribution of the EIB loans up to December 31, 1964, was 44 percent to industry, 29 percent to transport, 17 percent to energy, 7 percent to agriculture, and 3 percent to telecommunications.

The rate of interest applied by the Bank follows conditions on the capital markets. It was fixed at 5⅞ to 6¼ percent, varying with maturities, in October, 1964. Loans granted have had repayment periods varying from seven to twenty years.

The Bank lends to private enterprises as well as to public agencies. It normally does not require governmental guarantees but has done so in its loans to Greece, and it was expected to require such guarantees in its loans to Turkey and to overseas associated states of the EEC. The Bank frequently lends in association with other agencies, such as the Cassa per il Mezzogiorno in Italy.

Reference has been made above to the possibility of EDF

assumption of part of the EIB interest rate in loans to the associated overseas areas. This has similarly been assumed by the EEC member states in some of the lending to Greece and was expected to be done also in loans to Turkey. In a $6-million, twenty-year loan to the Public Power Corporation of Greece granted in March, 1964, the EEC assumed 3 percentage points of the 5⅞ percent interest rate; and the EEC assumed 3 percentage points of the 6¼ percent interest on a $10.3-million, twenty-year EIB loan granted in February, 1965, for irrigation in Greece.

With respect to loans to Greece and Turkey, the EIB has committed a five-year total of $125 million for Greece and $175 million for Turkey, pursuant to the EEC Association Agreements of these two countries. The amount for Turkey, however, was not to come out of the Bank's regular resources but was to be made available separately by the EEC member states. The $70 million committed by the EIB for the overseas associated areas during the five years beginning in mid-1964 has already been noted. Thus, besides the amounts that the EIB will lend for the less developed regions of the six industrialized member states of the EEC, it will administer a total of some $370 million in loans for other developing countries during the period 1964–69.

Other Regional Development Banks

The trend toward supplementing, through the creation of institutions of regional scope, the worldwide development financing provided under international auspices by the World Bank group has recently been extended to Africa and Asia. For Africa, besides the financing provided by the EDF, an African Development Bank formally came into being in September, 1964. And, in March, 1965, a resolution was adopted by the UN Economic Commission for Asia and the Far East, setting in motion machinery for the drafting of a charter for an Asian Development Bank. The membership and scope of the latter are still to be determined. The nature of the African Development Bank is described below.

The African Development Bank grew out of studies sponsored by the UN Economic Commission for Africa. An agreement to establish the Bank was adopted by a conference of African finance ministers held in Khartoum, Sudan, in August, 1963. Thirty-one African governments had signed the agreement by December 31, 1963, the deadline date for signature. The treaty entered formally into force on September 10, 1964, with the completion of the required number of ratifications.

The purpose of the Bank is to channel funds into major economic and social development projects and programs, particularly into projects of common concern and those designed to make the economies of African countries increasingly complementary and to bring about an orderly expansion of trade.

The Bank will attempt to mobilize and increase the flow of financial resources to Africa for the public and private sectors. The Bank also intends to provide technical assistance required for the study, preparation, and execution of development projects and programs.

The Bank has an authorized capital of $250 million, of which $203.1 million has been subscribed by the thirty-one African governments which signed the Treaty of Khartoum. The remainder is available for subscription by other African governments. One-half of the capital subscription is to be paid in over a period of four and a half years, the other half remains on call. The Bank is authorized to supplement its own capital by borrowing or by the sale of securities, and it may accept funds from governments and international financial institutions either for its general purposes or for financing projects sponsored by it.

The management of the Bank consists of a Board of Governors on which each member country is represented, a nine-man Board of Directors elected by the Board of Governors, and a President elected by the Board of Directors. Voting is weighted so that it is slightly less than proportional to capital subscriptions.

The Board of Governors has recently elected Mamoun Beheiry of the Sudan as the Bank's first President, and the Bank's headquarters will be in Abidjan, Ivory Coast.

United Nations

The financial agencies affiliated with the United Nations, i.e., those which provide capital assistance to the less developed countries on a global basis, are the agencies of the World Bank group, which are discussed above. In addition, the United Nations Organization itself and other of its specialized agencies regularly provide technical assistance on a worldwide basis, and they also engage in certain special relief operations. The technical assistance is not in the form of cash grants or loans but consists rather of the services of technical experts, of fellowship awards for study, and of demonstration equipment or equipment to carry out surveys and studies.

For one thing, there is a "regular program" of technical assistance which is financed out of the assessed budgets of the United Nations and certain of its specialized agencies. This is the smaller part of the technical assistance granted. It is separately listed in UN publications as amounting to about $9 million in 1963, of which $6.4 million

TABLE 14

Expanded Program of Technical Assistance—Pledges and Number of Contributing Countries, 1961–65

Year	Amount of Pledges, millions of dollars	Number of Contributing Countries
1961	41.8	91
1962	45.4	92
1963	50.1	105
1964	51.3	109
1965 (as of June 15)	54.0	107

were from the United Nations itself and the balance from the International Labour Organisation (ILO), the UN Educational, Scientific, and Cultural Organization (UNESCO), and the Food and Agriculture Organization (FAO).[61]

A larger part of UN technical assistance comes from the Expanded Program of Technical Assistance (EPTA), which is financed by voluntary contributions of governments. Compared with the $9 million of the "regular program" in 1963, the pledges to the "expanded program" in that year amounted to about $50 million. The number of countries that have contributed to the expanded program and the amounts of their pledges during the last five years have been as shown in Table 14.

The United States has regularly contributed about 40 percent of the total for both the regular and expanded programs. In 1965 its

[61] UN Office of Public Information, *Technical Assistance Newsletter*, August–September, 1963.

contribution to EPTA amounted to $22.7 million. Other contributors of $2 million or more were the United Kingdom, $4.8 million; West Germany, $2.7 million; Denmark, $2.6 million; Sweden, $2.5 million; Canada, $2.2 million; and the USSR, $2 million.

The projects financed by the expanded program of technical assistance are operated by the United Nations and specialized agencies for each agency's technical field. Besides the ILO, FAO, and UNESCO, these include the World Health Organization, the International Civil Aviation Organization, the World Meteorological Organization, the International Atomic Energy Agency, the International Telecommunication Union, and the Universal Postal Union.

Most of the project costs in UN technical assistance are expended on the services of experts which are provided to the recipient countries. About 5,000 experts are now (i.e., 1965) in the field. During the years 1960–64, about three-fourths of total EPTA project costs were for aid in this form, with about 18 percent going to fellowship awards and the balance allocated for equipment.

Another UN activity supported by voluntary contributions is the UN Special Fund, which was established in 1958 to assist less developed countries in "pre-investment" projects, i.e., in surveys of natural resources, in the establishment of training institutions, and in the development of research facilities. Its budget in 1963 amounted to $72.4 million and in 1964 to $85.4 million, also contributed to, to the extent of about 40 percent, by the United States. The Special Fund, like the technical assistance programs, operates on the basis of expert missions, the provision of equipment, and some fellowship awards rather than by cash grants or loans, but it puts greater emphasis on equipment and less on fellowship awards than do the technical assistance programs.

At its July–August, 1964, meeting, the UN Economic and Social Council recommended the merger of the UN Special Fund and the EPTA, forming a new organization to be known as the UN Development Program. The UN General Assembly approved this proposal at the end of 1965. It is hoped that this will result in an increase in contributions to the combined agencies to $200 million, compared with the goal of $150 million for 1965 and the actual contribution of $137 million for both EPTA and the Special Fund for 1964.

Aid-Coordinating Mechanisms

A significant aspect of the development and refinement of aid-giving techniques in recent years has been the constitution of different types of coordinating arrangements. Within the Soviet bloc, such coordination is mainly effected by the Council for Mutual Economic Assistance (CMEA), in which, at least until recently, the USSR exercised predominant control.[62] But Western development aid policies have developed piecemeal. For many years only the United States on the national and the World Bank on the international level were continuous providers of development aid on a worldwide scale. Britain and France—both of which had provided aid to their colonial empires for many years—continued to do so essentially within a closed circuit and with little interest in development aid outside their Empire and Commonwealth connections. As shown in previous sections, all this has gradually changed. The independent states which until recently were colonies in the British and French Empires have begun to look to other national and international sources of development aid, while Britain and France have begun to diversify their concerns with development aid on a broader international scale. In recent years, the increasingly prosperous states of West Germany and Japan have turned from aid-receiving to aid-giving partly under pressure from the United States, which has understandably sought to get her allies to participate in at least some of her growing burden of assistance to developing countries. The policies and terms of aid provided by individual donor countries have increasingly been coordinated with the corresponding policies of the World Bank and IDA, especially in the case of major joint projects. Virtually all the industrialized countries outside the Communist group are now joined in the Organization for Economic Cooperation and Development (OECD),

[62] There are many indications that, with the growing independence of the smaller European Communist countries, the coordinating and integrating functions of CMEA have decreased and that the individual member states, such as Rumania or Hungary, tend to pursue more independent national policies, including foreign assistance. If this trend continues, the evolution within the Communist bloc is, in some ways, opposite to that of the Western world. It is moving from closely disciplined integration to "polycentrism," whereas the West is making efforts to work out some measure of coordination between the many independent national aid-giving policies.

and most of these, in turn, are members of the aid-coordinating Development Assistance Committee (DAC) of the OECD.

As both the magnitude and the multiplicity of development aid requests increased, especially with the coming upon the scene of many new, economically weak states, the need to avoid conflicting aid policies and overlapping offers as well as requests became more urgent. It became equally urgent to avoid the danger of some of the potential aid-givers being played off against others, a source of both political tension and economic wastage.

Out of these needs and contacts there have developed, up to the present, several types of coordinating mechanisms:

The first is consortium aid, characterized by a continuing, though not formally institutionalized, mechanism of bringing the various— national and international—aid-givers to a particular country together in a common pledging exercise based on the recipient country's development program. The two types of consortia of this kind are the India and Pakistan Consortia conducted under the guidance of the World Bank and the OECD consortia formed for aid to Greece and Turkey.

A second type of coordinating mechanism is the consultative group. Such groups, both less ambitious and less closely organized than the above-mentioned consortia and involving no systematic pledging of funds, seek to coordinate external aid on the basis of specific projects or programs. Such consultative groups have been formed both under the auspices of the World Bank for Colombia, Nigeria, Tunisia, and the Sudan and, on a limited basis, also by the DAC of the OECD for East Africa and Thailand. As previously indicated, it is likely that this type of coordinating group will be extended to other countries at the initiative of the World Bank.

Third, there are broader general coordinating mechanisms, among donors or among both donors and recipients but not limited to single recipient countries, designed to act as clearing mechanisms for the exchange of information and, as far as possible, the harmonization and improvement of the policies of the different members. This type of coordination is represented by the Colombo Plan for Cooperative Economic Development in South and Southeast Asia, by the Inter-American Committee for the Alliance for Progress, and by the DAC of the OECD.

Still another type of coordinating mechanism, designed to effect a program of regional development of water resources, is found in the Lower Mekong Basin Project in Southeast Asia.

By way of illustration of these various types of coordinating mechanisms, the Aid-India Consortium and, more briefly, the OECD Consortia for Greece and Turkey, the Consultative Group for Colombia, the DAC groups for East Africa and Thailand, the Colombo Plan, the DAC, and the Lower Mekong Basin Project are described below.

THE AID-INDIA CONSORTIUM

The Aid-India Consortium was formed halfway through the Second Plan in August, 1958, when India was confronted with a serious foreign exchange crisis. Since then, the Consortium has met from time to time to discuss jointly the long-term question of the amount of aid which each country can provide in order to insure that India's development is not impeded for lack of external assistance.

Originally, the Consortium consisted of Canada, Japan, the United Kingdom, the United States, West Germany, and the World Bank, which looks after its secretariat as well. In May–June, 1961, France and IDA joined, and observers were present from Austria, Denmark, Norway, Sweden, and the IMF. In 1962, Austria, Italy, the Netherlands, and Belgium also became members.

The Consortium consists only of lenders. India is not a member, but an Indian representative is present at some of the meetings. The United States and the World Bank set the pace for contributions, the former as the biggest lender and the political leader of the West, the latter as the only lender which makes a comprehensive survey of the Indian program as a whole and which, as an international agency, commands universal respect and enjoys a position detached from the interests of individual parties.

Evolution of Attitudes. The evolution of the India Consortium reflects the general attitude of lenders and of India toward aid at various times. It could not be otherwise, for the Consortium is essentially a meeting place and joint pledging mechanism through which Western lenders coordinate their aid to India. The evolution of the attitudes can be broadly divided into three periods: (1) up to 1958, (2) 1958–59, and (3) 1960 and later. In the first period,

India was using her exchange reserves to finance a substantial part of the imports required for her development. During the second period, India was forced into seeking additional aid to meet an immediate balance-of-payments crisis. The lenders, especially those other than the United States, had still to become psychologically reconciled to assistance on liberal terms. They took time to appreciate the magnitude of India's needs and its capacity, as compared with other developing countries, to implement a large development program and, in general, to accept the proposition that developing countries could not afford to finance their growth with supplier credits.[63]

In May, 1961, the Consortium met for the first time, not to deal with an immediate crisis but to review India's foreign exchange requirements for the Third Plan period and to make decisions on the basis of "what additional aid should be committed by its members during the first two years of the Plan in order both to provide immediate support for India's balance of payments and to enable India to proceed in an orderly manner with the placing of new overseas orders for the Third Plan," according to a communiqué issued by the Consortium. The amount of aid announced at this meeting, the largest since the Marshall Plan commitment to Europe, and the manner in which it was agreed upon gave a clear indication that the United States had succeeded in impressing upon the other participating powers that the Indian Plan must be jointly underwritten.

By August, 1962, every major country in the Western bloc and almost every member of the EEC was represented in the Consortium, which has thus become practically the sole channel for pledges of Western aid. What started essentially as an emergency operation in 1958 with a substratum of political-cum-humanitarian motives has now become a semipermanent institution in the cases of India and Pakistan.

The Consortium at Work. The hard core of members in the India Consortium are Canada, Germany, Japan, the United Kingdom, the United States, the IBRD, and the IDA, and, latterly, France, Aus-

[63] See Alexander K. Cairncross, *International Bank for Reconstruction and Development*, Essays in International Finance, No. 33 (Princeton, N.J., International Finance Section, Department of Economics and Sociology, Princeton University, 1959), for a lucid statement of the notable disadvantages of such short-term arrangements.

tria, Italy, the Netherlands, and Belgium. At times, other governments, such as Denmark, Norway, and Sweden, sit in as observers. The IMF is always present as an observer.

The actual representatives of the governments making up the India Consortium tend to change. Sometimes the representative of a government is a permanent official in a home ministry; at other times, the representative of the government is the Executive Director of the World Bank for that country.

The kinds of problems with which the Consortium deals are of three types: (1) assistance in balance-of-payments difficulties arising from the execution of the Five-Year Plan, (2) the review of a new Plan, and (3) the actual commitment of finance to the Plan, which is always subject to final bilateral discussions with the Indian government.

It is noteworthy that the Indians are present for only part of the India Consortium discussions. In practice, the World Bank is the evaluator of the Plan and is in the best position to give an objective view of the Plan. In 1964, the Indian government prepared a memorandum for the Consortium which outlined the current status of the Plan and general conditions within the country. The proceedings of the Consortium receive very little publicity.

Assuming that the Consortium is dealing with a new plan or the requirements of an annual program (and not a crisis balance-of-payments problem), the work of the Consortium is somewhat as follows.

As has been indicated, the Bank has prepared an extensive review and evaluation of the Plan, and this evaluation is discussed between the World Bank and India. Then the individual Consortium members discuss the Plan, at which time changes of emphasis, priorities, and goals may be suggested. A kind of Quaker "sense of the meeting" determines which of these changes, if any, will be adopted and communicated to India. On the whole, it has been rare for any member country to suggest major changes in the Plan.

During the initial discussions for the Third Five-Year Plan, the aid which the Consortium members agreed to give covered only three years of the Five-Year Plan. In order to get the whole range of projects started, however, having regard for India's need to place orders and to make financial commitments, the Consortium agreed that their loans could be used for down payments on a whole range of projects involving equipment, services, and material, where a substantial part of the payments would come due in the fourth and fifth years of the Plan. In effect, the Consortium was binding itself to carry out additional payments that would have to be made by India over and above the amount which the Consortium members had committed for the first three years.

Estimates are given on the amount of aid which will be given by each country. If the pledges do not meet the goal, new efforts may be made by the chairman to increase the size of the pledges.

Eventually, the Consortium comes up with the total figure, which has generally been very close to the requirements of the Plan. The fact that this occurs is caused by a number of factors but most notably by the firm guidance of the World Bank. Other dialogues also take place, as for example, when the United States bilaterally puts pressure on one or several Consortium members to raise their contribution.

This is a genuine multilateral exercise even though the Indian officials are seldom present. A summary of the proceedings of the Consortium is circulated to member countries and is forwarded to the President of the World Bank for his information.

One of the important functions of the World Bank in the Consortium is to conduct a continuing investigation, both in Washington and in India, of the progress of the Plan and of the particular projects that are planned or under way. Only a few of the members of the Consortium themselves carry on this end-use evaluation; the others rely on the World Bank's periodic reports and the Bank's judgment of prudent and effective management of the resources made available by the Consortium.

One of the most difficult problems of the Consortium is the coordination of the different types of aid preferred by the various members, with the often-differing needs of India. Such harmonization is particularly difficult and urgent with regard to the terms of aid, the tying of aid to the donor country, and the issue of specific project versus general development aid. Thus, West Germany, France, and Japan have generally given extended commercial credits, while long-term loans usually come from the World Bank, the IDA, and the United States, and the United Kingdom has given partly long-term and partly short-term credits. Recently, however, the entire British pledge and about half of the German pledge have been on considerably more liberal terms. Again, while World Bank and the IDA aid is untied, that of all the national donors—except to the extent of about 25 percent in the case of German loans and some Dutch loans to India—is tied to national purchase requirements which often do not coincide with the desire of India to select both the best and the cheapest source of supply for particular items. In addition, India has a certain amount of leeway in the extent to which it can use Soviet-bloc loans as alternatives to Western loans.

By now, Indian procurement authorities have amassed considerable know-how on price and technical competence of the various industrial countries, and they attempt to negotiate with these countries to get from them the kind of equipment needed for their projects that will give the Indians maximum commercial advantage. The donor side also has its notion of what it wants to sell, which may well be based on such considerations as the availability of equipment from distressed industries. A time-consuming face-to-face negotiation is the inevitable result. Thus, the tying of loans to particular projects is not merely a unilateral act on the part of the donor. When the Indians deal or negotiate with countries like the United Kingdom, they know that the tying of loans to projects is inevitable. Therefore, they themselves are prepared to choose the projects that they want tied to the donor country's finance. However, about half of recent pledges by the Consortium have been in nonproject form.

In the Consortium meetings for the Third Five-Year Plan, India circulated among the donors its suggestions as to which projects should be financed by each donor. For example, India distributed the entire list of power projects to be carried out in the Third Five-Year Plan and, except for the projects to be financed by the World Bank, in which the orders are placed on the basis of international competitive bidding, showed the country from which financing and capital equipment for each project was to come (including some countries outside the Consortium).

The pledges for India's Third Five-Year Plan came to a total of $5.5 billion, distributed as in Table 15.

An important problem in the administration of aid to India is the time lag between pledges, authorizations, and disbursements. The process of Consortium aid is long and drawn out. It is not within the power of the Consortium per se to cut down the time lags, for aid from Consortium members is really on a bilateral basis. What the Consortium can do—and has done to a limited extent over the last several years—is to circulate notes about procedures and mechanisms of aid and thereby enable or persuade countries new to the aid business to rationalize their procedures and mechanisms.

TABLE 15
Indian Consortium Aid Pledges
(Millions of Dollars)

Country or Institution	1961–62	1962–63	1963–64	1964–65	1965–66
Austria	. . .	5	7	1	5
Belgium	. . .	10	10	. . .	4
Canada	28	33	30.5	41	41
France	15	45	20	20	20
West Germany	225	139	99.5	95	86
Italy	. . .	53	45	36	36
Japan	50	55	65	60	60
Netherlands	. . .	11	11	11	11
United Kingdom	182	84	84	84	84
United States	545	435	435	435	435
World Bank and IDA	250	200	245	245	245
Total	1,295	1,070	1,052	1,028	1,027

On the whole, the work of the Consortium is one of the more important social inventions that has come into being in the postwar world in the field of foreign aid.

OECD CONSORTIA

The OECD Consortia for Greece and Turkey have been managed and constituted outside the DAC, since Greece and Turkey are OECD members, while the DAC is an agency concerned with aid *from* OECD members to less developed countries outside the OECD group. The Greece and Turkey Consortia are managed in the OECD Secretariat outside the Development Department which services the DAC.

The Turkey Consortium has been very active in helping Turkey meet its large requirements of external assistance and has worked closely with Turkish authorities in recommending the shaping of internal economic policies and investment programs for the most effective utilization of the external finance and the achievement of orderly economic development. Of all international consortia, including those for India and Pakistan under the sponsorship of the World Bank, the OECD Turkey Consortium is probably the one that has worked most closely with the recipient country on its internal policies and programs. Its first year of operation was 1963, but Turkey had received considerable assistance in connection with its external financial problems on a somewhat coordinated basis from European and other creditors since the inception of its stabilization program in 1958.

The Greece Consortium, on the other hand, has not been very active, for a variety of reasons: the problem of external finance has not been as acute as that of Turkey, the sums required have been much smaller, and there has been a reluctance on the part of the recipient country in this case to have the Consortium concern itself with the country's internal policies. Although it has been in operation as long as the Turkey Consortium, the Greece Consortium has had no concrete accomplishments to date.

Both the Turkey and Greece Consortia were formally organized in July, 1962. The Greece Consortium consists of nine countries (Austria, Belgium, Canada, France, Germany, Italy, Luxembourg, the Netherlands, and the United States) plus the EIB and the IMF. The Turkey Consortium consists of these same nine countries plus five others (Denmark, Norway, Sweden, Switzerland, and the United Kingdom) as well as the World Bank, the EIB, and the IMF.

THE INTERNATIONAL CONSULTATIVE GROUP FOR COLOMBIA

The international consultative group constituted under the chairmanship of the World Bank for the coordination of external development financing for Colombia is illustrative of another type of coordinating mechanism.

Colombia had requested over a period of several years that the World Bank organize a consortium of the India and Pakistan type to obtain its external financing requirements. It approached the World Bank rather than the Inter-American Development Bank for this purpose because of close relations it had developed with the World Bank throughout the postwar period. Furthermore, it felt that the ability of the World Bank to tap sources of finance was greater than that of the recently created IDB. The World Bank eventually responded favorably to the proposal, though in modified form.

The international group that was formed was designated as a consultative group rather than a consortium. This designation was not a simple matter of detail but involved a question of principle. Instead of creating a consortium on the model of those functioning for India and Pakistan, in which a certain amount of financing is assured every year in accordance with the country's development plans and balance-of-payments projections, the World Bank was willing to sponsor a group which would have the sole function of coordinating foreign aid to Colombia. In other words, the group was to be constituted not for general development financing or for contributing to any nonfinanced gap in the development plan but rather for coordinating external aid on the basis of specific projects or specific programs of a more general nature. This did not mean that balance of payments or stabilization financing was to be excluded, but that such financing, in addition to the financing of specific projects, would be considered on an *ad hoc* basis without any advance commitments. The specific projects or programs were to be considered by the financing countries or agencies completely on their own merits.

The first formal meeting of the consultative group took place in Washington in January, 1963. The group is constituted under the sponsorship of the World Bank and consists, in addition, of the two Bank affiliates, the IFC and the IDA, together with the IMF, the IDB, the US government and the governments of Austria, Belgium, Denmark, Germany, Holland, Italy, Luxembourg, Norway, Sweden, Switzerland, the United Kingdom, Canada, and Japan. The most recent meeting of the consultative group took place in June, 1964.

The group's meetings are informal and do not involve entering into actual financing commitments. Projects and programs prepared under Colombia's Ten-Year Development Plan (1961–70) are reviewed, and the participants indicate the possibilities of their contributions. Actual financing proposals are negotiated directly between the Colombian agency involved and the particular foreign financing body to which it is presented. More general matters are also considered by the consultative group, such as the terms of financing and the burden of external debt service on Colombia's balance of international payments.

The World Bank has constituted a resident mission in Colombia, which works closely with the Planning Office of the Colombian government and with representatives of the United States and other governments and agencies on an informal basis. The mission considers with the Planning Office the relative priority and feasibility of different projects and assists in the preparation of a balanced list of projects for consideration by members of the consultative group.

DAC COORDINATING GROUPS FOR THAILAND AND EAST AFRICA

The coordination of aid at the level of individual recipient countries or groups of countries by the DAC has been limited and tentative to date. Only two DAC country coordinating groups are in existence, one for Thailand and the other for East Africa (Kenya, Tanganyika, and Uganda). It is doubtful that this type of activity will be expanded by the DAC.

These country coordinating groups are considerably different in nature from the country consortia (e.g., India, Pakistan) or the consultative groups (Colombia, Nigeria) constituted under World Bank sponsorship or the consortia (Greece and Turkey) constituted under OECD sponsorship but outside the DAC. The DAC country coordinating groups have not functioned as devices to obtain pledges of certain amounts of external financial assistance to meet targets set up by the recipient country. Their function has been rather to identify particular problems of the recipients with respect to the foreign assistance received by them and to seek solutions to those problems. Thus, the group for Thailand has concentrated on rationalizing and coordinating the technical assistance from numerous sources received by the country. The need for coordinating financial assistance was much less important in this case, since the sources of the financing and the projects financed were few in number, and coordination would not be facilitated by the constitution of a new, special group for this purpose. The group for East Africa has also been concerned with technical assistance problems, as well as others, including the important problem in that region of raising finance for local currency requirements.

These country coordinating groups consist of representatives of DAC countries and other donors (e.g., Australia, New Zealand, and the United Nations participate in the Thailand group) who meet under DAC sponsorship periodically in the recipient country or region itself or in one of the European capitals, such as Paris or London.

COLOMBO PLAN

The Colombo Plan for Cooperative Economic Development in South and Southeast Asia grew out of the 1950 meeting of the Foreign Ministers of the British Commonwealth. At this meeting, a Consultative Committee was set up to survey the development needs of the countries of South and Southeast Asia, to assess the resources available, and to provide a framework within which a cooperative international effort could be promoted to overcome the vast problems in this area. At its first meeting, in May, 1950, the Consultative Committee, consisting of Australia, Canada, Ceylon, India, New Zealand, Pakistan, and the United Kingdom, together with Malaya and British Borneo, recommended that the Commonwealth countries in the area draw up six-year development programs commencing from July 1, 1951. In addition, an institutional framework was established for the exchange of technical knowledge. Later in 1950, preliminary development programs were reviewed and embodied in a report that was published in 1951 with the title of "Colombo Plan for Cooperative Economic Development in South and Southeast Asia." The Commonwealth countries outside of the area gave some indications of the financial contributions they would make toward carrying out the programs proposed.

Subsequently almost all of the other countries in the area joined the Consultative Committee and, in addition, the United States and Japan became members. Today there are twenty-two member countries consisting of virtually all countries in the region, the industrialized Commonwealth countries outside the region—namely, the United Kingdom, Canada, Australia, and New Zealand—the United States, and Japan, as well as observers from the Economic Commission for Asia and the Far East (ECAFE), the World Bank, and the UN Technical Assistance Board.

The Council for Technical Cooperation in the Colombo Plan acts as a coordinator of technical assistance in the area. Aid is provided on a bilateral basis. The Consultative Committee and the Council thus provide a forum for an annual review of national and regional problems which assists both the recipients and donors in carrying out programs in the area. In recent years there has been an increase in technical cooperation among the countries within the area themselves. Total economic aid provided by Australia, Canada, Japan, New Zealand, the United Kingdom, and the United States to countries in the region from the beginning of the Plan through June, 1964, was $14.9 billion.

The Colombo Plan was one of the earliest efforts of cooperative regional development. It fostered planning and an understanding of regional problems by countries in the area, focused world attention on development problems in the region, and provided an opportunity for local development officials to meet and exchange views. Its significant contribution, in fact, lies more along these general, yet fundamental, lines than in any tight coordination of aid for development in the area.

THE DEVELOPMENT ASSISTANCE COMMITTEE OF THE OECD

A forum for the exchange of information, the harmonization and improvement of policies, and some degree of coordination with respect to aid to the less developed countries, exists in the DAC of the OECD.

The OECD was established on September 30, 1961, as a successor to the Organization for European Economic Cooperation (OEEC), which had successfully completed its task of administering Marshall Plan aid and of achieving the economic recovery of Europe from World War II. The OECD, consisting of eighteen Western European powers plus the United States, Canada, and Japan (later admitted to membership), turned its attention to continued cooperation for the achievement of optimum economic growth in member countries, for the expansion of world trade on a multilateral and nondiscriminatory basis and for the development of the less developed countries. The DAC of the OECD represents a continuation within the new organization of a Development Assistance Group, which had been formed in January, 1960, to achieve the same objectives of maximization of aid, as well as its coordination and more effective utilization, pending the establishment of the OECD. When the OECD was formed in September, 1961, the Development Assistance Group became the Development Assistance Committee of the OECD.

The DAC comprises the major capital-exporting countries of the free world. It includes fourteen countries (Australia, Austria, Belgium, Canada, Denmark, France, Germany, Italy, Japan, the Netherlands, Norway, Portugal, the United Kingdom, and the United States) plus the EEC, represented separately as a unit in its own right. The members participate to a large extent through representatives resident in Paris. The DAC holds about thirty meetings per year. The World Bank and the IMF participate as observers in most meetings except those constituting the Annual Aid Review. The IDB has been pressing for greater European participation in development financing for Latin America, and a DAC subcommittee, or "working party," has been set up on this subject in response to the Bank's initiative. The DAC met in September, 1964, with representatives of the recently established Inter-American Committee for the Alliance for Progress to explore possible means of cooperation with that agency.

The DAC, although consisting of representatives of governments, elects a chairman as an independent expert who does not represent any individual government. The Chairman, at present Willard Thorp of the United States, issues and publishes an annual report under his own responsibility which, in effect, is the end product of DAC's Annual Aid Review. The Development Department of the OECD Secretariat serves as the Secretariat of DAC.

The DAC does not itself administer any aid programs or disburse funds. Its purpose is to promote increased aid by its members on improved terms and to assist in coordinating that aid. It maintains under constant review and analysis the magnitude and terms of aid to the less developed countries, provides a forum for continual discussion of global problems relating to such aid and, as indicated earlier, has engaged to some extent in a program of coordinating aid for particular countries and regions. The DAC reviews only the aid programs of its members, i.e., the fourteen nations listed above and the EEC. It is, therefore, primarily concerned with bilateral programs, the multilateral program of the EEC via the EDF being the exception to the rule. It does not review in any direct fashion the activities of international lending agencies such as the World Bank or the IDB, although it *is* concerned with the contribution of its members to such institutions.

The heart of DAC's activities to date has been its Annual Aid Review. In this Review, which takes place over a period of several months, the members initially present statements concerning the nature of their aid programs in response to a questionnaire submitted by the Secretariat. These statements are analyzed by the Secretariat and are then presented individually, together with the analysis of the Secretariat, to the DAC, where they are subjected to intensive criticism and review. The annual report of the DAC Chairman is prepared on the basis of the Review and, in effect, consists of a summary of the Review and recommendations arising from it. The Chairman's report is submitted to DAC's consideration before publication, even though it is the report of the Chairman as an expert individual rather than that of the body as an intergovernmental committee. The Chairman's recommendations, however, take into careful account the views of the Committee. The Chairman's role is that of gently urging the Committee into positive positions, and his report essentially represents the views of the Committee without formally committing the governments that comprise it.

The 1964 Aid Review focused attention on numerous aspects of the assistance effort designed to lead to its strengthening. These relate to the expansion of the flow of assistance, further improvement of the terms and conditions of aid, steps to increase the developmental impact of the aid, including improved performance by the developing countries, improvements in technical assistance, more effective international coordination, tax incentive and guarantee schemes to promote the flow of private capital, and the implications of the recently concluded UN Conference on Trade and Development for the assistance policies and objectives of the DAC. The work of the DAC in the period ahead on these matters was to be organized around new subcommittees or working groups which were to be concerned with the magnitude of aid, or its supply-and-demand aspects, the amounts of external indebtedness and the debt burden of the developing countries, and the effectiveness of the various types of international coordinating mechanisms that have developed in the aid field.

The 1965 Aid Review adds to the continuing survey of these aspects of aid, a discussion of the level of aid, in the light of the 1 percent formula adopted in the UNCTAD of 1964 (with a table giving disbursements of assistance as percentage of national income) and of the "requirements approach" (projection of requirements of less developed countries needed to attain a certain pace of development), as put forward by Raúl Prebisch, Secretary General of UNCTAD.

The Review records the Recommendations on Assistance and Development Efforts and on Financial Terms and Conditions adopted by the DAC Committee in July, 1965.

These recommend, *inter alia*, that member governments should attain and, if possible, exceed the UNCTAD targets, give priority to technical assistance related to the special requirements of individual countries, adapt the level of assistance to the extent of effective mobilization of resources by less developed countries, relate the *terms* of assistance to the circumstances as well as to the "pursuit of appropriate economic, financial and development policies" by the recipient country, further soften and harmonize the terms of assistance in such a way that *all* DAC members would give assistance on the terms granted in 1964 by five members for a preponderant proportion of their aid, i.e., either as grants or as loans at 3 percent or less with repayment periods of twenty-five years or more and a weighted average grace period of new loan commitments of about seven years; that aid tying should be progressively reduced and, meanwhile, its adverse effects be softened by greater elasticity in its administration; and that the "project approach" should be supplemented by the recognition of the need "often to provide aid to meet the cost of imports other than those for particular projects as well as, on occasion, to finance the local costs of development."

LOWER MEKONG BASIN PROJECT

The Committee for the Coordination of Investigations of the Lower Mekong Basin, consisting of the four riparian countries, namely, Laos, Cambodia, Viet Nam, and Thailand, assisted by the ECAFE of the United Nations, was established in 1957 to promote, coordinate, supervise, and control the planning and investigation of water resources development projects in the lower Mekong basin.

The Committee receives technical advice from a high-level international Technical Advisory Board established by the UN Technical Assistance Administration in 1958 and consisting of engineering and technical experts. Day-to-day coordination of all component programs and arrangements for new assistance is carried out by a Secretariat which was established in 1959 and is headed by an Executive Agent.

The project will require roughly $2 billion over the next twenty-five years to cover electric power, irrigation, flood control, and navigation projects, both on the mainstream and on the tributaries.

As of January, 1965, total resources contributed or pledged to the Committee or the projects sponsored by it amounted to $67.8 million. Approximately $21.1 million, or 40 percent, has been for preinvestment work, and the remainder has been for construction. Almost half (45 percent) of these funds have been contributed by the member countries of the Committee, and the remainder has come from twenty cooperating countries, UN agencies, and other organizations. The contributions of the riparian countries have been in the form of appropriations, with $7.9 million going for studies and $22.2 million for construction. External contributions have been distributed almost equally between studies ($19.3 million) and construction ($18.4 million). About a third of the total external contribution has been in the form of loans, all for construction projects.

In connection with the Mekong Project, it is relevant to note the announcement by the President of the United States on April 8, 1965, that he would ask the U.S. Congress to approve a billion-dollar investment in Southeast Asia. Although he did not define the scope of the proposed investment, the president referred in his proposal to the potential of the Mekong River for providing water, food, and power. Presumably a large part of any such effort would be directed to Mekong Basin projects.

The Mekong Basin development program thus represents an effort under UN auspices to coordinate the exploitation on a regional basis of water resources potentially available to several countries in Southeast Asia. The program has moved only slowly up to the present in relation to its vast scope.

IV. Experiences of Selected
Aid-Receiving Countries

MUCH OF OUR RESEARCH has been concentrated on the experiences of selected countries in the receipt and use of aid. It is, of course, in such actual experiences that the methods and policies of the donor countries and institutions and the interplay between donors and recipients can be viewed in terms of how they work out concretely. The countries were selected for study with an eye toward assembling an array of experiences that would be generally representative of the various levels of development of the numerous aid-receiving countries, of the several broad regions of the world which are in the less developed category, and of the multiplicity of aid-giving institutions as they actually operate in practice in the field. Obviously, no selection of countries can be completely representative of the total world aid situation, since each country has at least some unique characteristics, but it is hoped that the selection we have made involves enough common denominators for it to be possible to view the foreign aid picture more or less as a whole on the basis of it.

Ten countries or groups of countries have been studied: two in Latin America, namely, Colombia and Chile; three in the Middle East and the south of Europe, namely, Israel, Greece, and Turkey; two in south Asia, namely, India and Thailand; and three in Africa, namely, Kenya, Tanganyika (now Tanzania), and Uganda, which make up what was formerly British East Africa, Senegal from French-speaking West Africa, and the Sudan. Every effort was made in these studies to take into account the attitudes of the aid recipients, along with those of the donors. The research was conducted primarily in the aid-receiving countries themselves, and, wherever practicable, qualified nationals or organizations of these countries participated in the work. Some of the country studies were written entirely by national individuals or organizations of the recipient countries.[1]

During the course of our research project, monographs on the detailed individual country studies were issued and distributed. These have constituted the principal raw materials for our work. In the present chapter, the experience with aid of each of the countries studied is analyzed in summary form. The sections that follow on each of the countries set forth the type of basic development problem with which it is faced, the characteristics of the aid it has received, the manner in which it has handled the aid, and the principal kinds of problems that confront it with respect to aid in the future. Viewing the aid picture in this coherent fashion on the basis of the individual overall country experiences makes it possible to appreciate the range of kinds of development situations with which foreign aid must deal.

Colombia

Colombia in many ways typifies the national economic situations and development problems to be found among the Latin American republics. Its population of about 16 million is growing rapidly at a rate of close to 3 percent per year and is clustered in a relatively small area of the country, although there is no serious problem of high population density. There has been, however, a marked trend of movement from rural to urban areas, which has aggravated the already serious deficiencies of housing and public services. National income per capita, estimated to amount to the equivalent of somewhat less than $300 per year, is at about the average level for Latin America as a whole, with the uneven distribution of income among the population which is also typical of the situation in most countries of Latin America.

Total national output has been rising at the rate of about 5 percent per year on the average during the past decade. The country is still, however, far from having achieved a steady, self-sustaining

[1] The studies of Colombia and Chile were conducted jointly with Raymond F. Mikesell, Associate Director of the Institute of International Studies and Overseas Administration of the University of Oregon.

pace of development. A ten-year development plan formulated for the years 1961–70 fixed the goal of an average annual growth rate of 6.5 percent during the period.

The achievement of the country's growth goals requires considerable public investments to provide economic infrastructure facilities and social services, as well as foreign exchange for the importation of capital equipment. Both public investments and the availability of capital equipment have been limited by the structure of the economy. Although Colombia has a relatively advanced and progressive system of taxation, it has been beset by chronic fiscal deficits resulting from its narrow tax base, which in turn reflects the generally low level of income and the concentration of income in a small sector of the population. While considerable advances have been made in industrialization through expanded production of finished consumer goods, there is little manufacturing of capital goods, most of which must come from abroad. The country's principal source of foreign exchange is coffee, which accounts for about three-fourths of total exports. Only limited progress has been made in the diversification of exports. Mineral resources are limited; petroleum is an important item of export, but it is only of secondary importance.

Because of the country's increasing import requirements associated with development, combined with its rigid export structure and the deterioration of its terms of trade, it has suffered from persistent balance-of-payments deficits. This is reflected in the decline during the last decade in the exchange value of the peso from 40 U.S. cents to less than 10 cents, as the price of coffee dropped to a level half as great as the price level at the beginning of the period. Substantial deficits in the current account of the balance of payments are expected during the next few years at least, as the objectives of the development plan are carried out. These deficits will have to be covered by capital imports, mostly in the public sector. After making allowance for new capital to offset the repayment of outstanding debt, net capital import requirements to cover the current account deficits are estimated as equivalent to close to a quarter of current account receipts of somewhat more than $500 million per year. International finance for the development of Colombia is thus of strategic importance.

NATURE OF AID RECEIVED

During the entire postwar period through 1960, Colombia received moderate, though fluctuating, amounts of international financial assistance. A substantial increase occurred during the period 1957–59, in connection with the funding of large commercial arrears that had accumulated during the several preceding years of declining coffee prices and financial mismanagement. Even with the large aid increases of 1957–59, however, net disbursements amounted to only slightly more than 10 percent of current exchange earnings, compared with the much higher requirements projected during the early years of the Plan period, as mentioned above. Since 1961 there has again been a large increase in the aid received by Colombia, though for different reasons. The present trend is a reflection of the inauguration of new international lending agencies, of increased emphasis on international assistance to Latin America under the Alliance for Progress, and of the more highly coordinated developmental effort within Colombia symbolized by its adoption of a Ten-Year Development Plan.

Total postwar public external loan authorizations to Colombia through 1960 amounted to some $645 million, gross disbursements to $501 million, and net disbursements to $273 million. The concentration of aid during 1957–59 is reflected in the portions of the totals which correspond to that short period of three years: $294 million of authorizations, $248 million of gross disbursements, and $163 million of net disbursements. Credits authorized during 1961 rose to close to $250 million, and although they have since subsided somewhat, they have continued at a much higher rate than earlier in the postwar period. By the end of 1964, the second year of existence of the international consultative group for external assistance to Colombia chaired by the World Bank, group members had committed a total of about $375 million in loans.

The principal sources of external financial assistance to Colombia up to 1961 were the Export-Import Bank of Washington, the International Bank for Reconstruction and Development, and the International Monetary Fund. The assistance was about half in the form of general balance-of-payments support and half for specific projects. The U.S. contribution to balance-of-payments support was via the EXIMBANK. Since 1961 the U.S. channel for balance-of-payments assistance to Colombia has shifted to its Agency for International Development, and there has consequently been a substantial easing of the terms of such assistance. The World Bank and IMF have both continued with active programs in Colombia, and the Inter-American Development Bank, which made its first loan to any country in February, 1961, has joined the ranks of lenders to Colombia. About 45 percent of the development financing committed in 1963 and 1964 came from the United States, another 45 percent from the World Bank, and the balance mostly from the IDB, with small amounts from other donor countries.

There was an early start in World Bank relations with Colombia. The first comprehensive economic survey mission organized by the Bank was sent to that country in 1949. From 1950, when the World Bank granted its first loan to Colombia, to the present, it has committed a total of $389 million to the country, and IDA has extended one credit, for $19.5 million. Since the beginning of 1961, World Bank activity in Colombia has intensified. The IDA credit was granted in 1961, and $210 million of the total of Bank loans have been committed since the beginning of 1961. Electric power and transportation projects have accounted for an overwhelming portion of the World Bank–IDA assistance: electric power loans have totaled $206 million, highway loans $86 million, and railway loans $76 million. The balance is made up of a $30-million loan for the improvement and expansion of the country's primary steel mill and $10 million in loans for agricultural machinery imports. In view of its close relations with the World Bank, Colombia requested the Bank to organize and chair the international consultative group for the coordination of external financial assistance to the country, which was formed early in 1963.

From the beginning of its operations early in 1961 to the end of 1964, the IDB committed a total of $107.5 million in loans to Colombia, about 60 percent out of its own resources and 40 percent out of the Social Progress Trust Fund administered for the United States. Most of the loans from its own resources have been on the hard terms of the Bank's "ordinary capital resources"; only $3.2 million has been loaned out of the Fund for Special Operations, for water supply, sewerage, and technical assistance projects. The "ordinary capital resource" loans have been mostly for public sector projects, including water supply and sewerage, electric power, a sodium carbonate plant, and ports. There was also one such loan, for $3 million, to the Private Investment Fund of Colombia's central bank, the Banco de la República, for re-lending to the private sector. This Fund has been assisted particularly by the U.S. AID. The Social Progress Trust Fund loans have been heavily for public housing projects and also for water supply and sewerage, farm credit, and higher education.

Loans for social infrastructure projects which started in 1961, represented a new departure in external lending to Colombia. Before the Social Progress Trust Fund was constituted in mid-1961, the trend was begun in loans by the Development Loan Fund, the predecessor agency of the U.S. AID. During 1961 the DLF authorized loans of $12 million to Colombia for low-cost housing and $8 million for agricultural colonization.

Balance-of-payments assistance to Colombia from the EXIMBANK of Washington consisted of loans of $60 million in 1957, $78 million in 1958 (in part a refinancing of the 1957 loan), $25 million in 1959 (which was never utilized), and $45 million in 1961. These loans were granted in conjunction with assistance from the IMF and loans from U.S. private commercial banks. They were all medium-term, having to be repaid over such periods as four, five, or eight years as a maximum, and contributed heavily to the country's burden of external debt service. The ratio of debt service to current exchange earnings ranged from 18 to 29 percent during the period 1958–61. Starting in 1962, balance-of-payments assistance from the U.S. government was taken over by the AID, and the terms of repayment eased considerably. A first loan of $30 million early in 1962 had a term of fifteen years and an interest rate of 3 percent. A second loan of $60 million authorized at the end of 1962 had a term of forty years, including a ten-year grace period, and bore no interest but only a ¾ percent service charge. Two loans totaling $60 million which were granted during 1964 had the same long maturity and low service charge during the grace period, but the charge was raised to 2 percent for the thirty-year repayment period.

Besides the AID's balance-of-payments loans to Colombia, which amounted to $150 million during the period 1962–64, most of its assistance has been in the form of loans to intermediate credit institutions. These have totaled $31.5 million: $7.5 million to the public low-cost housing institute, $10 million to the agrarian reform institute, $4 million to a public livestock bank, and $10 million to the Private Investment Fund previously mentioned.

The Private Investment Fund, which operates through the Colombian private commercial banking system and investment houses, was organized by the central bank to serve as a channel for international financing of private industrial projects. Besides the $10-million direct AID loan and the $3-million IDB loan, it has received the equivalent of $40 million in peso proceeds out of the AID balance-of-payments loans mentioned above and a credit of $1.4 million from the Netherlands.

The private sector in Colombia has, furthermore, been assisted by the International Finance Corporation, affiliated with the World Bank. To a considerable extent, this has also taken the form of financing via intermediate credit institutions. During the last few years, some five private development finance companies have been formed in Colombia, and almost half of IFC investments in the country have been investments in these companies. Total IFC investments have amounted to some $11 million, of which $4.7 million have been in such intermediate institutions.

ADMINISTRATION OF AID

One of the most important byproducts of public international lending to Colombia has been the stimulation of national economic planning in the country. This type of activity on a comprehensive basis was given its first stimulus by the World Bank survey mission of 1949. To the extent that it has continued and strengthened, it has been largely motivated by the prospects of foreign financial assistance, and it has been considerably influenced by international lending agencies. The latest expressions of the relationship between comprehensive national economic planning and foreign aid have consisted of the formulation at the end of 1961 of the Ten-Year Development Plan, its subsequent review by the Committee of Nine Experts of the OAS and by the World Bank, and the constitution in January, 1963, of the international consultative group for the coordination of external assistance to Colombia under the chairmanship of the World Bank.[2]

The National Planning Board, which is the body responsible for planning policy, and the Planning Department, which is the technical group for the function, serve as central points for the establishment of planning priorities, for the coordination of government policies, and for the centralization of requests for foreign financing. The functions are exercised in practice with a considerable degree of laxity, however, and there is much initiative carried out in a decentralized fashion by long-established administrative agencies with respect both to public investment and to the obtaining of foreign financing to assist in its financing. Nevertheless, the planning mechanism is the only agency with some degree of comprehensive responsibility and serves as a central point of contact for resident missions maintained in the country by the World Bank and the U.S. AID.

The administrative agencies for whose programs foreign aid is utilized consist both of regular departments of government, particularly of the national government, and of agencies and corporations with varying degrees of autonomy. The autonomous official corporation or institute has long been a popular administrative device in Colombia.

The principal regular department of the national government which has been involved in the administration of foreign aid is the Ministry of Public Works, in connection with the highway programs which have loomed so large in World Bank lending to Colombia. The Ministry of Finance, in connection with its responsibilities for general economic, fiscal, and foreign exchange policies, has, of course, also been concerned with foreign aid in various ways, particularly in negotiations with the IMF and the agencies of the U.S. government which have provided general balance-of-payments assistance. Such negotiations are conducted jointly with the central bank, which actually administers the assistance as part of its general control over foreign exchange transactions. Besides the central bank, the most important of the autonomous agencies involved in foreign

[2] The make-up and activities of the international consultative group for Colombia are discussed in Chapter III under the section on "Aid-Coordinating Mechanisms."

aid administration have been several electric power agencies, a national railways administration, agricultural and livestock banks, an agrarian reform institute, several telecommunications agencies, a ports administration, water supply and sewerage authorities, and a housing institute. All these have been in existence for varying periods of time to operate in the particular areas with which they are concerned and have received foreign aid as incidental to their general activities.

The official development bank or corporation, which has been of central importance in the administration of foreign aid in other Latin American countries such as Mexico and Chile, has not been of importance in Colombia. There has been such an agency, the Industrial Development Institute, which has been in existence in Colombia since 1940. It has been responsible for the formation of a relatively small number of large industrial enterprises, e.g., to produce steel, tires, and cement, but it has been chronically short of funds and has never assumed the prominent role in national economic life which has been played by the similar institutions in Chile and Mexico. As previously mentioned, however, important amounts of foreign aid have been channeled into Colombia through a variety of intermediate credit institutions: specialized banks and financial institutes (e.g., agriculture, housing), private industrial development finance companies, and the Private Investment Fund set up by the Banco de la República. The latter in effect involves the utilization of existing institutions rather than the creation of a new one, operating as it does through the central bank and the commercial banks. The private development finance companies have been favored by the World Bank group, in this case specifically through equity investments by the IFC.

There have been various differences between the lending agencies and the administering agencies over administrative and policy matters in the course of aid administration in Colombia. This has applied particularly to World Bank loans, which are perhaps less subject to political or other nondevelopmental motivations than bilateral loans. Furthermore, international agencies are in a somewhat better position than foreign national agencies to become involved in internal matters in the recipient country. Differences have arisen over political influences on administration of the railways, over contracting and auditing procedures in highway construction, and over rate policies for railway transport and electric power. These differences have generally been satisfactorily resolved. Improvements of administration and policy have been brought about, which might have been difficult to effect without the leverage of the conditions set to obtain the foreign financing.

It is of interest to note that World Bank loans for electric power in Colombia have been limited to the principal systems, serving such leading cities as Bogotá, Medellín, Cali, Manizales, and Bucaramanga. These loans have been granted to municipal or regional agencies which are quite autonomous of the national government. The smaller systems are under the control of a national electric power institute ("Electraguas"), which has not been operated quite as efficiently as the large local systems. The World Bank concentration on the larger systems may have been on the basis of a combination of economic priority and administrative efficiency. The first important international loans obtained by Electraguas came from the IDB in December, 1964, consisting of two loans for a total of $11 million. Thus, this regional lending agency supplemented World Bank electric power lending activity by taking over projects of lower priority.

Differences have at times remained unresolved. In one case, the U.S. government tried to get Colombia to set up a new type of institution, the system of savings-and-loan associations for housing, and earmarked a $5-million loan in 1961 from its Development Loan Fund for this purpose. This loan never materialized, because of the opposition of existing savings institutions in the country. No such system was organized in Colombia, although the United States has sparked its formation elsewhere in Latin America through financial assistance—in Chile, Peru, Ecuador, and Venezuela.

PRINCIPAL PROBLEMS IN AID

The issue of lending for specific projects versus general balance-of-payments financing has loomed large in international financial aid to Colombia. Colombian authorities have consistently argued for general balance-of-payments support because of the country's recurring foreign exchange crises and because specific project formulation and negotiation do not provide the amounts of exchange which are needed to meet the crises quickly enough. Lending agencies have been reluctant to provide the general type of financing—they have limited it in amount, at times have imposed short maturities for repayment, and have attempted to obtain agreements by Colombia to impose internal anti-inflationary policies. The need has been so great, however, that the general type of financing has been granted in increasing amounts and on more realistically lenient terms, although it has not entirely eliminated the inflationary and exchange pressures which keep recurring.

There has been some attempt in the general balance-of-payments financing to influence the course of investment in Colombia through the earmarking of some of the peso counterpart funds for certain purposes. An illustration of this is the channeling of some of these funds to the Private Investment Fund. While the short-run effect of such earmarking might be inflationary, the justification is the promotion of productive investment of a particular type which will contribute to development and be counterinflationary over the long run. In the absence of such earmarking, general balance-of-payments financing simply serves to cover a country's exchange deficit and so indirectly to finance the existing investment pattern, whatever that might be.

There has also been some attempt to link general balance-of-payments assistance to the tightening of anti-inflationary monetary and fiscal policies in Colombia. The lead in this respect usually has been taken by the International Monetary Fund in connection with its typical short-term balance-of-payments assistance. At times assistance from other sources has been combined with that from the IMF and has been made subject to Colombia's observance of IMF conditions. The separate balance-of-payments loans of the U.S. AID in recent years have also been conditional on Colombia's adoption of anti-inflationary measures. Colombian authorities have traditionally been conscious of the desirability of keeping inflation in check, and the country's record in this respect is favorable compared with the experience of other Latin American countries such as Brazil or Chile. Political factors have at times, however, made it difficult to apply sufficiently strict policies, and such factors appear to have been no less of an impediment to the carrying out of commitments undertaken to obtain external balance-of-payments assistance. This is illustrated by the announcement in mid-June 1965 that the World Bank, the IMF, and the U.S. AID were suspending further advances to Colombia, pending clarification of the government's intention to deal with pressing fiscal problems.

During some recent years Colombia's external debt service has constituted a particularly heavy burden on its current foreign exchange earnings. This has been because of the large representation in the debt of balance-of-payments financing repayable over short periods of time. The strict conditions were imposed by the lending agencies in an effort to force the adoption of austere anti-inflationary policies by Colombia, even if at the cost of slowing down development. This type of financing was granted especially in the late 1950s before the general liberalization of international development financing which occurred in the early 1960s. The total burden of the country's external debt service has been taken into consideration to a greater extent during recent years, particularly as its external borrowing has been approached in a more coordinated fashion through the international consultative group established under World Bank sponsorship.

A large part of the aid available to Colombia, especially that from multilateral agencies such as those of the World Bank group and the IDB, is available only for specific projects. The extent to which the country will receive such aid is obviously dependent upon its presentation of projects which are suitable for financing. Indeed, its general rate of development is also affected by the formulation of specific projects, since development in the last analysis is a function of investment. As in many other less developed countries, however, the tendency in Colombia has been for general planning to outrun specific project preparation. There is a considerable gap between the macroeconomic formulations in its long-run development plan and their translation into concrete investment projects. The gap is due to the highly imperfect nature of the planning on the one hand and to general defects of public administration on the other. Continuing attempts to have the process of planning closely woven into the fabric of the country's economic life have had only limited success. And the improvements in public administration which are necessary both for the planning itself and for the preparation of specific projects occur slowly. Some of the aid consists of technical assistance to make it possible to utilize greater amounts of financial assistance, but the speed of thorough project preparation continues as a principal problem in Colombia's foreign aid.

Chile

Chile is in a better situation than most other countries of Latin America in various aspects of its economic, social, and political development, but it is nevertheless beset by serious problems for whose solution substantial amounts of external assistance are required. Its population of some 8 million, increasing at about the same rapid rate of some 2½ percent per annum found generally in Latin America, enjoys a higher level of income and a more even distribution of income, particularly as a result of state welfare measures, than the average in the region. The extent of literacy and education is also greater than in most other Latin American countries, and Chile, with a broad range of highly developed political parties, enjoys a substantial degree of political democracy and stability.

On the other hand, Chile, like Colombia, is overwhelmingly dependent for its current earnings of foreign exchange on one commodity, in this case copper rather than coffee. Although copper has demand characteristics somewhat more dynamic than coffee, the foreign exchange which it has produced in Chile has not grown at a rate sufficiently rapid to provide the sums needed for development, and the commodity has been subject at times to pronounced cyclical fluctuations in international markets. As a consequence, the country has suffered from a persistent situation of balance-of-payments disequilibrium and exchange-rate depreciation, to which internal inflation, sparked primarily by official deficit financing, has also been a major contributing factor. During the past decade the economy has been in a situation of relative stagnation, with expansion barely keeping pace with the growth of population, and the level of income per capita is at about the level of the less developed countries of Europe, e.g., Spain, Greece, or Turkey.

The policy of deficit financing is a reflection of the low rate of domestic savings in the country, coupled with a tradition of government intervention to promote welfare and development. At the same time there has been a marked trend toward greater deficits in the current account of the balance of international payments. Because of both a balance-of-payments and a savings gap, capital imports have therefore been necessary to minimize the extent of inflation as well as to support an expansion of national output.

Chile's Ten-Year Development Program for 1961–70 established an annual average growth goal of 5.5 percent. This required an increase in the rate of investment from about 10 percent of national output to some 14 percent in 1961–65 and close to 17 percent in 1966–70. The achievement of these goals required a gross inflow of capital over the period equivalent to about a fourth of the country's current earnings of foreign exchange, with more of the capital required in the earlier part of the decade than in the second half, on the optimistic assumption that the growth and structural change goals would be achieved.

NATURE OF AID RECEIVED

Chile has received a large amount of external financial assistance during the postwar period, especially in connection with the efforts started in 1956 to stabilize its economy in the face of strong inflationary pressures. This is reflected in the present amount of public external indebtedness outstanding of somewhat more than $1 billion, or more than twice as much as the country receives annually from its current exports of goods and services.

During approximately the first decade, from 1945 through 1955, the external financing was of moderate proportions and highly sporadic from year to year. The level became substantially higher beginning in 1956 with the adoption of the stabilization program. The political regime that took office late in 1958 for a six-year period embarked on a deliberate policy of obtaining financial assistance from abroad to supplement the low level of internal savings and to promote economic development without inflation. This policy was re-emphasized in the 1961–70 Development Program adopted in 1960, and it has since been reasserted by the new administration that took office in November, 1964. During the four-year period 1960–63, official capital inflows amounted to $690 million gross and $530 million net of repayments.

More than half of the total financing, probably about 60 percent, has been for general balance-of-payments support or in the form of general program loans for economic development. The balance of 40 percent has been about equally divided between economic infrastructure projects and directly productive projects, with a smaller amount than either of these two categories for social infrastructure projects.

About three-fourths of the credits have come from bilateral sources, principally from the U.S. government through its EXIM-BANK and to a greater extent recently through the AID. There have also been some credits of importance from other governments, such as West Germany, the United Kingdom, and Canada, although they have represented only a minor part of the total. Private foreign sources have represented an important bilateral source of credit to official agencies in Chile, through suppliers' credits and private bank general balance-of-payments loans.

Prominent in the lending activity of multilateral agencies in Chile have been the IMF for balance-of-payments and economic stabilization assistance and the IBRD for assistance to economic infrastructure and a few mining and heavy industry projects. The IDA joined with the World Bank in one project, involving highway development, in order to ease the repayment terms. The IDB, since the beginning of its operations early in 1961, has become an important source of external financial assistance for Chile, having extended almost as much in loans as to Colombia, whose population is almost twice as large as that of Chile.

The U.S. AID has been granting Chile program assistance and similar loans annually since its establishment. These amounted to $40 million in 1962, $35 million in 1963, and $40 million in 1964; and in December, 1964, a loan of this type in the amount of $80 million was authorized for disbursement on a quarterly basis during 1965. The 1962 loan was granted to the Chilean Development Corporation for relending for economic and social infrastructure as well as for industrial and agricultural projects, with AID approval required for subloans above $100,000, but the others have had even fewer strings attached; i.e., the commitments regarding the use of the counterpart local currency have been quite general. All the loans have had forty-year maturities, but in the most recent commitment, what was formerly only a service charge of ¾ percent on the funds, in line with general U.S. policy, has been raised to 1 percent during the ten-year period of grace and 2½ percent thereafter. As a possible indication of its reluctance to limit all financing to general program loans, the AID also committed to Chile for 1965 the sum of $10 million "for mutually agreeable projects."

The U.S. EXIMBANK has been the most important single source of loans to Chile throughout the postwar period, accounting for about a fourth of the total. From 1945 through 1964, it authorized a total of some $420 million of loans to Chile. About a third of the loans have been general purpose loans, granted during the early postwar years for relending by the Chilean Development Corporation and later to the National Government and Central Bank to assist the general economic stabilization efforts. In some cases the stabilization loans have been part of joint financing with the IMF, the AID, the U.S. Treasury Stabilization Fund, and private banks. EXIMBANK loans of the latter type were authorized in the amount of $50 million each in 1963 and 1964. These loans carry hard terms; the 1964 loan was for a term of some eight years, including a two-year period of grace and at an interest rate of 5½ percent per annum. Outstanding among the specific projects assisted by the EXIMBANK is the mixed public-private integrated steel enterprise, the Companía de Acero del Pacífico (CAP); the Bank has granted a total of some $110 million in loans to this enterprise. Other activities assisted to a substantial extent have been copper and nitrate mining, electric power production, and railway modernization.

The World Bank has had a substantial volume of activity in Chile, though not quite to the same extent as in Colombia. Its total loans committed to Chile amount to $141 million plus $19 million committed by the IDA, the latest loan having been approved in February, 1965. Almost half the IBRD loans to Chile have been for electric power. The IDA loan was granted jointly with an IBRD loan for highways. Other activities assisted have been coal mining, pulp and paper production, and, in December, 1963, in connection with the new emphasis of the Bank, livestock development. Although no international consultative group has been established by the Bank for Chile as it has been for Colombia, the Bank appraised Chile's Ten-Year Development Plan. It also established a resident mission in Chile in June, 1962, to advise continuously on development planning. The IFC has had a modest amount of activity in the country, consisting of four loans in the total amount of $8.8 million for a copper mine and smelter, a flour mill and macaroni factory, a cement plant, and a pulp and paper plant.

Total loans to Chile by the IDB amounted to $101.9 million through 1964: $57.5 million out of its "ordinary resources," $9 million out of its Fund for Special Operations, and $35.4 million out of the Social Progress Trust Fund constituted by the U.S. government. A substantial volume of the Bank's loans has been granted for relending or administration by the Chilean Development Corporation. The "ordinary resource" loans have been for industry, mining, fisheries, petroleum refining, water supply, and irrigation. The Fund for Special Operations loans have been for farm settlement and agricultural development, and the Social Progress Trust Fund loans have been for water-supply projects, rural development, housing, and higher education.

ADMINISTRATION OF AID

Negotiations for the large amounts of external credits for general balance-of-payments support obtained by Chile have usually been conducted jointly by the Minister of Finance and the Central Bank. The Central Bank, which also administers these credits as part of its general function of administration of foreign exchange controls, is owned jointly by the central government and by private shareholders, principally banks. However, the power of the government in the Central Bank is decisive. Although the government does not have a majority on the Bank's Board of Directors, it has the power of veto in most questions of importance, and at times the Minister of Finance has also served as President of the Central Bank.

For external loans for specific projects, the pivotal agency in Chile is the Development Corporation (the Corporación de Fomento de la Producción, or CORFO), which also has some broader functions in connection with the country's receipt of foreign aid. CORFO is the oldest development corporation in Latin America. It was established in 1939 with the objectives of diversification of production, substitution of imports, and promotion of exports, especially in reponse to the severe decline in the country's mineral exports that occurred during the world depression of the 1930s. It is empowered to make direct investments in enterprises, to make loans to private or public enterprises, and to guarantee external loans. CORFO is also charged with the function of intervening in all negotiations for external credits. Although this is not uniformly observed in practice, CORFO is nevertheless the closest thing to a centralized agency in Chile for the negotiation of external credits. Negotiations for such credits are frequently conducted by CORFO's New York office.

CORFO's direct investment activities have resulted in many cases in the establishment of separate subsidiaries, the most important of which —ENDESA in electric power, CAP in steel, and ENAP in petroleum—have been recipients of substantial external loans. Its lending activities have made it a convenient vehicle for the administration of external lines of credit for relending to enterprises in a variety of fields. And external loans requiring a Chilean government guarantee are frequently guaranteed by this agency.

CORFO has been a very important institution in the strategy of economic development in Chile in quantitative as well as qualitative terms. Its investments represent about a third of total public investments, which in turn account for the substantial proportion of about half of total investments in the economy. Accordingly, it has been the obvious intermediate credit institution through which to channel external finance for development. There are no private development finance companies in Chile. The World Bank group, which tends to limit its loans and investments to such companies for reinvestment for general purposes, therefore, has not granted such assistance to Chile. The World Bank has, however, used CORFO as an intermediate channel for loans for specific sectors, such as its December, 1963, loans for livestock development. The general credit lines received by CORFO have come from the U.S. EXIMBANK and AID and from the IDB.

Besides its investment functions, CORFO has also been entrusted since its creation with the function of development planning for the Chilean economy. It limited its activity in this field to sectoral planning until the formulation of the comprehensive plan for 1961–70. Following the elaboration of this plan, CORFO served as the technical secretariat of an inter-agency committee (the Comité de Programación Económica y de Reconstrucción, or COPERE) established in 1960 as an advisory body for planning and programming and for the execution of plans and programs. In so far as external financing requirements in Chile have been defined through such sectoral and comprehensive planning, CORFO has thus been centrally involved in the process. However, the administration that took office in November, 1964, decided to separate the planning function from the promotional and investment activities of CORFO and to elevate the status of the planning function by centralizing it in the Office of the President.

The regular ministries such as the Ministries of Public Works, Agriculture, or Education have been much less important in Chile than the autonomous agencies as channels of investment and recipients of external development finance. They have accounted for only about a fourth of public investment and a fifth of external development finance. Besides the Central Bank of Chile and CORFO and its subsidiaries, important foreign aid recipients among the autonomous agencies have been the Chilean State Railways, public housing agencies, and various agricultural development agencies.

PRINCIPAL PROBLEMS IN AID

Chile has received substantial amounts of external financing in recent years, much of it as a general supplement to its inadequate internal savings and foreign exchange availabilities, to promote its efforts to stabilize the economy and achieve a more rapid rate of development. But the general economic impact of the assistance has been one of limited effectiveness. The rate of inflation has been slowed down from the peak increase in the cost of living of some 85 percent in 1955, but the extent of the control over inflation is uncertain, and prices rose by about 38 percent in 1964. And economic expansion has continued at only a slow rate; the average annual increase in gross national product during the period 1960–64 amounted to 3.4 percent, or less than 1 percent per year on a per capita basis.

The limited economic impact of the general external financing is, of course, a reflection of the merely supplementary role that such financing can play in any economy. The primary determinant of effective anti-inflationary and development measures is the complex combination of internal monetary and fiscal policies to keep demand in check and of other economic policies to effect the structural changes needed to unleash productive forces. The search for such solutions to make effective use of the external financing in the drive for self-sustained growth continues as a basic need in Chile.

In the large amount of external financing to which Chile has resorted since 1956, the country has burdened its balance of international payments with onerous debt service requirements. The reason has been the large amount of general balance-of-payments financing and suppliers' credits obtained at medium-term maturities. The medium terms have to some extent resulted from the type of institution from which the financing has been obtained, but in other cases they have been deliberately imposed by the lending agencies with the hope of pressing for the adoption of the type of measure needed to eliminate the causes of inflation and balance-of-payments disequilibrium. In any case, the terms have generally turned out to be unrealistic, and refinancing has later been required to avoid defaults. More recently, as the U.S. AID has entered the picture, more realistic repayment terms have been granted in the light of the time required to effect structural reforms.

The preparation of specific projects for external financing, to which the international agencies are largely limited and which many individual donor countries prefer, has lagged in Chile relative to the macroeconomic projections which make up its economic planning. This is the case despite the fact that Chile is more advanced than many other Latin American countries in the quality of its public administration for development, illustrated, for example, by its having set up the first development corporation in the region, which, as has been noted, has grown to be a very important factor in the economy. The paucity of such specific projects may not reflect administrative shortcomings—there have been numerous large projects in Chile which have received external assistance quite successfully—but rather excessively abstract planning techniques, the lack of entrepreneurship, or the instability of the general economic environment and its deterrent effect on long-term productive investment. In any case, a shortage of specific projects for external financing persists, and, if the balance-of-payments gap is to be closed, it will have to continue to be by much external financing of the program type. To help alleviate the problem, the IDB granted a loan of $3 million to CORFO in August, 1965, especially for the financing of feasibility studies and the preparation of specific projects.

Delays in the disbursement of loan commitments have at times given rise to dissatisfaction in Chile with the procedures of the lenders. This has occurred particularly when there has been a pressing need for the supplementation of foreign exchange availabilities. It usually is a reflection of failure to achieve a clear understanding with respect to conditions that may be imposed on general program loans. Such conditions may provide for the adoption of certain general policies or the undertaking of specific counterpart investments, which the borrower may accept under the pressure of the need for the foreign exchange assistance without a full appreciation of the implications of the conditions. Obviously, such conditions should be imposed on the basis of a realistic appraisal of their acceptability, or they should be interpreted in a flexible manner if the intention is for them to indicate a direction or emphasis rather than some specific content of policies.

Israel

Israel's development experience is unique among the capital-importing countries of the world. With a marked paucity of natural resources, a small market, and a rapidly increasing population, it has maintained one of the highest rates of national development in the world. During the short period since its creation as a state in 1948, annual economic growth has averaged 10 percent or better, to produce a level of income per capita estimated at nearly $1,000 in 1964. This income, widely distributed among the population, is close to the levels found in the developed countries of Western Europe.

The notable rate of economic development in Israel has been made possible by massive imports of capital, which the country has put to effective use in the achievement of its high levels of output and welfare. Much of the capital has come from unique sources which are not available to most other developing countries. It is perhaps in this sense, or on the basis of the relatively high levels of living which the country has achieved, that one must interpret its classification among countries "which are plainly in the stage of transition to economic self-support, and where economic aid can soon come to an end." This classification was made by the Administrator of the U.S. AID in a speech delivered on November 21, 1964.

Israel is, however, certainly by no means self-supporting in the sense of no longer being dependent on capital imports. Its current account balance-of-payments deficit continues at the high level of some $500 million per annum in relation to an annual level of imports of goods and services of some $1.2 billion; in other words, about 40 percent of its imports of goods and services are sustained by capital imports. Nor is it possible to support such a level of capital imports on conventional terms without an intolerable burden of debt service; it has been possible for Israel to sustain the large volume of capital imports which it has received throughout its history only because more than two-thirds of it has been in the form of unilateral transfers, requiring no repayment at all.

The problem of economic development aid to Israel is thus in a sense more akin to the problems in Europe that gave rise to the Marshall Plan than to the problems of other developing countries today. The country has achieved a level of income which puts it in the category more of the advanced rather than the underdeveloped nations, but it will continue to require substantial amounts of external assistance for a considerable length of time before its development can be genuinely self-generating. Failure to maintain a large volume of capital imports would endanger the high levels of well-being which have been achieved. And the country has demonstrated that it has the human resources and capacity for organization to put large amounts of capital to productive use.

NATURE OF AID RECEIVED

During the period 1949–60, net imports of long-term capital into Israel amounted to some $3.6 billion, or about the same as the total surplus of imports of goods and services over exports during the period. The annual amounts of capital imports ranged from $161 million in 1949 to $421 million in 1960, and they have increased during recent years, to some $520 million estimated for 1964. Although the sequential relationship cannot be as clearly established between capital imports and investments in the Israeli economy as between capital imports and the import surplus, investments are also of about the same order of magnitude. It is clear that the high rates of investment, amounting to more than 20 percent of national output, which have made possible the high rate of development, could not have proceeded without the imports of external capital.

Unilateral transfers accounted for some 70 percent of the total capital imports. For example, they amounted to $335 million out of the $520 million of capital imports in 1964. They have consisted principally of reparations and restitution payments from West Germany, transfers from international Jewish philanthropical institutions, gifts and transfers by individual foreigners and immigrants, and to a small extent U.S. government grants. Reparations payments by the German government, which accounted for close to a fourth of the unilateral transfers through 1960, are to be completed in 1966. Restitution payments to individuals in Israel started somewhat later than reparations and amounted to less in the early years. They reached an estimated peak of some $143 million in 1963 and are still to continue for several years, though at a dwindling rate. Direct U.S. government grants came to an end by 1962. The sales of surplus food by the United States for local currencies under the usual provisions of P.L. 480 have, however, continued, though at a reduced rate; total sales for the calendar year 1965 were scheduled at $34 million. It is thus obvious that the unilateral transfers component of capital imports as a whole is likely to be declining in the years ahead.

The remaining portion of some 30 percent of capital imports has been distributed among the bond issues by the Israeli government to individual purchasers, loans from the U.S. government, and loans from other governments, from international financing agencies, and from private banks and suppliers and private foreign direct investments. The ability of Israel to float bond issues abroad undoubtedly derives in part from motivations similar to those which have given rise to the contributions through the United Jewish Appeal. To a lesser degree this has also probably influenced the interest of private foreign investors in the country.

The first stage in the economic aid to Israel from the U.S. government consisted of loans from the EXIMBANK granted in 1949 and 1950, which totaled $135 million and were allocated on a flexible basis for financing developmental imports for various sectors of the

Israeli economy. There were no subsequent loans from the EXIM-BANK until 1958. In the intervening period Israel was granted a number of loans under U.S. mutual security legislation for the purchase of foodstuffs. Lending by the EXIMBANK since 1958 has all been for specific projects except for a $25-million loan in fiscal 1961 which was broadly allocated much like the early loans of 1949 and 1950. Total EXIMBANK lending to Israel since 1958 has amounted to the modest total of about $95 million; the most recent loans were $11.2 million for electric power and $4 million for petroleum refining in the first half of fiscal 1965.

The U.S. Development Loan Fund, the predecessor agency of the present AID, granted a total of $56 million in loans to Israel during its short life from 1958 to 1961. The volume of this lending was hampered by DLF's interest in financing large specific projects and the fact that Israel wanted to utilize German funds as quickly as possible. As it turned out, $21 million of the total was granted for specific irrigation and telecommunications projects, $20 million for relending by the Industrial Development Bank of Israel, and $15 million for broad sectoral utilization much like some of the EXIM-BANK loans.

The U.S. AID has committed a total of $110 million in loans to Israel since 1962, of which some $86 million have been broad program loans. The balance of specific project loans has been for electric power, copper production, and desalination of sea water. The most recent loans were granted in July, 1964, both program loans, one for $8 million to finance a variety of capital goods imports and $12 million for agricultural machinery and equipment. It is of interest to note that the terms of the latter loans have been much harder than the usual AID soft loan; both loans were for a period of twenty years, including a five-year period of grace, at an interest rate of 3½ percent per annum. Except for the interest rate, these terms could have been granted by the EXIMBANK.

The World Bank has granted Israel three large loans for the total amount of $74.5 million, the first of which was not granted until 1960: $27.5 million for the new port of Ashdod, $25 million for the potash- and chemical-producing Dead Sea Works Ltd., and $22 million for highways. With financing available from numerous other sources and available as general program financing, Israel did not approach the World Bank until the decline of some of the other sources was in prospect. The most recent World Bank loan, the one for highways, was authorized in October, 1962. There have been no loans to Israel from the IDA or investments from the IFC.

Modest amounts of medium-term loans have been granted to Israel by the governments of France, the United Kingdom, Finland, and West Germany. The Israeli government and public institutions have also received medium-term loans from private banks and suppliers in the United States, the United Kingdom, West Germany, Italy, France, Switzerland, Belgium, and Japan.

Because of the considerable proportion of unilateral transfers in Israel's capital imports, debt servicing has thus far not constituted so serious a problem as it would otherwise have been. It will, however, undoubtedly be a matter to reckon with in the future as loans come to constitute a larger proportion of the total of capital imports.

ADMINISTRATION OF AID

The institutions in Israel that deal with the organization of capital transfers from abroad and their local allocation are for the most part government ministries, but certain other public institutions also take part in the process. There is considerable   centralization through the Ministry of Finance, which is responsible for preparation and administration of the country's development budget, through which most funds for public investment are allocated. The Office of Economic Minister in the United States, working in conjunction with the Ministry of Finance and the Israeli Embassy in Washington, is of decisive importance in the actual conduct of negotiations for external assistance.

In preparing the development budget, the Ministry of Finance works closely with other ministries and autonomous agencies responsible for activities in the various sectors of economy; and, in view of the large extent to which public investments are financed by external sources of finance, most of these other agencies are involved too in the administration of foreign aid. The Ministry of Commerce and Industry is jointly responsible with the mixed public-private Industrial Development Bank of Israel for financial assistance to industry, which has been supported by loans from the U.S. DLF. The Ministry of Transportation worked with the Ministry of Finance in connection with the negotiation and investment of the World Bank loans for the development of the port of Ashdod and the Ministry of Labour for the extension of the road network. The Ministry of Development, which is responsible for the development of the outlying, less developed areas of the country, was involved in the negotiations relating to the World Bank loan to the Dead Sea Works enterprise, in the course of which government control of the firm was relinquished to private investors. In agriculture, institutions involved are the Ministry of Agriculture, the Water Planning Authority, the publicly owned Mekoroth Water Company, and the Jewish Agency. The Jewish Agency, which is the executive body of the World Zionist Movement, administers in cooperation with the government most of the receipts transferred to it from the United Jewish Appeal, which are devoted largely to immigrant housing and agricultural settlement projects. The general responsibility for public housing investments lies with the Ministry of Housing. The Prime Minister's Office also intervenes in public investment activities at times, though on a less regular basis and usually for projects of some special political importance.

The planning, negotiation, and administration of capital imports has thus been centralized to a large extent in the Ministry of Finance, backed up by various other ministries and official and semi-official agencies. With respect to general development planning, until recently long-term planning was done exclusively on a sectoral basis in the individual agencies concerned with various sectors of the economy. Comprehensive planning was limited to the short-term activity of annual budget formulation. A Planning Authority was established only toward the end of 1961, responsible to an Economic Ministers' Committee, presided over by the Minister of Finance. As a guide to policy, it was to view the country's economic prospects comprehensively over the medium-term future by preparing a four-year development plan. The Planning Authority also cooperates with individual agencies in working out specific investment proposals and in preparing economic policy proposals in such matters as foreign trade, wages, prices, fiscal and monetary controls, the encouragement of investment and savings, manpower utilization, and measures to increase productivity.

PRINCIPAL PROBLEMS IN THE RECEIPT OF AID

The rapid rate of economic development in Israel has been closely interwoven with its receipt of large amounts of capital assistance from abroad. One of its principal economic problems consists of the reduction of its heavy dependence on capital imports. This is, of course, a matter of basic economic development policy. Structural changes are required to correct the fundamental disequilibrium in the country's balance of international payments. And the closing of the gap between investments and domestic savings involves some restraint on the rapid advances in consumption. The task will be facilitated as the pressure to absorb large numbers of immigrants subsides. Obviously, it would also be much easier if it were possible for the country to diminish the extent to which it must devote resources to military readiness.

A substantial reduction in the dependence on capital imports will, however, take time. It will meanwhile be necessary to replace by new sources certain sources of such imports which have already been eliminated or are in the process of being eliminated. For example, German reparations and restitution payments plus U.S. government grants amounted to close to $200 million in 1960. Only restitution payments are continuing among these three sources, and they too will soon be completed. And since these special sources which are being eliminated consist of unilateral transfers, whereas the replacements will involve repayment liabilities, the terms of the new financing will have to be watched for their balance-of-payments service burden. This is particularly the case in view of the large amounts of capital imports involved.

Most of the aid that Israel has received has consisted of broad program assistance rather than assistance for specific projects, although there have been some important loans of the latter type as well. This, of course, reflects the special nature of the Israeli situation in terms of the unique sources of finance involved, the need for rapid assistance, and the highly developed nature of the administrative apparatus in the country for the handling of the aid. The emphasis on broad program assistance has continued even with the shift to the newer sources of finance, as illustrated by the large proportion of the U.S. AID financing which has been granted to Israel in that form. However, the shift to the newer sources which emphasize specific project financing involved some reorientation of Israeli practices by way of the preparation of projects tailored to meet the requirements of external lending agencies. This presented some problems in obtaining loans from the U.S. DLF and may explain the limited extent of World Bank assistance to Israel.

A very large proportion of the total external resources for investment in Israel has passed through government channels. This tendency has been inevitable in view of the special problems of the newly developing state. There can, however, be dangers of perpetuation of such control, with some faulty allocation of resources, beyond the time when it is no longer necessary for optimum development. Recognition of this problem is reflected in the willingness of the government to relinquish control to private investors of the large chemical producing enterprise, the Dead Sea Works Ltd., under the prodding of the World Bank, and in the creation of the Industrial Development Bank, with an increasing participation from the private sector, to allocate financial assistance to industry to a greater extent on the basis of economic and commercial criteria.

ISRAEL AS A DONOR OF AID

Israel ranks close to first among the countries of the world on a per capita basis as a recipient of external financial aid, but it is also a donor of aid in turn to other developing countries. The aid which Israel gives is, however, technical and instructional rather than financial. It does not give financial assistance as such, and the financial burden of its technical aid is relatively small, although the burden is not entirely inconsequential in such terms as scarce manpower.

Israel's technical aid program started fortuitously in 1956 in connection with a tour of several countries being made by a mission from Burma in quest of assistance for an agricultural settlement project. It was extended to Africa, specifically Ghana, in 1957 at Israel's initiative. In 1965 there were 700 experts in over thirty countries, in Africa, Asia, and Latin America, with a heavy concentration particularly among the newly emergent states of Africa. In addition, approximately 3,000 trainees from these countries attend courses of varying duration in Israel every year.

The program consists of the sending of experts and technicians for research and advisory work in the host countries, the provision of training for nationals of the latter in Israel as well as at their own locations, and to some extent of joint direct investments and operations in enterprises in the recipient countries. The costs involved in recruiting, sending, and maintaining experts is shared with the host government. The range of duration of their service is in most cases from two to twenty-four months. The largest number have been sent to Africa. The main fields in which they have worked have been agriculture, irrigation, medicine, education, and communications.

The costs of study in Israel are also jointly shared. This consists both of study in established institutions, as in medicine and agricultural engineering, and of the organization of special courses conducted in native or international languages, as in agriculture, family and community life, cooperatives, labor organizations, educational and vocational training, and administration.

Training centers have been established in some cases in the benefiting country manned by Israeli experts as well as by personnel from the country previously trained in Israel. This is a logical follow-up of the program of training in Israel, representing an attempt to transfer the know-how acquired in Israel to a wider section of the local population.

Joint-venture companies have operated mainly in transportation, construction, and the exploitation of water resources. The local partner is usually the government and the Israeli partner an official company or one owned by Histadrut (the influential General Federation of Labor). The Israeli interest is usually sold to the local partner after an initial period of organization and operations, the objective being to have the joint venture serve as a mechanism for the transfer of know-how. The motivation of Israel in these ventures, aside from the general political one, which also characterizes the technical assistance and training program, is the establishment of economic links that may serve its trading interests.

The technical assistance and training program is coordinated by an International Cooperation Department of the Ministry of Foreign Affairs. Various other agencies, such as the Ministries of Police, Communications, Agriculture, and Health, actually carry out the program. Capital investments in the developing countries are subject to the approval of an interdepartmental committee of the Ministries of Foreign Affairs, Finance, and Commerce and Industry.

Developing countries have shown a keen interest in these types of aid provided by Israel for a variety of reasons: Israel's own development experience, the adaptability of their environment of social institutions such as the General Federation of Labor and the cooperative and collective agricultural settlements, Israel's success in handling serious water and irrigation problems, the greater adaptability of Israeli experts compared with those from more highly developed countries, the absence of any possible taint of colonialism in the Israeli aid program, and Israel's own success in achieving harmonious living among peoples of highly divergent races and backgrounds.

Greece

Greece is one of the less developed countries on the European continent, having a level of income and welfare comparable to that in Spain or southern Italy. Its population of some 8.5 million has had a low natural rate of increase, and the size of the country's population has been affected in recent years by a substantial rate of emigration. It is estimated that some 120,000 members of the labor force left Greece in 1964 in view of a high rate of unemployment at home and employment opportunities elsewhere in Europe, e.g., in West Germany.

Greece became an associate member of the European Common Market in November, 1962, with a transitional period to last until 1984 before full membership is achieved. Its per capita income was estimated at $365 in the year of Greece's association, compared with a level of $1,265 in the full-member countries of the European Economic Community. This disparity is a reflection of the distance Greece has to travel to place itself on a competitive footing for full Common Market membership. Meanwhile, its association has given it a certain degree of preferential access to the Common Market and has made it eligible for capital assistance from the European Investment Bank.

The disruption in Europe caused by World War II was extended in Greece by a civil war that lasted through 1949. The massive foreign aid that Greece received, mostly from the United States following the proclamation by that country of the Truman Doctrine on the containment of Communism, was devoted to a large extent to direct military aid, indirect economic support of the military effort, and rehabilitation from the ravages of war before emphasis could be placed on long-term development. The strides that Greece has made are reflected in a comparison between the recent level of per capita income noted above and the level of some $50 per annum of such income estimated to have prevailed at the height of the civil war in 1947.

Nevertheless, serious economic problems remain. Despite the advances, the overall level of income is still far from adequate, and there are marked inequalities in the distribution of the income throughout the population and between rural and urban areas. Although total national output has been growing at the high rate of some 6 to 8 percent per annum, compared with a 1962–71 development plan goal of 6 percent, this growth has not been sufficient to effect any substantial reduction in unemployment. Manufacturing industry has failed to grow at target rates, and not much change has been effected in the low productivity structure of economic activities. Estimates of the size of the public investment gap and the balance-of-payments gap to be filled by capital imports for at least several years in the immediate future are on the order of $100 to $150 million per year. Imports, which attained a level of some $830 million in 1964, have grown much more rapidly than exports, which consist mostly of primary agricultural products such as tobacco, cotton, and fruit; and current receipts from invisibles (shipping, emigrants' remittances, and tourism) plus private capital imports have failed to close the balance-of-payments gap. Immediate balance-of-payments problems have been avoided largely by the contracting of substantial short-term and medium-term trade credits. And an inadequate domestic tax base and possibilites of internal borrowing make it difficult to close the public investment gap on a noninflationary basis without external resources.

NATURE OF AID RECEIVED

From about the end of World War II through 1962, Greece received a total of some $4.1 billion in foreign aid. Direct and indirect aid for military requirements amounted to somewhat more than $1.6 billion. Slightly more than half of the total, or $2.1 billion, consisted of economic aid on a grant basis. The small balance consisted of economic aid in the form of loans ($237 million) and reparations for war damage ($133 million from Italy and Germany). These capital imports for the public sector were supplemented by a small amount (about $70 million) of private foreign direct investment, pursuant to an incentives law (No. 2687) adopted in 1953, and some inflow of speculative private capital.

Economic grant aid was particularly large up to the early 1950s designed to support the military effort against the Communist guerrillas and to assist in the economy's rehabilitation from war. It accounted for close to half of total capital imports from 1945 through 1952 and declined to about 30 percent of the total from 1953 through 1962. Except for some specialized loans during the first few postwar years, public external loans did not figure in the capital movements until 1959. There were no such loans during the period 1950–58. The inflow of capital in the form of loans averaged about $25 million per year during the period 1959–62.

The United States accounted for the overwhelming majority of the foreign aid to Greece: $3.4 billion out of the total $4.1 billion, consisting of $2.1 billion of economic aid and $1.3 billion of military aid. Besides the reparations payments by Italy and West Germany, other bilateral assistance has consisted of loans from European countries, primarily from West Germany. Except for a large program from the UNRRA early in the postwar period and NATO military aid, assistance from international agencies has been minimal. There have been no loans from the World Bank and IDA and only two investments by IFC, amounting to a total of $2.1 million.

The current trends in aid to Greece include a shift from grants to loans, a diversification of bilateral sources with a reduction in the overwhelming participation by the United States, a move toward more assistance from multilateral sources, principally the EIB, and a greater emphasis on loans for specific projects rather than for the support of the general investment budget or general balance-of-payments equilibrium. Since 1962 the United States has made it clear that it considers Greece to have emerged from the situation of requiring aid on concessionary terms. U.S. technical assistance to Greece came to an end in 1961. As transitional measures, the United States has continued to make agricultural surpluses available for sale to Greece against local currency, under the provisions of P.L. 480; and in July, 1963, the U.S. AID approved a $10-million program loan, repayable in dollars over twenty years at an interest rate of 2 percent per annum. Also, in August, 1963, the AID granted Greece a specific project loan of $21.6 million for electric power, at a term of twenty-five years and an interest rate of 3½ percent per annum. The EXIMBANK, however, with its conventional hard loan terms, is to be the source of any future U.S. loans to Greece. And the United States took the initiative in the spring of 1962 for the formation, under OECD auspices, of an international consortium for assistance to Greece in order to press for the diversification of the sources of aid for that country.

The OECD consortium for aid to Greece was formally organized in July, 1962, with the participation of nine countries: Austria, Belgium, Canada, France, West Germany, Italy, Luxembourg, the Netherlands, and the United States. The consortium has not been very active by way of arranging for firm commitments of particular levels of assistance on an overall basis. It may be noted that the World Bank does not participate in this consortium. As previously noted, there have been no World Bank operations in Greece. However, following the settlement of a prewar public debt of Greece to Britain and a visit in June, 1964, to Washington of the Greek Minister of Coordination, it was announced that Greece would thenceforth be eligible for World Bank assistance.

By virtue of Greece's association with the European Common Market late in 1962, it became eligible to borrow from the EIB. The Bank committed a five-year total of $125 million for loans to Greece, of which $50 million was to be allocated during the first two years. By May, 1965, it had allocated $36.5 million in eight loans, $17 million for road programs, $6 million for an electric power transmission line, $10 million for irrigation, and $3.5 million for industry. The most recent loans are the irrigation loan, authorized in February, 1965, at a term of twenty years and an interest rate of 6¼ percent, of which the EEC agreed to assume 3 percentage points, indicating a recognition that Greece is not quite ready to assume all external loans on conventional hard terms, and the industrial loans for cement and fertilizers, authorized in May, 1965, at an interest rate of 6 percent and a term of twelve years.

ADMINISTRATION OF AID

The primary comprehensive responsibility for the administration of foreign aid in Greece is vested in a Ministry of Coordination. Working closely with the Ministry on overall foreign aid questions is the semi-autonomous Foreign Trade Administration. Both agencies date back to the early postwar period, when the U.S. aid program was at its peak, and were created at the suggestion of the United States. Indeed, by agreement between the two governments, the post of Executive Director of the Foreign Trade Administration has been held by Americans, in order to alleviate the pressures on Greek personnel for the allocation of scarce exchange resources.

The Ministry of Coordination was given the role of formulating and coordinating national economic policy, including central control over budget planning and execution as well as foreign aid and foreign economic policy. It is this Ministry which has developed the various long-term economic plans which Greece has been formulating since 1959. The Foreign Trade Administration continues to administer controls over Greece's foreign trade, but these controls have been largely eliminated since the application in 1953 of financial stabilization measures including the devaluation of the drachma to its present exchange rate of 30 per U.S. dollar. The Executive Director of the Foreign Trade Administration continues to be an American national, though now by unilateral decision of the Greek government rather than by agreement with the U.S. government. The Americans who have held this post have been individual experts in the employ of the Greek government and not representatives of the U.S. government. With the changing nature of U.S. and European aid programs, the Executive Director of the Foreign Trade Administration has become adviser to the Minister of Coordination on aid questions. In this capacity he assists in negotiations for new aid programs and has advised and assisted other public agencies such as the Public Power Corporation and the Economic Development Financing Organization (EDFO) on the uses of their development loans.

The Public Power Corporation has complete control of the electric power sector in Greece and has been one of the principal recipients of external financial assistance for specific projects in the country. It is an officially owned corporation which was established in 1950 and organized with the advice of a specialized American firm of power consultants contracted by the Greek government for this purpose as well as to develop a power production plan. It operates with complete autonomy, although its internal financing is supplied by the state. The Public Power Corporation has received substantial loans from the governments of the United States, West Germany, France, and Italy and from the EIB.

The EDFO was established by the government in 1954 as a development bank for the granting of long-term loans for productive projects in the private sector. It succeeded an earlier Central Loans Committee jointly established in 1948 by the Greek and U.S. governments to channel aid funds to the private sector. The EDFO received its resources from the Greek government as well as from U.S. aid agencies. It concentrated its loans to a relatively few projects, mostly in mining, hotel operation, and manufacturing. In an effort to stimulate more productive investment in the private sector, a new Hellenic Industrial Development Bank was recently formed by the government at the end of 1964 with a capital of $150 million, into which the EDFO was absorbed as it had previously absorbed the assets of the Central Loans Committee upon its own creation in 1954.

PRINCIPAL PROBLEMS IN AID

Aid to Greece in the form of general support of the investment budget and of balance-of-payments equilibrium has largely come to an end. There is no longer the need for external assistance to contain and alleviate a pressing emergency of the type that existed early in the postwar period. Continued development in the face of structural and institutional deficiencies in the economy is still, however, dependent on external assistance, at least as a supplement or catalyst for the mobilization of domestic resources.

The public investment budget has since the late 1950s expended increasing sums on infrastructure. Limitations have, however, appeared in the form of an inability in the last few years to achieve investment targets. It has been increasingly difficult to find adequate sources of noninflationary funds to finance these expenditures because of a narrow tax base and the undeveloped state of the internal capital market. Furthermore, the balance-of-payments equilibrium has been more apparent than real, since it has been financed to a considerable extent by suppliers' credits and an inflow of speculative capital. Thus, there is a continued need for overall external financial support, but it is likely to be available mostly only for specific projects.

The success of the Public Power Corporation in formulating and carrying out, with external support, specific investment projects is, however, unique in Greece. There is no comparable efficiency in the rest of the government services. Large public works are often badly planned and suffer from delays in execution or excessively high costs. Greece is thus confronted with administrative difficulties in organizing its development needs in the form of feasible individual projects which are acceptable to international lending agencies. The result has been that few new aid requests on a project basis have been forthcoming, while general foreign support for the investment budget is steadily diminishing.

With the bulk of economic aid available in the past on a grant basis, Greece has had no problem of external debt servicing. The problem is beginning to emerge, however, with the increasing volume of suppliers' credits which have been assumed in recent years. Development assistance must be provided on terms that will permit servicing of the debt during the period of development. This is a matter which should be of concern to the debtor country and to its creditors alike.

Although it has been in existence for more than two years, there does not seem to have been any disposition on the part of the OECD consortium for aid to Greece to come to grips with the problem with which it is to deal. Greece continues to have a development problem reflected in the low level and uneven distribution of its income, its high rate of unemployment, the structural inadequacies of its economy, and its administrative deficiencies. With the commitment for it to become gradually integrated into the mainstream of the European economy, a more concerted international effort would seem to be in order to assist in overcoming the obstacles to its development.

Turkey

Turkey is the other country besides Greece for which the United States organized an aid program pursuant to the Truman Doctrine of 1947. Unlike Greece, however, Turkey continues to be one of the countries on which the United States is still concentrating heavily in its foreign aid. The level of per capita income is somewhat lower in Turkey than in Greece, and its balance-of-payments disequilibrium is much more marked than that of Greece. The OECD has also organized an international aid consortium for Turkey as it has for Greece, but the Turkey Consortium has been far more active. Turkey, like Greece, has acquired associate membership in the European Economic Community and as one consequence has also received a five-year commitment of $175 million in loans from the EEC to be administered through the EIB.

Per capita income for Turkey's population of some 30 million is at a level of somewhat less than $250 per annum, and income is quite unevenly distributed throughout the population. The population is growing at the rate of about 3 percent per year, and it is consequently necessary for total output to grow at a high rate in order to achieve improvements on a per capita basis. Gross national product in Turkey increased at an average rate of 5 percent per annum in the decade ended in 1962, and the growth target in Turkey's first Five-Year Plan, covering the years 1963–67, was fixed at 7 percent per annum. The target was slightly exceeded during 1963, the first year of the plan, but it was not achieved in 1964, when growth proceeded at a rate of slightly above 5.5 percent for the year.

Turkey's balance-of-payments disequilibrium continues to be a critical problem. For the plan period 1963–67, the current account deficit is estimated to amount to an annual average of about $250 million, with little progress anticipated in its reduction by the end of the period. This deficit represents close to 40 percent of the average level anticipated for imports of about $640 million per year. In addition, foreign debt payments during the period are estimated at an average of some $115 million per year. With private foreign capital imports projected at a level of only some $25 million per year, it is obvious that substantial external assistance is required to close the payments gap. The OECD Consortium for Turkey, organized in July, 1962, has been most active in helping Turkey meet its large external assistance requirements and in advising Turkey on the most effective utilization of the assistance. The general program assistance requested of the Consortium by Turkey for 1965 amounted to $250 million.

The economic rationale of aid to Turkey was summarized as follows by the OECD in its August, 1964, review of the economic situation in that country:

First, there are the heavy requirements for re-financing foreign debt. Second, experience has shown that Turkey needs considerable external assistance even when net productive investment falls to very low levels. One fundamental reason is that imports and domestic output are far from being close substitutes in the present conditions of the Turkish economy. Thus, any policies aimed at reducing consumption would have to go to extreme lengths before the current deficit was substantially cut. This is hardly conceivable, given the very low living standards of the great majority of the population. In any case, productive investment would have to be cut long before the current external account approached a balance. With the present fast population growth, it is indeed only by increasing productive investment and maintaining it thereafter at a high level that a reduction in the balance of payments deficit and of the corresponding needs for foreign aid will become possible in the future. It is, therefore, imperative to ensure an adequate inflow of foreign aid under appropriate conditions, if the development problems of Turkey are to be solved.

NATURE OF AID RECEIVED

At the end of World War II the Turkish government requested a loan of $500 million from the United States to help finance imports of capital goods for development. This represented a marked change from the highly nationalistic attitudes which had characterized Turkey's policies during the interwar period. The response to the request was, however, limited. U.S. credits to Turkey during the entire period 1945–47 amounted to only a little more than $50 million. Furthermore, the help extended to Turkey following the proclamation of the Truman Doctrine was almost entirely military, and U.S. assistance did not amount to a great deal through 1949. Initially, Turkey's efforts to launch an ambitious economic development program with foreign assistance under the aegis of the Marshall Plan were rejected by the OEEC and the United States as being outside the reconstruction scope of the Plan. Thus, Turkey did not receive much foreign assistance during the early years of the postwar period.

External foreign aid to Turkey started in earnest during the period 1950–54. Economic aid from the United States and World Bank loans constituted the principal sources of medium- and long-term external financial resources obtained by the country, which amounted to an annual average of about $120 million during this period. During the first part of the period, much of the aid was to help finance infrastructure projects, such as in coal and power. The World Bank organized one of its first comprehensive survey missions for Turkey, the report of the mission having been published in 1951. It helped Turkey establish its privately owned Industrial Development Bank in 1950 and extended loans to the Bank. Indeed, all World Bank loans as such to Turkey to date, i.e., excluding IDA and IFC assistance, were committed during the period 1950–54. This consisted of a total of $63.4 million, including $18 million for the Industrial Development Bank, $16.3 million for ports, $3.9 million for silos, and $25.2 million for a multipurpose electrical power, flood control, and irrigation project.

The government, however, started to follow inflationary economic policies in the financing of investments after 1950, resulting in the beginning of substantial current account deficits in the balance of payments, over which policies a falling out occurred between Turkey and the World Bank in 1954. The government requested the World Bank to withdraw its resident mission from the country. There was also increasing concern over the irresponsible financial policies of the government on the part of the OEEC and the U.S. government, and some cutbacks were effected in the volume of U.S. aid. Nevertheless, the loose economic policies continued, and there was some recourse to medium-term suppliers' credits to help finance balance-of-payments deficits.

The ensuing period of the second half of the decade up to the military coup of May, 1960, was one of continuing inflationary and foreign exchange crises, fed largely by the politically oriented desire of the government to keep the boom conditions going. The government was successful in obtaining increasing quantities of foreign financial assistance, which rose from the annual average of some $120 million in 1950–54 to about $200 million per year during the period 1955–59. Throughout the period, the government was plagued by the need to repay large amounts of accumulated debt as well as to meet current balance-of-payments deficits. A large part of the aid was in the form of U.S. government grants and agricultural surplus shipments under P.L. 480 paid for in local currency. The situation came to a head in August, 1958, in an agreement with the OEEC, the IMF, and the U.S. government for them to provide economic assistance upon Turkey's adoption of a stabilization program, including a devaluation in the exchange rate from 2.80 Turkish lire to 9 Turkish lire per U.S. dollar. During the subsequent year or two up to the military revolution of 1960, however, it became apparent that little effort was being made to carry out the fiscal and financial restraints called for by the stabilization program.

Drastic measures were taken soon after the 1960 revolution to balance the budget and the accounts of state economic enterprises. The inflationary lending by the Central Bank to state economic enterprises for investment purposes was stopped. A new Planning Bureau was established. Measures were adopted to increase direct taxation. Public international development financing continued at a high rate, amounting to about $200 million in 1961, about 60 percent of which came from the U.S. AID and most of the remainder from West Germany and other European sources, but it proceeded under more orderly conditions. By 1962, the first Five-Year Plan, for 1963–67, had been formulated, and the OECD Turkey Consortium had been formed, not only as a fund-raising venture but also with a considerable involvement in the internal economic and investment policies of the recipient country.

The World Bank group resumed activity in Turkey in 1962. Indeed, in recognition of the Turkish balance-of-payments problem, loans were made available under the concessionary terms of IDA rather than the conventional terms of the Bank. The IDA loans have included three loans amounting to a total of $20 million to the Industrial Development Bank, a $20-million loan to continue the irrigation phase of the multipurpose project for which the World Bank had about a decade earlier committed a loan of $25 million, and $24 million for electric power. Except for the irrigation loan, the proceeds of these loans were to be re-lent on conventional terms by the Turkish government to the operating agency involved, although the government obligation to IDA was on the usual IDA concessionary terms. In 1963 the IFC acquired $920,000 of equity interest in the Industrial Development Bank, thus linking all three World Bank group agencies in assistance to that institution.

Recent U.S. AID loans to Turkey have included a general program loan of $35 million and a power loan of $31.3 million in fiscal 1963; a general program loan of $70 million and $61.5 million in specific project loans for electric power, highways, railroads, and industry in fiscal 1964; and a general program loan of $70 million to be utilized during the calendar year 1965 as well as a $5.9-million irrigation loan.

Members of the OECD Turkey Consortium besides the United States and the World Bank are the European Investment Bank and thirteen donor countries (eleven from the European continent, the United Kingdom, and Canada). West Germany, France, and Italy have been the most active of these other sources in extending loans and credits to Turkey.

ADMINISTRATION OF AID

The administrative organization in Turkey for the receipt and coordination of aid has been subject to various changes which have to some extent paralleled the changes in the nature of the aid itself. Initially, in 1948, an Organization of International Economic Co-operation (OIEC), attached to the Ministry of State, was established as a liaison office between the United States and the OEEC, on the one hand, and the various establishments of the Turkish government which were to utilize the aid, on the other. It was not, however, given any clear-cut functions in aid programming, allocation, or coordination, and conflicts soon arose with the Ministry of Foreign Affairs because of overlaps with the latter's general responsibility for the conduct of foreign relations.

In 1952 the OIEC was moved from the Ministry of State to the Ministry of Foreign Affairs, although no change was enacted in the authority of functions of the agency. Nevertheless, the Ministry of Foreign Affairs assumed a much more active role than had previously been played by the aid liaison organization, which in turn created frictions with agencies with substantive operating responsibilities such as the Ministries of Finance, Commerce, and Industry. Foreign aid programs were formulated and carried out by officials of the Ministry of Foreign Affairs, who were frequently not aware of their full implications. For example, arrangements were made for the importation of agricultural surpluses with payment in local currency without regard to the impact on domestic production.

In connection with the stabilization program of 1958, an Economic Coordination Committee was formed under the chairmanship of the Minister of Coordination and with participation by the Ministers of Foreign Affairs, Finance, Commerce, and Industry. The Ministry of Coordination had been established in 1957 to coordinate all economic activities of the government, including foreign aid, but it was not endowed with any administrative organization. The Minister of Coordination was in effect a political figure acting on behalf of the Prime Minister. The constitution of the Economic Coordination Committee represented a forward step in the programming and coordination of foreign aid, but it was never properly organized and soon became inoperative. Individual ministries continued to operate in this field on their own. For example, while negotiations were being carried on for the consolidation of Turkey's external debts pursuant to the stabilization program, the Ministry of Foreign Affairs independently concluded a $50-million bilateral credit with Italy. The committee set up for the purpose of coordination was not even kept informed of these negotiations.

After the revolution of May, 1960, the Economic Coordination Committee was abolished, and the OIEC was moved from the Ministry of Foreign Affairs to the Ministry of Finance. This was in recognition of the responsibilities of the latter ministry for overall economic and fiscal policies and of the need to integrate foreign aid policy into general economic policies rather than to carry it out merely as a phase of international relations. However, the situation continued to be far from satisfactory. Individual ministries often made applications for technical and financial aid directly to the U.S. Aid Mission in Turkey or to representatives of other countries. The applications which were accepted in principle were then transmitted to the OIEC in the Ministry of Finance for final ratification. The latter agency continued to play essentially a passive role. It was only with the creation of the Planning Organization in September, 1960, that an attempt was made to formulate a coherent foreign aid policy for the whole government.

The Planning Organization, attached to the office of the Prime Minister, established a Permanent Committee for the formulation of overall foreign aid policies under the chairmanship of the Under Secretary of Planning and composed of the Director of the Treasury, the Head of Economic Affairs in the Ministry of Foreign Affairs, the Director of Foreign Trade in the Ministry of Commerce, and the Director of the Central Bank, with a permanent secretariat. The purpose was to make it possible for individual ministries and agencies to follow a commonly agreed line and to give consistent and clear instructions to delegations negotiating problems related to international financing with foreign governments and international agencies. The powers of the committee were enlarged in March, 1962, and it was designated as the Inter-Ministerial Committee for Foreign Economic Relations. The secretariat was, however, transferred from the Planning Organization to the Ministry of Foreign Affairs, which could give rise once again to the same type of jurisdictional squabbles which have characterized attempts to coordinate foreign aid administration in the past.

The Industrial Development Bank of Turkey, created in 1950, is an outstanding example of the success of the World Bank in promoting the formation of privately owned development banks in the less developed countries. There was at first considerable reluctance in Turkey to set up the Bank outside the public sector, but it was finally agreed to and the share capital was put up mainly by existing private banks. The Bank has since financed a significant portion of private industrial investment in Turkey and has played an important role in acquainting the industrial community with better techniques of investment planning and in raising the standards of business management. It has received more than $55 million in external financial assistance from the World Bank, IDA, the IFC, and the U.S. government.

PRINCIPAL PROBLEMS IN AID

Turkey has received a large volume of external financial assistance during the postwar period and continues to be in the forefront of countries on which foreign aid is being concentrated today. This is reflected in the high priority being accorded to Turkey in the U.S. foreign aid program, in the active role being played by the OECD Consortium in the rounding up of a large volume of aid to Turkey, and in the five-year commitment of aid by the European Economic Community via the EIB in connection with Turkey's recent attainment of associate membership in the EEC. The volume of aid required is defined in relation to the large balance-of-payments gap from which the country suffers and to a considerable extent has been defined in these terms throughout the postwar period. While it is true that external aid is required to close the gap, the basic problem is to make certain that the aid does not serve merely as a palliative and that it is primarily assisting in the promotion of development. The closing of the balance-of-payments gap is achieved as an incidental feature of the assistance, but it is not its primary function. There is now a greater awareness of this in Turkey than ever before.

Concentration on external assistance to meet balance-of-payments problems more or less on an emergency basis was characteristic of Turkish policy during much of the postwar period. Thus, at times the country failed to come to grips with the need for discipline in internal economic policy to keep inflation in check and to proceed with development on an orderly basis. Promises of changes of policy and declarations of good intentions were repeatedly made, only to be repeatedly ignored or discarded. External assistance may be a necessary supplement, but it cannot substitute for the mobilization of domestic resources, without which successful development cannot be achieved.

Besides the need to relate external assistance to sound general internal economic policies and developmental investments, the Turkish experience also illustrates the problems that arise when the terms of aid are not appropriately related to the pace of development. Indeed, the two aspects are not unrelated to each other. Turkey accumulated large volumes of suppliers' credits as an alternative to assistance on adequate terms of repayment which at times was cut back by potential donors because of Turkey's refusal to adopt disciplined economic policies. The result was not only that economic development was not being served but also that intolerable burdens of debt were accumulated. Debt moratoria and refundings were the only alternatives to outright defaults. One of the problems of this aspect of external financing as well as of the others previously mentioned is, of course, the complex of motives involved on the donor as well as the recipient end, not all of which are concerned primarily with the promotion of development. Lax economic policies on the part of recipients may be made possible because donors are prepared to support them for a variety of reasons. A multinational consortium may assist in this respect, but it is by no means a panacea.

The haphazard and disjointed way in which the coordination and allocation of foreign development financing was carried out in Turkey during most of the postwar period was to some extent a reflection of the lack of any overall comprehensive economic planning. With the creation of a Planning Organization in 1960 and the formulation of the first Five-Year Plan in 1962, this difficulty was in part eliminated. It is still, however, not an easy matter to subject numerous ministries and independent agencies, each with important economic and investment programs, to the discipline of a coordinated approach for the entire country. Besides, the decentralization of initiative in public administration is not an altogether undesirable feature. The problem is one of finding the right balance in the complex relationships involved in the government apparatus.

Administrative difficulties occur not only in the relationships among various government agencies but also in the operations of some individual agencies themselves. While the specific project approach in international development assistance may not be a guarantee of overall development, since it does not involve control over all resources or elements involved in the development process, it may be helpful in connection with the improvement of administrative practices in individual agencies. The problem of effecting administrative or policy changes in the face of internal political opposition may be facilitated if it is posed as a condition for obtaining external financial assistance. And the external agency may be in a position to couple technical assistance to this end with its financial assistance. This has occurred in Turkey, for example, in the assistance provided by the U.S. government for the country's road programs.

In general, in Turkey there still exists as a holdover of the approach followed during the 1950s, something of an attitude of excessive hope with respect to the results to be achieved from foreign aid. The attitude has been that most problems of development can be solved if a sufficient volume of foreign assistance is obtained, whatever its form or source. This attitude tends to deflect from the basic fact that it is primarily through internal efforts that economic development can be achieved and that foreign financing can play only a marginal part in the process. Nevertheless, this proper role of foreign assistance is recognized by Turkey's Planning Organization, which has expressed the country's aim as being "to move progressively towards a balance in external payments over the fifteen-year period" (i.e., 1963–77) and which holds the hope that "once the plan targets have been realized towards the end of the Second Five-Year Plan period (i.e., 1972), development efforts can be pursued without recourse to any exceptional aid."

Senegal

Senegal, a nation which has a population of more than 3 million inhabitants, obtained independence in 1960 after many years of French colonial administration. Although, like most other newly independent states, it is beset with numerous economic, social, and political problems, it has embarked upon independence from a level of development that in many ways shows considerable advance and promise for the future. Its gross national product is estimated to represent a yield in the neighborhood of about $200 per capita, a figure well above the lowest range for the less developed countries. In recent years its output has been increasing at the rate of some 3.2 percent per annum. Targets for development were set forth in a Four-Year Development Plan (1961–64), which has now been completed. A Second Four-Year Plan (1965–69) was approved by the National Assembly in June, 1965. Planning is not new to Senegal. The first planned development program for the country was drafted by the French following World War II as part of France's own Ten-Year Plan.

In 1958 Senegal began work on what became its first post-independence Four-Year Plan. This Plan was approved by the National Assembly in May, 1961. Its goal was an 8 percent annual increase in the gross national product and a gross investment equal to 15 percent of the gross national product.

The Four-Year Plan (1961–64) called for various structural reforms and the creation of a number of development institutions. Great emphasis was put on rural programs. Centers were established to provide technical assistance on the local level. Others were created to develop an awareness on the part of the peasant in relation to his country, its politics and economics, and its problems. A new development bank was set up. An Agricultural Marketing Office began operations with the purpose of intervening in the marketing of agricultural products and improving the importation and distribution of equipment and other items necessary to agricultural production. Great importance and emphasis were given to cooperatives, and the role of the middleman in agriculture was reduced. Other programs in the Plan provided for roads, housing, education, industry, and health services.

The Plan called for investments of over 90 billion CFA francs (approximately $367 million). Some 28 billion CFA francs ($114 million), or about 30 percent of total investments, were to come from external sources. This was about the same order of magnitude as the flow of such funds into the country since the end of World War II. During the seventeen-year period 1946–63, the total amount of external assistance received by Senegal is estimated to have been some 116 billion CFA francs ($473 million), or an annual average of 6.8 billion CFA francs compared with the 7 billion average provided for under the Plan.

THE PATTERN OF EXTERNAL ASSISTANCE

The total volume of public external assistance to Senegal in the period 1946–63, estimated at 116 billion CFA francs ($473 million), included net subsidies paid by France for Senegalese peanuts. (The net figure is derived by deducting from peanut subsidies estimated payments above world market prices by Senegal for French goods.) About 80 percent of the total, if one includes the subsidies, has been in the form of grants which have been utilized to help finance technical assistance and investments in basic social overhead facilities. Most of the balance has been in the form of low-interest, moderately long-term loans. A small fraction has consisted of equity investments in public and private enterprises.

France has accounted for 101 billion CFA francs out of the total of 116 billion. All its assistance has been in the form of grants except for 20 billion CFA francs of loans from the Caisse Centrale de Coopération Économique and 484 million CFA francs of equity investments. The sources of the grants have been FIDES during the period of colonial status and FAC since independence; FAC replaced FIDES as the budget line for French external assistance upon the granting of self-government to most of France's colonies. The policies for administration of both these funds have been set by various committees of the French Government and carried out by the Caisse Centrale. The Caisse Centrale, a semiautonomous public corporation, has been the most flexible agency of French external aid. All French public loans to and virtually all public equity investments in Senegal have come from this source. The Caisse has been instrumental in the organization of development institutions in Senegal, in whose equity it has invested and through which it will be channeling more of its assistance in the future.

The European Development Fund has been the second most important source of external assistance for Senegal, although it is a poor second to France, accounting for only 9 billion CFA francs. The Fund has been in operation, however, since 1959. All of its assistance has been in the form of grants for technical assistance and social overhead investments. As constituted for the period 1963–67, under the new EEC Convention with Associated States the Fund will continue to make assistance available to those States as grants, although provision has been made for the administration of 15 percent of its total resources as loans. The Caisse Centrale of France is the paying agent for the Fund.

The small balance of some 6 billion CFA francs (about $25 million) of external assistance to Senegal has come from the United States, West Germany, and the United Nations. Agreements for technical and economic cooperation have also recently been signed with other countries, including the Soviet Union, Poland, Yugoslavia, Tunisia, Denmark, and Israel, although it is unlikely that there will be any appreciable increases in bilateral aid for Senegal from sources other than France.

French aid policies tend to be flexible and pragmatic. This is partially explained by the fact that the overwhelming bulk of French assistance has gone to former French territories, where the

French are familiar with the problems and leading personalities in each recipient country.

On its annual visit from Paris, the FAC team is able, after reviewing dossiers and meeting with the relevant officials, to agree "in principle" on the financing of particular projects without requiring detailed project presentations. This is a most helpful procedure in short-staffed recipient countries because it enables them to concentrate on the detailed preparation of those projects which will be financed once they are presented.

Project aid presents a problem to countries which have many small projects. FAC has developed a technique for providing general-purpose grants which can finance numerous small projects or schemes.

France appears less concerned than other sources of aid about the relative roles of public and private enterprise in development. The fact that France has its own development plan also provides it with an insight into the problems of planning in many of the developing countries.

French aid motivations in Senegal run the gamut of cultural, moral, political, and commercial considerations. In addition, there is the momentum which develops when aid programs have gone on for many years. The French Embassy, the local Caisse Centrale office, the FAC Mission, and the French Military Mission are all very active, each with its own particular purposes within the total flow of French aid.

The European Development Fund gives project-oriented grant assistance limited to public overhead and infrastructure projects. The forms of assistance will be expanded under the new EEC Convention to include loans, technical assistance, and technical cooperation. Recognizing that Senegal and other recipient countries need more people to assist in drafting requests for assistance, the new activities of the EDF will include providing experts to assist in the preparation of aid requests.

The EDF analysis of projects is done within a national framework and is quite thorough. This has proved useful both in keeping down project costs and in contributing to balanced development.

EDF funds come from the six member states of the EEC. Most of these funds are spent in former French territories. This has created a few problems, for it has resulted in French contractors getting the bulk of EDF construction contracts. Disturbed because their nationals were not getting a fair share of the EDF contracts, various EEC members voiced their complaints. The EDF tried to solve the problem by holding a meeting in Brussels to which they invited contractors from all the EEC countries. These contractors were advised of the EDF program and encouraged to bid on EDF projects. Subsequently, bids were requested for a road construction project in Senegal. French contractors living in Senegal submitted bids which were 40 percent lower than their previous bids for similar work, and they received the contract. Thus, the threat of international competition apparently had the effect of substantially reducing costs.

Belief that a strong Africa will mean a strong Europe has been one of the underlying reasons for the establishment of the EDF. Increased development in Africa will mean increased exports of goods and services from Europe, and the new EEC Convention assures a most most-favored-nation status to all member states in relation to each of the Associated African States.

All UN assistance has been in the form of grants, in connection with some of which matching local contributions are required. The specialized agencies have supplied experts in many fields. The Special Fund has concentrated on training institutions, a minerals survey, and Senegal River development. The political and commercial motivations found in bilateral assistance programs are, of course, absent from UN assistance.

U.S. assistance, for the most part, has been in the form of grants of surplus rice which was sold locally. The local currency proceeds are invested in mutually agreed social overhead and infrastructure projects. U.S. aid policy in Senegal supplements in a minor way French and EDF assistance and provides the United States a presence.

German assistance has come primarily in the form of a $6.1-million, fifteen-year loan utilized for construction of roads. Two grants have been made for social overhead projects. A prime motivation of German aid appears to be the desire to create goodwill so that German commercial interests will be in a good position once discriminatory barriers are removed as a result of the new EEC Convention.

As previously noted, the bulk of external financial assistance received by Senegal has been in the form of grants, although there has recently been a trend toward a greater portion of loans, both in the definition of requirements by the Senegalese and in the policies being adopted by Senegal's principal sources of foreign aid. Considering Senegal's need for technical assistance and training and for capital projects which are not directly revenue-producing, the justification for grants is clear. It is also proper that more finance be made available through loans as more revenue-generating projects can be carried out and as the fiscal structure of the country strengthens. The terms of these loans, however, should be fixed so that the total repayment burden on the country's presently weak balance of international payments structure will be manageable.

All the bilateral assistance which Senegal receives—mostly from France—is tied to the procurement of goods and services in the assisting country; i.e., the proceeds may not be spent freely abroad, with the exception of loan assistance from Germany. The one loan that Senegal has received from Germany, however, was an exceptional one and is not likely to be repeated. The tying of EDF assistance is somewhat broader, relating to all the EEC countries. Thus, in effect, the proceeds of all aid received by Senegal must be spent in France, except for the aid proceeds, of secondary importance, which must be spent in the European Economic Community. In the light of the political and commercial pressures and balance-of-payments problems in aid-giving countries, it is futile simply to urge that the practice of tying aid be abandoned; tied aid is better than no aid. The example cited above, however, of the reduction of project costs by a French contractor under the threat of competition from other EEC contractors should be enough to illustrate the desirability of donor countries' at least observing strict competitive practices with respect to the execution of aid contracts on the part of their own national suppliers and contractors.

ADMINISTRATIVE MACHINERY FOR AID

Senegal has a number of specialized public or mixed public-private financial and development institutions to help carry out its economic and planning policies, some of which are very useful vehicles for the channeling of external assistance. Some date from colonial times, while others have been developed or reorganized with French assistance since independence. The Caisse Centrale de Coopération Économique, the principal administrative agency for French overseas assistance, has been instrumental in the development of these institutions, in some of which it holds a minority equity position. The Caisse Centrale has also transferred more and more of its loan transactions to the Senegalese institutions. Principal among them, as vehicles for the receipt of general external financial assistance, have been the Senegalese Development Bank and the Credit Populaire du Sénégal, which were merged to form the Banque Nationale de Développement du Sénégal in June, 1964. The Development Bank, which was the administrative agent for expenditure of the nation's capital budget, extended loans and invested in enterprises on an equity basis. The Caisse Centrale held 22.5 percent of the Bank's stock. Although it had a variety of powers, the Bank engaged for the most part in short-term lending to agricultural cooperatives. The Credit Populaire du Sénégal owned up to 40 percent by the Caisse Centrale, was heavily involved in agricultural lending before the establishment of the Development Bank, and made loans for commercial, industrial, and artisan activities, as well as for housing. SICAP, a specialized low-cost housing institute, has received substantial amounts of external assistance, principally from the Caisse Centrale. There is also a Mutual Fund for Rural Development, for granting financial assistance for small village development projects.

While this range of institutions is impressive for a country that has only recently gained independence, they present a number of problems. There is an insufficiently clear relationship between the various activities of these institutions and the goals of the Plan, especially as regards agricultural diversification and industrial development. The line of demarcation between the functions of the two principal general financial institutions, the Senegalese Development Bank and the Credit Populaire, was not well enough drawn. There was also the question of how wise it was to proliferate agencies in a country where administrative talent is very scarce. With these problems in mind, Senegal decided to merge the two principal institutions and to establish different departments within the new body.

Although a considerable start has been made by Senegal in the structural changes called for by its Four-Year Plan, there have been certain short falls in relation to Plan targets. Private capital investment is far below its anticipated level, to some extent as a result of apprehensions among private investors concerning economic policy intentions of the newly independent government, probably also because of the political crisis that occurred at the end of 1962, and perhaps because the targets set for the private sector in the Plan were too ambitious in the light of the limited capital and entrepreneurial ability available in the country. Investments for administrative overhead purposes have been substantially greater than the planned level. Also, investments programmed for directly productive projects have lagged in relation to investments in social overhead and infrastructure projects.

A substantial portion of Senegal's investments, as previously noted, are financed with external aid funds. As is the case in most countries, however, the major part of the investments must come from mobilization of internal resources. The carrying out of the investment projects, through matching resources that are obtained from abroad or otherwise, has placed a strain on Senegal's fiscal situation. This is true for its current budget as well as its capital budget. In addition to the local resources that must be spent on the investments themselves, there are new fixed claims on the current budget that arise from the operation and maintenance of new capital projects. This has become a problem particularly in connection with the many new roads that have been constructed in recent years. This public finance problem, which exists in most developing countries, will be aggravated in the case of Senegal by the termination of the French subsidy that has been paid for years for the purchase of Senegalese peanuts and by the withdrawal of French troops stationed in Senegal. These have constituted important sources of revenue for the government.

Another important problem for Senegal arises from the scarcity of trained manpower. Immediately following World War II, most Senegalese development projects were found in the Ten-Year Plan, which was drafted in Paris. From 1949 on, more and more projects were drafted in Senegal by French experts. This pattern continued down to independence. Since independence, the Senegalese have been playing a greater role in drafting their own projects. French technical advisers and advisers from other aid sources continue to make important contributions in setting up projects. It will be some time, however, before Senegal can carry out this technical work unaided.

The problem of coordinating aid programs in Senegal has arisen in recent years as the sources of aid have become somewhat diversified, and informal suggestions have been made that the various donors of aid to Senegal should work more closely together. It was hoped that this would prevent duplication of efforts, lead to the sharing of information, and promote the discussion of common problems. These suggestions have not been followed. Coordination takes place, if at all, on an *ad hoc* basis.

The principal stumbling block to coordination appears to be the choice of a leader for the group. The French, because of their long historical relationship with Senegal and their paramount position in the field of aid, feel that they should head the group, but other sources consider leadership of an international aid-coordinating group by one nation, particularly the metropolitan power of a former colony, politically undesirable. Coordinating groups elsewhere are generally headed by an international agency such as the World Bank, DAC, or OECD. A logical and feasible leader of such a group for Senegal would seem to be the EDF or some other organ of the EEC.

Although it has not been possible to form any comprehensive aid-coordinating group, the Senegalese themselves have managed to coordinate the efforts of more than one source in relation to particular projects; and the French, the United Nations, and the EDF have cooperated jointly on a number of projects.

PRINCIPAL PROBLEMS IN AID

The Senegalese have expressed a number of opinions relating to external assistance. Some of the more common attitudes are the following:

1. Aid is given more for the benefit of the donor than for the recipient. It has permitted the United States to dispose of surplus commodities, found markets for French goods and services, and permitted the Germans to lay the groundwork for the sale of German goods.

2. By giving aid on a project basis, the donors cause distortions in the Plan. Donors give the kind of assistance which is easiest for them

rather than the kind necessary for Senegal. This is true even though Senegal has a comprehensive development plan with a timetable. In this manner the donors rather than the Senegalese government determine the pattern of development.

3. The expenditure of loan proceeds, which must be repaid by Senegal, are also carefully regulated by donors of such loans. This caused one prominent commentator [3] to state a preference for loans on foreign money markets because Senegal would be free in utilizing the loan proceeds.

4. The complex time-consuming procedures of sources of aid make it extremely difficult to keep to the timetable of the Plan.

5. Too much external assistance has gone into infrastructure and social overhead projects and not enough into productive projects. Aid in this form is a kind of neocolonialism which keeps Senegal dependent upon external powers.

6. Social overhead and infrastructure products become fixed charges to the government in relation to operating costs and maintenance. They seldom produce revenue. It has been suggested that these recurrent costs should also be met by external aid sources.

7. If the external sources of aid were serious about assistance to developing countries, they would concentrate their attention on the prices of primary products, so that Senegal and others could develop on their own resources. The Senegalese would prefer to develop on their own resources. Short of this, they want assistance without conditions in order to develop at their own pace in their own direction.

With respect to the first point, the relevant question would seem to be the benefit of the aid to the recipient. This need not necessarily be mutually exclusive with respect to benefits derived by the donor.

The second criticism points up the need for developing a proper coordinating mechanism not only for the activities of the various donors but also in relation to national economic plans. The recipient country should obviously play an important role in the coordination.

[3] Michel Dembèle, Chief of the Financial Division of the Senegalese Plan Organization, "Les problèmes de financement du premier Plan Quadriennel," in a special issue of *Développement et civilisations* on "Sénégal 'an 2' par lui-meme," December, 1962.

With respect to the third point, the fact of the matter is that private international money markets are simply not open to flotations by most of the less developed countries. It has been necessary to develop special mechanisms in the postwar period to promote the international flow of capital, especially to facilitate economic development.

Every effort should obviously be made to overcome unnecessarily burdensome procedures in the aid administration process.

It is of course necessary to keep a proper balance between infrastructure and social projects on the one hand and productive projects on the other, but the latter cannot proceed too rapidly without the former, especially in a country such as Senegal. Indeed, the tendency in foreign aid circles until recently had been to concentrate too much on "bankable" productive projects without giving sufficient attention to the creation of the underlying conditions that will ultimately induce more productive projects.

There is a reluctance on the part of aid donors to provide straight budgetary support for current operating expenditures on the ground that the aid will not be effective unless the prime effort in a development program is internal. There is, nevertheless, some flexibility in this respect, depending upon the special circumstances of individual countries, and in any case the important consideration is a proper balance between total national effort and external assistance, whether for investment or for current operations.

Finally, the issue of "trade versus aid" raised by the last point is one which is very much occupying the attention of the leading nations of the world. An international conference on trade and economic development prepared under UN auspices was held in the spring of 1964. In the case of Senegal, with a typical monoculture of an agricultural product with not very dynamic demand characteristics, the problem is further aggravated by the termination of the subsidies the French have been paying for Senegal's peanuts as a result of the new EEC Convention. There is certainly no easy answer to the problem of increasing the exchange earning capacity of the less developed countries, but in any case it seems unthinkable that this capacity could be increased in the short run for most such countries to the point that aid would no longer be required. Also, while aid is still being granted, no source of such aid appears disposed to provide it on blank-check terms, although the paternalism tends to diminish as the recipient country demonstrates its abilities to invest funds well. Furthermore, aid-claimant countries should recognize that aid-donor countries are subject to conflicting political pressures at home that sometimes require compromises in the application of policies.

Senegal's foreign aid requirements will continue to be substantial in order to achieve the goals of its economic development plans. France will undoubtedly continue to be the primary source of external assistance. The European Development Fund has already committed a slightly larger amount for its total program of assistance during the next five years than during its operations to date. Other sources of assistance, such as the World Bank group and the African Development Bank, can also be tapped to a greater extent in the future. With a concentrated effort to perfect the deficiencies in the carrying out of its economic plans and with a proper coordination and application of the foreign financial assistance available to supplement its own resources in relation to these plans, Senegal will undoubtedly be able to quicken its rate of economic and social development.

Sudan

Sudan, a nation with a population of slightly more than 12 million inhabitants, obtained independence in 1956 after almost sixty years of rule by the Anglo-Egyptian Condominium. A coalition civilian government was overthrown by the military in 1958 as a result of a downturn in the economy and fear of intervention by the Egyptians. The appearance of calm under military rule was shown to be misleading by the return to rule of a civilian coalition government following the overthrow of the military at the end of 1964. Political tensions, which may have an important effect on development, still exist. One of the centers of discontent is the southern Sudan. Economically undeveloped, less educated, culturally different, these people have been demanding more autonomy or separation from Sudan. In the cities secularism is impinging on the domain of the religious-oriented Muslim political groups.

Cultural change and political conflict have been given impetus by a series of development programs, and at the same time development efforts have received support as a result of political and cultural changes.

Sudan's development efforts have resulted in a rise of 5 to 6 percent annually in the gross domestic product, bringing it to $1.1 billion or $93 per capita in 1962. Targets for future development have been set forth in a Ten-Year Development Plan.

The current Plan, covering the period from 1961–62 to 1970–71 (July 1–June 30), was preceded by a number of five-year capital development programs instituted and prepared primarily by the British following World War II. The current Plan calls for an annual growth in gross domestic product of 5 percent and a level of gross investment calculated at 13 percent of gross domestic product for 1961–62. It is a comprehensive plan both to create the infrastructure and social overhead projects which will permit more rapid expansion in the future and to diversify agriculture and create industry to provide the funds for future development.

Total investment expenditures under the Plan amount to $1.6 billion, with close to 60 percent of total investments in the public sector. More than 36 percent of Plan investment expenditures, or $584.3 million, is expected from external sources. (This figure includes debt service during the plan period.) External assistance is relatively new to Sudan, with the first such assistance coming in 1958 following the failure of the cotton crop.[4]

EXTERNAL ASSISTANCE

Over 60 percent of Sudan's export earnings arise from cotton and cotton products exports. This dependency on one crop created serious problems in 1957, when almost none of the crop was sold. A $62-million positive balance of trade in 1956 was turned into a $46.5-million deficit in 1957. Pests destroyed the 1958 cotton crop, and 1958 saw another $46.5-million deficit in trade balances.

At the time of these cotton problems Sudan was engaged in a number of large development schemes which were eating into foreign exchange reserves. Trade deficits cut foreign exchange reserves down to the danger level and Sudan sought external assistance.

[4] Sudan borrowed on the London market in the 1920s to finance the Gezira Project. See Robert F. Meagher, *Public International Development Financing in Sudan* (New York, Columbia University School of Law, 1965), pp. 77–79.

The IMF made a short-term stand-by loan and the United Kingdom and West Germany supplied medium-term export credits. These were followed by aid agreements with the World Bank, the United States, the Soviet Union, Yugoslavia, Kuwait, and the UN Special Fund.

From 1946 through June, 1963, Sudan received public loans and grants totaling $292.4 million. Aside from a $5.6-million grant given by the United Kingdom in the late 1940s in appreciation of Sudan's war effort and $500,000 of UN technical assistance, all of this assistance was received after the 1957 cotton crisis.

Almost 75 percent of the total assistance has been in the form of loans, and the rest has been grants. Two-thirds of the assistance has been from bilateral sources and one-third from international sources. Five-sixths of the grants and over 60 percent of the loans have come from bilateral sources and the remainder from international sources. For the five-year period ending in June, 1963, Sudan has averaged $58.5 million of external assistance obligations per year.

The United States and the UN Special Fund and specialized agencies have been responsible for virtually all of the grant aid to Sudan if one excludes the $5.6-million grant made by the United Kingdom in the late 1940s. Close to 40 percent of all loan assistance has come from the World Bank and the IDA. The other sources of loan capital are clustered together with each source giving from 7 to 12.8 percent of the total. The United States and the World Bank have each given approximately one-fourth of all assistance flowing to the Sudan. If the IDA figure is added to the World Bank total, the joint percentage moves up to 30 percent. The other sources are clustered with the highest percentage from any other source being only 11.5 percent.

World Bank assistance has been particularly welcomed in Sudan because of its reputation for objectivity, thoroughness in project analysis, and nonpolitical nature. The Bank has played an important role through its economic analyses of the economy, its appraisal of the ten-year development program, and its loans. Furthermore, the Bank has encouraged West Germany to invest in the Roseires Dam, has secured an expert group to analyze the Sudan Railways, and has established and chaired a Consultative Group for assistance to Sudan.

In 1957 the first World Bank mission to Sudan analyzed the economy and decided that irrigation and Sudan Railways deserved highest priority. Over the next four years the Bank made three loans to Sudan totaling $74 million. These twenty-to-twenty-five-year loans, at 5 ⅜ to 6 percent interest with three-to-seven-year periods of grace, have been fundamental to Sudan's development. The high level of World Bank experts has acted as a backstop to the understaffed Sudanese Civil Service. It is doubtful that any national group could have been as successful as the Bank's Mission to study the railways. Many blunt truths have to be spoken about administrative matters, and the Bank Mission was not hesitant in this respect.

The World Bank has mixed its own hard loans with soft loans from the IDA, and in addition the Bank has been able to attract other sources of capital to join in the financing of projects. The Roseires Dam Project is an example of both these points. The Bank's $19.5-million loan at 5 ¾ percent for twenty-four years with seven years' grace was combined with an IDA loan of $13 million for fifty years at ¾ percent with a ten-year period of grace. The Bank encouraged West Germany to look into the project; and, relying on the Bank's project analysis, the Germans provided an $18.4-million, 4 ¾ percent, twenty-year loan with a five-year grace period. The three parties have entered into an Administrative Agreement under which the World Bank administers the drawdowns on all three loans.

The UN specialized agencies, in spending $4.9 million, supplying 274 experts, and awarding 234 scholarships, have done a great deal to supplement the understaffed Sudanese Civil Service. Experts have been utilized in general administration, labor, education, agriculture, health, civil aviation, and meteorology. Sudan is one of the few countries which has used the United Nations to supply technical assistance on a payment basis. This technique permits countries having funds but limited ability to recruit experts to turn to the UN for such recruitment. The experts are then paid by the country requesting the assistance.

Seven of the ten Special Fund Projects are for training and for research institutes, thus supplementing existing facilities.

U.S. aid totaling $74.7 million has been provided. During the foreign exchange crisis foreign exchange was provided on a grant basis to permit Sudan to import necessary goods; project assistance, also on a grant basis, has been provided to assist the existing cadre and to develop new staffs, primarily in education, agriculture, transportation, public utilities, and industry; development loans for the Industrial Development Bank ($2 million) and an industrial sewerage system ($3.8 million) were made under extremely favorable terms to Sudan to ease pressure on the balance of payments. They run for forty years with a ten-year period of grace at an interest rate of ¾ percent. Another loan, for $10 million, has been made to an American entrepreneur for construction of a textile mill. It was a fifteen-year loan at 5¼ percent interest including a three-year period of grace. There are no local sources for this large a loan, and at the time 15 to 30 percent of Sudan's imports were cotton piece goods and textiles, in spite of the fact that Sudan's principal crop was cotton. Lastly, the United States has provided commodities, chiefly wheat and wheat flour, to ease pressures on foreign exchange reserves for food imports.

The Sudanese find U.S. aid procedures extremely cumbersome and time-consuming. Although they appreciate the reasons for American thoroughness, they don't have the staff to satisfy American demands for detailed presentations.

The Soviet Union opened a $22-million credit for the Sudanese government at the end of 1961. Under the agreement this credit was tied to a list of projects. Each credit is for twelve years, commencing from the date the project goes into operation. Interest has been set at 2½ percent. Preliminary surveys have been completed, and the Soviets are beginning the construction of canneries at Wau and Kerima, a milk-processing plant at Babanosa, and an onion-drying and -processing plant at Kassala. Some Sudanese officials question whether sufficient agricultural products will be available for the plants to operate at a reasonable utilization factor and whether adequate markets for some of the products can be developed in a reasonable time.

West Germany was one of the first countries to come to Sudan's assistance after the 1957 cotton crisis by making an untied $6-million credit available to finance imports needed for development projects. This was a medium-term credit with repayments to be made within four years of each drawdown. Interest was put at 5½ percent. The second loan was made in conjunction with the World Bank and IDA for the Roseires Dam. It was a twenty-year loan of $18.4 million at 4¾ percent. The interest rate was a full percentage point below the interest charged by the World Bank on the same project. Germany has also provided $2 million of grant aid for agricultural projects, a technical training institute, research on forestry, research on malaria, and a printing press. In addition Germans have supplied approximately $16 million worth of suppliers' credits for a sugar factory and a hydroelectric project. Negotiations have been going on for a loan to the Industrial Bank. The conditions of this proposed loan have been criticized by the Sudanese on the same terms they criticize the U.S. loan to the same Bank; i.e., there is too much supervision by the lending agency. In the case of the German loan, it has been proposed that each subloan by the Bank must be approved by the Kreditanstalt. In the American loan, provision is made for such approval for all loans over $100,000.

The United Kingdom has provided Sudan with two credits tied to the import of British goods. Each loan is for $14 million. The first credit, however, was to be repaid in five years, whereas the second credit runs over a twenty-year period. Interest in both cases was set slightly above the cost of money to the British Treasury, i.e., at premiums of ¾ percent for the first credit and ¼ percent for the second credit.

There is some feeling in the Sudan that the British are giving less than Sudan expected in light of their long relationship. One of the reasons may be that the United Kingdom has concentrated its assistance to Commonwealth members and Sudan decided not to join the Commonwealth.

Yugoslavia provided Sudan with a $15.4-million credit in 1959 to enable Sudan to make contracts with Yugoslavian economic organizations for the delivery of capital goods on a credit basis. No credit is to be for more than eight years, and interest is charged at the rate of 3 percent per annum. To date credits have been utilized for a tannery, a cardboard factory, four coast guard patrol launches, and two new cargo ships. Approximately $9.8 million has not yet been allocated to particular projects.

Sudan became the first recipient of a loan from the newly created Kuwait Arab Economic Development Fund. The Fund gave Sudan a $20.1-million loan for the development of Sudan's railways. It is a fifteen-year loan with interest at 4 percent.

The Netherlands, Italy, and France have each provided Sudan

with suppliers' credits, and Japan has provided some technical co-operation in the form of experts.

About two-thirds of Sudan's Public International loans are for periods of fifteen years or more. Interest rates range all the way from ¾ percent to 6 percent with 25 percent of the loans at rates of 3 percent or less and the rest clustering about 5½ percent except for the Kuwait and one of the German loans at 4 to 4¾ percent.

ADMINISTRATIVE MACHINERY FOR AID

Sudan has no one group charged with securing external assistance. When the 1957 cotton crisis arose, various emissaries were sent abroad to find capital. With the establishment of the Ten-Year Plan, the Ministry of Finance and Economics was reorganized and the Permanent Under Secretary for Planning in the Ministry assumed the responsibility for finding sufficient external assistance to satisfy the Plan's requirements. Contacts continue to be made by many individuals. When President Abboud visited the United States and subsequently the United Kingdom, one of the items on his agenda was requests for additional foreign aid.

In order to assist Sudan to coordinate assistance from all possible donors and at the same time to maximize Sudan's aid receipts, the World Bank took the initiative to coordinate aid assistance to the Sudan by forming a Consultative Group. Ten countries and three international organizations (Belgium, France, West Germany, Italy, Japan, the Netherlands, Sweden, Switzerland, the United States, the United Kingdom, IBRD, IDA, and IMF) attended the first meeting of the Group in November, 1963, and they were joined by Canada, acting as an observer.

At the first meeting of the Group the World Bank analyzed Sudan's Ten-Year Plan and its progress. This was followed, in the second meeting, in January, 1964, by a report of the Permanent Under Secretary for Planning, who outlined the state of the economy, the major problems relating to the Plan, and a list of projects for which Sudan was seeking external assistance. In addition to project assistance, he requested a general-development loan. Kuwait joined in as an observer at the third meeting in June, 1964.

The Industrial Bank was organized to assist in the establishment, expansion, and modernization of private industrial enterprises in the

Sudan and to encourage and promote the participation of private capital, both internal and external, in such enterprises.

During the Bank's first sixteen and one-half months of operation, through December 31, 1963, it received 121 applications for its financial, technical, and managerial assistance in the establishment or the expansion and modernization of industrial private enterprises. The Bank approved twenty-one loans totaling about $1.8 million. A little less than two-thirds of the Bank's loans were to cover foreign exchange costs of projects. In an effort to avoid imposing the entire foreign exchange burden of developing industry on the current balance of payments of the country, the Bank sought external assistance.

Both the United States and West Germany have shown interest in the Bank. The United States has made a loan to the Bank and is providing it with technical assistance, and West Germany is completing negotiations for a loan.

Industry makes up less than 2 percent of Sudan's gross domestic product. It is a sector where, in spite of many problems, there can be substantial development. The Bank has an excellent opportunity to act as a catalyst in this field.

PRINCIPAL PROBLEMS IN THE RECEIPT OF AID

The substantial flow of external assistance in recent years has been essential for Sudan's current rate of economic development. Substantial development problems remain, however, and external assistance has brought with it another series of problems. The development problems were summarized by the Minister of Finance and Economics in his 1964–65 budget speech as follows:

It cannot be doubted that the extremely high investments on development in the last two years have not only contributed to the drain on our foreign and local resources, but also greatly accentuated the physical bottlenecks and the other strains and stresses on the economy. The obstacles to development are numerous and varied. The shortage of capital is only one of them. There are other real hindrances which money alone cannot overcome, the dearth of skilled manpower, deficiencies in public administration, elements of social resistance and maladjustments in the economic structure are cases in point.

External assistance problems revolve around three main points: the amount of assistance, the detailed presentations required by the donors with each loan request, and the terms and conditions of the assistance.

The Sudanese contention that the amount of external assistance has fallen short of their goals is questioned by the principal donors. The formation of a Consultative Group consisting of the principal donors of the Western bloc has resulted in a continued inflow of assistance. Sudan has had an opportunity to present a picture of its financial needs to most of the potential donors at one time.

Detailed project presentation raises two problems. The first relates to the fact that each source of assistance requires detailed project presentations to be made before providing aid. The nature of the presentation varies from source to source. Sudan does not have sufficient trained staff to prepare these multiple presentations within the time limits set by the Plan. Sudan is, however, being assisted in this respect by the World Bank and AID. The second problem relates to the fact that most assistance is tied to projects. The Sudanese Plan is an integrated whole with interrelated sections. Balanced development is based on a sequential completion of projects. Many of these projects are small or in fields which donors find to be unattractive. In general, donors prefer large projects which will be identified with the source of assistance. This results in a lack of external finance for many small but important projects. To prevent unbalanced development, Sudan has suggested that donors supply a part of their assistance in the form of general-development loans. This assistance would then be used for small projects and subprojects in the Plan. This has not proved to be a popular suggestion with the different providers of aid. Only one country, and that a small donor, has agreed to make a general development loan.

Sudanese officials have stated that political conditions have not been a source of problems in relation to external assistance. Other conditions, however, are viewed by them as being troublesome. The tying of the expenditure of aid to purchases in the donor country has annoyed the Sudanese because it results, at times, in less value to the Sudanese per aid unit. It is unlikely that the United States, the Soviet Union, the United Kingdom, or France will modify their policies in relation to this condition. Sudan will be forced to follow the procedures of other recipient countries in searching for the most economical source and then attempting to secure assistance from this source or, as an alternative, getting less than full value for their external assistance. A substantial proportion of external assistance to Sudan from the World Bank, IDA, Kuwait, and West Germany has been untied. Another condition which is considered irksome is the requirement that subloans of the Industrial Bank have to be approved by the West Germans or the Americans, depending on which assistance is being used. The U.S. agreement requires approval for all loans over $100,000, whereas the draft of the German loan proposes approval for all subloans.

Sudan is a relatively new aid recipient and, as such, has not developed substantial problems in this area. It will benefit from the experiences which the various donors have had in other countries. It still has some time before debt servicing will become a major problem. Sudan is already enjoying the long-term, low-interest soft loans of the IDA and AID. The Consultative Group should be of assistance in alleviating some of the potential problems by maximizing available resources, avoiding multiple presentations of aid requests, and standardizing aid conditions.

India

India, with a population of over 470 million, is faced with one of the most complex development problems in the world. Following independence, India decided that the most rational approach to development would be through five-year development plans, and in 1951 the First Five-Year Plan was initiated. At that time, per capita national income was estimated at $55, the population growth rate was about 1.7 percent, the industrial sector was relatively undeveloped, and gold and foreign exchange reserves stood at a little more than $2 billion. A major goal of the planners was to raise the per capita income to $110 over a twenty-five-year period. This was equivalent to annual increases in per capita income of 3 percent. Even such a modest gain was recognized as a strain because of population increases.

India recently completed its Third Five-Year Plan. Each Plan has been comprehensive and has been directed toward balanced growth. Public spending has increased progressively under each Plan from $4.6 billion in the First Plan, to $9.6 billion in the Second Plan, to an estimated $15.8 billion in the Third Plan.

India's national income grew by 42 percent during the decade of the first two Five-Year Plans. From 1961 to 1964 there was no increase in per capita income after a 16 percent rise during the first two Plans. Consecutive bad monsoons and an increase in the annual population growth to 2.5 percent (approximately 12 million additional people per year) were contributing factors to the recent poor results. Estimates for 1964–65 indicate an increase in per capita income of 2.5 percent.

Agriculture accounts for about half of India's national income and supports roughly 70 percent of the population. Yields per man and per acre are among the lowest in Asia. During the First Plan, major emphasis was placed on agricultural development, and the average rate of increase in agricultural production was 4.2 percent. Emphasis was shifted to heavy industry in the Second Plan, and the average rate of increase in agricultural production dropped to 3.9 percent. During the Second Plan a major foreign exchange crisis confronted the government, and agricultural production received more attention. For the Third Plan, the average rate of increase of agricultural production was approximately 2 percent—four years of inadequate rain and insufficient fertilizer were contributing causes in this decline. The 88.5 million tons of food grain produced in 1965 was far below the 100-million-ton goal of the Plan.

Industrial production has increased rapidly. Using 1956 as a base year, the Index of Industrial Production climbed to 168.8 in 1963–64. From the beginning of the First Five-Year Plan in 1951 to 1963–64, steel production increased fourfold to 4.3 million tons, electricity increased from 6 million to 26 million kilowatt-hours, and coal production almost doubled, from the 1951 total of 35 million tons to 66 million tons. With new industry there has been an increased demand for imports of capital goods, replacement parts, and raw materials, which has eaten up most of India's foreign exchange reserves.

India's gold and foreign exchange reserves dropped from over $2 billion at the beginning of the First Plan to under $600 million at the beginning of 1965. Since $420 million of gold is required by statute to act as cover for Indian currency, approximately $160 million is left in free foreign exchange reserves. India's $2 billion of annual imports is not matched by exports, and the annual trade deficit runs over $800 million per year. This situation may have a negative secondary effect in relation to foreign private capital investment, which the government has recently begun to woo in earnest. A recent newspaper story [5] reports that Western-owned refineries have been asked to accept Soviet crude oil because the Soviet Union will accept payment in rupees. In addition, this report goes on to say, "The Government is also approaching foreign companies here to try to persuade them to postpone the repatriation of present profits and thus ease the pressure on exchange reserves."

Limited savings and reserves have forced India to seek external financial assistance.

NATURE OF AID RECEIVED

India has been the largest recipient, among the less developed countries, of international financial assistance. (On a per capita basis however, India ranks very low.) This aid has increased particularly since mid-1958, when the Aid-India Consortium of Western bloc donor countries and agencies was constituted. External assistance utilized during India's First Five-Year Plan (April, 1951–March, 1956) amounted to only 2.28 billion rupees and increased to 14.67 billion rupees during the Second Five-Year Plan (April, 1956–March, 1961). External assistance requirements during the Third Five-Year Plan (April, 1961–March, 1966) were estimated to be 32 billion rupees, or about double the utilization during the two previous Five-Year Plans combined. By the end of the Third Five-Year Plan, India had received more than 50 billion rupees in external aid, or more than $10 billion.

The external aid has been of increasing significance in connection with India's attempts to achieve rates of economic growth in excess of its population growth. The large volume of assistance during the Third Five-Year Plan was equal to the total of imports during this period for investment plus some for consumption; in other words, the external financial assistance has financed at least all imports in excess of those required for maintenance of the economy at current levels of activity.

[5] New York *Times*, Feb. 15, 1965, p. 39.

The prospect is that the present high level of external assistance in the amount of more than $1 billion per year ($1,027 million was committed by the Aid-India Consortium for 1965–66, the last year of the Third Five-Year Plan) will be required for at least another decade before the relationships among local production, exports, and imports will have been strengthened to the point where adequate economic growth can be more self-propelling. For example, it is estimated that imports for investment during the Fourth Five-Year Plan (April, 1966–March, 1971) will have to amount to at least 35 billion rupees to satisfy growth requirements, and it is unlikely that exports will do more than keep pace with the somewhat increased requirements of imports for maintenance. The estimated total of 35 billion rupees is somewhat higher than the 32 billion rupees of external assistance under the Third Plan. Thus, if India is to continue to grow even at the modest rate that it has been able to achieve, which still leaves much to be desired considering the very low levels of living of its vast population, the massive aid from more fortunate countries in a position to provide it will have to continue. Various aspects of this basic problem in today's international relations are considered below.

India is an exception to the general situation in nations which have emerged from colonial status since the end of World War II with respect to the sources of external assistance in the initial phase of their independence. In most cases, the aid is provided by the former metropolitan power. Thus, the bulk of the large amount of external aid granted by France has been to its former colonies, and British aid has similarly been concentrated on former British colonies. But the scope of India's aid requirements and the importance of the country have been far too great for its external assistance to have come primarily from Britain. Even the management of the international consortium for aid to India, which in and of itself does not mean the provision of large sums of capital assistance, has been entrusted to a multilateral agency, the World Bank, rather than to any single nation. While Britain is cooperating fully in aid to India, it has provided only a minor part of the total, certainly less than 10 percent.

To the extent that economic assistance to India has been dominated by any single source, it has been by the United States, which has supplied about 55 percent of the total. This has resulted from the sheer magnitude of the task as well as from the nature of some of the assistance required. The volume of external assistance needed by India has been beyond the capacity of multilateral agencies such as the World Bank, just as European reconstruction requirements were after World War II, and the primary source then too became the United States. Furthermore, there has been no multilateral international mechanism for the provision of assistance in the form of agricultural commodities for current consumption, which has constituted about 30 percent of total aid to India, while the United States had huge surplus supplies of such commodities.

The motivations for U.S. aid to India have been a mixture of various factors. Aside from the humanitarian motivation of rendering assistance, to alleviate distress as well as to promote development, to such a vast single segment of the world's population, the basic motivation has undoubtedly been political and strategic in the context of the world ideological conflict between East and West. The objective in this sense has, however, not been the attainment of short-run strategic advantages such as are hoped for when aid is primarily in support of a military effort. After the failure of U.S. foreign policy to prevent a Communist revolution in China through an assistance program that was mostly military, the strategy has been to provide economic aid which in the long run will strengthen the Indian social and political structure. The fact that as much as 55 percent of U.S. aid has been in the relatively painless form of the provision of surplus agricultural commodities does not detract from the fact that much of such assistance, in effect, amounted to gifts. In recent years the United States has taken the lead among donor countries in making loans available on very lenient terms. The commercial motivation of providing aid to assist the export industries of the donor country, while not completely absent in the case of the United States, has been of secondary importance. The tying of its loans to purchases in the United States during the last five years has been a response to its balance-of-payments deficits and the outflow of its gold and is a far more complex matter than merely the gaining of trade advantages.

The increasing size of the task of assistance to India, the U.S. balance-of-payments difficulties, and the ability of other Western-bloc countries and institutions to participate in the assistance effort—all contributed to the establishment of the international consortium to coordinate aid to India. The consortium, which was a pioneering effort and inspired similar arrangements for aid to other countries, was a necessary intermediate step between sheer and somewhat chaotic bilateralism at one end of the spectrum and the unlikely though theoretically tidy administration of all aid through multilateral channels at the other. With virtually every major country in the Western bloc represented, the consortium has made it possible to meet the levels of assistance required in overall terms and to give some measure of assurance of commitments on an advance and continuing basis. It has elicited additional aid from some laggard donors and has helped to achieve a liberalization of repayment terms needed in the light of the Indian situation. At the same time, it has permitted flexibility of the detailed relations between India and the numerous individual donors.

The consortium has been managed by the World Bank, which, together with its soft-loan affiliate, the IDA, has been the second most important source of Western-bloc aid to India after the United States. Though well behind the United States in the magnitude of its assistance, the IBRD (plus IDA) had nevertheless provided as much as $1 billion by mid-1964. Important as this contribution is in quantitative terms, the influence of the IBRD in India has been proportionately even greater in other ways, especially by virtue of its pivotal role for the entire Western bloc in reviewing India's comprehensive development plans and in managing the consortium. Also, the IBRD has brought its influence to bear on the administration of aid within India. Thus, the establishment of the privately owned Industrial Credit and Investment Corporation of India (ICICI) as a channel for industrial financing resulted from the Bank's influence; without it, the channels for such financing would have been exculsively public.

The sources of aid to India have been augmented by substantial aid from the Soviet Union and several other countries of Eastern Europe, which have contributed some 10 percent of the total. This aid has been concentrated in industrial development projects, the most important of which has been the Bhilai steel project in the public sector. More of the same aid appears to be in the offing with the announcement of a Soviet offer to finance the Bokaro steel project. An agreement for a $211-million, 2½ percent, twelve-year loan for the first phase of the project is reported to have been signed in January, 1965. The Soviet credit followed the withdrawal by India of its financing request to the United States for this project after it became clear that the U.S. Congress would not sanction such a large loan for a state-owned steel mill in India.

Thus, all the principal sources of international capital assistance, Western and Eastern, bilateral and multilateral, have become involved in a mammoth effort of assistance to India, the single most important claimant nation. With the continuing large and varied requirements of India for external assistance and with the broad range of motivations and practices among the donors, there is the prospect of much scope for continued participation by the various donors.

India has received about 90 percent of its total aid from the Western-bloc powers but has not had any military or political alliance with the West. It has pursued a policy of nonalignment with one or the other bloc in the East-West struggle and has jealously guarded its desire for a foreign policy independent of both. The aid that it has received, except for the last two years following Communist China's incursions on its northern border, has not been military, although the economic aid that it has received has, of course, indirectly permitted India to divert some of its own resources to the maintenance of its military establishment.

There has been some objection expressed in the West from time to time with respect to certain foreign policy actions of India but never to the point where correction of the actions was posed as a *quid pro quo* for economic aid. Thus, while there were some threats of this type in relation to India's annexation of Goa, they did not materialize, and India's action in Goa was carried out without any effect on external aid. The controversy in the West with respect to India's acceptance of aid from the Soviet Union in the form of MIG airplanes or a factory for their production did not apparently lead to any conclusive results one way or the other.

At the same time, the Soviet Union, after initial hesitation, decided to grant aid to India. Both East and West have come to accept the genuineness of India's neutrality and to believe that their position would be prejudiced by having a country as large as India be entirely dependent on the other camp. Aid has consequently been concentrated on contributions to India's long-term development.

Communist China's military action on India's northern border in the fall of 1962, which also accentuated the strategic and ideological differences between Communist China and the Soviet Union, has given a new political aspect to aid for India. Military aid to India has since then been forthcoming from the United States and Britain, as well as from the Soviet Union, and there is the prospect of a combination of aid from the two camps in the presence of a common threat rather than in competition with one another.

India, because of its strategic position and genuine neutrality, has thus been able to convince the donors of aid that their contribution to India's development is desirable without exclusive military or political alliances.

The aid that has been provided to India is a complex mixture of technical assistance grants, sales of agricultural commodities for local currencies, most of which are in turn re-lent on a long-term basis and to be repaid in local currencies, short-term suppliers' credits, medium-term loans, long-term loans, loans on which repayment begins before disbursement is completed, loans bearing virtually no interest at all, and loans with rates of interest on a fully commercial basis. What they all have in common is that India is enabled to obtain goods or services without having to pay for them out of current exchange earnings. In some cases, there is no obligation to pay at any time, in other cases, the repayment terms are no more favorable than for credits normally obtained in business relationships, and in still others, the terms are subsidized by donor governments so that they are easier than commercial terms. Obviously, only those forms of provision of goods or services from abroad that require either no payment or repayment on more favorable than commercial terms can properly be considered aid. The rest are simply international movements of capital.

By no means all the massive movements of capital from abroad into India can be considered aid, but, in light of the difficulties of India's external economic position, there has been a growing realization that there is a need for international capital movements on terms which can properly qualify them as aid. About 10 percent of the total to date has consisted of outright grants, and another 30 percent of commodity assistance, much of which is akin to grants. There has been a move away from grants, but commodity assistance continues. With respect to the 60 percent made up of loans, there has been an appropriate softening of terms in recent years, especially from the United States and the IDA.

The large increase in loans to India has meant that the burden of their servicing has moved up from 3 percent of the country's export proceeds in the First Plan period (1951–56) to 12 to 13 percent at the present time in the middle of the Third Plan period (1961–66). It was obvious that this could not continue for long, and the response was the softening of terms by the United States and the IBRD, the latter shifting its loans to India to the IDA. Even with these softer terms, it will not be until the late 1960s that there will be an easing of the service burden.

The IDA terms of fifty years for repayment and an interest or service charge of ¾ percent per annum are the softest, followed by the forty-year term of the U.S. Agency for International Development. AID loans initially also bore a service charge of only ¾ percent per annum, but this has been raised in its most recent loans to 2½ percent after the first ten years. Under the pressure of the United States and the IBRD in the Aid-India Consortium, other donors have been prevailed upon to lengthen their maturities somewhat, but their interest rates are still at about the commercial level of 6 percent. The Soviet interest rate is low, at 2½ percent per annum, but its loans must be repaid within twelve years, which is burdensome for an economy with the uncertain balance-of-payments prospects that India's has.

The Indian case more than any other has drawn attention to the need for lenient repayment terms in international assistance programs if they are to be large enough to have an impact on development.

ADMINISTRATIVE MACHINERY FOR AID

Prior to 1958, foreign aid played a comparatively minor role in Indian development plans. The Indian government developed no elaborate procedure either for securing or coordinating external assistance. The initiative for aid tended to come from the various donor countries. India showed a preference for World Bank assistance, and any efforts made by the government were thus directed toward this source.

It was only after the seriousness of the foreign exchange crisis became apparent in 1957, and India began to realize the nature and magnitude of its obligations, that India began to make a concerted effort to obtain external assistance. In mid-1958, a senior civil servant visited London, Washington, and Bonn to impress upon the respective governments the nature, extent, and urgency of India's foreign exchange needs. The President of the World Bank also carried on informal discussions in the United States and the United Kingdom on behalf of India. These actions led to the formation of a consortium of Western-bloc countries and the World Bank in August, 1958. The World Bank is chairman of the consortium. Initially, the consortium was concerned with providing enough funds to bring India out of its immediate foreign exchange crisis. Subsequently, it has developed into a coordinating committee of aid for India, known locally as the "Aid to India Club."

The members of the consortium informally advised India that they would consider Third Plan aid requirements actively and sympathetically. With the drafting of the Third Five-Year Plan (1961–66), India, for the first time, drew up a plan based explicitly upon the expectation of a large amount of foreign aid. The World Bank prepared an extensive review and evaluation of the Plan for the consortium. The direct foreign exchange requirements of the Third Plan were estimated in the Draft Outline published in July, 1960, at $5.5 billion, excluding over $1 billion of commodity imports under the U.S. P.L. 480 program.

At the end of May, 1961, a meeting of the consortium was held to pledge assistance for the Third Plan. A total of $2.4 billion was pledged for the first two years of the Plan. In June, 1963, another $1.05 billion was pledged for the third year of the Plan. In May, 1964, an additional pledge of $1.03 billion was made, and in April, 1965, another $1.03 billion was pledged for the final year of the Third Plan.

By August, 1962, every major country in the Western bloc and almost every member of the EEC was represented in the consortium, which has thus become practically the sole channel for pledges of foreign aid to India from Western-bloc countries. What started essentially as an emergency operation in 1958 with a substratum of political-cum-humanitarian motives has now become a semipermanent institution.

Soviet-bloc aid does not come into India through the consortium. It continues on an *ad hoc* basis in the form of trade and economic assistance agreements.[6] Almost all the aid is in the form of credits. The Soviet Union accounts for approximately 85 percent of these credits.

India has had two major industrial financing institutions until 1964, when they were joined by the new Industrial Development Bank. The IFC was established in 1948 as a statutory corporation which gives mainly long-term mortgage-type rupee loans to large and medium-sized concerns, organized as public limited companies or cooperatives. Most of its loans have gone to sugar, paper, cotton, textiles, chemicals, and metal products. Recently, it has gone to some extent into foreign currency loans.

The ICICI was registered as a joint stock company in January, 1955, encouraged first by the U.S. aid mission in India and later by the World Bank. Although the government has no participation in its share capital, one of its principal shareholders is the Life Insurance Corporation, a publicly owned body. In addition, the government has advanced the ICICI 275 million rupees in loans. U.S., UK, West German, French, and Japanese interests have participation in its share capital. Its principal business is to give foreign currency loans and to underwrite public issues. It also gives mortgage-type rupee loans and subscribes directly to share capital. Most of its assistance has gone to paper, chemicals, iron and steel, vehicles, machinery manufacture, and electrical equipment.

The original reason for setting up ICICI seven years after the establishment of the IFC was that the U.S. aid mission and the World Bank—both averse to lending to publicly owned institutions—wanted to sponsor and finance a private nonstatutory body which, among other things, would transact business which IFC could not at that time take up under its charter. Over the last few years private

---

[6] See, in more detail, Chapter III.

business has expanded and diversified so rapidly and foreign exchange has become so scarce that both IFC and ICICI have had to widen their spheres of activity, thus resulting in some overlap. Both the IFC and the ICICI have been recipients of foreign exchange loans. The IFC has received loans from the U.S. DLF and AID, the German Kreditanstalt, and the French and Japanese governments. ICICI has received the bulk of its loans from the World Bank. Smaller sums have come from the U.S. DLF and the German Kreditanstalt. By lending to these financial institutions, these sources of external finance have put the problem of lending to specific Indian industries into the hands of those who are best qualified to deal with such questions.

PRINCIPAL PROBLEMS IN AID

The bulk of the aid made available to India is tied by the donor country. The proceeds of the loans must generally be spent on goods and services purchased exclusively in the donor country. Virtually the only loans that are untied in this respect are those from the IBRD and IDA.

The reasons for the tying of aid by countries vary. In the case of the United States, where the effects are greatest in India because of the size of its program, the primary reason is its balance-of-payments deficits. In other cases, aid is tied to improve the donor's trading position in the Indian market, which is of vast potential. Part of West Germany's aid—which is in a very strong balance-of-payments position—is untied, but with the expectation that most of the proceeds will nevertheless be spent in West Germany. In the case of Soviet aid, the policy orientation is paramount. All economic transactions are part of a state-directed economic plan and of state policy. The tying of loans means not only the purchase of USSR equipment but the continued servicing by technicians which the Soviet Union can supply and direct to work abroad far more easily than corresponding Western enterprises.

From the point of view of the recipient country, there are obvious disadvantages to the country of tying aid. By virtue of the restriction on the area of possible purchasing, competition is limited and there are the consequent undesirable effects on prices as well as on quality, specifications, and the range of goods obtainable. Furthermore, if the tying donor has not been a traditionally important trading partner of the recipient, delays may arise because of the need to locate appropriate new suppliers and because of the unfamiliarity of the users of capital equipment with new specifications. These disadvantages have all prevailed in the case of U.S. loans to India for the purchase of capital equipment and have therefore reduced the value of the aid. Indeed, considerable amounts of aid offered by the AID have remained unused for substantial periods because of these difficulties. On the other hand, of course, if the untying of the aid were to result in a lower volume of aid because of balance-of-payments pressures, the results might be still more undesirable. Tied aid is obviously better than no aid at all.

In the absence of basic compelling reasons such as persistent balance-of-payments problems, the general rule should be the granting of capital aid on an untied basis with respect to the country of expenditure. This was the case with U.S. development loans prior to 1959. If bilateral aid were generally untied, individual countries would be hard put to justify tying their aid. Exceptions could be made, by general agreement, for countries in a balance-of-payments deficit position on the basis of criteria that should not be too difficult to work out.

This general rule should not, however, be applied so as to interfere with the maximizing of the volume of aid. Additional aid above certain levels could be provided on a tied basis if that were to raise the total volume. For example, this is a technique that has been worked out in Britain, where tied aid above that in regular foreign aid programs is granted to finance the sale of output of industries with surplus productive capacity.

This type of reversal of present policy would not be easy to achieve, of course, considering the various national legislative processes involved, nor could it be effected for India alone. The most obvious vehicle for achieving an international agreement of this type is the DAC of the OECD.

The major part of the aid made available to India has been tied to specific projects and programs, and only a minor part has been available for the financing of general import requirements. Donors have been reluctant to have their aid diffused over the entire Indian investment program and identified only as general "aid to India."

They have wished to see it related to specific projects or programs, partly because of interest in being involved in particular sectors of economic activity and partly because of a belief that their aid would thereby be more effective in relation to India's development.

As the magnitude of India's exchange problem and aid requirements has grown, however, there has been an increasing need for more generally available foreign exchange that can be quickly utilized, and donors have been expanding the amount of aid made available in this form. For example, more than half of the loans to India by the U.S. AID has been for broad import requirements, and up to half of the total pledges for the last year of the Third Five-Year Plan made at the April, 1965, meeting of the Aid-India Consortium were not necessarily tied to specific projects and may be made available for general import requirements. In some cases, even though a loan is tied to a specific project or program, the foreign exchange proceeds of the loan may be available for general imports by virtue of the fact that the expenditures on the project are mostly local currency. The 1961 IDA roads loan is an illustration of the liberal attitude in this respect now adopted by the World Bank.

The tying of assistance to specific projects and programs, aside from extraneous considerations such as commercial or prestige motivations, is essentially a matter of confidence in the economic programs and policies of the recipient country. While it is recognized that the granting of aid for specific projects releases resources in the recipient country for other, perhaps less desirable, uses and that the tying of aid to projects cannot assure development unless there is control over all investment and economic policies, there is a feeling that at least the desirable specific projects are being carried out when aid is tied to projects. This is perhaps less compelling a consideration in the case of India than in other countries, in view of its respected public administration, development planning techniques, and general economic policies. There is no feeling, for example, in the case of India that foreign exchange will be squandered on unnecessary imports or that it will be used to shore up a negative balance-of-payments position caused by internal inflationary policies. Although there may be differences in view between donor countries and India on specific elements of its Five-Year Plans, there is satisfaction with the general nature of its development effort and confidence that general foreign exchange provided will be used to promote development. The very definition of aid requirements in relation to comprehensive national economic plans contributes to that confidence.

The issue of attempting to influence Indian policy in favor of private enterprise has arisen in lending for industrial projects by the United States and the World Bank. There has been no such issue in loans from these sources for infrastructure purposes, such as electric power and transportation, where there is no dispute with respect to the active role that must be played by government in a country such as India. Other Western-bloc donors, having themselves a much larger public sector in economic life than the United States, have been much less concerned with the doctrine of public versus private enterprise in India. And it goes without saying that the issue is not at all relevant in the case of the Soviet bloc.

The leading case involving a disagreement of this type between the United States and India has, of course, been the Bokaro steel project. In other instances in India, e.g., in fertilizers, the United States has made loans to public-sector enterprises, and it was presumably the very large size of the Bokaro project that tipped the scales in this case. While there is by no means unanimity in the United States with respect to the appropriateness or effectiveness of a policy of not lending for public-sector industrial projects, it became apparent that the negative view would prevail in the United States with respect to assisting Bokaro, despite the fact that the private sector in India favored the project. To avoid an official refusal, India withdrew its request for assistance. The result, of course, has not been to stop public enterprise in steel in India. India is now considering an offer of assistance for it from the Soviet Union.

The issue of public versus private enterprise in steel in India is partly a pragmatic matter rather than an issue of doctrine. There is substantial private participation in the industry alongside the public participation. Public enterprises have been assisted not only by the Soviet Union but also by Britain and West Germany, but the magnitude of expansion required in steel in India is beyond the capacity or interest of local private enterprise. As for foreign private enterprise, even if it were prepared to take the large risks involved, it would undoubtedly not be acceptable on doctrinaire grounds. Steel is looked upon in India pretty much as a public utility. And it is generally taken for granted that public utilities are no longer an appropriate field for private foreign investment in the less developed countries. Thus, there appears to be little justification, either logical or practical, for the view that has prevailed in the United States toward the Bokaro project.

The World Bank has gone even farther than the United States in that it has made no loans at all for public-sector industrial projects in India. And it has utilized its influence in various ways to encourage a favorable attitude toward private enterprise in India. Thus, it was instrumental in the establishment of the privately owned ICICI, to which it has granted substantial assistance, rather than to the officially owned IFC. Nevertheless, the latter has received substantial assistance from the DLF and the AID of the U.S. government.

Thus, the efforts of the United States and the IBRD to influence India favorably toward private enterprise have been of doubtful consistency and effect. India appears to have gradually developed a pattern of coexistence which gives considerable scope for both public and private enterprise in its economic life. The private sector still comprises by far the major part of India's economic life; in 1960–61 it generated 90 percent of the country's total output. But this conceals the dominant role played by the state, not so much through the direct control of enterprises as by the direction of national planning and the vital administrative controls over foreign exchange and purchase, employment, import quotas, and other factors on which the conduct of economic activities depends. Such controls are indispensable in a country that must allocate priorities in development to insure a minimum standard of living for its teeming masses. But this necessity underlines the crucial importance of adequate training and efficiency in public administration.

Despite the sophisticated level of economic planning and public administration in India, there are numerous problems remaining to be solved in the more effective and more rapid utilization of the amounts of aid committed to the country. The sheer size and complexity of the program make it a difficult one to administer. The difficulties are most pronounced in the portion of aid which is tied to specific investment projects. It is obviously much easier to administer commodity aid programs, which are simply a matter of organizing distribution mechanisms. Lags in the utilization of specific project commitments aggravate the scarcity of foreign exchange and delay the favorable effects hoped for on the balance of international payments.

There are inadequacies in preinvestment studies, in the budgeting of foreign exchange requirements, in maintaining targets during the execution of projects, and in the coordination of the activities of all the official agencies and dependencies that may be involved.

There are, of course, no easy answers to such problems, which are not unique to the administration and utilization of foreign aid but are a reflection of the tremendous burden on public administration in general, from which foreign aid and administration cannot be divorced. What is needed perhaps is more delegation of authority within the civil service so that some of the pressure is removed from the key administrators. In addition, there should be more emphasis on the practical aspects of carrying plans out more efficiently relative to the attention that is paid to the formulation of the plans themselves. The entry of the government into industry has also changed the nature of training required for civil servants engaged in these undertakings. These activities require civil servants trained in, or at least aware of, the manifold problems of management, accounting, and other aspects of business. This is important not only for the conduct of public enterprises such as India's publicly owned steel mills but also for the many complex and vital planning decisions. They often involve cooperation with foreign and international public institutions as well as private investors. Precisely because so many vital economic decisions must, in a country like India, be a matter of public rather than private decision, development of a civil service that has a practical as well as a theoretical understanding of the conduct of business is likely to pay dividends well out of proportion to the financial investment involved.

Thailand

Surrounded by countries in various stages of strife and instability, Thailand stands out as one of the few countries in southeast Asia with a considerable degree of economic and political strength and stability.

Thailand is unique in southeast Asia by virtue of never having been under colonial rule. As a result, the country does not exhibit the sensitive, highly nationalistic attitudes and complexes that are found in many countries which have been under colonial rule. On the other hand, the country has no cadre of civil servants who have been trained under colonial administration over the past hundred years as in India, nor have public services been highly developed; and deficiencies in public administration have constituted a problem in the utilization of international development financing.

Agriculture is the occupation of over 80 percent of Thailand's 29 million inhabitants. Production is high, and the country is not over-populated. In 1964 Thailand became the leading rice-exporting country in the world. Thailand has an export economy, with exports accounting for about one-fifth of the national output. Rice accounts for 35 percent of export revenue, followed by rubber (19.4 percent), maize (8.5 percent), tin (7.9 percent), and jute and kenaf (3.65 percent). These figures reflect the change in recent years from a dependency on rice and rubber alone.

Commodity price fluctuations continue as a major problem for Thailand. For example, during the drop in rubber prices in 1961, the total export value of rubber, which accounted at that time for a fourth or more of the country's exports, dropped by 25 percent. The government has utilized two approaches in attempting to solve this problem: diversification of agriculture and the encouragement of industrial investment.

During the years 1951–64 the average annual rate of growth of the gross national product was 5.2 percent, one of the highest in southeast Asia. At the end of 1964, the gross national product was estimated at $3.1 billion, for a per capita product of approximately $100. In recent years, the rate of growth has passed the 6 percent target set by the Six-Year Development Plan (1961–66). The rate of population increase is around 3 percent. Inasmuch as Thailand has a large surplus of basic foodstuffs, the population is not subject to the hunger found in many other Asian countries. Areas in Thailand such as the northeast, however, remain quite a bit behind the level of the rest of the country.

In 1959, following the advice of foreign advisers, Thailand established the National Economic Development Board (NEDB) which drafted Thailand's First Six-Year Plan during 1959 and 1960 to cover the period 1961–66. Before the completion of the first three years, revisions were made in the targets for the final three years. Owing to political and strategic reasons, a special development plan was drafted for the northeast within the framework of the Six-Year Plan.

Thailand's foreign exchange reserves have increased by over $200 million since 1955 to the present level of more than $600 million, and some have questioned the need for continued aid to Thailand. The buildup of reserves to some extent reflects the foreign aid of the past, which has been heavily in the form of grants. On the other hand, these reserves, which amount to the value of one year's imports at the present rate, would not go very far toward financing the direct and indirect foreign exchange requirements of a stepped-up development program. At the same time, there are a number of political and strategic reasons for Western-bloc countries to see that Thailand develops as rapidly as possible.

THE NATURE OF AID RECEIVED

Thailand has received more than $1.1 billion of external assistance from 1946 through 1964. Over 43 percent was in the form of U.S. military grant assistance. Economic assistance from bilateral and international sources totaled $654 million, consisting of $320 million, or 49 percent, in the form of grants and $334 million, or 51 percent, in the form of loans.

The World Bank, the United States, and West Germany have been the principal suppliers of external assistance to Thailand. Excluding military assistance, the United States has provided about $400 million of assistance, and over 70 percent has been in the form of grant aid. The World Bank has made thirteen loans totaling $204 million, and West Germany has provided more than $38 million, with four loans accounting for $36.25 million. Grant assistance has come from the UN Special Fund ($9 million), the specialized agencies of the United Nations ($8.6 million), and UNICEF ($4.3 million) and from various Colombo Plan countries, including Australia ($7.5 million), the United Kingdom ($1.7 million), and Japan ($1.5 million). Aside from the first three sources, all other assistance has been in the form of grants.

Until 1950, Thailand's development was almost completely based upon the resources of its own economy. Stable economic and political conditions and its ability to repay loans made Thailand one of the earliest recipients of international development financing, especially from the World Bank. In 1950, the Bank made three loans to Thailand, and from 1950 through 1954, the World Bank was the largest aid contributor to the country. The United States and the specialized agencies of the United Nations also began their assistance programs in Thailand in the early 1950s. The British Commonwealth countries held their first meeting on the Colombo Plan in 1950. Thailand attended early meetings as an observer and in 1954 became a full member of the Colombo Plan. Thailand also entered into a military assistance pact with the United States at that time and became a founding member of the Southeast Asia Treaty Organization as well.

Following the fall of North Viet Nam to the Communists in 1954, the amount of economic assistance from the United States increased sharply. It climbed from less than $10 million per year to over $40 million in fiscal year 1955 and reached a high point of $49.4 million in fiscal 1959. It has slowly declined since that date. In fiscal 1964 it was set at $12.6 million—all in the form of grants. U.S. loans, which have totaled about $100 million, have been for commodity imports, irrigation projects, a slaughterhouse in Bangkok, a dredge for the port, an electric distribution system, an electric power plant, roads, a telecommunications network, and a few other items. More than 45 percent of the grants have gone into transportation projects, including highways, airfield construction, and a railway repair shop. Health and sanitation projects received 11 percent of the assistance, followed by agriculture and natural resources (9 percent), industry and mining (7 percent), education (6 percent), and public administration (6 percent).

Australia has been the leading provider of aid from Colombo Plan countries (if one excludes the United States). It has provided more assistance than all of the other Colombo Plan countries together. This $7.5 million has included railroad cars, ambulances, diesel locomotives, a screening and crushing plant for lignite, and feeder roads.

West Germany entered the aid picture in 1962 with a $25-million credit which has been fully utilized in three separate loan agreements for the Industrial Finance Corporation of Thailand, an irrigation project, and an extension of a railroad line. Late in 1964, a German loan of $11.25 million was made for a fertilizer plant. In addition, West Germany has provided over $2 million in grants for a number of training centers, surveys, and equipment.

World Bank loans have been directed primarily to infrastructure. Two loans have gone for electric power, four loans for irrigation, three for the railways, two for the port, one for highways, and one for the Industrial Finance Corporation.

The foreign aid received by Thailand has not followed any single, comprehensive pattern. A large part of the aid has been in response to the political and strategic situation in southeast Asia as an important theater of operations in the Cold War, some has consisted of financing of specific social overhead projects in isolation, and there have been a great variety of largely uncoordinated technical assistance in numerous specific areas. This helter-skelter pattern of foreign assistance reflects to some extent the limited effectiveness to date of national economic planning in the country, as previously noted, but also derives from the differing motivations of the various donors.

The World Bank, the Special Fund of the United Nations, and the specialized agencies of the United Nations have the goal of economic development as their primary consideration. The motivations of the United States are more complex. Political and strategic considerations are important factors. As we have seen above, U.S. aid rose markedly after the Communist take-over of North Viet Nam. Thailand is a strategic center and a member of SEATO. These facts doubtlessly limit the United States in approaching aid from a purely developmental point of view.

In more recent years, Australia, Germany, and Japan have shown an increased interest in Thailand. Australia and Japan have commercial, economic, and political motivations in providing assistance to Thailand. Japan is attempting to assert prewar leadership in Asia and to find markets for its expanding industrial activities. (Recently Japan offered Thailand $7 million worth of suppliers' credits.) Australia, faced with reduced European markets owing to the EEC and with the growing realization that it must become a more active part of Asia, has increased its assistance to Thailand. West Germany, with its expanding economy, has been put under pressure by members of the DAC of the OECD to give more foreign aid. In addition, Germans have an historical trade relationship with Thailand. Thus, they have increased financial and technical assistance to that country.

Although there has been little or no formal coordination to date among the providers of capital assistance to Thailand, there has been some cooperation between particular donors, and steps are under way to increase such cooperation generally.

In conformity with their general pattern of attempting to work rather closely together, the U.S. aid agencies and the IBRD have done so in Thailand. When the IBRD made the Yanhee loan for electric power generation, conditions were included relating to an expanded distribution system and an increase of interim power in the Bangkok area. Although the agreement did not specify that such assistance should come from the United States, the United States did extend loans for these purposes.

The whole UN complex of organizations works rather closely together. The IBRD, ECAFE, the Special Fund, and the offices of the specialized agencies tend to help one another in supplying information and in assessing proposals and personalities within each country.

Much would be gained if the U.S. AID mission worked more closely with the specialized agencies of the United Nations. There has been some complementary activity in this direction. For example, the DLF of the United States required as a condition of its loan for a dredge that Thailand carry out a siltation study. This was done subsequently by the Special Fund of the United Nations. When domestic agricultural pressure in the United States prevented it from granting additional assistance to Thailand for rice development, the Special Fund of the United Nations stepped in and set up a program in this field.

Some coordination automatically occurs by virtue of the extensive knowledge on Thailand possessed by the IBRD and the United States. When various countries send missions to Thailand to look into commercial and developmental problems, they invariably meet with the IBRD resident representative and frequently with members of the U.S. AID mission.

In order to bring about more coordination in technical assistance projects in Thailand, the United States suggested that the DAC of

OECD hold a meeting to discuss this and related questions. The first meeting was held in May, 1962, and has been followed by subsequent meetings. A DAC Coordinating Group in Thailand emerged from these meetings. This has resulted in an increase in the exchange of information among the donors of assistance, which has been beneficial to all concerned. In 1963 and 1964 the group published annual Compendiums of Technical Assistance to Thailand.

The terms on which aid has been extended to Thailand have not imposed any undue burden of repayment on the country's future resources. A large part of the aid, at least from the United States, has been in the form of grants involving no repayment at all. Loans have been granted with comfortably long maturities by the principal lenders, the IBRD, the United States, and West Germany; and the United States has, in addition, granted a considerable amount of soft loans in the sense of even longer maturities or with repayment in local currency, which gives loans the characteristic of being virtually grants.

The IBRD has given terms to Thailand ranging from fifteen to twenty-five years. Interest rates have been prime commercial market rates, varying from 3¾ to 5¾ percent. These loans have permitted from twenty-two months to six years for the first repayment of principal. All repayments are made in the currency of the loan. Procurement is effected on the basis of worldwide bids.

U.S. loans to Thailand have ranged from ten to forty years. Interest rates have been from 3 to 5¾ percent. First repayment of principal has been deferred for eight months to five years. The United States has had legislative authority to accept repayment for all loans except EXIMBANK loans in local currency. A higher interest rate was charged when repayment was to be made in local currency. Under the legislation establishing AID, however, it has now become the policy to require repayment in dollars. Until 1962 only one non-EXIMBANK loan required repayment in dollars, i.e., the DLF loan for the slaughterhouse. When repayment is made in local currency, the proceeds are usually reallocated to the Thai government for further development projects. Since the end of 1959, U.S. assistance has been tied to procurement in the United States.

The German loans are scheduled to be repaid over periods of eighteen to twenty years with a six-year period of grace before the first repayment of capital. Interest rates range from 3 to 6 percent, and the aid is not tied to procurement in West Germany.

There are thus obvious advantages for Thailand to continue to look to these sources for future aid rather than to utilize the much less favorable source of supplier credits.

The conditions attached to loans relating to the soundness of their administration have been particularly successful in the case of the World Bank. Bilateral sources of assistance find it somewhat more difficult to impose such conditions for a variety of reasons: there is the political factor of the delicacy with which relations between sovereign states must be handled, extraneous motivations such as strategic considerations can dilute the bargaining power of the donor, and bilateral funds are usually derived from governmental appropriations and there may be somewhat less concern with the protection of the investment than in the case of the IBRD, which is very much concerned with the quality of its portfolio because of its reliance on private capital markets for its resources.

Agreements between the IBRD and the Thai government reflect the Bank's concern with sound administration and the protection of its investments. To assure the most economical and proper use of its loan funds, the Bank requires worldwide bidding for equipment purchases. The Bank or its agents supervise the bidding. When they are not satisfied with the procedures, as, for example, in a bid on locomotives for Thailand, they refuse to permit the use of Bank funds for the purchase. The Bank also reserves the right to approve engineering consultants who supervise the execution of projects.

If the Bank is not satisfied with the administrative organization for use of the loan, it frequently insists that there be some designated change as a condition of the loan. In Thailand this resulted in an independent Port Authority, Railroad Authority, and National Energy Authority. The Bank also protects its investments by imposing conditions relating to financial policy of the borrowing agency. In public utilities, the Bank requires that the rate structure be sufficient to service the debt and to build up reserves for maintenance and expansion. This was true in Thailand in the cases of the port loans, railway loans, and the Yanhee electric power loan. Budgetary practices and other internal administrative details, such as requiring the creation of a Central Personnel Division in the railroads of Thailand, have also been conditions of the IBRD loans.

In the DLF and EXIMBANK loans to the Metropolitan Electricity Authority, these U.S. agencies had the advantage of the conditions already negotiated by the IBRD in the Yanhee loan. They also financed technical assistance contracts which were concerned with administrative improvements.

Such conditions, in addition to achieving the objective of protecting the investment of the donor, also have the desirable effect of improving administration in the recipient country. The improvement of administration even when desired locally may otherwise be very difficult to achieve for political or other reasons, and the leverage exerted by the disinterested leading agency may be the necessary ingredient to bring about these changes.

Two projects sponsored by ECAFE and involving Thailand to some extent have attracted worldwide interest as regional development ventures. These are the Mekong River Project and the Asian Highway Project. The Mekong Project, for the multipurpose development (navigation, irrigation, power, and flood control) of one of the largest rivers of Asia for the use of Cambodia, Laos, Thailand, and Viet Nam, has attracted contributions from numerous states outside the region to surveys and studies made in connection with the river. The complete development of the Mekong River will take several decades. Up to now, most of the survey parts of the project have been completed. The Asian Highway Project is basically a program to coordinate the national planning of roads and the standardization of road signals among the various countries of the region. The Asian Highway is expected to begin in Djakarta and to terminate in Teheran. There is no regional financing involved, since the idea is to have each national state responsible for building its own section, which would add to the other national sections to make the Asian Highway. This approach thus illustrates the possibility of harmonizing national planning to achieve regional benefits.

The formulation of regional development projects such as these has been hampered to some extent by the deficiencies of economic planning in the region. While some countries such as India are quite advanced in this respect, most other Asian countries as yet do not have anything like India's elite corps of planners. ECAFE has suggested that there be established an Asian Institute for Economic Development, and at a conference held in Bangkok in August, 1962, such an institute was launched. It held its first class in 1964.

Under the stimulus of the foreign aid of the last decade or so, the outward façade of Bangkok has changed radically, rural areas have been opened up by new highways, and Thailand continues as a relatively prosperous country compared with all of its neighbors except Malaya. However, major developmental problems remain. In areas such as the northeast, these problems are of major proportions; the country in general still has an inadequate level of living, and there is need to step up the rate of growth.

ADMINISTRATIVE MACHINERY FOR AID

Within the Thai government two institutions were charged with the responsibility of negotiating for the allocation of external assistance to various projects which the government of Thailand wished to carry out: the Bank of Thailand and the Thai Technical and Economic Committee (TTEC). The former dealt with the World Bank and the latter with the United States. The Bank of Thailand, which is the central bank, continues to carry out negotiations with the World Bank on behalf of Thailand. The Committee was dissolved and transferred into the structure of the NEDB upon its formation in 1959. There it is found as a Sub-Committee of the Executive Committee of the NEDB known as the TTEC, and its task is to consider and carry out work pertaining to international economic and technical cooperation (except, in practice, from the World Bank). The Sub-Committee has a secretariat known as the Office of Thai Technical and Economic Cooperation. It consists of the staff from the old Committee, which had been dissolved. The major function of the Sub-Committee is the development of foreign aid resources and the planning and implementation of foreign aid projects. The Program Division of the Office has sections concerned with U.S. aid, Colombo Plan aid, and UN and Third Country aid.

Another subcommittee of the NEDB Executive Committee with functions related to aid is the Foreign Loans Sub-Committee (FLSC), which was charged with the responsibility of keeping foreign loans within ceilings established by the Ministry of Finance. It is essentially a foreign debt management body concerned with the amount and terms of debt incurred by the country. All foreign loans are supposed to be approved by the FLSC, although in practice this is not always done.

The finalized budget consists of projects which will be financed wholly with domestic funds and projects which will be financed in whole or in part with foreign funds. With respect to the latter, the TTEC is the responsible agency of the NEDB for securing the foreign aid involved. The Planning Office, which is part of the Secretariat of the NEDB, when drawing up the annual program, holds discussions with the TTEC and various donor agencies to see whether or not various projects will be able to attract foreign assistance. TTEC also discusses these projects with various lending agencies. A general picture develops as to which projects will receive support. These projects are included in the annual program. There are some projects which find their way into the annual program as a result of discussions with potential donors of aid by individuals both within and outside the government. These projects may be introduced either by the Planning Office or the Council of Ministers. There have been occasions when a donor of aid initiated a project by discussing it with the Planning Office, the TTEC, the ministries, or other Thai bodies. Thus, projects included in the annual program may be initiated by an agency of the Thai government, by private individuals, by government officials, or by the donors of aid.

The way in which a foreign aid project becomes a part of the annual program will frequently, but not always, determine how it will become finalized. If the TTEC was involved with it initially, it will probably carry on the negotiations and finalize the agreement with the assistance of the technical people of the ultimate ministry or para-statal body. If the project was initiated by a minister, he may carry out the negotiations himself. We have come across one instance where a private foreign national initiated a project and, after receiving the approval of the Thai government, made the initial approach to the foreign source of capital.

The administrative machinery for aid is undergoing some change as a result of the establishment, early in 1964, of a Ministry of National Development. The TTEC has become the DTEC, or Department of Technical and Economic Cooperation, within this ministry. External assistance for the private sector has been channeled through the Industrial Finance Corporation of Thailand (IFCT). The IFCT was established in 1959 to assist in the establishment, expansion, or modernization of private industrial enterprises and to encourage the participation of private capital, both internal and external, in such enterprises. The paid-in share capital was originally 6.1 million baht ($290,000), was increased to 17.4 million baht ($828,000) in 1963, and was finally increased to 30 million baht ($1.43 million) in 1964. Thais hold 46 percent of the shares, foreign shareholders 41 percent, and the IFC 13 percent.

In addition to its paid-in share capital, the IFCT has loan capital amounting to 157 million baht ($7.55 million). Of this amount, 48 million baht ($2.3 million) has been provided on favorable terms by the government of Thailand, partly from counterpart funds arising from U.S. government assistance; the equivalent of 57 million baht ($2.74 million) has already been arranged in the form of a DM 11 million loan available in foreign exchange by the Kreditanstalt of West Germany; and the equivalent of 52 million baht ($2.5 million) has been provided through a World Bank loan.

The IFCT, after some early organizational problems, has become an important stimulant to private sector investment and expansion.

PRINCIPAL PROBLEMS IN AID

Planning in Thailand is primarily a budgetary exercise. It is therefore of limited effectiveness in setting up goals for the economy and in organizing a national effort to achieve them. Since private investment accounts for about two-thirds of the total investment in the economy, there is obviously a need for planning to go considerably beyond its work in the public sector to be effective. Nevertheless, the start that has been made is of considerable importance for the development of more orderly and rationalized procedures for public expenditures and for influencing the pattern of private activity.

Once the decision was made to draft a Plan, the government demanded that it be prepared immediately, and in the rush to get the Plan onto paper, various aspects were not thought through adequately. However, the analysis was considerably more systematic and the account taken of the relationships of the various aspects of the Plan more sophisticated in the revision for the second three years of the Plan period. Furthermore, the decentralized approach in the recent development of planning by regions may lead to more realistic planning.

Inadequate and low-quality statistical data and the small number of experienced and well-trained middle- and top-level personnel make planning a difficult task. Statistical experts from abroad plus international training programs are, however, beginning to reduce these problems. To attract the best people into government, there will have to be a review and change in salaries and other amenities of the civil service.

Another problem in planning in Thailand is the excessive interjection of political considerations into the formulation of priorities for projects. Obviously, in Thailand, as elsewhere, vested political interests cannot be entirely eliminated; but to the extent that they govern economic analysis, the scarce investment resources available to the country will be misallocated and economic development will be impeded. Abuses of this type can damage relations with the external donor agencies and can lead to public disillusionment with respect to the expectations raised by the planning process.

Problems have arisen as a result of allegations that some Thai officials have not acted in the public interest in utilizing foreign funds for various development projects. Specific instances have related to the purchase of locomotives under the IBRD loan, the use of suppliers' credits rather than IBRD funds for highway construction, and the possibility of malpractices in connection with the construction of a new airport. In addition, there have been problems relating to the nonuse of military airports and the diversion of civil aviation facilities to military purposes. If there is validity to such charges, these malpractices obviously tend to discredit foreign aid internationally and in the long run tend to damage the national interest of the recipient countries. In addition to steps that can be taken internally to correct such abuses, greater coordination of aid among the donors and greater harmony with national planning objectives can serve to safeguard against practices that defeat the purposes for which the aid is given.

Since 1950 a large number of foreign assistance projects in Thailand, though by no means all, have been initiated by the donor countries and organizations. This is not at all surprising in veiw of the early stage of development of the country and the consequent shortcomings of public administration and planning. More recently, as the Thai Technical and Economic Cooperation Office, the Economic Planning Office, and the Budget Bureau have augmented and improved their staff, more and more of the initiation of projects has been coming from the Thais. The need for the training of program and development officers capable of preparing projects in the necessary detail to satisfy potential donors of assistance is obvious. The initiation of projects by donor countries and organizations may or may not be conducive to the carrying out of projects with appropriate priorities. There is a natural tendency for particular donors to emphasize those activities in which they are specialized.

The continuity of aid and its appropriate integration into national development plans can be promoted by the stationing of permanent representatives of donors in the recipient country. This can at the same time, however, create problems of coordination and priority if the representatives are too numerous and too specialized. The United States, the IBRD, and the specialized agencies of the United Nations have representatives stationed in Thailand who are specifically concerned with the aid programs. The United States has an elaborate organization with specialists in many of the different spheres of government and private activity, e.g., education, industry, and community development. The specialized agencies of the United Nations are able to use experts within ECAFE when the need arises. The IBRD keeps one man in Thailand and brings in experts before granting any particular loan. Recently, the IBRD has provided several experts to the government to assist in planning.

The large organization of the U.S. AID mission raises the question as to whether this large field force results in an effort to develop a program in each field where the United States has an expert, whether it is of overall high priority or not. Each year each section is asked to submit proposals for the next fiscal year, and individual officials with particular specializations might prepare programs which may not be of an overall high priority. It is true that these programs are supposed to originate in the recipient country and that overall priorities should be determined by the U.S. Mission Director in cooperation with the recipient country. When national planning is weak, however, national priorities will also be ill-defined, and there are not many recipients who reject gifts which may be useful.

East Africa

Within the past four years, the former British territories of East Africa—Kenya, Uganda, Tanganyika, and Zanzibar—have achieved independence. In 1964, Tanganyika and Zanzibar merged their governments to form the new Republic of Tanzania.

Each of these newly independent countries is predominantly agricultural with a low per capita income, subject to fluctuating commodity prices and almost completely dependent on external financial assistance to carry out its development program.

In Uganda and Tanzania, two-thirds of the gross domestic product is derived from agriculture and primary products. Kenya is somewhat less dependent on agriculture, with only slightly more than 40 percent of the gross domestic product coming from agriculture. Kenya has, to a greater extent, developed wholesale and retail trade, transport and storage, and industry, each of which constitutes a little more or a little less than 10 percent of the gross domestic product. In all three countries, agricultural products and primary products constitute over 90 percent of the value of exports. In Uganda, cotton and coffee are the most important cash crops, accounting for 60 percent of the country's export earnings. Other cash crops include sugar, sisal, groundnuts, tin, and livestock. In Tanzania, sisal, cotton, and coffee constituted close to 65 percent of Tanganyika's export revenue, with sisal alone accounting for one-third of the total. Zanzibar has an economy almost completely dependent on the export of cloves. Tanzania also exports diamonds and gold, which account for almost 10 percent of export revenue. Coffee, sisal, tea, and pyrethrum are Kenya's principal exports.

The population of the three countries together is over 26.4 million, with 10.1 million in Tanzania, 9.1 million in Kenya, and 7.2 million in Uganda. Population has been increasing at the rate of 3 percent per year in Kenya, 2.5 percent per year in Uganda, and 2.2 percent per year in Tanzania.

Uganda's per capita gross domestic product in 1963 was about

$64. Real per capita income has grown by only 1 to 2 percent per annum over the past ten years. In Tanganyika the gross domestic product estimates since 1954 show an annual growth rate in real terms of 3½ to 4 percent as a whole and 1½ to 2 percent on a per capita basis. In 1963 the per capita gross domestic product was estimated at $67. After stagnating for a few years, the gross domestic product of Kenya increased by 6.5 percent in 1963, which was higher than any year since 1957. The real per capita income increased by more than 3 percent to a little over $81.

The British instituted planning in East Africa during and immediately after World War II. Ten-year plans were a prerequisite for Colonial Development and Welfare (CD&W) assistance. These early plans were primarily a list of public sector capital projects. Each of the territories experimented with plans of varying length as well as different institutional arrangements for plan formulation and execution. The latest plans of each of the countries: Uganda (1961–62 to 1965–66), Tanzania (1964–65 to 1969–70), and Kenya (1964–70) are comprehensive plans covering both the public and private sectors. Each has instituted a new planning organization.

Economic development in the East African countries is held back by a severe shortage of both trained manpower and capital resources. When the conditions of limited physical resources, fluctuating commodity prices, and special problems such as the tsetse fly, which covers large areas of Tanzania's best potential cattle land, are added, one can appreciate that it will take a considerable period of time before these countries will reach the take-off stage of self-sustaining growth.

Prior to the independence of the East African countries, there was high hope that these countries would form an East African federation. Although some lip service is still given to the idea, it does not appear that any concrete steps will be taken to implement this idea in the near future; indeed, recent trends have involved a weakening of the force for federation.

The lack of political unity has not prevented the East African countries from operating a common market and common services. By way of a central legislature with limited powers and the East African Common Services Organization, the East Africans run a common railroad and harbors, post and telegraph services, airways, a university, merchant shipping, meteorological services, and research. In addition, they administer common customs, excise, and income tax laws. The common market has prevented the promotion of fiscal or administrative barriers to the movement of goods and productive facilities among the East African countries. A common external tariff for imports and a common taxation structure have been the operational tools in the structure. Over the years, strains have developed within the common market because Kenya tended to attract the bulk of industrial investment. An attempt at industrial licensing for all of East Africa was unsuccessful. In early 1964, Tanganyika threatened to withdraw from the common market. Meetings were held in Kampala, Uganda, however, and on April 29, 1964, the three countries agreed to a series of measures to rectify trade imbalances and the common market remained intact.[7]

In recent years, investigations have been made in relation to the possibility of establishing a central bank either for East Africa or for each country. No decision had been reached on this matter as of the end of 1964. Tanzania has printed new currency, however, and has stated that they will probably put it into circulation in July, 1966.

THE PATTERN OF EXTERNAL ASSISTANCE

East Africa has received more than $708 million of external assistance from 1946 through mid-1964.[8] Grants make up approximately 52.6 percent of the total. About 72.6 percent of all assistance has come from the United Kingdom, followed by the United States with just less than 12 percent and the World Bank Group (IBRD, IDA, IFC) providing over 10 percent. West Germany, the UN Special Fund and specialized agencies, China, and the Soviet Union have supplied the rest.

Prior to independence, the East African Territories received most of their assistance from the United Kingdom. The United Kingdom also acted as a guarantor on four World Bank loans totaling $46.4 million. The United States and the UN Special Fund and specialized agencies all had small assistance programs in East Africa prior to independence.

[7] The "Kampala Agreement" has been reprinted in *International Legal Materials*, III, No. 6 (November, 1964), 1106 *et seq.*
[8] UK assistance has been calculated only through March, 1963, U.S. assistance through June, 1964, and World Bank assistance through 1964.

External assistance to the countries of East Africa has increased in recent years both because of increased assistance from the United Kingdom and because of new sources of aid. For example, UK assistance to Tanganyika jumped from $10.9 million in 1960–61 to $27.2 million in 1961–62 and $30.5 million in 1962–63. The same pattern was evident in Kenya and Uganda. Part of this increase is to provide for transitional expenses and will not be repeated. Part is to provide funds for retaining and/or pensioning former British civil servants. In addition, each country has received a special allocation at the time of independence. West Germany, China, and the Soviet Union are new sources of assistance in the area.

More than $514 million of UK assistance has been given to the East African countries through March, 1963, with almost 60 percent being in the form of grants. Prior to independence, it was concentrated in CD&W allocations. These funds were for a whole range of development activities, including administration and surveys, communications, economic aid, and social projects, as well as research. All but $4 million of the $172.5 million provided from CD&W was in the form of grants, with Kenya receiving $57.1 million, the East African Common Services Organization $47.8 million, Tanganyika $43.1 million, Uganda $20.4 million, and Zanzibar $4.4 million.

When the traditional source of colonial finance in the form of guaranteed London market loans dried up in the late 1950s, the United Kingdom introduced the Exchequer loan as a new source of debt capital. These loans were made as general development loans to finance projects in development plans which had already received prior approval in London. Interest is at ¼ percent above the Treasury borrowing rate, and the general length of these loans is twenty-five years. Eleven Exchequer loans totaling $114.5 million have been made in East Africa from 1959 to April, 1963. Kenya and Uganda have each received four loans, Tanganyika two, and the East African High Commission (now known as the East African Common Services Organization) one.

Kenya has been the recipient of colonial grants and loans of $86.8 million for the maintenance of administration commencing with the 1954 emergency. Of this amount, $70 million was in the form of grants and the remainder in loans. Both Kenya and Tanganyika have required grants-in-aid from the United Kingdom in recent years.

These are provided to balance the Current budget (as distinguished from the Capital, or Development, budget).

CD&W assistance and colonial grants and loans are made only to dependent territories. With the dawn of independence, UK assistance is now being given through different UK budgetary headings.

In July, 1961, the Department of Technical Cooperation (DTC) took over the Foreign Office, Commonwealth Relations Office, and Colonial Office responsibility for providing technical assistance to developing countries. The major DTC-aided program has been the Overseas Service Aid Scheme (OSAS), which took effect in 1961. Its purpose is to enable overseas governments and administrations to retain the services of expatriate experts until local officers can take over. OSAS provides about one-quarter of the total cost of expatriate officers' pay, allowances, passages, pensions, and compensation payments. Over 8,000 officers in East Africa were covered by the OSAS in 1963. Tanganyika has received assistance from DTC in its first two years of operations valued at $12.3 million, followed by Uganda, $10.6 million, and Kenya, $10.1 million.

Commonwealth loans and grants have recently been introduced into the area. This assistance is provided for development expenditure, and other purposes and part or all of the assistance may be used to cover local costs. Tanganyika has received $17.9 million of loans and $4.5 million of grants under this form of assistance. Uganda has received $5.6 million divided equally between loans and grants. In 1963–64, $31.6 million, or two-thirds of the total funds allocated under this title, were scheduled for East Africa.

The Commonwealth Development Corporation, a public corporation set up by the UK government with all its capital in the form of loans from the UK Treasury, has as its main purpose the assisting of the economic development of Commonwealth countries which have achieved independence since 1948. It provides funds either on a loan or equity basis to private enterprises, governments, or statutory bodies. As of December 31, 1963, the CDC had thirty-four projects in the East African countries. Kenya had nineteen projects with CDC commitments of $31.5 million, Uganda two projects and $4.4 million, and Tanganyika thirteen projects and $23 million.

The United States gave intermittent assistance to East Africa from 1948 onward. In the early years it took the form of basic surveys, training agricultural officers, and the provision of some road construction and transportation equipment. The United States also agreed to the utilization of Marshall Plan and other counterpart funds for financing various revolving loan funds in East Africa. In 1953, two port loans totaling $6.7 million were made for the development of Mombasa and Tanga ports. These were twenty-five-year loans at 5 percent with repayment in local currency. In 1961, the DLF made a $1.9-million loan to Tanganyika for the construction of a road. It was a twenty-year loan at 3½ percent, repayable in dollars. There was strong opposition within Tanganyika to accepting a loan tied to U.S. procurement, and, after a great deal of negotiating, it was decided that Tanganyika could apply these loan proceeds to imports from the United States without tying these imports to the project, thus releasing an equal amount of foreign exchange for building the road.

Total U.S. assistance to East Africa through June, 1964, has amounted to $83.8 million, divided between loans ($27.7 million) and grants ($56.1 million). Included in this sum is $25.8 million of commodity assistance in the form of grants. Most of it was supplied after the 1961 floods. Tanganyika received $15.3 million of this assistance, Kenya $9.4 million, and Uganda $1.1 million. The U.S. loans have tended to be soft loans, i.e., long maturity and low interest rates. The pattern established in the DLF loan discussed above has been followed with other loans in East Africa, reducing the friction over tied loans. The United States still prefers project to general-development loans.

The Peace Corps, with a group of engineers, surveyors, geologists, and nurses, is operating in Tanzania.

The World Bank has made four loans to East Africa, totaling $46.4 million. Each of these loans was made prior to the independence of any of the East African states, and all were guaranteed by the United Kingdom. The earliest was a $24-million loan in 1955 to the East African High Commission for use by the East African Railways and Harbors Administration. This was followed in 1960 by a $5.6-million loan to Kenya for African farmers and feeder roads in these farm areas. In 1961, Uganda received an $8.4-million loan for the extension of electric power transmission and distribution systems. The last Bank loan was made to Kenya in 1961. It was an $8.4-million loan to help finance the development of farmlands in the former white highlands for resettlement primarily by African farmers.

Some recent loans to East Africa have come from the IDA, with its longer terms and lower interest rates. There have been four such loans. Tanganyika has received two of these loans: a $4.6-million credit to assist the government in enlarging the secondary school system and a $14-million credit to help finance the construction or improvement of light main roads in various parts of the country. In 1964, Kenya received a $2.8-million credit to re-lend to the Kenya Tea Development Authority for the expansion of tea production by African smallholders. Later, in the same year, Kenya received an additional $4.5-million credit to carry out road improvements in various parts of the country. The IDA credits are on its standard terms of fifty years with a ¾ percent service charge and a ten-year period of grace. Three of the Bank's loans were for a twenty-year period, and one was for ten years. The IFC has also had activities in East Africa. In 1960 it purchased $2.8 million of 7 percent debentures and convertible income notes in the Kilombero Sugar project. In 1964 the IFC increased its investment to $4.7 million with $700,000 in the form of equity and $4.0 million in loans. Purchase of equity was made possible by an amendment to the IFC Charter between the time of the first and second investment. In 1965 the IFC committed $3.5 million in loan and share capital in Mulco Textiles Ltd., a new Ugandan company established to build and operate a major textile mill at Jinja near Lake Victoria.

The UN Special Fund has made grants to East Africa totaling $13.4 million. Uganda has five projects utilizing $3.9 million of Special Fund grants, Tanzania seven projects utilizing $5.6 million, and Kenya six projects employing $3.9 million of Special Fund assistance. About half of the projects are for training institutes, and the rest have included mineral exploration, ground-water studies, sheep raising, and irrigation studies.

The specialized agencies of the United Nations have sent over 370 experts to East Africa since 1953 and spent over $3.1 million. Tanzania has received the lion's share of the assistance, with 238 experts and assistance valued at $2.4 million.

West Germany sent both public and private missions to East Africa in 1961. Both Kenya and Tanganyika were offered credits of $10 million. Early loan agreements negotiated under these credits in Kenya included smallholder settlement projects, extension of tea cultivation, road construction, installations for sewerage and water supply, and an investment in the newly organized Development Finance Company of Kenya. In Tanganyika, loans have been made for an extension of a railway line, agricultural projects, and an investment in the Tanganyika Development Finance Company. A German mission visited Uganda at the end of 1962, and West Germany has now agreed to invest in the new Uganda Development Finance Company. German loans have maturities up to fifteen years, with five-year periods of grace, and interest rates ranging from 3.35 to 4.5 percent per annum.

In 1964, the Soviet Union, mainland China, and East Germany had begun to offer assistance to East Africa. China has offered Kenya a $3-million grant in convertible currency and a $15-million interest-free credit. The credit is to be drawn down by 1969 and repaid within ten years from 1975 in exports from Kenya or in convertible currency. Tanganyika was offered a $28-million interest-free credit and Zanzibar a $14-million interest-free credit. Tanzania has been offered a $2.8-million grant. In mid-1964, the Soviet Union announced that it would give Kenya a 200-bed hospital, a clinic, and a technical college for 1,000 students and, in addition, provide technological instructors. The USSR has also promised to assist in building a textile mill, a fish cannery, a fruit-processing factory, a sugar factory, and a radio station.

In December, 1964, Uganda and the Soviet Union signed an economic and technical cooperation agreement. The Soviet Union will assist Uganda in establishing a cotton textile factory, a tailoring workshop, a center for training for mechanized agriculture, a meat refrigeration installation, and a dairy factory. A long-term Soviet loan of $15.4 million will go toward road construction.

East Germany agreed, in September, 1964, to provide Zanzibar with $2.4 million worth of light industrial goods and machinery for food production, to help establish a state building enterprise, to set up a brick factory, and to supply sixteen fishing vessels over the next three years.

ADMINISTRATIVE MACHINERY FOR AID

Each of the East African countries have recently revised its administrative machinery relating to aid. Prior to independence, the

Colonial Office in London and the Treasury in each of the territories were the key institutions dealing with aid. The Colonial Office kept the territories advised of new sources of external assistance and generally provided background data on how to go about obtaining it. The Colonial Office advised the territories to make applications for assistance from different sources and reviewed the requests before passing them on to the ultimate source. The Treasury in each territory was responsible for deciding on how much assistance was needed and then for attempting to obtain it, with help of the Colonial Office. Missions were sent to a number of countries in Asia, Europe, and North America to sound out governments in relation to financial and technical assistance. Special sections were established with each Treasury to keep abreast of the developments and changes in the various sources of external assistance. Officials were sent from each of the territories to the Economic Development Institute of the World Bank to familiarize themselves with available sources of external assistance, to learn how to draw up loan requests to the World Bank and the IFC, to meet officials from other countries with similar problems, and to spend a concentrated period of time thinking about and discussing development problems.

With independence, each of the East African countries moved the responsibility for external aid into the Planning Office. In Uganda, there is a financial planning and external aid branch under the direction of the Development Secretary. In Tanzania, there is a new Directorate of Development and Planning, where it is hoped that carefully studied projects will be developed to attract external assistance. In Kenya, there is a new Ministry of Economic Planning and Development; and one of the two Chief Financial Officers will, with his staff, be responsible for external aid negotiations, both technical and financial. It is quite likely that the respective Ministers of Finance and Development will still be the focal point of aid negotiations. Each of the countries of East Africa appreciates how dependent it is on external assistance and will take all steps which it considers necessary to attract external assistance.

Both prior to and subsequent to independence, many individuals hoped that the Economic Advisory Unit of the East African Common Services Organization could act as a central point for assistance to East Africa. Unfortunately, this idea has never been practicable. Each of the East African countries has established two financial institutions relating to industrial development. The Uganda Development Corporation, the National Development Corporation (Tanzania), and the Industrial Development Corporation of Kenya are each government-owned bodies. They were established to facilitate the industrial and economic development of each of the countries concerned by promoting and assisting in the financing, management, or establishment of new and established enterprises and in conducting research in industrial and mineral potentialities of the countries. They may invest by way of debt or equity capital.

The other set of institutions are known as the Development Finance Company of Kenya Ltd., the Tanganyika Development Finance Company Ltd., and the Development Finance Company of Uganda Ltd. Each of these companies is jointly and equally owned by the CDC, the local development corporation, and the German Company for Economic Cooperation and Development, or Deutsche Gesellschaft für Wirtschaftliche Zusammenarbeit (Entwicklungsgesellschaft) mbh. The theory behind having two institutions is that there are some projects which may be handled better by a wholly government-owned corporation, e.g., projects with political significance, projects to carry out planned policies, investments in utilities, projects where the government does not want outside partners, and smaller enterprises where there may be more risk than a privately oriented group would want to assume. The jointly owned development companies handle projects which are primarily profit-oriented; the local governments have brought in outside partners for capital, know-how, and business contacts. In addition, the presence of internationally known and trusted groups within the development company provides a certain amount of psychological security to potential investors unfamiliar with the developing country. These new companies are just getting under way.

PROBLEMS OF AID

Ideally, the East African governments would like external assistance to be in the form of general-development grants, untied to the source of procurement and available for local and external costs. They would like to secure assistance by filling out one standard form for all sources of assistance and receive a final reply within a relatively short time. Capital assistance would be accompanied by technical assistance. Reality falls short of these standards.

General-development assistance is favored in East Africa because it permits each government to carry out its plan as drafted. When assistance is limited to projects, it is frequently impossible to convert many of the elements of the plan into projects, and this leads to distortions of the plan. Project assistance is preferred by all of the sources of aid. It makes their aid identifiable and also makes it easier to sell the aid program within their own governments. Some sources have attempted to get around this problem by defining "project" very broadly. Others, such as the United Kingdom, have provided East Africa with general-development loans in the form of Exchequer loans. Others, however, are hesitant about following the lead of the United Kingdom, which has had long experience in these countries, is aware of the personalities and problems, and has a large number of its own nationals acting as advisers and civil servants in these countries.

The tying of procurement to the country of the source of aid creates problems of higher prices and the use of unfamiliar products. The United States, pleading a balance-of-payments problem, and the Sino-Soviet bloc countries tie their assistance to their own domestic products. The United States has attempted to minimize the tying of aid by permitting loans to be spent on "development" imports even if they are not used in the project for which the loan is made.

Most sources of aid require that external assistance be utilized only for foreign exchange costs. This presents a formidable problem in East Africa. For example, in Tanzania, "it seems likely that only some £22.5 million will be raised in local currency out of a total capital requirement of the government and parastatal organizations during the Five-Year Plan of £102 million, including a local currency requirement of rather more than £50 million."[9] The various sources of aid are exploring ways to overcome this problem, and the United States is currently permitting over 50 percent of its assistance to be utilized for local costs in these countries.

The various sources of external assistance require different kinds and depths of information to sanction assistance. This puts a great burden on the few individuals in each government charged with preparing aid requests. It would save a great deal of time and effort if the donors would standardize the information required.

[9] *Tanganyika Five-Year Development Plan, 1964-70*, p. 89.

Each of the East African countries is short of well-trained individuals in almost every field. There is need for individuals to prepare aid requests, and there is need for individuals to supervise the various projects in the different Plans. Capital assistance, to be useful and well utilized, must, for the present, be supplemented with technical assistance.

V. Some Cases of Projects and Programs
Assisted by External Financing

TO ILLUSTRATE in detail the application in practice of public international financing to assist developing countries, a selection is presented in this chapter of seven cases of projects and programs so assisted. These cases have been selected from the country monographs to which reference is made in the preceding chapter. The selection covers Latin America (Colombia and Chile), Israel, South Asia (India and Thailand), and Africa (the Sudan). The practices of several donor countries (the United States, the United Kingdom, and West Germany) and international agencies, especially the World Bank, are represented. And the activities assisted include specific projects in the development of economic infrastructure facilities (highways and railways) and industrial activities (steel, chemicals, and textiles), as well as a case of general balance-of-payments support.

The cases in Colombia involve World Bank assistance to the railways of that country and balance-of-payments support provided jointly by U.S. agencies, private banks, and the IMF. The case in Chile is one of assistance to the railways from bilateral sources, principally the EXIMBANK of Washington. The Israeli case involves a large chemicals-producing enterprise that was moved from public to private control and then obtained substantial assistance from the World Bank. In India, the set of cases is that of assistance to three officially owned steel enterprises by the USSR, the United Kingdom, and West Germany. The Thailand highways case includes assistance from the United States as well as from the World Bank. And the case from the Sudan is that of a substantial U.S. loan for the development of a large textile enterprise in the private sector.

With this variety of countries, donor agencies, and projects or programs, many of the types of policies pursued and problems found in the administration of public international development financing can be discerned in these cases.

The World Bank Loans to the National Railways of Colombia [1]

This study concerns the negotiation and implementation of three World Bank loans totaling about $46 million, made over the period 1952–60 for the extension, integration, and improvement of the Colombian National Railways. The principal contributions of the loans were the linking of Bogotá and other major inland cities to an Atlantic port and the integration and rehabilitation of the eastern and western railway systems. Construction of the Atlantic Railroad began in January, 1953, but the entire line from the upper Magdalena to the Atlantic coast port of Santa Marta was not completed and in operation until late 1961. Three separate loans are involved, those of August, 1952, June, 1955, and September, 1960, and there has been a continuous relationship between the World Bank and the Colombian National Railways, dating from the first World Bank mission to Colombia in 1949 to the present time. In June, 1963, the Bank authorized a fourth loan to the Colombian Railways, in the amount of $30 million, at a term of twenty years and an interest rate of 5½ percent. This was to finance the purchase of rolling stock, rails, and other equipment during the first two years of a ten-year program of modernization.

BACKGROUND OF THE LOANS

When the World Bank mission under the direction of Lauchlin Currie visited Colombia in 1949, special attention was given to transportation and power, and the mission's report laid the basis for subsequent loans by the Bank for railroads, highways, and electric power, the principal fields for which World Bank financing has, in fact, become available for Colombia. Some of the major difficulties with the railway system at the time of the negotiations on the initial

[1] By Raymond F. Mikesell, Associate Director, Institute of International Studies and Overseas Administration, University of Oregon, based on a case study prepared by Rafael Isaza at the Centro de Estudios sobre Desarrollo Económico, Universidad de los Andes, Bogotá, Colombia.

loan are apparent from the fact that cargo from the Atlantic ports of Baranquilla and Santa Marta to Bogotá or Medellín had to be brought up the Magdalena River to Dorada or Puerto Berrío and thence transferred by rail to the inland cities. The Magdalena River is not navigable throughout the year beyond the city of Puerto Wilches, however, so that during certain seasons of the year there was no means of shipping cargo from Bogotá to either an Atlantic or a Pacific port even by a combination of rail and water. Indeed, the original project to be financed under the first World Bank loan was to solve this problem by a line which would connect Bogotá with Gamarra; this would have provided year-round transportation, even though it meant a combination of rail and water shipment to the Caribbean coast.

Another obvious deficiency was the absence of a link between Bogotá and some other cities on the eastern rail system and, more importantly, between Bogotá and the western rail system, which joins such important centers as Medellín and Cali with the port of Buenaventura on the Pacific coast. Since highways were poor and inadequate across the mountains separating these two important economic areas, the economic integration of the country was being held back. Finally, even if these important links had been forged by the extension of rail lines, the facilities themselves were too diverse for the creation of a unified national railway network. The gauges of the railways were not uniform, thus necessitating the use of different types of equipment and even reloading in cases where lines came together. Thus, it was necessary to standardize the gauge in the creation of an integrated system. In addition, each geographical division had its own administrative personnel, its own repair shops, and its own locomotives and rolling stock. Some of the lines were owned by the national government, others were owned and administered by departmental governments, and still others were privately owned. In the west there were three lines: one starting at the Pacific port of Buenaventura and connecting with the Antioquia Railroad, a second linking Cali with Popayán and a third linked the city of Manizales with the Pacific railroad. The eastern system included four separate lines, all linked to Bogotá. In addition to the eastern and western systems, there were five isolated lines, two of which, the Santa Marta–Fundación and the Bucaramanga–Puerto

Wilches lines, now form a part of the integrated national railway system.

The idea of a railroad connecting Bogotá with the Atlantic coast and of establishing a link between the eastern and western railroad systems which would have provided Bogotá with a railroad link both with the major cities of the West and with the Pacific coast port of Buenaventura had been cherished for many years, and, indeed, it was under discussion before the turn of the century.[2] In 1945 the Colombian Congress passed a law authorizing the construction of several new railroad lines, including one starting at Pasto in the southern part of Colombia and running to Cartagena on the Atlantic coast. In addition, the Congress approved the construction of a line from Barbosa to Bucaramanga and another uniting the eastern and western systems by the construction of a section from Ibagué on the eastern side of the mountains to Armenia on the west. In fact, this latter section is still under consideration. The Colombian Congress did not, however, appropriate sufficient funds for the carrying out of these ambitious plans. Thus, one of the first tasks of the 1949 World Bank (Currie) mission was to review the several existing plans for achieving the twin objectives of providing a year-round route to the Atlantic and of linking the eastern and western railway systems.

Although the Currie mission was in agreement with the plan for linking existing roads with a down-river port from which all year around water transport to the Atlantic coast would be possible, it recommended, in place of the government's plan to join the Bogotá–Barbosa line with the Bucaramanga–Puerto Wilches line, the construction of a new line alongside the Magdalena River between Dorada and Puerto Wilches and passing through Puerto Berrío. The mission based its recommendations on the following considerations:

1. The construction costs of the alternative projects, the government's proposed Barbosa–Bucaramanga line and the mission's proposed Dorada–Puerto Wilches line, were believed to be similar, or at least the latter would not be substantially higher than the former.

[2] Carlos Dues Lehmann, "El Ferrocarril del Atlántico," *Construcción Colombiana*, No. 4 (April–May, 1961), p. 24.

2. Because of fewer curves and gentler slopes over the Dorada–Puerto Wilches route, operating costs would be lower.

3. The Dorada–Puerto Wilches line would link the eastern and western systems at Puerto Berrío and accomplish the dual purpose of providing a rail link between Bogotá and the important western industrial centers, such as Medellín, and the latter with a rail link to the all-year river port of Puerto Wilches.

Both the World Bank and the Colombian government accepted the basic recommendations of the Currie mission, thereby establishing a general basis for the project which was to be financed by the first World Bank loan.

THE LOAN NEGOTIATIONS

The Currie mission report was transmitted by the World Bank to the Colombian government on July 27, 1950. Shortly thereafter, the government appointed a nongovernmental, nonpartisan Economic Development Committee to assist the government in formulating an overall development program based on the Currie report and to recommend steps to be taken for the execution of the program. One member of the Bank's staff and two consultants who had been members of the World Bank mission (including Currie) returned to Colombia as advisers to the Committee. All the recommendations of the Bank's mission with respect to railroad transportation were approved by the Committee for Economic Development, which began work in September, 1950. These recommendations included (1) the construction of the Magdalena Railroad along the lines indicated above, (2) the reorganization of railroad administration, (3) better maintenance of the equipment, (4) the standardization of lines with differing gauges, and (5) the abandonment of some sections whose operations would be uneconomic and that could not be connected with the major sections of the railroad system.[3]

At the end of 1950, the Colombian Ministry of Public Works signed a contract with a Canadian engineering concern, Lockwood, Kessler and Bartlett, to study the route of the line and to serve as consultants during the construction period. The Canadian firm pre-

[3] República de Colombia, Comité de Desarrollo Económico, *Informe Final, September, 1950–August, 1951* (Bogotá, Imprenta Banco de la República), pp. 141 ff.

pared a report on both the technical and economic aspects of a new railroad line between Dorada and Gamarra, the latter city being some 116 kilometers further north on the Magdalena River than Puerto Wilches, the terminal suggested by the Currie mission report. The Lockwood report was presented to the World Bank in support of the application for a loan. But before approving the application, the Bank wanted an additional report and recommended that the Madigan-Hyland Company prepare a study on the project. Following a report by Madigan-Hyland and further study by representatives of the Bank, a $25-million loan was approved on August 26, 1952, $20 million of which was to assist in financing the construction of the proposed line between Dorada and Gamarra and $5 million to be applied to the construction of railroad repair shops at Bogotá. Both the Madigan and Lockwood firms were requested to continue as consultants and work on the construction of the line from Dorada to Gamarra, a distance of 380 kilometers, begun in January, 1953.

While this work was under way, however, it was decided that an effort should be made to find financing for a continuation of the line from Gamarra to Fundación, where it would link up with the existing line from Fundación to the Atlantic port of Santa Marta. Not only would the new section avoid reloading between rail and riverboat at Gamarra, which would add considerably to the cost of transportation, but it would avoid the additional cost of construction of docks and loading facilities at the river terminal. Both the consulting engineers hired by the Colombian government and the Bank's staff approved the extension of the line, and, on June 15, 1955, the Bank approved a second loan of $15.9 million to the Colombian National Railways to finance imported equipment and services needed for the construction of the 300-kilometer line from Gamarra to Fundación, improvements in the existing road of 100 kilometers to Santa Marta, the construction of terminal facilities at Santa Marta and at Ciénaga, where the railroad and the Barranquilla highway intersect, the purchase of rolling stock for use on the extension, installation of ferry slips, and the purchase of a ferryboat and tractor-trailer units. The purpose of these latter expenditures was to link the railroad with a ferry connection across the Magdalena River to Barranquilla. It was expected that the entire line, including the sections financed by the loans of 1952 and 1955, would be completed by 1958.[4] Actual completion was delayed until 1961.

As is the usual practice of the World Bank, loan financing was provided for covering only the foreign exchange costs of the commodities and services required for the project. As of June 30, 1962, $39.2 million out of a total of $40.9 million authorized under the two loans had been disbursed. The total cost was estimated at 600 million pesos, and the loan component, according to this estimate, at the then-current rate of exchange represented about 42 percent of the total, while the remainder was covered from domestic sources. However, a full accounting of the costs of completing the railroad lines and the terminal facilities and repair shops is not available.

When the program for the improvement and extension of Colombia's railroad systems began, not only was their equipment incompatible with through traffic service from one line to another because of differences in gauges of the track, but the equipment, including locomotives, freight cars, passenger cars, and maintenance facilities, was all in very poor condition. Most of the locomotives were steam, and seventeen distinct types of locomotives were represented among the total of sixty in operation in the sections leading from Bogotá to the north and northeast. Thus, to complete the program of integration and to provide an efficient rail system, Colombia needed new equipment. This was recommended by the original World Bank mission, and studies of requirements were made by the consulting firms. Thus, on September 20, 1960, the World Bank made a loan of $5.4 million to the new Atlantic Railroad (the new name for the system) for the purchase of sixteen diesel locomotives, about thirty freight cars, parts to rehabilitate passenger coaches, and shop equipment. Of the total estimated cost of $6 million, local currency costs of $600,000 were to be met by the Colombian government.[5] The 1963 loan of $30 million, as indicated above, was for purposes similar to those of the 1960 loan.

As to the terms of the loans, amortization payments on the 1952 loan of $25 million were to be made over the period 1957–78 at 4¾ percent interest on the unpaid balance; the 1955 loan of $15.9 mil-

[4] IBRD Press Release No. 404, June 15, 1955.
[5] IBRD Press Release No. 652, Sept. 20, 1960.

lion is repayable by installments beginning in 1958 through 1980, again at 4¾ percent; the 1960 loan of $5.4 million is repayable over the period 1962–75 at 5¾ percent. These are more or less standard terms for the types of World Bank loans involved, and there is no evidence of any difficulties arising over the terms. Except in the case of the 1952 loan, portions of the loan representing the early maturities were sold to private U.S. financial institutions.

CONDITIONS IMPOSED BY THE BANK

The World Bank does not approve loans solely on the basis of an examination of the general desirability of the project but requires technical engineering studies, the preparation of budgets based on cost estimates by accountants and fiscal experts, and studies of the economic feasibility of the projects covering the direct and indirect benefits in relation to costs. The Bank staff also makes a study of the balance-of-payments position and prospects of the country in order to evaluate the capacity of the country to service the loan. Even after a loan is approved on the basis of more detailed studies, actual disbursements are made only for specific imported commodities and for the payment of services of foreign engineering and consulting firms directly related to the project. The Bank usually recommends that the services of reputable consulting firms be employed on a continous basis in order to advise the borrowing agency on day-to-day technical problems and other matters as they occur. Finally, the Bank expects the borrowing agency to maintain a continuous relationship with members of the Bank's staff, including the making of progress reports.

One of the important conditions imposed by the World Bank in connection with the railroad loans was an administrative reorganization of the railroad systems so as to provide both a centralized administration of the systems to be integrated and the establishment of an autonomous board of directors and management which would be relatively independent of political influence and of changes in the political control of the government.

At the time of the World Bank mission in 1949, the national railway system was organized as a branch of the national government under an administrative council of which the Minister of Public Works was chairman. Not only was the chairman a political appointee and subject to change with each shift in the national administration, but the other members of the council appointed to represent industry and agriculture were also changed frequently, and only two members had any significant continuity of tenure. In its report, the World Bank mission recommended that the national railways should be vested in a public railways corporation with a board of directors who would be given full responsibility for the operation of the railroads.

In the reorganization of the administration of the Colombian National Railways in 1953, a board of directors was established which was responsible for integrating and bringing under a central management the various sections of the railroad previously controlled by various governmental bodies and private corporations. While the administration has been centralized to a considerable degree, the Antioquia railroad line is still owned and managed by the Province of Antioquia, but negotiations have been going on to incorporate this line into the national system.

In its recommendations for the reorganization of the railroads, the Bank was anxious that the national railway system be operated as an independent commercial concern, even though ownership was in the hands of the central government. Although the Colombian government is ultimately responsible for the debts of the National Railways system to the Bank, funds made available to the railway system for the reconstruction and extension of the line from both World Bank and Colombian government sources should be repaid by the railroad out of its net earnings. Throughout the period prior to 1960, however (and probably since that time), the Colombian National Railways incurred losses, although these losses declined each year between 1956 and 1959. The ability of the railroad to repay this debt is, of course, linked to the rates charged by the railroad for passenger and freight service, but, as in the case of other public service enterprises, the rates charged are subject to government control, and changes must be approved by the Ministry of Development (Ministerio de Fomento). In the case of the first two loans, the World Bank did not establish any specific conditions with respect to rates. When the third loan was applied for, however, that for financing new equipment for the line, the Bank imposed the condition that the rates charged for the services must be increased so that the earnings of the railroad system would be sufficient not only to cover operating expenses but to provide an amount sufficient for debt retirement and service charges. The reorganization also provided for an improvement in the accounting methods employed, and the Madigan-Hyland consulting group helped to initiate better accounting procedures.

As will be noted below, the recommendations of the two outside consulting firms, Lockwood and Madigan-Hyland, with respect to the location as well as other aspects of the construction of the line, led to considerable controversy with Colombian engineering and other groups in the country. For this reason the World Bank requested specific Colombian congressional approval of the first loan and the conditions attached thereto.

ECONOMIC EVALUATION OF INVESTMENT PRIORITIES

The Currie mission report of 1950 gave a high priority to the allocation of capital for the extension and improvement of Colombia's transportation system, both as a means of reducing costs and for providing adequate services essential to the growth of the Colombian economy. Leaving aside the difficult problem of allocating the share of investment in transportation in the total volume of investment resources, both internal and external, which were expected to become available for Colombia, there is the problem of allocating investment expenditures among the various types of transportation, including railroads, highways, waterborne shipping, and air transport. In considerable measure, the first three are substitutes for one another, and to this extent, estimates of relative costs in relation to the volume and efficiency of the services are relevant for determining the proper allocation of investment resources. In addition, there are certain indirect economic effects on economic development which accrue from the location of the transportation system, whether it be a highway or a railroad. Thus, new transportation facilities may be important factors in the development of a rich agricultural region as yet little exploited.

There is no evidence that the World Bank mission determined the total amount of investment funds for allocation to transportation, as against other uses of capital set forth in its overall program, on the basis of an elaborate development programming model. The total amounts suggested for investment in the fields of transportation and power, the principal purposes for which World Bank loans have been made to Colombia, were arrived at on the basis of providing reasonably adequate services in these areas in relation to projections of demand and taking account of efficiency and cost. To some extent the allocation of investment funds between different forms of transportation was determined by the nature of existing facilities and the physical characteristics of the country. Thus, only in certain situations were alternate forms of transportation, e.g., improved or extended highways, railroads, or waterborne facilities, regarded as alternative uses of capital and decisions made on the basis of economic considerations. Thus, for example, it was determined that a railway paralleling navigable portions of the Magdalena River should be constructed as against an improvement of the existing system of a combination of rail and waterway transport.

As has been noted, the Currie mission recommended basic changes in the original Colombian government plan for the integration of the railroad system and the linking of the rail system with the year-round navigable portions of the Magdalena River. The Currie mission's recommendation provided a link between the eastern and western systems without the building of the costly line across the mountains between Ibagué and Armenia. Also, the Currie mission's proposed line provided a more direct link between the industrial center of Medellín and year-round navigation to an Atlantic port. Finally, an important advantage of the railroad as constructed is to encourage the development of the rich agricultural lands of the lower Magdalena Valley. Recent studies have been made regarding the potentialities of this region and the large amount of unexploited land which the construction of the railroad, plus certain feeder highways, should help bring into commercial use for grazing or crops. It is worth noting that one of the areas designated for colonization under Colombia's land reform program, and financed in part by a loan from the DLF, is located in the Magdalena Valley along the new Atlantic Railroad line.

Studies were made by both the Lockwood engineering firm and by the consulting firm of Madigan-Hyland as to the relative costs per mile for hauling freight by rail as against river transport, and estimates were made of the volume of traffic which would be served by the proposed lines. An economic analysis of the proposed projects also had to take into account the expected diversion of traffic from existing transportation facilities, the projected expansion of total traffic with the growth of the area, and the impact of new transportation facilities on the development of certain areas. Naturally, there was room for differences in judgment regarding estimates of this type, and these were reflected in criticisms of the conclusions of the outside consultants by Colombian engineers and economists.

PROBLEMS ARISING DURING THE IMPLEMENTATION OF THE
LOAN PROJECTS

Mention has already been made of the fact that progress on the construction of the new Atlantic line was always behind schedule; the line required over eight years to complete instead of the four years originally contemplated. Moreover, actual work did not begin on the line until January, 1953, nearly three years following the submission of the Currie report. Some of the delay was due to unforeseen technical difficulties and changes in routing made necessary by conditions of the terrain. Much more significant, however, were the delays occasioned by political developments within Colombia and differences of opinion between Colombian engineers and the external consultants, which had certain political repercussions. There were also minor misunderstandings between the World Bank and local officials, but these did not appear to be especially serious. During the period between the signing of the first loan agreement with the World Bank and the completion of the line in late 1961, four governments were in power in Colombia, and local political disturbances were a frequent occurrence throughout the period. The Rojas Pinilla regime came into power through a *coup d'état* in 1953 and was overthrown in 1957, following which a democratically constituted government was installed. Whenever a new government comes into power, there is not only a break in continuity occasioned by the change in officials responsible for policy decisions, including the provision of funds for continued operations, but each new government also wants to review existing plans and initiate certain changes. In addition, local violence mainly in the form of attacks by bandits have at times been responsible for delays in construction operations.

The basic recommendations of the Currie mission for a railroad line paralleling the Magdalena River, as opposed to the government's earlier plans, occasioned considerable opposition even though the recommendations were accepted by the government in power in 1952. Opponents of the incumbent government argued against the substitution of rail for river transport or at least a duplication of facilities along the same route. Such criticism was largely, however, of an uninformed and prejudicial nature which tended to reflect political opposition to the government more than anything else.

More significant was the criticism of the reports of both the Lockwood and of the Madigan-Hyland consulting firms by the Colombian Society of Engineers.[6] The Lockwood report to the Bank with respect to the proposed route of the line was based mainly on aerial photographs. It was believed with some justification that the swampy, lake-studded terrain and its implications for construction costs had not been adequately considered by the consultants. When construction began, certain of the criticisms of the Colombian engineers proved to be correct. Partly as a consequence of the criticisms of the Lockwood report, the Bank requested an additional study and recommended that the Colombian government engage the Madigan-Hyland Company to prepare a report on the economic justification of the project before the loan application was approved. In addition, the Bank requested that the Colombian Congress formally approve the loan agreement with the World Bank, although at the time the government possessed discretionary power to negotiate such agreements, since the country was in a state of siege. This delayed completion of the loan negotiations, since the Congress did not approve the loan contract until late in 1952.

Another criticism of the project by Colombian engineers related to the projected amounts of freight which the new line was expected to handle and to the anticipated cost per ton-kilometer of the freight to be transported. The Madigan-Hyland report had forecast that by 1956 one million tons of freight would be transported annu-

[6] Sociedad Colombiana de Ingenieros, *Anales de Ingeniería* (Bogotá, Editorial Minerva, August–September, 1953), No. 641, pp. 122–48.

ally over the new road. This amount included the river cargo expected to be diverted to the railroad and imports coming through Buenaventura on the Pacific, and rerouted through the Atlantic ports. The consulting firm estimated that 80 percent of the freight in and out of Bogotá would be diverted to the new railroad. As it turned out, this estimation of the portion of the traffic diverted from other types of transportation was too high, and the expansion of traffic on the railroad must depend more on the growth of trade between the Magdalena Valley and other regions. The estimates of the cost per ton-kilometer of rail transport of the Lockwood consulting firm were substantially lower than those of the Colombian engineers, which, in turn, were based on experience under existing lines. Thus, while the Lockwood firm maintained that the new railroad could earn a profit on the basis of the same rates charged for waterborne traffic, the Colombian engineers predicted heavy losses for the new system. The fact is that the railroad system of Colombia has shown a loss in every year for which data are available, but this may have been a consequence of both inefficient management and inadequate rates.

Colombian engineering opinion is clearly shown in the following excerpt from the proceedings of their second annual convention in 1953:

But the most important point . . . is related to the studies on the economic justification of the Magdalena railroad made by the firms Lockwood and Madigan. These two studies are so erroneous and contradictory that what one can deduct logically from them is that the railroad along the Magdalena River should not be constructed.[7]

While it has been alleged that the opposition of the Colombian Society of Engineers to the reports of consulting firms arose mainly from the fact that the consulting firms were foreign, the critical views of the Society were of a technical nature, and, on some points, they apparently proved to be correct. Some members of the Society were convinced of the practicality of the project as recommended by the Currie mission, while others favored the original governmental proposal for the construction of the Ibagué–Armenia section and of the Barbosa–Bucaramanga line. Certainly, failure to obtain the World Bank loan for the construction of the line would have been

[7] *Ibid.,* p. 132.

harmful to the interests of Colombian engineers, since a number of Colombian engineering firms were employed for constructing various sections of the railroad.[8] Foreign companies were engaged mainly for the construction of bridges.

While the Colombian engineers' objections were mainly technical, they did provide ammunition for purely political attacks against the government in power at the time the first loan agreement was signed. Conceivably, some of this opposition might have been avoided had a well-known Colombian engineering firm been asked to participate in the preparation of the preliminary reports and to cooperate with the foreign consulting firms in ironing out any differences before the reports went to the World Bank and to the Colombian government.

Another problem which arose during the period of implementation of the loan agreements was the failure of the officials of the National Railway system to keep the Bank informed regarding the progress of the construction and of changes in plans with respect to the various projects which made up the total program which was financed jointly by the Bank and from governmental sources. Apparently this failure arose out of a misunderstanding on the part of the railway officials, who were under the impression that in providing information to and collaborating with the consulting firm of Madigan-Hyland, they were satisfying the requirements stipulated in the loan contract with the Bank. In other words, the railroad officials apparently did not distinguish between the consulting firm, which had been engaged upon the recommendation of the Bank, and the Bank itself. Close collaboration with the Bank, including the provision of adequate reports, was necessary, first, because the Bank disbursed loan funds only as they were needed for foreign exchange expenditures on commodities and services required by the program and, second, because the Bank's assistance was made available in the form of three separate loans, the second and third of which depended upon the successful carrying out of the previous loan agreements. This error in interpretation continued during the period covered by both the first and the second loans, and it was not until

[8] Before construction began in 1953, several Colombian concerns were commissioned to undertake portions of the work under a "cost-plus" arrangement. Later, in 1955, contracts were changed to a system of fixed contract prices.

application was made for the third loan that the problem of liaison and reporting between the railroads and the officials of the Bank was straightened out.

In the course of interviews with railroad officials acquainted with the implementation of the loans, it was apparent that the officials were often confused in consultations between officials sent by the Bank, on the one hand, and members of the consulting firms, on the other. In addition, many of the experts sent to Colombia were not familiar with the language, and misunderstandings arose because of having to converse through interpreters.

As a condition for the making of the third loan, the Bank recommended that the services of a reliable auditing firm be obtained to improve the accounting systems employed by the various sections of the road which were still not fully integrated. It has been reported that differences of opinion arose between the Colombian government officials and the financial consultants engaged for this purpose.

COLOMBIAN ATTITUDES TOWARD THE LOANS

Aside from the technical criticisms expressed by the Colombian Society of Engineers regarding the location of the railroad line recommended by the Currie mission and the cost estimate made by the Lockwood firm, certain additional critical attitudes were expressed by knowledgeable people who were interviewed. One respondent expressed the view that the Bank, in financing both highways and railroad transportation in Colombia, failed to take a comprehensive approach to the entire transportation problem and that there was some misallocation of capital resources involved in building both highways and improved or additional rail facilities over the same routes. It was suggested that the construction of secondary and feeder roads, which would link outlying areas to the railroads, would have been more beneficial and would have avoided costly duplication of facilities.

Certain criticisms were also expressed regarding the personnel of the consulting firms as well as the experts sent by the Bank. It was alleged that some of them showed little interest in becoming acquainted with the social and political conditions in the country and that their effectiveness was reduced because they could not speak the language. Also, many of the experts were in the country for only a short time, and by the time they had become reasonably acquainted with Colombian institutions and the individuals with whom they were working, they left the country for other assignments. Some respondents also questioned the high cost of the services of the consulting firms, which were believed to be out of line with the contributions made by them. These criticisms, however, did not imply that the railroad loans were not beneficial to the country, and even those who originally opposed the basic outlines of the plan for extending and reorganizing the National Railways system have now become reconciled.

ECONOMIC CONTRIBUTION OF THE RAILWAY LOANS

The major objectives of the loans, namely, the linking of the interior with a means of transportation to the Atlantic ports, usable throughout the year, and the integration and rehabilitation of the major railways systems, have been achieved. The conditions established by the World Bank in making the loans undoubtedly hastened improvements in management and operating efficiency as well as in accounting procedures. In addition, the insistence by the Bank on increases in rates charged for freight has reduced operating losses and hence the subsidies paid by the government to the railway system. On the other hand, the latest available figures show that the National Railways system is still "in the red," and, in addition, traffic has not expanded by the amount initially estimated by the consulting engineers. The railways are expected to start earning a net income by about 1967, after covering all costs including depreciation. Available records indicate that a somewhat smaller volume of traffic has been shifted from waterborne to rail transportation than had originally been estimated. In addition, the amount of local traffic generated by the construction of the line through the relatively undeveloped portions of the Magdalena Valley has not as yet achieved the estimated potential. The improved highways made possible in part by other World Bank loans have perhaps diverted some freight to highway trucking. In the case of passenger service, there has been a decline in both the number of passengers carried and the passenger-miles traveled over the Colombian railway system. This decline is probably due entirely to the increased motor vehicle traffic made possible by the improvement in the highway system and to the large expansion of airline traffic.

It is clear, therefore, that a full evaluation of the contribution of the railway loans can be assessed only by taking account of the developments in other forms of transportation. Such an assessment should also include an analysis of the relative costs in relation to benefits, direct and indirect, of the several types of transportation.

Balance-of-Payments Loans to Colombia, 1954–62 [9]

A large proportion of the public external loan disbursements to Colombia during the postwar period, perhaps over half if the most recent disbursements are included, has taken the form of balance-of-payments financing. By balance-of-payments loans, we mean loans made available for general use in financing imports of goods and services or for debt refinancing—as opposed to loans for financing specific projects or programs within a country and where there is close supervision of the use of the funds made available for the agreed purposes.[10]

This study deals with a series of balance-of-payments loans to Colombia over the period beginning with Colombia's first IMF credit in 1954, to the AID loan agreement of December, 1962, together with the circumstances which gave rise to the loans and their contribution to the solution of Colombia's economic and financial problems. Two things might be said at the outset regarding this study. First, Colombia's basic balance-of-payments problem is still

[9] By Raymond F. Mikesell, based on a case study prepared by Jorge Franco Holguín, Economic Consultant, Bogotá, Colombia.

[10] In most cases public external loans for specific projects are made available to finance only the imported components of the projects, and the funds are disbursed as foreign exchange is needed for commodities and services designed to implement the agreed projects. In some cases, however, all or a portion of the foreign loans are used for projects involving local currency expenditures. This was true, for example, in the case of the Development Loan Fund loans to the Instituto de Crédito Territorial and the Caja de Crédito Agrario. Even though the loan agreements provided that the dollar exchange be converted into pesos, however, the loan funds were made available only as needed for implementing the agreed projects or programs and under supervision by the lending agency. Thus, such loans should be regarded as project rather than balance-of-payments loans, even though the dollars made available in the first instance for conversion into pesos were free for payments to the United States for any purpose.

unsolved, and the government will undoubtedly continue to request, and probably receive, additional balance-of-payments loans. Second, Colombia's experience in recent years has by no means been unique in Latin America. A number of countries, including Argentina, Brazil, and Chile, have also received a high proportion of their external assistance in the form of balance-of-payments loans, and the factors surrounding their balance-of-payments difficulties include many of the same elements that are found in Colombia.

The following is a summary of the external public loan financing in the form of balance-of-payments loans received by or authorized for Colombia over the period 1954–62:

1. A series of standby credits from the IMF, of which $140 million had been drawn as of the end of February, 1963, and $40 million had been repaid.

2. Credits from the EXIMBANK of $60 million in July, 1957; $78 million in May, 1958; $25 million in November, 1959 (not drawn upon); and $44.9 million in May, 1961.

3. A $30-million loan from the AID early in 1962 and a second loan authorization of $60 million from AID in December, 1962.

In addition to the balance-of-payments financing from external public agencies, ninety-day acceptance credit liens totaling $30 million were made available by U.S. commercial banks in 1957 and renewed in 1958 and 1959, an additional $25 million in commercial bank credits was made available in 1958, and balance-of-payments loans by U.S. commercial banks totaling $44.9 million amortized over a three-year period were made available to the Banco de la República (Colombian central bank) in 1962. Since these commercial bank credits were negotiated on the basis of agreements reached with the EXIMBANK and other public agencies and were in some cases a part of a "package" arrangement involving both public and private credits or the refinancing of old ones, they cannot be separated from a history of public balance-of-payments financing.

It is not feasible to consider separately each of the balance-of-payments credits indicated above or the circumstances surrounding them, since in some cases two or more credits constituted a related package. Moreover, these credits cannot be considered properly outside of the context of Colombia's economic and financial history over the past decade. Consequently, we shall deal with the complex pattern of Colombia's external balance-of-payments financing mainly within the context of a functional and chronological description and analysis of Colombia's external financial developments since 1953.

While Colombia's balance-of-payments crises, which have led her to seek emergency or balance-of-payments financing from time to time, have usually been occasioned by an accumulation of commercial arrears and current debt service payments in excess of the country's ability to deal with them out of current earnings, inability to meet the commercial arrears or debt service payments, on the one hand, and external financing requirements for maintaining essential imports, on the other, cannot be separated. This is true, first of all, because the accumulation of commercial arrears reduces the willingness of foreign suppliers and financial institutions to extend new credits or turn over old ones and, second, because the necessity of meeting current indebtedness in order to avoid defaults and further impair the nation's credit would at times have necessitated a sharp cutback of imports. Since most imports involve credit transactions of varying maturities, the basic problem lies in the relationship between imports of goods and services, on the one hand, and exports and net long-term capital imports, including direct private investments, on the other. There is, in addition, the element of capital flight, but this is also heavily dependent upon what might be called the *basic* balance in the international accounts.

GENERAL ECONOMIC AND POLITICAL FACTORS

We may list the basic causes of Colombia's chronic balance-of-payments disequilibrium in recent years as follows:

1. The rapid industrialization directed almost entirely toward production for domestic consumption rather than production for export.

2. The slow growth of exports in relation to the rapidly expanding demand for imports which accompanied industrialization and investment in economic overhead projects.

3. A heavy dependence upon one major export commodity—coffee, the world price of which has been highly unstable.

4. A relatively small rate of inflow of long-term foreign capital.

5. Improper monetary, fiscal, and foreign exchange policies.

A full discussion of the structural factors in the pattern of Colombia's economic growth, including the direction of industrialization, the structural rigidities in agriculture which have resulted in low productivity and inelasticity of supply for the growing domestic market, and the failure to diversify exports, would lead us into a comprehensive analysis of the Colombian economy and its development, which is beyond the terms of reference of this study. Nevertheless, it should be kept in mind that these factors are basic to an understanding of Colombia's external disequilibrium and provide an explanation of why monetary and fiscal restraints have often been ineffective except over short periods of time, or have proved to be incompatible with economic growth.

THE INSTABILITY OF THE COFFEE MARKET DURING 1953–62

Paradoxically, Colombia's balance-of-payments crises beginning in 1957 to the present time have been in considerable measure a by-product of the period of relatively high coffee prices beginning in 1953 and ending with a sharp fall in the latter part of 1957. Coffee prices and, hence, export proceeds from Colombia's major export have shown chronic instability. During the immediate postwar years, this instability manifested itself in decreased plantings and cultivation as a result of the low prices prevalent during and immediately following World War II. These years of low planting led after a five-year period (the usual gestation period for coffee) to reduced output in 1953–54, which was further aggravated by the 1953 frosts in Brazil. Thus, the monthly average price for Colombian (Manizales type) coffee in the New York market rose from $0.56 per pound in April, 1953, to $0.91 in March, 1954, a rather significant rise if account is taken of the fact that a one-cent increase per pound of coffee means an increase of about $8 million in Colombia's export earnings.[11] Coffee prices declined from the high levels reached in the spring of 1954, falling to $0.60 in January, 1955, but they reacted strongly again, maintaining an average of around $0.70 during 1956 and the first eight months of 1957, following which they dropped to the levels of the first months of 1953 (around $0.54). Thereafter, they tended to decline to a low of $0.39 at the

[11] During the past four decades, coffee has accounted for between 60 and 80 percent of total export earnings of Colombia.

end of 1962. The signing of the International Coffee Agreement in September, 1962, had some steadying effect on coffee prices. While the coffee agreement prevented further decreases in coffee prices, which in the light of the long-run demand-supply situation were otherwise likely to decline further, a significant rise in prices to anything like the levels achieved in the mid-1950s is most unlikely.

POLITICAL AND ECONOMIC DEVELOPMENTS IN COLOMBIA, 1953-57

In 1953 Colombia was torn by civil strife between the two tradi-tional parties, the Liberals and the Conservatives, and the Conserva-tive government then in power was faced with almost insurmount-able difficulties in governing the country. The governmental crisis culminated in June 10, 1953, in a military *coup d'état*, and General Rojas Pinilla assumed dictatorial powers. The new regime had a favorable reception from the civilian population, which was weary of civil strife and welcomed the restoration of peace and order. Al-though economic conditions were quite favorable, the new govern-ment acted in a dictatorial manner and gravely mismanaged the economy of the country. Economic deterioration coupled with growing opposition to the harsh dictatorship led to the overthrow of the Rojas regime in May, 1957, by a new political movement under the leadership of Alberto Lleras Camargo, a member of the Liberal party. Lleras achieved a reconciliation with the Conservative party headed by Laureano Gomez, and after a transitional govern-ment by a military junta (June, 1957–August, 1958), Lleras was elected President under a new national front government.[12]

The principal shortcoming of the Rojas government on the eco-nomic side was its failure to adopt effective monetary and fiscal policies appropriate for dealing with the wide fluctuations in coffee prices over the 1953-57 period. The effect of the sharp rise in prices on the Colombian economy was already evident by the end of 1953. This was recognized by the then Minister of Finance, Carlos Villaveces, who stated that "as a result of the increase in coffee prices, coffee income has been increasing more than in other

[12] Under the new system of government the two parties collaborate in the cabinet and all offices of the state on a fifty-fifty basis. Alternation of the presidency is obligatory, and in 1962, once the Lleras term came to an end, a Conservative President, Dr. Guillermo Leon Valencia, acceded to power. The basic justification for this new system was to put an end to the civil strife.

activities and this might create disequilibrium. Besides, the balance of payments may show (by the end of the year) a surplus of 200 million pesos which might cause inflationary pressure." [13]

The failure to curb the excessive monetary demand during the period of high and rising receipts from coffee exports led to an increase in import demand which was accompanied by the government's abolition of the existing prohibited import list. Later on, the government sought to restrict imports of luxury goods, but it was not successful in preventing a level of import demand which not only fully utilized the increased foreign exchange earnings but gave rise to a very heavy backlog of commercial import indebtedness. That this happened during a period when Colombia's exchange earnings were the highest in history can only be explained by (1) the existence of fiscal and monetary policies which permitted a large expansion in monetary demand and (2) the willingness of foreign exporters and financial institutions to grant Colombian importers more credit than was warranted by the prospective economic condition of the country after taking account of its heavy dependence upon an unstable world market for coffee. In the light of the history of fluctuations in the price of coffee, economic policy in Colombia should have been directed toward the accumulation for foreign exchange reserves during this period of increased export earnings. Instead, Colombia's international reserves actually declined by $95 million in 1955. Imports were permitted to grow at an even faster rate than the rise in exports so that there were current account deficits financed mainly by accumulation of commercial arrears during the 1954–56 period in spite of the relatively high export earnings.

The accumulation of external commercial debt led the Rojas government to tighten exchange and import controls at the end of 1956 and the beginning of 1957. It would also appear that private capital flight took place on a considerable scale in 1957 and 1958. The adoption of restrictive import policies was a significant factor in the general popular movement for the overthrow of the Rojas regime. Fortunately, the transition to the new government was made without violence, but the military junta government inherited the serious economic and financial problems created in considerable

[13] Carlos Villaveces R., *Memoria de Hacienda 1954* (Bogotá, Imprenta Nacional, 1954), p. 111.

measure by the Rojas regime and made more difficult by sagging coffee prices.

ECONOMIC POLICIES OF THE MILITARY JUNTA—AUGUST 1957–58

The military junta government was faced with an extremely difficult economic situation. External coffee prices continued to decline (the average price for Manizales type in New York was $0.52 in 1958 as compared with $0.64 in 1957 and $0.74 in 1956), settlements on the commercial arrears had to be made, and a monetary and fiscal policy was needed in order to restore internal and external stability. Stock was taken of Colombia's external commercial arrears, and to everyone's surprise it was estimated to have amounted to about $490 million as of the beginning of 1957. About half of this amount arose out of the deficits incurred during the period 1954–57; the other half corresponded to the normal credits granted by foreign suppliers to Colombian importers. Since payments had been stopped at the end of 1956, the entire amount had to be negotiated before normal import credits could be reestablished. The repayment of this commercial debt, together with Colombia's deteriorating exchange position, forced the new government to take strong measures in the exchange field.

In June, 1957, the government approved two basic decrees: (1) Decree 105 authorized the government to negotiate loans with a view to refinancing the commercial backlog; (2) Decree 107 devalued the peso from the existing multiple exchange rates (2.50 pesos per U.S. dollar plus varying exchange taxes) to a single fluctuating selling (import) rate and a special coffee-buying (export) rate of 6.10 pesos per U.S. dollar minus a special new 15 percent tax. In addition, two distinct exchange markets were created, one for merchandise transactions at the official exchange rate indicated and another for invisibles, which was completely free at a fluctuating rate. The 15 percent tax on coffee exports, together with a new 10 percent tax on all remittances abroad, both to be paid in dollars, were destined to finance the repayment of the accumulated and consolidated commercial debt.

This new exchange policy was reinforced with the introduction of three import groups: a completely free list which included some basic capital goods and raw materials, a list of prohibited nonessential goods, and a list for which special licenses were required. In addition, prior import deposits (the amount depending on the relative need for the good to be imported) and strong monetary restrictions were imposed with a view to curbing import demand.

At this juncture not only the government but also public opinion was in favor of the new economic policy and particularly of consolidating and making arrangements for the repayment of the commercial debt. Serious negotiations for a settlement were therefore initiated, although some attempts had been made earlier.

SETTLEMENT OF THE COMMERCIAL DEBT

It is important to analyze the negotiations for the settlement of the commercial debt accumulated during the Rojas regime not only because they throw light on the financing problems of Colombia but also because they gave rise to the first balance-of-payments credits which the country received. These credits, however, were not confined to the settlement of the commercial debt, and other balance-of-payments loans will also be described and analyzed.

Since the commercial backlog had already become a serious problem by the end of 1956, the Rojas government took the first step for a settlement by approving Decree 10 of 1957, which authorized payment by the Banco de la República of the larger part of the commercial debt accumulated up to December 31, 1956. This was to be done by making a cash payment of 60 percent of the indebtedness and issuing negotiable promissory notes for the other 40 percent. These notes, which had a maturity of thirty months starting on April 1, 1957, at 4 percent interest, were registered with the U.S. Securities and Exchange Commission. Once the registration was approved, the first (60 percent) cash payments, amounting to $82 million, were made out of the foreign reserves of the Banco de la República. The first issue of the promissory notes was made in April, 1957, and payments proceeded satisfactorily to cover approximately $55 million.

Decree 10 of 1957 was important not only because it was the starting point in the settlement of the commercial debt but also because it converted purely private debts into public debts. Since the government and the Banco de la República undertook the repayment obligation, they required importers to pay the Colombian peso equivalent of their dollar import indebtedness to the Banco.

SPECIFIC SETTLEMENT ARRANGEMENTS

As time went by, the government, having undertaken the obligation to repay the commercial debt, made various types of settlements with different groups of creditors. On the basis of the authorizations granted by Decrees 10, 105, and 107, the following settlements were made:

Settlements through the Colombian Stabilization Fund.[14] Many Colombian importers had been authorized to obtain official foreign exchange but had not received it and therefore had paid foreign suppliers with free-market dollars. The Banco de la República decided to repay the pesos which the importers had used to buy the free-market dollars, thus canceling the claim the importers had on official exchange. In this way the Bank settled nearly $76 million, which in fact was not being claimed by foreign suppliers but rather by Colombian importers who had already made payments with funds acquired through the free exchange market at rates substantially higher than the merchandise import rate.

Settlement of Freight Charges. The same system described above for settlement of the debts for merchandise already paid with free dollars was employed for freight charges. Fifty percent of the freight charges was authorized for payment in official exchange, and where importers had paid the charges in free dollars, they were given the right to draw 4.95 pesos from the Stabilization Fund for each U.S. dollar equivalent of foreign exchange paid. In this way nearly $7 million in claims was settled.

Colombian Commercial Banks. Some Colombian banks had paid free dollars for imports for which they were entitled to obtain official exchange. Arrangements were made with five banks under

[14] The Stabilization Fund is an agency of the Banco de la República created by Law 7 of 1935. The basic object for which it was created was that of stabilizing government bond prices and intervening in the exchange market. During World War II it was given the function of administering German and Italian properties confiscated by the government. Later on other functions were assigned to the Fund such as administering the proceeds of prior deposits and financing departments and municipalities. These functions have now been transferred to the Banco de la República.

which a portion was paid immediately in dollars or pesos and the rest in installments.

Petroleum Companies. Authorizations for official exchange totaling approximately $22 million had accumulated in favor of the International Petroleum Company for imports of fuel, freight charges, and remittance of profits. Settlement was made by cash payment of $3.4 million and the remainder in forty-eight monthly dollar promissory notes of the Banco de la República.

Maritime Companies. A number of maritime companies were authorized to receive payments in official exchange for freight charges; settlements were made with these companies consisting of cash payments and promissory notes for the remainder.

Capital and Dividends. The arrears on capital and dividends of foreign enterprises for which official exchange had been authorized were settled: (1) with a 20 percent dollar cash payment and thirty-six monthly dollar promissory notes for the remaining 80 percent, (2) with a 20 percent dollar cash payment and 80 percent repayable in pesos at the 4.70 rate, and (3) 100 percent repayable in pesos at a 4.95 rate. In this way nearly $30 million was settled.

Settlement of European Debts. The following special settlements were made with European countries and firms:

Philips.—On October 18, 1957, an agreement between N.V. Philips Glocilampenfabricken and N.V. Philips Telecommunicatie Industrie, and Philips Colombiana S.A. and Industria Colombiana de Productos Eléctricos was entered into by which the debt of the Colombian firms for imports up to December 31, 1956, was fixed at approximately $22 million. The Banco de la República offered a special settlement of 20 percent cash in dollars and 80 percent in pesos at a rate of 4.70 pesos per U.S. dollar. This settlement was accepted.

Ericsson.—The debt with the Ericsson Company of Sweden was estimated in October, 1957, at $4.3 million, and the Banco de la República made a settlement with this firm providing for 20 percent payment in dollars and the rest to be paid by shipments of coffee to Sweden.

Sweden.—In November, 1957, a contract was signed between the Banco de la República and representatives of the Exporters Association of Sweden for the settling of arrears for imports received before May 1, 1957. Preliminary studies estimated the arrears at $4.8 million. The settlement consisted of a 20 percent cash payment in dollars and 80 percent in thirty-six monthly promissory notes which were issued with payments beginning in February, 1959, at 5 percent interest. The total amount settled came to nearly $3.3 million.

The Netherlands.—An agreement was signed between the Banco de la República and representatives of various Dutch banks by which debts in arrears were paid 20 percent in dollars and the rest (80 percent) in monthly promissory notes at 5 percent interest.

Other European Countries.—Similar arrangements were made with other European countries providing for 20 percent payment in cash and 80 percent in thirty-six monthly promissory notes. The settlements that were made are shown in Table 1.

TABLE 1

Colombian Settlements of
Commercial Debts with
Selected European
Countries

Country	*Date of Settlement*	*20 Percent Cash Payment, thousands of U.S. dollars*
Belgium	Dec. 2, 1957	3,896
England	Dec. 5, 1957	10,974
France	Dec. 5, 1957	4,616
West Germany	Dec. 19, 1957	12,486
Switzerland	Jan. 2, 1958	3,967

Latin America. Settlement of the arrears with Argentina, Brazil, Costa Rica, Cuba, Curacao, Chile, Panama, Peru, Dominican Republic, Trinidad, Uruguay, and Venezuela was made on a straightforward basis with 100 percent payment in cash by the Banco de la República. For debts of more than $1 million with Mexico, the 60 percent–40 percent plan was employed.

LOANS FROM THE EXPORT-IMPORT BANK, THE AGENCY FOR INTERNATIONAL DEVELOPMENT, AND U.S. COMMERCIAL BANKS

Since the Colombian effort to pay all the accumulated commercial debt referred to above was proving too heavy a financial burden and since a rapid rate of repayment would have reduced the already low exchange earnings available for imports, the Colombian authorities approached the EXIMBANK and U.S. commercial banks for financial assistance. Negotiations were initiated in the second half of 1957 by Martin del Corral, manager of the largest commercial bank in Colombia, representing the Colombian government. At first there was considerable resistance from the EXIMBANK and the private commercial U.S. bankers to financing a country which had accumulated such large commercial arrears and had followed such an unwise financial policy. As time went by, however, they became convinced that the drastic political change that had taken place in Colombia also meant a modification of its economic policy in the direction of financial responsibility. On that basis, and also in the belief that forcing the new government of Colombia to assume too heavy a financial burden might endanger the political transition and social stability, the EXIMBANK decided to grant the financing requested. On August 19, 1957, the EXIMBANK authorized a $60-million loan with an amortization period of four years at 5½ percent interest. A group of U.S. commercial banks granted credits up to $30 million for ninety-day acceptances at a 5 percent interest rate. These credit lines were renewed for nearly $26 million in 1958 and 1959 and finally canceled in 1959.

The main condition placed on disbursements of these loans related to the employment of the funds received. Of the $60-million EXIMBANK loan, $29.4 million was to be used to cover payments for imports made from January 1 to June 30, 1957, a period not covered by the 60 percent–40 percent debt settlement arrangements, $16.1 million was made available for a portion of the 60 percent cash payment, and the rest, $14.5 million, for redeeming the promissory notes used to settle 40 percent of the commercial arrears. The commercial bank loans were to be utilized, $23.3 million for the 60 percent cash payment and $6.7 million for payment of the (40 percent) promissory notes.[15]

In April, 1958, a high-level Colombian financial mission went to Washington to request additional balance-of-payments financing. Negotiations were initiated with the EXIMBANK without too much success, and diplomatic channels were used in which the mission im-

[15] New balance-of-payments loans were granted by U.S. commercial banks to the Banco de la República in 1962 for a total of US$44.9 million with an amortization period of three years and a 5¾ percent interest rate (three banks charged 6 percent).

pressed high U.S. officials of Colombia's urgent need for new balance-of-payments assistance in order to avoid an economic recession and grave social disturbances. Subsequently negotiations with the EXIMBANK proceeded somewhat better on a purely technical basis, and after a protracted period the Bank authorized a new balance-of-payments loan of $78 million (eight years, 5¾ percent interest) in June, 1958, which was in part a refinancing of the $60-million loan granted in 1957. An additional $25 million was provided by a group of U.S. commercial banks.

The basic condition on the utilization of the new EXIMBANK loan was that it be used for capital goods imports only, the Banco de la República having to submit a list to the EXIMBANK of the goods imported to the extent of $6.5 million per month.[16] Although this condition seemed sound, it did not necessarily change the total composition of Colombian imports, since the loan proceeds simply liberated for importing other goods funds which would otherwise have been used for capital goods imports.

In 1959 the Colombian authorities felt again the need for balance-of-payments assistance because the heavy repayments on the commercial debt reduced the country's exchange availabilities for essential imports. In addition, coffee prices continued to fall (averaging $0.4221 per pound as compared with $0.6394 per pound in 1957 and $0.5234 per pound in 1958). In view of these conditions, the Colombian government appointed a team composed of the Colombian Ambassador in Washington, the manager of the Banco de la República, and the Chief of the Planning Department to negotiate new balance-of-payments assistance with both the IMF and the EXIMBANK. The negotiations took a long while because a disagreement arose between the foreign lending agencies and the Colombian negotiators as to the amount that the country needed to maintain essential imports. In reality the disagreement centered around the problem of the internal effort the country should make in meeting its external debt out of its own resources.

After protracted negotiations, the International Monetary Fund authorized a standby credit for $41.25 million in October, 1959. This standby credit was not utilized in 1959 or 1960 and expired in

---

[16] Some difficulties arose in relation to the submission by the Banco of the monthly reports to the EXIMBANK.

October, 1960. A new standby of $75 million was granted in November, 1960, of which $65 million was utilized in 1961. Negotiations with the EXIMBANK came to a standstill because of the conviction of the Bank's officials that Colombia was not in need of further balance-of-payments assistance at that time. But in November, 1959, following the new standby agreement with the IMF, the Bank changed its position and authorized a $25-million credit (four years, 5½ percent interest, with payments to begin in January, 1964) to finance capital goods imports. This loan was granted on the condition that the IMF standby credit granted in the preceding month be utilized first. Since this basic condition was not fulfilled, the loan was never disbursed and was later canceled. Both of the credit lines served as an additional support to Colombia's credit position and undoubtedly influenced the financial policy of the country and the willingness of foreign suppliers to provide additional credits. An additional loan was authorized in 1960 as part of the $70-million social package loan in which the EXIMBANK provided $45 million and the DLF $25 million. This package was first authorized in August, 1960, with a preliminary allocation of funds for specific projects in the field of social development; the EXIMBANK funds were to be used for roads, municipal services, and agricultural machinery and the DLF funds for agricultural colonization and housing. Since the projects were not ready and the Colombian government insisted on using the funds for the financing of general imports, a new series of negotiations took place. In May, 1961, the Colombian view was accepted, and the EXIMBANK portion of the loan was converted into a balance-of-payments loan for financing imports. The peso counterpart of the loan was to be used for social projects, principally in the agrarian reform program. This loan, for $44.9 million, was to be used for capital goods imports, and had a five-year maturity and 5¾ percent interest with repayments to begin in August, 1963.

The $44.9-million loan of 1961 illustrates some of the basic issues in external financing to Colombia. The initative in requesting the social package loans was taken by the U.S. Ambassador to Colombia. The Ambassador, together with the head of the ICA mission and the chief of the Colombian Planning Office, negotiated the loans in Washington in quite a hurry because an OAS meeting was taking place in Bogotá (at which the Act of Bogotá was drafted), and the clear intention of both the U.S. and Colombian governments was to have the loan agreement announced before the meeting was to take place. In this sense it was a "political" loan, and since the uses for which it was initially destined were not clearly determined, it was not surprising that the terms of the loan were changed. The change in the character of the EXIMBANK portion of the loan was the work of the Colombian President, who, even though facing heavy opposition from the Colombian Congress for not utilizing the loan earlier, waited for the change in the U.S. administration that took place in 1961 in order to renegotiate the loan and achieve what he considered the country needed more than project financing, that is, balance-of-payments assistance.

The EXIMBANK has not granted further balance-of-payments assistance to Colombia. The country's requirements in this field, however, continued almost unchanged, and new negotiations were undertaken for further assistance (1962), this time between the newly created AID and the Banco de la República. Difficulties in these negotiations arose in relation to basic balance-of-payments data and the amount of assistance Colombia needed, so that AID decided to send (end of 1961) an expert to determine Colombia's balance-of-payments and external debt position and the amount of financing required for 1962. The expert worked in the Banco de la República in close collaboration with experts at the Banco. On the basis of this study, the Banco negotiated a $30-million loan which was authorized by AID early in 1962. The terms of this loan were very favorable (fifteen years, 3 percent interest rate), particularly in view of the still heavy repayments Colombia had to make on its balance-of-payments financing. It was fully utilized during 1962.

On the basis of that experience and more precise balance-of-payments estimates, a new balance-of-payments loan was requested from AID at the end of 1962 for the year 1963. The negotiations were undertaken with AID by the Colombian Ambassador in Washington with no serious difficulties, except that the conditions for the utilization were more stringent and specific than on previous occasions. Thus, under the loan agreement of December, 1962, it was provided that

The U.S. Agency for International Development would make available $30 million when Colombia's proposed exchange reforms were formally adopted, and another $30 million after steps are taken to carry out a fiscal and monetary stabilization program. These fiscal and exchange measures are expected to yield sufficient Colombian funds to help finance economic and social projects which will implement the nation's development plan. . . . Funds loaned by AID would finance imports of essential goods and services from the United States needed to support the planned high level of economic activity. Local currency generated by sale of the imports would be used to finance development, largely in the private sector.[17]

The new $60-million loan authorized by AID in December, 1962, embodied quite generous terms: amortization over forty years with a ten-year grace period and no interest charge except for a commission equal to ¾ percent. On the other hand, it was clear that AID intended to condition the disbursement of the funds on the achievement of specific fiscal and monetary and exchange reforms to be undertaken by the Colombian government. In this connection, mention was made in the AID press release announcing the loan authorization that on November 7, 1962,

The Colombian Congress received several measures intended to help the country move forward in its self-help development program. These measures would permit taxes on certain products and revise the inheritance tax. The pending tax measures would increase Colombian government revenue by the equivalent of $100 million per year.

This reference to measures pending in the Colombian Congress was apparently designed to serve notice on the Colombian Congress that the availability of the second $30 million would depend upon the enactment of these measures.

INTERNATIONAL MONETARY FUND BALANCE-OF-PAYMENTS FINANCING

The second major source of Colombia's balance-of-payments financing after the U.S. government (EXIMBANK and AID) has been the International Monetary Fund. By the end of 1954, when the coffee price declined slightly from its all-time high in March of that year, the Colombian authorities, seeing that a more than normal backlog of debt was accumulating, requested a drawing from the International Monetary Fund for $25 million to cover a portion of the import indebtedness. It is surprising that the Fund decided to grant

[17] See Agency for International Development, Press Release 110, Dec. 19, 1962.

this loan at a time when Colombia had an abundance of foreign exchange and when there was so much financial mismanagement. Probably the reason behind the Fund's decision was that it believed that by granting the credit it could exercise some influence on Columbia's financial policies.

In June, 1957, shortly after the Rojas government was overthrown, the IMF granted a standby credit of $25 million to Colombia, of which $5 million was utilized in 1957 and another $10 million in 1958; the remainder was not utilized. It is important to note, however, that the agreement with the IMF regarding Colombia's stabilization program, which constituted the condition for the $25-million standby credit, was an integral part of the arrangement under which the $60-million EXIMBANK credit, together with the $30 million in acceptance credits provided by U.S. commercial banks in 1957, was authorized. As has already been noted, a new standby agreement was entered into with the Fund in October, 1959, for $41.25 million, followed shortly by a credit of $25 million from the EXIMBANK. Neither this standby credit nor the $25-million EXIMBANK credit was utilized. The utilization of the EXIMBANK credit was conditioned on a prior utilization of the October, 1959, IMF credit. Since Colombia's official gold and foreign exchange reserves declined rather sharply during 1960, it is surprising that the standby credit of October, 1959 (and consequently the $25-million EXIMBANK loan), was not used. This was presumably because of some disagreement between the IMF and the Colombian government over the carrying out of the stabilization agreement with the IMF.

In November, 1960, a new standby agreement for $75 million was reached with the IMF, of which $65 million was utilized during 1961. This standby agreement expired in November, 1961, but a new standby credit of $10 million was arranged in January, 1962, $7.5 million of which was utilized in 1962. In January, 1963, another standby agreement was reached with the Fund amounting to $52.5 million, of which $27.5 million was utilized early in 1963. It is quite likely that the understanding between the IMF and the Colombian government, which accompanied the January, 1963, standby agreement, was related to the agreement under which the $60 million in AID funds, authorized in December, 1962, was to be utilized.

The economic situation of Colombia deteriorated sharply in 1962 owing to a relaxation of the strict monetary policy. The IMF called the attention of the authorities to the deterioration that was taking place on a number of occasions but was only partially heeded. By October, 1962, once the transition to a new national front government (conservative) had taken place, it became apparent that an "agonizing reappraisal" was urgently needed. The government then proceeded to take the necessary measures: it devalued the currency, consolidated the fiscal deficits of 1961 and 1962 which it had financed through the Banco de la República, and applied a rigid control on private bank credit.

The Fund missions advised the government on the new economic policy adopted but were only partially successful. While the exchange, fiscal, and monetary policies were in general well oriented, they were largely offset by a general wage increase decreed by the Congress. In addition, prices began to increase rapidly even before the November, 1962, devaluation owing to excess liquidity and the budget deficits. It seemed, however, that there was no other way open for the government.

The IMF has imposed rather stringent conditions on the standby credits granted to Colombia. Before signing a standby agreement, the country has to accept a financial program under which the exchange, monetary, and, to some extent, fiscal policies are clearly delineated. The aim has been monetary stability and exchange unification, but performance has nearly always fallen somewhat short of these objectives. It has been extremely difficult to follow the standby programs closely in view of an explosive social and political situation.

Drawings of dollars and other foreign exchange under the standby credits are subject to repayment (repurchase) if and when the international reserves of the Banco de la República increase and, if this is not the case, three years after the original purchase operation. The interest charges increase with the length of time the credit is outstanding.

ECONOMIC CONTRIBUTIONS OF THE LOANS

The principal contribution of the balance-of-payments credits from the EXIMBANK, U.S. commercial banks, the IMF, and AID was to enable Colombia to refinance a large accumulation of commercial arrears totaling about $490 million at the beginning of 1957 and to make repayments on both the commercial arrears and the loans specifically contracted to finance the commercial debt settlements, totaling nearly $390 million from the beginning of 1957 through October, 1961. Since most of the external financing received was either short-term or intermediate-term (up to eight years' maturity), the vast bulk of the net repayments over the period 1957–61 was, in fact, financed out of export earnings and indirectly by capital imports made available for financing imports of goods and services.

The net impact of the debt repayments on import capabilities is somewhat difficult to determine. This is true, first, because of the erratic behavior of Colombia's official gold and foreign exchange reserves, which rose from $131 million at the end of 1956 to $212 million at the end of 1959, declining again to $149 million at the end of 1961, and, second, because it is difficult to distinguish external financing made available specifically for commercial debt retirement and other external financing (much of it of a balance-of-payments variety), which was made available in order to help Colombia maintain essential imports in the face of a combination of declining proceeds from coffee exports and the debt payments. Colombia's merchandise imports declined sharply from the level of $657 million in 1956 to $416 million in 1958–59, but rose again to $557 million in 1961, thereafter declining to $492 million in 1962. The behavior of Colombia's merchandise imports has not, however, followed the pattern of her merchandise exports, especially since 1958. In recent years the pattern of imports has been affected not only by export earnings, debt repayments, and new capital imports but also by new commercial indebtedness, which had risen to $236 million by December, 1962. This level of commercial indebtedness is by no means negligible when compared with the annual rate of Colombia's imports and its holdings of gold and foreign exchange reserves, which amounted to about $120 million at the end of 1962.

Apart from the new commercial indebtedness, Colombia's debt-service obligations, including interest and principal on both public loans and old commercial indebtedness, appear to have been reduced to manageable proportions. Fortunately, the two loans made by AID during 1962 (especially the $60-million loan authorization of December, 1962) provide for very generous repayment terms and will not constitute a significant burden on Colombia's balance of payments.

An important question with respect to the repayment of the commercial arrears and the assistance provided from external sources is whether Colombia undertook too heavy a burden in repaying the bulk of the accumulated debt within a period of less than five years. As has already been mentioned, the actual burden on import availabilities of the debt refinancing and repayment is difficult to determine, but a rough estimate for the period of 1957–61 is an average of $75 million a year. This is not a negligible amount for a country with average yearly exports of about $450 million. Two alternative courses would have been open to Colombia in dealing with the debt. One would have been to impose much stiffer terms on the creditors, say, requesting them to accept ten-year promissory notes for the entire debt. The other alternative would have been to obtain long-term external financing, involving loans with maturities of ten or fifteen years. The former alternative would have greatly impaired Colombia's national credit standing, with consequent effects upon both direct foreign investment and ability to obtain long-term capital. At the same time, Colombia would have been forced to take measures to maintain imports within current foreign exchange availabilities, plus what she might receive in the form of project loans from external assistance agencies. The second alternative, that of providing Colombia with sufficient long-term financing to pay off accumulated commercial arrears, would have virtually eliminated the ability of public external financing institutions to bring pressure on Colombia to establish monetary and fiscal reforms. In addition, increased confidence given to foreign suppliers would have enabled Colombia quickly to reconstitute an even higher level of commercial indebtedness.

Whatever may be said about the contribution of the external loans for refinancing Colombia's commercial indebtedness and the provision of additional balance-of-payments loans to enable her to maintain imports in the face of declining export proceeds, it is clear that Colombia's basic balance-of-payments problem is far from solution, either in the short run or, more particularly, over the long run. It might even be argued that the balance-of-payments assistance given Colombia has delayed actions which might have been taken for dealing with the more deep seated structural problems in Colombia's economy, of which the balance-of-payments deficits are but one manifestation.

On the other hand, it can be argued with equal cogency that constructive reforms are not likely to take place in an atmosphere of social and political chaos. The basic solution of Colombia's balance-of-payments problem is bound up with broad development policy and development planning. The revenue system must provide income to meet growing costs of government and to provide local currency for public investments. Excessive credit must not simply be restrained, but new credits plus funds derived from savings and from capital imports must be directed into private and public investments which have the highest priorities for the achievement of Colombia's development goals. This aim, along with encouragement and mobilization of domestic savings, can be achieved only by reasonable price stability and the avoidance of price disparities which lead to a misallocation of investment resources.

Finally, new sources of export earnings must be promoted, and this can only be achieved if the Colombian authorities provide at least the same incentives as those granted to import substitutes, often for less essential or upper-middle-class goods. Moreover, those industries which are designed to produce import substitutes should be those in which Colombia has some comparative advantage, perhaps arising from the use of local materials or the relative abundance of labor. Thus, the adoption of a policy for promoting exports and reorienting import substituting industries is imperative for both a solution of the long-run balance-of-payments problem and the achievement of self-sustaining growth.

ATTITUDES TOWARD THE BALANCE-OF-PAYMENTS LOANS

As has already been mentioned, the commercial debt settlement arrangements and the negotiation of external assistance for this purpose, beginning with June, 1957, coincided with the transition period from the overthrow of the Rojas dictatorship to the restoration of a democratic government. While the restrictive policies forced on the Rojas government by the deteriorating balance-of-payments situation in late 1956 and early 1957 brought further resentment against the government and contributed to its overthrow, the austerity policies adopted by the military junta and later by the Lleras government, which came to power in August, 1958, were accepted and understood. Thus, the new government was able to convince the public that the misguided policies of the dictatorship had created conditions which made it imperative that the country tighten its belt so that the legacy of debt and general financial mismanagement could be liquidated. It was also understood that since the dictator had squandered valuable foreign assets during the coffee boom, imports had to be restricted during the period of declining coffee prices. Somewhat harder to accept in some circles was the necessity of the sharp devaluation which occurred in 1957.

After a time, however, it became more difficult for the public to accept austerity measures by placing the blame on the overthrown dictator. The government has had to contend with strikes and various demonstrations of discontent, as it has sought to apply restrictive measures. There has been some resentment by more knowledgeable people against the IMF and the U.S. government for requesting fiscal and monetary restraints as a condition for loans. There is also apparently some feeling that the conditions attached to the loans, together with their relatively short maturities, "forced" Colombia to pay a large proportion of its accumulated indebtedness with its own resources. It is true, of course, that the first $60-million loan from the EXIMBANK (1957) was granted under the condition that the funds could be used only for payments to U.S. exporters on the basis of a plan whereby 60 percent of the commercial indebtedness was to be paid in cash and 40 percent in promissory notes of rather short maturities. On the other hand, the basic settlement plan and negotiations for settlements with various external creditors were decisions of the Colombian government itself, and, in its loan application, it requested assistance from the EXIMBANK for implementing these settlements. There is no evidence that either the U.S. government or the IMF dictated the terms of Colombia's commercial debt settlement arrangements. The only thing that could be said is that the first loan of $60 million from the EXIMBANK had a rather short maturity, but the following year a loan of $78 million was provided, partly to refinance the 1957 loan, and this loan not only provided for repayments over 5½ years but the first payment was not due until December 1, 1961.

It still might be argued, of course, that the burden of heavy re-payments of the commercial arrears over the period 1957–61 could have been avoided by larger external refinancing loans with quite long maturities and low or no rates of interest, such as the AID credit authorization of December, 1962. This alternative, however, gets us back to the basic question of the kinds of policies that the Colombian government would have followed had it not been under considerable pressure both because of the heavy debt payments and the continued needling by IMF officials, and perhaps by the EXIM-BANK as well, to live up to the terms of the stabilization agreements. But the argument that the settlement agreements, together with the terms of financial assistance, held back Colombia's development, since they reduced exchange availabilities for capital goods and other essential imports, must be qualified on two grounds: rather generous balance-of-payments assistance, apart from the loans specifically designed to finance commercial arrears, were provided, and there is no guarantee that a higher level of imports would have promoted a higher rate of growth.

If a criticism can be made of the IMF and other external assistance authorities during the period 1957–61, it is that they placed too great emphasis on monetary and fiscal restraints as the basic means of dealing with Colombia's balance-of-payments difficulties, rather than on fundamental structural changes and the reorientation of investment and foreign trade policy along the lines suggested above. The agreement of December, 1962, between AID and the Colombian government, together with the other self-help provisions of the Punta del Este Charter, appear to give greater emphasis to the structural factors which are basic to the long-run solution of Colombia's balance-of-payments problem.

*External Financing for the Modernization of the
Chilean State Railways System* [18]

This study is concerned mainly with the negotiations relating to a loan by the EXIMBANK of Washington to the Chilean State Railways Company (Empresa de Ferrocarriles del Estado). While plans had

[18] By Raymond F. Mikesell, based on a case study by Carlos Hurtado, prepared at the Instituto de Economía, University of Chile, Santiago.

been formulated for the modernization of Chile's railroad system in the early 1940s, and efforts to obtain public international financing credit were initiated in 1956, formal negotiations with the EXIMBANK did not begin until the fall of 1960; and on November 10, 1960, the EXIMBANK authorized $30 million to finance a portion of Chile's program of railroad rehabilitation. The actual loan agreement was not signed, however, until August 1, 1961, and provided for a credit of $20 million, the proceeds of which covered the purchase of diesel locomotives and parts ($13 million), rolling stock ($2 million), track renovation ($2 million), communications ($900,000), and miscellaneous equipment ($2.2 million).

This loan is of special interest because of the multiplicity of sources from which the Chilean railways company sought—and, in some cases, actually obtained—external financing for the modernization of their railroad system and also because it provides an illustration of a loan by a public financing institution which was motivated by the desire both to assist U.S. exporters and to provide development assistance to Chile. Most of the negotiating problems arose out of the EXIMBANK's interest in promoting U.S. exports rather than from conditions imposed on the borrowing institution with respect to such matters as the soundness of the railroad rehabilitation plan, the rates charged for transport services, or the organization and financing of the borrowing institution.

THE CHILEAN RAILWAYS SYSTEM

Chile is united by a railroad system, most of which is operated by the Chilean State Railways, which extends from Iquique in the north to Puerto Montt in the southern part of the country.[19] Chile's railway network takes the form of a north-south line paralleling the Pacific Ocean, with branches extending on either side of the principal trunk line. In the northern part of the country, the lines developed principally as a means of transporting minerals to the seaports, and it was not until the 1920s that these east-west lines were united by a longitudinal line for the purpose of facilitating internal trade in the northern part of the country. In the case of the railroad lines

[19] There are several railway lines in both the extreme northern and southern portions of the country which are outside of the integrated network. Among these is the Chilean portion of the railroad line from Arica on the Pacific Coast to La Paz, Bolivia.

south of Santiago, development took a different pattern. The longitudinal line was extended south, uniting the capitals of the various provinces with Santiago and the port city of Valparaíso, while the east-west branches were added bit by bit as appendages to the longitudinal line. Thus, the development of the railroad network south of Santiago tended to respond more to the needs of internal commerce, while development in the north was largely export-oriented. The Chilean railroad network developed piece by piece almost without interruption from the middle of the nineteenth century until 1945, after which only small additions to the routes were made. It is one of the best systems in South America but has undergone considerable deterioration since World War II. Moreover, the trend for the future should be a gradual elimination of certain portions of the network which carry little traffic and where highway transportation is more economical.

Presently the length of first line track in operation is nearly 9,000 kilometers, of which more than 6,500 kilometers is operated by the Chilean State Railways and another 1,044 is also government-owned. Approximately half of the trackage lies south of La Calera (a city near the coast somewhat north of Santiago); the southern portion of the network serves the most populous portion of the country and is the most important part of the system. The most important private railroad is the Antofagasta and Bolivian Railway, Ltd., which owns 10 percent of the total trackage. Other private railways are owned principally by the mining companies.[20] Although the bulk of the railway lines are operated by the Chilean State Railways, the network is by no means integrated. For example, most of the traffic north of La Calera goes on 1-meter gauge lines, while the main trunk line to the south is 1.676-meter gauge. There is comparatively little interchange between the northern and the southern sections. In addition, many of the branches on the southern system have a gauge which differs from that of the main trunk line. Until recently at least, most of the locomotives and rolling stock were antiquated, and renovation of the rails and the roadbed, as well as modernization of the signaling equipment, was urgently required for efficient service.

[20] For more detailed information, see Merwin L. Bohan and Morton Pomeranz, *Investment in Chile* (Washington, D.C., U.S. Department of Commerce, 1960), pp. 194–98.

In addition to the need for modernization and standardization of equipment and rolling stock, the Chilean State Railways had been faced with serious economic and administrative problems. Owing to the lack of adequate highways, the railroads had an almost complete monopoly on overland transportation up to the end of World War II and operated without losses. A substantial degree of governmental interference with respect to the rate structure, the type of service rendered, and the selection and promotion of personnel has contributed to high costs, and, since 1945, there has been an inability to compete with highway and air transportation. Even though the general level of rates charged has not kept up with the rising costs as a consequence of inflation, the rate structure has tended, until recently, to be a function of the value of the product, so that industrial products paid a rate per ton-kilometer substantially higher than that paid by agricultural and forestry products. Thus, truckers were able to compete favorably with the railroads for high-valued goods, not only because of lower rates but because they could provide faster and more flexible door-to-door service. Therefore, the railroads found themselves in the position of hauling the bulk of their cargo at rates which did not cover average costs. They also lost much of their passenger traffic to buses for short and medium distances and to the airplanes for long-distance transportation, especially in the case of passengers who previously had used first-class and sleeper accommodations on the railways. The railways also inherited a system designed in some cases to serve regions of low traffic density with branches and a large number of railway stations along the lines. Once lines and stations had been established, it was politically difficult to abandon them. Also, the fact that many branches on the southern system have a gauge different from that of the main line has led shippers to use highway transportation for moving their goods either to the main line or all the way to their final destination.

While the Chilean State Railways enterprise is authorized by its basic legislation to establish rates sufficiently high to compensate for its expenses, in practice, political pressures on the government, which must approve the rates, against raising rates and against reducing costs through the elimination of featherbedding and of uneconomical lines, stations, and passenger service in certain areas have resulted in large deficits which constitute a heavy drain on the national budget. In spite of rapidly rising costs, nominal freight rates were actually held constant between 1959 and 1962. Nevertheless, the State Railways on their own initiative actually decreased rates through reclassification of product categories and by making special agreements with certain shippers so as to confront sharply increased truck competition. Increased truck competition with traditional railway traffic has been the principal element in increasing railway losses since the end of World War II. In general, the State Railways have tried to maintain their historical position by cutting rates rather than by eliminating uneconomical services. The poor financial condition of the railway system in turn has made it difficult to obtain funds for improvements and modernization which would have lowered costs and bettered its competitive position.

PLANS FOR MODERNIZATION OF THE RAILWAYS

Beginning with 1946, proposals were made to the government either by the Chilean State Railways or governmental commissions for the rehabilitation and modernization of the railway system. For the most part these proposals were not acted upon, but in 1953–54 the Ministry of Agriculture and the Chilean Development Corporation (CORFO) prepared an eight-year agriculture and transport development program. [21] The railroad portion of this plan provided for an investment of $127 million (about equally divided between local currency and foreign exchange expenditures) and contemplated the electrification of the route between Santiago and Chillán (406 kilometers of the main trunk line to the south) and the route between Santiago and Cartagena on the coast. The plan also included expenditures for track renovation, signal equipment, and rolling stock. On the basis of this plan, the Chilean government in 1956 sought a credit from the World Bank for financing of a broad program for the development of both agriculture and transportation, including railroads, highways, water shipping, and ports. Presumably, the World Bank was approached for assistance in financing this elaborate eight-year plan, since the plan was prepared during 1953

[21] See *Agriculture and Transportation Development Program* (Santiago, Ministerio de Agricultura y Corporación de Fomento de la Producción, 1954), two vols. (mimeo.).

and 1954 as a direct consequence of the recommendations of a mission organized by the World Bank and the UN Food and Agriculture Organization.[22] Negotiations with the World Bank did not result, however, in any loans being made either for transportation or agriculture on the basis of this plan. This was not because the Bank was not interested in lending to Chile at that time. The World Bank made a loan to a Chilean public power company (Endesa) on November 1, 1956, and two loans to private coal mining firms on July 24, 1957, all of them through CORFO. Unlike Endesa, whose operations have been relatively free from politics, the Chilean State Railways could not come to terms with the Bank, perhaps because the Bank took the position that, until substantial changes were made in the organization and management of the railways which would make the system relatively independent of political influences, it would be unwilling to consider loan applications.

In the absence of public international credits, the Chilean State Railways, faced by the urgency of modernizing its operations, contracted with a group of Italian firms in 1957 for the electrification of the road from Santiago to Chillán, and private supplier's credits were provided for the initiation of the project. With the assumption by Jorge Alessandri of the presidency early in 1959, the government took a renewed interest in the problem of the railways, both because the large subsidies interfered with the government's financial stabilization plan and because a more efficient railway system constituted an important aspect of the government's development program for the economy. This concern led to the formation of a governmental transport commission in April, 1959, charged with the duty of preparing an investment program for all transport media. The Minister of Economy and Finance, Roberto Vergara Herrara, requested that the State Railways prepare a draft investment program to cover the period 1960–64, in part because of the expectation of receiving foreign credits for the railways.

The program drafted by the State Railways was announced by the President of the Republic in a radio address in September, 1959, and was included in a statement by Vergara to the Chilean Congress in October of that year. This original program was analyzed closely

[22] See Mission's Report, *The Agricultural Economy of Chile* (mimeo.), December, 1952.

by the government's transport commission. It was modified extensively in a revised version prepared by the State Railways in August, 1960. It was this modified draft which was presented by the State Railways to the EXIMBANK in the fall of 1960 as the basis for a loan application. The final report of the government's transport commission was not completed until January, 1961, and was published in June, 1961, as a part of the Ten-Year Development Plan of CORFO. This latter plan was a reduced version of that given to the EXIMBANK but was nevertheless criticized by the World Bank Mission, which examined the Ten-Year Development Plan, as being too ambitious.

SUMMARY OF THE CHILEAN STATE RAILWAYS INVESTMENT
PROGRAM OF 1960 [23]

The modernization and rehabilitation plan for the Chilean State Railways, which accompanied the application for a loan from the EXIMBANK, provided for six basic categories of expenditures (see Table 2). The categories included: (1) the electrification of certain portions of the network; (2) the replacement of steam engines with diesels in certain other portions; (3) the renovation of the road, which involved the acquisition of rails, the importation of machinery for strengthening the roadbed, and substantial installation expenditures; (4) the acquisition of new rolling stock for both freight and passenger service; (5) the acquisition and installation of new signal and communications equipment; and (6) a variety of other types of equipment which do not fit into the categories above.

The total foreign exchange costs estimated in the plan amounted to $99 million, while the local currency expenditures were estimated at 109.8 million escudos, or a total of 213.9 million escudos in all (equivalent to $203.2 million U.S. at the then current rate of 1.053 escudos to one U.S. dollar). The investment plan was to be com-

[23] The most recent investment plan for the Chilean Railways is contained in the comprehensive Ten-Year Development Plan for Chile, completed in 1961 and reviewed by the OAS Panel of Experts. It is not the same as that presented in August, 1960, by the Chilean State Railways to the EXIMBANK, although there are a number of features in common. The Ten-Year Plan takes into account the relationship between railway investment and other forms of transportation, including highways and their relationship to other aspects of the development program for Chile. See *Programa Nacional de Desarrollo Económico, 1961–1970*, Corporación de Fomento de la Producción, Santiago.

pleted in six years beginning in 1960, at an average annual rate of 35 million escudos per year.

TABLE 2

Plan for Modernization of Chilean State Railways:
Principal Categories of Expenditures

	Foreign Exchange Expenditures, millions of U.S. dollars	Local Currency Expenditures, millions of escudos	Total,* millions of escudos
Electrification	38.2	12.5	52.6
Dieselization	18.8	. . .	19.8
Route renewal	19.2	43.6	63.8
Rolling stock	9.8	46.0	56.3
Signals and communications	9.2	7.2	16.9
Other equipment and machinery	3.8	0.5	4.5
Total	99.0	109.8	213.9

* In 1960, at the time this plan was presented to the EXIMBANK, the value of the escudo was 1.053 escudos to the U.S. dollar.

Source: Ferrocarriles del Estado, Santiago.

Although the total six-year investment plan was presented by the railroad officials to the EXIMBANK, the actual application for an EX-IMBANK credit was for only $30 million, or less than one-third of the estimated foreign expenditures. In part, this was because other sources of credit for large portions of the program had already been arranged for. For example, the electrification of the Santiago–Chillán road and the renovation of the equipment for the line between Santiago and Valparaiso (totaling $23.4 million) had already been contracted with a consortium of Italian firms, and the acquisition of rails ($15.7 million) had been negotiated with Japanese firms. While this still left $60 million out of the $99 million of foreign exchange expenditures to be covered under the entire plan, there was evidently not complete agreement within the government regarding certain portions of the plan, so that the request from the EXIMBANK was scaled down to $30 million. For example, that part of the plan which provided for the electrification of sections of the railroad south of Chillán, involving a foreign exchange outlay of over $13 million, was abandoned. It is also evident that some parts of the plan for the Chilean State Railways were under review by CORFO and other government agencies engaged in the preparation of the Ten-Year Development Plan for Chile. For example, passenger service on many portions of the line might well be abandoned in favor of bus transportation; such a program would reduce the requirements for coaches.

HISTORY OF NEGOTIATIONS WITH THE EXPORT-IMPORT BANK

Discussions with international lending agencies on the basis of the 1960 investment plan for the Chilean State Railways were conducted early in the fall of 1960, even before the completion of the studies by the Commission which had been designated to formulate the development plan. In addition to the strong interest of President Alessandri in dealing with the problems of the Chilean State Railways, considerable initiative was taken by Roberto Vergara Herrera, the Minister of Economy and Finance, both in promoting the modernization program for the State Railways Company and in seeking international credits for this purpose as early as 1959. In the United States, the Chilean government was represented in the negotiations by the Chilean Ambassador, Walter Muller, and a representative of the Chilean State Railways Company in New York, Enrique Barraza.

On August 31, 1960, the director of the Chilean State Railways sent Barraza a memorandum which contained the fundamental elements of the modernization plan, as a basis for discussions with international credit institutions in Washington. Copies of this document were transmitted to the EXIMBANK, the World Bank, and the DLF. Apparently, discussions were first undertaken by the Chilean Ambassador and Barraza with the DLF, in the course of which they expressed to the director, Vance Brand, their desire to obtain from the DLF financing for certain equipment and construction expenditures in Chile. They were told by Brand that the DLF could not finance the local currency expenditures and, furthermore, that the DLF would consider the financing of purchases of equipment in the United States only in cases where hard-loan sources of financing, such as the World Bank and the EXIMBANK, were unavailable.

In the course of the initial discussions with the World Bank, the Chilean representatives sought refinancing for the credits which had been made available by the consortium of Italian firms. This was impossible, since it is a firm policy of the Bank not to provide refinancing for old indebtedness. The World Bank did, however, express an interest in considering financing for the modernization program, but not without a thorough study of the State Railways development plan in relation to the general transportation requirements and plans of Chile. Had discussions with the World Bank gone further, the Bank undoubtedly would have also concerned itself with the level and schedule of transport rates and fiscal deficits and perhaps, in addition, with the management and administrative independence of the Chilean State Railways. Since the Chilean State Railways corporation was not concerned with or prepared to wait for a thorough examination by the World Bank of the relationship between the railway modernization plan and Chile's transport system as a whole and, in addition, the Chilean government perhaps wanted to avoid lengthy negotiations regarding loan conditions relating to rates, deficits, and management, discussions with the World Bank terminated in favor of those with the officials of the EXIMBANK...

Negotiations with the EXIMBANK moved quite rapidly, and, in fact, the Bank requested a specific loan application for its consideration shortly after inquiries had been made, evidently sooner than the Chilean representatives had expected. While political considerations may have played some role in the haste with which the Bank acted in announcing the credit authorization, it is more likely that the Bank was motivated primarily by the desire to promote U.S. exports and by considerable pressures from U.S. equipment firms. The EXIMBANK had been making generous credits available to Chile during 1960, including a $10-million earthquake reconstruction loan of May 27, 1960, a $15.6-million loan of August 18, 1960, to the Pacific Steel Company, a $42-million credit authorization of October 6, 1960, to a Chilean power company, and, shortly following the credit authorization for the railways, a $15-million balance-of-payments loan on January 19, 1961. In the light of this history, it is difficult to conclude that a quick decision on the railway loan was necessary for a special political impact at a critical moment, although there was certainly a desire on the part of the U.S. government to support the Alessandri regime on general grounds and because of its economic stabilization efforts, which had been hampered by the severe earthquake in the spring of that same year.

U.S. corporations hoping to benefit by a credit to Chile, including General Electric, General Motors, and other producers of railway engines and equipment, were well aware of the intention of the Chilean State Railways to seek financing for their modernization program before any approach was made to the EXIMBANK. In fact, the State Railways Corporation had issued tenders for bids for diesel locomotives and other equipment, including signaling equipment, in advance of their approach to the EXIMBANK. Thus, the Bank had received numerous inquiries from U.S. exporting firms after the Chilean tenders were out, and the Bank had a definite desire to assist the exporters in obtaining large orders from the Chilean State Railways. Of course, this could have been dealt with on the basis of exporter credits, but such credits tend to have shorter maturities, and, in the absence of a large project loan arrangement, the Chilean State Railways might well have purchased more of their equipment elsewhere. In fact, this was what had happened in the case of the electrical equipment which was obtained from the Italian firms in 1957 and of the rails from the Japanese firms early in 1960. In addition, following the earthquakes of May, 1960, several European governments offered long-term credits on liberal terms.

LOAN AGREEMENT OF AUGUST, 1961

The credit authorization was approved by the Export-Import Bank on the basis of the six-year development plan for the modernization of the Chilean State Railways, but the $30-million credit was designed to cover only certain items in the program, including (1) dieselization ($18,845,000), (2) equipment and materials for the renovation of the lines ($1,941,800), and (3) signal and communications equipment ($9,238,954) (see Table 3). As explained earlier, other foreign purchases required by the plan had either been contracted for, as in the case of the electrification, or were eliminated from the plan for the time being. In addition to the amount and the general purposes for which the loan would be used, the credit authorization stipulated the rate of interest (5 ¾ percent) and the repayment terms (twenty-four semiannual installments beginning October 31, 1963). The next step was the drafting of the actual loan agreement, much of which contained standard clauses found in all EXIMBANK agreements of this type, including the conditions of

TABLE 3

Items Presented by the Chilean State Railways for Financing by EXIMBANK *under the Credit Authorization of November, 1960, and the Loan Agreement of August, 1961*

Items	Initial Request under Authorization of November, 1960	Final Authorization under Loan Agreement of August, 1961
Electrification		
Equipment	. . .	$307,560
Freight	. . .	29,440
Subtotal	. . .	337,000
Dieselization		
Locomotives	$18,845,000	11,415,000
Parts	. . .	1,140,000
Freight	. . .	350,000
Subtotal	18,845,000	12,905,000
Track renovation		
Equipment and parts	1,941,800	1,847,699
Freight	. . .	206,301
Subtotal	1,941,800	2,054,000
Rolling stock, total		2,000,000
Signaling and communications		
Signaling	8,298,000	. . .
Communications	940,954	900,000
Subtotal	9,238,954	900,000
Other		
Equipment	. . .	1,530,000
Contingencies, freight, etc.	. . .	274,000
Subtotal	. . .	1,804,000
Total	$30,025,754	$20,000,000

disbursement, documentation, and repayment. The loan agreement provided for a guarantee of repayment by the government of Chile and a written guarantee by the Chilean Minister of Finance that the local currency expenditures required by the program for railroad modernization would be available.

We shall not be concerned with such details of the loan agreement as the method of payment for goods and services required or the nature of the documentation relating to the credit operations and other items which are more or less traditional in Export-Import Bank loan agreements. And while there were consultations on some points and petitions for modification, relatively little difficulty arose in reaching an accord on the draft loan agreement which had been originally prepared by the Export-Import Bank and submitted to Barraza on November 30, 1960. The basic problem which led to a reduction in the amount of credits to be made available by the EX-IMBANK from $30 million to $20 million, and the consequent change in the list of items to be purchased, arose out of the incompatibility between the tying of EXIMBANK funds to purchases of equipment and services from the United States, on the one hand, and the soliciting of bids for the same equipment from firms throughout the world, on the other. Notification of the solicitation of bids for acquisition of the various items to be imported under the railway modernization program, without restriction as to source, was given long before the EXIMBANK had been approached for a loan. Bids that had been received were opened in December, 1960, some weeks *after* the announcement of the credit authorization from the EXIMBANK. The making of purchase decisions involved some problems for the State Railways and for the Chilean officials who were making arrangements for the loan in the United States. If the contracts were given to European or Japanese suppliers on the basis of lower bids than those submitted by U.S. suppliers, coupled with generous credits, the EXIMBANK would, of course, not finance the purchases. At the same time, it was felt that a substantial portion of the EXIMBANK credit would have to be utilized, or the EXIMBANK might cancel the entire credit authorization.

The difficulties facing the Chilean officials were further compounded by a press campaign which criticized both the Chilean government offiicals and the United States.[24] It was argued that the EXIMBANK credit was provided, not as a means of helping Chile but as a consequence of pressure on the part of U.S. firms to obtain contracts. It was pointed out that the State Railways Corporation was not in a position to judge bids impartially, since the EXIMBANK credit was available for use only in the United States. The press also raised

[24] Much of the criticism appeared in the left-wing, opposition Santiago newspaper, *Las Noticias de Ultima Hora*, which published articles on Dec. 1 and 2, 1960, dealing with the decisions regarding the bids and the credit granted by the EXIMBANK.

the question as to why the bids had been opened *after* rather than *before* the loan was requested from the EXIMBANK. In other words, why were the decisions regarding the purchases not made first and the credits negotiated afterwards? The press articles pointed out that European and Japanese firms had incurred considerable expenses in supplying bids on a number of items, and that this was quite unfair to these firms if it were known that they had no opportunity to obtain the contracts to begin with.

The foregoing discussion does not imply criticism of either the State Railways or the EXIMBANK in regard to the timing of the announcement of the loan authorization and the opening of the bids. It was customary to make purchases of equipment on the basis of bids open to all sellers, and consideration of bids would include both price and credit terms. U.S. suppliers would not be in a position to offer generous credit terms unless they were assured of EXIMBANK financing, and, hence, they could not act with respect to bids until after the loan authorization. There is no evidence that the State Railways requested bids from European and Japanese firms for the sole purpose of forcing U.S. firms to lower their prices and with no intention of accepting the bids that would be made. The only basis for criticism would be if, in fact, the EXIMBANK had led the State Railways officials to believe that the entire line of credit would be canceled if not all the equipment were purchased in the United States. Apparently, the chief difficulty arose as a consequence of confusion with respect to this issue.

In a press conference early in December, 1960, Fernando Gualda, Director of the State Railways Corporation, stated that decisions on the bids would not be affected by the granting of the loan and that the credit available from the EXIMBANK was only one of the factors which would be taken into account. Moreover, it was in the interest of the Corporation that North American suppliers be subjected to competitive bidding from other countries as a means of getting them to reduce their prices. Serious doubts regarding the procedure were also expressed by the Chamber of Commerce of Santiago to the Director-General of the State Railways in a letter of December 27, 1960. In this communication, the Chamber urged that the EXIMBANK credit not be allowed to influence the decisions on the bids received. On January 12, 1961, the Director-General answered the letter and reaffirmed that decisions on the bids would be made exclusively on the basis of the advantage to the Corporation.

It is believed that a political approach was made to the U.S. State Department through the Chilean Ambassador to enable the Railways Corporation to negotiate a change in the draft agreement with the EXIMBANK to conform to the bidding procedure without a cancellation of the loan authorization. It was apparently felt that the U.S. Department of State, for reasons of foreign policy, would want to avoid cancellation of the credit and could bring pressure on the EXIMBANK to change the agreement even in the face of strong pressures against such procedure by the U.S. suppliers. On April 4, 1961, the Chilean Railways Corporation requested a modification of the loan agreement involving a reduction in the amount of the loan from $30 million to $20 million. It was made known that a part of the locomotives in the amount of $6 million would be acquired from France under a credit provided partly by the French government ($1.5 million at 3½ percent interest for fifteen years) and the remainder by the suppliers ($4.5 million at 6 percent with a ten-year maturity). The signal equipment would be obtained from an English firm for about $3.5 million, the credit being advanced by the British government at a rate of interest of 6½ percent payable over the period 1965–71. In the case of both the locomotives and the signal equipment, the bids were substantially lower than those submitted by the U.S. suppliers. In the case of locomotives, the savings amounted to approximately $1 million and, for the signaling equipment, approximately $2 million.

The elimination of that portion of the locomotives in the original loan request which was now to be provided by France, plus the elimination of the signaling equipment to be provided from Britain, left the total amount at several million dollars less than the $20 million now requested, and it was necessary to add new items to reach $20 million. On April 21, 1961, the EXIMBANK gave its approval to the general reduction in the credit authorization to $20 million but refused to finance some of the items which were now requested in order to bring the total purchases from the United States up to $20 million and asked for clarification regarding the significance of others. Full agreement on all of the items in detail was apparently reached at the time of the final signing of the loan agreement on August 2, 1961 (see Table 3 for items in final loan agreement).

A delay in the signing of the agreement occurred because the governmental decree, which authorized the Director of the Chilean State Railways Corporation to contract the credit with the EXIM-BANK under a guarantee by the Republic of Chile, was not forthcoming until August 1, 1961.

The Dead Sea Works Ltd. in Israel [25]

HISTORY OF THE COMPANY

The Dead Sea Works Ltd. was established in June, 1952, for the exploitation of the mineral wealth of the Dead Sea. Its predecessor was the Palestine Potash Company, Ltd., founded in London in 1929 and owned by Jewish private capital. The Palestine Potash Company received a concession from the Palestine Mandatory Government and built two plants on the Dead Sea—the first at Kallia on the northern shore, which is now in Jordanian territory, and the second at Sdom at the southern extremity of the lake.

Being motivated by national and Zionist ideals of developing a deserted area in Palestine, the owners of the Palestine Potash Company were ready to bear the very substantial risk involved in the implementation of this project. The company operated for many years without profits, and in only a few years did it have very small profits. Its output in both plants was below 100,000 tons per annum of a low-grade potash. In 1947, it was decided to expand the southern plant and equipment was actually ordered. Yet, though it arrived during the same year, it was never put into operation. The War of Liberation of 1948 caused the company serious damage. The plant at Kallia was occupied and destroyed by the Jordanians while the plant at Sdom—though remaining in Israeli territory close to the frontier of Jordan—was cut off from the center of the country, since the only transportation route to it is by barge to the north shore of the Dead Sea, which is now under Jordanian control. As a result, production was suspended, most of the staff deserted the place, and the plant was neglected.

Toward the end of 1948, the Minister of Finance appointed a

[25] By Chaim Ben-Shachar, Hebrew University, Jerusalem.

committee to examine the various possibilities for operating the plant at Sdom. The committee was headed by the director of the Bank Leumi Le-Israel,[26] who was favorably disposed toward private enterprise, but the majority of the committee had an opposite view on this issue. After some deliberation, the committee decided to recommend that the government intervene directly.

The Palestine Potash Company had opposed the appointment of this committee, arguing that the mere existence of such a committee would hamper seriously the possibilities of raising foreign private capital to operate the southern plant. The government waited until 1951 to give the company an opportunity to raise private capital for the rehabilitation of the plant. The company made serious efforts in both England and the United States and succeeded in interesting several foreign investors. All of them withdrew, however, after hearing the talk about possible nationalization. Since the company's efforts to raise the capital did not materialize, negotiations were initiated in October, 1951, between the government and the Palestine Potash Company for the taking over of the southern plant by the government. The negotiations were conducted by the Minister of Finance and the Development Division of the Ministry of Commerce and Industry.[27] In 1952, following the formation of a new enterprise called the Dead Sea Works Ltd., an agreement was signed between it and the Palestine Potash Company, transferring the southern plant to the new company, in return for which Palestine Potash received shares and debentures of the new firm.

PRODUCTION PROCESS AND OUTPUT

Dead Sea Works Ltd. exploits the minerals of the Dead Sea. Its chief product is potash, which is of considerable importance for agriculture and is becoming more important with the growing use of fertilizers. In the process of potash extraction, there are a number of byproducts, the most important of which are common salt (sodium chloride), calcium chloride, magnesium chloride, and magnesium bromide. Not all these byproducts were actually exploited by the company.

The production process used by the plant is based on the pump-

[26] The largest commercial bank in Israel.
[27] Which later became the Ministry of Development.

ing of Dead Sea water to shallow pans, where it undergoes evaporation, during which part of the common salt precipitates to the bottom of the pans. The remaining brine is transferred to other pans,
where the carnallite, which is the raw material for potash manufacture, is deposited. The concentrated brines in the pans serve as raw
materials in the production of various other chemicals.

The production of carnallite is the first stage of potash production. The second stage takes place inside the refinery, where the
material is upgraded to the commercial chemical grades.

Production was resumed in 1953 at the existing plant on a small
scale. The first years of operations were unsuccessful, owing to
technical difficulties in production, lack of trained personnel, and
unsatisfactory management. Although pans were expanded and a
new refinery, with a capacity of 135,000 tons per annum, was built,
output grew at a very slow rate.

The persistent failures of the company during this period led to
the setting up of an inquiry committee, appointed in 1956 by the
Ministry of Development. The committee found evidence of poor
planning, poor financial management, lack of trained technical staff,
lack of uniform production procedures, and inadequate financial resources.

Although administration improved with the appointment of a
new managing body in 1955, the company remained unprofitable
because of the large investments carried out under very difficult
conditions and because of its comparatively small capacity. The lack
of profits, in spite of the considerable improvement in administration, personnel, and production and marketing procedures, caused
management to propose a far-reaching expansion program which
was presented in 1958.

FINANCIAL ORGANIZATION PRIOR TO EXPANSION

When Dead Sea Works Ltd. acquired the potash plant in 1952,
the share distribution of the new company was as shown in Table
4.

The founders' share A, held by the Israeli government, conferred
upon it 51 percent of voting rights at general meetings and the decisive influence upon management. The founders' shares B, held by
the Palestine Potash Company, conferred upon it 16 percent of the

voting rights but participation to the extent of one-third in the profits of the company. The company's charter, moreover, stated that no changes in the equity structure of the company might be made without the agreement of the founders' shares B (i.e., of the Palestine Potash Company).

TABLE 4
Dead Sea Works Ltd.:
Distribution of Shares

Type of Shares	No. of Shares (I£I each)	Shareholders
Founders' share A	1	Government of Israel
Ordinary shares	2,129,988	Government of Israel
Founders' shares B	1,220,000	Palestine Potash Company
Ordinary shares	310,000	Others
Ordinary shares	12	Signatories of incorporation memorandum (government)
Total	3,660,001	

The Palestine Potash Company also received debentures of Dead Sea Works Ltd., in the nominal amount of I £390,000. These carried interest at the rate of 5 percent per annum and were linked to the U.S. dollar at the exchange rate of I £1 = $2.80. Furthermore, the Palestine Potash Company was credited with various other payments, so that the total amount it received was I £2,468,439.

Since the formation of Dead Sea Works Ltd., the government has been its main—indeed, almost its sole—source of new capital. Most of the financing was provided in the form of long-term loans from the development budget, and the ratio of such loans to the company's paid-up capital constantly increased. On March 31, 1962, on the eve of the company's reorganization, the government's investments in the plant reached 75 percent of the total I £52 million put at the company's disposal in all forms. The proportion of paid-up capital constantly decreased, and as of March 31, 1962, it was only 7.3 percent. This was an extraordinarily high financial leverage.

In 1960, when the Dead Sea Works Ltd. presented its expansion program to the World Bank its production capacity reached 160,000 tons of potash per annum, and actual annual output was 135,000 tons.

EXPANSION PLAN

To expand the output of potash substantially, a complete change in the methods of exploitation was required. There was no more dry land for any expansion of the existing pan system. Therefore, the program called for a utilization of the southern shallow portion of the Dead Sea as a large evaporation pan and for converting the existing system into one of concentration pans for the production of carnallite. This was not a new idea. The Palestine Potash Company had already asked a Dutch company to examine such a possible project, although it had never been carried out. The principal innovation of the new management was not in the expansion of potash production but in planning the production of an assorted line of other chemical products.

The Dead Sea Works Ltd. contracted with the Construction Aggregates Company of Chicago for the preparation of an engineering estimate for a dike system on the Dead Sea. After careful exploration and continuous testing, Construction Aggregates recommended enclosing an area of 41 square miles, which would increase the capacity of potash production to 900,000 tons.

With natural gas becoming available from a newly found deposit in Zohar, about 17 miles away, it became possible to produce potash through a new process of crystallization (the "hot leach" process). The plan called for a power plant and a new refinery with a capacity of 400,000 tons per annum (with the possibility of increasing it to 900,000 tons per annum), which would produce higher quality products both chemically and physically. The Stearns-Roger Corporation of Denver, an experienced company which had built most of the potash plants in the United States, was charged with the initial engineering estimates.

Having completed the survey of the dike system and the initial engineering estimates for the plant, the Dead Sea Works Ltd. worked out an economic analysis of the project, expanding it to include the byproduct production of bromine, bromine compounds, table salt, and magnesite. Although this expansion called for a very large investment, the project showed good profitability prospects and constituted a very important source of foreign exchange earnings for the country.

To confirm the technical aspects, a Dutch firm was called in to examine the dike system, and Stearns-Roger Corporation was charged with the detailed engineering of the potash plant. The company also worked with other reputable companies in examining the production of the various byproducts proposed.

Total investments under the plan were at first estimated at $55 million, but after changes in the list of products and the scope of the plant, the investment was estimated at $71.5 million, with the following breakdown:

Investment	Millions of Dollars
Potash	48.4
Dike system and concentration pans	27.1
New refinery	15.2
Other investments	6.1
Common salt	0.3
Bromine and bromine derivatives	2.2
Magnesite	6.2
Running-in costs	0.2
Working capital	8.8
Interest paid during period of construction	5.4
Total	71.5

NEGOTIATIONS FOR FINANCING THE EXPANSION PLAN

Even before the final estimate of the cost of the project was made, it became clear that the amount required to finance it would be considerable, in both local and foreign currency. The government of Israel, jointly with the company, decided that this would be a suitable project for which to explore possible international and foreign sources of financing. During 1958, while the technical study of the expansion was in process, the Ministry of Finance discussed the problem of financing with various other government departments, although no final conclusions were reached and no financial reorganization was as yet decided upon.

The decisive push to the financial plan was given at the World Bank Conference in the fall of 1958, as a result of unofficial talks between the Governor of the Bank of Israel and the President of the World Bank, during which it was suggested that the Israeli government could submit a request for a loan for a specific project. Following these talks, it was decided to submit to the World Bank three alternative proposals for loans: the Ashdod harbor project, the Dead Sea Works expansion project, and a proposal for a loan to the Industrial Development Bank of Israel. The third proposal was rejected in the initial stages. Thereafter, it became the objective of the Israeli agencies involved to obtain the other two loans. The Ashdod harbor project was felt to have the better chance of approval. The Dead Sea Works project was also attractive, however, since it offered good chances of expanding exports of potash and other chemicals to a volume of some $30 million per annum, while assuring considerable profits.

Both projects were submitted to the first delegation of the World Bank to visit Israel. It was hoped that some two-thirds of the investment (then estimated at $55 million) in the expansion of potash production would be financed by a World Bank loan and the remaining third by private investment in the potash company's shares by Israeli and foreign investors.

In March, 1960, Dead Sea Works Ltd. completed the World Bank questionnaire customarily sent to applicants for loans, stating the relevant information concerning the company itself and the expansion project. This report included a financial and technical analysis of the existing situation, an account of the expansion program, and a fifteen-year forecast of income and cash flow.

No clear plans were made for dealing with the project in case the World Bank should not approve a loan to finance it. In Ministry of Finance circles, which were dealing with the financing plan, the view was expressed that without the World Bank loan the project could not be implemented. On the other hand, economists in various other government offices felt that since it had been proven that the expansion project was profitable and generally desirable, the necessary financing should be found, even if this meant resorting to other sources.

In May, 1960, the President of the World Bank visited Israel and indicated that the World Bank might be ready to consider the financing of the Dead Sea Works project, in addition to granting a loan for the construction of the Ashdod harbor, provided certain conditions were met.

The capital structure of Dead Sea Works Ltd. would have to be changed, and the Israeli government would have to give up its majority of the company's shares as well as its majority voting rights. This condition was in accordance with the general policy of the World Bank, which encouraged private ownership of industrial undertakings and did not support government industrial enterprises. Most of the negotiations between the World Bank and the government centered on this subject, about which there was lengthy bargaining. During the negotiations there was a lively public discussion of the whole issue of government ownership of the Dead Sea Works in Israel. The Minister of Development, who represented a left-wing socialist party in the government coalition, demanded that the government retain its control of Dead Sea Works Ltd. for the following reasons: the Dead Sea is a repository of natural wealth belonging to the state and should not be handed over to private ownership; the profits likely to be reaped from the potash project are large and only government ownership could assure their reinvestment in the development of the country; the doubts expressed concerning the ability of governments to administer business undertakings do not apply to Israel, which had already proven its capabilities in this sphere; and public opinion, both in Israel and abroad, would regard the demand of the World Bank as an attempt to exert political pressure on a sovereign state, and this was undesirable from the point of view both of the World Bank and of the Israeli government.

The Minister of Finance, however, had an opposite opinion on this issue. He stated that the government had to dissolve its control of various economic enterprises in order to encourage foreign private investment in these undertakings and thus help meet the needs of economic development. The Minister of Finance suggested that the government should adopt a policy of selling existing government enterprises to foreign private investors and investing the proceeds in new economic ventures, which were vital to the economy but too risky to attract private capital. The attitude of the Minister of Finance prevailed in the government, which decided to terminate its control in the Dead Sea Works.

The World Bank urged that private capital from Israel and foreign sources participate in the financing of the project to a sizable extent. At its recommendation, the project was turned over to two United States investment banking institutions—Lazard Frères of New York and the First Boston Corporation—with requests for participating in its financing. Both these institutions had a worldwide reputation and prestige, and it was felt that their participation was likely to attract the necessary private capital. The two banks negotiated on the project as a single body, and the negotiations with them were very lengthy.

It was proposed, at first, that the two American investment banks would raise some $20 million in the project by underwriting shares of Dead Sea Works Ltd. They were not ready, however, to negotiate before making a complete survey of the Dead Sea Works and the project. They asked the consulting firm of Arthur D. Little to prepare this survey. A careful and comprehensive examination of all the technical, commercial, and financial aspects of the company and the expansion project was carried out. Although the report recommended some technical improvements, it reached the conclusion that the marketing and profit prospects were attractive. Negotiations were then started between the two American investment banks and an Israeli team headed by the Governor of the Bank of Israel and including the Director-General of the Ministry of Finance, the Director-General of the Ministry of Development, and the Managing Director of the Dead Sea Works.

With the aim of attracting their own customers to invest in the Dead Sea Works, the two American investment banks insisted on having both the advantages of equity investors and the protection of creditors. Therefore, they suggested that the Dead Sea Works sell them "capital notes," i.e., notes redeemable by annual payments with the option by their holders to convert them into common stock before they were fully redeemed, at a value equal to the nominal price of the stock regardless of its appreciation. The banks also demanded that their United States dollars invested carry a premium of 33⅓ percent above the official exchange rate.[28] It was emphasized by the banks that only under these conditions would they be able to attract foreign private capital.

This method of financing was not accepted in Israel, and the pro-

[28] I £2.40 per $1, as compared with the official rate at that time of I £1.80 per $1.

posal was finally rejected. After the failure of these negotiations, various alternative methods were considered, such as raising the necessary funds from direct investments by Jewish business interests and institutions. Under the arrangement finally agreed upon, the company was to raise more equity capital by floating new shares through local banks and receive a $10-million loan from a private American commercial bank. Combined with the company's own resources, this would meet the World Bank conditions of terminating the majority equity ownership of the government and insuring a sound financial basis.

FINANCIAL REORGANIZATION

The following financial program was finally crystallized through negotiations with the World Bank:

Sources	Millions of Dollars
Loan from the World Bank	25.0
Loan from the private American bank	10.0
Deferred interest loans from government of Israel	1.2
Short- and medium-term loans	4.8
Interest on loans and deposits	2.1
Share issues	15.0
Internal sources (retained earnings and depreciation)	20.5
Total	78.6

Uses	
Investment in the project (breakdown as given above)	71.5
Interest on shares issued	2.8
Short- and medium-term debt redemption	3.2
Replacements and renewals	1.1
Total	78.6

The financial reorganization carried through in June, 1961, included the following operations:

1. Share capital was increased from I £3,660,001 to I £57,600,000, comprising 30,600,000 "A" shares and 27,000,000 ordinary shares, all of I £1 each. The only difference between "A" shares and the ordinary ones is in regard to dividends during the first five years.

2. All shareholders received one "A" share for each of their old shares.

3. The debt owed to the government of Israel, amounting to I £ 38,717,748, was converted into 26,939,999 "A" shares and into I £ 11,777,749 of junior debentures [29] carrying interest at 5 percent per annum and linked to the U.S. dollar at the I £ 1.80 = $1 exchange rate.

4. The government transferred to the Palestine Potash Company a further 2,806,000 "A" shares, as well as 610,000 junior debentures, in compensation for the decrease in its control as a result of the reorganization. For the same reason, the government also allocated 344,000 "A" shares and 360,000 junior debentures to the other shareholders.

5. Consequently, the Israeli government received, in addition to its 2,130,001 old shares, a further net amount of 23,789,999 "A" shares and 10,807,749 junior debentures. The government's holding was thus reduced from 58 to 45 percent of the company's share capital. Moreover, the government agreed to limit its voting rights to 35 percent by depositing all its holdings in excess of 35 percent with the Bank of Israel, which is to hold them in trust.

As a result of these operations, the equity ownership of Dead Sea Works Ltd. immediately following the reorganization is as shown in Table 5.

TABLE 5
Dead Sea Works Ltd.:
Distribution of Shares
Following Reorganization

	Thousands of Israeli Pounds	Percent
"A" shares held by government	25,920	45.0
"A" shares held by Palestine Potash Co. Ltd.	4,026 [a]	7.0
"A" shares held by others	654 [b]	1.1
Ordinary shares	27,000	46.9
Total share capital	57,600	100.0

[a] 1,220 for the old shares and 2,806 from the government allocation.
[b] 310 for the old shares and 344 from the government allocation.
[29] Junior to the World Bank and the American bank loans.

In settlement with the Palestine Potash Company and with other shareholders, the distribution of the junior debentures was as given in Table 6.

TABLE 6
Dead Sea Works Ltd.:
Distribution of Junior
Debentures Following
Reorganization

	Israeli Pounds	Percent
Government of Israel	10,807,749	91.8
Palestine Potash Company Ltd.	610,000	5.2
Other shareholders	360,000	3.0
Total	11,777,749	100.0

The reorganization also affected the composition of the Board of Directors. There are fifteen directors, of whom fourteen are elected by the shareholders. Of these, only five (i.e., 35 percent) are elected by the government. The fifteenth director is the Managing Director of the company.

Simultaneously with the financial reorganization, the company was granted a concession. Previously, it had been operating without a concession. The law governing this concession was passed by the Knesset, which is the supreme legislative authority, in contrast to the normal practice that concessions are granted by the executive authority. This was done in order to stress the permanence of this concession, thus reducing the risks to foreign investors. The concession runs until 1999. Under its terms, the company will pay royalties to the government totaling 5 percent of the ex-works value of all its products starting in April, 1964.

WORLD BANK LOAN

Immediately following the financial reorganization, the World Bank approved its $25-million loan to the Dead Sea Works company. This loan was granted for fifteen years, redemption being in twenty-one equal semiannual payments starting in November, 1966, and ending in November, 1976. Interest is at the rate of 5.75 percent per annum, with 0.75 percent on balances not withdrawn. The loan will be utilized solely for purchases and expenditures within the framework of the expansion project as presented to the World Bank and only for expenditures in foreign currency. Regular reports on the implementation of the project must be made to the World Bank.

The World Bank loan is secured by a first specific mortgage on the entire area in which the Dead Sea Works company is working (excluding the Dead Sea). The mortgage also covers all the company's and its subsidiaries' rights and concessions. Other securities include a specific charge on all the company's equipment and possessions. Besides, there is a floating charge on all the company's assets, including good will. The borrower must execute all the insurance transactions necessary for the implementation of the project. Neither the borrowing company nor its subsidiary companies may increase their long-term debt without the World Bank's approval until the plans have been fully implemented. The company's debt on the date of the completion of the project must not exceed its paid-up capital plus retained earnings. The borrowing company must not declare any dividends or bonus shares (except as regards its liabilities on shares already issued) unless these are from profits accumulated after March, 1961. It is also obliged to maintain at least a 1.25:1 ratio between current assets and current liabilities by March, 1968. No sum exceeding $250,000 may be invested by the company outside the project without the specific approval of the World Bank, unless the investment is within the framework of the expansion project. The remaining terms of the loan relate to the implementation of the financial reorganization, including the receiving of an additional loan from the private American bank, and the floating of share issues.

To complement the agreement between Dead Sea Works Ltd. and the World Bank, the latter also signed a guarantee agreement with the government of Israel on June 11, 1961. Under this agreement, the government undertook to permit tax-free interest and redemption payments and to guarantee the company's debentures.

PRIVATE AMERICAN BANK LOAN

After the failure of the negotiations with Lazard Frères of New York and the First Boston Corporation, it was decided to raise $15 million by selling shares in Israel. This reduced the amount required in the form of loans from private foreign banks to approximately

$10 million. The Bank of Israel approached a certain American bank with which it has had financial connections, and, after rapid negotiations an agreement was reached in July, 1961, under which the American bank loaned the Dead Sea Works $10 million. The terms of this loan include quarterly interest payments at the prime rate of the bank plus 1 percent, always providing that the effective rate does not exceed 6 percent per annum and does not fall below 5 percent per annum. The loan is to be redeemed in annual payments of $2 million, starting in 1965.

NEW SHARE ISSUE

Even in the early stages of the financial planning, it was clear that part of the necessary financing could be supplied by selling shares to the public. Information available at that time concerning the capacity of the securities markets led, however, to estimates which put the amounts which could be raised in this manner at a low figure. Only later, when actual contacts were made in Israel and abroad, did it become clear that there were possibilities of successfully floating a relatively large issue.

The agreement concerning the floating of this issue was signed with a consortium of local banks which included all the major Israeli banking institutions. The issue totaled I £27 million ($15 million), but only I £7.5 million worth of I £1 shares were sold through the Israeli stock exchange in Tel Aviv, the remaining I £19.5 million being purchased directly by various investors in Israel and abroad.[30] In the market, the shares were sold at a 7 percent premium, i.e., at 107 percent of their nominal value.

These shares carry interest at 5 percent per annum, linked to the U.S. dollar at the I £1.80=$1 exchange rate, for the first five years— which are the construction years for the project. In this connection, the government claimed that there was no justication for the new ordinary shares to receive an income during the period of construction, while the "A" shares were to receive no income during this period. The government also opposed the company's demand that it should pay no interest on its debentures during these five years. After negotiations, the following agreement was reached: the new shares were to receive 5 percent during construction. "A" shares will

[30] Investors abroad purchased I £8.3 million ($4.6 million) worth of stock.

not receive dividends during construction but dividends will accumulate during the period and be paid out over a period of years after the construction is completed; and although the interest due on debentures held by the government will not be actually paid during the construction period, it will constitute an additional government loan to the company at 5.75 percent per annum.

The new issue of ordinary shares is regarded as an "approved" investment under the Law for the Encouragement of Capital Investments. Accordingly, the income tax on interest paid on these shares during the first five years and any dividends that will be paid later cannot exceed 25 percent. Moreover, foreign investors are protected against double taxation.

Before the issue was floated, a publicity campaign, without precedent in the Israeli securities market, was launched. It was stressed that the new shares were an excellent long-term investment. The objective was to prevent speculation in these shares and sharp fluctuations in their stock exchange quotations. Priority for allocations was given to purchasers ready to undertake not to sell their shares for as long a period as possible. Small investors were likewise given priority, as were employees of Dead Sea Works Ltd., who were even given loans to enable them to purchase shares.

REINVESTMENT

One of the important items in the financing plan is the company's internal sources of funds during the period of expansion. To estimate the extent of these sources, the company projected a cash flow estimate. The main items in the cash flow report constituting sources of financing are earnings after taxes, interest earned during the period of expansion, and various depreciation funds.

PROGRESS IN CONSTRUCTION

With the signature of the agreements assuring the various sources of funds, work began on the first stage of implementing the expansion project. Funds accruing from the sale of ordinary shares were deposited with the Accountant-General, and were used in part to redeem current liabilities.

The international tender for the construction of the dam and the evaporation pans was published in 1962. There was a great demand for experts in this branch of construction at the time because of a disaster in Holland, and the offers made were on the expensive side. American companies offered lower bids than European companies. If the tender had been limited merely to the United States, however, the feeling is that the bids of the American companies might have been significantly higher. The two lowest bids were those of the Construction Aggregates Company and of the Kaiser and Macco Corporation. Initially, the tender committee accepted the bid of the Construction Aggregates Corporation, which was the lowest, but it was later decided to include the Kaiser and Macco Corporation to the extent of 20 percent each, as against 60 percent for the Construction Aggregates Company. The reason for this step was the desire to associate with the project additional internationally known companies with extensive know-how.

Supervision of construction was entrusted to a Dutch company which specializes solely in supervising the execution of such construction projects. The construction work is being carried out by a staff hired by Construction Aggregates and Kaiser and Macco. This enables the Dead Sea Works to avoid increasing its own administrative and technical staff, which might have caused personnel problems and inefficiency later, after the undertaking had been completed. On the other hand, it meant that the company had to pay a larger part of these expenses in dollars.

SUMMARY

The special characteristics and the significant aspects of the financing of the Dead Sea Works expansion project can be summarized as follows:

1. In contrast to many cases that may be cited in Israel as well as in other developing countries, in this case an undertaking controlled by the government was transferred to private control.

2. The government acted as intermediary and guarantor in the negotiations between foreign suppliers of funds (both public and private) and the local concern.

3. Though slightly more than half of the financing was supplied from abroad, control remained vested in the Israeli owners. Of the $78.6 million of financing, $39.6 million (50.4 percent) was supplied from abroad (the World Bank—$25 million; the private American

bank—$10 million; shareholders—$4.6 million). Of the 57,600,000 shares, 47,274,000 (78.6 percent) are held by the Israeli owners (45 percent by the government, 1.1 percent by old shareholders, and 32.5 percent by new ordinary shareholders).

These results would most likely not have been achieved without the significant participation of the World Bank in the financing of the project.

Aid for the Rourkela, Durgapur, and Bhilai Iron and Steel Plants in India [31]

ROURKELA IRON AND STEEL PLANT

Modern steelmaking in India dates back to the first decade of the century, and during the interwar years the number of units rose to three (two of the plants, Tata's and SCOB, being in the private sector and a small plant in Mysore being owned by the then Native State) and output in the industry progressed at a steady, if not always satisfactory, pace. In the course of World War II, demand and output increased. Expansion of steelmaking capacity was therefore a natural concern of newly independent India, and as early as 1948 two firms of consultants, one from the United States and the other from the United Kingdom, were asked by the government of India to report on the possibilities of setting up a steel plant in India with an annual capacity of 500,000 tons of ingots. The fact that India was (and is) one of the cheapest producers of pig iron in the world and the fact that India had become a substantial importer of steel provided the general economic justifications.

Burdened as India then was with the problems of maintaining her administrative system in the wake of British departure and those arising from partition, the Indian government did not act on the favorable report of the consultants, and the First Plan did not contain any proposal in this regard. Moreover, estimates of demand made by a Technical Mission of the World Bank in cooperation with Indian authorities in 1952 indicated a prospective shortage in supplies (after taking into account expansion schemes in the private sector) of only 400,000 to 500,000 tons in 1958. Thus, Indian thinking continued to

[31] By R. K. Hazari, University of Bombay, and S. D. Mehta, Economic Commission for Africa.

be geared to a 500,000-ton plant, and this was the basis of fruitless initial explorations in both the United Kingdom and the United States, for technical and financial collaboration.[32]

Interest shifted to Western Germany, and after some preliminary soundings the Secretary of the then Ministry of Production visited Western Germany in 1953. A memorandum of association was worked out between the Indian representative and two West German producers—Fried Krupp, Essen, and Demag Aktiengesellschaft, Dursburg—without involving, it appears, the West German government. The West German combine were appointed consultants for a 500,000-ton integrated iron and steel project (for a fee of 21 million rupees), and the project was estimated to cost 800 million rupees. Equity participation by Krupp and Demag was visualized, rising upwards in proportion to the volume of purchases of equipment in West Germany, to an eventual maximum of 95 million rupees (in Deutsche Marks).

The consultants submitted a preliminary project report in May, 1954, and after acceptance by the government of India, this was followed by a detailed project report in 1955. Both reports were based on a 500,000-ton plant.

Meanwhile, the demand estimates of the World Bank team were called into serious question as another survey assessed the demand for steel in 1960–61 at 6 million tons of ingot steel (4.5 million tons of finished steel), indicating a projected gap between scheduled private sector expansion schemes and estimated final demand four to five times as large as the estimate made only two years earlier. This induced the Government of India (GOI) to ask the consultants to prepare a revised version of the detailed project for a million-ton plant. This was completed before the end of 1955 and was accepted early in 1956.

Certain other changes were also made. The government decided that it did not wish German equity participation. The Industrial Policy Resolution of April, 1956, including iron and steel among industries "the future development of which will be the exclusive responsibility of the State," [33] was casting its shadow before its

[32] Estimates Committee, *Thirty-third Report*, dealing with the three public-sector steel projects, 1958–59, p. 4.
[33] Industrial Policy Resolution, Govt. of India, April 30, 1956, para. 7.

formal appearance. Furthermore, although Krupp and Demag continued as consultants, the responsibility for insuring coordination of suppliers during the construction period passed from Krupp and Demag, who were to have been specialist working partners with some equity stake, into the hands of inexperienced civil servants who comprised the Board of Directors of Hindustan Steel Ltd., the government company which had been formed in January, 1954, for the Rourkela project. The commitment to the care of Hindustan Steel Ltd. of the two other public sector steel plants—Durgapur and Bhilai—in March, 1957, added to the administrative burden.[34] With the denial of equity for Krupp and Demag, the responsibility of managing the immediate post-construction phase also passed from the West Germans on to Hindustan Steel.

In brief, the position in early 1956 was this: a million-ton integrated iron and steel plant was to be set up in the public sector at an estimated cost of 1,200 million rupees, with an estimated foreign exchange content of 890 million rupees, the equipment for which was to be bought in Germany.[35] Krupp and Demag were to be consultants to the project. The Indian Rourkela project authorities were to arrange for civil engineering work and designs. The plant as a whole was expected to go into operation by the end of 1959. From the earliest stage, it had been decided to use the LD process for conversion of pig iron into steel and to manufacture mainly flat steel products.

The first problems arose when the site had to be changed and enlarged to accommodate the increase in capacity and several by-product plans that had not been contemplated initially. The estimates of earthwork involved moved up drastically, as it was found that rock excavation had been seriously underestimated. Procedural delays at the government level were supplemented by frequent delays in receipt of detailed plans. In the absence of sufficiently detailed preparatory work, the placing of contracts was delayed, and contracts frequently went to inexperienced contractors. The gov-

[34] At Durgapur, however, coordination was achieved through a consortium arrangement; and at Bhilai, the Russians were in effective charge.
[35] In purely legal terms, equipment could be purchased anywhere. In practice, "it is not unlikely that it was originally intended that the purchases would be made from Germany" (Estimates Committee, *Thirty-third Report*, p. 18), and on the record, the bulk of the contracts have been placed in Germany.

ernment did not find it easy to coordinate supplies from thirty-five German suppliers (and their subcontractors), and the provision to look after ocean transportation from North German ports was difficult for the GOI to manage in spite of the fact that most West German deliveries were on schedule. In addition, Rourkela changed its General Manager five times in six years. Also, there had been insufficient preparatory work on the ancillaries—township, ore mines, water supply arrangements, etc.

Two general consequences ensued: costs increased sharply. The estimate had risen up to 1.28 billion rupees before the end of 1956 [36] and by August, 1957, cost estimates were put at 1.7 billion rupees, including foreign exchange components of 1.22 billion rupees.[37] By 1962, estimates appear to have exceeded 2 billion rupees,[38] and the completion of various sections of the plant was delayed. At the end of 1957, the first revision of the target dates indicated a delay of some four months, in terms of the last main section of the plant. By the time the Estimates Committee reported in February, 1959, a further six months' delay was reported, stretching the total delay to ten months. As of the end of 1962, the last major section (namely, the cold-rolling mill) had not quite been completed, thus extending the time lag to a minimum of thirty-six months.

As each section went into production, the Germans handed operations over to Hindustan Steel Ltd. after having proven its capacity to produce as per specifications.

Other weaknesses in the organization of the Rourkela project kept some output at low levels. Thus, it was reported in 1961 that out of the three blast furnaces, one could not be put into operation "unless the slag ladles ordered quite some time ago arrive," [39] and the remaining two furnaces were "producing only about 33,000 tons a month as against 60,000 tons of pig iron proved at the time they were taken over from the Germans." [40]

There was a grave shortage of skilled workers, technicians, and

[36] *Second Plan*, p. 396.
[37] Statement by the Minister for Steel, Mines and Fuel in the Lok Sabha on Aug. 13, 1957.
[38] Inferred from the aggregate investment estimates given in *Programmes of Industrial Development, 1961–66*, p. 9.
[39] K. Sankarasubramanyam, *The Public Sector, a Hindustan Times Survey*, p. 22.
[40] *Ibid.*, p. 23.

sectional heads. The training programs at times proved to be inadequate. The maintenance of the plant was below par, as spares were in short supply—sometimes because the significance of import orders was not appreciated in the license-issuing branches of the government—and because maintenance staff did not have adequate authority to act to prevent troubles. The plant had to contend with raw materials which varied in quality, and sometimes, as in the case of coal, there were deficiencies because other plants had not been brought into production as scheduled. It was also found that some West German supplies of machinery and equipment were not up to specifications. To add to all these points, labor morale was poor, and there was considerable absenteeism, lack of discipline, and over-staffing. There were also inadequate communications and transportation facilities.

The net effect of all these factors was to raise costs, both capital and current, to reduce output, to damage the plant,[41] and to create an air of pessimism and an atmosphere in which Indians sought to denounce the basic quality of the West German plant. It was stated, at the ministerial level, that Rourkela could not be rated with the other two steel plants.[42]

The German reaction was one of astonishment. Eventually, these feelings were embodied in the Solveen Report, whose amended version was described as "the most searing indictment of inefficiency and mismanagement in the annals of steel-making." [43] At one stage, in early 1962, the Development Aid Committee of the Bundestag decided that the Third Plan expansion of Rourkela to 1.8 million tons of ingot capacity should not be undertaken until after the plant, as installed, had reached its optimal levels of production.[44]

Luckily for Rourkela, Subramanian, the new Minister for Heavy Industries, came into office early in 1962. His first reactions were a break from the bureaucratic quagmire of elaborate defenses for every complaint and he demanded better performance at Rourkela with additional powers to the General Manager to match his responsibilities. Steadfastly, the Minister refused to be drawn into the ap-

[41] The Solveen Report, prepared by the West Germans, estimated the cost of setting things right at some 100 million rupees.
[42] Swaran Singh, the Minister for Steel, in a speech in 1961. Reported in Sankarasubramanyam, *The Public Sector*, p. 20.
[43] *Times of India*, May 14, 1962.   [44] *Financial Express*, June 3, 1962.

portionment of blame between the Germans and India, asserting that what really counted was measures to bring back to health "the sick child," as he described Rourkela. The overcentralization of powers and functions in Hindustan Steel Ltd. was reduced under a general reorganization which took effect from July 1, 1962. Moreover, the new Minister laid down targets—while providing action along the lines of the Solveen Report [45]—for the management of Rourkela to fulfill.

As early as May, 1962, reports from Rourkela were encouraging. Initially proven levels of production were being regained and records were being established. And in October, 1962, the plant produced 88 percent of the finished steel output for which it had been designed. The "sick child" had become almost normal, and attention was being directed to future growth.

Rourkela began as a commercial transaction between West German steelmakers and the Indian government. It remained so until the exchange crisis in 1957, which resulted in a generally favorable Western response to Indian needs. The Indian Finance Minister visited Bonn in October, 1957, and broached to the German government the subject of refinancing Rourkela payments. The favorable reactions to this move crystallized into the first aid transaction.

An agreement was signed on February 26, 1958, for postponement of payments to various German contractors (thirty-nine names were specified in an Appendix to the agreement) which would mature between November 1, 1957, and March 31, 1961, but did not cover any increases in amounts falling due by September 30, 1958, owing to escalator clauses. The procedure involved the issue of promissory notes by the Government of India in lieu of payments in Deutsche Marks to the German firms when the liability of payment arose within the time limits specified. For payments made by promissory notes prior to the signing of the Agreement but falling within the period laid down, the government could issue fresh promissory notes as from the date of the agreement, namely, February 20, 1953. These notes, when issued, were negotiable by the supplier concerned in West Germany.

The notes bore interest at a distinctly commercial rate of 6 per-

[45] Among other things, the West Germans provided more technicians to work the plant.

cent and an additional fee of 0.3 percent for service and administrative charges, and were redeemable by the Government of India three years after the date of issue, as already indicated, in Deutsche Marks. The maximum limit for the issue of notes was fixed at 660 million DM, a sum which presently is equivalent to 777.9 million rupees.[46]

Simultaneously, it was made clear in the Agreement that this rather non-aid-like transaction, on the face of it, was only "a preliminary postponement of payment obligations." [47]

In the second half of 1960 two rather complex arrangements were worked out for extension of repayment periods for promissory notes issued earlier (Table 7).

TABLE 7
Rourkela Steel Plant:
Extension of Repayment Periods
for Promissory Notes

	Notes Maturing by March, 1961 millions of DM	*Notes Maturing April 1, 1961– Dec. 31, 1961 millions of DM*
1. Amount	147	202
2. Cash payment required	49	20.2
3. Repayment arranged for (1 − 2)	98	181.8
4. Extension of further 8 years (4 years + 4 years at India's option in case of March, 1961, notes)	49	90.9
5. Extension of further 12 years (4 years + 8 years at India's option in case of March, 1961, notes)	49	90.9

Source: *External Assistance*, 1960, p. 46.

This mix of commercial terms and the desire to aid, however, underwent a change, presumably at the urging of the government of India. The previous arrangements were replaced by two agreements

[46] Explanatory Memorandum, General Budget, 1963–64, p. 161. The changes reflect in the main the effect of revaluation of the Deutsche Mark in March, 1961.
[47] Preamble to the Agreement.

—one signed on January 30, 1961, and the other signed on April 29, 1961.

The first agreement was for 98.36 million DM between the two governments—and with an additional contract with the Kreditanstalt, the actual agency through which the refinancing took place —to meet obligations from maturing promissory notes issued by the government of India under the first, 660-million-DM credit, broken up according to dates as follows:

40.22 million DM	for obligations maturing on January 31, 1961, and covered by promissory notes executed by the Government of India.
58.14 million DM	for obligations maturing between January 30, 1961, and March 30, 1961 and covered by promissory notes executed by the Government of India.
98.36 million DM	

The loan was to be used by the Kreditanstalt for discharging the commitments under the promissory notes, on the dates specified, on behalf of the government of India, the interest rate charged being 5 ¾ percent, 0.55 percent less than the combined interest and service charge under the 660-million-DM credit. The entire credit was repayable in a single installment, four years from the date of signing, on January 30, 1965.

The above agreement, from the government's point of view, was a gain in the sense that the cash portion of repayments (49 million DM) was avoided and a loss inasmuch as the maximum repayment spread was lowered from being between eight to twelve years to just four years. In any case, it recorded the stretching of a portion of Rourkela credit of 660 million DM to seven years in the aggregate.

The second refinancing agreement recorded even more gains for the government by lengthening the repayment period. The 10 percent cash payment for promissory notes maturing during a somewhat longer period than was originally agreed upon—namely, for notes maturing between April 1, 1961, and March 31, 1962—remained, and the amount was somewhat larger at 230 million DM instead of 202 million DM. The loan was granted in the form of a redeemable loan, under a separate contract with the Kreditanstalt, one-half of the amount involving repayment spread over April, 1965, to the end of March, 1974, or, in effect, a repayment spread of twelve and a half years. The other half of this loan—103.5 million DM [48]—was given for the time being with a lump-sum maturity of four years with the assurance within the agreement that "The Government of the Federal Republic of Germany will endeavor to ensure that a corresponding period of maturity will in due course also be stipulated for the second half of the loan." [49]

The particular notes to be redeemed under this loan were left to be determined by the West German government, and the rate of interest was settled at 5¼ percent.

The net result was that interest rates had come down from 6.3 to 5.25 percent and repayment spreads gone up to fifteen and a half years (including three years under the original 660-million-DM credit).

In the course of 1962, another similar agreement was undertaken involving 101.2 million rupees, or roughly 90 million DM.

Two further points need to be made about West German financing of the Rourkela project.

First, there is reason to believe that a large portion of the general credits for capital goods granted by West Germany also went into the financing of the Rourkela project. As much as 200 million DM may have gone into this extension of initial financing, a large part of it in the ancillaries and some for the steel plant proper. Thus, West German aid for Rourkela may be estimated at 860 million DM—or 1 billion rupees—out of the eventual cost of the project of over 2 billion rupees, including the foreign exchange component of probably around 1.45 billion rupees. The West Germans have, therefore, financed half the cost of the project proper and a little less than 70 percent of the foreign exchange costs.

Secondly, to the extent to which Rourkela's current needs as distinguished from capital costs—70 to 100 million rupees—are also being met from some recent credits, the share of Rourkela in the West German aid program is higher. The total position, as of March, 1963, may be estimated as follows:

---

[48] 230 million DM less 10 percent (23 million DM) in cash constitutes the real refinancing, i.e., a loan of 207 million DM. One-half of the latter is 103.5 million DM.

[49] Article I, para. 2, of the Agreement.

Credit		Millions of rupees
Total West German credits		2,494.0
Out of which (a) *initial* financing		
for Rourkela:		
1. Under the Rourkela credit	777.9	
2. From other credits (est.)	220	
3. For current needs	70 — 100	
	1,067.9 — 1,097.9	
Out of which (b) for refinancing:		
1st prolongation credit	111.6	
2nd prolongation credit	273.8	
3rd prolongation credit	101.2	
	486.6	
Total of Rourkela credits (a + b)	1,554.5 — 1,584.5	
Therefore, share of Rourkela in the		
West German credit total, approximately		63 percent

As part of its help for the Third Plan, West Germany indicated willingness to carry its aid for Rourkela further by a 280-million DM credit (333.4 million rupees) to be made available in 1963–64 and following years.[50]

DURGAPUR IRON AND STEEL PLANT

Negotiations for British financial and technical collaboration in the setting up of an integrated iron and steel works were started by the Birlas, the well-known Indian industrial group, some time in 1954. The resulting proposals involved private equity participation to the extent of only 10 percent in an investment anticipated to amount to 1 billion rupees. This proposal was turned down by the government of India on the ground of unsound finance. Later, the future development of the iron and steel industry came to be reserved for the state.

Although the Birla proposal was turned down, the government of India was interested in an expansion of steel capacity, faced as it was in 1954 with a demand estimate for steel that was a multiple of the World Bank Technical Mission's projected gap in Indian steel supplies. Acting through the consultative mechanisms of the Colombo Plan, the government of India invited to India a mission of British steel men under the leadership of Sir Eric Coates.

[50] *External Finance*, 1961, p. 41.

The Coates Mission reviewed the problems, economic and techlical, connected with the establishment of another million-ton integrated iron and steel works in the public sector, in addition to the plants decided upon at Rourkela and Bhilai. The report of the Mission was ready by August, 1955, and its general acceptance by the government of India led to the formation of the Indian Steelworks Construction Company (London), Ltd. (ISCON), a consortium of thirteen British firms interested in the supply of plant, equipment, and services for Durgapur. A delegation from ISCON visited India to discuss details of handling the contract by a single agency and submitted a preliminary report and estimates in January, 1956. In July, 1956, final estimates and specifications were received. After examination, a contract was concluded in October, 1956.

The contract was a package deal for the supply of the plant; and ISCON, for a fee of 150 million rupees, was to perform the various technical services involved in the construction and setting up of the plant on a "turnkey" basis. The machinery was to be purchased by India through competitive bidding, although it seems to have been understood all along that the plant, in the main, would be British. The responsibility for the first engineering works was with Hindustan Steel Ltd.

The Second Plan had visualized Durgapur, as a whole, to be commissioned by December, 1960, but the contract indicated July, 1961. This target date, for the plant as a whole, was exceeded by nine or ten months. The factors responsible for the delays in the case of Durgapur have not aroused the wide discussion that occurred in the case of Rourkela. Except for the problems of coordination, which in the present case were handled by ISCON, the explanations for the delays seem to be broadly similar, though less intensive. Nevertheless, here too there have been reciprocal recriminations, with the Indians harping on defects in machinery and ISCON playing up delays in construction, deficiencies in planning by the project authorities and in the civil engineering works. The main ground for complaint against Durgapur does not, however, arise from the relatively small scale of delays. Estimates of total cost were initially put at 1.15 billion rupees, out of which 720 million rupees was the foreign exchange component. By August, 1957, the figures had moved up to 1.38 billion rupees and 920 million rupees, respectively. In the middle of

1961, the total cost figure amounted to over 1.8 billion rupees. And, according to the *Programs of Industrial Development, 1961–66*, total costs seem to be finally settling for 2 billion rupees, with a foreign exchange cost of 1–1.1 billion rupees.

The main causes of the increase in costs at Durgapur are, broadly speaking, similar to those at Bhilai and Rourkela—underestimation of civil engineering work, inadequate preparatory work on the ancillaries, lengthened gestation periods due to failures in coordination, and occasional additions to the physical content of the plants, such as the coal tar distillation plant at Durgapur. The escalation clauses in the contract for Durgapur, it is claimed, have worked out more unfavorably than at Rourkela.

Durgapur has provided the single largest export order ever to be secured by British industry—£50 million in terms of the 1957 estimates.[51]

The first UK financing for Durgapur was of a strictly commercial nature and was, in fact, organized through a syndicate of five London banks (namely, Barclays, Lloyds, District Bank, Glyn Mills, and Martins Bank) managed through Lazard Frères, a merchant banking company. This financing seems to have been in negotiation almost from the placing of the contract with ISCON. The credit was made conditional on the fact that the contract with ISCON was for goods with an F.O.B. value of not less than £55 million, as well as an initial payment in sterling to ISCON of 10 percent of the F.O.B. value of the goods.

The credit itself was for a sum of £11.5 million, and drawings were to take place according to a schedule established over a period of more than three and a half years. Amounts not drawn on the scheduled dates could be carried forward, but not beyond the final date of the schedule. Interest was levied on the total amounts drawn, on a day-to-day basis of balances, at a rate 1 percent above the UK bank rate in effect from time to time, subject to a minimum rate of 4½ percent.

The credit could be used either on a payment basis (which involved several checks and authorizations) or on a reimbursement

---

[51] *Economic Cooperation between India and the United Kingdom*, UK Central Office of Information, August, 1961, p. 9. The actual amount has been much higher.

basis through the UK branch of the Reserve Bank of India. The government of India preferred the latter.

Repayment was laid down in a schedule of amounts and arranged as semiannual installments commencing on January 1, 1962. The period of repayment from the dates of drawings amounted to five years or less.

The utilization of this relatively small amount of 153.3 million rupees, or one-fifth of the value of the contracted goods spread over three and a half years, did not present any problems.[52] Repayment has begun and amounted to 80 million rupees up to March, 1963, and was to be completed in 1963–64.[53]

The "bank rate plus 1 percent" clause meant at one stage an effective interest rate as high as 8 percent, just as the reduction of the bank rate to 4½ percent has implied a lowering of the interest charge in the last phases of the contract.

The Durgapur credit of the Export Credits Guarantee Department (ECGD) was authorized on June 30, 1958. It seems to have been induced by the exigencies of servicing the largest export order, as well as by somewhat belated concern for India's foreign exchange problems. The amount involved was £15 million (200 million rupees), to be used for financing the F.O.B. value of equipment shipped or to be shipped from the United Kingdom in furtherance of the ISCON contract. The interest payable is that applicable to similar loans from the UK Consolidated Fund at the time of the drawing, plus an administration charge of ⅛ percent. In practice, this has worked out to between 5⅜ and 5¾ percent.

The procedure for drawing is by the sale of promissory notes to the ECGD by the government of India. The government of India agreed to repay in four equal annual installments of £3.75 million each, starting on July 1, 1966.

This credit—agreed upon almost two years after the awarding of the contract to ISCON and applicable to equipment shipped as well as to be shipped and further comprising a small part of the total foreign exchange expenditure on the project—was also capable of the

---

[52] The total foreign exchange expenditure on Durgapur came to 790 million rupees by March, 1960. See V. K. R. V. Rao and Dharam Narain, *Foreign Aid and India's Economic Development* (Bombay, Asia Publishing House, 1963), p. 46.

[53] Explanatory Memorandum, General Budget, 1963–64, App. XIV, p. 165.

quickest utilization. The government of India had drawn the entire amount by the middle of March, 1959, so that the total repayment spread became somewhat longer than ten years.

These are the only two credits in the UK aid program directed exclusively at the initial Durgapur project. The third Durgapur transaction is for the extension of the Durgapur project in the Third Plan period. The repayment periods of the first two credits average 7½ years and their composite rate of interest above 6 percent.

The hard positions on repayment periods and amounts—the United Kingdom has never relaxed on interest charges—are, however, considerably modified with respect to Durgapur by drawings from other, later loans and credits. While precise figures are not available, another 300 to 350 million rupees from these later credits have been directed to the financing of Durgapur. This estimate plus the loans specifically given for Durgapur would bring up the proportion of aid in foreign exchange financing to somewhere between 65 and 70 percent of the total, a level comparable to the rate of West German financing in Rourkela.

It was proposed to extend the capacity of Durgapur to 1.6 million tons of ingots during the Third Plan. This was estimated to involve investment of 410 million rupees in foreign exchange and at the Aid-India consortium meeting in May–June, 1961, the United Kingdom indicated loan assistance of £20 million (266.7 million rupees) but with a repayment spread of twenty-five years. This credit has since been authorized in a higher amount—293.3 million rupees.

BHILAI IRON AND STEEL PLANT

In September, 1954, there were reports that the USSR had offered an integrated steel mill of 1-million-ton capacity on credit, repayable in convertible rupees at 2½ percent (about one-half of the interest then charged by the World Bank and the United States on infrastructure loans), to be wholly owned and managed by the Indian government and with a guarantee of completion in about three years. In the same month, India invited a team of Soviet specialists to study the technical aspects of a new steel mill. Two months later, in November, a Soviet team arrived in India to make the study. In January, 1955, the team recommended the setting up of a steel plant of 1-million-ton ingot capacity to manufacture mainly railway materials and structurals. In the course of inter-government negotiations, India, it is reported (although the report has not been confirmed), refused to accept a dismantled steel mill from Czechoslovakia and a second-rate mill previously rejected by China. In February, 1955, the credit agreement was signed. Thus, within five months of the Indian approach, the USSR sent out a technical survey team, prepared and negotiated an interim report, and signed an agreement for a project then estimated to have a total cost of 1.1 billion rupees and a USSR export component of 434 million rupees.

Under the agreement, the USSR undertook to design and provide the most up-to-date equipment (worth 434 million rupees F.O.B. USSR ports) for a 1-million-ton ingot plant to produce mainly railway and structural materials. In addition, India had to pay 25 million rupees for the detailed project report, drawing designs, and other technical services. Repayments were to be made in rupees over twelve years computed as from the date of each consignment. The USSR agreed to use these rupees for purchases in India but reserved the right to convert the outstanding rupee balance into sterling. Final agreement on construction of the plant was contingent upon Indian acceptance of the detailed Soviet project report to be submitted within nine months after selection of the site. The USSR agreed to receive one or more Indian delegations to observe the operations of a plant similar to the type to be built in India. The USSR was to be paid up to 8 million rupees in the event of Indian rejection of the report, while Indian acceptance of the report had to be conveyed within three months of its submission.

The agreement clearly spelled out the division of responsibility between the Indian government and project authorities, on the one hand, and Soviet authorities, on the other. India was to complete arrangements for raw materials, transport, water supply, civil works, internal procurement of equipment, administration, and financing. The USSR undertook the responsibility for supply of equipment at world competitive prices, supervision of construction, commissioning and operations, performance of individual items and the plant as a whole, provision of adequate Soviet personnel at USSR cost to supervise and advise, for up to three years after commissioning of the plant, training of Indian personnel for designing and operations in the USSR and at the site, and liabilities in connection with infringement of patent rights. The USSR also undertook to provide a Chief Engineer who would coordinate all Soviet activity in relation to the project and to commission the project satisfactorily in two phases by the end of 1958 and 1959, subject to absence of delays on the Indian side, regarding which it retained the right to call attention to delays and ask for implementation of suggestions. It also agreed to hand over all drawings and blueprints without additional charge.

The agreement, like all other subsequent agreements with East European countries, did not require any payment by India for royalty or fees for know-how. The agreement was of a package nature, with the USSR combining the supply of technical consultant services, detailed working drawings, equipment, and finance. There was no question of preparing designs or specifications for tenders:

In Russia design organizations are independent of the manufacturing organizations. Therefore, though the agreement was for the consultancy service as well as for supply of equipment, the arrangement was said to have all the advantages of independent consultancy as well as of a well-coordinated and integrated approach to the problem.[54]

The entire agreement was negotiated on the Indian side by a committee of selected senior civil servants (against only one civil servant in the case of Rourkela). The Soviet preliminary project report was considered by a team of twenty-five experts. A delegation of eleven official and nonofficial experts visited the USSR to inspect representative steel works and factories manufacturing metallurgical equipment. This team made certain suggestions which were accepted by Soviet consultants in preparing the detailed project.

The agreement did not specifically mention the amount of the credit, but the payments due from India were put down under at least four headings: (1) cost of plant to be supplied by the USSR, excluding sintering plant, estimated at 434 million rupees F.O.B. USSR ports; (2) payment of 25 million rupees for project report and drawings; (3) an amount to be agreed upon later for salaries and expenses of Soviet personnel; and (4) payment for "separate

[54] Estimates Committee, *Thirty-third Report, 1958-59*, Lok Sabha Secretariat, February, 1962, pp. 21-22. The Committee did not come across any criticism of the agreement or its working with respect to the consultation service for the project.

contracts for prices . . . of equipment . . . not covered by the terms of this Agreement." The final credit amount came to 647 million rupees.

In March, 1956, a supplementary agreement was signed to provide for training of 300 Indian skilled workers and 135 engineers in the USSR (later increased to 686 in all) and of 4,500 unskilled workers and 500 engineers in India. The highest number of Soviet personnel at the plant was 843, which was reduced to 170 on commissioning of the plant and to less than 100 in 1961. The salaries and expenses of Soviet personnel employed by the project were paid for by India. Through March, 1961, 50 million rupees were paid to Soviet engineers on this account. There were significant delays at the Indian end in selecting personnel for training, especially in design work, but the presence of a large number of Soviet personnel eventually prevented disruption of the construction and operation schedule in a large measure.

The importance which the USSR attached to completion of the project on schedule was indicated in a number of ways; apart from the speed at which the preliminary work was done, expert assistance was provided and schemes drawn up for training of Indian personnel. The credit agreement excluded development of the Rajahara iron ore mine, which was left wholly to India. In November, 1957, this work was also taken up by the USSR when India found itself unable to develop the mine in time to feed the plant. At the Soviet end, Prime Minister Khrushchev himself took a personal interest in the fulfillment of contracts by the hundred-odd organizations concerned with the project. At one stage, when transport bottlenecks in India threatened to hold up delivery of equipment at the site, Khrushchev cabled Prime Minister Nehru for the latter's personal intervention in removing the bottleneck.

Competent technical opinion, in India and elsewhere, has rated the Bhilai plant very high. Among other things, it has been said that Bhilai "is better designed for continuous production than anything I have seen either in the U.S.A. or in Russia proper."[55] Not only was the construction of Bhilai completed sooner than the other two

[55] Earle C. Smith, Chief Metallurgist and Director of Research, Republic Steel Corporation of the U.S. Quoted by Sankarasubramanyam, *The Public Sector*, p. 26.

public-sector plants (although not on schedule), but as the figures in Table 8 demonstrate, its production potential has been more quickly realized.

TABLE 8

Output of Bhilai, Durgapur,
and Rourkela Steel Plants,
1961–62 and 1962–63
(Millions of Tons)

	1961–62	1962–63
Bhilai	0.79	1.06
Durgapur	0.46	0.73
Rourkela	0.35	0.70

In addition, Bhilai attained profitable operations earlier than Rourkela and Durgapur. Thus, in 1960–61 Bhilai yielded a profit of 15.3 million rupees as compared with losses of 23 million rupees for the two other plants.[56]

Nevertheless, investment costs at Bhilai have followed the same upward curve as other public sector plants, rising from an initial estimate of 1.1 billion rupees to nearly 2 billion rupees finally. The plant as a whole has met with similar delays, though on a significantly lower scale, so that full commissioning was delayed by nearly eighteen months as compared with the target date of end of 1959.

The terms of repayment, reckoned from the date of each consignment, required beginning of the repayment as early as 1956–57. A little more than a quarter of the credit had been repaid by March, 1961, as shown in Table 9.

The schedule of early repayment has obviously been onerous from the Indian point of view. Subsequent agreements have recorded easier terms, including substantial grace periods.

Enthusiastic Soviet nursing of the project continues. The credit agreement for financing expansion of Bhilai to a 2.5-million-ton ingot capacity during the Third Plan (1961–66) was signed as early as September, 1959. The total cost of Bhilai expansion in the Third Plan was estimated at 1.66 billion rupees, of which the foreign exchange cost (including cost of Soviet personnel) is 610 million rupees. The allocation out of the September, 1959, credit for this

[56] Information based on a Hindustan Steel publication.

purpose was 750 million rupees. In June–July, 1961, Soviet organizations submitted a detailed project report on the expansion. Most of the design work was done at Bhilai under the guidance of Soviet experts. Hindustan Steel was to employ 200 Soviet engineers and technicians to look after the expansion. Although training of Indian per-

TABLE 9

Repayment of the Bhilai Credit

Year	Annual, millions of rupees	Cumulative, millions of rupees
1956–57	1.5	1.5
1957–58	12.7	14.2
1958–59	43.3	57.5
1959–60	54.7	112.2
1960–61	55.1	167.3
1961–62	64.0	231.3
1962–63 [a]	98.0	329.3

[a] Revised estimates, inclusive of 54 million rupees due in 1963–64, proposed to be repaid a year earlier.

sonnel was not covered by the expansion agreement, the USSR indicated its willingness to undertake this work. A contract for the expansion project was signed in February, 1962. There are preliminary indications of Soviet aid for an expansion of the project to a capacity of 3.5 million tons during the Fourth Five-Year Plan, 1966–71.

Highway Programs in Thailand [57]

In Thailand, the United States and the World Bank have been the principal sources of assistance for the country's highway programs. The U.S. assistance has been particularly extensive.

U.S. ASSISTANCE

The United States has had a large number of highway programs in Thailand. From 1951 through 1954, American assistance to Thai highways consisted of technical assistance and a small amount of construction equipment. Assistance was directed to improvement of a specific list of the most critically needed highways, most of which

[57] By Robert F. Meagher.

were included in later programs. In 1954 the political climate in Viet Nam and Laos led to an expansion of the highway programs. Beginning in 1955, the U.S. aid mission and the Thai government, working jointly, developed a comprehensive plan for a basic highway system. This provided for eight primary highways. As the United States became involved in the highway program, various needs became evident and resulted in the following U.S.-sponsored and financed activities: heavy equipment training school, a highway bridge replacement program, a highway materials survey, a highway equipment pool, technical assistance to the Thai Highways Department, and an evaluation of the transportation system requirements. These programs supplemented the engineering and construction principally of the following highways and road programs: the Northeast, or Friendship, Highway; the East-West Highway; the Bangkok-Saraburi Highway; the Korat-Nongkai Highway; and the Bangkapi road program within Bangkok. The Northeast and East-West Highway programs are discussed in detail below.

During the period from 1951 to 1962 a total of $107.6 million of U.S. economic aid was obligated to the transportation sector of the Thai economy, of which $83.8 million, or 77.8 percent, was spent on highway programs. These grants were supplemented by substantial Thai contributions. More recently, U.S. assistance for highways has been granted in the form of loans. In May, 1965, AID authorized a $20.6-million loan, at an interest rate of 3½ percent and a repayment term of twenty-five years, including a five-year grace period, for a road to link the Friendship and East-West Highways; this was matched by a local currency appropriation by the Thai government equivalent to $16.9 million. Also, the EXIMBANK of Washington is providing a loan of $19 million for the Bangkok-Sriracha Highway.

Northeast, or Friendship, Highway. Following the fall of North Viet Nam to the Communists and the occupation of two provinces of Laos by the Communist-led Pathet Lao, Thailand's defense and strategic importance became an immediate concern of the U.S. government. There had been a military aid program to Thailand since 1951, and the Thais had received equipment and training from the United States. With the major threat to Thailand from a military point of view considered to be from the northeast and with no existing highway into the northeast capable of carrying the traffic imposed by modern mechanized military forces, it was considered necessary for military operations in this area to undertake a road program. The Thai military forces had been furnished transport to support field operations, but such vehicles could not be properly utilized unless the road facilities were improved. The Northeast Highway represented a major start in the direction of adequate tactical and logistic support of troops in this area of high strategic value. The Thai armed forces were not capable of supporting operations in this area by air transport, and both rail and road facilities were necessary to accommodate military loads.

In addition to these military reasons, the northeast section of Thailand was and still is the most economically depressed area in the country, and it was believed that a highway would help in its development by providing communications with the large market area in Bangkok and its environs. In addition, it was hoped that the highway would provide the means to tie the people of the northeast more closely to those in the central plains area and thus strengthen their relations with the economic, political, and cultural life of the country.

The Thai government was consulted, and agreed on the construction of a road from Saraburi to Ban Phai (192 miles) as soon as possible, the most critical section being the section between Saraburi and Korat (100 miles).

It was decided that U.S. engineering and construction firms would be used for the work because the Thais did not have the capacity to undertake a job of this magnitude, considering the type of construction planned and the shortness of time. This was to be the first highway constructed in Thailand with modern mechanical methods of construction. It was hoped that it would serve as a model for other primary highways and that there would be firsthand training for the Thais in the application of these techniques and methods. Owing to the urgency of the situation, the U.S. Mutual Security Agency waived the requirements for competitive bids and comparative proposals for the construction and engineering, and permitted a negotiated contract with an engineering firm (Sverdrup and Parcel Engineering Company) and a construction firm (Raymond Construction Company).

An initial preliminary estimate of $7.5 million was made for the cost of constructing the 192 miles of road from Saraburi to Ban Phai. Half of the road involved new construction through difficult terrain, and the other half involved largely bridge repairs. This estimate was a first quick estimate made in Bangkok based on such information as was available in Thai government surveys and plans. Before any contracting was undertaken, however, an engineering reconnaissance survey was made by the Raymond Company and by Sverdrup and Parcel. This survey resulted in a new estimate of $22 million. On this basis it was decided to build only the first 100-mile stretch from Saraburi to Korat. Further upward revisions in design criteria to meet military requirements, and general worldwide construction cost increases were reasons given for a subsequent revised estimate of $22 million for the first 100-mile stretch. The actual cost of the construction was $20 million. With deduction of equipment and parts transferred to the East-West Highway, however, the net cost was $15.7 million.

The engineers and construction contractors arrived in Thailand in August, 1955, and the highway was dedicated on July 10, 1958.

Regularly employed engineers and technicians of the Thai Highway Department were assigned to the Northeast Highway project from the beginning in order to gain experience. One group of Thais was given the job of acquiring right-of-way for the road and quarry sites. This group also handled relationships with Thai citizens along the road, involving the location of culvert pipes in rice paddies, the location of entrance roads, and crossings for railroads. A second group was assigned to the project for specific jobs in which additional manpower was needed. They were used primarily in survey parties and in drafting and design work. A third group consisted of recent graduates in civil engineering from Chulalongkorn University in Bangkok, who were sent to the project for training as well as to assist in the work. These young men were rotated through location and construction, surveying, drafting and design, soils and materials testing, and inspection of construction. Most of the men were doing satisfactory work within six months and fitted into permanent positions within a year. In addition to the training program, there was an observation program for highway officials. The Thai personnel that participated in the training and observation program consisted of thirty-seven working engineers, thirteen working technicians, twenty-four visiting Division Engineers, ninety-seven visiting District Engineers, one Chief of Surveys, and six Chulalongkorn engineering students. In addition, 1,500 Thais were trained in various phases of operation of equipment, maintenance, repair, welding, and quarry operations.

At the time that construction began on the Friendship Highway, there were many critics. Putting aside the military factors which were not necessarily evident to observers at the time, their criticisms related to the standards and specifications and the economic importance of the highway. Critics argued that the wheel base load was too high and that there was no need to round out the curves and reduce steep grades as much as was being done, for the cost was too high for a country in Thailand's stage of development.

The road has now been open for seven years. It was built under the U.S. standard that a primary road should be adequate for fifteen years. If anything, it appears that the standards may have been too low. The road is already beginning to feel the effects of overloaded, fast-moving vehicles. It is not yet possible in Thailand to control traffic loads on highways. Although the rules have been established, it has not been possible to enforce them.

Agricultural production in the area of the new highway, which has shortened the distance between Bangkok and Korat by 90 miles is booming. New crops of maize and kenaf have been introduced, and a new livestock industry has sprung up. In addition, small industries are beginning to develop near the road. The most recent traffic density charts indicate that the Friendship Highway has quickly become one of the most heavily traveled highways in Thailand. At present, average traffic is over 2,000 vehicles per day.

East-West Highway. While the construction of the Friendship Highway was under way, discussions were held between the Thai government and the U.S. government about the construction of a road from northern Thailand to northeast Thailand. There had never been an all-weather road connecting these two sections of the country. One of Thailand's armies had headquarters in Pitsanuloke in the northern region and another had its headquarters in Korat in the northeastern region. It was considered necessary to have a road which would be capable of carrying these military forces and equipment from northern to northeastern Thailand. This was a primary consideration in the joint agreement between the two governments to go ahead with the construction of the East-West Highway. In addition, it was believed that there would be other byproducts from the construction of such a road. It was believed that this sparsely populated area contained mineral resources and large tracts of timber and that it had farming possibilities. Development of these resources would be encouraged by the construction of a road in the area. Moreover, the UN Economic Commission for Asia and the Far East had proposed a Trans-Asian Highway, and this was to be a Thai link in such a highway.

When initially considered, the East-West Highway was planned to run from Pitsanuloke to a point near Dansai; but these plans were changed subsequently, and the amended proposal was for a road from Pitsanuloke to Lomsak (about 75 miles). It was hoped that this road would then be continued to Khon Kaen (near Ban Phai), thus linking northern and northeastern Thailand.

The same construction and engineering contractors that built the Friendship Highway were retained to build the East-West Highway. Acting on a letter of intent, in anticipation of a contract, a reconnaissance of the Pitsanuloke area was made by members of Sverdrup and Parcel Engineering Company and the Raymond Construction Company in December, 1956. The actual contracts were signed in October, 1957. The engineering contract was subsequently amended to include services for a bridge reconstruction project on other highways, a preliminary highway location study from Lomsak to Khon Kaen, and a bridge over the Nan River at Pitsanuloke.

The final inspection and acceptance of the completed 75-mile road took place in January, 1961. The bridge over the Nan River was completed in early 1963. The project has cost approximately $17 million, plus over $300,000 for the Nan River Bridge.

Location and design work on the Friendship Highway was ahead of construction, and this made it possible for the transfer to the East-West Highway area of an experienced crew of engineers and the use of equipment on hand. The letter of intent provided for the free transfer of men and equipment between the two contracts. Both contracts were administered from the same Bangkok office, and economies were made possible through a central management and through the ability to transfer personnel and equipment freely between the contracts. U.S. aid missions like to enter into negotiated contracts with engineers and construction companies which have done a good job in the area. It saves time and is usually economical, and the mission is relatively sure of what they are getting. Congress is wary, however, of such arrangements,[58] fearing possible conflicts of interest, favoritism, and higher prices.

Like the Friendship Highway project, the East-West Highway provided for training of Thai personnel. A total of forty-one graduate engineers, ten technicians, and thirty-one student engineers worked on various aspects of this contract. The graduate engineers and technicians were all from the Thai Highway Department. The construction corporation also trained 3,679 manual workers and 399 administrative personnel.

In August, 1960, the engineering feasibility study and cost estimates of constructing a road of primary standards between Lomsak and Khon Kaen were presented to the Thai government and the U.S. aid mission. The estimated length of this road was 147 miles through some mountainous terrain, and the estimated construction cost was $19.8 million. At that time it was decided not to continue the road to Khon Kaen. Inasmuch as the principal purpose of constructing the road was military, one may conclude that there was a change in attitudes in relation to the military priority for the road. Discussions on the continuation of the highway to Khon Kaen have been revived recently, and it is possible that the project may move forward at some time in the future.

To a limited extent the road has opened up a corn-growing area. A major limitation on more activity along the road has been the fact that it is not linked to any major market area. The recent AID loan for $20.6 million mentioned above is for a 175-mile north and south road to link the East-West Highway at Lomsak with the Friendship Highway at Saraburi. This may increase the economic importance of the existing road. In addition, feasibility studies are being carried out by the World Bank and AID on roads from Chumpae to Khon Kaen and from Lomsak to Chumpae, respectively. After these feasi-

[58] "Foreign Aid Construction Projects—Hearings before a Sub-Committee of the Committee on Government Operations," U.S. House of Representatives, 85th Congress, 2nd session (November, 1957–June, 1958).

bility studies are completed, the Thais will probably ask for design and construction studies for these roads and eventually for financing from these or other sources.

Technical Assistance from the United States. In retrospect, U.S. technical assistance to Thai highway programs appears to have been *ad hoc.* As problems arose, the Americans sought an organizational or administrative solution.

The Highway Department, as such, did not receive much attention until assistance had been coming to Thailand for a number of years. Transportation Consultants, Inc., carried out an evaluation of Thailand's transportation system requirements and issued a report in September, 1959. They were extremely critical about the operation of the Highway Department and its operational and administrative divisions. Charles Upham Associates worked directly with the Highway Department from 1957 to 1962. This group advised the Department and supervised the training of Thais in highway system planning, in location, in preliminary surveys, in plans and specifications, in construction, in highway maintenance, in soils and materials, in equipment, and on a technical library. In April, 1962, the Public Administration Service (PAS) made a report on the organization and administration of the Department of Highways. Aside from general critical comments on the internal organization and administration, this report made specific reference to the inadequate provision for highway planning and maintenance. PAS pointed out that traffic and safety engineering were largely ignored and that there were insufficient shop facilities and equipment. They found fault with budgetary, procurement, and inventory procedures and controls and suggested an administrative reorganization of the Department. As part of the current IBRD loan, a British firm of consulting engineers is advising the Thai Highway Department's division of design, construction, and maintenance.

Under the Highway Bridge Replacement Project, Thai and American technicians found that the replacement of bridges would open up more than 2,400 miles of existing highway to heavy commercial traffic. The plan proposed the replacement of 1,011 bridges which had made the highways hazardous or precluded their use entirely. Except for two sections of highways, all necessary engineering, including design and supervision of construction, was provided by the Royal Thai Highway Department. At the start of the project, there were only seven contractors in Thailand known to have the equipment, financial backing, and technical background for doing such work. As a result, the Royal Thai Highway Department found it necessary to build fifteen of the first bridges itself. Eventually seventy-eight contractors were considered capable of assuming responsibility for contracts and actively participated in the program. Construction came to be done entirely by independent local contractors, who bid competitively for the work. The last of the 1,011 bridges was completed about the end of 1963.

The Friendship and East-West Highways were rush projects primarily justified on a security basis. Nevertheless, large numbers of Thai engineers and construction workers received valuable training in highway engineering and construction by being associated with these projects. This experience has permitted Thai engineers of the Highway Department to perform the engineering for the entire Korat-Nongkai Highway in the northeast, which was constructed by Thais and completed late in 1964. There is still a shortage of trained highway engineers and construction workers in Thailand, but Thailand is growing more self-sufficient in this area with each passing year.

Evaluation of U.S. Aid. U.S. aid and technical assistance has concentrated on highways more than on any other field. This assistance has had a number of objectives: establishment of central government contact with isolated populations; military access to remote areas, economic development of particular areas, and a desire to help the Thais to become self-sufficient in this fundamental sector of their economy.

In relation to two of the major roads, Friendship Highway and the East-West Highway, the principal motivation for the projects was military, although this purpose was not made public at the time the projects were approved. If the motives for a project are unknown, it can make analysis difficult and misleading. In relation to these two roads, Friendship Highway was a great economic success in addition to being of military use. Such was not the case with the East-West Highway. In this case the analyst is presented with an expensive highway running from a town of 3,000 to a town of 300, with only minimal economic activity resulting from the construction. Within the context of a military decision, this may have been justifiable; from the point of view of development, it was not.

When nondevelopmental aspects of a project are paramount and when the interest of the donor in a project is as great as the recipient's, the donor has less control over the project. It is in this kind of situation where one is most likely to find malpractices and corruption. There are no such allegations in relation to the above projects.

Although the urgency for the completion of the two major highways resulted in construction by Americans, the United States did not ignore the technical-assistance training function offered by these projects. Many Thais were trained on these projects and are now putting this experience to use.

The results of U.S. assistance have, in general, been favorable. There are still a number of organizational problems in the Highway Department, and road maintenance programs seem to have fallen short of expectations. On the other hand, the Highway Bridge Construction Program and the large number of trained highway engineers and construction workers have fulfilled some of the objectives of U.S. assistance. The network of primary roads, which were largely on paper eleven years ago, are quickly becoming a reality thanks to external financial and technical assistance.

WORLD BANK ASSISTANCE

A first approach to the World Bank in 1952 for a loan to Thailand for the construction of major roads was not successful. In 1960, the government of Thailand made another approach to the Bank for a survey of the highway network, and this approach resulted in the granting of a loan in June, 1963. A World Bank team visited Thailand in March–April, 1961, and, together with Thai officials, made a detailed analysis of existing highways and steps which would be required to bring these highways to modern standards. A recent study states, "In a very real sense highway planning by the Department of Highways dates from the creation of this technical working group." [59] The Bank study indicated that three-quarters of the highway system was in need of rehabilitation and/or improvement.

[59] "Report on Organization and Administration of the Department of Highways," Public Administration Service, Report Number M-10, April, 1962, p. 33.

In 1962, the World Bank was approached for a loan to finance the construction of part of the roads program suggested by its 1961 mission. Another Bank mission visited Thailand in July, 1962. The program discussed relates to the rehabilitation and construction of seven highways:

1. Songkla–Naradhivas (in the extreme south).
2. Chiengmai–Lampang (in the northwest).
3. Loey–Khon Kaen (north-northeast).
4. Udorn–Nakorn Panom (in the extreme northeast).
5. Nakorn Pathom–Chumporn (near Bangkok to the south).
6. Nakorn Srithamaraj–Kantang (south).
7. Saraburi–Nakorn Sawan (near Bangkok to the northwest).

The contemplated program includes final engineering, construction, supervision, advisory engineering, training of Thai engineers abroad, instruments, and other sundry items. The program is to be carried out in three phases from 1963 through 1970. During the first phase, the final engineering and construction of two highways will take place, namely, Songkla–Naradhivas and Chiengmai–Lampang. At the same time, final engineering will take place on all of the other highways except Saraburi–Nakorn Sawan. During phases two and three, all seven highways will be completed. To carry out all these programs, it is expected that the Thai government will have to borrow over $70 million for the foreign exchange costs.

During the course of these negotiations, the World Bank teams gave priority to reconsructing and completing the Nakorn Pathom–Chumporn road. They were advised, however, by the Highway Department that this road was in rather good condition from Nakorn Pathom to Prajuab (about halfway) and that the Highway Department therefore believed that it should not be included in the first phase of the Bank program. Discussions continued, and the World Bank team reduced the priority on this road but kept it in the program. The program was finalized, and the Bank team returned to Washington.

Later, however, negotiations were reportedly undertaken by Thailand with a private American group for the extension of an interest-free, seven-year supplier's credit of up to $33 million for the engineering, construction, and/or reconstruction of the highway from Nakorn Pathom to Prajuab, despite the indications regarding its priority that had been given to the World Bank and a higher cost for the road under this arrangement. For a time this incident threatened to endanger the possibility of a Bank highway loan, but the incident and consequently the danger have since been eliminated. The Bank granted Thailand a highway loan of $35 million, at a term of twenty years and an interest rate of 5½ percent, on June 11, 1963.

CONCLUDING OBSERVATIONS

The major difference between U.S. and World Bank assistance to Thailand's highways has related to the motives underlying the assistance. The primary goal of U.S. assistance was military, although, at least in the case of the Friendship Highway, there were substantial economic byproducts flowing from the new road. The World Bank's goal was limited to development purposes.

An interesting problem might have developed if the reported negotiations for a supplier's credit had arisen in relation to one of a series of roads being financed by a U.S. loan rather than one being financed by a World Bank loan. The Bank, with its goals limited to economic development, has much greater freedom to cut off assistance if it is dissatisfied with the way a government is conducting its internal affairs in relation to development than is the United States with its diverse motives.

Another important distinction between these sources of aid relates to the tying of U.S. aid to American goods and services. This policy has been in effect since 1960. World Bank assistance is allocated for goods and services procured as a result of worldwide bidding.

With the completion of the roads presently contemplated, Thailand will have undergone a major change in its transportation network. Vast areas of the country will be within easy contact for the first time in the history of Thailand. In addition many new areas will now be exploited because there is a way to evacuate goods to the markets.

Sudan American Textile Industry Co. Ltd.[60]

This case study presents a brief history of the development, financing, and operation of the Sudan American Textile Industry

[60] By Robert F. Meagher.

John Theodoracopulos Co. Ltd., which is popularly known as SATI.

BACKGROUND

Prior to independence, Sudan had no large-scale industrial enterprises. Cotton and gum arabic provided the overwhelming proportion of foreign exchange. Virtually all manufactured goods were imported. Following independence, there were increasing demands for modernizing the country. It was recognized that this would be expensive and would require the importation of foreign equipment. In attempting to select industries, textiles were an obvious choice, for although Sudan was a country rich in cotton, it had no textile industry. Each year Sudan imported £S12–13 million of textiles. If Sudan had its own industry, these foreign exchange costs would be saved.

In late 1957 and early 1958, the U.S. and Sudanese governments discussed the possibility of U.S. aid to Sudan. The parties signified their decision for a program in an agreement signed on March 31, 1958. A U.S.-financed textile mill was one of the possible projects discussed by the parties.

The idea of a Sudanese textile mill was carried back to the United States and discussed in various entrepreneurial circles. One entrepreneur, John Theodoracopulos, decided to look into the scheme, provided that the DLF would give a long-term loan for the project. The DLF advised that they would be interested in financing such a project provided that their standards could be met.

Theodoracopulos, a ship-owner, with a reputation for entrepreneurial ability, had two consulting groups review the project. He then organized SATI and had it incorporated in Sudan on November 10, 1958, with an authorized capital of £S1 million in 10,000 ordinary shares of £S100 each. On the same date, by an order of the Sudan government, the company was classified as an "Approved Enterprise" under the terms of the Approved Enterprise (Concessions) Act of 1956.

Approved Enterprises are authorized to receive the following benefits for the purpose of assessing business profits tax:

1. Depreciation at double the normal rates for five years.
2. Profits up to 5 percent on the capital employed are exempt

from the tax and additional profits are taxed at one-half of the standard rate for five years.

3. Any net loss incurred over the five-year period of relief is treated as a loss incurred in the fifth year of relief.

4. Any dividend paid during the five-year period of relief is tax-exempt.

The Act also provides for these additional benefits:

1. Exemption from import duties on machinery, tools, and equipment up to the time of the full establishment of the industry.

2. Exemption from import duties on building materials not manufactured in Sudan and on raw materials.

3. Permission for the entry into Sudan of technical personnel.

4. Repatriation in transferable sterling of foreign capital and profits thereon and bona fide savings of foreign employees.

The company was also advised that protection against foreign competition would be sympathetically considered on its merits by the government when necessary.

THE DLF LOAN

Following SATI's organization, a formal request was submitted for a DLF loan. Prolonged negotiations were carried on, and the proposed loan agreement went through many drafts. Principal issues during the negotiations included the capitalization of the company, the technical consultants for the factory, and the control by the DLF of expenditures of funds from other sources. The Loan Agreement was signed on May 22, 1959. The Agreement provided for an eighteen-year $10-million loan at 5½ percent interest per annum, conditioned upon SATI's raising $10 million of matching capital from other non-public sources. April 1, 1964, was designated in a subsequent amendment to the Agreement, as the date for the first of twenty-nine semiannual repayments of principal. This followed by six months the first payment of interest.

At least $2.5 million of the matching capital had to be in the form of equity capital. The remainder could be in debt or equity in the form of cash, in irrevocable letters of credit, or in eligible items other than services which formed part of a DLF-approved list. The value of the eligible items had to be within the DLF-approved level.

DLF and matching capital funds were to be used for financing the reasonable costs of acquisition, importation, and installation of such equipment and materials and services required to carry out the project. The expenditure of all of these funds, including matching capital, required prior approval, in writing, of the DLF. No goods or services either coming from Communist countries or carried on Communist ships could be financed from these funds and 50 percent of the gross tonnage of the imported eligible items were to be transported on U.S. ships, if they were available.

DLF funds could not be used for items ordered or contracted for prior to the signing of the Agreement, working capital, or local costs. No such limitations were placed on matching capital funds except that only the first year of working capital could come from these funds. Incorporation and organizational costs could also be financed out of matching capital.

In addition to SATI, three guarantors signed the Agreement with DLF: National Shipping and Trading Corporation, John Theodora-copulos, and the Vascona Compañía Naviera S.A. The last company is the principal shareholder of SATI and is wholly owned by Theodoracopulos. The guarantors have effective voting control of the issued and outstanding shares of SATI. They agreed jointly and severally to guarantee payment of SATI's obligations arising from the DLF loan, to assure private contributions to SATI of equity and loans to match the amount of the DLF loan, with SATI to provide funds for any costs over and above the $20-million estimated cost of the factory, to provide semiannual reports to the DLF on their financial status and at once in case of serious changes in their status, and not to reduce their consolidated net worth below the outstanding amount of the loan. At the date of the Agreement, they warranted that their unencumbered and freely disposable consolidated assets exceeded $15 million. As additional security, DLF secured a mortgage on SATI property and plant.

In return for the DLF loan, SATI agreed, among other things, to the following conditions: to maintain books and records on the expenditure of the DLF and matching capital funds; to provide quarterly reports containing information requested by the DLF on the status of the textile plant, the source and terms of the matching capital, any other matters relevant to the project; not to incur any indebtedness, excluding matching capital, for over a period of one year without the prior consent of the DLF; to maintain current assets at $1 million over current liabilities for the first two years after completion of the factory and at $2 million subsequent to that; to provide detailed plans and specifications of the project satisfactory to DLF; to enter into contracts with consulting engineers and firms for design, procurement, construction, and installation mutually acceptable to the parties; to provide a list of mutually acceptable eligible items and their costs and to include the uses to which the working capital would be put; and to provide satisfactory evidence that matching capital had been contributed. They warranted that they would carry out their operations with due diligence and efficiency following sound technical and engineering practices, employing competent and experienced management, and that all items supplied with DLF or matching funds would be used only within the Sudan during the life of the loan. Further warrants stated that no commission, fee, or payment of any kind had been or would be paid to any person, firm, or corporation in connection with the application which resulted in the making of the loan by the DLF, except for bona fide professional or technical or other comparable services and that these payments would be promptly declared.

March 31, 1963, was agreed on as the date for completion of the project. Final requests for letters of commitment were to be made by September 30, 1962, and the final disbursements made by March 31, 1963.

THE MATCHING CAPITAL

The matching capital consisted of $2.5 million of equity capital and $7.5 million of suppliers' credits. The equity was offered by Vascona Compañía Naviera S.A. on November 17, 1959. The minutes of the company state that these funds were received on April 8, 1960. The suppliers' credits were granted by a British Consortium consisting of the English Electric Co. Ltd.; Platt Bros. (Sales) Ltd.; and Maples, Ridgeway and Partners, Ltd., under a contract dated December 19, 1959. The total price payable under the contract was £5,933,583, of which £2,678,571 was a credit to be paid in nine equal semiannual installments commencing on February 28, 1963, at 5½ percent per annum on the decreasing balance.

SATI OPERATIONS AND PROBLEMS

Construction of the factory was begun in 1959. Installation of the plant and machinery commenced in 1961, and, after test runs at the end of that year, production started in February, 1962. A second shift was added in May, 1962. Bleaching and finishing operations were commenced by mid-November, 1962, and dyeing started in May, 1963. The company hoped to add a third shift by the end of 1963.

The first payment of interest came due to the Consortium on August 31, 1962, and was paid. The second payment, including principal and interest, was due on February 28, 1963. The company saw that it might not be possible to meet the second payment, and a meeting attended by representatives of SATI, the British Consortium, and the U.S. AID (the successor agency to the DLF) was held in London in February, 1963, to discuss SATI's financial position. The British Consortium agreed to defer their payment until May 31, 1963. The AID agreed to capitalize all interest due up to April 1, 1963.

Once SATI's major creditors learned of the company's financial difficulties, they carried out analyses of its operations. These analyses were presented in the form of two separate audit reports. The first, prepared by the British Consortium's chartered accountants, was delivered on May 31, 1963. The second, carried out by AID-retained auditors, was presented in August, 1963, and included SATI's balance sheet as of June 30, 1963. These reports painted a very gloomy picture of SATI's operations. Taken together, they explain the source of the company's difficulties. Major problems related to the cost of cotton, the sales price of cloth, dumping of foreign cloth, failure of the government of Sudan to provide adequate tariff protection, overestimation of the efficiency of the plant in its early years of production, poor management, and the use of too high a quality of cotton. These problems were heightened by an extremely high debt/equity ratio. The audit reports also pointed up a number of shortcomings in relation to the supervision of the loan by the creditors.

When the feasibility study was carried out in relation to SATI, it was estimated that cotton could be purchased at 7 piastres per pound and that the prevailing sales price for cloth would continue. Neither assumption proved to be correct. The price of cotton moved up to 9 piastres per pound—an increase of 28 percent. At the same time the price of cloth dropped by 25 percent. These were the principal factors in SATI's difficulties.

These factors were exacerbated by the fact that the government of Sudan had not instituted protective tariffs to aid this new industry. Egyptian and other cloth flooded the market and prices fell. Domestic political considerations were such that the government did not want to introduce tariffs which would raise the price of a staple product, used by virtually everyone in the country, by at least 25 percent. The cloth from the United Arab Republic was in part payment for outstanding debts which might never be paid in any other manner, and it was decided not to stop this flow. In addition, there appears to have been some resentment over the size of the potential profits which Theodoracopulos would make.

The cotton used by SATI was of a higher quality than was needed for the cloth market of Sudan. The raw cotton cost was 47 percent of the final selling price, which is much higher than normal. The government would not, however, permit the import of cheaper quality cotton from India or elsewhere.

The technical experts were overoptimistic in their appraisals of the operating efficiency of the plant in its early years. They did not give sufficient weight to the absence of auxiliary services in developing countries. They overlooked the absence of training schools, the fact that labor turnover would be high, and the fact that shift labor was uncommon in Sudan. The experts had assumed a production of 70 million yards of cloth, whereas the chartered accountants scaled this down to 55.2 million yards. The difference between the figures was caused by estimates of a 75 percent loom efficiency as against 90 percent, 22.5-hour working days per month instead of 24, loom speeds of 190 p.p.m. rather than 200 p.p.m., and the fact that the specifications for cloth required more picks per inch than the original estimates.

The chartered accountants suggested a new managerial structure and a change in the basis for the management fee. It was hoped that decreasing the size of the expatriate staff and increasing the local staff could reduce the labor cost per yard to SATI by 20 percent. SATI's financial structure was so heavily weighted on the debt side that there was little money left for working capital, and there was a constant pressure to meet current obligations. Among other things, this caused SATI to attempt to market its cloth without offering credit to the local merchants. This went against prevailing market practices and reduced the interest in SATI cloth. In addition, SATI violated the DLF loan agreement by having the guarantors pledge their already-pledged assets to local Sudanese banks in return for overdraft facilities.

As of May 31, 1961, the chartered accountants gave this picture of SATI's financial condition:

Original capital:		
Share capital		£S 887,100
AID loan (original)	3,500,000	
Interest capitalized on AID loan	385,000	3,885,000
English electric credit		2,625,000
		£S7,397,100
Cost to SATI of its land, buildings, machinery, transport, etc.	6,536,478	
Of which the following was not yet paid	230,000	6,306,478
		£S1,090,622
It has incurred fees and expenses with formation, construction, management, and training and interest on the loan, and credit during the construction period as follows:		
Charged to fixed assets account (including £S 385,000 AID capitalized interest)	1,146,733	
Charged to preliminary expenses	163,387	1,310,120
Giving deficit of		£S 219,498

The foregoing excludes the balance due on fixed assets, trading losses already incurred, any further losses to be incurred in the period of reorganization, and increased working capital.

SATI must be assured of permanent capital of £S2.4 million broken down as follows:

Deficit of original capital	£S 219,498
Stocks	1,450,000
Outstanding capital expenditures	230,000
Provision for further loss during reorganization	200,000
Trading losses to February 29, 1963	304,521
	£S2,404,019

The chartered accountants pointed out that the need for permanent capital could be reduced to £S1,083,315 if the outstanding credits with the banks (£S700,500) and the Sudan government (£S620,204) could be deferred.

They concluded that SATI could be viable only if (1) the Sudan government was prepared to create conditions which would enable an infant industry to grow up by giving it assistance and protection against mature foreign competition so that it could sell its products at a price which would enable it to meet its obligations and earn a reasonable profit, (2) AID and the Consortium were prepared to give a period of grace in relation to SATI's obligations, (3) existing credits and bank facilities could be retained on a revolving basis, and (4) there was a fundamental reorganization of the management structure of SATI.

Prior to the deadline of May 31, 1963, set in the February Moratorium Agreement, it was clear that SATI would not be able to meet its payments on the loan or the credit. A second meeting was held in May in London to decide on what further steps should be taken.

At this meeting the creditors voiced their dissatisfaction with SATI's operations. They decided that John Theodoracopulos should be replaced and that his interest should be bought out. In return for his withdrawal, the creditors agreed that there would be a new moratorium on the debt; they would make representations to the government of Sudan on behalf of SATI in relation to tariffs, import quotas, credit for Sudanese cotton, and sundry other matters; they would not require Theodoracopulos to account for unaccounted expenditures from the equity capital; and they would give Theodoracopulos $1.54 million of notes which would be paid after other creditors were repaid. The $1.54-million figure was arrived at after an audit showed that more than $1.54 million of the equity capital, all of which had been put up by the Theodoracopulos group, had been expended on SATI operations. It was believed that following this procedure the factory would continue to run, and the creditors would minimize their risk of loss. These general points were accepted in principle by all the parties and the creditors began work on the formal document embodying these points.

From August 9 through August 14, conferences took place among the creditors, the government of Sudan, and representatives of SATI. Some of the points discussed during this period were reduction of the price of raw cotton, the replacement of Sudanese cotton by cheaper cotton, the sales price of SATI's cloth, the provision of cotton to SATI by the Sudanese government on credit, an increase in SATI's equity through stock purchases by the U.S. and Sudanese governments, the possibility of increasing working capital through a UK Export Credits Guarantee Department or U.S. P.L. 480 loan, a loan from Barclay's Bank, and the possibility of buying out the Consortium's interest at a discount. These meetings were inconclusive.

In addition to the Consortium and AID, the government of Sudan was an interested party, for it had not been paid for cotton delivered to SATI by the Sudan Ministry of Agriculture. This debt with interest amounted to over £S2 million by the fall of 1963.

THE PROPOSED UNDERSTANDING FOR FINANCIAL REORGANIZATION

Commencing in late October and continuing until February, 1964, meetings were held in Khartoum among SATI, the Consortium, AID, and the government of Sudan. The parties came to sufficient agreement to draw up a proposed understanding for reorganization of the company.

Under this proposed understanding, Vascona Compañía Naviera S.A. and John Theodoracopulos were to relinquish any rights to any present or future shares of SATI, and they relinquished any right to take part in the management of SATI. In return, Vascona Compañía Naviera S.A. were to become a deferred creditor in respect of £S550,000 ($1.54 million), and no accounting was to be made of expenditures by SATI from the equity capital exceeding $1.54 million. This credit was to be evidenced by a note which will mature for payment on July 1, 1980. Thus, the Theodoracopulos group was to receive a deferred credit in return for an amount of money which is less than the creditors were certain that the group put into the enterprise. As deferred creditors, they were not to receive principal prior to the full payment of the Consortium, AID, and the government of Sudan debts, and in no event were they to receive anything prior to 1967.

As of October 31, 1963, SATI's principal debts were as follows:

Sudan Ministry of Agriculture
For cotton lint 1961–62 crop, together with
interest, approx.   £S   613,531.833
For cotton lint 1962–1963 crop, together with
interest, approx.   1,430,000.000
Total   £S2,043,531.833

AID
For money advanced under loan agreement
dated May 22, 1959 $ 9,978,133.70
For interest accrued due up to April 1, 1963,
and agreed to be capitalized   1,259,355.99
For interest on principal and capitalized interest for the period from April 1, 1963, to
October 31, 1963, approx.   350,000.00
Total $11,587,489.69

The Consortium
For the unpaid balance of the price of goods
and services delivered and performed under
Construction Agreement dated December 19, 1959   £2,678,571.00
For interest on the unpaid balance for the
period August 31, 1962, to February 28,
1963, and agreed to be capitalized   73,660.00
For interest on the unpaid balance and capitalized interest for the period from February 28, 1963, to October 31, 1963, approx.   100,000.00
For extras and additions arising under the
said Construction Agreement together with
interest, approx.   220,000.00
Total   £3,072,231.00

For the unpaid balance of the price payable
under a separate Agreement for the Construction of SATI's hostel   £   14,757.00

Under the settlement each of the above parties agreed to accept payment for part of their debt in equity shares and part in non-interest-bearing convertible notes.

The mechanics were set forth as follows: existing share capital was to be reduced by canceling 8,869 outstanding shares owned by the Theodoracopulos group; 45,700 new ordinary shares of £S100 each were to be created; and the government of Sudan, the U.S. government and the Consortium were to subscribe for 3,500, 3,500, and 2,000 shares, respectively. The remainder of the shares were to be placed in reserve for the following purposes: for issue to Sudanese private investors (1,000), for issue to a management company (750), in case the government of Sudan, AID, or the Consortium exercises its conversion rights (35,950), and as a general reserve (129).

Payment for the shares was to be made by the creditors as set-off against debts due, by Sudanese private investors in cash, and by a management company in the form of services rendered.

On the "settlement date" the creditors were to accept the resignation of all of the members of the Board of Directors of SATI. A new Board was to be constituted, consisting of two persons nominated by the government of Sudan and three persons nominated jointly by AID and the Consortium. No one in the Theodoracopulos group was eligible for membership on the Board.

To determine the amount of the full debt of each of the parties, it was agreed that interest was to continue to accrue until a "settlement date." This date was twenty-one days after the date of the order of the Supreme Court of Sudan sanctioning the formal arrangements for the settlement of the debt.

The payment of that amount of debt still outstanding after the set-off in the form of common stock was to be settled as follows:

Government of Sudan. The 3,500 shares to be accepted by the government of Sudan were valued at £S350,000. Sudan was to accept non-interest-bearing convertible notes with a face value of up to £S1.65 million. These notes were to be paid in ten equal semiannual installments commencing on October 1, 1974. All of the debt remaining after taking into account the stock and the notes was to be paid within twenty-one days after the "settlement date" as defined above.

AID. The 3,500 shares to be accepted by the AID were valued at £S350,000. AID was to accept non-interest-bearing convertible notes with a face value up to £S1.65 million ($4.71 million). These notes were to be paid in ten equal semiannual installments commencing on October 1, 1974. All of the debt remaining after taking into account the stock and notes was to be paid in dollar promissory notes bearing 3¾ percent interest per annum. There were to be thirteen notes of equal amounts, and they were to be paid semiannually commencing on April 1, 1967.

The Consortium. The 2,000 shares to be accepted by the Consortium were valued at £S200,000. The remaining Consortium debts were defined as the principal debt, the Consortium debt for extras, and the separate agreement for the construction of SATI's hostel.

The shares which were to be accepted by the Consortium were set off against the principal debt. The remainder of the principal debt was to be secured by two sterling non-interest-bearing notes valued at £148,809.5 each, maturing on April 1, 1973, and October 1, 1973, respectively, and the balance of the Consortium principal debt was to be secured by sixteen sterling promissory notes bearing 5½ percent interest per annum and payable semiannually commencing on April 1, 1965. One-half of the debt for extras was to be paid to the Consortium within twenty-one days after the "settlement date." The other half of the debt for extras was to be secured by a sterling promissory note bearing 5½ percent interest per annum maturing on June 30, 1965. The entire debt relating to the Agreement for the construction of SATI's hostel was to be paid to the Consortium twenty-one days after the "settlement date."

On the "settlement date" the Consortium was to produce an estimate by a chartered accountant of the fair and reasonable additional financing charges which the Consortium would have as a result of the arrangements under this settlement, and SATI was to issue to the English Electric Company its non-interest-bearing promissory notes for the amount of such estimate or £120,000, whichever was smaller, and maturing for payment on October 1, 1979.

The government of Sudan was to guarantee the payment of 40 percent of the principal and interest payable to the Consortium under this settlement.

The parties also discussed the future operations of SATI. Two matters received particular attention: additional financial assistance to SATI and protection and assistance by the Sudanese Government to the company. Within three months after the "settlement date," both the government of Sudan and AID were each to lend or procure the loan to SATI of £S500,000 at 3 percent interest per annum payable semiannually in twelve equal installments commencing on April 1, 1968. The Consortium was, within three months after the "settlement date," to enter into a contract with SATI for the sale to SATI of spare parts and additions to equipment supplied under the Construction Agreement to a total value not exceeding £625,000. Additional equipment was limited to 25 percent of the total value of the new contract. All orders had to be placed before December 31, 1965, and payment for each order was to be 10 percent with the order, 10 percent against shipping documents or warehouse receipt, and 80 percent in eight equal successive interest-free, semiannual payments, secured by SATI's promissory notes, 40 percent of which were to be guaranteed by the government of Sudan and issued against the documents, commencing on June 30, 1967. The government of Sudan was to exempt all of these goods from customs and other import duties. The government of the Sudan was to take all steps necessary to insure that SATI could sell its current stock of finished goods at no less than the current price. In addition, the government was to take further steps to insure that SATI would be able to sell its future production at prices which would cover the full cost thereof and generate sufficient funds to enable it to meet the payments becoming due from time to time to the government, AID, and the Consortium.

Both the government of Sudan and AID stated in the proposed understanding that it was their mutual desire that SATI should be a privately owned company and that neither of them intended to exercise the conversion rights which would be attached to their non-interest-bearing notes in order to hold further shares themselves.

REVISION OF THE PROPOSED UNDERSTANDING

In February, 1964, the proposed understanding was approved by the Sudanese Council of Ministers. It was not signed, however, because the new Minister of Finance and Economics wanted an opportunity to review the understanding. In April, the Minister raised a number of questions and asked for additional data. AID answered the questions and provided the data. In August, the government of Sudan decided against accepting equity in SATI, and in October, a new proposed understanding was drafted, incorporating suggestions from each of the parties.

AID and the Consortium agreed to accept the shares which the government of Sudan no longer wanted. The AID agreed to increase the proposed equity holdings by £S200,000 and the Consortium by £S150,000, bringing their total holdings to £S550,000 and £S350,000, respectively. These amounts are to be offset against the debts presently outstanding. In the case of the Consortium, the remaining debt of £S2,539,686 will be repaid in twenty-two equal semiannual installments commencing June 30,1966. This loan will bear interest at the rate of 5½ percent on the declining balance. AID's remaining credit of £S3,762,427 will be repaid in thirty-four equal semiannual installments commencing June 30, 1967. Here again, interest will be at the rate of 5½ percent on the declining balance. Both of these debts will be secured by notes, a substantial portion of which will be convertible into ordinary shares if this should prove to be necessary.

The government, which will not be a shareholder, will lend SATI £S2,500,000. £S1,500,000 will be utilized immediately to repay a portion of the existing cotton credit of £S2,103,270. The balance of the cotton credit, £S603,270, will be repaid in six equal semiannual installments commencing June 30, 1966. The £S2.5-million loan will be repaid in thirty equal semiannual installments commencing June 30, 1969. With respect to both the cotton credit and the new loan, interest will be at the rate of 5½ percent on the declining balance. The loan from the government is to come out of P.L. 480–104(g) counterpart funds. The loan of £S2.5 million will leave SATI with £S1 million of additional working capital.

Theodoracopulos will receive a £S300,000 note payable from 1973 to 1983. Although interest will be set at 5½ percent commencing July 1, 1968, no payments will be made until 1973, because it is anticipated that the net profits, together with the balance carried forward, will be insufficient in the years 1968 to 1972 to permit current payments of interest. This £S300,000 note is considerably below the £S550,000 note promised to Theodoracopulos in the Moratorium Agreement. The parties believe, however, that he will accept the reduced amount.

It is understood that the government has confirmed their statement that they will take steps to insure that SATI will be able to sell its future production at prices which will cover the full costs thereof and generate sufficient funds to enable it to meet the payments becoming due from time to time to the government, AID, and the Consortium.

At the end of 1964, the military government was turned out of power, and a new civilian government took its place. There were no indications as of January, 1965, on how the new government views the revised proposed understanding.

OBSERVATIONS AND CONCLUSIONS

Although it is difficult to reconstruct the early history of SATI, it is clear that the United States believed that a large industrial project would be helpful to the Sudan government at a time when both governments feared that the Egyptians were threatening to subvert the government of Sudan and when the government was commencing a program of diversification.

The choice of Theodoracopulos as the recipient of a DLF loan for a textile mill seemed at first blush to be unusual. He was not a textile man. He had no special competence in Sudanese affairs. Apparently, he was selected because no textile people were interested in the project. But it is not known whether any attempt was made to find anyone in the textile industry. We have been advised that it was important to find an entrepreneur willing to invest in an area where there had been almost no prior industry. Theodoracopulos was such an entrepreneur.

The Greek textile experts retained by Theodoracopulos are an established group with a good reputation in their field. One might question, however, why they suggested such an expensive and modern plant for the Sudan. The chartered accountants, in retrospect, believed that a more moderate enterprise would have been more appropriate.

The overestimation of the productive capacity of the plant by the experts was the result of social, economic, and political factors. Estimates of the price of cotton and the sales price of cloth were based on the then-current prices in Sudan projected over the future years. An influx of cloth from Egypt as part payment of a debt to Sudan and an increase in the price of Sudanese cotton wiped out all of the anticipated profits.

The failure on the part of the experts to recognize and deal with local mores was a contributing factor. There was an overestimation of skills and education and a failure to appreciate that an innovation such as shift labor requiring some to work after 5:00 P.M. would be resisted. When the second shift was instituted, SATI was faced with a rapid rate of turnover of staff, making it extremely difficult to develop a trained staff.

The problem of cotton and cloth prices as well as tariff protection might have been handled somewhat differently. The DLF could have required a decree from the government of Sudan specifying the conditions under which a tariff would be imposed and/or an agreement on the pricing of cotton and/or the pricing of cloth. Although the U.S. government is generally opposed to interfering with the market mechanism in the private sector, it has required government assurances from governments in relation to other loans such as the Volta River Project. It cannot be stressed too often that the techniques and mechanisms of developed countries cannot be applied to developing countries. Each country must be treated *sui generis*.

The optimistic report of the technical consultants probably accounts for the lopsided debt/equity ratio. Not only was the ratio high at 87.5/12.5 percent, but in addition, the $7,500,000 credit from the Consortium was a medium-term loan under which the first interest payment was to be made less than three years after the signing of the credit agreement, and the first repayment of principal was to take place thirty-eight months after the signing of the agreement. Thus, SATI was required to begin payments on the credit before it had completed its first year of operation. The DLF loan agreement also provided only six additional months for the first payment. These conditions are even more onerous when one recognizes that SATI had little or no working capital and local procedures required financing of the merchants by the manufacturer.

Additional financial pressures arose because of the manner in which the Theodoracopulos group handled the equity. The group informed the DLF that the equity capital was in a Swiss bank. As of June 30, 1963, the auditors stated that they had satisfactory evidence that approximately $1.54 million of the equity capital had been brought into the company. SATI refused to permit the Swiss bank to let the auditors examine the account in which the equity capital was kept. In the Agreement of May, 1963, the creditors agreed not to force an audit of these accounts if the Theodoracopulos group would accept deferred notes for only $1.54 million. The group agreed, and this was the arrangement in the proposed understanding. Subsequently, in the revised understanding, the amount was reduced to $840,000. The DLF Loan Agreement provided that the DLF was to receive full information on the receipt of the matching capital which included the equity. In addition, they were to receive information on the expenditures of the loan and the matching capital. If DLF received this information, it was not transmitted to the auditors.

There is another point which is not clear and relates to the security offered by the guarantors. A number of allegations have been made including the fact that the guarantors sold off part of their pledged assets without informing the DLF and that they offered already pledged assets to local banks as securities for additional loans. This suggests that the reporting system employed by the DLF in relation to the pledged assets was inadequate. In addition, when SATI ran short of funds, it does not appear that the guarantors were approached to put up more funds as required by the DLF agreement. It is doubtful whether there were sufficient pledged assets to cover SATI's debts. If so, they were not sold, and the DLF did not take action before default occurred.

The merger of the DLF into the new AID in 1961 may account for some of these problems. It created a great deal of chaos when many loan officers were replaced and/or transferred, and it was some time before order was restored.

The new proposed understanding will remove the Theodoracopulos group from the scene. Their loss, though not total, will be substantial. Their investment, which has been estimated at more than $1.54 million, will be repaid in the form of $840,000 worth of notes, on which they will draw interest of 5½ percent from 1968 to 1984.

The first interest payment will be made in 1973, and the 1984 payment will make up for the first four years when interest will accrue but not be paid.

SATI continues to run, and AID and the Consortium will soon become its shareholders. It is understood that the creditors hope to be able to sell their shares to a private group as soon as possible. They have no desire to be in the textile business.

The creditors will protect their investments under the proposed arrangements. The loan of P.L. 480 funds will alleviate some of SATI's working capital problems. One wonders, however, whether the proposed debt schedule will not be too heavy for SATI over the next few years. It is quite likely that both AID and the Consortium will have to convert some of their notes into equity. Even presuming that this occurs, SATI may very well find itself back in a difficult financial position in 1967. The new proposed understanding includes a provision that the government of the Sudan will insure that SATI will be able to sell its future production at prices which will cover the full cost thereof and generate sufficient funds to meet the payments becoming due to the various major creditors. These provisions may be sufficient to see SATI through, but it is certain that there will be many tense days before SATI gets over the hump.

It is now more than seven years since the United States first discussed a textile mill for the Sudan. Today, Sudan has the most modern mill in Africa, but it still has a long way to go before it will be the most efficient mill. There were a number of difficulties resulting from incomplete analysis of the society before the venture was commenced. The capital structure of the company was too heavily weighted on the side of debt capital. This financial structure tended to limit the company's operations. The management selected to run the plant showed many of the weaknesses of promoter groups which are not experienced or interested in long-term industrial operations. Insufficient concern was directed to the role of the government of Sudan when setting up the project. Inadequate provisions were made for tariff protection, the pricing of cotton, and the finished cloth. The reporting system of the DLF was inadequate to protect the interests of the United States both in relation to the matching capital and in relation to the security pledged by the guarantors. The new proposed understanding appears to afford satisfactory protection for the creditors. It still appears, however, to be too burdensome in relation to SATI's ability to pay over the next few years. If the Sudan government's agreement in relation to prices can be converted into profitable sales, these fears may prove to be unjustified.

VI. Principal Policy Issues

General Nature of International Financial Development Aid

THE PURPOSE of the public effort in international development financing in the broadest economic terms is to make resources available to the less developed countries over and above what they have as a result of their own efforts, plus the investment resources they receive from abroad on a normal commercial basis. The total resources at their disposal, in the absence of this effort, consists of their own output, to the extent that it is available for use at home, plus commercial foreign investments. Total resources constituted in this way have hitherto generally been inadequate, given the amounts that must be devoted to current consumption, to permit the level of investments necessary to achieve acceptable targets of economic growth. In the absence of what has come to be loosely known as foreign "aid," the level of investments can be increased only at the expense of consumption, although it is, of course, possible to promote growth by making investments more efficient rather than by increasing them.

Except for the latter qualification, however, it is the level of investments which is the primary determinant of growth; and investments and consumption together account for the total use of resources. Where consumption is already low, there are serious limits to how much it can be reduced to release resources for investment. And where total resources are small, investments are generally limited to low levels. Hence, there has been the public effort to increase the flow of resources to the less developed countries so that they can increase investments while they maintain levels of consumption which are generally acknowledged to be too low to be reduced. The hope is, of course, that a process of growth will be generated which will permit increases of consumption, as well as increases of investment out of the increments in output themselves, with an eventual elimination of the dependence on the external supplements.

The international public effort in development financing which has been mounted in the postwar period is an acknowledgment of the fact that international capital movements to the less developed countries would be inadequate on the basis of a laissez-faire approach. This does not mean that the public effort must consist entirely of movements of public capital that have their origin in the governmental appropriations of donor countries. To be sure, a large part of the effort does consist of such capital movements, but the effort can take other forms. Measures can be directed to inducing private international investments and capital movements by improving the investment climate—through the provision of governmental guarantees or insurance, special tax incentives, or devices for settling investment disputes. And some of the capital that is provided by public authorities can be raised through voluntary participation by the private sector in response to official guarantees or subsidies, rather than through taxation. The essence of international financial development aid lies in the fact that it is a reflection of a deliberate public effort to raise the flow of resources to the less developed countries, whatever form the effort takes, above the flow that would take place autonomously.

CRITERIA OF AID

It is, of course, difficult, if not impossible, to establish a clear distinction between the flow of financial resources to the less developed countries that results from international aid and that which is autonomous. In the spectrum of types of such flows, one extreme is represented by the use of resources that would not be available except as "aid" and the other by the use of resources that would be available even in the absence of any "aid" effort. But it is virtually impossible to determine how much of what passes as strictly public "aid" would be available on other grounds and how much strictly private investment or financing is available as a response, even though a very loose and indirect one, to the emphasis and encouragement of public authorities. There is thus a large middle area of resources that flow to the less developed countries whose relationship to the aid effort is indeterminate.

There is in any case no need for purposes of policy to make any such clear distinction if the basic premise is accepted that purely autonomous capital flows are insufficient and that there is need for an aid effort. What is important in the first instance is the magnitude of the total flows of resources in relation to the amounts needed to promote development. It is generally accepted that an aid effort is needed to achieve an adequate magnitude in the flow of resources.

Another dimension of the question of what constitutes aid relates to the terms on which the resources are provided. Whether a country is receiving aid for development is a matter not only of the supplementary resources over and above those available from its own efforts but also of the terms on which it must return the resources, if at all, to the donors. The range extends from grants, which do not have to be returned at all, to loans that must be repaid at interest rates and maturities no more favorable than the customary ones in commercial transactions. The latter is not aid at all if it involves no concession for the recipient in relation to what it can obtain from commercial sources. Even such loans, however, might be considered aid if the situation of the recipient is such that it could not obtain the supplementary resources at the commercial price or indeed at any price at all.

The terms of the resources made available are also relevant to the question of what is aid from the point of view of the donor. The resources of donors can be put to a variety of uses at home or abroad, at certain rates of return. If the return on an investment of resources in a less developed country is as favorable to the donor as any other use to which it might put the resources, the donor is making no sacrifice in providing the resources, and there is consequently no "aid" element in the transfer as far as the donor is concerned. From the point of view of the donor, the extent to which it is "aiding" less developed countries is a matter of the degree to which the terms on which it provides resources are less favorable to it than in alternative uses.

The issue of what should properly be considered as international financial development aid is thus difficult to resolve definitively, since one criterion is the cost to donors and another the benefit to recipients, at times without any apparent connection between the two. What may involve a great cost to the donor may be of little benefit to the recipient; conversely, a transfer of resources involving no cost to the donor may be of great benefit to the recipient. Whether or not the investment of resources received from abroad proves to be of benefit in the economic development of the recipient may be entirely unrelated to the cost to the donor of providing the resources.

The focus in the first instance should be on the provision and use of supplementary foreign resources in magnitudes and on terms which permit increased development. This cannot, of course, be achieved without regard to the cost to the donors. From a global point of view, however, the costs to the donors should not be judged apart from the benefits in the development of the recipients. Certainly, as a practical matter, the attitudes in donor countries toward the costs are undoubtedly influenced by the effectiveness with which the aid is utilized. The costs, however defined, may loom larger or smaller, depending upon the confidence of the donors in what the aid is achieving.

The general attitude toward what may be considered as development aid which has been implicitly or expressly adopted in international councils concentrates on the magnitude and terms of the transfer of resources to less developed countries, without attempting very rigid definitions. The OECD, made up of the Western bloc powers, most of whom are on the donor side of the international aid effort, regularly surveys the "flow of financial resources to less-developed countries," excluding only loans of one year or less in maturity and including private investments, though stating them separately from movements of public capital. A similarly comprehensive approach is used by the fourteen-member aid donor Development Assistance Committee of the OECD, although, being concerned more exactly with the concept of "aid," the DAC arbitrarily eliminates from the flow loans with a maturity of five years or less. Both, however, include in the flow figures which take into account all loans above the respective lower limits of maturity regardless of how high their interest rates might be. This is not to say that these agencies consider all resource movements that fit into their arbitrary definitions as equally aidlike. The DAC indeed has done much to press for a liberalization of the terms of the more onerous loans. But this approach on the basis of the flow of financial resources does reflect the statistical, and even the conceptual, difficulties of defining international financial "aid" very exactly. The emphasis of the OECD and DAC is placed on the volume in which resources move with at least a minimum of delay in the rate of repayment. Beyond that, they have been much concerned with raising the "aid-quality" elements in the flow of resources.

Even the recipient-country-dominated 1964 UN Conference on Trade and Development (UNCTAD) viewed "aid" as broadly as does the OECD. In its Resolution on Growth and Aid, in which it is recommended that "each economically advanced country should endeavour to supply . . . financial resources to the developing countries of a minimum net amount approaching as nearly as possible to 1 per cent of its national income," financial resources are defined to include government lending for periods exceeding one year and all long-term private capital, the latter not being any further defined with regard to maturity.[1] Although a more rigid definition in terms of the effort on the part of donors, perhaps excluding private capital, might have been expected from UNCTAD as compared with the donor-oriented OECD, here too the initial emphasis is on the total magnitude of resources available to the less developed countries on the basis of quite a minimal effort on the part of the donors. Elsewhere, to be sure, e.g., in a resolution on "Terms of Financing," which is discussed below, there are numerous recommendations calling for easy terms of repayment, but the definition for purposes of the minimum target set with respect to the volume of assistance takes the same broad approach as does the OECD in its statistical evaluations.

Motivations and Attitudes of Donors

Economic aid is provided in a considerable variety of forms and programs which have arisen in response to diverse and complex motivations on the part of the donors. The desire to promote the long-run economic development of the recipients is only one of these motivations. It is, therefore, not surprising that the purposes of

---

[1] United Nations, *Proceedings of the United Nations Conference on Trade and Development*, I, 44.

economic development are not always served by what qualifies as external economic aid. Indeed, even if the objective of donors were exclusively to promote development, this would still be true to some extent in view of the highly complex nature of the development process.

MULTILATERAL AID AGENCIES

The decision in 1944 to create the IMF and the World Bank was to avoid the economic chaos which had followed World War I and to see that there would be a concerted effort to establish monetary stability and to provide funds for the reconstruction of countries devastated by the war and the development of countries which were entering into a period of modernization. These were the principal motivations in the creation of these institutions, and they were backed by the major participants.

International organizations such as the World Bank group, the Inter-American Development Bank, and the Special Fund and other agencies of the United Nations have the promotion of economic development as their exclusive aim. Representing no one nation, requiring no support in votes on political issues in the UN General Assembly, and not being involved in military relations or confrontations with other nations, these agencies can pursue their single-minded purpose and have not generally been criticized for their motives; but they are responsible for the flow of only about 10 percent of world external assistance. Nevertheless, there has been some attribution of extraneous motivations even in the case of the international agencies. For example, the World Bank, by far the most important international institution in terms of total resources, has been criticized because of its prejudice against public-sector industrial projects. The Bank has admitted that it has held this position, though not on doctrinaire grounds. Furthermore, there are indications of some modification of this attitude. In a recent speech, the President of the Bank stated:

We have been reluctant to finance State-owned industrial enterprises primarily because of the great difficulty of assuring that they would be managed on a businesslike basis, free of political pressures. We are quite aware, nonetheless, that in some of our member countries, and especially in the newer ones, a shortage of private savings and of industrial entrepreneurship harshly limits what purely private capital can accomplish. We are therefore embarking upon a re-examination of our policies as applied to such cases to see whether there are ways, other than through completely private ownership, in which effective management of industrial ventures can be assured.[2]

BILATERAL AID AGENCIES

The origins of bilateral assistance, which is still an overwhelming proportion of the total, were primarily in ideological battles following World War II. The Soviet Union was supporting the Communist groups, and Western Europe and the United States were supporting a democratic-pluralistic form of government. During this period these struggles were most intense in areas bordering on the Soviet Union and China. There were a civil war in Greece, threats against Turkey, the occupation of the Iranian sector of Azerbaijan, guerrilla warfare in Burma, Viet Nam, Malaya, Indonesia, and the Philippines, and deep-seated friction in India and Pakistan following the partition of the subcontinent. There were difficult social problems of land tenure, caste, and class throughout these countries. To add to the unrest, many had just become independent, and the others were demanding their freedom. The scene was one of political, economic, and social turmoil. It is within this context that one must view the flow of external assistance to understand some of its origins and some of the forces that still motivate it.

U.S. Aid. American assistance to developing countries commenced, after President Truman's Inaugural Address of January, 1949, under the Mutual Security Administration. The title of the agency was the clue to its principal objective: to maintain external and internal security in addition to promoting economic development in the long run. Critics of assistance to developing countries have often complained of the waste of huge sums totaling in the neighborhood of $100 billion of U.S. assistance and the poor results obtained from this large flow of assistance. John Nuveen, a former Director of Marshall Plan assistance to Greece, directed himself to these critics in a recent article [3] by analyzing the flow of major U.S. foreign assistance from July 1, 1945, through March 31, 1961. The

---

[2] Address by George D. Woods to the Economic and Social Council of the United Nations on March 26, 1965 (reprinted by World Bank), p. 7.
[3] "Social and Political Aid," in Goldwin, ed., *Why Foreign Aid?*

total aid figure was $83.9 billion, and "the amount of money appropriated for the economic development of the underdeveloped countries has only been about $6 billion, not $100 billion."[4] He noted that total appropriations to the developing countries during this period amounted to $34.3 billion, but $27.1 billion went to military assistance and defense support and another $1.9 billion was spent on such things as administration, international agencies, and miscellaneous items.

In the 1950s American aid was directed primarily to short-term Cold War objectives. Development was secondary. The aid program was presented to Congress annually as an anti-Communist crusade. This approach presented a number of problems. The American public was conditioned to believe that Communism was *the* reason for giving aid. This idea made it difficult to justify assistance to Latin America or Africa. Leaders in these areas were wont to comment wryly that it was necessary to encourage the Communist Party in order to become eligible for American assistance. There was a greater emphasis on military than on economic aid, and the economic aid that was furnished was administered with little concern for the underlying requirements for the long-run development of the beneficiary countries. The maintenance of political stability and the political *status quo* in the countries aided were the objectives of U.S. aid policy. If, as in India, there was a government with a developed civil service and the ability to plan, some development aid commenced. But even in India there were problems when India refused to align itself publicly with American views of the world. American congressmen denounced the Indians, and the U.S. Secretary of State found Indian neutralism to be immoral. For those countries less fortunately endowed than India with administrators and enlightened leaders, security and stability rather than development were the goal of U.S. aid policy.

The confusing of these short-term objectives with development created domestic problems in relation to U.S. aid. Critics of the program used figures of total aid, regardless of how much was for development, to show how much the United States had given and then attacked the government because so little had been accomplished in the way of development. The inevitably long-run nature of the

[4] *Ibid.*, p. 48.

development process was ignored. Poverty continued in all areas, and both recipients and the U.S. aid program were accused of waste and corruption. Few realized how little money had been earmarked for development. And, with the justification of the aid program on the basis of short-term anti-Communist objectives, it was difficult to defend the developmental rationale whenever some short-term objective failed to be achieved.

A shift in emphasis away from short-term objectives toward long-run development was begun with the creation of the DLF in 1957. The DLF was empowered to make long-term loans at concessionary interest rates, and it could accept repayments in local currencies of borrowing countries. The DLF had a staff which differed from and was independent of the rest of the aid program. Following the 1960 presidential election, the aid program was analyzed and major revisions were made. Development lending was integrated with the other aid programs, and economic development became the major goal of the newly created AID. The Alliance for Progress also came into its own during this period, and with the Alliance, public recognition was given to the principle that social change was a fundamental part of economic development. Efforts were also made under the Alliance to involve recipient leaders in the decision-making process in relation to aid. By fiscal year 1964, almost 80 percent of economic aid funds were directed to economic development.

Today U.S. economic assistance is given as development loans, development grants, supporting assistance, EXIMBANK loans, and in the form of surplus agricultural commodities under P.L. 480. The first two categories are for economic development programs. Supporting assistance is provided to countries which are allocating a part of their own funds to military purposes. This assistance is to enable them to carry out economic projects which could not be carried out otherwise, as a result of the diversion of resources to military activities. The Export-Import Bank was established to promote the export of U.S. goods, and this is still the primary motive of the Bank, though the effect obviously also includes a considerable contribution to development. P.L. 480 serves a dual purpose in U.S. policies. First, it provided surplus food to developing countries at advantageous terms. Second, inasmuch as these surpluses must be purchased by the United States government even if they are not utilized under P.L. 480, the government saves the cost of storing such surpluses. The burden to the United States is minimal, but the benefit to the recipient countries can be substantial.

A large proportion of the American public supports foreign aid for purely humanitarian reasons. There is a long-standing tradition in the United States of charitable contributions. Many of those who support foreign aid are the same people who support hundreds of charitable funds within their own country, who gave money in the early 1920s to aid victims of an earthquake in Japan long before the phrase "Cold War" had entered into their vocabulary, and who have supported mission schools and hospitals throughout the world.

Commercial motivations are satisfied both through the tying of U.S. AID loans and through the loans from the EXIMBANK. In the wake of these programs American goods and services had found new markets.

Although the strategy of U.S. aid has changed, the overall objectives have not. Short-term strategy now tends to be separated from long-term strategy. Programs for nondevelopmental purposes are now limited to countries on the Sino-Soviet periphery. Strategy elsewhere is aimed at the underlying political objectives through long-term development contributions.

French and British Aid. French and British aid on a regular basis began immediately after World War II, when it was provided to colonies. Prior to this time, the economic development of these areas was based on the internal resources of each colony alone. Economic policies were guided by colonial civil servants, and trade links insured that the metropolises would benefit from aid expenditures. Political objectives and administrative prerequisites and safeguards were all built into the system. With these other considerations well in hand, aid was concentrated on economic development.

Following the independence of their colonies, France and Britain continued aid under existing patterns. Slight changes were made in the names of various aid programs, the proportion of loans to grants increased, more so in English-speaking areas than in French, and British and French consultants continued to dominate economic policy-making.

There is less dependency on the former colonial powers in some ways but more in others. Nigeria and Ghana are developing their own policy-makers. In French-speaking Africa, there may be even more dependency on France now than there was before independence. This has been brought about by ambitious development programs in countries which have limited physical and human resources. The French have about 50,000 experts working abroad— almost all in Africa—and some 30,000 are teachers. In this way one of France's aid objectives—spreading the influence of French civilization—is being carried out.

The commercial objectives of French and British aid are satisfied by the tying of virtually all aid to the source of the aid. Even if this aid was not tied, it is quite likely that the period of colonial occupation would have developed preferences for goods from the former colonial power. For example, today one finds most of former French Africa drinking wine and former British Africa drinking beer.

The French and British still direct most of their assistance to former colonies. They continue to play an important role as consultants in policy-making in these areas, especially in Africa. This has meant that there was less need to worry about strategic and political considerations in their aid policies. Over the years these areas have, for the most part, developed a general outlook not too dissimilar from that of France and England. In recent years, however, both France and England have begun to move toward a greater dispersion of aid. This will raise for each of them the complex problems of utilizing aid for political and strategic reasons in areas where they have not exercised control or influence over a period of time.

Germany and Japan. The two other principal Western-bloc suppliers of economic assistance to developing countries are West Germany and Japan. As defeated countries following World War II, they had no colonies in which to continue aid programs and none of the resources to engage in the kind of aid program established by the Western powers. Both countries were recipients of substantial amounts of American capital, but for some years now their rehabilitation from the war has been complete. West Germany is among the more prosperous countries in the world, whereas Japan is still a net importer of capital with a relatively low per capita income.

Neither of these countries was eager to become a donor of foreign aid on concessionary terms. West Germany was more or less pressured into doing so by other members of the Development Assistance Committee. For the most part, German assistance has been in the form of medium- and some long-term loans and suppliers' credits. Interest rates have been relatively high. The primary motive of this assistance appeared to be the securing of new markets for German goods. In the last few years, however, the terms of German aid have "softened," and German loans have achieved more aidlike characteristics. Japanese assistance has followed the German pattern with even more emphasis on export promotion. Virtually all Japanese assistance has originated in loans from the Japanese Export-Import Bank. In 1961, however, Japan created the Overseas Economic Cooperation Fund to provide credits on softer terms than the Export-Import Bank. To date very few credits have been issued by this new institution. Japan is interested in recapturing markets which were lost following the war. Commercial motivations dominate Japanese aid policies.

Communist Aid. Sino-Soviet aid originated probably largely as a response to Western assistance. Owing to the inability of the Soviet Union to match the magnitude of Western assistance, it provided technical and capital assistance on a credit basis and warned the developing countries that no one ever provides assistance without expecting something in return. Their assistance has similar motivations to Western aid. They have chosen their recipients with care and have tended to concentrate their assistance in nonaligned countries such as India and Indonesia. Economic development and social change may assist the Soviet Union in its long-term political goals. One student of Soviet aid discussed this matter as follows:

Until a certain degree of industrialization has upset the traditional social and economic structure of an underdeveloped country to such a degree that, for example, there is already a marked drift of population from rural areas to the towns and a social vacuum is becoming increasingly apparent, Communism has little chance, since its broad appeal can only be to those whose traditional bonds have been loosened by the process of industrialization. If this line of thought is pursued the Soviet Bloc aid policy may certainly be regarded as a means of gradually creating the conditions required for the spread of Communism in underdeveloped countries. In other words, the idea that the worse economic and social conditions are, the better are the chances of Communism gaining ground, requires some modification in the case of underdeveloped countries, because any material progress beyond their present level will increase the social vacuum and thereby provide more favourable conditions for Communism to operate in.[5]

Soviet aid is tied and it has opened many new markets for Soviet goods. Communist Chinese assistance is beginning to expand, but it is still limited both in magnitude and operational areas. It has opened new markets for Chinese goods and has permitted China to enter into competition not only with Western sources of assistance but also with Soviet assistance.

Thus, there are diverse motivations for the granting of aid by the various donors, with a somewhat unique mixture of several motivations in the cases of individual donors. Aid is given to gain strategic advantages in the prosecution of the Cold War. It is given as a remnant from the colonial period of earlier positions of supremacy of certain donors in recipient countries. Humanitarianism also figures as an important force in the willingness of affluent societies to assist in bringing up the level of the poorer ones. Some aid is given for short-term economic advantage, as in the promotion of exports through tied aid and in the opening up of trade channels through the undertaking of programs of aid in new countries by donors not previously represented. And there is the long-run economic advantage to be gained by the favorable effect on international trade of the growing prosperity of the developing countries.

An understanding of these diverse motivations of the suppliers of aid points up some of the problems in assisting economic development through foreign aid. A country which is interested in finding new markets for its goods may hinder rather than aid development. The same effect may result from aid granted for short-term political objectives rather than for development goals. As a practical matter, however, it must be recognized that there will always be diverse motivations related to the giving of economic assistance, and the

[5] Klaus Billerbeck, *Soviet Bloc Foreign Aid to the Underdeveloped Countries* (Hamburg Archives of World Economy, 1960), p. 90.

principal goal should be to minimize the conflict, if any, between these objectives and economic development. In the United States, Senator Fulbright, the Chairman of the Senate Foreign Relations Committee, has suggested [6] that the United States should give most, if not all, of its development loans through the World Bank and its subsidiary organizations for multilateral administration. The Jeanneney Report in France suggested that by 1975, 25 percent of French aid should go through multilateral channels. It is presumed that both were motivated by the desire to see more aid devoted to economic development and less to short-term political objectives or at least by the desire to separate the two types of aid more clearly. Indeed, as experience has been accumulated in the process of foreign aid, there has been a trend toward a clearer separation of the objectives of the various types of aid even in bilateral programs, with a gain for the type whose avowed primary objective is the furtherance of economic development.

Magnitude of Aid

The long-term trend in the flow of capital resources to the less developed countries over the past decade or more has been upward, although the level has been more or less constant since 1961. The movement of official capital has been responsible for the increase. Although there have been various measures to encourage the flow of private capital, thus far private capital movements have at best been merely stationary; to the extent that a trend is discernible at all in private capital movements, it is a declining one. Whether or not the magnitude of the flow of total capital resources is adequate is a question, on the one hand, of what the needs of the recipients are and, on the other, of what the donors can be expected to contribute. Some attempt has been made to provide answers to these difficult questions in the international attention that has been directed to development aid.

ESTIMATES OF REQUIREMENTS OF DEVELOPING COUNTRIES

Various estimates have been made by official agencies and qualified private observers of the overall amount of foreign capital re-

[6] New York *Times*, June 3, 1965, p. 13,

quired annually by the less developed countries.[7] The starting point for most of these is a certain goal of growth of national income, in most estimates stated as being in the vicinity of 2 percent per capita annually. Estimates of capital requirements needed to achieve such goals are then made on the basis of such relationships as capital-output ratios or the amount of capital needed per worker. Estimates of domestic resources are then deducted from the total investment requirements to arrive at the foreign capital required. Such estimates all essentially attempt to measure the requirements in terms of the gap between a desirable amount of investment and the volume of domestic savings available in the less developed countries. A group of experts under UN auspices, using 1949 as a reference year, estimated the annual foreign capital requirements at $8.5 billion (excluding mainland China and Mongolia), for the period 1950–60. One private estimate for about the same geographic area, using 1953 as a base year, amounted to $6.5 billion, while another, using 1959 as the point of departure, amounted to $7 billion. A more recent private estimate, starting with 1961, estimated the annual requirement at $5.7 billion through 1971.[8] To the extent that the figures may be considered comparable,[9] it is of interest to note that the actual movement in 1963 of financial resources to the less developed countries of close to $10 billion, cited in Chapter II, is in excess of all of these estimates. The President of the World Bank, however, in a presentation to the DAC in July, 1965, is reported to have stated that the underdeveloped countries could productively use from $3 billion to $4 billion a year more in aid than is currently being provided by donor governments.[10]

As pointed out in Chapter II, the definition of the financial problem of the less developed countries, which was presented to the 1964 UN Conference on Trade and Development, was in terms of their

[7] Cf. United Nations, *Capital Development Needs of Less Developed Countries*, Sales No. 62. II. D. 3 (New York, 1962).

[8] *Ibid.*, p. 14.

[9] The UN report cited states that "one incidental conclusion of this review concerns the ambiguity—conceptual as well as statistical—that still surrounds many of the terms in current use, including such seemingly simple ones as 'development capital' and 'economic assistance.' As a result, serious difficulties are encountered in making quantitative estimates of past capital movements." See p. 52.

[10] New York *Times*, Aug. 4, 1965. These figures are also used in the IBRD, *Annual Report*, 1964–65, p. 62.

balance-of-payments gap rather than the investment-savings gap. The balance-of-payments gap projected for 1970 (in 1959 prices) was $20 billion, to achieve the UN Development Decade goal of an annual growth rate in national income of 5 percent. It was not suggested, however, that this gap was to be closed by capital imports. Capital imports would be called upon to close part of the gap, but one of the main points of convening the UN Conference was indeed to set in motion measures to permit the less developed countries to earn more of their own way in the development process by increased exports of goods and services. No attempt was made to define the magnitude of the capital import requirements, and it is therefore not possible to compare the results of this global balance-of-payments approach to estimation of development aid requirements with the investment-savings approach used in the other estimates mentioned above.

AID TARGETS FOR DEVELOPING COUNTRIES

Nor did UNCTAD attempt to define any precise magnitude of aid requirements, although it stated that the current flow is inadequate. Indeed, it even questioned the adequacy of the 5 percent growth target formulated for the UN Development Decade. In its resolution on growth and aid,[11] the Conference recognized "the wide concern expressed regarding the inadequacy of the growth target of 5 per cent per annum for the United Nations Development Decade" and the fact "that in recent years rates of growth of national income of developing countries in the aggregate and per capita have been generally unsatisfactory." It then drew attention to the total import capacity of the less developed countries, including but not isolating the capital import requirements, by recommending that

the import capacity resulting from the combined total of export proceeds, invisible earnings and capital inflow available to the developing countries, taking into account the evolution of prices, should rise sufficiently and the measures taken by the developing countries themselves should be adequate to enable these higher rates of growth to be achieved.

The view of the Chairman of the Development Assistance Committee, consisting of the principal aid donor countries, is similarly that there is "no one figure which could purport to give expression

[11] United Nations, *Trade and Development*, pp. 43–44.

to the needs for assistance by all the less-developed countries. These needs differ greatly from country to country and are susceptible of rather rapid change within each country." [12] There is also recognition in this quarter that the current effort is insufficient. In his recommendations, the DAC Chairman pointed out in September, 1964, that "fresh initiatives and new impulses are needed to secure a further substantial expansion of assistance to the less-developed countries." [13]

The aggregative approaches to the issue of the magnitude of aid are, of course, gross oversimplifications. Even if it is assumed that only the variables which are taken into consideration in the models, whether in the investment-savings gap approach or the balance-of-payments or any other analytical approach, are the significant ones for the achievement of growth and development, the variables are numerous and the relationships are highly complex. The fragile structure on which the models are based depends upon many arbitrary assumptions. The reliability of many of the assumptions is subject to question, and the entire structure can thus become easily open to doubt. This is true even in attempting to define the aid requirements of a single country, and the margin of error becomes obviously far greater when the attempt is made to define the requirements globally.

Nevertheless, the aggregative attempts to define the magnitude of aid requirements serve a useful, if limited and not altogether scientific, purpose. They give some quantitative scope to the question of what the size of the international aid effort should be, although they by no means assure the achievement of the growth goals which are posited, even if the general order of magnitude is met. They provide some quantitative frame of reference within which to consider the conduct of foreign aid programs. Despite all their acknowledged shortcomings, the macro-economic definitions of aid requirements serve as a point of departure in the formulation of international policies for assistance to groups of countries as well as to individual countries. The ten-year, $20-billion requirement of external assistance to carry out the objectives of the Alliance for Progress between the United States and the Latin American republics is illustrative of the former. Obviously, the success of the Alliance for Progress depends upon many more complex factors than merely the

[12] OECD, *DAC 1964 Review*, p. 14.   [13] *Ibid.*, p. 91.

amassing of $20 billion of external capital over a ten-year period, but the definition of the aid requirements in this way has served as a useful rallying point and stimulus in the effort to achieve the development implied in the program.

On the individual country level, the magnitude of aid requirements is usually an integral part of long-term national development plans. The definition of total aid requirements in national plans has been brought particularly into play as a policy matter in countries such as India and Turkey, for which international aid consortia have been constituted. The consortia are indeed devices for the pledging of specific amounts of aid to the recipient country by the various donors, and so by their very nature presuppose a definition of the country's total aid requirements. Nevertheless, the consortium technique has not been extended to many countries. Although it is being increasingly recognized as desirable to coordinate the programs of the numerous sources of aid for individual recipient countries, the consortium has for the most part given way to the international consultative group. The international consultative group is a looser sort of arrangement and concerns itself less than the consortium with the total aid requirements which the recipient country may have defined. Among the countries surveyed in some detail for this study, Colombia is illustrative of this more flexible approach. In such cases, more attention is paid to aid requirements for specific projects or programs than to any total definition of aid requirements. In other cases, indeed, such as the DAC coordinating group for Thailand, the concern is with special problems such as technical assistance rather than with capital resources at all.

Even where no international groups of donors have been formed to assist individual recipient countries, the latter have usually defined their external capital requirements in one way or another, in some cases in relation to the balance-of-payments gap and in others through some variant of the investment-savings gap approach. Such definition has become an integral feature of the comprehensive national economic plans which more and more countries are coming to formulate. The process of definition of aid requirements as part of the national plans serves as a guide for policies aimed at mobilizing resources, both domestic and external, to carry out the plans and to achieve national objectives.

With the magnitude of aid requirements by recipients being as imprecise and indefinite a matter as has been indicated, it is not surprising that the contributions that should be made by the donors, constituting the other side of the same coin, have been no more exactly defined. Reference has been made to the UNCTAD recommendation that there be a minimum net flow of resources to the less developed countries in the amount of 1 percent of the national income of the developed countries. As has been pointed out, this covers private as well as public capital, though the amounts are stated as being on a *net* basis, i.e., over and above the requirements for repayment or repatriation of previously invested capital. Furthermore, it is to be noted that the target is stated as a minimum, with obviously no upper limit. This point is especially worthy of mention, since there is a tendency for such figures to be loosely considered as a goal rather than as a lower limit. The DAC has adopted the 1 percent goal in a resolution adopted in July, 1965.[14]

The 1 percent goal had to a large extent been achieved by 1961, but it has faltered since then with the stationary level of aid and the increases in national income of the developed countries. The Jeanneney Report on foreign aid prepared for the French government found that the principal donor countries in 1961 provided resources to the less developed countries in amounts equivalent to the following percentages of their gross national products, including both private and public capital:[15]

United States	0.97 percent
France	2.41 percent
United Kingdom	1.32 percent
West Germany	1.17 percent

The showing for public capital alone was as follows:

United States	0.72 percent
France	1.78 percent
United Kingdom	0.66 percent
West Germany	0.88 percent

---

[14] OECD, *DAC 1965 Review.*
[15] Ministère d'État chargé de la Réforme Administrative, *La politique de coopération avec les pays en voie de développement*, Annexes, July 18, 1963, p. 121.

Although the 1 percent goal was adopted by DAC in July, 1965, the UNCTAD resolution calling for the minimum 1 percent of national income was adopted with the abstention of nine countries; the Final Act of UNCTAD does not indicate which countries abstained in the vote on this resolution, but it seems safe to assume that they were the same nine which voted against the liberal resolution on terms of financing.[16]

The formulation of a goal for the volume of assistance as a percentage of the national output of the donor countries means, of course, that the volume of assistance would automatically rise as economic growth proceeded in those countries. Thus, the Jeanneney Report concluded that it seems reasonable to assume that France could maintain public aid at the level of some 1.5 percent of GNP, which would permit a doubling of the aid volume by 1975 on the basis of the expected growth of GNP.[17] This suggestion, however, has never been officially adopted by the French government.

In the United States, there is some recognition of the significance of the aid burden expressed as a ratio to GNP. In presenting the request to Congress to authorize military (about a third of the total) and economic assistance in the amount of $3.38 billion for the fiscal year 1966, the U.S. administration pointed out that "it represents the smallest burden on the American taxpayer: one-half of one percent of our GNP (compared with two percent of GNP at the height of the Marshall Plan), and 3.5 per cent of the federal budget (compared with nearly 12 percent seventeen years ago)." [18] The flow of resources from the United States which constitute economic aid by DAC standards is actually higher than the amount indicated above of $3.38 billion. The flow of economic aid in 1964 amounted to $3,534 million, as indicated in Chapter II. The amount of military aid included in the fiscal 1966 request to Congress is more than offset by the economic aid for which annual legislative authorization is not required, namely, loans by the Export-Import Bank and sales of surplus agricultural commodities for local currencies.

[16] Belgium, Canada, Germany, Italy, Japan, the Netherlands, Switzerland, the United Kingdom, and the United States; see United Nations, *Trade and Development*, pp. 43–44.
[17] *La politique de coopération*, I, 70.
[18] U.S. AID and U.S. Dept. of Defense, *Proposed Mutual Defense and Development Programs FY 1966*, p. 5.

Donor countries have shown considerable reluctance to assume commitments to provide any particular amounts of aid on a continuing basis. It has been noted that the French government has not adopted the Jeanneney Commission recommendation for a volume of public aid in the amount of 1.5 percent of GNP. The U.S. Congress has repeatedly turned down Administration requests for long-term aid authorizations. Important segments of assistance are provided on bases other than through fixed appropriations, as in the lending by the U.S. EXIMBANK or lending by the UK Export Credits Guarantee Department, which is designated as "below the line" expenditure, i.e., expenditures not financed by specific appropriations but rather by Treasury borrowings or general Treasury surpluses. These segments are, therefore, not constituted as any fixed amounts, as occurs with annual appropriations. The reluctance to undertake any fixed continuing commitment reflects the desire by donors to exercise greater control over their aid expenditures than they feel would be possible under a commitment to provide certain magnitudes of aid over a period of years. It poses serious problems for recipients, however, by virtue of the constant uncertainties with respect to the continuity of aid.

The expression in broad aggregates of how much aid should be provided by donors also presents difficulties on other grounds. As has been indicated, resources of a considerable variety all qualify as "aid" under the broad definition used in connection with the 1 percent of GNP criterion. This presents problems in evaluating the relative efforts being made by the various donors: countries contributing the same percentages of their GNP are judged to be making the same effort, even though one might be providing all grants and the others all medium-term, high-interest loans. Furthermore, the same fixed percentage of GNP for all developed countries fails to take into account the fact that some are more highly developed than others: Japan, with a per capita GNP of perhaps a fifth that of the United States, should not be expected to be contributing the same percentage of its output to assistance as the United States. A similar point to the latter one was made by the U.S. Administration in justifying to the Congress its program request for fiscal 1966:

The U.S. contribution (including P.L. 480 surplus agricultural commodities) represents less than one percent of the GNP in a country where per capita GNP now exceeds $3,000 a year. The developing countries' own contribution to their progress represents about 12 per cent of GNP, in countries where GNP per capita averages about $145 a year.[19]

The magnitude of aid provided by donor countries is frequently viewed in terms of the "burden on the taxpayer." [20] This is, of course, because so much of the aid is in the form of public capital which has been raised by taxation. As has been noted repeatedly, however, a substantial, though still not increasing, portion of assistance to the less developed countries also is in the form of voluntary movements of private capital, in response to official incentives or otherwise. This type of aid may, of course, be a "burden on the economy" of the donor, but it is usually only indirectly or minimally, if at all, a "burden on the taxpayer." Increased attention has been paid in recent years to the prospects for raising the magnitude of aid through the relatively painless approach of tapping the private sector as a source of finance for the aid effort. This is by no means entirely new; the World Bank, the oldest of the international lending agencies, from the very beginning of its operations has relied heavily as a source of funds on borrowings in private capital markets against the backing of its subscribed capital. Although the results are not yet apparent, there has been a growing awareness recently of the great potential in such alternatives to the method of direct recourse to public treasuries for aid resources. The devices include official guarantees for private export credits; official insurance schemes, both national and possibly international, for private direct investments; institutional machinery for the settlement of international investment disputes; credits against tax liabilities for new investments in less developed countries; and guarantees and subsidies for private portfolio capital investments, as in the Horowitz Proposal discussed in Chapter III. A vigorous pursuit of these indirect approaches to the problem of raising the magnitude of aid opens the possibility of a considerable augmentation of the resources provided out of tax revenues and diminishes the tendency to think of aid as a burden on the donor.

The adequacy of the magnitude of aid, assuming a willingness on the part of donors to provide it, is in the last analysis a matter of the

[19] *Ibid.*, p. 3.
[20] See Robert E. Asher, *Grants, Loans, and Local Currencies—Their Role in Foreign Aid* (Washington, D.C., The Brookings Institution, 1961).

effectiveness with which it is utilized in promoting growth and development. One view which is fairly widely held, at least in some donor quarters, is that the primary bottleneck in development is not the magnitude of available aid but the existence of projects and programs suitable for financing. It is contended that the availability of aid is such that no appropriate projects or programs need go begging for lack of financing. The critical question in this connection is that of what is "suitable" or "appropriate" for financing. During recent years there has been a considerable liberalization in the attitude of donors in this respect, involving a greater willingness to provide finance for purposes broader than just specific projects and for projects or programs of a social character in addition to those which are purely economic. This type of question is related to the development performance of the recipients themselves, a subject to which we turn our attention at this point.

Aid in Relation to National Planning and Performance by Recipients

Successful development requires the positive will and involvement of the developing country. No amount of external assistance can do the job alone, and, in fact, such assistance generally plays a relatively minor role. With the potential demand for external assistance substantially exceeding the supply, donors have become increasingly concerned about the development efforts of recipients: measures taken to gain popular support for their efforts, programs to mobilize capital through new savings or tax plans, the organization of public administration and education, and the amelioration of social problems.

The accent on self-help presents major problems for countries which are far from approaching the "take-off" stage. These countries, which include a large number of the newly independent African states, are in serious need of assistance to define their problems and to mount a development effort. Their public administration is weak and illiteracy almost universal. They may have only a few people trained in economics and few if any of these with experience. They are not equipped to absorb foreign aid unless technical assistance is provided first. In the more developed countries, differing ideas of donors and recipients with respect to the content of self-help are likely to raise allegations of intervention in the internal affairs of the developing country. Nevertheless, the World Bank, the OECD, the IMF, and the United States have been instrumental in getting countries to make major internal reforms or to undertake far-reaching stabilization programs.

The emphasis on self-help of developing countries has found one expression in the proliferation of planning activity which has occurred during the postwar period. External assistance has been used to give impetus to planning. The British and French urged planning on their colonies and made it a condition precedent to development assistance. The United States has imposed similar conditions for the receipt of external assistance under the Alliance for Progress. The World Bank, although not requiring comprehensive country plans as the basis for assistance, has nevertheless encouraged planning in its various country studies carried out by expert missions.

This emphasis on planning has resulted from the belief that it would lead to quicker development and the optimal use of aid funds. Prior to setting up plans, few countries were aware of their physical or human resources, they had no idea of how fast they might grow, and they had never considered alternative allocations of investment funds. Planning involved governments to a greater extent in development.

These planning exercises, by indicating how much could be done with internal resources, gave a basis for aid requests based on a pre-determined rate of growth. Planning and the studies related thereto provide a country with a picture of where it is and enable it to decide on where it will go and how fast.

Plans can act as a focal point for coordinated external assistance through the mechanism of consultative groups or consortia. When donors have an overall picture of the development efforts of a country, they can decide among themselves how to distribute their relative aid.

Planning and the studies related thereto tend to make effective the demand for both technical and capital assistance. In the early stages, there is a need for competent individuals to get the relevant studies under way, to suggest institutional and organizational structures, and to draft the plan document itself. Once drafted, the ideas must be turned into concrete projects, which in turn must be put into operation; and these operations also require external technical and capital assistance in most cases.

External involvement in planning varies in relation to the stage of development of the assisted country. The early plans initiated by France and Britain in Africa were almost completely drafted by non-Africans. The fact that these were colonial territories made this point unimportant at the time. With independence, however, there is more concern with the approach of the planners. Many African countries are still unable to rely exclusively on their own nationals to draft plans. Some have permitted virtually all of the assistance for planning to continue to come from the former colonial power. This has been particularly true in former French West and Equatorial Africa. Others have used assistance from new sources. At times confusion arises when experts with very different approaches are introduced into the planning process, as in one African country where French, British, and Yugoslav experts are concerned with the same plan. In Thailand in recent years American advisers have been replaced by World Bank advisers, reflecting to some extent a preference for international assistance but also the desire of the bilateral donor to avoid commitments to finance plans and projects which their advisers helped to draft.

Foreign aid sometimes disturbs planning priorities by offering to finance projects which are not included in a country's plan. Realizing that the proferred assistance may be of use, recipients may be reluctant to reject it even though it may distort plan priorities. Such a possibility tends to be minimized when recipients coordinate their external assistance through a single body.

Plans, however, vary widely in quality. When faced with an ill-conceived or poorly constructed plan or the absence of a plan, donors must use their own analyses to understand the need and effect of assistance on overall development. The United States and the World Bank have evolved elaborate techniques for this purpose. The Bank evaluates each project in relation to its own detailed analysis of the country's economy. The United States has developed a country-by-country strategy based on its own analysis of the recipients' resources, objectives, and economic indicators. These alternative techniques are by no means comprehensive, but they minimize the problems generated by an *ad hoc* approach to development.

The presence of plans has not automatically meant that they were well received and supported by donors. Donors with set ideas about how development should take place are not easily induced to support different approaches. Disagreement may focus on the approach to planning priorities within the plan or even on particular projects. Furthermore, donors may not feel equally well equipped to handle all kinds of projects. Thus, countries may find that they have set up an approach to development which may or may not receive external support. The fact that external experts are involved in the planning process minimizes but does not eliminate this problem. When differences arise over particular projects, such as placing an industry in the public or private sector, recipients may attempt to play one donor off against another. This is particularly possible in countries which are considered to be politically important in the Cold War, such as India or Egypt. However, Soviet bloc resources for aid are not vast, and this is not a tactic which can be overplayed.

Some of the African countries depend almost exclusively on external assistance for their development projects. These countries are in a difficult position if parts of overall schemes cannot attract financing, for they have no internal resources to allocate to the missing link. For example, one source of assistance may agree to build a school, but unless funds are also forthcoming for a water supply and a road, it may be impossible to go ahead with the scheme. When a country has development resources of its own, the problem is just one of integrating and allocating the domestic and external resources.

Plans at times give countries a false sense of confidence. Some countries tend to believe that, once ideas are put on paper, development will flow automatically. Frequently, insufficient attention is given to the coordination of public investments called for by the comprehensive plan, the preparation of specific projects to carry out the investments, and the formulation of appropriate economic policies to induce productive private investments. The preparation of comprehensive medium or long-term master plans is merely a first step. Planning is a continuous process that has to be woven into the fabric of national economic life to be effective; the preparation of one-time blueprints by itself does not necessarily contribute to the process. The emphasis on planning by aid donors, though it was never intended to be misinterpreted in such a superficial way, has to some extent resulted in mere lip service of this type to the planning requirement.

Thus, the increased efforts of aid donors to employ standards of self-help and to encourage planning have created new problems. They have, however, also concentrated more attention on the fundamentals involved in development. These standards should produce quicker development results and assure the donors of a better use of their funds.

Financing for Specific Projects and General Development Financing

The increasing tendency to relate external assistance to comprehensive national planning and to the definition of total aid requirements by recipients has resulted in a greater degree of flexibility on the part of donors in providing financing for more general purposes than those implicit in specific projects. The limitation of financing to specific projects that qualify under the criteria of the lending agencies would in many cases result in a volume of assistance below the total aid requirements perceived by recipients; and specific project financing has, therefore, been supplemented by more general financing to help close the balance-of-payments gap of recipient countries. Furthermore, there may be particular needs, such as current budgetary support in some instances or the full utilization of existing industrial capacity in others, which do not lend themselves to the specific project approach.

Assistance for specific projects generally is defined as assistance for the construction or expansion of particular new capital facilities, such as roads, electric power stations, factories, or low-cost housing. The essential point is that such assistance is utilized to augment the capital stock of the recipient country in some specific, clearly identifiable way. There is a variety of types of assistance for other purposes—for current budget or general investment budget support, for emergency balance-of-payments assistance, for general balance-of-payments supplementation in support of development programs, for the importation of certain categories of capital goods —but it is convenient to distinguish broadly only between the two categories of specific project financing and all other, more general development financing, since the policy issue between donors and recipients, to the extent that there is one, hinges on this difference.

Donors tend to favor specific project financing. The international agencies, such as the World Bank Group and the Inter-American Development Bank, indeed limit their assistance almost exclusively to specific projects, although there has been some relaxation in this respect in the recent period. An outstanding example is represented by the $90-million and $100-million credits to India granted by IDA in June, 1964, and August, 1965, to permit the importation of components and materials by certain capital goods industries so that they might fully utilize their capacity, rather than for the creation of any new capital facilities. The lines of credit granted to national development banks and corporations by international agencies, as well as by donor country agencies on a bilateral basis, are akin to specific project loans. They are for the same types of purposes ultimately and may be considered to be a way of financing specific projects on a wholesale basis. The United States, West Germany, Japan, and the Soviet-bloc countries also favor specific project financing in their bilateral programs. The trend toward a greater portion of general development assistance in the aid of the United States is not a negation of this preference; it is less a matter of positive conviction than a response to the failure of recipients to come forward with sufficient specific projects. The United Kingdom and France, and especially the latter, are somewhat more disposed to give general development assistance because of the greater need for it by the areas where their aid is concentrated and because of their closer involvement in the affairs of their recipients by virtue of the background of colonialism.

Recipients, on the other hand, tend to favor more of the general type of development financing, although they are not entirely unmindful of some of the advantages of specific project financing and of the pressures on many financing agencies to limit themselves to financing of this type. Thus, the opposition by recipients to specific project financing was qualified in the UNCTAD expression on the subject by stating that *"as far as possible,* development loans should not be tied to particular projects." [21] This statement was contained in the resolution on Terms of Financing, which was adopted by a vote of 81 to 9, with 25 abstentions, the 9 negative votes and the 25 abstentions including the principal aid donors. The desire for more aid in the form of general development financing is evident also in the cases of each of the ten recipient countries surveyed in this research project, whose aid experiences and problems are summarized in Chapter IV.

Specific project financing is favored by donors because of their feeling that they are contributing in this way to the carrying out of investments of high priority in the development of the recipients. Besides, specific project financing provides the opportunity to influence the administrative and financial conditions under which recipient countries develop and operate strategic sectors of their economies. This is viewed as desirable not only because of the favorable effects on development but also because it enhances the reputation for effectiveness of the financing agencies, thereby facilitating future contributions by taxpayers or investors. Indeed, the advantages in this respect are not felt only by the donors—there is considerable appreciation of this type of contribution on the part of recipients, since it tends to strengthen the hand of professional developers against the influence of irresponsible politicians. Specific project financing also facilitates the association of technical with capital assistance and stimulates the mobilization by recipients of domestic resources for high-priority purposes. And it permits bilateral donors to "show the flag," by having their assistance identified with tangible facilities. The Soviet Union has been particularly successful in having its aid identified with spectacular projects such as the Bhilai steel mill in India or the Aswan Dam in Egypt.

Many recipients, on the other hand, consider it an illusion to believe that the financing of specific high-priority projects contributes more to development than general financing. Specific project financing releases resources of the recipient for other purposes, and the specific project financing thus indirectly finances the marginal project of lowest priority in the country's total investment program. This can be avoided only if there is complete control of a

[21] United Nations, *Trade and Development*, p. 45.

country's investment program, which would constitute a completely impractical and unacceptable intrusion by donors into the domestic affairs of recipients. Furthermore, the preference of donors for certain types of projects and their imposition of certain types of conditions may distort rather than enhance investment priorities. To qualify for the financing, recipients may place emphasis on projects that meet the requirements of the lending agencies but which may not be of high priority in relation to their needs. Thus, because of the tendency of many donors to finance only the direct foreign exchange requirements of projects, there is a compelling reason for recipients to carry out projects with a high foreign exchange content, regardless of their priority status on other grounds. The specific project approach may also distort priorities by its emphasis on new fixed capital investment; at times foreign exchange assistance may be needed much more for other purposes, such as the full utilization of existing capacity. The specific project approach is most disadvantageous when combined with aid tied to purchases in the donor country, which is now characteristic of most bilateral aid; the range of selection among competitive suppliers for the recipient is the narrowest under these circumstances. This disadvantage can be considerably mitigated, however, by the possibilities of communicating and bargaining, which have been greatly enhanced under recipient country consortia and consultative groups. Finally, there is objection by recipients to the specific project approach on the ground that it imposes an undue burden on their limited administrative resources in attempting to meet the project formulation and documentary requirements of donors.

Viewed positively, the more general type of development financing is favored by recipients because it helps them meet requirements that cannot be met by project financing: it permits them to work out investment priorities without extraneous considerations, it speeds up the utilization of external assistance, and it diminishes some of the undesirable effects of country tying of aid.

In practice, both types of financing are being provided, with an increase in the more general financing relative to the specific project type. The more general financing is provided especially under bilateral programs. At the same time, considerable assistance is being granted to recipients to improve their performance in project preparation and to help close the gap between their general planning and the translation of plans into specific, concrete projects. The pre-investment financing provided by the UN Special Fund is illustrative of this type of assistance. Such assistance is also evident in the activities of the World Bank and the Inter-American Development Bank and in some of the technical assistance activities of bilateral aid agencies, such as the U.S. AID and the Caisse Centrale of France.

The concern of donors with the results of general development financing is essentially a question of the quality of the development effort of recipients. For example, such assistance often takes the form of emergency balance-of-payments support which may sanction undesirable monetary, fiscal, or investment policies of recipients, with doubtful effects on development. This raises the question of the extent to which it is appropriate or possible for donors to intervene in the economic policies of recipients in connection with the aid which they are providing. Consideration is given to this issue next.

Administrative, Financial, and Economic Conditions of Aid

In an effort to see that aid funds for specific projects or programs are well utilized and that the supported undertakings bring forth the best returns, the donors of aid frequently insist on various administrative and financial conditions in the underlying agreement between the parties. The practice in general program aid or emergency balance-of-payments assistance has usually been to require commitments to some changes in fundamental economic policies and institutions. Such conditions have been imposed by both bilateral and multilateral donors with varying experiences and degrees of success.

The imposition of administrative conditions is usually directed toward making the project or program work as efficiently as possible and assuring that the funds are used in the way intended. Many of the conditions are routine and provoke little comment on the part of the recipient. In this category one might include the right of the donor to inspect the project and audit the books, the condition that all goods provided will be used on the designated project within the recipient country, and the provision of progress reports by the recipient to the donor. At times, however, there has been objection to reporting requirements. For example, the United States has required the Industrial Finance Corporation of India, in connection with loans extended to it, to provide quarterly reports, annual reports, and special reports on the transportation of goods in ships of U.S. registry. Some of the Indian officials involved have resented such requirements as constituting undue supervision of an institution with a long history of competent operation.

With respect to the increasing trend of lending via national development banks, the conditions requiring prior approval of subloans granted by development banks out of the proceeds of large external loans granted to them have caused complaints in some cases. Some recipients feel that such conditions reflect on their integrity and ability as lenders, and, in addition, they consider it to be a cumbersome, time-consuming procedure. The latter complaint has been met in part in some countries by delegating the authority of approval of subloans to representatives of the donor who are stationed within the recipient country. This was done by the United States in the Sudan, where, however, West Germany still required subloans to be approved at the headquarters of the lending agency. The condition of prior approval has also been limited in some cases by requiring prior approval only for subloans above a certain amount, e.g., subloans for over $100,000 in the case of a U.S. loan to the Industrial Bank of Sudan. Despite such criticisms, most recipients recognize the advantage of this indirect lending for specific projects via development banks over direct lending from the agency abroad, which is not practicable at all for small projects. The donors might accomplish the same goal that they seek with a prior approval process for subloans if they used spot checks on subloans or a postauditing procedure.

Competitive international bidding for goods and services, although generally favored by most sources of aid, has raised some questions. The more advanced developing countries are interested in some cases in the use of domestic goods and services in projects externally financed. It is reasonable to suppose that domestic suppliers should be allowed some advantages in bidding, since they cannot be expected to be as efficient as suppliers in developed countries and since it is desirable to encourage their participation because of the stimulus thereby afforded to development. The difficulty lies in knowing where to draw the line between excessive and reasonable protection and encouragement of local participation. Furthermore, where local suppliers are used, the external financing becomes available as free exchange, which some donors complain is then used by recipients without regard to international competition. On the other hand, recipients complain that international agencies have at times administered the bidding in such a way as deliberately to exclude local participation and to force unnecessary foreign exchange expenditures on projects. The problem is to find the appropriate balance between lower costs and the specific use of foreign exchange, on the one hand, and somewhat higher costs and the freeing of foreign exchange for more general use, on the other.

More delicate policy questions are raised when the donor is convinced that the personnel in charge of a project should be changed, that a program ordinarily managed by a ministry should become an autonomous agency, or that a particular department should be reorganized before the assistance is authorized. Recipient governments are not always opposed to conditions imposed by providers of aid. As a matter of fact, at times they are able to institute desired reforms by stating that these reforms are conditions precedent to the receipt of aid. The reorganization of the Colombian Railways administration, insisted on by the World Bank, is a case in point. A more difficult question arises when the recipient either disagrees with the donor or feels that internal conditions will not permit such a course of action, a situation which could mean the rejection of the proffered assistance.

The development of a working relationship between the recipients and the various sources of aid tends to limit misunderstandings on the part of both parties. With the passage of time, the recipients begin to understand the value of the rationale behind many of the conditions, and the donors are also able to be less rigid as they begin to understand the capabilities of the recipients.

Financial conditions are sometimes attached to economic assistance to insure a satisfactory return on the investment. There may be requirements to raise electricity or transportation rates in power or railroad loans, conditions concerning the numbers or categories of personnel employed, or an insistence that an industry be moved from the public to the private sector for financial reasons. These are frequently highly controversial conditions. In Uganda there were very strong debates within the Uganda Electric Board when the World Bank required the UEB to raise its electric power rates. The Bank imposed this condition because it saw no other way for the UEB to meet its debt service charges, accumulate reserves, and be in a generally sound financial situation. The Bank also pressed for other financial reforms, including a requirement for depreciation of assets which were installed but not in use, to give a more accurate picture of the financial status of the company. The Bank stood firm in its demand for these conditions and the UEB, having no alternative source of financing, accepted them. The arguments in a situation such as this frequently turn on differing views on the part of donors and recipients regarding how costs should be distributed over a society.

To preserve the underlying security for their loans, some donors have at times included a condition which requires recipients to obtain their consent prior to entering into any additional external loans. The closer coordination of external assistance through international consultative bodies or consortia diminishes the need for such a condition as a formal requirement.

When a country is involved in a major financial or economic crisis, the terms on which it can secure assistance may include conditions relating to fundamental economic policies and conditions. These crises may involve strong inflationary pressures or the inability to service debt. Turkey, Brazil, Chile, and Colombia, among others, have had these kinds of problems. During the crisis it is usually possible to get agreement on the imposition of conditions relating to credit controls, a prohibition on suppliers' credits, limitations on public finance expenditures, or the introduction of tax reforms, but it may thereafter be difficult to keep a country to the accepted conditions. The imposition of such conditions is usually more palatable when it is done by an international organization, such as the IMF or the World Bank, rather than on a bilateral basis. At times the task is entrusted to the IMF by a major donor country, whose aid may be contingent on an agreement by the recipient with the Fund.

But even in such cases there is not always smooth sailing. Illustrative are the temporary ruptures of relations which have occurred at times between the World Bank and certain countries, such as Turkey and Brazil. While adherence to the conditions is by no means assured even when they are imposed under international auspices, the chances for adherence under such circumstances are obviously greater because of the involvement of most of the major donors. In any case, such broad conditions create many more difficulties than administrative or financial conditions relating to specific project assistance. It must, nevertheless, be recognized that such conditions, when appropriately fixed on a multilateral basis, are not intended to interfere with the prerogatives of sovereign states but to insure that the environment will be conducive to development. The prospects for expanding general development financing are inhibited when it proceeds mostly under political pressures to bail countries out of emergencies, with little positive effect on the pace of development.

Technical and Capital Assistance

External economic assistance for development is provided in the form of both capital resources, i.e., goods, and technical assistance through the provision of the services of specialized foreign personnel or the training of nationals. The focus of the present study has been on capital, or financial, assistance. The field of technical assistance, though also of great importance to development, has a host of unique problems of its own, and no attempt has been made to deal with them here in any systematic way. The two fields of financial and technical assistance cannot be entirely separated, however, and a consideration of the problems of financial assistance is not complete without taking into account its relationship with technical assistance.

In the evolution of development assistance during the postwar period, the first emphasis was indeed given, to a large extent, to technical rather than financial assistance. Thus, the U.S. program of development assistance can be said to have started with the enactment into legislation in 1950 of the Point Four Program, under which the United States undertook to transfer some of its technical know-how to less developed countries. At that time there was not yet any disposition to come to full grips with the problem of providing a complete program of development assistance, and the bilateral program of the United States was limited to technical aspects, except for the resources incidentally provided under the export financing programs of the Export-Import Bank. Otherwise, U.S. financial resources for development were provided through its participation in the World Bank. It was not until 1957 that the United States embarked on a development financing program of its own through the establishment of the DLF. France and the United Kingdom, meanwhile, in their assistance to present and former colonies, also laid much stress on technical assistance because of the great need of these countries for trained manpower. And the United Nations, too, developed its technical assistance programs early in the postwar period.

The later expansion of development assistance to include substantial financial resources was not at the expense of technical assistance. Indeed, the financial programs made the need for technical assistance more evident than ever before and served to reinforce the technical assistance programs. When the U.S. AID was created in 1961, recognition of the relationship between technical and financial assistance was given through the centralization of both functions in the new agency. The UN Special Fund started operations in 1959 to provide technical assistance designed to facilitate the granting of financial assistance by other agencies. And international financing agencies, such as the World Bank Group and the Inter-American Development Bank, stepped up their own technical assistance activities in support of their primary lending function. Thus, the evolution has been in the direction of a greater merging of the two types of assistance. Nevertheless, to a considerable extent financial assistance and technical assistance continue to be independently run, and the question remains as to whether all that is possible or desirable is being done for the coordination of the two types of assistance so as to contribute to the greatest possible extent to development.

The need for technical assistance may, of course, be quite independent of capital assistance, and to that extent there may be no need to coordinate the two. In many of the newly independent countries, one frequently finds very few trained individuals, and there are pressing needs for planning, financial, and administrative specialists, quite apart from the need for capital. In these early stages of development there is usually also a need for surveys in many fields, e.g., manpower, minerals, education, industry, and health. Technical assistance programs to meet such needs can be administered quite independently of any capital assistance programs.

This is also the case for some of the requirements of countries which are more highly developed. Economic growth is not always dependent on additional capital. The existing stock of capital can frequently be put to much better use through measures that do not involve the investment of additional capital. Technical assistance intended for such purposes can also be administered quite independently of capital assistance.

Thus, there is some justification in principle for the administration of technical assistance programs by agencies, whether national or international, which are quite separate from those which provide financial assistance. In accordance with this justification, one finds separate agencies for technical and capital assistance in West Germany and France, and at various times the same was true in the United States and the United Kingdom. It was apparently, however, the feeling that it was desirable to coordinate technical and capital assistance more closely, and this feeling led to the merger of the two functions in the newly created U.S. AID in 1961 and in the UK Ministry of Overseas Development in 1964. And the merger of the UN technical assistance programs and Special Fund and the possible conversion of the Special Fund into a Capital Development Fund are illustrative of a similar trend among international agencies, as are the undertaking of technical assistance programs by essentially financial assistance agencies such as the World Bank, the Inter-American Development Bank, and the African Development Bank. There is in practice such a close intermingling of technical and capital assistance that it appears best for both types of assistance to be provided by the same agencies, and there is certainly a great need for close coordination of the two when separate agencies exist for one reason or another.

In the more primitive economies, the initial phase of technical assistance is followed by a period when the recommendations of the advisers are to be carried out. At this stage there is, of course, a need for capital, but there may also be a considerable concurrent increase in the need for technical assistance. The new capital investments themselves give rise to the need for operatives, some of whom must be supplied from abroad while others are being trained at home.

The much debated question of the ability of the developing countries to absorb capital assistance is also to a large extent a question of technical assistance. Limits on capital-absorptive capacity are largely a result of deficiencies in trained manpower to formulate and carry out investment projects, which can be corrected through technical assistance.

Another factor which limits the effectiveness of technical assistance where it is divorced from capital assistance is the reluctance of sources of capital assistance to accept surveys and reports of technical experts from other agencies or countries. For this reason, it is prudent as a practical matter to coordinate technical and capital assistance from the beginning of projects.

The UN Special Fund makes a special effort to coordinate its essentially technical assistance type of function with capital assistance. When carrying out surveys which may require capital assistance, the Fund requests recipient governments to advise whether provision is made for such investment in its development plan or whether it wishes the Special Fund to provide the services of an adviser to assist in exploring sources of investment capital.[22] Furthermore, the Fund has used the World Bank as an executing agency in relation to nine of its projects, and six of these completed projects subsequently received follow-up investment from the Bank.[23]

More of this kind of mutual reinforcement by the two types of assistance would undoubtedly be useful. Technical assistance may have the most impact when it is combined with actual investment programs and results in putting new capital to use. And capital assistance is most effective when it is carried out with full recognition of the human element in the development equation.

Aid for Social Projects

As the volume of international development assistance has expanded in recent years, the proportion of aid granted for social, rather than purely economic, projects has also increased. This is

---

[22] UN Special Fund Document SF/PGL/1, June 1, 1964, p. 18.
[23] Draft report of the Thirteenth Session of the Governing Council to the Thirty-ninth Session of the Economic and Social Council, SF/L.117.

illustrated by the U.S. Social Progress Trust Fund, which has been administered by the Inter-American Development Bank, by the devotion to social projects of a substantial part of the resources of the European Development Fund, and by recent loans for education by the World Bank and IDA.

During the four years 1961–64, the Inter-American Development Bank committed slightly more than $450 million, or close to 40 percent of its total loans, out of the Social Progress Trust Fund, for housing, water supply and sanitation, agricultural settlement (in which the rationale is more social than economic), and higher education. Although the total of $525 million in the Social Progress Trust Fund is not to be augmented, the Bank will continue lending for such purposes primarily out of its substantially enlarged Fund for Special Operations. In his annual address to the Board of Governors in April, 1965, the President of the Bank stated that "it must place increasing emphasis on the concept of a development balanced between economic and social investments."

The first European Development Fund committed close to $190 million, or also almost 40 percent of its total aid commitments from 1958 to August 31, 1964, to social projects. These included education and training, health, water supply systems, and town planning. Assistance for social projects is being continued by the second Fund, which was constituted in June, 1964.

In an address to the Economic and Social Council of the United Nations in March, 1965, the President of the World Bank stated that

the crucial importance to economic development of an adequate educational system hardly requires emphasis, but the shocking deficiencies of education in terms of economic development may not be so widely recognized. . . . While the Bank and IDA combined could never hope to provide any significant proportion of the very substantial finance required for education, I think we can help point the way to solutions for some of the key problems. To do so, we are financing strategic projects that will help to fill gaps or otherwise assist in breaking bottlenecks in educational systems. Beginning with an IDA credit in 1962 to enlarge the secondary school system in Tunisia, we have now advanced more than $52 million for educational projects, including a recent credit of $20 million to Nigeria. Many projects related to education are now in our pipeline.

The particularly new departure in the developments indicated above is the provision on a larger scale of capital assistance as distinct from technical assistance for social purposes. Some capital assistance for such purposes had always been available to some extent in a number of bilateral aid programs, such as those of France, the United Kingdom, and the Soviet Union; but the World Bank had previously limited itself to loans for economic projects, and U.S. assistance for social purposes had been mostly technical rather than capital assistance. Since the establishment of the Development Loan Fund in 1957, however, the United States has also provided some bilateral capital assistance for social projects. For example, in the fiscal year 1964, the U.S. AID committed loans in the amount of $106.5 million, or close to 15 percent of its total development loan commitments, for health and sanitation, education, and housing.

As stated in the pamphlet on Principles of Foreign Economic Assistance published by the Program Coordination Staff of the U.S. Agency for International Development (1963, p. 30), "economic development is not the sole aim of A.I.D.'s development assistance program, A.I.D. is also concerned with the social welfare, broadly conceived, of the population which it assists." The AID is, therefore, prepared to assist in the financing of social projects such as the construction of housing and health facilities because of their contribution to social welfare, even though "some of them do not necessarily promote economic efficiency in the short run." It does, however, recognize that they may contribute to economic growth in the long run:

Measures which contribute to the physical well-being and work capacity of a population are forms of social self-help which may help promote economic efficiency. Examples are the extension of housing, provision of better health facilities including the training of doctors and construction of hospitals, legislation for the prevention and control of disease, and improvements in water supplies and in sanitation facilities.

The classification of social projects as being eligible for external capital assistance which is reflected in these policy changes of recent years has resulted from new attitudes toward development and aid for development in a number of respects: investments in "human resources" have come to be regarded as just as important as investments in capital equipment in order to promote economic growth, direct support for social progress is now increasingly accepted as a necessary counterpart to economic growth, and a considerable modification of the principle that social projects should be financed only out of local resources has come to be accepted.

In the last analysis, the purpose of economic growth is to make it possible to achieve better conditions of human welfare for more people, in the form of better health, higher levels of education, improved housing, greater financial security, improvements in conditions of property ownership, and better conditions in other aspects of levels of living. At the same time, however, these various elements in levels of living are instruments in the growth process. They are desirable not only as ends in themselves but also as means to achieve economic growth, with the result that in turn their achievement is enhanced and reinforced by virtue of their contribution to growth. In technical economic terms, they make it possible to utilize existing physical capital more productively, or, put in another way, they serve to lower the capital-output ratio so that given amounts of investment in physical assets will yield higher amounts of output. Labor becomes more productive the better it is nourished, clothed, housed, and educated and the more incentive it has to participate in the process of production. This view of social development as a key growth sector has recently found expression in the creation in Geneva of a new UN Research Institute for Social Development, whose main field of inquiry is the "interaction of social and economic factors, and its relationship to economic development." [24]

The direct approach to social progress as a goal, concurrently with measures to promote economic growth, is best illustrated in the Alliance for Progress for Latin America. In this connection, reference has already been made to the Social Progress Trust Fund established by the United States. Besides measures designed to promote economic growth, great emphasis is placed in the principles of the Alliance as ends in themselves on housing, agrarian reform, conditions of labor, education, health and sanitation, and equitable taxa-

---

[24] Hans W. Singer, "Social Development: Key Growth Sector, Philosophy, Plans, and First Results of the U.N. Research Institute," *International Development Review*, March, 1965, pp. 3–8.

tion. The philosophy of the approach in the Alliance to social progress was stated as follows by the Committee of Nine Experts named as a review body under Alliance procedures:

During the 19th Century there was first an accumulation of capital, after which came a process of distribution of income aimed at achieving effective social progress. Nowadays, it is felt that economic and social development can and should be synchronized. This is the fundamental principle of the Alliance for Progress. The Charter of Punta del Este establishes that national programs should simultaneously further economic growth and social progress, in order to attain ambitious goals in both fields during this decade. Naturally, this is based on a maximum effort by the countries in the mobilization of domestic resources and on timely external aid in amounts and under conditions suitable for the achievement of the proposed goals. . . . If resources are insufficient to cover simultaneously investment in the economic and social fields in order to reach the goals set forth in the Charter, the Committee does not believe that social investment should be undertaken only with what is left after economic investments have been made that will assure an annual per capita rate of income growth of 2.5 percent. The Committee believes that a careful estimate of social investments should be made, seeking in any event a volume sufficiently large so that the new benefits attained will increase proportionally more than the growth of the population.[25]

The view that external loans should be limited to economic projects had been justified largely on the ground that only such projects could yield the increment in national output out of which the loans eventually would have to be serviced. In an even stricter interpretation, the position was sometimes taken that even the economic projects financed should be limited to those with a favorable effect on the country's balance of international payments, since the repayments of loans had to be transferred into foreign exchange. In the broader view which has come to be accepted, there is recognition of the need to service external loans out of general increments in national output and more specifically out of increased availabilities of foreign exchange. At the same time, however, it is recognized that the increases in output and in foreign exchange are in the last analysis dependent on the country's total development program and not merely on those projects which are externally financed. The eli-

[25] *Report of the Panel of Experts to the Inter-American Economic and Social Council* (Washington, D.C., Organization of American States, 1962), pp. 21-22.

gibility of projects and programs for external loans is now determined by their place in the total development program, the mix of both foreign and domestic resources in the aggregate financing of the program, and the contribution of the total program, including the social projects, to the viability of the international economic position of the country.

Although these broader views of the role of social projects in development and of their eligibility for external financing have gained acceptance, such projects still constitute only a minor part of the projects financed from abroad. Such financing is justified more as a catalytic agent to stimulate the mobilization of domestic resources and the creation of institutions to carry out social investments than as a fixed proportion of total requirements. There is still a marked preference by lending agencies for projects with a direct impact on economic efficiency and growth. Nevertheless, the rigid approach that was characteristic of earlier years of the postwar period has come to be liberalized to a considerable degree.

Tying of Aid to Purchases in Donor Country

The tying of aid to purchases in the donor country limits the full play of international competition and hampers the freedom of choice in procurement by the recipients. Recipient countries are, therefore, generally opposed to it, although they recognize some of the compelling reasons for the practice. It was with some qualification that recipient countries went on record against the tying of aid at the 1964 UNCTAD Conference in Geneva. The UNCTAD Resolution on Terms of Financing,[26] after pronouncing itself against the tying of development loans to particular projects, set forth the following principle on country tying:

Loans for purchases of capital equipment or nonproject assistance, should not ordinarily be tied to purchases in donor countries and, keeping in view the desirability of flexibility to developing countries in the procurement policies, should be available for use in best markets and, particularly, in the markets of recipient and other developing countries. In any case, they should be available for purchases in countries with

[26] United Nations, *Trade and Development*, p. 45. This Resolution was adopted by a vote of 81 to 9, with 25 abstentions, the negative votes and abstentions being those mostly of developed countries (including the Soviet bloc).

convertible currencies. Moreover, in all cases of tied loans where the recipient country can show that the required equipment and goods are available at cheaper rates or better terms elsewhere, the Governments should intervene either to bring down prices and regulate conditions of supply or, where this is not feasible, to transfer the funds for other purchases in donor countries at competitive rates or, failing that, to release them for free purchase in the best market from the point of view of the recipient country.

The most onerous combination is the tying of aid both to specific projects and to purchases in the donor country. Under this combination, the competitive possibilities are limited to a narrow range of goods. Country tying becomes somewhat less objectionable in program financing, since the range of goods to be purchased is much broader and there are possibilities of substitution. This increases somewhat the competitive element of purchases.

The extent to which aid-tying actually forces trade into unnatural channels is, however, limited. As viewed by the Chairman of the DAC, "there is no doubt but that a very large part of the assistance would continue in its present channels even if there were no requirements with respect to purchase." [27] The strong orientation of many countries in Latin America toward the U.S. market, of French-speaking African countries toward France, and of Commonwealth countries toward the United Kingdom would be the same even without the tying of aid. Aid-tying must certainly, however, have some effect in the distortion of trade channels, since obviously "there would be no need for the aid-tying requirement if it did not on occasion substitute required channels for international competitive markets." [28]

Probably the most compelling circumstance in the increasing trend toward country tying of aid is the balance-of-payments problem of the United States, the largest donor, which has led to the application of this practice in its development lending since 1959. Other principal donors have shown no disposition to move toward an untying of aid so long as there is little chance that aid funds made available bilaterally by the United States will be spent outside of that country. Thus, the call by the DAC Chairman in September, 1964, for "a fresh move to reverse the present tendency of increased aid-tying" through joint action by donors even if such "action had

[27] OECD, *DAC 1964 Review*, p. 50.   [28] *Ibid.*

to be confined to those countries which do not have major balance-of-payments problems"[29] appears not to have evoked much of a response from DAC member countries.

The balance-of-payments reason for the tying of U.S. aid, though perhaps the one with the most pervasive effect at the present time, may turn out to be temporary. There are, on the other hand, political and commercial reasons for country tying of aid which are probably of a more enduring character. Most aid of the Soviet bloc is tied, both to specific projects and to the donor country, largely because the donor country wants its aid to have a positive effect on its political relations with the recipient. The tying of the aid of France also has political motivations. The bulk of France's aid goes to French-speaking Africa, and its recent limited extension to other areas, such as Latin America, is also politically oriented.

Much aid is, however, tied for very definite commercial reasons. EXIMBANK loans have, of course, always been tied; that Bank, with its clear legislative mandate to promote U.S. exports, has never been empowered to grant loans in any other form. Even the aid administered by the U.S. AID, which is tied primarily for balance-of-payments reasons, is "sold" by the Administration to the legislature to a large extent on commercial grounds. In the presentation to Congress of the AID program for fiscal year 1966, after pointing out that "the U.S. procurement policies followed over the past four years have minimized the drain of our assistance programs on our balance of payments," the Administration cited the fact that "another result of AID's procurement policy is a substantial export business for American private enterprise."[30] Many congressmen are undoubtedly much more mindful of some of their export-oriented constituents than of the U.S. balance-of-payments position in voting for aid so long as it is tied to purchases in the United States. And the appreciable portion of aid given in the form of tied suppliers' credits, some under government guarantees, and tied official loans by European countries and Japan are also given primarily for commercial reasons.

The channeling of aid through international agencies is the principal method of administering aid on an untied basis. This is one of

[29] *Ibid.*, p. 51.
[30] *Proposed Mutual Defense and Development Programs FY 1966*, p. 17.

the reasons that many recipient countries prefer aid from such agencies. And, by the same token, it is probably the chief reason that militates against any substantial increase in the proportion of aid that donors are willing to provide through international agencies. Yet, even here, devices have recently been developed to combine the practice of aid-tying with administration by international agencies. For example, the Inter-American Development Bank has recently convinced some nonmember donor countries, such as Canada and Spain, to turn over to it for lending funds in trust which are, for the most part, tied to purchases in the particular donor country.

As previously noted, the undesirable effects of aid-tying can be mitigated by having more aid in the form of program assistance relative to aid for specific projects. This can also be done by concentrating the aid of particular donors on projects and commodities for which their conditions of supply are competitive. Countries, such as India, which receive aid from a considerable number of sources, in fact, do bear this criterion in mind in their aid negotiations and so are able to minimize the effects of limited competition. Donor countries can also contribute to this same end by procedures for maximizing competition among their own suppliers of commodities or equipment which are financed under aid programs. And at times they may even grant waivers of tying requirements under special circumstances in which the tying is particularly onerous to the recipient.

While there is no doubt that untied aid is preferable to tied aid and that every effort should be made to move in the direction of untying aid as circumstances permit, the volume of aid available at present is undoubtedly greater than it would be if it had to be provided on an untied basis. The forces which oppose aid in some donor countries, such as the United States and France, are probably considerably disarmed by the provisions which tie aid to purchases from domestic suppliers. Given such political realities, the most productive immediate approach seems to be in the direction of methods to diminish the adverse effects of the tying of aid. Tied aid, especially if administered with a consciousness of the need to maximize the impact on development, is obviously better than no aid at all.

Terms of Repayment

One of the major problems of international development aid which faces the community of nations today is the ability of the recipients to maintain the increasing volume of debt service which is accumulating as the volume of lending expands. It was concern with this problem that led to the creation at the beginning of the present decade of the International Development Association (IDA) as a soft-loan affiliate of the World Bank and to the consolidation of soft-loan terms upon the reorganization of U.S. aid through the establishment of its AID. Under the impetus of these developments, the loan terms of other donor nations have also been eased, and provision has been made for some concessionary lending by other international agencies, such as the Inter-American Development Bank.

Despite these measures, the problem has by no means been solved. The question of the burden of debt service is a cause of continuing concern and a subject of continuing study by DAC, the World Bank, UNCTAD, and the U.S. government.

The DAC, in a resolution on the Terms and Conditions of Aid adopted in April 3, 1963, noted "with concern the rapid increase in recent years of the external debt service liabilities of developing countries" and the "substantial discrepancies between the terms of aid from various DAC members." [31] It recommended that DAC members "relate the terms of aid on a case-by-case basis to the circumstances of each under-developed country or group of countries" and "make it their objective in principle to secure a significant degree of comparability in the terms and conditions of their aid"; the latter "would involve a liberalisation of the terms adopted by some members." The resolution suggested that the members consider providing an appropriate "mix" of hard loans and soft loans or grants. The *DAC 1964 Review* noted that "a certain amount of progress has been made in the past year in easing the terms on which loans are provided" but indicated that the whole program of debt-servicing difficulties was continuing to receive active consideration in the DAC. Indeed, in July, 1965, the DAC adopted resolutions on the terms of aid that in certain respects went even beyond

[31] OECD, *DAC 1964 Review*, pp. 44, 97–99.

UNCTAD recommendations noted below: [32] as a goal to be realized in three years, 80 percent of all government aid should be provided as grants or as loans maturing in twenty-five years or more, at interest rates of 3 percent or less and with interest-free grace periods of at least seven years.

Pursuant to the DAC resolution of 1963 on Terms of Aid, as well as a request by the Secretary-General of UNCTAD, the World Bank published in 1964 an analytical and statistical study of *Economic Growth and External Debt*.[33] This is the most recent in a series of studies in which the Bank has kept the problem under review.[34] The study focuses attention on the factors which determine a country's ability to service foreign debt, pointing out that in the last analysis they can all

be reduced to only one: a high level of investment that yields a high rate of return. Once this is achieved, the rest will take care of itself: if the rate of return is high, the plough-back will also be high; if the plough-back is high, output will grow quickly; if output grows quickly the balance of payments will tend to show structural strength which will facilitate external debt management.[35]

Nevertheless, there are no generalized answers to the question of what the prescription for aid terms should be for any given country: "Only by systematic country-by-country studies in depth can answers to these questions be given, at least in part." [36]

The principles which should govern the terms of aid were spelled out in the resolution on Terms of Financing adopted by UNCTAD, with the affirmative votes of 81 recipient countries, the negative votes of 9 donor countries, and the abstention of 25 other donors.[37] According to that resolution,

as far as possible, aid should be a blend of grants and loans. . . . Repayments should be spread over a considerably long period which should normally be not less than twenty years, and with a certain grace period, taking into account the specific nature of goods. . . . Interest rates for

[32] OECD, *DAC 1965 Review.*
[33] Dragoslav Avramovic and associates, *Economic Growth and External Debt* (Baltimore, Johns Hopkins Press, 1964).
[34] Cf. Dragoslav Avramovic, *Debt Servicing Capacity and Postwar Growth in International Indebtedness* (Baltimore, Johns Hopkins Press, 1958); and Dragoslav Avramovic and Ravi Gulhati, *Debt Servicing Problems of Low-Income Countries, 1956–58* (Baltimore, Johns Hopkins Press, 1960).
[35] Avramovic, *Economic Growth*, p. 194. [36] *Ibid.*, p. 195.
[37] United Nations, *Trade and Development*, pp. 44–45.

development loans should take into account the repayment capacity of the borrowing country. Endeavour should be made that they should not normally exceed 3 per cent and, where this is not feasible, waivers of interest should be considered to meet this objective.

Furthermore, the principle was recommended that

some part of repayment of loans may be accepted in national currencies of the debtor countries, . . . [and] where loans are repayable in convertible currencies and are tied to purchases in donor countries, ways and means should be devised . . . for the repayment of such loans in mutually determined commodities and manufactures produced by the debtor country.

In another resolution on the problem of Debt Service in Developing Countries,[38] adopted by 109 votes with 11 abstentions, UNCTAD called upon the international financial agencies to "consider the possibilities of adapting their organizations and procedures with a view to improving the terms of their transactions, keeping in view the particular problems of developing countries," and for an increase in the resources available to IDA "to provide assistance to developing countries on terms with a minimal burden of debt service" through the transfer of a "reasonable portion of the net earnings" of the World Bank at the end of each fiscal year and through "contributions on a continuing basis . . . by the member Governments to the maximum extent possible."

In a report released in April, 1965, the U.S. AID analyzed the dangers of the growing burden of external debt service and urged Congress not to impose severer terms on U.S. loans. The report pointed out that

in the last 10 years, the debt-service burden has increased so rapidly that it has cancelled out much of the growth in total aid. In 1955, 8 per cent of external assistance received was offset by debt service. In 1964 debt service offset 30 per cent of external assistance.[39]

Furthermore, the burden was expected to worsen with a continuation of present loan rates:

debt servicing costs to the underdeveloped countries will climb from $.8 billion 10 years ago to nearly $7 billion a year by 1975. In terms of export earnings, repayments will cost the underdeveloped countries

[38] *Ibid.*, p. 46.   [39] New York *Times*, April 6, 1965.

13.6 per cent of their foreign exchange income by 1975, compared with 3.7 per cent in 1955 and about 10 per cent now.

Grants, Hard Loans, and Soft Loans

It is ironical that U.S. Marshall Plan aid to European countries was mostly in the form of grants, while the shift of U.S. aid to the less developed countries, whose ability to repay is generally inferior to that of Marshall Plan recipients, was accompanied by a gradual change in the terms of the assistance from grants to loans. The major exception to this in U.S. aid is, of course, the grantlike disposal of agricultural surpluses for local currencies, but this is due to unique domestic circumstances. To be sure, the shift to loans in U.S. aid was largely to soft loans. At first, "softness" meant repayment in local currencies; later it meant long terms and low interest rates but repayment in foreign exchange. The softness of the terms has diminished in recent years, however, as interest rates have been raised and maturity periods have been shortened. The hardening of U.S. loan terms has resulted from the conviction of legislators that this is a "sounder" basis on which to extend loans because it is conducive to greater discipline in their utilization on the part of recipients. There has also been the objection that soft terms by the United States have been a means of subsidizing the recipients for the harder terms exacted by other lending nations. This objection should be effectively countered by the realization of the aid term goal adopted by DAC in July, 1965. As noted above, there is a keen awareness among the administrators of U.S. aid that the mix of the various forms of aid must be related to the balance-of-payments prospects of the recipients and that an increasing proportion of soft terms is required if an intolerable burden of debt service is to be avoided.

French aid, which is second in volume only to that of the United States, continues to be heavily weighted on the side of grants. The main reasons for this are, first, the past colonial status of most of the countries aided, second, the low or delayed yield of the social and economic infrastructure requirements of these more underdeveloped countries, and, third, the recognition of balance-of-payments difficulties. The forms in which British aid is provided are subject to much the same influences and factors as French aid, although more of British aid goes to stronger countries and to that extent is on somewhat harder terms. The British government, however, announced at a Commonwealth Prime Ministers' Conference in June, 1965, a new policy of extending loans free of all interest or management charges to poorer countries. It was expected that about half of British loans granted in the future would be interest-free.

At the other end of the spectrum among the major Western-bloc donors are West Germany and Japan, whose terms even of official loans are not too far removed from commercial terms. Their outright grants are limited to technical assistance and social projects, which constitute only a small portion of their assistance to less developed countries. They too, however, have made some provision in recent years for loans on softer terms, in response to international pressures. Still, the Japanese seriously question the wisdom of making any international resources at all available on concessionary terms. To some extent, this position is a reflection of Japan's own relative economic standing, but it also results from the view that world economic development is best served by financial discipline.

The more-or-less typical 2½ percent, twelve-year loan from the Soviet bloc is concessionary in relation to the interest rate, though not more so than the AID type of U.S. loan and much less so than IDA loans. The maturity is, of course, much less favorable than that of most Western lending. And grants constitute only a very minor portion of Sino-Soviet aid. Soviet countries frequently arrange to accept repayment in the products of the projects assisted. This is attractive to the less developed countries in so far as it gives them an assured outlet for products which they might otherwise have difficulty in marketing abroad. This matter of the treatment of exports from the less developed countries is, however, a general trade question, to which much attention is being paid separately in UNCTAD.

One of the factors which contributes to the debt-servicing problems of the less developed countries is short- and medium-term suppliers' credits, which have increased in recent years. The flow of such credits has been stimulated by officially sponsored, competitive guarantee or insurance schemes in developed countries designed to promote their exports and is abetted when less developed countries encounter difficulties in obtaining financing for their imports on more favorable terms. On the one hand, capital-exporting countries take action to limit "unfair competition" in export credits by agreeing to fix maximum maturities, while, on the other, they recognize the desirability of lengthening the maturities of loans to help countries with heavy external debt-servicing burdens.[40] In view of the commercial motivations on the donor side, suppliers' credits are much more easily obtained than long-term development loans, which may be conditioned on the careful working out of investment priorities.

Recipient countries sometimes take the easy way out, resorting to suppliers' credits when they cannot reach agreement with developmental agencies on investment priorities. Chile's financing of the requirements of its railroad modernization program through bilateral sources rather than the World Bank, discussed in a case study above, is illustrative. Such devices sometimes possibly aggravate the debt-service burden of the recipient country and also distort its investment priorities and result in higher costs. This occurred under the irresponsible policies of the Rojas Pinilla dictatorship in Colombia in the mid-1950s. At least one electric power project of doubtful priority and feasibility was carried out in that country because suppliers' credits were available for it; in this instance, the priorities of a national electric power development plan were not respected, and, in the absence of international competitive bidding, investment costs were undoubtedly higher than they would otherwise have been.

Nevertheless, suppliers' credits constitute a time-honored mechanism in the financing of international trade. Despite their drawbacks, they cannot entirely be replaced by long-term financing for purchases on international competitive terms. Considerable study, caution, and cooperative international efforts are required to resolve the complex problems associated with suppliers' credits. An UNCTAD resolution adopted without dissent [41] recommended that such a study should be undertaken by the World Bank.

How far financial assistance should be granted on concessionary terms or be repayable at all depends in the last analysis on the amount of aid required and on the effectiveness with which it is utilized. Relevant questions are the extent to which output of the

[40] Cf. OECD, *DAC 1964 Review*, pp. 47–48.
[41] United Nations, *Trade and Development*, pp. 50–51.

recipients increases as a result of financial aid and whether changes in the structure of the balance of payments are brought about to permit repayment in foreign currencies. There are no easy, generalized answers to this type of problem. But there is an increasing awareness of the problem in the international community, which makes it possible to guard against the prospect of demoralizing defaults and to make adjustments in terms and in repayment schedules when required by the compelling circumstances of development.

Multilateral and Bilateral Aid

The Chairman of the U.S. Foreign Relations Committee, Senator Fulbright, recently advocated the increased multilateralization of American foreign aid. In taking this position, he joined other experts, such as those on the Jeanneney Commission, which reviewed French aid policies. Implied in these suggestions is the belief that multilateral aid is more concerned with the objectives of economic development than the bilateral sources, which are under constant pressure to implement the more varied objectives of a national government.

Some sentiment exists in the United States for a greater multilateralization of aid, as illustrated by the adoption by the U.S. Senate of a provision in the foreign aid bill for fiscal year 1966 that up to 15 percent of the funds provided for development loans may be channeled through the World Bank and its affiliates, provided they are matched by the other member countries. The amount theoretically involved under this provision is, however, small, amounting to only about $117 million. Any substantial increase in U.S. contributions to international organizations raises questions in relation to the balance of payments and the contributions of the United States relative to the contributions of others. The general policy in international organizations is not to tie aid funds. Thus, an increase in economic assistance through international organizations could conflict with the U.S. policy of tying aid. With respect to the second point, the United States provides 30 percent of the capital of the World Bank and has voting power comparable to its contribution. If only the United States increased its assistance, the U.S. voting rights might increase and thereby diminish the international character of the organization. The problems of tied aid and voting rights can, to some extent, be avoided by setting up special funds in trust to be administered by the international organization. This course has been pursued by the Inter-American Development Bank in relation to Canadian and American contributions.

Other obstacles which impede multilateralization of aid include the special historical ties between donors and certain recipients and the related matter of political and strategic interests of donors in supplying aid; the desire of donors to "show the flag" in relation to projects assisted; and the greater possibilities of tying aid on a bilateral basis, which donors find desirable for commercial and political reasons besides balance-of-payments reasons. Also, certain forms of aid, such as the sale of agricultural surpluses for local currencies and export financing, do not easily lend themselves to multilateralization by their very nature.

Public opinion polls in France have shown opposition to multilateral as opposed to bilateral aid, including opposition to the 25 percent target for multilateral aid suggested for 1975 by the Jeanneney Report. There is not a much greater disposition toward multilateral aid in the United Kingdom, West Germany, and Japan. The latter two countries, in the process of reestablishing themselves following defeat in World War II and seeking new markets, seem inclined to have the source of their assistance clearly identified, and thus one would not expect strong support on their part for multilateralism.

Although the volume of aid could remain the same whether it is multilateral or bilateral, it seems reasonable to assume that legislators would continue to be willing to allocate more funds to institutions which are controlled by their nationals.

Apart from the political difficulties, multilateral aid is generally viewed as being more effective than bilateral aid because multilateral funds are loaned on an untied basis and are free of political, commercial, or other extraneous motivations. The management of multilateral lending agencies is more effective because of their greater autonomy, continuity, and freedom from political influences. Multilateral agencies are also better able to bring their influence to bear toward more efficient use of aid by recipient countries and to apply genuine development criteria to their financing assistance. Multilateralism also tends to lead to greater participation by recipient countries in the aid process; they are, after all, subscribers to and members of the multilateral agencies. Furthermore, small donors can be brought into the stream of aid much better by making their resources available through multilateral agencies rather than by setting up bilateral programs.

Although some recipients show a marked preference for multilateral aid because it is untied and is considered to be less political, other factors can modify this leaning. Some recipients, who through skillful and energetic efforts have received relatively high inflows of aid, fear that a strengthened multilateral agency focusing on worldwide priorities might reduce their relative share of the total. In addition, the centralization of the sources of aid would limit the recipients who maximize their assistance by playing donors off against each other. Also, the centralization of aid through a single source might put too much power in the hands of a few aid administrators. Another disadvantage of multilateral aid is that most of it is in the form of loans, with the notable exception of the European Development Fund. As debt-servicing becomes a more serious problem, recipients would probably prefer to maintain their bilateral grant sources of assistance. Multilateral loans, e.g., from IDA, are, however, being offered on terms which approach grant assistance, and there is a growing trend from grant assistance to loans among bilateral donors.

Recent discussions on the proposed UN Capital Development Fund indicate that multilateralization of aid in and of itself does not satisfy many recipients. They are interested in playing a greater role in deciding on the terms and conditions of the assistance, and they have suggested that such decisions should be made on the basis of each country's having one vote in the formulation of these policies. This matter is discussed in more detail below.

It can be argued to some extent that bilateral aid can be more innovative and flexible than multilateral assistance. It is perhaps easier to develop new ideas within one government than it is to obtain the consent of many.

A technique which has been employed more and more in recent years is the international administration and coordination of bilateral assistance. The approach which is used in the Mekong and Indus River projects, in the consortia and consultative groups sponsored by the World Bank and the OECD, and in the activities of the European Development Fund and the Alliance for Progress combines many of the advantages of both forms of assistance. These coordinating mechanisms and the problems related to them are discussed below.

It is apparent that assistance will continue to be provided from both multilateral and bilateral sources. Although there are good reasons for a greater multilateralization of aid and some trend toward more of this type of aid, it is not likely that it will constitute even as much as 25 percent of the assistance provided in the near future. Much imagination and flexibility have been demonstrated, however, by the international community in developing new techniques to combine the best features of both types of channels for aid.

Techniques of Coordination

The proliferation of sources of aid has given impetus in recent years to the creation of a variety of aid-coordinating institutions and mechanisms. This has included organizations designed to coordinate policies on a broad and general level, as well as devices for the coordination of aid to specific recipient countries. Within the two categories distinguished on this basis, there are additional variations. On the general level, the Western donors have joined in the DAC to coordinate their policies; the Inter-American Committee on the Alliance for Progress has brought together recipients and the principal donor to carry out a cooperative program for a particular region; and the UNCTAD, consisting not only of Western donors and less developed recipients but also of the "centrally planned economies" of the Soviet bloc as well, in a way qualifies as an aid-coordinating mechanism by virtue of having adopted numerous resolutions relating to the principles and practices of international financial aid. The variety of aid-coordinating mechanisms on the individual recipient country level is illustrated by the fact that such mechanisms have been constituted for seven of the ten recipient countries whose aid experiences have been studied in detail in the research for this report (see Chapter IV)—World Bank consultative groups for Colombia and the Sudan and a World Bank consortium for India, OECD consortia for Greece and Turkey, and DAC coordinating groups for Thailand and East Africa. And the latter types of country-coordinating groups do not exhaust the list—the latest addition is the Inter-American Development Bank consultative group, inaugurated with the constitution of the first such body for aid to Ecuador in June, 1965.

These numerous types of coordinating mechanisms illustrate the complexity and variety of situations to be dealt with in the aid-giving process. Just as aid is likely to continue being dispensed by a host of multilateral and bilateral agencies, and indeed in view of that very circumstance, the coordinating mechanisms necessarily take a variety of forms. The various types of mechanisms serve different purposes, and no single type has any claim to exclusivity.

The recipients are not represented in the DAC, but the purpose of that organization is to effect a confrontation of policies among the Western donors with the objective of maximizing their contributions and harmonizing terms on liberal bases. The recipients are represented in the Inter-American Committee on the Alliance for Progress because the purpose there is to influence domestic development policies, in addition to promoting a flow of external resources. And there is the broadest type of representation of donors and recipients in UNCTAD, where the purpose is to mount a global effort to solve the problems of financing development in the broadest terms.

On the country level, the consortia represent the tightest type of coordinating mechanism, involving as they do the pledging of specific amounts of external assistance on a regular, annual basis. They are, however, limited to India and Pakistan under World Bank sponsorship and to Turkey under OECD sponsorship (the OECD consortium for Greece has not been operative). These consortia to a considerable extent had their origins in emergency situations, and the countries for which they are being continued are of key importance in the world aid effort and highly strategic from the political point of view. In the subsequent development of country-coordinating arrangements, the consortium technique was abandoned in favor of the looser consultative group. In the consultative group there is no continuing commitment to supply any given amounts of aid, although there is an expression of positive interest and intent by virtue of the very existence of the group. The DAC coordinating groups are the least formal of them all, and their scope has been limited: the coordinating group in Thailand has concerned itself mostly with technical assistance to that country, and the group for East Africa has met only sporadically and does not appear to have taken any definite shape. The Inter-American Development Bank-sponsored type of consultative group, as illustrated in the first one constituted for Ecuador, has introduced a novel element by including some countries which are net aid recipients themselves but which are nevertheless capable of providing some technical assistance to others; thus, the Ecuador group includes five other Latin American republics and Israel in connection with the technical assistance aspect of its activities.

With the increase in the number of newly independent countries entering the scene as claimants for aid and with the increasing variety of sources of aid, it is not surprising that the coordinating mechanisms have come into being. Indeed, the limited number of country-coordinating groups which have been established thus far is probably a reflection only of the still dominant position of one or a few donors in aid to particular countries. Thus, there appears to be little need for such formal groups when it is only the United States and the World Bank which need to, and can easily, consult with one another informally with respect to financial assistance to Thailand or with France and the European Development Fund with respect to assistance to Senegal. But the need for coordinating mechanisms will increase as many recipient countries shake some of these relatively exclusive ties and turn to more diverse sources of assistance. And the trend toward a greater diversification in the sources of assistance is being strengthened by the principal donors as well. The very existence of the European Development Fund itself is due to France's desire that the European Economic Community share the aid burden in Africa. And the United States pushed for the creation of DAC and has vigorously supported the multinational aid coordinating groups for the same sort of reason. In its presentation of the 1966 aid program to Congress, the U.S. AID pointed out as a positive achievement that "during fiscal year 1966, 85 percent of all AID development loans in Asia and Africa will be committed through these multinational consortia or consultative groups." [42]

The policy of the World Bank is to pursue vigorously the forma-

[42] *Proposed Mutual Defense and Development Programs FY 1966*, p. 14.

tion of additional consultative groups of capital-exporting countries and international agencies interested in the development of particular countries. The President of the Bank affirmed this policy strongly in an address to the UN Economic and Social Council in March, 1965, as follows:

> These groups offer the developing countries the prospect of an orderly and timely flow of development assistance from all aid-giving sources, directed to priority needs. They offer the donor agencies the opportunity to consult effectively among themselves and with the recipient country on means of strengthening development efforts of the country concerned.
>
> We have recently come to a decision in the Bank to redouble our efforts in this respect. We plan to take the lead, insofar as practicable, in organizing consultative groups where they promise to be of some advantage, and we have started conversations with member governments on this subject. We no longer intend to wait until a developing country has a reasonably well-defined economic program before considering the formation of a consultative group. Our principal criterion will be whether the activity of such a group may significantly improve the prospects for a better development effort in the country concerned.
>
> To organize and effectively serve a significant number of consultative groups will call for great effort on the part of the Bank and will require current, intimate and detailed knowledge of the economies, plans and problems of each of the developing countries involved. I believe, however, that the resulting give-and-take of ideas, finance and technical aid may well produce an important breakthrough, enhancing the performance of receiving countries and inspiring new confidence in those who supply assistance.[48]

There is little dissent with respect to the desirability of country-coordinating groups. The limitation which results on the recipient country's ability to play off one donor against another is more than offset by the achievement of order out of chaos and by the concentrated attention paid to the needs of the recipient involved. But the success of the effort, and indeed of aid itself, is dependent on effective performance by the recipient and by a sympathetic tailoring of the coordinated contributions of the donors to the aspirations of the recipient. This involves a delicate relationship between the recipient and the donors in the coordinating group, for which there are no

[48] Address by George D. Woods, President of the World Bank and Its Affiliates, to the Economic and Social Council of the United Nations, March 26, 1965, pp. 12–13.

facile prescriptions. However, the constructive and conciliatory spirit that has guided the groups which have been functioning to date augurs well for the success of the numerous additional ones likely to be constituted in the future.

Channels for Receipt of Aid

The effectiveness of the contribution of international financial aid to development is to a considerable extent dependent on the nature and quality of public administration in the recipient countries. The aid is channeled through various types of organizations in the recipient countries; and the efficiency with which they carry out their functions, in general, naturally also affects the effectiveness of external aid. There is substantial variation in the quality of administration in the developing countries of different backgrounds and at varying stages of development which have been studied in our research—ranging from the well-developed civil service and apparatus of public administration in such countries as India and Israel to newly independent countries with great dependence on foreign administrators, such as Senegal or East Africa, while other countries, such as Chile, Colombia, Greece, Turkey, or Thailand, are between these extremes. The tasks of the donors of aid are, of course, facilitated where there is effective control and administration by the recipient countries. But public administration has evolved differently in different countries, and the donors for the most part must adapt to the various situations which they find. Solutions to the problems of administrative deficiencies can be worked out only on an individual country basis and must be tailored to the peculiarities of the individual countries.

INSTITUTIONAL PATTERNS IN DEVELOPING COUNTRIES

Close centralization of foreign aid administration in Israel is through the Ministry of Finance and the Office of the Economic Minister in the United States, in keeping with the highly developed teamwork among public officials and agencies which is generally characteristic of that country's public administration. In addition to the participation of the centralizing offices, the specific investing agencies for whose programs foreign assistance is destined usually are also involved in the negotiations with the sources of the funds. Thus, the donors can be confident that the programs they are assisting are developed carefully both in themselves and in their priority status in relation to total national programs. This type of optimum combination of the advantages of both centralized control and decentralized initiative is, of course, facilitated by the small size of the country, by its highly developed sense of national purpose, and by the background of training and experience which its officials have had.

The problems of administration are much greater in India owing to the size and complexity of the tasks of development, although the country has a highly respected corps of British-trained public administrators who gained experience under British rule. The administrative paths for aid donors to follow are simplified by virtue of the strong national planning operation, as well as by the prototype international aid consortium for the country. Nevertheless, there are deficiencies in the coordination of public programs, in the carrying out of preinvestment studies and in the formulation of projects, in the administration of economic controls such as that over foreign exchange utilization, and in the execution of investments themselves, which impede the effective utilization of foreign aid. Administrative procedures in India can be officious and arduous, and there is a need for greater emphasis on the practical aspects of carrying out investments. Particularly in view of the importance of state-owned enterprises in certain fields, there is a need for the development of more "management-mindedness" among public officials. Such deficiencies in Indian public administration and their effect on the application of foreign assistance are illustrated in the difficulties encountered by the large steel mill projects which have been carried out with British, German, and Soviet help.

In the Latin American countries studied, many of the projects assisted are carried out through autonomous public corporations which operate in certain sectors of the economies. In Colombia this includes electric power enterprises, specialized banks, railways, water supply and sewage enterprises, and an agrarian reform institute. In Chile a number of such corporations have spun off as specialized subsidiaries or affiliates of a national development corporation with broad responsibilities, which is one of the oldest of its type found in the less developed countries of the world. This has occurred in electric power, petroleum, and iron and steel. Besides, there are important public corporations which have developed independently of the development corporation, such as the Chilean State Railways. Such corporations are favored because of their more businesslike attitudes and greater immunity from political pressures than regular government departments.

At times, sources of aid have been successful, in connection with their assistance, in pressing for a separation of the functions involved from regular government departments and for their administration by autonomous agencies, as occurred in the case of the World Bank loans for the Colombian railways. Attempts have also been made in these countries, with varying degrees of success, to centralize in single agencies control over the formulation and negotiation of aid requests. This has been attempted in Colombia with only limited success through the country's National Planning Office, although the centralization has been abetted recently as a result of the activities of the international consultative group for aid to that country. The centralization has been somewhat more complete in Chile because of the strong position of its development corporation, CORFO, but even in that country, there is a tendency for autonomous agencies, such as the State Railways, to go their own way in aid negotiations.

The greater looseness of control in the administration of foreign aid noted in the cases of Colombia and Chile is even more marked in the case of Turkey. In the course of the history of foreign aid to that country, there have been sharp jurisdictional disagreements among such agencies as the Ministry of Foreign Affairs, the Ministry of Finance, and the operating agencies. There has been a frequent shifting of centralizing responsibilities, but insufficient powers have been given to the agencies designated from time to time to exercise the control. For the last five years, there has been an attempt to centralize the process through an interagency committee under the Planning Organization, but there is still some conflict, e.g., with the Ministry of Foreign Affairs in relation to its responsibilities for the conduct of foreign relations.

In Greece there has been considerable centralization in a Ministry of Coordination, but there are serious deficiencies with respect to the development of strong administrative units to carry out sectoral responsibilities. The Public Power Corporation in Greece, which was established early in the postwar period under U.S. prodding, is an outstanding example of an effective public administrative body and has been a channel for much foreign assistance. This type of organization is not duplicated in other fields, however, and public works execution and administration, as well as the volume of aid for specific projects, suffer as a result.

In Thailand responsibility for aid administration has been centralized in two agencies—the central bank for loans from the World Bank and an Office of Thai Technical and Economic Cooperation for aid from other sources. The latter had been a subdivision of the country's National Economic Development Board and has been moved to a recently created Ministry of National Development. Nevertheless, there has been considerable dispersion of aid-seeking initiatives by various government offices outside of this structure. In the African countries—Senegal, East Africa, and the Sudan—there has been centralization of responsibility for aid in the various national planning offices. The international consultative group for the Sudan has helped in the focusing of the administrative responsibility, and France has fulfilled a similar function in Senegal, in view of its predominant position in aid to that country. In some activities, such as railways and ports, the East Africa Common Services Organization has served as a central channel for the provision of aid to the three countries of that region.

The donors of aid are at times convinced that a particular body in a recipient country should be subjected to certain changes or that new institutions should be created for the aid to be effective. It has already been indicated that donors have at times been instrumental in having new autonomous public corporations set up to administer programs more effectively. There has been a substantial degree of positive influence of this type by aid donors on the institutions of recipient countries. The United States was instrumental in the creation in Greece of a Central Loans Committee in 1948 to channel aid funds to private projects. This agency has since undergone a considerable metamorphosis, and has recently emerged as the Hellenic Industrial Development Bank. The Caisse Centrale of France has been responsible for the establishment of the National Development Bank of Senegal and its predecessor agencies, in which it indeed holds a minority equity position, as well as for other specialized agencies in that country. The World Bank has been instrumental in the creation of independent port, railroad, and power authorities in Thailand and of development banks in Turkey and India.

In such situations, the recipient country has usually become convinced of the desirability of adopting the change proposed and has not done so merely to fulfill a condition necessary to obtain the aid. In some instances, however, the efforts by donors to induce certain changes have proved abortive. One example is the attempt by the U.S. Development Loan Fund to induce Colombia to establish a system of savings and loan associations for housing. Indeed, a DLF loan authorization was committed for such an institutional arrangement, but it never became effective because of the opposition of existing savings organizations in the country. This example points up the need for donors to work sometimes within the framework of strongly entrenched institutional traditions in recipient countries, although, as indicated, this by no means implies that no institutional improvements or changes are ever possible.

Another example of an abortive attempt by an aid donor to change a deep-seated institutional tradition in a recipient country is provided by the failure of India to conclude an aid arrangement with the United States for its Bokaro steel enterprise. The precedents here were provided by the Rourkela, Durgapur, and Bhilai steel plants, all in the public sector, and the determination by the government of India to proceed with Bokaro also in the public sector, especially since private interests in India indicated their inability to carry out a project of the size involved. The result of the U.S. refusal to finance a state-owned steel mill was not the abandonment of the recipient country's institutional arrangement but a shift in the source of the aid—from the United States to the Soviet Union. On the other hand, a change in the institutional arrangement, involving a shift from public to private ownership, resulted in the case of the Dead Sea Works enterprise in Israel from the urging of the World Bank. This is particularly impressive in view of the strong role of public enterprise in the context of Israel's development effort, but the authorities accepted the shift as being in the country's interest.

With respect to the issue of public and private sectors as channels for aid, UNCTAD pronounced itself against discriminatory treatment of public enterprises. In its resolution on Needs of the Public Sector in the Transfer of External Resources to Developing Countries, adopted by 117 votes to 1, with 1 abstention, the Conference recommended the following principles:

I. Governments of developed countries should take appropriate account of the needs of the public sector in developing countries, in particular:

(a) By not discriminating between enterprises of the public sector and private enterprises, with regard to the financial and commercial treatment;

(b) By giving technical assistance to enterprises and institutions of the public sector of developing countries on an equal basis to that granted to the private sector;

(c) By creating for their enterprises favourable conditions for industrial and agricultural cooperation with enterprises of the public sector of developing countries, in matters relating to licenses, purchase of spare parts, semi-manufactures, intermediate products, etc., from the developing countries and to other forms of joint efforts resulting in industrial and trade progress in developing countries;

II. International institutions, agencies, bodies, etc., and in particular financial institutions, should endeavour to assist without discrimination the public sector of developing countries in accordance with the development plans of these countries.[44]

DEVELOPMENT BANKS AND CORPORATIONS

Increasingly important for receipt and administration of aid in virtually all developing countries is the national development corporation or finance company. Such institutions constitute a device through which external resources can be brought to small and medium-sized enterprises, especially in the private sector. They make external loan proceeds available to numerous borrowers much more effectively than outside institutions can. They thus constitute a type of financing which is intermediate between the general development financing and specific project financing which have been discussed above.

The wide variety of such institutions found in the recipient countries studied in our research is illustrative of their wide variety in general. Each of the countries has one or more of such institutions. In

[44] United Nations, *Trade and Development*, p. 50.

Colombia there is the publicly owned, rather weak Instituto de Fomento Industrial, as well as five privately owned development finance companies which operate on a regional basis. It is the latter which have received external assistance, especially from the IFC. In Chile there are no privately owned development finance companies; the public Corporación de Fomento has been an important channel for external financing, especially from the World Bank, for specific projects or programs. In Israel there is the mixed public-private Industrial Development Bank, which was created to move the administration of development budget funds for industry from the Ministry of Commerce and Industry to an autonomous agency and is becoming increasingly private in character. It has received loans from the U.S. DLF. In Greece there is the public Hellenic Industrial Development Bank, created at the end of 1964 by way of reorganization of the Economic Development Financing Organization, which in turn was established in 1954 as an outgrowth of the Central Loans Committee set up in 1948. These institutions have served as a channel for U.S. aid.

In Turkey there is, in the Industrial Development Bank, an outstanding example of such an institution established in the private sector, over some initial objections by the host country, at the suggestion of, and with financial assistance from, the World Bank. In Senegal the public Banque Nationale de Développement, with minority participation by the Caisse Centrale of France, is the latest version of earlier organizations set up with French assistance. In Sudan the Industrial Bank is also a public institution, which has received assistance from the United States and is in the process of being assisted by Germany. In India the genesis of and assistance to the Industrial Credit and Investment Corporation of that country are similar to those of the World Bank-sponsored Industrial Development Bank of Turkey. In addition, there is in India a government-owned Industrial Finance Corporation, which has been assisted by the United States, Germany, France, and Japan. In Thailand the Industrial Finance Corporation is privately owned by national and foreign interests, with a minority participation by the International Finance Corporation. It has received additional assistance from the World Bank, the United States, and West Germany. In each of the three countries of East Africa a national development finance company has been established with joint and equal ownership by the local government, through its national development corporation, the Commonwealth Development Corporation, and the DEG of West Germany.

These development banks are sometimes slow in their utilization of the general external credit lines made available to them, for the most part because of the insufficiency of projects in the country which can be financed and a lack of entrepreneurship. In certain cases, as in India, there has been very strong demand for the facilities of the development banks, since they have been re-lending external credits for imports, for which the foreign exchange is otherwise difficult to obtain. The exchange risk in loans out of the proceeds of foreign lines of credit is usually passed on to the ultimate borrower by development banks. This might seem to be a deterrent, especially when the borrowing is for local currency expenditure requirements. The deterrent of the exchange risk is usually offset, however, by the inflationary tendencies in many less developed economies, which make it profitable to borrow even if the foreign exchange value of loans must be maintained during periods of exchange depreciation.

There is a considerable degree of flexibility among donors in providing assistance to public and mixed public-private development corporations as well as to private development finance companies. The World Bank group, however, which by June, 1964, had extended close to $300 million of assistance to eighteen development finance companies in sixteen countries, prefers companies which are privately owned:

It is the experience of the World Bank and IFC that development finance companies are most likely to operate successfully if their ownership is predominantly private. This appears to be the best way of assuring continuity of sound investment policies and experienced management, so that operations will be conducted on sound business lines and by reference to economic rather than political criteria. Examples are numerous of publicly controlled development banks that have failed in their purpose because their investment decisions were dictated mainly by political considerations.[45]

Other donors, such as the U.S. AID, the Caisse Centrale of France, and the UK Commonwealth Development Corporation, have ex-

[45] International Finance Corporation, *Private Development Finance Companies,* Washington, D.C., June, 1964, p. 3.

tended assistance to such institutions even though government-owned. This is in recognition of the lack in many countries of entrepreneurship in the private sector, which it is precisely the task of development banks to stimulate. In many cases, such as the newly independent countries of Africa, there may be no alternative to the establishment of development banks by the governments.

International assistance to national development institutions is provided in the form of loans as well as equity investments. Positions in equity, on a minority basis, are taken by such donors as the IFC, the Caisse Centrale, and the Commonwealth Development Corporation. This makes up for deficiencies in local risk capital. At times it is done as part of a syndicate operation in which various foreign investors take up shares, which makes for a closer relationship between the outside source of capital and the development bank and facilitates the provision of other types of assistance besides the equity investment itself. A byproduct of such equity participation in national development companies is that the international corporation may join with the local development company in making other assistance separately available to individual enterprises in the country. The intermediate investment in the development company, however, is becoming the increasingly popular mechanism for making international public capital available for private enterprises in recipient countries.

Aid and Regional Development

Most of the international financial aid has been provided to finance projects and activities which are carried out within national borders without regard to the possibilities of integration on a regional basis. There is, however, an increasing consciousness of the role that can be played by international financial assistance in connection with the growing trend toward regional economic integration. The principal hampering factor in this respect to date has been the difficulty of achieving international agreements and planning of integration schemes and projects. The providers of financing have not generally taken the initiative in this connection; they have generally accepted as given whatever progress nations or groups of nations have made in multinational approaches to development.

The potential of regional development has nevertheless been recognized by both DAC and UNCTAD. In discussing the conditions for the effective use of assistance in his 1964 review, the DAC Chairman stated that

it is important to note that increased stress is being placed on the possibilities of regional groupings. In part, this is because the populations or the variety of resources in a number of countries are too small to permit production or market development on an efficient scale. Thus regional trade arrangements can aid in development. Furthermore, regional planning can be economical in meeting transportation requirements as well as other common needs such as universities and research centres.[46]

The DAC Chairman recommended that

in view of the limited size and resources of many of the less-developed countries, efforts by them to promote economic integration, regional planning, and common service organisations should be encouraged. This whole subject should be examined more closely by the D.A.C.[47]

UNCTAD, in a resolution on Regional Development adopted without dissent, expressed the belief

that development on a regional basis can be of material help in enabling developing countries to obtain the benefits of economies of scale for efficient production, marketing, research and trade generally, . . . that a proportion of assistance [should] be provided to developing countries, where possible and appropriate, through, or in association with, regional bodies such as the Inter-American Development Bank and the African Development Bank, [and] that the Secretary-General of the United Nations, in consultation with the President of the International Bank for Reconstruction and Development, regional economic commissions, regional development banks and other appropriate regional bodies, [should] be asked to study the problems of regional development and report to the General Assembly of the United Nations at its twentieth session.[48]

The developed nations at UNCTAD, however, generally either dissented or abstained with respect to a resolution on the creation of a Regional Development Fund, adopted by a vote of 78 to 11 with 27 abstentions, which requested the convening of a committee of experts to study "the feasibility of establishing a fund, where appropriate, for aid to developing countries for the purpose of financing

[46] OECD, *1964 Review*, p. 54.   [47] *Ibid.*, p. 95.
[48] United Nations, *Trade and Development*, p. 48.

long-term capital projects with particular emphasis on regional and/or sub-regional development projects without prejudice to bilateral arrangements." [49]

It is the regional financing institutions in particular in which, quite naturally, most stress is being placed on the financing of projects of regional scope. Much is hoped for along these lines from the recently created African Development Bank, and the proposed Asian Development Bank. The European Investment Bank in a sense is contributing to regional integration in the commitments it has set aside for Greece and Turkey on the basis of their associate membership in the European Common Market. The fundamental justification for EIB financing in Greece and Turkey is to strengthen those particular parts of the region in preparation for their eventual full membership in the Common Market.

There is an acute awareness of the desirability of promoting regional economic integration in the Inter-American Development Bank, although the accomplishments have been limited to date. The Bank has set aside $30 million of its ordinary resources for lines of credit to national agencies which finance the export of capital goods to other countries within Latin America. In connection with the Central American Common Market, it has approved loans in the amount of some $14 million to the Central American Bank for Economic Integration for relending for projects of regional interest and a loan of some $2.9 million for coordinated programs of the five Central American universities. The Bank has carried out studies of the feasibility of integrating the border zones between Colombia and Venezuela and between Colombia and Ecuador. The Colombia-Venezuela study gave rise to a loan of some $3 million to a Colombian electric power agency to finance, among other things, a connection of electric power facilities between bordering states in the two countries. The Bank established in mid-1965 a Latin American Integration Institute, with headquarters in Buenos Aires, to engage in research and training in this field.

The activities in this respect of the Inter-American Development Bank, like those of other agencies, have been hampered by the slow progress of integration under the procedures of the Latin American Free Trade Association. The Bank itself has repeatedly pronounced

[49] *Ibid.*

its favorable disposition toward integration, and Felipe Herrera, its President, has been one of the foremost spokesmen for the movement.[50] He joined with three other leading Latin American economists (Raúl Prebisch, Director General of the Latin American Institute for Economic and Social Planning, and Secretary General of UNCTAD; José Antonio Mayobre, Executive Director of the UN Economic Commission for Latin America; and Carlos Sanz de Santamaría, Chairman of the Inter-American Committee on the Alliance for Progress) in drafting in the spring of 1965 *Proposals for the Creation of the Latin American Common Market*.[51] These proposals were prepared in response to a request from the President of Chile to these four international officials "asking them to present their views regarding methods of speeding up the economic integration of Latin America." In addition to proposals concerning trade and other policies, this document includes proposals for a regional investment policy in industry, agriculture, transportation and communications, and electric power. In connection with such regionally coordinated investments, the report recommends that the

Inter-American Development Bank should channel a considerable part of its resources into these investment programmes without thereby giving any less attention to the financing of national development. As the integration policy gathers momentum, however, more extensive resources will have to be forthcoming, either from additional contributions made to the Bank for this purpose, or from funds from other sources. The Inter-American Committee on the Alliance for Progress is destined to play a leading role in coordinating these various kinds of financing.[52]

In Asia regional development projects have been promoted by the regional economic commission of the United Nations for that area, the Economic Commission for Asia and the Far East (ECAFE). One illustration is the multipurpose Mekong River Project involving the four riparian countries of Cambodia, Laos, Thailand, and Viet Nam. Another is the Asian Highway Project, designed to link and standardize national roads in a continuous international highway

[50] E.g., see Felipe Herrera, "Political and Economic Aspects of Latin American Integration," an address delivered before the Colombian Society of Economists, June 12, 1964; copies can be obtained from the Division of Information of the Bank.

[51] Obtainable from the Inter-American Development Bank.

[52] *Ibid.*, p. 18.

from Viet Nam to Iran. And the Asian Development Bank itself, which is conceived of as an instrument to promote regional economic cooperation, is also a promotion of ECAFE. An outstanding example outside of ECAFE of international cooperation in Asia to carry out a project of multinational scope is the Indus River scheme being carried out under the sponsorship of the World Bank.

An early example of a regional approach to development was the Asian Economic Development Fund established by the United States under the Mutual Security Act of 1955. The Fund was under the control of the President of the United States and allocations were primarily for regional purposes in the form of loans. In 1958 this program came to an end.

Regional economic integration in Africa has had an uncertain course. The achievement of independence, on the one hand, has to some extent had the effect of economic fragmentation along national lines, as in the case of the separation of Senegal from the former French West African Federation and later from the Mali Federation and in the weakening of the Common Market and integration forces in Kenya, Tanzania, and Uganda, or what was formerly British East Africa. Most foreign aid to Africa has consequently been for purely national plans and programs, though there has been some significant assistance for projects of regional scope, such as the World Bank loan of $24 million in 1955 and $38 million in 1965 to the East African Railways and Harbours Administration. Nevertheless, the hope that the East African Common Services Organization might serve as a focal point for external economic assistance to the countries of the region was never realized, and development corporations and development finance companies were set up on a purely national basis in each of the three countries. On the other hand, the UN Economic Commission for Africa has been pushing the planning of some projects on a regionally coordinated basis, as in the iron and steel, textile, and other industries in various countries of West Africa; and the African Development Bank itself is expected to operate in such a way as to promote regional economic integration on the continent.

Undoubtedly the potential for the dispensing of aid for projects of regional scope has been little exploited. The external financing agencies have on the whole remained passive in this respect, reacting to initiatives arising elsewhere rather than acting on their own initiative. These agencies could probably exert considerably more leverage than they have to the end of positively influencing planning and development along regional lines over the opposition of uneconomic national vested interest. Beginnings along these lines are already discernible, expecially among the international financing agencies of regional scope.

New Proposals for International Organization of Aid

Multilateral capital assistance to developing countries has come primarily from the World Bank group, in which the developing countries play a minor policy role. To increase their role in multilateral assistance, the less developed countries advocated at the UNCTAD the creation of a UN Capital Development Fund, under the control of the General Assembly, with each country having one vote. They have been supported in this position by the centrally planned economies, which are not members of the World Bank Group.

The desire for a UN Capital Development Fund on the part of recipient countries is not new. For many years they urged the formation of a Special United Nations Fund for Economic Development (SUNFED), and this proposal is but a new variation of the SUNFED scheme. The World Bank, with its careful and thorough approach to development lending, has been a long-time target of developing countries. These countries are members of the Bank but under its system of weighted voting they can be outvoted by the developed countries. The increasing debt-service burden of developing countries led to the formation of the International Development Association. IDA satisfied the criticisms relating to the terms of World Bank loans but weighted voting kept its policies beyond the control of the developing countries. Thus, in 1962, the Economic and Social Council and the General Assembly asked the Secretary-General of the United Nations to prepare a report on attitudes of various member governments on a UN Capital Development Fund.

Developed countries have, for the most part, opposed the formation of a UN Capital Development Fund. In their opinion such a Fund is unnecessary because of the existence of the IDA, and they oppose the proliferation of international aid organizations. They also argue the new Fund would divert money from existing UN programs and lead to the duplication and fragmentation of efforts, which would in turn increase the problem of coordination. Implicit in their position is the desire to have continued influence in the use of the assistance which they provide. The Fund, as proposed, would minimize this influence.

A few of the smaller capital-exporting countries have been favorably disposed toward a Capital Development Fund within the United Nations. They have proposed the expansion of the UN Special Fund, however, on the ground that a new Capital Development Fund was not likely to attract the necessary financial support from those countries who were in a position to make large contributions. They also stated the belief that the extension of the Special Fund into the field of capital development "would have the double advantage of ensuring the better coordination of pre-investment and investment activities and of minimizing overhead expenses." [53]

The less developed countries, in supporting the formation of a Capital Development Fund, have referred to the need for more funds to finance economic development and the necessity of obtaining those funds under more liberal arrangements with respect to utilization and repayment terms. It is their opinion that "a variety of financial institutions tends to increase the total financial resources available." [54] And in their opinion it is both good ethics and good economics for the economically advanced countries to give a substantial and rising volume of development assistance.[55]

The centrally planned economies have supported the establishment of a capital development fund. These countries are not members of the World Bank group and at present provide only bilateral capital assistance. There has been no indication, however, of the magnitude of assistance which might be forthcoming from these countries if a new Fund were to be established.

There has been a great deal of discussion on the structure of a

[53] *Financing of Economic Development, United Nations Capital Development Fund,* UN Document E/3790, June 14, 1963, p. 3.
[54] *Economic Development of Under-Developed Countries: Establishment of a United Nations Capital Development Fund,* UN Document A/5536, Sept. 24, 1963, p. 3.
[55] *Ibid.*

new Fund, the principal question being whether the Fund should be a new institution or an extension of the functions of an existing institution. Recognizing that a new Fund might not receive much support, many advocates of a Fund agreed that the best that could be hoped for was the expansion of an existing institution. Both IDA and the UN Special Fund were considered in this connection. Supporters of an expanded Special Fund pointed out that it was an existing UN body with a relatively equitable political balance in the make-up of its Governing Council, and it had the advantage of support by some capital-exporting countries. The capital-exporting countries reiterated their support for IDA, but the recipients argued that IDA would be acceptable only with the following fundamental changes in its structure:

it would have to be placed under the political control of the General Assembly if it were to become a United Nations Fund; it would have to become open to membership of all state members of the United Nations, and the specialized agencies; and all states would have to enjoy equal voting power.[56]

Opposition to the expansion of Special Fund activities came from the donor countries on the additional ground that the Special Fund was short even of the resources considered essential and urgent for the fulfillment of its responsibilities in the preinvestment field.

The proposed Capital Development Fund was discussed at the UNCTAD Conference, and two resolutions were passed in relation to it. They read as follows:

UNITED NATIONS CAPITAL DEVELOPMENT FUND *

The Conference

While noting the hopeful initiatives that have been proposed for extending the scope of the United Nations activity in development finance.

1. *Recommends* that the United Nations Capital Development Fund should start its operations at an early date to finance on favourable terms in all developing countries, especially in countries at an earlier stage of development, national and regional development plans, programmes and projects, particularly in the field of industrialization.

2. The resources of the United Nations Capital Development Fund should be derived from voluntary contributions.

* The Conference adopted this Recommendation by a roll-call vote of 90 to 10, with 16 abstentions.

[56] *Ibid.*

GRADUAL TRANSFORMATION OF THE
UNITED NATIONS SPECIAL FUND *

Referring to the note by the Secretary-General of the United Nations entitled "Transformation of the Special Fund into a United Nations Capital Development Fund: A study of the practical steps involved,"

Considering the objective of channelling more development assistance through the framework of the United Nations,

Considering that, if and when a merger between the Expanded Programme of Technical Assistance and the Special Fund is decided, such a merger may result in:

(a) Increased total resources being made available for development purposes;

(b) Greater administrative efficiency and better utilization of resources,

Believing that it would be appropriate to consider an extension of the terms of reference of the Special Fund into the field of investment proper in accordance with General Assembly resolution 1936 (XVIII).

1. *The Conference recommends* to the Governing Council of the Special Fund that it continue to give consideration to:

(a) Enlarging its activities in assisting governments, which so request, to find the necessary financing to implement the recommendations of Special Fund pre-investment surveys; and

(b) Broadening its criteria so as to include increased financing of demonstration projects, thereby playing an effective role as a bridge between pre-investment and capital investment;

2. *The Conference recommends* to the Governments participating in the Conference to take, in the light of paragraph 1 above, a constructive attitude to a gradual transformation of the United Nations Special Fund, so as to include not only pre-investment but also investment proper, as referred to in General Assembly resolutions 1219 (XII), section III and 1936 (XVIII), as additional resources become available;

3. *The Conference recommends* that the Fund should be authorized to accept additional contributions for the purpose of following up its pre-investment activities, provided that the Governing Council of the Special Fund is satisfied that such expenditure for this purpose will not unfavourably affect Special Fund financing of pre-investment needs;

4. *The Conference also recommends* that particular emphasis be placed on: (a) the channelling of any investment resources, which the Special Fund may have at its disposal as a result of action taken in conformity with paragraphs 2 and 3 above, to areas not adequately covered by other capital supplying facilities; and (b) ensuring that action taken under

---

* The Conference adopted this Recommendation by a roll-call vote of 89 to 5, with 22 abstentions.

these paragraphs would not unfavourably affect Special Fund financing of pre-investment needs.[57]

The note by the Secretary-General referred to in the second resolution quoted above considered the financial requirements, institutional changes and possible guidelines for the gradual transformation of the Special Fund. It was noted that over the years the figure of $200–250 million per annum has been the suggested figure for a capital development fund. Although capital development needs have since increased, other institutions such as the IDA have been formed, and this figure was used as a basis for dicussion. In focusing on areas where direct capital investment is needed and where, at the same time, financing by this Fund could be particularly appropriate and effective, it was concluded,

Among such areas are, first, those related to major United Nations programmes and activities . . . and, second, the sponsoring of, and participation in, consortia for the financing of development projects to which other public and private bodies would presumably contribute substantially larger resources than the fund itself.[58]

These new activities, in the opinion of the UN Secretary-General, might best be handled by utilizing a different operational approach to the old and the new activities. The report suggests a separation of the accounts of the two activities in order to permit voluntary contributions for preinvestment surveys and/or capital assistance to be earmarked, thus permitting the contributors to support only those activities they desired to support.

The following possible priorities were suggested for the expanded Special Fund:

(a) participation in the financing of the World Food Programme and other special development activities of the United Nations family;

(b) development financing aid in geographic areas in which the United Nations has undertaken special responsibilities;

(c) financial participation in appropriate projects with other United Nations-sponsored financial institutions, such as the African Development Bank;

(d) management of special capital resources which might be estab-

[57] United Nations, *Trade and Development*, I, 47, 48: Annexes A.IV.7 and A.IV.8.

[58] *Financing for an Expansion of International Trade*, E/Conf. 46/66, March 9, 1964, p. 4.

lished within the United Nations for such fields as industry, housing, science and technology, literacy, etc.[59]

The report concludes that "the ability of the United Nations family to assure the effective orientation and implementation of its technical assistance and pre-investment activities would be enhanced by the addition of capital investment functions." [60]

The principal capital-exporting countries, both in the Western and Communist blocs, either abstained or voted against the expansion of the Special Fund's activities. The Soviet bloc voted in favor of the establishment of a Capital Development Fund, whereas the Western bloc opposed it.

The multiplicity of aid organizations raises the question whether some of them might be merged and integrated. As can be seen from the discussion above, some countries believe that there is a need for new institutions, to serve particular needs. The major capital-exporting countries, who in the last analysis are the sources of most of the funds for new institutions, are somewhat divided on this question. The Western bloc seem on the whole to be satisfied with their bilateral programs and existing international organizations. France has suggested, however, that a larger proportion of European assistance should be channeled through European institutions, such as the European Development Fund and the European Investment Bank. This is presumably because the United States and the United Kingdom play a dominant role in the World Bank group. The Soviet bloc, excluded by choice from the World Bank group, has no multi-lateral capital assistance institution. It has supported the establishment of a UN Capital Development Fund but has given no indication of how much financial support it would give to such an institution.

The multiplicity of lending agencies has led to a certain specialization of functions and activities. This has its advantages in developing expertise in different kinds of operations. Its principal limitation is the integrating and coordinating of assistance from different sources. Most lenders have integrated some technical and capital assistance in their respective programs. The lack of capital assistance in the UN operations gives a certain appeal to the proposal of an extension of the Special Fund's work into this field.

The UNCTAD Conference has pointed up the frustration and

[59] *Ibid.*, p. 8.   [60] *Ibid.*, p. 9.

unrest in many of the developing countries in relation to their development. They feel left out of aid discussions which have a direct bearing on their development. These frustrations are partially eased by the regional organizations in which they have a greater voice such as the Alliance for Progress, the Inter-American Development Bank, and the African Development Bank. Even in these organizations, however, they are dependent upon capital being provided by the capital-exporting countries. One of the positive aspects of the UNCTAD Conference was that it made the developed countries aware of the depth of the frustrations of the recipient countries and may lead to a resolution of some of the underlying problems which would in turn ease the tensions. At the root of the problem is the desire for a more equal division of the world's resources among the world's people.

VII. The Future of International Development Aid

AFTER less than twenty years of continuous growth as a new and increasingly important field of public international relations, international development aid has now reached a critical turning point. Aid to the developing countries—on the part of both international financial institutions and the world's richer countries—must either continue to grow at an accelerating rate, or it will fail. Not only has there been a vast and explosive increase in the number of new states, but these belong overwhelmingly to the category of "very poor" countries; they are at the very bottom of the scale of economic development. Nationhood and independence bring with them claims to economic development which have hitherto been submerged and raise new expectations, which increase the gap between reality and aspirations. As Escott Reid points out in his forthright and incisive essay, *The Future of the World Bank*,[1] the average income per head in the rich countries is going up by about $50 per year, in poor countries by about $2.50 per year, and in the very poor countries by about $1.50 per year.[2] The disparity is in part a result of the fact that the population trend in the low-income countries has been upward and the trend in the rate of growth of production has failed to keep pace. Reid's estimate that "if aid from rich countries to low-income countries is to be decisive, the rich countries must pour into the low-income countries a much greater flow of men, materials and skills,"[3] is shared by responsible administrators and students of de-

[1] International Bank for Reconstruction and Development, September, 1965.
[2] Under the classification prepared by the Statistics Division of the Economics Department of the World Bank, very poor countries are defined as those with a per capita GNP of less than $100 (US); poor countries are those with a per capita GNP of $100–$249 (see Reid, *ibid.*, p. 60).
[3] *Ibid.*, pp. 11–12.

velopment aid everywhere. Reference has been made in this study, for example, to the recommendations of the French Jeanneney Report and to the recent White Paper of the British Ministry of Overseas Development, both of which agree that, relatively and absolutely, in terms of the overall magnitude of aid, as well as in terms of the share of the gross national product of the rich countries to be allocated to aid, the present phase is not the beginning of the end but rather the end of the beginning. The World Bank and IDA Report for 1964–65 [4] estimates, on the basis of an expert study, that over the next five years, the developing countries could on the average absorb some $3 to $4 billion more external aid per year.

Magnitude of Aid

Yet, at this very time, there are distinct signs, in all the major aid-giving countries, of a backward swing of the pendulum, of skepticism, indifference, or lassitude. Strong pressures toward, at best, a stabilization of the present level of aid or even a reduction of aid, are considerable in the United States, France, and West Germany. Financial factors such as the U.S. balance-of-payments problem—which is not acute in either France or West Germany—provide only a part of the explanation. The pressure is perhaps most serious in the United Kingdom, where the recent White Paper of the new Ministry of Overseas Development eloquently states the case for an expansion of foreign aid, against the background of a chronic economic crisis, which restricts Britain's capacity to implement this plea. In the United States, West Germany, and France, the predominant sentiment is one of disillusionment with the political dividends of foreign aid or impatience with the patent need to view foreign aid as a very long-term problem. The recent aid statistics show overall a holding of the line in most cases.

Terms of Aid

The problem of magnitude is closely allied to that of the *terms* of aid. The burden of interest and capital repayments grows from year to year. The need for a drastic softening of the terms of aid has be-

[4] *Annual Report of the World Bank and IDA, 1964–65*, Washington, D.C., p. 62.

come urgent. Even if aid terms are softened, gross aid will have to grow for some time to keep *net* aid constant. As the British White Paper puts it, "it has gradually come to be recognized that many developing countries cannot pay interest at market rates, repay capital, and, at the same time, maintain an adequate rate of development. They are faced with an increasing burden of debt, which pre-empts a larger and larger amount of their earnings of foreign exchange." [5] This view is echoed with regard to the member countries of the Development Assistance Committee, by the *1965 Review* of the DAC Chairman, although with emphasis on the need to differentiate the terms of aid, according to the state of progress and development reached by a recipient country. That aid must be provided on easy terms is also the view of the World Bank–IDA Annual Report for 1964–65.[6] In response to these needs several of the major aid-giving countries have indeed softened their terms significantly in the last few years. Interest rates were progressively reduced by France, the United Kingdom, West Germany, and Italy, while some of these countries, as well as Canada, granted longer average maturities. The DAC aims at extending the combination of significantly lower interest rates, significantly longer maturities, and grace periods to all of its member countries; and the British White Paper frankly states that interest-free loans must be provided in appropriate cases, together with grants. Yet these hopeful developments are countered by the reverse evolution in the United States, which accounts for almost 60 percent of the total aid given by DAC countries. In the United States, political pressure in Congress since 1964 has led to an increase of minimum interest rates from 0.75 to 2.5 percent. On the international level, the recent increase in the funds of the IDA has significantly but insufficiently strengthened the World Bank group's capacity to make more loans on softer terms. With present IDA resources of $300 million a year, Reid estimates, "The net contribution of resources from the Bank and IDA to the very poor countries would go up from about 10 cents a head to about 21 cents a head. The poor member countries would still, however, be receiving almost nothing from the Bank and IDA."

Until now, about half of the total U.S. aid has consisted of com-

---

[5] Ministry of Overseas Development, *Overseas Development: The Work of the New Ministry*, Cmnd. 2736 (August, 1965), Sec. 96, p. 35.
[6] P. 60.   [7] Reid, *Future of the World Bank*, p. 39.

modities for which payment is made in local currency (P.L. 480) and thus approaches—at least with respect to the foreign exchange burden—grantlike conditions. And as U.S. agricultural surpluses have recently declined [8] considerably, it becomes increasingly likely that future food aid will be given on the same terms as aid in general. In any case, it is clear that a major and sustained public educational effort will have to be made in the years to come. In all the countries of the Western world—whether as individual providers of aid or as members of the World Bank group—it will be necessary to point out the illusoriness of "tough" terms, their self-defeating character. A defaulting debtor, or a debtor so burdened with obligations that he cannot use development aid for development, is not a good debtor from any point of view.

A decision to increase the total volume of aid, especially to the poor and very poor countries,[9] and at the same time to soften the terms of aid—both in bilateral loans and through larger member contributions to IDA [10]—is not primarily a question of economic feasibility. All of the countries of the Western world have continuously expanding economies and a steadily rising standard of living. As John Nuveen points out in his essay quoted earlier in this book,[11] the amount of U.S aid devoted effectively to economic development purposes has only been about $6 billion over a period of nine fiscal years (1953–61). This figure contrasts with a gross private domestic investment in the United States during 1951–59 of $522 billion. Taking into account the relative populations of the United States and of the less-developed countries, "the amount we have given or invested to raise the economic level of the people in the less-developed nations on a per capita basis is ⅛ of one per cent of what we have spent on our own development." [12]

A United Nations Capital Development Fund?

The creation of a new Capital Development Fund, under the auspices of the United Nations, has been a persistent demand of the

[8] New York *Times*, Oct. 31, 1965, p. 1.

[9] Reid, *Future of the World Bank*, p. 60.

[10] The latter, in Reid's view, should at least be trebled from the present annual level.

[11] "Social and Political Aid," in Robert A. Goldwin, ed., *Why Foreign Aid?* (Chicago, Rand McNally, 1962), pp. 46 ff.

[12] *Ibid.*, p. 54.

poor member countries for a good many years; it has with equal persistence been turned down by the Western aid-giving countries, which provide the bulk of economic aid bilaterally and through the World Bank group. The demand was articulated again with the votes of the seventy-seven countries that constituted themselves into a bloc of the less developed world at the Geneva UN Conference on Trade and Development of 1964.

The answer to these requests given by the Western aid-giving countries is that there are more than enough institutions designed to provide development aid and that the creation of a new institution does not increase the amount of actual aid by one penny. There is, however, one contingency in which the creation of such a new capital fund might be desirable—that of a cooperative effort in development aid between the Western world and the Soviet bloc. A few years ago such a joint effort would have appeared utopian because of the intensity of the political conflict. Yet the political configuration of the world has changed drastically in recent years. The bipolarity of the Cold War has given way to a far more fluid situation, in which there is much less unity left either within the Communist world or within the Atlantic group of nations. One aspect of the change is increasing pressure towards expansion in the trade relations between the Eastern and Western group of nations. The fact that the USSR sent observers to the Constitutive Conference of the Asian Development Bank indicates the possibility that at least in certain areas, and for limited purposes, joint efforts are not inconceivable. But only if such cooperation should reach the dimensions of joint contributions to a UN Capital Development Fund would the creation of yet another development aid agency make sense. It might avoid the psychological and ideological difficulties of the USSR's and other Communist states' joining the World Bank group, which has acquired a predominantly Western and non-Communist orientation.

Development Planning in the Underdeveloped World

It is obvious from the many studies of aid-receiving countries which form the basis of the present volume, as it is from the observations of many experts deeply sympathetic to the needs and objectives of development aid, that, in order to make development aid effective, a major and continuing effort is required on the part of the aid-receiving countries. Even if the present trend of a steadily widening gap between the rich and the poor countries is reversed, and even if the volume and terms of development aid in the decade to come should, contrary to the present trend, be greatly improved, a quick bridging of the enormous gap between the small number of developed and the increasingly large number of very underdeveloped countries cannot be expected. The gap must be measured not only in terms of wealth, of differences in the national product, the average income per capita, or other aspects of the standard of living. It is perhaps even greater in terms of the availability of long-term capital and above all of the technical, administrative, and educational infrastructure, without which ordered and steady development cannot take place. The tragedy of the underdeveloped world in our time is heightened by their acceptance, under very different circumstances, of a combination of nineteenth-century nationalism and twentieth-century welfare-state ideology. Together, they have created conditions and aspirations that impede rather than foster the steady growth and development of the less developed countries and, in particular, of the many new states. The past decade of development aid has shown how prolonged and arduous are the major objectives of moving from a simple rural agricultural economy to a diversified export economy, including indigenous industry; developing from an almost total lack of skilled administrators, scientists, technicians, teachers, and workers to a society self-sufficient in these skills; and, finally, advancing from a society replete with inequalities, in which the overwhelming majority of the people are poor, and often a very small minority very rich, to one in which a greater degree of equality and sharing of benefits prevails. The need to retard the attainment of the third objective in favor of the first two is a most bitter pill to swallow:

Out of their poverty, out of their very scarce resources of materials and skills, the low income nations will have to squeeze out a greater proportion for economic development. They will have to be willing to postpone indefinitely the prestige projects, which may be big dams, or steel plants, or nuclear powered plants, or international airlines, or new capital cities, if these yield a low rate of economic return. . . . [T]he political leaders of the poor countries know . . . that if their country is to lift itself out of its poverty they must hold down increases in con-

sumption by the poor, they must put off doing much to reduce inequalities and inequities among regions and among groups within regions, they must sacrifice today's goods for tomorrow's hopes.[13]

The experiences of the last decade, and in particular the detailed
studies of the experiences of selected capital-receiving countries
which have been the core of the Columbia Law School's research
project, appear to indicate three major needs:

First, a sober and realistic adjustment of economic development
planning to goals that are realizable in terms of the country's conditions and ways of living, economic as well as social, in terms of
available human resources and in terms of capital resources seen in
relation to national income and the prospects of export. This certainly means the abandonment of prestige and "status" projects
which have no economic justification or put an undue strain on the
resources of the country at the expense of more realistic development projects. It also means, positively, a shift of emphasis, especially in the many countries which have not yet reached the "take-
off" stage, to improvement of agricultural techniques and support
for small and medium business. Only a few countries have realized
that the improvement and modernization of agricultural techniques
and productivity is often a more practical process of development
than sudden transition to industries for which the infrastructure, the
capital resources, and the human skills are lacking. Moreover, the
majority of the new states are based on village or tribal communities, which can organically develop small-scale business or cooperative schemes but not large-scale industries.[14]

The second connected need is more emphasis on human resources. This not only means greatly increased provision on the
level of the World Bank, the UN Special Fund, and the other international agencies, as well as in the aid programs of the aid-giving
countries, on technical assistance in the widest sense—planning
schemes, administrators, teachers, scientists, technicians, and others;
but it also means close coordination of the technical training pro-

---

[13] Reid, *Future of the World Bank*, pp. 49, 55.
[14] A legal corollary of this need is the establishment of business associations
that correspond to the social and economic structure of these countries. An
example is the new Ghana Companies Act drafted by L. C. B. Gower of
London, which provides for incorporated partnerships and thereby departs
from the English Companies Act.

grams with the gradual and planned development, based on the social traditions and habits as well as the economic needs of the country.

It is greatly to be welcomed that two of the most recent authoritative documents, Reid's study for the World Bank and the White Paper of the British Ministry of Overseas Development, as well as the recent *DAC Reviews* clearly recognized this need. Much progress has already been made. What remains to be done is most clearly shown in the sections on "technical co-operation" of the *DAC 1965 Review* and in the three sections (XI–XIII) devoted to recruitment and voluntary service, economic services, education, training, and public health in the British Government's White Paper of August, 1965. The implementation of these objectives means greatly increased human involvement. Many more specialists from the aid-giving countries and the international agencies will have to spend prolonged periods in developing countries. There must be a corresponding readiness of the receiving countries to cooperate and a readiness to accept, for prolonged periods, the services of foreign experts, including notably those of the ex-colonial masters. This appears to be easier now that most of the new countries in Asia and Africa are moving from the immediate period of intense post-independence nationalism to a more balanced appreciation of their long-term needs and a more dispassionate appreciation of the benefits that citizens of other countries can bring to them.

And, third, the developing countries will not be able to bypass for much longer the urgent need to coordinate their own development plans to a much greater extent that has been the case. Ambitious schemes have been proposed, and new institutions have been created —the rapidly expanded Inter-American Development Bank, the more recent African Development Bank, the Asian Development Bank, which has just been organized, and the common market plan for five small Central American republics and a much looser free-trade plan for a larger number of Latin American countries. But in East Africa the three states which have for nearly half a century been joined by Britain in a common market based on freedom of internal tariffs, a common currency, and common railway, postal, and air services, far from progressing toward a closer federation, have actually marched backward. Tanzania will soon have its own separate currency, and this is likely to lead to a complete disintegration of the common currency. It is with great difficulty that even the remaining features of the common market are being maintained. More ambitious schemes for wider joint African economic planning have so far remained on paper. Even if the many new states that have emerged, especially in Africa, should be able to retain political independence, it is obvious that they will have to engage in far more cooperative economic planning than hitherto. Development aid may well become more and more dependent on progress in this field.

The extent to which the developing countries will be willing to comply with all the aforementioned requirements, and especially with the need to subordinate narrow nationalistic aspirations to wider needs and visions, will very largely depend on the degree of communication not only among themselves but also between them and the aid-giving agencies. Some observations on this crucial problem of communication are made below.

Public and Private Enterprise in the Developing Countries

None of the developing countries, old or new, has adopted a philosophy of complete state socialism. But all of them have mixed economies, in which public development corporations and other state enterprises play a major part. This is usually the result of a mixture of conviction and necessity. In most of the new countries, all or most of the basic industries are state-owned. In this they do not differ greatly from some of the older countries, such as Britain or France. In the past, the definite refusal both of the United States and of the World Bank to give aid to publicly owned industries other than in the infrastructure sector has caused obstacles and frictions. Thus, the refusal of the U.S. Congress to finance the Indian Bokaro Steel Mill Plan, despite the declaration of the Indian Chamber of Commerce that no private capital would be available in India to finance this project and despite the conviction of the Kennedy Administration after years of study that the United States should support it. This did not stop India from proceeding with the project, which will now be financed by the Soviet Union. The World Bank, too, has supported private but not state-owned steel mills in India.

In most of the newer countries, and especially the poorest, responsible private venture capital is scarce or nonexistent. In some of them, such as Uganda, a public development corporation has had considerable stimulating effect on the development of small and medium industries. The approach to the aid-worthiness of public and private enterprise should be based on pragmatic tests, not on dogma. It is greatly to be welcomed that authoritative voices have been raised in favor of such an approach, and that the new leadership of the World Bank has endorsed it. Thus, World Bank president Woods recently stated that

> We have been reluctant to finance State-owned industrial enterprises primarily because of the great difficulty of assuring that they would be managed on a businesslike basis, free of political pressures. We are quite aware, nonetheless, that in some of our member countries, and especially in the newer ones, a shortage of private savings and of industrial entrepreneurship harshly limits what purely private capital can accomplish. We are therefore embarking upon a re-examination of our policies as applied to such cases to see whether there are ways, other than through completely private ownership, in which effective management of industrial ventures can be assured.[15]

In the view of many of the developing countries, the Bank's former ideological bias against public ownership of manufacturing industry was interpreted as a sign of the domination of the Bank by "predilections and prejudices peculiar to the United States." [16] And Cairncross, a former director of the Bank's Economic Development Institute and presently Economic Adviser to the British Treasury, said in 1959 that "a European observer, living in a mixed economy, cannot altogether share the ideological hostility of the Bank to public enterprise and manufacturing industry, although he may recognize its imperfections." [17]

[15] Address by George D. Woods to the Economic and Social Council of the United Nations on March 26, 1965, reprinted by World Bank, p. 7.

[16] Reid, "Future of the World Bank," p. 21.

[17] Alexander K. Cairncross, *The International Bank for Reconstruction and Development*, Essays in International Finance, No. 33 (Princeton, N.J., International Finance Section, Department of Economics and Sociology, Princeton University, 1959), p. 22.

The present more flexible attitude comes closer to the sense of the resolution on "Needs of the public sector in the transfer of external resources to developing countries," adopted by 117 votes to 1 with 1 abstention at the 1964 Geneva Conference on Trade and Development.[18] It thus helps to lessen the political and psychological gap between the developed and the developing countries. In practice, a high proportion of development financing will continue to go to the basic utilities and services which both the United States and the more orthodox World Bank view concede to be a proper sphere for the public sector.

A greater flexibility with respect to the functions of public and private enterprise might also facilitate future limited aid collaboration between the West and the Communist powers, e.g., through regional development banks. Finally, collaboration between public and private enterprise will facilitate the use of bipartite and multipartite joint ventures between developed and developing countries.

Joint Ventures

Transformation of former branches or wholly owned subsidiaries into partnership associations assures not only the participation of local capital and manpower in a joint enterprise but also to a greater extent channels part of the revenue into the host country. In some enterprises of this kind, public and private capital of different countries have gone into partnership association with the host country. A notable example is the $200-million LAMCO Iron Ore Project in Liberia. Here, the government of Liberia, as owner of the iron ore, has 50 percent of the shares in a giant enterprise in which the other 50 percent are held by a consortium of Swedish, American, and Canadian foreign interests. A separate partnership arrangement provides for 25 percent of the capital to be supplied by the U.S. Bethlehem Steel Company, which in return obtains the right to a corresponding ratio of the output and pays half of its net revenue in taxes to the government of Liberia. These partnership arrangements are supplemented by purchase contracts with various American, German, and other foreign consumers of iron ore; and the capital basis is further strengthened by loans from two governmental institu-

---

[18] United Nations, *Trade and Development*, I, 50, Annex A. IV. 13.

tions, the U.S. EXIMBANK and the German Kreditanstalt für Wiederaufbau, as well as a minor loan by the private Chase Manhattan Bank.

On a minor scale, the Tanzanian Kilombero Sugar Scheme represents partnership collaboration between private Dutch firms, the publicly owned British Commonwealth Development Corporation, the IFC and local public and private Tanzanian interests.

Communication between Donors and Recipients

One of the most important parts of Reid's essay is his emphasis on what he calls "the Bank's diplomacy." By this he means a need for constant communication, on all levels, between the World Bank Group and the countries to which it gives loans. He rightly stresses the delicacy of these relations, particularly the difficulty of maintaining needed control over development planning and the economic use of the aid resources without offending the recipient countries' sensibilities. He calls for resident missions in all recipient countries, headed by experienced senior officers who have a sense of diplomacy as well as a knowledge of the country in which they reside. It is only on the basis of such continuous contact and a climate of mutual confidence that the necessary direction over the conduct of the developing countries' economies can be exercised.

On the donors' side important strides toward closer communication and coordination have been made in recent years. The World Bank has led the way through the establishment of the Aid-India and Aid-Pakistan Consortia, which have functioned successfully for a number of years and provide a machinery for constant contact between the major Western donor countries and the World Bank and provide the opportunity for contact between the consortium and the planners and other government officials of the recipient countries. A lesser form of coordination—without advance pledging—has been practiced through consultative groups, which, as stated earlier in this book, it is the World Bank's intention to extend greatly. Parallel efforts (which have been discussed in Chapter III) have been made by the OECD and the DAC. No less important is the link which associate membership in the European Economic Community provides between the French-speaking and some other

African states, on the one side, and the founding members of the EEC, on the other side.

Another hopeful development is the association of donor and recipient countries through functional development schemes. In the Indus River Valley Project, India and Pakistan are collaborating in the constructive solution of one of their major areas of strife with the World Bank and a considerable number of Western countries, including the United States. In the Mekong River scheme, four neighboring countries which in many ways are politically antagonistic to each other—Cambodia, Laos, Thailand, and South Viet Nam —continue to collaborate in the development of the potentialities of this river. In this they are assisted by the contributions of other countries, under the general auspices of the United Nations.

Finally, regional development banks, provided they follow the pattern of the Inter-American Development Bank and the new Asian Development Bank rather than that of the African Development Bank can associate donor and recipient countries in a common organization.

Tying of Aid

Despite the obvious disadvantages that tied aid has for the developing countries and despite the proposals made in the United States by Senator Fulbright and in France by the Jeanneney Report for a shift from tied bilateral to untied multilateral lending, the prospects of any significant change are very small. For various political, financial, and other domestic reasons none of the donor countries—Western or Communist—is likely to reverse the trend of the tying of aid to purchases within the donor country. This increases the significance of aid consortia or consultative groups because group lending somewhat enlarges the area of freedom of choice by the aid-receiving country. Within the group of national lenders, the recipient can choose the products or commodities which it can obtain under the relatively most favorable terms. This freedom of choice is, however, limited by the size of the donor country's contribution. Thus, India can choose between purchases in the United States, West Germany, or Japan only within the total limits of their respective aid commitments. As a long-term objective, the untying of aid, either by concurrent national policy decisions or by increasing shifting to multi-lateral aid, must remain a major goal.

Aid and Trade

The developing countries have stated with increasing emphasis, particularly since the Geneva Conference on Trade and Development, that the only really effective form of aid in the long run is an improvement in the terms of trade, enabling them to earn their living and their foreign exchange by exports.

In the course of the three-month Conference, many complaints were aired and many concrete suggestions were put forth. The principal problem was to find ways to increase the export earnings of the developing countries. This was closely related to the problems of the terms of trade and fluctuating commodity earnings. Proposals were discussed for new international commodity agreements and an international insurance fund to stabilize prices. In addition, developed countries were also asked to remove quotas and tariffs on imports from developing countries, both for primary products and manufactured and semi-manufactured goods, on a nonreciprocal basis. These were but a few of the many important items discussed at the Conference.

In the short time since the conclusion of the Conference, the newly organized UN Trade and Development Board has already held general meetings. The World Bank has completed its thoughtful study on Supplementary Financial Measures and will soon complete a study on suppliers' credits. Solutions to the underlying problems will obviously take years of painstaking work and negotiations. One can be encouraged that systematic studies of the problems are finally under way.

The foregoing brief survey of major problems has sought to pinpoint some of the most crucial issues that face the developed as well as the developing nations in the coming decade. The decisions that face both groups are not exclusively questions of economics. They are political decisions in so far as they depend on basic choices as to the kind of world to be built; they demand courage and sacrifice by all parties. They demand a long-term view rather than short-term perspectives. Even on the most optimistic assumptions, the problems of development remain gigantic. But unless issues such as the ones outlined in the preceding pages are faced frankly and courageously, there is little hope for the solution of a problem that in worldwide importance ranks second only to the danger of humanity's self-destruction by nuclear war.

Bibliography of Selected References

CHAPTER II

Organization for Economic Cooperation and Development. Development Assistance Efforts and Policies in 1961. Paris, September, 1962.

—— Development Assistance Efforts and Policies, 1963 Review. Paris, September, 1963.

—— Development Assistance Efforts and Policies, 1964 Review. Paris, September, 1964.

—— Development Assistance Efforts and Policies, 1965 Review. Paris, September, 1965.

—— The Flow of Financial Resources to Countries in Course of Economic Development, 1956–1959. Paris, 1961.

—— The Flow of Financial Resources to Countries in Course of Economic Development in 1960. Paris, 1962.

—— The Flow of Financial Resources to Developing Countries in 1961. Paris, 1963.

—— The Flow of Financial Resources to Less Developed Countries, 1956–1963. Paris, 1964.

United Nations. International Flow of Long-Term Capital and Official Donations 1951–1959. New York, 1961.

—— International Flow of Long-Term Capital and Official Donations 1959–1961. New York, 1963.

—— International Flow of Long-Term Capital and Official Donations 1960–1962. New York, 1964.

—— International Economic Assistance to the Less Developed Countries. New York, 1961.

—— The United Nations Development Decade: Proposals for Action. New York, 1962.

—— World Economic Survey 1962. Part I, The Developing Countries in World Trade. New York, 1963.

—— World Economic Survey 1963. Part I, Trade and Development: Trends, Needs and Policies. New York, 1964.

CHAPTER III

United States

Committee to Strengthen the Security of the Free World [The Clay Committee]. The Scope and Distribution of United States Military and Economic Assistance Programs. Report to the President of the United States. U.S. Department of State, Washington, D.C., 1963.

Export-Import Bank of Washington. Annual and Semi-Annual Reports to the Congress. Washington, D.C.

The Foreign Assistance Program. Annual Report to the Congress for Fiscal Year 1964. Washington, D.C., 1965. [Publication also available for earlier years.]

U.S. Agency for International Development, Program Coordination Staff. Principles of Foreign Economic Assistance. Washington, D.C., 1963.

U.S. Agency for International Development and U.S. Department of Defense. Proposed Mutual Defense and Development Programs FY 1966, Economic: Agency for International Development; Military: Department of Defense, Summary Presentation to the Congress. Washington, D.C., 1965. [Publication also available for earlier years.]

U.S. Congress, Senate. Foreign Aid Program—Compilation of Studies and Surveys. S. Doc. No. 52, 85th Cong., 1st Sess. (1957).

U.S. Department of State, An Act for International Development: A Summary Presentation, June 1961. Department of State Publication 7205. Washington, D.C., 1961.

France

Caisse Centrale de Coopération Économique. Les operations du F.A.C., du F.I.D.E.S., du F.I.D.O.M. et de la Caisse Centrale de Coopération Économique en 1963. Paris, 1964. [Publication also available for earlier years.]

French Embassy in the United States, Information and Press Service. France—Aid and Cooperation. New York, 1962.

——— French Economic Assistance in West and Equatorial Africa—A Decade of Progress—1948–1958. New York, 1958.

"Méthodes de l'assistance bilaterale entrangère." *Journal officiel de la République Française du Conseil Économique et Social*, No. 4, 1962.

Ministère d'État chargé de la Réforme Administrative. La politique de coopération avec les pays en voie de développement. Rapport de la Commission d'Étude instituée par le Decret du 12 mars 1963, soumis au Gouvernement le 18 juillet 1963. Paris, 1963.

Overseas Development Institute Ltd. French Aid: The Jeanneney Report. An abridged translation of "La politique de coopération avec les pays en voie de développement." London, 1964.

Postel-Vinay, A. "La Caisse Centrale de Coopération Économique," *Bulletin de liaison et d'information de l'Administration Centrale des Finances*, No. 27, 1964.

"Principes et méthodes d'une politique française d'aide et de coopération à l'égard des pays en voie de développement," *Journal officiel de la République Française du Conseil Économique et Social*, No. 44, 1962.

"Relations avec les pays en voie de développement," *Journal officiel de la République Française du Conseil Économique et Social*, No. 17, 1960.

Triboulet, Raymond. Cinq ans de Fonds d'Aide et de Coopération— Rapport sur la coopération franco-africaine. Ministère de la Coopération, Paris, 1964.

United Kingdom

Commonwealth Development Corporation. Report and Accounts 1964. London, 1965. [Publication also available for earlier years.]

Commonwealth Development Finance Company Limited. Eleventh Annual Report and Accounts, Year Ended 31st March 1964. London, 1964. [Publication also available for earlier years.]

Export Credits Guarantee Department. ECGD Services. London, 1964.

H.M. Treasury. Aid to Developing Countries. Cmnd. 2147. London, September, 1963.

Ministry of Overseas Development. Overseas Development: The Work of the New Ministry. Cmnd. 2736. London, August, 1965.

Overseas Development Institute Ltd. British Aid, Government Finance. London, 1964.

———— British Aid, Survey and Comment. London, 1963.

West Germany

Deutsche Gesellschaft für Wirtschaftliche Zusammenarbeit [Entwicklungsgesellschaft] mbH. Annual Report Covering the Year 1964. 1965. [Also available for 1963.]

Kreditanstalt für Wiederaufbau [Reconstruction Loan Corporation]. Annual Report Covering the Year 1964. Frankfurt am Main, 1965. [Publication also available for earlier years.]

Twelve Years of German Development Assistance. [Reprint of twelve-part series in *German International*.] Druck- und Verlagshaus Heinz Möller, Bonn, 1964.

White, John. German Aid. Overseas Development Institute Ltd., London, 1965.

Japan

White, John. Japanese Aid. Overseas Development Institute Ltd., London, 1964.

Sino-Soviet Bloc

African-American Institute, Inc. *Africa Report*, X (January, 1965), 40.

Berliner, Joseph S. Soviet Economic Aid. Praeger, New York, 1958.

Billerbeck, Klaus. Soviet Bloc Foreign Aid to the Underdeveloped Countries. Hamburg Archives of World Economy, Hamburg, 1960.

Bykov, A., "CMEA and International Economic Cooperation," *International Affairs* (Moscow), II (1964), 68.

Carnett, George S., and Morris Crawford. "The Scope and Distribution of Soviet Economic Aid." In U.S. Congress Joint Economic Committee, 87th Cong., 2d Sess. (1962), Dimensions of Soviet Economic Power, p. 457.

Choa, W. F., "China's Economic Aid to Developing Countries," *The China Mainland Review* (Hong Kong), I (June, 1965), 13.

Franck, Peter G. Afghanistan between East and West. National Planning Association, Washington, D.C., 1960.

Goldman, Marshall I. "A Balance Sheet of Soviet Foreign Aid," *Foreign Affairs*, XLIII (1965), 349.

———— "Soviet Trade and Aid," *Challenge*, XII (1963), No. 3, 30.

Kaser, Michael. COMECON, Oxford, London, 1965.

Korbonski, Andrzej. COMECON, *International Conciliation*, No. 549. Carnegie Endowment for International Peace, New York, September, 1964.

Horvath, Janos. "Moscow's Program: The Performance So Far," *East Europe*, XII (1963), 8.

Malenbaum, W. The East and West in India's Economic Development. National Planning Association, Washington, D.C., 1960.

World Bank Group

International Bank for Reconstruction and Development. Articles of Agreement. Washington, D.C., 1945.

———— Policies and Operations of the World Bank, IFC, and IDA. Washington, D.C., 1963.

———— Some Techniques of Development Lending. Washington, D.C., 1960.

———— The Economic Development Institute 1965–66. Washington, D.C., 1965. [Publication also available for earlier years.]

———— The Horowitz Proposal: A Staff Report. Washington, D.C., 1965.

———— World Bank and IDA, Annual Report 1964–65. Washington, D.C., 1965. [Publication also available for earlier years.]

International Bank for Reconstruction and Development, International Development Association. 1964 Annual Meetings of the Board of Governors, Summary Proceedings. Washington, D.C., 1964. [Publications also available for earlier years.]

International Development Association. Articles of Agreement. Washington, D.C., 1960.

International Finance Corporation. Articles of Agreement. Washington, D.C., 1956. [As amended by resolution adopted 1961].

—— 1964–65 Annual Meeting of the Board of Governors, Summary Proceedings. Washington, D.C., 1965. [Publication also available for earlier years.]

—— Ninth Annual Report 1964–65. Washington, D.C., 1965. [Publication also available for earlier years.]

International Monetary Fund and International Bank for Reconstruction and Development. *The Fund and Bank Review, Finance and Development*. Washington, D.C. [quarterly].

Reid, Escott. The Future of the World Bank. International Bank for Reconstruction and Development, Washington, D.C., 1965.

Weaver, James H. The International Development Association. Praeger, New York, 1965.

Indus Basin

International Bank for Reconstruction and Development. Indus Basin Development Fund Agreement. Washington, D.C., 1960.

—— Indus Supplemental Agreement. Press Release No. 64/10. Washington, D.C., April 8, 1964.

—— Indus Water Treaty Signed. Press Release No. 650. Washington, D.C., Sept. 19, 1960.

U.S. Congress, Senate, Committee on Foreign Relations. "Total Commitments to Indus Basin Development Fund." Hearings, Foreign Assistance, 1965, 89th Cong., 1st Sess., (1965), p. 15.

Inter-American Development Bank

Inter-American Development Bank. Activities 1961–1964. Washington, D.C., 1965.

—— Fifth Annual Report, 1964. Washington, D.C., 1965. [Publication also available for earlier years.]

—— General Information. Washington, D.C., 1962.

—— Proceedings, Fifth Meeting of the Board of Governors, Panama, April 1964. Washington, D.C., 1964. [Publication also available for earlier years.]

—— Social Progress Trust Fund, Fourth Annual Report, 1964. Washington, D.C., 1965. [Publication also available for earlier years.]

Pan American Union. Agreement Establishing the Inter-American Development Bank. Washington, D.C., 1959.

European Development Fund and European Investment Bank

Communauté Économique Européen. Fonds Européen de Développement. *Situation mensuelle des projects en exécution*. Brussels [monthly].

European Economic Community. Convention of Association between the European Economic Community and the African and Malagasy

States Associated with That Community and Annexed Documents. Brussels, 1964.

European Investment Bank 1958–1963. Brussels, 1964.

European Investment Bank. Annual Report 1964. Brussels, 1965. [Publication also available for earlier years.]

International Legal Materials. Regulations of the European Development Fund. Washington, D.C., July, September, 1965.

Ripoche, P., "Le Fonds Européen de Développement," *Les Banques de Développement dans le Monde*, I (1964), 241. Statute of the European Investment Bank, Brussels, 1958.

African Development Bank

Economic Commission for Africa. Report of the Committee of Nine on the General By-laws of the African Development Bank, ADB/I/BG/2. Addis Ababa, July 30, 1964.

—— Report on the Establishment of the African Development Bank. E/CN.14/310. Addis Ababa, Dec. 4, 1964.

—— The African Development Bank: An Instrument for African Development. E/CN.14/ADB/30. Addis Ababa, April 10, 1964.

United Nations. Agreement Establishing the African Development Bank, Preparatory Work, Including Summary Records of the Conference of Finance Ministers. U.N. Pub. Sales No. 64.II.K.6. New York, 1964.

United Nations Technical Assistance

United Nations, Technical Assistance Committee of the Economic and Social Council. Annual Report of the Technical Assistance Board for 1964. New York, 1965. [Publication also available for earlier years.]

United Nations Technical Assistance Board. "A Statistical Summary of Activities from July 1950–June 1965," *Technical Assistance Newsletter*, June–July, 1965. [Publication also available for earlier issues.]

Colombo Plan

Chancellor of the Exchequer. "The Colombo Plan for Co-operative Economic Development in South and South-east Asia," *Annual Reports of the Consultative Committee*, London, 1964.

Department of Technical Cooperation. "Technical Cooperation under the Colombo Plan," *Report for 1963–64 of the Council for Technical Cooperation in South and South-east Asia*, London, 1964. [Publication also available for earlier years.]

United Nations Special Fund

United Nations Special Fund. Annual Reports of the Governing Council to the Economic and Social Council of the United Nations. New York.

—— Annual Reports of the Managing Director to the Governing Council. New York.

—— Costs of Projects Approved by the Governing Council May 1959–January 1965. SF/Reports, Series B, No. 7. New York, Jan. 31, 1965.

—— Project Guideline No. 1. SF/PGL/1. New York, June 1, 1964.

Lower Mekong Basin

United Nations Economic and Social Council. Annual Report for 1964 of the Committee for the Coordination of Investigations of the Lower Mekong Basin. E/CN.11/679. New York, Feb. 1, 1965. [Publication also available for earlier years.]

Organization for Economic Cooperation and Development

See publications listed for Chapter II.

CHAPTER IV-V

Reports by Columbia University School of Law on Public International Development Financing:
1. Public International Development Financing in East Africa (Kenya, Tanganyika, Uganda), January, 1962.
3. Public International Development Financing in Turkey, November, 1962.
4. Public International Development Financing in Thailand, February, 1963.
5. Public International Development Financing in Israel, March, 1963.
6. Public International Development Financing in Colombia, June, 1963.
7. Public International Development Financing in Senegal, November, 1963.
8. Public International Development Financing in Chile, March, 1964.
9. Public International Development Financing in India, July, 1964.
10. Public International Development Financing in Greece, September, 1964.
11. Public International Development Financing in Sudan, April, 1965.

CHAPTER VI

Arnold, H. J. P. Aid for Developing Countries. Dufour, Chester Springs, Pa., 1962.
Asher, Robert E. Grants, Loans, and Local Currencies—Their Role in Foreign Aid. The Brookings Institution, Washington, D.C., 1961.
Avramovic, Dragoslav. Debt Servicing Capacity and Postwar Growth in International Indebtedness. Johns Hopkins Press, Baltimore, 1958.
—— and Ravi Gulhati. Debt Servicing Problems of Low-Income Countries, 1956–1958. Johns Hopkins Press, Baltimore, 1960.

Avramovic, Dragoslav, and associates. Economic Growth and External Debt. Johns Hopkins Press, Baltimore, 1964.

Basch, Antonin. Financing Economic Development. Macmillan, New York, 1964.

Benham, F. Economic Aid to Underdeveloped Countries. Oxford University Press, London, 1961.

Black, Eugene R. The Diplomacy of Economic Development. Harvard University Press, Cambridge, Mass., 1960.

Coffin, Frank M., Witness for Aid, Houghton Mifflin, Boston, 1964.

Feis, Herbert. Foreign Aid and Foreign Policy, St. Martin's Press, New York, 1964.

Galbraith, John Kenneth. "A Positive Approach to Foreign Aid," *Foreign Affairs*, XXXIX (1961), 444.

General Confederation of Italian Industries. Public Financial Aid to Developing Countries. Rome, 1961.

Goldwin, Robert A., ed. Why Foreign Aid? Rand McNally, Chicago, 1962.

Liska, George. The New Statecraft. University of Chicago Press, Chicago, 1960.

Little, I. M. D. Aid to Africa. Overseas Development Institute, Macmillan, New York, 1964.

―――― and J. M. Clifford. International Aid. Allen & Unwin, London, 1965.

Mason, Edward S. Foreign Aid and Foreign Policy. Harper and Row, New York, 1964.

Montgomery, John D. The Politics of Foreign Aid. Praeger, New York, 1962.

Morris, James. The Road to Huddersfield. Pantheon, New York, 1963.

Organization for Economic Cooperation and Development. See listing for Chapter II.

Shonfield, Andrew. The Attack on World Poverty. Random House, New York, 1960.

Society for International Development. *International Development Review*. Washington, D.C. [quarterly].

―――― Motivations and Methods in Development and Foreign Aid. Proceedings of the Sixth World Congress of the Society for International Development. Washington, D.C., 1964.

―――― *Survey of International Development*. Washington, D.C. [monthly].

United Nations. The Capital Development Needs of the Less Developed Countries. Sales No. 62.II.D.3. New York, 1962.

―――― Trade and Development, Final Act and Report. E/Conf.46/141. New York, 1964.

United Nations Conference on Trade and Development. Towards a

New Trade Policy for Development. E/Conf.46/3. New York, Feb. 12, 1964.

United Nations Economic and Social Council. Financing of Economic Development. United Nations Capital Development Fund. E/3790. New York June 14, 1963.

—— Transformation of the Special Fund into a United Nations Capital Development Fund: A Study of the Practical Steps Involved. E/3934. New York, July 8, 1964.

United Nations General Assembly. Economic Development of Under-Developed Countries, Establishment of a United Nations Capital Development Fund. A 5536. New York, Sept. 24, 1963.

U.S. Agency for International Development. See listing for Chapter III.

Wolf, Charles. Foreign Aid: Theory and Practice in Southern Asia. Princeton University Press, Princeton, N.J., 1960.

Index

Abboud, Ibrahim, 214

Adela Investment Company, 54, 124

Afghanistan: aid flow from Sino-Soviet bloc, 35, 85; from USSR, 89

African countries: EEC Convention of Association with, 124, 127, 128, 199, 201, 207; planning in relation to aid, 402

—aid flow to: *1960–63*, 32, 34–35 *(table)*; per capita aid, *1963*, 33, 34–35 *(table)*; bilateral aid, *1963*, 36, 37 *(table)*; from U.S., 46; from France, 54–58, 60, 61, 199; from West Germany, 74; from Communist China, 85, 86; from Sino-Soviet bloc, 85, 86; from USSR, 89–90; from EIB, 124, 125, 130; from EDF, 124–30

—see also East Africa

African Development Bank, 5, 56, 57, 91, 131–32, 208, 414, 446, 447, 464, 469

Agency for International Development (AID), 23, 39, 238, 408, 413, 444; Technical Cooperation Development Grants, 50; functions, 386, 414

—loans, 48, 424, 427, 428, 435; *1963* commitments, 49 *(table)*; defined, 49–50; *1961–63*, 51; *1966*, 52; to Colombia, 156, 157–58, 162, 276, 290–91, 294, 298; to Chile, 166–67, 169, 171; to Israel, 175, 178; to Greece, 184; to Turkey, 191, 192; to India, 225, 229, 230, 232; to Thailand, 239, 246–47, 348, 353; to Sudan American Textile Industry Co., 363, 365, 366, 369, 370, 372, 376; for social projects, 417; tying of, 422; repayment terms, 426–27

—see also Development Loan Fund

Agricultural surpluses, 26, 49, 50, 174, 183, 191, 201, 205, 221, 224, 226, 386–87, 397, 427, 431, 460; see also Food for Peace Program, Public Law 480 (U.S.)

Agriculture: IDA and IBRD loans for, 100, 101 *(table)*, 102; IDB loans, 119–20, 120 *(table)*, 168; EDF grants, 126; EIB loans, 130; AID loans, 175; loans to Sudan, 213; aid to Thailand for, 236, 237

Agriculture Trade Development and Assistance Act, see Public Law 480 (U.S.)

AID, see Agency for International Development

Aid-India Consortium, 62, 82, 106, 136, 137–42, 219, 220, 222, 225

Aid-Pakistan Consortium, 62, 106, 136, 434

Aid-receiving countries, see Recipient countries

Albania, aid to China, 86

Alessandri, Jorge, 303

Algeria: EDF grants to, 126

—aid flow to: *1960–63*, 34 *(table)*; per capita aid, *1963*, 34 *(table)*; from Sino-Soviet bloc, 35, 85; from France, 55, 59, 60

Alliance for Progress, see *under* Latin America

Argentina: IBRD loan to, 103–4

—aid flow to: *1960–63*, 35 *(table)*; per capita aid, *1963*, 35 *(table)*; from Japan, 79

Ashdod, port of, Israel, 176, 177, 319

Asian countries: Economic Development Fund, 449